THE SOCKET GREENY SAGA

TONY BERTAUSKI

BERTAUSKI STARTER LIBRARY

BOOK 1

For the search.

PART I

Virtualmode: an alternate reality where there is no pain. No consequences.
No fear. A place that is numb and safe.
Not cold, but empty.

1

No Rime or Reason

Your entire life can change in one day.

It's not like my life didn't need it. Basically, I lived a life of killing time. I was zoning out on a steady diet of video games and energy drinks. The only thing that made school even slightly bearable was getting into a fight at the end of the day. Sometimes, the sound of a nose crunching made life worth living. Even if it was my nose.

The day my life went inside-out started like any other day. I got to study hall just before the bell rang. Chute was reclined with her eyes closed and the transplanter discs behind her ears. Her red ponytail was hanging over the seat. Streeter had already crossed over. He was lying back with a grin on his face and his fingers laced over his belly.

I stuck the transplanters behind my ears. They sucked at the soft skin under my earlobes. My small hairs stood up and a spot quivered in my head like a tuning fork. The numbing took over.

There were no lights in the darkness behind my eyelids. No colors. A deadening sensation oozed down my neck and consumed me. Sound faded and the outside world drifted away. Temperature became nonexistent. I left my skin behind and my awareness—whoever *I* am—was drawn into the Internet and transplanted into virtualmode.

For a moment, I drifted in darkness with the falling sensation. This was the place where most people failed to enter virtualmode. They couldn't handle the drifting. Virtualmoders knew how to ride the in-between like a wave.

I entered my sim that looked pretty much like my skin, except for the hair. I liked my sim bald. Back in the skin, my hair was past my shoulders and white as snow. Don't know why it didn't have color.

Darkness took form. First, there was an empty room with lumpy, colorless furniture. The gray walls turned into wood paneling with frosty windows. Cheap sofas, frayed rugs covered the floor and monstrous deer heads looked down from mounts, their glassy eyes reflecting the fire in the hearth. Above the fireplace was an enormous moose head.

The flames flickered over the dry wood, occasionally licking the old stone around it. The top of the mantel unfolded and a tiny woman, with blond hair and sweeping curves, stepped out and crossed her perfectly smooth legs.

"Can't feel the heat?" she asked. "Upgrade your gear with Dr. Feelers' tactile attachments. Dr. Feelers puts you in control of the nervous system inputs; you can feel as little or as much as you like. Fire too hot? Turn it down by—"

"Off." Chute's sim was taller than her skin. It was leaner and more dangerous. "Dr. Feelers don't work," she mumbled, even though she was rubbing her hands in front of the fire.

A giant barbarian came out of the next room, with a wooden chair that looked tiny in his hand. Streeter's sim was ten feet tall, muscles bulging off his neck and rippling down his arms, with a bloody axe dangling from his hip. I always thought he should just go the whole nine and wear a loincloth. Dude was four feet tall in the skin, the shortest high school sophomore who ever lived, but in virtualmode he was a god.

He kicked the sofa away to make room and sat in the chair that groaned and splintered but somehow held him. Control panels emerged from the floor and wrapped around him like mission control.

"What're we doing here?" I asked.

"We're going to get our kill on."

"I just got pardoned for fighting. We get caught, just stamp my suspension."

"Don't worry, Buxbee's out of town." Streeter's rich voice vibrated off the walls. "That substitute has no idea where we're going. I set up a false scenario. As far as anyone's concerned, we're reliving Desert Storm for history class."

I looked at Chute. "Did you know we were doing this?"

"He didn't tell me. If you were in class on time, he wouldn't have told you, either." She turned her head, the ponytail whipping around. "That's the way he does it."

"All right," Streeter sang to himself. "If you're wondering where we are, I hacked us into a world—"

"Whoa, wait a second." Chute held up her hand. Her sim looked like it had never seen the sun. "I don't think we need to be hacking into anything, Streeter. You got caught last time and we don't need to be wandering around some protected world *while we're in class!*"

His bushy eyebrows knitted together like enormous caterpillars. "First of all, I didn't get *caught* last time, someone ratted me out. And they couldn't prove I hacked anything so, technically, I wasn't caught. Secondly, stop being a wuss. Right, Socket? Right?" He smacked me with a fist the size of a basketball. "We're in, we're out, no harm, no foul or whatever else jocks say before a game. We're not getting caught. Besides, this place is one hell of a ride. I hacked in the other night just for a little taste and me likey."

I didn't care one way or the other. I never wanted to admit it to Streeter, but I was getting a little bored of virtualmode battles. So was Chute, I could tell. But Streeter lived for it, so I shrugged.

Streeter smiled. "All right, good. This place is called the Rime. It's a bunch of twelve-year-olds with rich parents. I say we vaporize their asses down to bare data and harvest all their experience points. They aren't worth shit, but who says we can't have a little fun."

"Twelve-year-olds?" Chute said. "Seriously?"

"Yeah, seriously. We ain't got time for a real battle. It's just a little quickie, come on."

The monitors lit up. Streeter scanned them, mumbling to himself as he surveyed the environment outside the cabin. Chute was already sitting on the couch, with her arms locked over her chest, checking her emails. She wasn't going to talk, so I figured I'd check mine, then changed my mind. There'd just be a thousand unread emails and I wasn't going to read them. Besides, there was likely a video message from Mom with the worn-out face, telling me she wouldn't be home tonight. Again. So I sat next to Chute and zoned out for a while.

"You all right?" Chute said.

"Yeah, I'm all right. You?"

"Something's bothering you."

Life was bothering me, but I couldn't explain that to her. It was just one of those days, but I could never hide it from Chute. She looked right through me.

Streeter clapped his hairy-knuckled hands that sounded like paddles and smiled, his teeth big and square and chipped. "Let's shred some twelve-year-old ass."

"Don't say it like that," Chute chimed.

Our clothes shifted and changed, turned white speckled with browns and blacks, and hung like rags. A battle staff appeared in Chute's hands. Evolvers materialized on my belt, simple handles that looked less threatening than Chute's pole but, once activated, transformed into any weapon I visualized.

A clean-cut kid appeared at the door. "Are your weapons weak? When you need to destroy and do it fast, think the Canonizer." He held up a pistol with an oversized barrel. "It's rapid, compact, and requires a fraction of the code—"

We walked through the apparition and his cheesy weapon onto the front porch. The boards were gray and weathered like the sky. The cabin was buried in a dense forest. A narrow path at the bottom of the steps carved between the snow-crusted trees. My breath came out in long clouds.

I could feel it all the way back to my skin and it felt cold. Maybe it was my imagination, or maybe I was just nervous. Or maybe things were about to get really weird.

2

SHADOWPLAY

MY GUTS WERE EVERYWHERE.

I was staring at a gray sky streaked with snowflakes blowing like tiny bullets, remembering two words. *True Nature.* Someone whispered them into my ear just before something happened.

Everything seemed so unreal, like time was moving in slow motion. The sky was like a steel sheet that concealed the sun. It looked cold. There were shouts and the howling of wind, but even that was blotted out by a high-pitched whine inside my head like I'd been knocked out with a concrete block.

Puttylike goo bubbled and burped from gaping holes in my chest and my stomach was just plain gone. Instead of intestines, the ground was splattered like someone dropped a brick in a bucket of paint.

Just my sim. For a second, I forgot I was in virtualmode, afraid that was my skin smeared on the ground. *Why am I still here? If I died in battle, I should've been kicked back to the skin. And why can't I remember anything?*

I was on a frozen tundra with snowy dunes rolling all the way to the horizon and pointed snow-capped mountains in the far-off distance, but where I was lying, it was bare ground like some sort of fiery meteorite filled with gray ooze exploded. There was a shadow in the white landscape, slipping among the scoured snowdrifts like a tattered ghost fleeing the scene of a crime. Suddenly, a giant blocky-toothed barbarian was leaning over me, his face crisscrossed with pink scars. Streeter's lips were moving, but I barely heard the words.

"Bail out! Code bail out!"

A girl slid across the ground and elbowed him out of the way. Somehow, her cowl stayed pulled over her head, but her red hair spilled out. "Get us out of here, Streeter!"

"What d'ya think I'm doing?"

"You're standing there with your thumb up your ass!" She cradled my head and bit her lip against the wind that was biting back. "I told you, Socket, I told you," she said, not so quiet, "I told you we shouldn't let him hack us in here. I told you something would go wrong." She held up her hand; my guts dripped off in the wind. "You knew it, too."

Maybe I did, but I always felt like something was wrong. With me. With the world. Everything.

Streeter was screaming and cursing. Something wasn't working. Bail out always took us back to the skin. "I told you, Streeter," Chute shouted, "now those Rimers got us locked in here until they shred our sims to goop! We'll be lucky if they don't report us to the cops!"

"Just shut up. Let me think for a second!"

Streeter stomped around, muttering to himself, thinking out loud before falling on the ground and hunching over something in his hand.

"What happened?" My voice echoed in my head.

"We don't know," Chute answered. "Something exploded." She glanced down at my farting chest wounds. "We don't know how that happened."

The shadow ghost was back, playing peekaboo in the snow as it weaved in and out of the ground, its body flapping madly. I pointed at it now standing beside Streeter, but Chute pushed my hand down. "Try not to move, it's only going to screw up your sim. It's going to take like a month to fix as it is." She bit her lip again but not against the wind, this was more about Streeter.

"That thing." I nodded at it. "Who is that?"

She looked. "What thing?"

"That shadow."

She looked again but only shook her head.

"He's delirious." Streeter was now sitting with his legs folded, poking at something in his hand.

"It's right there," I said, pointing again.

"Look, there's no shadow sim." He waved his hands right through it. *How could he not see it?*

"It's right next to you."

"You're brain damaged. Shadow sims can't stabilize in this environment, so just relax, I'll get us out of here."

"You better," Chute said.

"You're such a wuss," he replied.

"And you're dead meat if you get us suspended."

"Relax, we're not going to get caught by that lame-ass substitute; he doesn't know his bunghole from a hole in the ground. I guarantee he doesn't know how to monitor virtualmode activity. And the cops would be here already if the Rimers were going to report us, so just freaking relax, all right." He snorted, shaking his head, probably thinking, *Wuss.*

But they were missing the obvious. There was a shadow standing right in front of us and only I could see it. And now each time the shadow moved, I felt a tug somewhere *inside*, all the way back to my skin that was sitting in study hall.

Chute closed her eyes, shaking her head. I took her hand. She was probably reclined in the study hall with the same worried frown crunching the freckles between her eyebrows. I could almost feel her skin tense up. And then I realized I *could* feel it. I could feel her hand cupped inside mine. It was warm and shaky. And the bits of sleet and snow stung my cheeks. Each time I felt the tug of that shadow moving around, I could feel more, like I was a vessel filling up from the inside.

I should've been having a full-blown freak-out. Feeling something in virtualmode? But I felt Chute's fingers scratch me as she lifted my head. I could smell the fragrance of her hair snapping in my face like fine whips.

"This is weird," I said. "I can feel you."

"What?" Chute put her ear closer to my lips.

"You guys want to stop playing boyfriend/girlfriend for like two seconds and help me?" Streeter said.

"I'm sorry," Chute shouted, "do you need some help? Here." She scooped up a handful of liquid guts and splattered it along Streeter's backside. "Anything else?"

He looked over his shoulder. "That really wasn't necessary."

While those two argued, I rubbed my fingertips together, feeling the brittle texture of my fingerprints and the arctic wind bite my exposed skin. My senses sharpened quickly, but it went beyond that. I felt the ground under my back and the snowflakes drive across the snowdrifts, like I was becoming part of the environment, plugging into the ground. I sensed the surroundings like they were my own body and the cold was no longer cold and the wind no longer windy because I was the cold and I was the wind. I felt the shadow sweeping around me. It felt so familiar, like seeing someone I once knew.

I felt the ground tremble. Felt the bodies growing from the frozen soil beneath the blanket of snow before I actually saw them emerge like blackened sunflowers.

I yanked Chute's flapping sleeve and jerked my head in the direction of the disturbance. She looked over and sat up straighter. The wind knocked her hood off; her long hair whipped sideways. "We're screwed."

The sunflowers transformed into small, stout warrior thugs with beards and bushy eyebrows, with battleaxes and long swords they gripped with sharpened claws. There were a hundred of them that slowly worked toward us through the snow. Seemed like the wrong sort of warrior sims to have in a world of snowdrifts, but they'd get to us eventually.

Streeter leaped up and pulled his staff out of the snow. It was as thick as a tree trunk topped with spikes with bits of skin and hair and brains. He looked at the sky like he was studying the weather, then bowed in prayer. An electrical field crackled around the spikes and dark clouds rolled out of the gray sky like smoke pushing through holes from the other side. I could feel my hair stand on end. Streeter rammed the staff on the ground and lightning bolted down, frying every one of the tiny warriors in their tracks, leaving behind smoldering holes.

"That's called a shit storm," he said.

"There's more coming," I said.

"Yeah, well, I can't keep pulling lightning out of my ass; it takes too long to power up." He jerked his head at Chute. "Why don't you do something?"

"What do you want me to do?" Chute answered. "I'm a healer."

"Oh, yeah. I almost forgot." He stared at my dripping chest cavity and rolled his eyes. "You're doing great."

"That's it." She was on her feet, reaching into her sleeve. Streeter held out his hands, not trembling or in surrender but begging her to rethink. Chute pulled a long, slender staff from her sleeve, impossibly long to fit inside her cloak, and spun too quickly for the barbarian to do anything. The pole flexed under the velocity of her swing and it cracked on the back of his legs, making a sound like a textbook dropping flat on a desk.

"Socket!" Streeter dropped on his knee. "You better stop her!"

"I'll show you how much I suck!" Chute dropped three more quick shots on him, deftly avoiding his half-hearted attempt to snatch her. She flipped over him and drove the staff into his back, driving him face first into the snow. "Who sucks now, douche bag!"

Streeter could've knocked her halfway across the tundra if he wanted to. Sometimes he did, but most of the time he let her get it out of her system. Sometimes I broke it up and sometimes I watched their spats play out and they always ended with one of them damaging the other's sim and then cursing each other for all the trouble. This time, I didn't do anything because I was *feeling it*. I felt Chute's muscles tense, Streeter's knees throb. And this time I stopped them not by stepping between them. I stopped them with a thought.

[Stop.]

Chute was in mid-strike, ready to put a hole through Streeter's right lung, when the thought struck her and her body obeyed as if the thought was her own. She looked around, like someone had whispered it to her, but I simply willed her to step off Streeter. Streeter looked up, his scraggly beard powdered with snow. They could feel something, too. They could feel me inside them. And then they watched my stomach begin to rebuild itself, regenerating simulated flesh, filling the holes in my chest until my body was whole again.

Streeter got on his knees and looked at Chute. "I owe you an apology."

"I didn't do anything." Her mouth barely moved. "How'd you do that?"

The shadow walked up behind her and through her and stood between us, its ghostly form snapping in the wind. I sat up and looked at my hands, unsure if this was virtualmode or a dream.

"Do I know you?" I asked the shadow.

Streeter and Chute looked at each other. Streeter said, "I think he's having a stroke."

"Socket, are you all right?" Chute asked.

But I didn't hear her words. I felt them, understood them like they were my own. I penetrated everything in this world, felt the tree limbs blowing on the mountaintops and the squatty warriors emerging in the distance again. I was everything except the shadow. I got up without much effort, like I levitated onto my feet.

[You've known me your entire existence.] The thought was in my head, but it was not mine. It came from the shadow that had no face.

"Did you do this to me?" I raised my hand, rubbing my fingertips. "Are you making this happen?"

"You're starting to worry me." Chute stepped through the shadow and stopped so the two were superimposed, making her fair complexion a shade darker. "We need to get you back to the skin."

"Yeah, get off the crazy train, Socket," Streeter huffed, gripping the staff with both hands. "I'm going to need some help for the next wave."

"Who are you?" I asked.

The shadow didn't gesture, shrug or say anything. It remained superimposed over Chute's worried expression. Whatever she said after that was lost in the wind. The familiarity of the shadow had a taste and a smell, some sort of presence not generally associated with one of the five senses. I felt it like a thought or an intuition.

"Did you heal me?" I asked.

[You were never broken.]

"Socket, you're freaking me out, here," Chute said.

"I ain't got time to wait for him to come back." Streeter charged past me and my crazy rambling. The tiny Nordic warriors were black as tar, staining the snow as they shoved through the drifts. They were close enough to hear their snarling. Streeter let out a war cry, the same one he let loose before every clash, the same howl that Chute said made him look like a drama queen, and charged ahead to meet them head-on, bringing down the spiked club to crush the first one's skull.

Something squirmed in my belly. I had the vision of a bright star twinkling inside my stomach. A spark that, for a moment, blinded me. I felt my mind wrap around it and fuse with it.

And then things slowed.

Things stopped.

I could see in 360 degrees as if every particle of snow that hung sparkling in midair like tiny Christmas ornaments were my eyes. I did that. I was the one that willed the world to stop, for the wind to die and everything in it to take a time-out while I could think. I didn't intend for things to actually stop, but that's what I wanted and that's what happened. I took one of the snowflakes between my finger and thumb, studying the crystalline detail. It began to melt and water dripped down to my knuckle.

It was dead silent. Dead still.

The shadow was standing in front of Chute. Without the wind, his form shimmered like smoky particles loosely clinging together. I opened my mouth, trying to figure out what the familiar flavor was, trying to figure out just who the shadow was. And then a thought came from somewhere deep inside, some place that had been stored in the lockers of a three-year-old toddler. I was in a bathroom and smelled the scent of a man shaving at the sink. It was a safe smell. The man rinsed the razor and smiled down at me.

I couldn't bring myself to say it, couldn't say the word that I identified with this essence I was experiencing because the man that was shaving was dead. He died when I was five.

"What the hell is going on? Is this some sort of goof?"

I reached for the shadow, but my hand waved through the wispy form, and as it did, the essence tasted stronger, tingling all the way to my stomach, wrenching me with a helpless sense of falling, almost dropping me to my knees. But the essence was unmistakable. *Father.*

[The time has come to know who you are.] The thought had a distinct tone, but it was unlike the voice I remembered as my father's. *[For you to know your true nature.]*

Time wasn't to be measured in that still moment. The hands on a clock would not be moving. At some point, I stepped forward and merged with the shadow, and the essence filled my emptiness, those pockets I did not know existed. Emptiness that yawned inside and sometimes pissed me off, made me sad and pissed me off at being sad. Emptiness for my dad dying and emptiness that he left me to figure things out on my own. Emptiness for having to look at the emptiness in my mother's eyes. Emptiness that left me awake at night, staring at the ceiling, wondering what the hell was the point of living. And now I didn't feel those things. I felt so present. So complete.

When the ground trembled, I realized I'd closed my eyes. The shadow was no longer there. And the ground continued to shake. The snow vibrated and the statue-like sims of Chute and Streeter shook, too. I no longer felt connected with them or the rest of the environment.

On the horizon, the ground broke open and snow spilled inside a widening crevasse that snaked towards me, ripping the ground like

God had grabbed both ends of the world and decided to pull it apart. I watched the rip race under my feet. The falling sensation was back in my stomach because this time I was falling for real, down into the empty blackness that tasted like essence, that sixth sense, only this time it tasted steely and hard.

Blackness was all there was. No sim. Just falling.

I felt the hot needles of my sweaty skin sticking to the armrests of the study hall chair. I opened my eyes back in my skin. A silver ball hovered in front of me. Its surface gleamed like polished metal with a red eyelight beneath the surface. "The three of you must follow," the lookit said.

I was firmly planted in the seat, but still felt the falling.

3

Perp Alley

"JUSTIN HEYWARD STREET," the lookit announced.

"You know, middle names are so unnecessary," Streeter said, sitting forward and rubbing the feeling back into his face.

"Anna Nancy Shuester," the same lookit announced. Chute quickly did the same as Streeter.

"Socket Pablo Greeny." Its red eyelight shot right into my eyes. "The three of you are to follow."

Honestly, I still wasn't sure where I was. I gripped the armrest like my chair had been dropped from a cargo plane. I was still trying to return to my skin. I felt out of sorts, like half of my awareness was somewhere else. Back in my sim?

The lookit wasn't going to wait. It was about to call security when the room suddenly erupted. All the virtualmoders sat up, groaning and cursing, ripping the discs from behind their ears. The lookit's eyelight was spinning, recording the hundreds of study hall sound infractions. It blazed around the room, trying to get control, then called for security and returned to the front row. The substitute teacher was watching a music video, looked up and closed his laptop.

"The three of you must follow," the lookit repeated.

I could barely feel my legs when I sat forward. Chute hooked her finger around mine and led me up the steps like the living dead. The queens, rats, burners, gearheads, jocks and goths and anyone else that couldn't thought-project into virtualmode looked up from their laptops and tablets and stared at us. Virtualmoders were all back in their skin.

"Did you do this, Streeter?" someone shouted. "Did you crash virtualmode?"

"Psssht. Noooo." He wasn't guilty, not this time. Streeter walked faster as wads of paper came flying.

PERP ALLEY CONSISTED of five plastic chairs against the wall. A heavy door with wire-imbedded glass was across from the plastic chairs and behind that were the offices of the dean of boys, the dean of girls, various assistant principals, and the principal. This trip had the dean of boys stamped all over it.

I was feeling better after walking down the hall. The lookits wouldn't let us talk and that was all right, it gave me some time to think. Streeter had already asked what the hell happened. *What happened? I was haunted by a ghost, that's all. Oh, did I mention it was my dead dad? Yeah. Oh, and I stopped time and connected with the entire universe and experienced a moment of spiritual oneness. Any questions?*

Once we sat, I told them about the shadow, that time seemed to stop and the world split open, that it must've been some special weapon the Rimers set off, and blah, blah, blah, I don't know what happened, either. Crazy shit happens all the time in virtualmode.

"The world split open?" Streeter asked.

I described the black crevasse.

"That's serious, Socket. I mean, if you fell inside that rip, you could be disembodied, your awareness floating somewhere in the in-between forever and ever. They did a special on Discovery, virtualmoders that lay there like vegetables for months and months after they got swallowed in a crash."

I didn't bother telling him I did fall in.

Chute was looking more through me, sort of like a cop looking for the truth. I buried my face in my hands when the room started spinning. I wasn't falling, but both my feet weren't exactly on the ground. Chute rubbed my back. I just wanted off the ride.

"I want revenge," Streeter said.

"Just stop," Chute snapped. "We hacked into their world and they taught us a lesson and that's the end of it. Besides, you said it yourself, we crashed the world, so it probably doesn't even exist anymore. You should be worried they'll find us and make us pay for it."

"Naw, they'll have safeguards against a hiccup like that; it'll snap right back together. Besides, those shitheads aren't going to report us because they were duping. Those little black things were automated versions of a dupe to avoid detection, like empty manikins with a single mission. They probably blew up Socket. Hell, we could report *them* to the cops and have *them* arrested for duping. But that wouldn't be any fun. I'd rather make them pay."

"They can dupe if they want to, it's a private world."

"Um, hello. Duplicating is illegal, in any form or fashion. Read your virtualmode code laws: Any attempt to duplicate your identity, whether for business, recreation or just plain whatever, is not allowed under any circumstances. Period, the end. You know it, I know it. I don't give a shit if they did it in their dreams. You can't dupe."

"I really don't give two craps," Chute said. "Why would anyone care what they do in their world? Stupid."

He walked several steps away, scratching his thick shag of brown curls like he needed a time-out from stupidity. When he returned, he had an intense look of concentration that flattened his face, making him look more like a frog than usual. He said slowly, "You don't listen in class, do you? First of all, I'm just going to ignore the improvement in safety that virtualmode laws have done, just forget all that. The world is going digital, Chute. In five years, half the world's population will be able to virtualmode, creating a digital reality with digital bodies and digital homes and everything, get it? People will be doing business from their homes, commerce and manufacturing and colleges will all be in virtualmode. If people start duplicating their identities, how the hell are you going to know what's real and what's not? You won't! So you can't dupe, Chute. Get it? You want to write that down so you don't forget? No. Duping. Period."

Chute jumped out of her seat and shook her finger right in his face. "Don't take that tone with me. I don't live and breathe for the virtualmode like you, so I don't know the stupid laws. Next time you talk like that, I'm stuffing you in a locker."

Streeter surrendered. "Hey, don't take your sexual frustrations out on me. I didn't blow Socket's mind." He snapped his fingers. "Socket, come back from the dead, buddy. Anytime now."

I looked at Streeter snapping. I shook my head, returning from a dreamy state. *I'm back in the skin,* I had to remind myself. Maybe Streeter was right. There were already studies suggesting that excessive virtualmoding was causing a disconnect between mind and body, where one would have a hard time distinguishing between reality and fantasy.

I needed a three-day suspension. Maybe stay off virtualmode the whole time. Streeter would bitch, but I needed a break.

Flip-flops slapped from around the corner and a girl with short, black hair flip-flopped in our direction. Streeter stared up at her with his tongue about to roll out. She had to walk around him, flicked her eyes at Chute rubbing my back, and went into the administrative office, but not before a sudden drop in altitude pulled my stomach through the floor. I hung onto the chair for dear life.

[Socket Greeny, in trouble again? Shocker.]

"Did you hear that?" I said. "Did you hear what she was thinking?"

Chute clenched my arm tighter. Streeter and Chute looked at each other, exchanged knowing glances; then he sat on the other side of me. "Dude, you sure you're all right? I mean, you're starting to scare me a little with the wacky talk. You sure your nojakk isn't flaring up." Streeter tapped his cheek. "You hear me now? Hear me now?"

My cheek vibrated and I heard him through the nojakk seed imbedded in my cheek. But I heard the girl thinking. A thought was a thought, not a goddamn voice chiming from a nojakk. I waved him off and buried my face in my hands again.

"Listen, buddy." Streeter dropped his hand on my shoulder. "You're not hearing voices or thoughts or stopping time. You're just in a fuzzy area right now, reconnecting with the skin. It happens all the time; don't press it. Take some deep breaths, in with the good air, out with the bad." Streeter demonstrated deep breathing. "Don't crack on me. I need you."

"You're not taking him back to the Rime," Chute said.

"Don't be hasty. And you're not his mom."

I did take some deep breaths and did feel better. This was like a bad dream that took longer than usual to fade. The office door opened. The secretary stuck her head out. "All right, y'all. Mr. Carter wants to see you now."

We got up. I felt fine but suddenly realized I was mad-crazy starving. I could feel my ribs poking through my shirt, like I hadn't eaten in days. Maybe I was getting a bit hypoglycemic. There was a girl in my social studies class that was hypoglycemic and she had symptoms like that. Maybe she forgot to mention the hallucinations. And thought-reading.

"Not you, Socket," she said. "Your mother will pick you up at the curb in a few minutes. You need to go right out."

"My mom?"

"She called right after y'all got caught doing whatever you were doing, and said you have a family emergency. Don't worry, you're still going to be suspended."

"Oh, man." Streeter stepped away from me like he might get infected.

I watched the two get escorted inside and past the secretary's desk. Chute turned and pointed at her cheek, mouthing the words *call me.* Streeter and Chute wouldn't be feeling too bad about their fate. Streeter lived with his grandparents and he would make up a story as to why he was home and they would believe it. Chute's dad would be upset, but he was always easy on her. But my mom?

Shit storm.

4

IN THE MOODY

MOM PULLED into the parking lot. Her car was a silver, square thing. It didn't look like any model I'd seen on the road, certainly not one Ford or Chevy manufactured. It came from work, and like most things concerning her employer, I was clueless.

She was looking at the soccer field, where a bunch of students were testing hovering jetter discs. Some new company donated them to the school, said the jetter boards had antigravity boosters that could carry three hundred pounds and they wanted the virtualmoder students to learn how to ride them. They said they were sponsoring a new game that would revolutionize sports. Tacket or tagghet or something like that. Ordinarily, that would get my interest, but anything that had to do with school and/or school spirit was immediately off my to-do list.

When I got in the car, she handed me two breakfast bars in white wrappers. "How'd you know I was hungry?"

She didn't answer, just eased through the parking lot. I tore open the first one and nearly swallowed it without chewing. My mouth filled with saliva and my stomach roared. It was like a shot of adrenaline tingling under my scalp. I chewed the second bar and laid my head back. Finally, I felt back to my skin. *What the hell are in these things?* The wrapper had no writing on it, no label, and no ingredients. I licked the inside of it.

We were on the interstate heading towards Charleston. Mom gripped the wheel like it offended her. The skin over her knuckles pulsed. But she grabbed everything that way: coffee mugs, doorknobs, and little soft, innocent puppies. She stared blankly through the windshield. Maybe I was in trouble, I wouldn't really know for a while. We didn't talk about things that involved feeling.

That's the Greeny way.

I tapped up music on my nojakk and watched the traffic.

HALF AN HOUR LATER, we started over the 2.5-mile, cable-stayed bridge that crossed over the Cooper River. "We going shopping or something?" I asked.

She readjusted the stranglehold. "I'm taking you by the office."

"Awesome," I muttered. I didn't want her to hear that, but it was so silent in that car you could hear a sand flea fart. But she didn't take the bait, just kept her eyes ahead with one hand on the wheel and the other tucked under her arm. She was hiding her right hand.

"Thought you quit that," I said.

"Nothing wrong with a moody," she answered.

She fidgeted in her seat, then calmly put the moody cube in her purse and drank from a bottle of water. Her thumb was red and swollen. I knew about moody cubes, heard the warnings in school every day. Some company convinced the FDA that a little black square could stimulate dopamine production by relaying messages through the nervous system, and relieve symptoms of depression and anxiety. They argued that because the brain was essentially a poppy field producing *natural* happy sedatives, it was nothing like narcotics.

The FDA said sure, but it should at least be prescribed and the company responded, *Yeah, we're okay with that.*

I sometimes pressed her into giving up the habit because that couldn't be good. But sometimes I couldn't stand that dead-zone look on her face and just let her get some relief. I looked back out the window and watched the ships below, wishing I could smell the water or the salty South Carolina breeze, but there was nothing getting inside that car. It's like we were sealed inside a tomb.

MOM DROVE THROUGH DOWNTOWN, waiting more often for College of Charleston students and tourists than actual traffic. We passed the art dealers and law offices and souvenir vendors and old retired horses pulling antique-looking carriages full of New Yorkers and Midwest-erners listening to the driver, sitting backwards on the front, telling ghost stories and rehearsed jokes about the good old South and the charm of the Holy City.

Her office was a block past the regal steps of the Custom House. It was just a simple black door wedged between an art gallery and a chocolate shop. No sign hanging on a rod perpendicular to the building or a window to see inside, just small letters on the door. *Paladin Nation, Inc.*

They were in desperate need of an advertising agency; they were barely a step up from a manhole. In fact, if you didn't look right at the door, you didn't notice it. I walked past it three times once. Mom slowed up to the curb just as a man stepped out of the door. A young guy in good shape with a proper haircut opened the car door for her. He didn't bother with me.

Mom waited at the office door. She pushed her hair behind her ear, it fell back, and took a deeper breath than usual. I thought she was more distant than usual. In fact, she felt cold. No, she *tasted* cold, like some sort of essence. I shook it off. Didn't want to go there. I'd been grounded in my skin for a whole hour and preferred it that way. But I couldn't help noticing her coldness brought a taste of sadness with it. Sometimes I didn't even feel related to her, like she was just a stranger watching over me, like I was some sort of orphan. *Good times.*

———

THE DOOR LED UP creaky steps to a tiny room. There was a receptionist area behind a counter with a computer, desk, and files, but there was never anyone there.

Mom told me to wait for her, she'd be right out, then went through the only door to the left of the receptionist area. I never went beyond that door. I had a vague memory of going beyond once with my dad when I was real little, but there wasn't much but a short hallway with three doors. The only thing I remember after that is a blue light and then I fell asleep, dreaming of caves and jungles.

I sat in the waiting room and slouched down. No magazine rack, no television or pictures of beaches with birds. I crossed my arms and laid my head back and closed my eyes, but the slightest motion in my stomach made me bolt upright. Not going there. Nope.

I slid my fingers over the black iHolo strap around my wrist. An image illuminated above the strap like a holographic screen no matter which way I turned my wrist. I pushed the icons around, looked at a playlist I'd put together earlier that week, and uploaded it to the nojakk, then booted up the music. While an acoustic guitar echoed inside my head, I went to my email and noticed the news headline.

International Virtualmode Blackout.

The story began in a virtualmode network hub inside a warehouse with a single aisle going between lines of blue, pulsing orbs, five feet in diameter and encased in clear boxes, with lab technicians wearing white coats and hardhats inspecting them. I'd seen portals before; the school had one in a basement below the Pit. It was the powercell that transported a user's awareness into virtualmode. I'd heard physicists explain how the intense power and density of portals allowed them to transcend time and space and interact simultaneously. Trippy shit. But no one cared how they worked, just that they worked.

"Sometime around 10:43, Eastern Standard, virtualmode experienced its first blackout," a reporter's voice announced as the lab technicians observed the portals. I turned the music down and sat up. "According to sources, a surge from somewhere in the world caused an international crash of all virtualmode worlds. Authorities say the balance of power has been restored and that normal activity has resumed, although there seems to be some confusion as to where the surge originated."

That's when the rip occurred. Did I make the whole thing crash? *Impossible.* Those portals were like a thousand nuclear reactors doing some sort of cold fusion. How in the hell—

Zzzzzsthhhp.

The iHolo image scattered for a second.

I shut down the music and felt the floor shudder. It came from the door. I was remembering the blue light again when the door opened and Mom was followed by a man. She stood to the side and let him pass. I jumped up.

The man walked fluidly. He was a bit older than Mom. His hair was streaked with gray and his face clean-shaven, what most women would call a handsome man with a smoldering attraction. He stopped only a few feet away, but the room was so small he couldn't get much farther away. I wondered if I should bolt for the stairwell just in case a mugging was about to go down.

But then I *tasted* a taste, an essence. It was deep and sort of minty. Potent. I'd experienced that before. Maybe seen this guy before. Behind the door?

I looked at Mom. Christ, no one was saying anything. This was beyond awkward. The man was looking through me, studying me, like a doctor without the stethoscope and white coat. If he asked me to take my shirt off, it was going to be stairway city.

"It's a pleasure to meet you, Socket." He extended his hand. I shook it. "Now that you're grown up."

I nodded, wondering why it felt like I was meeting the president.

"My name is Walter Diggs."

"Nice to meet you."

"It's been a while since I saw you last, but I'm sure you don't remember. You were only that big." He put his hand down, the universal sign for a short person.

I was struggling with the memory of going through the door when I was *that big* and linking it to the minty essence, but the memory ended up in caves and jungles. Then I remembered colored bats coming out of the trees. A real messed-up dream.

"I knew your father," Walter said. "He was a fine man, he was. I was damn proud to have known him. No one could replace someone like Trey Greeny."

Oh, shit. Is this the stepfather talk? I'm not trying to replace your father, Socket, no one could. But I'm in love with your mother and you're going to have a new baby brother. Now go clean your room, asshole.

Walter started laughing. He looked over at Mom, who returned his laughter with just barely a flicker of the corner of her mouth. He looked back at me. It was getting weird.

"What I'm trying to say is if you're half the person your father was, you'll have a lot to offer the world. But I suspect you're twice that."

"Thank you, Mr. Diggs, but I'm not sure what any of this means."

"Things are a little sketchy, I know. But it'll make sense real soon. Your mother is going to take you to meet some people in our facilities."

"I don't even know what you do." I shuffled back until my leg hit the chair.

"You will, soon." *Wink.*

No one winks when something really shitty is about to happen. Right? "Should I be worried right about now?" I looked at Mom. She was still cold. Walter offered a smile that, compared to Mom's, was like the sun.

"I can't tell you how happy I am to see you grown up. I look forward to working with you." He squeezed my shoulder, made eye-contact with Mom, and then was through the door from where he came, closing it behind him.

Mom opened the door to the stairs.

"Wait, what just happened?"

"There's a lot to explain," Mom said. She was itching for that moody. "I'll tell you everything on the way."

"We're not going with him?" I asked.

"The facility is a long way from here," she said. "But it won't take long to get there."

"We're flying?"

"No."

Now what in the hell does that mean?

5

Wormholed

THE PARKING ATTENDANT was waiting out front with the door open. Mom took the first left turn and then another left down a narrow alley wedged between tall buildings. No one would notice it from the street, and if they saw it, wouldn't think to drive a car down it. It ended at a brick wall and backing out would seem impossible without swiping a door handle. There was a garage door on the left, which would've been directly below the office.

I had a feeling we were going wherever minty-man Walter Diggs went, although getting back in the car for a trip around the block made no sense. Mom had a whole life of secrecy. When she wasn't home, I'd go through her files and look under her mattress and through her closet to find out what she was doing. Now the jig was up and I was minutes away from everything. I always thought it would be more fun to find out.

The garage door opened and she eased into the lightless space as the door closed behind us. "This is going to feel funny," she said.

"You mean funny, ha-ha?" I answered. I was starting to squirm. The falling feeling was coming back.

"We're going through a wormhole, like a puncture in the fabric of time and space."

"Where we going?" I said, almost casually. Why not? Today wasn't making any sense, why not finish it with a trip through a rip in time. And space.

Mom laughed, sort of. It was mostly a hiccup, but not a smile, and certainly no joy.

A door in front of us began to open, blue light spilling out. "Close your eyes," she said. "And make sure your tongue is pushed against the roof of your mouth."

The blue light engulfed me. I clenched my eyes shut, grabbing onto the door. I felt like one of those cartoons getting steamrolled flat as paper. Thought I was going to scream, then puke. I didn't see blue. I didn't see anything. My lungs were burning and I gulped for air, drooling on my shirt when I realized we were through.

"Oh, Jesus," I blurted.

It was night. We were still in the car, although it wasn't moving. Instead, we were idling on a flat piece of ground with miles of boulder-strewn wasteland ahead of us without a road in sight. At the far end was a sheer-faced cliff. The full moon revealed streaks of ochre like ancient bloodstains. It stood like a monolith, like God had plopped down a massive block of granite and said, "End of the world, assholes."

"This society has existed for as long as history's been recorded." Mom took a breath and touched the center panel. Lights appeared on the speedometer; holographic images illuminated the dash with maps and data and green dots and red dots and bullshit that looked more like a fighter jet than car. "We protect humankind from extinction."

"From what?"

"Once upon a time, it was natural disaster and plague and wars. In this era, the threat of extinction comes from humans." Her eyes appeared deeper set in the moonlight and the glow of the instruments. "Humankind lacks understanding. As a species, we are still in our infancy. Our potential is limitless, but first we must survive to realize it."

"Are you one of them?"

"In a way."

"What's that mean?"

"It means the answer is complicated. There's a lot to understand; you'll have to be patient. For now, just know that we can do things that normal people can't."

She touched the control panel. Something thumped beneath the car. And then we were moving forward, only we weren't rolling. We were hovering. The car was flying. Not fast like spaceship fast, it was more like a slow hover that crossed over the impossible terrain. The wheels had folded beneath the car. No one was getting across this ground without one of these.

"You got to be shitting me."

"Watch your language, Socket."

I sat back, realizing I was still holding onto the door. We were halfway to the red cliff when I relaxed. "What's this place called?" I asked. "This club, or society."

"The Paladin Nation."

"This is it, here?" I pointed at the looming cliff.

"No, it's all over the world. This is just one of the compounds."

I watched the cliff get closer. "We're not in South Carolina anymore."

She almost smiled, I could feel it.

THERE WAS no door in the side of the mountain. Instead, we passed through it, like it was only an apparition, into an enormous cavern. Mom touched a few buttons on the console and the car gently sank to the ground.

The cavern was dome-shaped, complete with authentic dripping stalactites. *Caves and jungles? Maybe that wasn't a dream.*

Mom pushed the steering wheel up and locked it out of the way. She gathered items from the backseat. I still hadn't let go. I had just taken my first ride in a flying car, hit a transportation wormhole, and now I was parked inside a mountain somewhere in the world that had mountains.

A large, gray sphere emerged from the wall. Several more appeared, floating inches above the ground like supersized lookits. They took positions around the car, waiting.

"Servys," Mom said. "Technology is a bit more advanced here. You're going to see some things that don't exist in the outside world yet." She had her thumb buried in the moody again. A look of eerie relief was on her face.

"I wish you'd stop that."

She closed her eyes, pushing her thumb in deeper. "There's so much to do, Socket. I just need to catch my breath."

"You don't have to save the world."

She tucked her hair behind her ear with her free hand. "Sometimes the world needs you and you have to be there. You'll understand one day. And I hope you find more strength than your mother."

I gently pulled her thumb from the moody, red and swollen. "You're plenty strong."

"Let's hope so."

She opened her door and stepped out. I turned to mine—a silver man was at the window. He had no face.

6

Faceless

HIS EGG-SHAPED HEAD WAS FEATURELESS. No eyes or nose, mouth, ears or chin. Just a smooth egghead with an eyelight pointed at me.

"Welcome to the Garrison, Master Socket." He waved a silver hand. "Do you need help exiting the vehicle?"

If I hadn't seen the colors move on his face, I would've sworn a real person said it. He looked like he was from a movie, standing six feet tall on two legs: A humanoid mech. The arms and legs were sinewy like an Olympian. And to top things off, he wore a loose plum-colored overcoat, sleeveless, cinched at the waist. But sure, why not. This was already shaping up like a dream, why not send in the flying dragons.

Mom was out of the car, explaining something to him. The servys repositioned themselves around her. One went to the back of the car and returned with her briefcase firmly gripped by an arm that had grown from its spherical body. The robe-wearing silver mech pointed at me. I was still grabbing the door. So far I'd looked at everything through the safety of a window. Getting out was another level. I reluctantly opened the door.

I've been here before.

It was the smell. Pleasantly musty and wet. Ancient. I was here long, long ago. Maybe it was take-your-kid-to-work day. I always thought it was a dream. Same cave, same smell.

"Socket," Mom said, "this is Spindle." The silver mech placed his hand on his belly and gestured with a small bow. "He's my assistant. He'll be your guide for the day."

"You're leaving?"

"I have to attend an urgent meeting." She touched my arm, like an apology. "Afterward, we'll meet in my office."

"Are you kidding me? You're just going to leave me here with... with..." Spindle's eyelight stared at me. "You can't do this to me, Mom. This isn't right. I've got crazy things in my head and you're flying a car and then there's the wormhole." I paced around, thinking about taking a hit from her moody. "This is bullshit."

"Don't curse." Her left eye ticked. "We'll discuss it later. In the meantime, Spindle will escort you to security assignment. You're going to like him. You'll be safe."

Oh, great. Telling me I'll be safe meant I was in danger, like when someone says they ain't scared means they're really scared shitless. But Mom wasn't prone to signs of affection. It didn't happen often, so I was caught by surprise when she gently placed her hand on my cheek. "I'll see you in a couple hours."

[It'll be all right.]

That's what she was thinking. Instead of telling me where I was and why, she just wanted me to know it was all going to be all right. The last time she said that, she took me to the doctor for shots. While I waited, the nurse told me we were waiting on *a little stick,* then rammed a needle in my ass. I would've preferred a better explanation, then and now, but her touch and smile seemed to be enough for the moment. What else was I going to do? I didn't know how to fly that car, and even if I did, where the hell was I going?

Mom was off to the only door in the cavern. The door slid open and closed behind her, leaving me with the muscular android.

"Do you have any questions?" Spindle asked.

His posture was friendly, his face bubbly yellow and orange. He was completely unaware I had just been squeezed through time and space for the first time like a birthing canal. But he waited patiently, the eyelight glowing, like a video game character waiting for my response.

"Okay. Ummm... where am I?"

"You are in the Garrison. It is one of many global training grounds of the Paladin Nation."

"Right. The Paladin Nation." I glanced around the cave. "Why haven't I heard about this place until about three minutes ago?"

"There are many things you have not heard of." He gestured to the servys still bobbing around us. "Nanoplastine technology, for instance. These servys are composed of cellular-sized nanomechs that make up a generic round body, much like the cells of your body. A processor is located at the core and can shift the cellular nanomechs into whatever form is necessary. Very useful. Humanity has not been granted access to this technology yet."

"What, you don't like to share?"

"Many discoveries are still considered too dangerous. When the circumstances are right, they will be released."

"These Paladins," I said, "they're human?"

"That is correct."

"What gives them the right to horde all this stuff?"

"The Paladin Nation is a much more evolved race of humans. The general public cannot be trusted with such power. It would be like giving a gun to a two-year-old child. In the hands of a responsible adult, a gun can be used safely. However, a two-year-old child would likely harm himself." He pushed his shoulders back and tilted his head. "Does that make sense?"

"But adults still shoot each other, so I'm not sure the gun analogy works."

"That is why it is a perfect analogy. Even guns are used irresponsibly. Can you imagine what the same people would do with some of these magnificent advancements?"

Spindle waited for my response. His facial colors were muted yellow, fading back to silver. He turned to the servys. His face jumped with dark blues, but he said nothing out loud. The servys drifted back to the walls and merged through them as if the openings were all there, just masked with the illusion of rocky walls.

"If you have no more questions, we can proceed to security assignment. We can begin our journey with a friendly gesture." He held up his hand, fingers spread. "Stick it, Master Socket."

I looked at his expectant hand. "Do what?"

"Stick it." He shook his hand. "It is a friendly handshake that kids do. You stick it."

I held up my hand like his, expecting something like a high five.

"No, no, you stick your fist in the palm of my hand."

I did like he said, only in slow motion. *Where's this going?* He wrapped his soft, fleshy fingers around my fist and shook. "Do you see?" he said. "You stuck it."

"What, you mean, like, Paladin kids are doing this?"

"No, kids in society. Kids like you do this, yes. I hope I did it right. It is a friendly gesture. Did I do it too soon? Should we be better acquainted before such customs?"

"I'll be honest, I never heard of it."

"You have not?" His head looked yellow again, splattered with specks of black. "My data says this is very popular."

"Where'd you get the data?"

"The data originated from a teenage website named Pops. It is rated the number one virtualmode website for teenagers in your age bracket."

"There's your problem. Pops is for little teeny girls and boys wanting to meet their favorite boy bands and movie stars. About as stupid as it gets."

"Is that true?" The colors changed. "I will have to rewrite my database."

"Good idea. And don't ever do that gay handshake again."

"Please do not curse, Master Socket. It is unbecoming of you."

"I didn't curse."

"I believe you did when you used the term 'gay' as a derogatory reference."

Now the colors on his faceplate were dark. I was being scolded by a robot. And he wasn't moving until I complied, I thought. "Yeah, okay. No problem. Consider the word erased."

"Very good." The faceplate brightened. He stepped aside and gestured to the door. "Let us proceed to security assignment."

WE WENT through the same door as Mom. It was an elevator.

"This is a leaper," Spindle said. "It will take us to any part of the Garrison in a matter of seconds. It can move as fast as two hundred miles per hour."

"Two hundred? We'll be pancakes."

"Not to worry. Antigravity floaters offset the velocity. You will not feel motion." Spindle stepped inside. "This is the main mode of transportation within the Garrison. Centuries ago, when the Paladin Nation was in its infancy, these were just tunnels. Technology has advanced."

"Yeah. No shhhi... no kidding. I take it this thing wouldn't go anywhere without clearance."

"You would not be here if you did not have clearance." It seemed like he was refraining from laughing at something so stupid because, clearly, you're not getting here without a wormhole and a flying car. "Spindle, access code 0452B. Security assignment room, level 1. Prepare for new arrival."

There was a sharp pang in my stomach, and then it was gone. The door opened to a short, doorless hallway. So far I'd been in a cave and now a white hallway. For all the technology, Paladins weren't flashy.

Spindle started down the corridor and stopped halfway. "Here we are."

"Where?"

"Doors are composed of plasmic particulates creating the illusion of a solid surface." He pushed his hand through the white wall in front of us. "Much like the cliff you drove through."

I knocked on a solid wall. "It's not working."

"That is because you are touching the wall." His face lit with sunny yellows, shaped a little like a smile. *Dumbass.*

"Are you laughing at me?"

"Laughing? I do not experience emotions, Master Socket. However, it does appear odd you are trying to push through a wall when the doorway is right next to you."

"Yeah, well, I don't see a doorway."

"Not yet." He walked through the wall, poking his head out several seconds later. "Are you coming?"

"I'm not used to walking through walls."

"Here." He extended his hand. "I am programmed to assist you."

An odd color lit his face. He lightly pulled me through—like a sheet of frigid air—into a large room. It was empty and sterile. How exciting. Let me guess, dinner is white rice with water.

"This is the security assignment room. I will assign you level one access. If you will have a seat, I will start the process very soon."

"You mean, on the floor?"

Spindle crossed the room in five steps. As he did, it reshaped. A chair emerged from the wall. End tables popped out of the floor. The white walls turned dark green with burnt orange trim. Pictures formed on the walls with views of oceans and deserts. A window appeared with a view of scenic mountains, a flock of birds passing by.

"Now that's what I'm talking about." I sat on the chair and felt it reform to fit my body, leaving me weightless. "This room... it's made from the same stuff as those servys?"

"Yes." He was busy with a control panel on the wall. "Our rooms can suit any purpose. I hope you are comfortable. We will begin in a minute."

A vase emerged from a table with flowers. I took a white daisy and sniffed. It smelled like a flower. The room was a regular room in any house across the world, yet it wasn't. It was buried in a mountain made up of tiny cell-sized robots that made a flower smell like a flower and a window overlook a mountain. I could dig this.

"Can I ask you something?" I said.

"You may ask me a question at any time, Master Socket."

"What's my mom do?"

"She is the commander's assistant."

"Commander? You mean this is like a military?"

"It is not a military, but it has order. There is protocol. Any society must have rules and it must have leaders. Commander has been traditionally used."

"So my mom, she's a Paladin?"

The eyelight circled to the back of his head and focused on me while his hands continued to work. "No, Master Socket. Paladins have inherent abilities that she does not possess. She has developed some mild extrasensory powers, but she is a civilian, and she is vital to the Paladin Nation. Has she not told you these things?"

"We don't talk a whole lot."

"But she is your mother." He stopped working. "Your caregiver."

"She's been a little busy. Since Dad died."

His face sparkled. "I knew your father."

"You did?"

"Yes." His eyelight drifted upward, thinking. "Your father was a remarkable man. He was head of mech design and maintenance. Your father was involved in my prototype design and personally worked on my bodyshell."

"He was a Paladin?"

"He expressed Paladin traits, much more than your mother, but never fully realized them. He worked in the Garrison and was not often involved in missions. The Paladin Nation has been watching to see if you would inherit his traits. I believe you caught them by surprise."

"What's that mean?"

"All the details will be revealed to you soon."

My dad died for a secret agency and no one ever told me. That's super. No doubt she knew I was next in line to follow in his footsteps. What else did Mom have in the family vault?

I buried my face in my hands and took a deep breath. *I want off the crazy train.*

"Was he a good father to you?" Spindle asked.

To me? He was asking like my father was a good father to him. Did he think we were brothers? I shook my head, my voice echoing through my hands. "I guess. I don't remember much."

"I remember your father quite well, from the very first day he ignited my awareness panel." His eyelight drifted up again. He was lost in thought for several seconds while colors flashed on his face. "We spent every day together in the beginning, perhaps the entire first year of my existence. He worked on my programming to perfect my learning impulse. After that, I saw him once a week. That is unusual, you realize, for a creator to remain after programming is complete. Your father did that."

He had that drifting look again.

"You miss him?" I said.

"Miss him? I am not sure what you mean."

It feels like there's something missing, that's what. It's longing. Sadness. It's all of the above. "It feels... empty."

"Empty?" He contemplated that, feeling his belly with his hand. His face brightened in a *got it* moment. "There is something missing. A... hole in my awareness. Not a hole, but an..." His eyelight focused on me. "*Emptiness.* Yes, I do sense that. I do miss him, Master Socket. Thank you for teaching me."

The colors on his face ran through the full spectrum, brighter and brighter. I didn't consider emptiness something he needed to thank me for. For me, it ached. But for Spindle, it was obviously something joyous to experience. *Whatever.*

He turned back to the control panel, then said, "If you hold still, a body print is being scanned and a security access level assigned."

Tiny shock waves started at my feet and ended at the top of my head. The control panel folded back into the wall. The pictures, vase and flowers dissolved. I stood and the chair disappeared. The room was empty once again.

"You have been assigned level one access." Spindle walked through a dim arching outline on the wall. I could see the doorway now. No more walking into walls for me. I followed him into the hall.

"You should be able to see doorways to rooms you have clearance to enter," Spindle said. "Do you see them?"

There was a similar outline that simulated a doorway at each end of the hall. I nodded. "Got it."

"Good," he said. "Agent Pike is waiting."

"Agent Pike? Who's that?"

"He will be conducting your preliminary evaluation."

"Whoa, wait a second. I thought we were going to Mom's office. I don't know anyone named Pike."

"All potential cadets are evaluated for potential traits upon arrival. It is the first assignment after security clearance."

"I'm a cadet? Wait, when did that happen? I didn't sign up for anything."

Spindle remained absolutely still, assessing the conversation. "Why do you think you are here, Master Socket?"

"I don't have a clue."

Long pause, again. "You were assigned to the Garrison because you exhibited exceptional abilities that need to be assessed."

"When the hell did I do that?"

His face darkened, but he let the *hell* word slide. "It will all be explained to you after the preliminary evaluation. However, it is imperative that we remain on schedule. You need to report to Agent Pike immediately."

I grabbed him as he turned. "Wait, I'm not going anywhere until you tell me what's going to happen at this... evaluation."

"Agent Pike is a minder; he has extraordinary psychic ability. He will assess your potential."

"So I *am* a Paladin?"

Pause. "That is up to Agent Pike to decide." He stepped quickly before I could grab him again. I was trapped in a short hallway inside a mountain about to meet a man named Pike. *It's just a little stick, Socket.*

We walked into a leaper at the other end of the hall. "We will be traveling at 189 mph in a northwest direction exactly 33 degrees above ground level, covering 5,133 feet. Are you ready?"

Hell no. A falling sensation twisted my gut.

"We have arrived."

It was another short hallway, a gray archway at the far end. Spindle walked with his shoulders square, his head held high. My knees were unreliable, but I forced myself to follow. I wanted to hold his arm, but I wasn't going to look like a pussy. Even if I felt like one.

"You will have to enter alone," Spindle said. "I will wait here."

I brushed my fingertips across the chilly gray archway. "So you're saying he's just going to ask questions, nothing else?"

"Yes," Spindle said. "And assess you."

Assess me. Goddamn, I don't like the way that sounds. "Where's Mom?"

"She is sorry." His fluid voice faltered, just a bit. "She is very aware of you."

Was that supposed to calm me down? Don't tell me the truth or I'll freak out. I was turning numb and couldn't stop nodding.

"Agent Pike." Spindle patted my shoulder. "He is waiting."

The weakness in my knees was now in my chest. If I waited any longer, I was going to fill my shorts. As I saw it, there was no choice. Nowhere to run. *The nurse never says the shot's going to hurt. She'll say it's just pressure, that's all you'll feel.* I put my foot through the archway, felt Spindle's hand slip off my shoulder, and plunged to the other side. *But we all know that shot's going to hurt like hell.*

7

PIKED

PRESSURE.

It was around me as soon as I entered, wrapping around my body and dimpling my skin like a golf ball. A frail man sat on a chair, his hands on his thighs. Stubble shaded his scalp. His narrow sunglasses partially wrapped around his head, the lenses convex and black.

"Have a seat." His voice was clipped, cold and dry.

A similar chair emerged from the floor in front of him. I pulled it away. We didn't need to sit that close. Tiny cracks appeared around his mouth. *More pressure.*

[Agent Pike has mental pressure at level one. The subject is feeling discomfort, but seems to be controlling his nerve response unconsciously.]

The thought was in my head. I looked around the room, white and empty, and there was no one here except me and this gecko-looking nutjob.

Agent Pike twitched. Nothing noticeable. His eyebrows lifted a few microns. How did I notice that? *Gecko.* There, it happened again. He heard me. *Is that right, Mr. Gecko?*

"I am Agent Pike," he said, no warmer than his greeting.

A servy emerged from the wall. Three arms grew from the middle of its body. I pulled my arm away. It stopped and turned its eyelight to Agent Pike.

"The servy simply needs to monitor your vital signs and take a few samples. It will be painless."

The eyelight returned to me. I could've fought the thing, but they were going to get samples one way or another. I had the feeling I was going to need all my strength by the time this "evaluation" ended. One of its arms wrapped around my elbow, turning it numb. The other two arms touched various parts of my back, neck, and chest.

"You performed an unauthorized timeslice today at 11:25 a.m.," Agent Pike said.

"Yeah, I didn't do anything."

"Timeslicing is a stoppage of relative time. Since this incident, you have heard random thoughts. Has this not happened to you?"

I don't like this guy.

"We know this to be true, but your cooperation will make this transaction easier."

He didn't need me to answer. He *wanted* me to answer. So I nodded. Fine. There's your *transaction*, weasel.

The servy pulled its rubbery arms off and merged back into the wall. Three spots of blood beaded on my arm. *Blood, skin, tissue, muscle. You forgot a chunk of brain.*

Agent Pike's eyebrows shifted again. *More pressure.*

The dimpling sensation was deeper, more intense. I grabbed the bottom of the chair. A line of sweat popped up on my lip. That last wave went deep, like the dentist forgot to numb me before drilling.

"Only Paladins have the ability to cease relative time," he said. "It is not magic. We have the ability to alter our metabolism to move and think infinitely faster than the ordinary human, to *experience* time stopping. The ability can be performed only in short bursts before the body consumes all its energy. You were very hungry after timeslicing, were you not?"

He paused. *We know this to be true.*

"Your timeslicing ability was activated by an unknown presence that approached in the form of a shadow. This person was traced to the Garrison, but we do not know the identity." His nostrils flared, blowing hot air. "Tell me who the shadow is."

I barely remembered what happened; how would I know who the shadow was? This guy was a moron if he thought—

My eardrums popped. The air thickened.

"You are sixteen years old." Agent Pike's voice was now unusually loud, slightly echoing. "Paladin cadets do not timeslice until they are twenty. Your activation is an anomaly." His lips moved softly, no more than a whisper, but the words rang. "WHO ARE YOU, SOCKET GREENY?"

[Agent Pike, back down the mental pressure.]

His stare locked me in the chair. I couldn't move. It was a full-blown seizure. The chair legs rattled.

[Agent Pike! You are ordered to back off! The subject is unstable; you must stop the pressure immediately!]

A black tunnel collapsed around me. My head split. No, not my head. *My mind.* Pike went looking for answers. Psychic fingers pushed inside like cold spikes. I let out a howl that died in the dense air. Memories hurtled out of the blackness, falling at random. Things I'd forgotten played like movies.

Two years old. Dad pulled me from the car and Mom came around. The room was large and dank. Musty. *The parking cave.* Dad carried me and his footsteps echoed. A man greeted him. Shook his hand.

"He's showing signs," Dad said.

The man ruffled my hair. His breath minty. I hid my face in Dad's shoulder. "We'll keep an eye on him," the man said.

Icy pain cut me. Pike dug deeper.

I was four, holding Dad's hand. The carnival lights illuminated the night that smelled like straw and sugar. I ate something fried on a stick. Dad tore off a piece, popping it in his mouth. "You want to go on that one, Socket?" he said.

A capsule ride shot straight up, disappearing above the lights.

"Trey," Mom said, "I don't think that's a good idea. He'll get scared."

I held his rough hand and we climbed inside the capsule. It was humid and smelled like puke. We strapped into the seat and I was thinking Mom was right. I grabbed Dad's arm when we blasted off, burying my face in his coat.

"It's all right, Socket," he said. "It'll be all right."

Mom was waiting for us when it was over. She was wringing her hands, but she was smiling. *Smiling.*

Pike plunged deeper. Memories popped like bubbles, overlapping each other. Confusing one with the other. I was spinning. Faces passed. Days went by. The memory wheel stopped.

I was five. The colorless sky was cold.

Men were dressed in dark uniforms with white gloves, standing in line. They lowered a casket into the ground, a flag draped over it. Dirt thudded on the lid. A few people cried, but most were expressionless, like soldiers that knew the line of duty. Mom was dressed in black. Her face was sallow. Eyes were sunk in the dead zone.

A man rustled my hair. "Your father was a good man."

His breath was minty. My stomach was hard and cold; that block of ice I would carry the rest of my life had already formed.

Memories fell faster, each one stacking on top of the next. Pike flipped through them like playing cards, each one ripped from somewhere dark and quiet. The catalogue of my life reeled in front of me.

I was tearing.

He was coming in. I couldn't keep him out. I wasn't big enough to contain him.

The memory of the Rime appeared, fast-forwarded to the shadow. The view was fading. Pike grappled with the memory, trying to bring it into focus. His mental fingers grew colder. Sharper.

WHO IS THE SHADOW?

It just hurt.

Too much.

"You are not authorized to enter this room!" Pike slithered out of my mind.

I was back in my skin, slumped in the chair. Empty and violated. Several people entered the room, emerging from the seemingly solid walls. Their hair was short. Their uniforms tight and black. Two of them wore black glasses. They stepped on each side of Pike like bookends. Pike jumped up, his chair falling back and dissolving. Spindle wrapped his arms around me and kept me from falling.

"You were ordered to back down twice!" Mom shouted. "YOU WILL NOT BREAK HIM!"

"I am in charge of this preliminary!" Pike retorted with equal venom. "You have no right to be in here!"

"He is my son!" Mom shot back. "And this has become a psychic lynching! You were not authorized to probe deeply!"

"There is a traitor in the Garrison. I will use whatever methods necessary."

"This preliminary is over. You will be removed from this assignment."

His face reddened. "I am primary minder. I decide methodology. I assess traits; my decisions are final. Understand, *civilian,* I will not go."

"You can have this conversation with the commander, if you like, but either way, we are finished."

Pike turned; the glasses slipped, revealing white eyeballs. No iris. No pupil. He fixed his glasses and stared at Mom, but she didn't flinch. She stood in front of me, her hands clenched. Veins pulsed in Pike's neck. Tension hissed.

"Try it." Mom stepped closer to him, her nose almost touching his. "Go on, get inside me and try it."

The room charged with static. Her hair floated out.

"If you dare to penetrate my mind, you will not see the outside of a prison cell for eternity, I will see to that personally, Agent Pike. If you do not contain yourself in the next few moments and leave this room, I will bring a team of minders in here to incapacitate you for the rest of your life. If you don't believe me, then try it." Her lips were very thin. "Back. Down."

The vein throbbed on Pike's neck. A bead of sweat rolled down his temple. He calmly adjusted his black glasses. He sucked air between his teeth, took his time turning, and glided through the wall. The two black glasses-wearing men followed as did three black suits. Two men stayed in the room, hands behind their backs. At attention.

My mind was still cleaning up the memories Pike uncorked, trying to put them in their rightful places. They swirled like papers finding their way back to the ground.

"Get him to the infirmary," Mom said to Spindle and the men. "I want a medical minder to begin decompression wave therapy immediately. Have the medical mechs monitor his vitals and administer sedatives but do not put him to sleep. Once normal brain activity resumes, I want him asleep for twenty-four hours. All activity is to be sent to my office; keep me updated of every second, Spindle. And I mean every second."

A stretcher floated inside the room. Servys laid me on it and guided it down the short hall to the leaper. Mom and Spindle walked alongside.

"I will be updating Commander Diggs with what just happened," she said. "Contact all my appointments for the rest of the day and reschedule for tomorrow."

"But you have an appointment with the director of—"

"I don't care," she said. "I need some time with the commander."

I took her hand. It was hot. Wet.

She pushed her hair back. The rigid muscles loosened along her jaws and around her eyes. She stopped the stretcher before it went inside the leaper, squeezed my hand and pushed the hair off my forehead.

"You made it," I croaked.

She nodded, feeling my forehead. She whispered, "Get some rest." She stood back. "I'll be with you soon."

We moved onto the leaper. She watched from the hallway. She would not rest. Not tonight. There was too much to do.

PART II

Time does not exist.
There is only the present moment.

The past and future are merely thoughts about the present moment. If you think about it, you have already missed the point. One must live life in the present moment to be real; otherwise, your life is a collection of thoughts.

No different than data.

8

PRESERVED

WEEKS PASSED. Then months. Instead of getting on a bus for school and falling asleep in front of the TV, I was somewhere else in the world, where they administered tests and I went to sleep on a weightless bed, looking out so-called windows with views of canyons, oceans or whatever scenic view was on tap for the night. Sometimes I forgot it was just a picture, that few things I saw were actually real. Then again, I wasn't trying to think all that much. If I really thought about what was happening, I'd unravel. So I did what they told me, went where they wanted me, and shut up for once.

I thought a lot about Pike. Not so much the part where he tried to rip my mind in half, I tried to forget that part, but the question he asked: *Who are you?* I thought he meant to find out if I was a spy or something, but I kept hearing it a different way. *Who am I?* I thought I was some sixteen-year-old latchkey kid growing up in a broken home. I figured I'd end up drilling holes in sheet metal for a living and die in a retirement home. Not exactly the American dream, but there were worse fates.

But now who am I? Really, *who am I*? Does anyone *really* know who they are? Are we just a collection of behaviors we learned as babies that run us around like wind-up toys? Or does anyone know why we're here? Is there a purpose to any of this besides getting a piece of gold and a boat and a hot wife to put on it? There has to be more to life than just this.

I sat in my little room sometimes, pondering all that, but I always ended up on that one question: *Who am I?* Somehow it didn't feel like it had an answer, but it was a question that had to be asked. Over and over. If I didn't ask it, I felt crazy. And I had to hang onto every shred of sanity I could because this place made little sense. And everything I thought I was didn't exist anymore. *So who am I now?*

MY TESTERS WERE NEVER the same person. Sometimes a man, sometimes a woman. Never Pike. Thank the lord in heaven. They were never friendly, never rude. They took blood samples, tissue samples, made me run, walk, do push-ups, and asked some of the goofiest questions I've ever heard. "Have you ever noticed cockroaches following you?"

"What?"

He or she would ask the question again, almost as if they just wondered if I liked vanilla or chocolate ice cream.

Sometimes the interviews were more formal. We would face each other in chairs; they'd ask questions, I'd answer. Sometimes they would ask if I saw certain colors or heard a certain thought. Sometimes I did. I felt psychic pressure, but nothing like what Pike did; that was like a grown man trying to squeeze his fat ass into a baby's onesy. The testers would ask me to *open my mind* and asked what came up. The first couple times I sat there and daydreamed. The third time, I *saw* something. It was like my mind had become a three-dimensional staging area. A reddish object appeared.

"What did you see?" the tester asked.

"An apple."

The tester said nothing. Wrote nothing down. But I was right. He was thinking of an apple and I saw it.

The next day, I knew how to read thoughts. That's right, I could look into someone's mind and see what they were thinking. I could even shut the thoughts out if I wanted. It wasn't doing me a damn bit of good around the Paladins, who had full control of their thoughts. Opening my mind to them was like trying to find out what a wall was thinking. But I could read their thoughts if they let me.

"How do I stop time?" I asked.

The tester sat quietly, hands on his thighs. "You will have to look deep inside yourself," he said, calmly, softly, almost mechanically. "Inside there will be a metaphorical mechanism, a symbolic trigger, you can use to alter your metabolism. Some experience this as a spark found in the solar plexus."

I closed my eyes, focusing on my gut. I remembered that sparkly feeling I had at the Rime, the first time I sliced time. I searched this part of my being but felt nothing but chaotic energy. I imagined I was a traveler hunting a valuable gem, flying through inner space. Lights blurred past, curled out of my grasp like hyper fireflies. I went after them, one direction then the other, but they were nothing but tiny lights. No spark.

"You cannot chase it," the tester said. "You must allow it space; then it will appear."

So I sat there. Minute after minute went by. Pretty soon I was thinking of lunch because the food in that place was outstanding. I could order just about—

"Bring your focus back."

I went back to my midsection and let the fireflies do their dance. They stopped running away and began circling around me. Faster and faster they went, streaking inner space with curves brilliant and lasting. There was a twinge. My ears pricked with excitement. A bright light sparked. It was small and intense, like a quasar glowing somewhere inside. I brought all my awareness to this tiny flare.

"There." The tester barely spoke. "Wrap yourself arounddd…"

My hands involuntarily clenched. The spark grew brighter. Brighter, still. And then it happened. The spark ignited, engulfing me in a psychic blast. When I opened my eyes, the tester was still, his mouth partially open, caught in mid-sentence. I looked around the room for more proof, but I turned cold. And hungry.

"You are not strong enough to sustain a timeslice." The tester was standing over me with the hint of a grin. "But you found it. Nicely done."

NO ONE WOULD TELL me what they were looking for when they tested. Told me nothing, in fact. Not who the Paladins were or what they were trying to protect the world from. Mom was the least helpful. I saw her more in those months than I had the previous year, but she had only one answer for every question: "I can't tell you anything right now, Socket."

I thought about Streeter and Chute a lot. We'd been friends forever, like family. Chute and I were, as Streeter put it, a girlfriend-boyfriend thing. I missed them both. Maybe I should've missed her more. I tried to call them, but the nojakk no longer worked. The Paladins had shut it down. Standard procedure. Maybe they were afraid I'd call and say *You'll never guess where I am! I can stop freaking time!* I probably would've.

I wondered if they were worried. Not so much Streeter, but Chute. What was she going to think when she heard I was a freak? Who was I kidding? She was never going to find out. She might never see me again, even if Mom said I would see her soon. *Soon.* That was as specific as she got. That could mean *never.*

In between tests, Spindle and I played games. We played chess with holographic pieces and ping-pong on a table that materialized from the floor, complete with paddles and ball. He taught me a game called Reign. The animated pieces moved around seven levels of chessboards and chopped each other to pieces. Blood would squirt and the pieces would die moaning. Very cool.

I was restricted to the transforming rooms, leapers and corridors. No matter what shape or form they became or what illusory views I could see through the windows, it was stuffy. It beat school, yeah. And it beat sleeping in front of the TV on empty pizza boxes. But no matter how big the room, I was still inside a mountain. I hadn't seen the sun in a long time. Pictures of it, sure, but not the *real* thing.

"YOU HAVE BEEN CLEARED to enter the Preserve," Spindle announced in the third month, I thought. For all I knew, we weren't even on a twenty-four-hour schedule anymore. He waited for me outside a testing room, where a man had asked if I could move a set of round objects with my mind (he gave me ten minutes, but all I did was stare at them and wonder what he did for fun). Stupid.

I stepped quickly to keep up with Spindle, his gait so smooth and effortless. "Recreation is important," he said. "I think you will enjoy this very much."

We stepped inside a leaper.

I didn't know what a Preserve was, but it had to be better than staring at balls that wouldn't move. "No more tests?"

"You have no more tests today." The colors formed a rough smile on Spindle's face.

The leaper opened. I expected another white room, maybe a view (real or not) of the hills. At the very least, I'd hoped we might go out to the field Mom drove (or flew) across when she brought me to the Garrison. At least it was wide open. I just wanted to feel the wind on my face. We didn't go there; we went someplace so much better. We stepped outside where the sun was bright, the air humid and earthy. We were in the outside world, but one where I'd never been. One I never thought possible.

No illusion this time.

We emerged from the side of a cliff. From our vantage point, the tropical forest had been carved out of the mountain like a stone bowl. Trees, birds, palms... the whole deal.

"The Preserve is a man-made, enclosed environment supporting the growth of over ten thousand botanical species." Spindle spoke louder to clear the screeching call of a toucan or howler monkey or something else wild. "In addition, there are numerous exotic species of birds, mammals and aquatic creatures."

"Enclosed environment?" Blue sky was peeking between the clouds. "You mean that's not real?" My heart sank.

"Do you see those?" Spindle pointed to a barren limb on top of a large tree. "Those are magnashield generators disguised as part of the tree. There is one every five hundred square feet. They power an overhead force field that encloses the Preserve. Nothing can get in. Nothing can get out."

"How big is this place?"

"Five point two square miles. It is primarily used for research. Many medical breakthroughs that have been discovered here will soon be made available to the public. Right now, I would like to take you to the entertainment sector."

Spindle stepped onto a dirt path that went around an enormous banyan tree. The trail beyond the tree was ten feet wide with a thick layer of leaves. Trees enclosed the humid path. Secondary paths split off now and again, darker and narrower. Things scurried along the undergrowth while small monkeys watched from above. One hung from a thick vine and screeched. Colorful birds teased him.

I'd been in places like that on a much smaller scale. We went on a field trip to a greenhouse conservatory with butterflies and lizards. Plants bloomed in all sorts of colors, shapes and sizes, attracting bugs of equal strangeness. None of us said anything but *whoooaaaaa* for the first five minutes; then we threw pebbles at turtles chilling on a log. But this was way beyond that.

Spindle stopped along the way, describing plants, pointing at animals, and gave me the brief history of things he found interesting. I reminded him I was in high school, not college. But he was having too much fun, his faceplate all sunny and sparkly, so after a while I let him do his thing.

We hiked for miles before stopping on a ledge and looking into the deepest part of the Preserve. There, surrounded by lush forest, was a large oval field of the greenest grass.

"Here it is." Spindle swung his arms out as if I'd won the grand prize. "It is a fantastic sport, a test of navigational skills, strength, agility, accuracy and teamwork. I am not one for guarantees, Master Socket, but I would wager it will be more popular than lacrosse, football, and soccer combined." His face lit with red, yellow and orange. "Tagghet."

"The game with jetters?"

"Yes. The technology has been in commercial production for a year. Perhaps you have seen it at your school."

"I've heard a thing or two."

"You have not played?" he asked.

I just stared.

"Then follow me."

The path switched back and forth. We dropped fifty feet in elevation before reaching the edge of the field. Spindle knelt on one knee and ran his hand over the grass.

"It is good fortune for a tagger to pause and touch the field before walking on it," he said.

"It is?"

"It is always good fortune to pause." He gestured to the spot in front of me.

"I'm no tagger, so I don't think so."

Spindle's feet sank in the lush, dense grass. The blades were narrow, the tips each holding a bead of moisture. Like living shag.

"This is nice," I said.

"I knew you would like it." His face sparkled. "The scent is quite grand, is it not?"

"You can smell?"

"I have olfactory sensors equivalent to a Labrador retriever."

I dropped to one knee and spread my hand over the turf, letting the wet tips tickle my palm. I wanted to lie on it and stare at the clouds like I used to with Chute and Streeter. We used to lie in my backyard, pointing at clouds and naming them; it was just us. Sometimes Streeter would have to go home and Chute stayed. She'd ask if I could read her mind, tell her what she was thinking. *You wish you had bigger boobs.* She left a red mark on my chest because I was probably right. Back then, there was no one else. No one judging, no one watching. We made up stories, laughed and played, and when we were ready to go home, we did. No one was there to tell us, *Go here, now here. Make those stupid balls move with your thoughts.*

"If you are ready, we can explore the rest of the Preserve," Spindle said. "There are some magnificent features."

"Spindle, could I go alone?"

"You do not like my company?"

"That's not it, no... it's just... I just need to clear my head. I mean, my whole life changed in a single day and I'm still not sure I'm digging all this. I need to get lost for a while and sort things out. You know what I mean?"

"You want to... go without me?" His face turned dark blue. "I thought we would spend the afternoon together. There are many interesting things to visit. Creatures you have never seen. I was, perhaps, looking forward to showing them to you."

"Another time, huh? I'm sure I'll be here a few more weeks." *Or months. Years. Forever.*

He held out his hand and helped me up. "Of course. If you need help, I will come."

He said that like a Paladin angel. If things were just that easy in real life. *Is this real life?*

"I suggest you strike out on the path to our right. It will take you to an artificial sinkhole and a breathtaking water feature."

Spindle stood at the field's edge and watched me walk across the turf. I waved before entering the dense jungle. He waved back. Now if I could just see the clouds.

9

BATTY MAN

I WAS LOST. Big time.

I could blame Mom for never putting me in Boy Scouts, but there was no badge for this. I made the mistake of leaving the trail. The trees all looked alike. My arms were scratched bloody. I sat on a rotten log to rest until fire ants stung the hell out of me. My legs were covered with welts. I went a bit farther, heard a stream, and went barefoot, stepping carefully on mossy stones. The cold water was a relief. I found a dry boulder. Checked for fire ants.

I was in a tropical forest. I couldn't see the sky, but it was still exactly what I had in mind. The lookits were somewhere and they were watching. At least, for once, it didn't feel like it. I was as close to alone as it was going to get. I was picking my nose, a full knuckle deep, and feeling pretty good about it. Until someone giggled.

"Who's there?" I called, oddly wondering if I could convince them I was just scratching my nose.

Something in a tree. Something bright red. A whole crew of things scrambled into the thick canopy, flashes of yellow, blue and purple. They crossed from tree to tree like squirrels. I splashed after them until the stream got deep and I went back on land. Spots of sunlight penetrated the trees ahead. I maneuvered around a tangle of vines and peeked through the leaves. It was a clearing, of sorts. A massive stone slab with patches of moss and snaky cracks. A huge tree was on the far side, its branches as big as tree trunks. The bark was twisted and sinewy, smooth and gray like a well-crafted relic. *Quite grand.*

The tree was without a single leaf, but alive with color. Thousands of bright-colored creatures squabbled along the branches. Some crawled over each other, some wrestled, and others rested quietly. They didn't have feathers; they looked like bats, but their colors were like poison dart frogs.

Several of them hovered near a guy at the base of the tree. Spindle didn't warn me about other people in the Preserve. In fact, it was the first normal-looking person I'd seen who wasn't asking lame-ass questions. He didn't look like he belonged here. His hair was long and his clothes ragged. He held up his hand and the creatures grabbed it. A fluorescent pink one hung by its long sharp tail.

I stayed in the trees and crossed the stream, not bothering to take off my shoes. I hustled through the ferns and over rocks to a soft patch of leaves until I was a lot closer. The colored things were still there, but the guy was gone. They had little arms and legs and their tails swished like whips. They had snouts. *Caves and dragons. That was not a dream.*

I needed to get closer. I turned—he was behind me.

I fell through the branches onto the open slab and crawled backward. He stepped out of the trees. His skin was bronze from the sun, his hair bleached. And he wasn't a guy, he was more like a kid. Older than me, maybe, just out of high school. College?

"Who are you?" I said.

He flicked his sandy hair out of his eyes. His eyes... they were the eyes of a dead fish. He listened, holding out his hand. I didn't move. He shook his hand, insisting I take it, so I reached up. He squeezed firmly and yanked me close. *Jesus, he hasn't showered in forever.*

He wouldn't let go. His pupils were much too large. He pulled me closer. Pressure gripped my entire body. I wanted to shake out of it, but his eyes fixed me in place. They were deep holes. He let go. I stumbled, too dizzy to run.

"*Are you all right?*" someone said on my nojakk.

My nojakk was working. I tapped my cheek several times. "Hello?"

"*Pivot would like to know if you are all right.*"

The blind guy had his face to the sun. Something moved over me like a thousand dishrags snapping on a clothesline. It was the things from the tree, slapping their leathery wings, stirring the dust at my feet.

"*Can you speak?*" I heard again.

A golden flying thing was on the guy's shoulder, its tail curled around his neck.

"You said that?" I asked.

"*I did,*" the golden thing said without moving its mouth.

"How'd you do that... wait, you talk?"

"*I do.*"

I stroked my cheek. "How'd you get my number?"

"*We're good with technology.*" The golden thing shrugged. "*I did a simple scan and decoded your nojakk. You really should upgrade your passcodes.*"

"Scanned it with what?"

"*It's a mental scan. You wouldn't understand.*"

I'm reading thoughts and stopping time. Now there's talking... things. Sure, why not. "What are you?" I said. "Like a dragon or something?"

"*Phhsssh.*" Its lips flopped around, exposing rows of sharp teeth. "*We're grimmets, hailing from the edge of the Milky Way. My name is Sighter.*"

Grimmets. *Hmmmm.* Tiny dragons speaking on nojakks, apparently with their mind. We missed that species in biology class. And from the Milky Way? We missed that in astronomy. Of course, we never covered timeslicing in physics. I reached for Sighter, wanting to poke him, make sure he was real. He snapped my finger with his tail, like a wet towel.

"CHRIST!" A red line swelled across my knuckles. I put it to my lips. "Why'd you do that?"

"*We're not pets.*"

"Well, tell him that, you're sitting on his shoulder."

"*I like him.*" He wrapped his tail around the blind guy's neck again. "*But Pivot doesn't own me, boy.*"

"My name is Socket."

"*I know.*"

"Then why'd you call me boy?"

"*I just met you.*" He rolled his bulging eyes. "*Do I have to explain everything?*"

"Listen, three or four months ago I was living a normal life, now I'm reading thoughts and stopping time and you look like a golden dragon that did some sort of"—I waved my hands over my head frantically—"*mental scan* to steal my passcodes and now you're talking to me without moving your lips." We stared at each other, deadpan, until I said, "So, yeah, explain everything."

Pivot's eyes remained unfocused, but his lips moved. Sighter nodded.

"*Fair enough, boy,*" Sighter said. "*Follow us.*"

We went to the tree. It wasn't growing in the stone slab after all, but against it. The slab dropped off, and below, maybe fifteen feet, was a pond. The tree was rooted in that. Pivot sat against the tree and Sighter climbed to the top of his head. Hundreds of grimmets peeked out of hiding places along the branches, their eyes glowing.

"*We came to help awaken the human race.*"

"This gets better every day," I muttered.

"*You don't think Earth is the first planet in the universe to make a mess out of their evolution, now do you?*"

"I didn't even know there was life on other planets."

Sighter shook his head. "*You have so much to learn, boy.*"

"I just got here. Remember?"

The grimmets fluttered around Pivot like needy butterflies,

fighting to be the next to swing on his fingers. Sighter stood on his shoulder, monitoring the fracas, waving them off when they got too pushy.

"So who are you?" I asked the blind kid. "Your name is Pivot, right?"

No answer. Then all the grimmets looked up. Their eyes grew wider. Brighter. They scattered like bugs, finding stones to sit on, branches to hang from. Sighter crossed his arms. They weren't looking at me. They looked over my shoulder.

SOMEONE STRODE across the stone slab. He was about my age. Each one of his steps landed softly and purposefully. His hair was black, properly cut. His one-piece suit was loose fitting, green and beige. It may have been the colors of the jungle, but it was too clean to belong in the Preserve.

"Salutations," he said. "I see they have finally let you out of the box."

I was still taking in the camouflaged onesy and the strange way he walked. It was almost like he did it perfectly. Whatever that means. Guess he figured I was confused. He jerked his thumb over his shoulder, not taking his eyes off me. "The Garrison. They finally let you out. It can get quite stuffy in there, no?"

Not a single grimmet stirred. Pivot sat quietly, unnoticed. My gut sparked like a fire alarm just went off.

"I hope you don't mind, but I believe it is high time we met." He extended his hand. "I'm Broak."

I shook it. He squeezed my hand tightly, then quickly let go and rubbed it on his thigh.

"Your name is Broak?"

"Indeed, it is," he said, tipping his head. "I named myself. Didn't care for the name I was given, decided I needed something more regal and fitting. It is a combination of two of the greatest Paladin warriors ever to live: Braiden Alexander Faber and Stoak Glacial

Ginshen. Braiden and Stoak." He pronounced each word crisply. "I am Broak."

"How about that," I stated.

Broak locked his gaze on me. I felt pressure surround me, pushing against my head. I set my feet, prepared for what might come next, but the probing was exploratory, not penetrating. It ran over my skin, under my chin, through my scalp.

"You have an unusual name, as well," he said. "Dear Socket."

"There's no dear. Just Socket."

"I see." Broak was humming to himself. Waiting.

"I don't think the name comes from anything," I said. "My parents liked tools."

People usually laughed at that. Not Broak. Maybe I should've made something up about a great warrior named Craftsman. He still wouldn't have laughed.

"You are creating quite a stir, you know." He narrowed his eyes. "The whole Paladin Nation is abuzz about the new find. I had to see you with my own eyes."

I filled an awkward silence with a laugh. He talked funny. "What's the big *stir*?"

"Well, for one, you are sixteen years old and timeslicing, my dear friend. That is quite abnormal. And so far your preliminary evaluations are soaring. Only one cadet has ever had higher scores than you." He smiled. Teeth perfect.

"And that would beeee... you." I gave him a chance to fill in the blank—he was obviously proud—but he let me do it.

"Do not feel disappointed. I am a product of genetic engineering. New and improved, one might say."

"You timeslice?"

"Oh, no. I will begin timeslicing when I'm twenty, that's the normal progression. You see, the body isn't prepared for such stress while it is still developing. At twenty, you are adept physically as well as mentally. You realize you are lucky to have survived your acci-dental timeslice." He smiled again. A little too big. "Premature timeslicing can drain the life from you, starve you to the end. It is a good thing you are here for us to guide you."

"I'm thrilled," I said, thinking of my first day.

He opened his mouth wide and laughed. It sounded unnatural. Like he practiced laughing.

"Pike got a little aggressive in your preliminary, yes, I heard. You handled it quite well, though. Most cadets leave something like that unconscious. You, on the other hand, actually spoke. Quite impressive, indeed."

He looked me up and down again, walking around me. Grimmets scurried out of his way. He made a full circle, nearly stepping on Pivot. "Could you tell me something?" Broak held my hair and let it fall off his fingers. "Why is your hair so unkempt and lacking of color?"

This guy was way into my personal space. And he was holding my hair. That was... *unnatural.* My stomach tightened and sparked. Broak put his hands up like he felt a warning. *I surrender.* He rubbed both hands on his pants.

"Pigmentation disorder." I took a step back.

"I have never heard of such a thing. You are not albino, how is that possible?"

"I live in South Carolina, but I'm standing in a jungle somewhere in the world where there's mountains. How's that possible?"

Suddenly, saying I lived in South Carolina didn't feel right. *Do I live here now?*

He stopped observing and narrowed his eyes. "You are intriguing, dear Socket. Take any other sixteen-year-old, drive him through a wormhole and introduce him to a brutal minder like Pike and, well, he'd be crying for mommy. You, on the other hand, behave as if this happens every day. You are quite extraordinary."

"Not like I had a choice."

"No. You didn't." His smile faded from his smooth face. No sign of whiskers.

"How old are you?" I asked.

"Same as you. Do you find that odd?"

"You seem pretty okay with all this yourself."

"That's because I was born here. I'm a Paladin breed. I was made to do this. You are a genetic mutation and that's why so many Paladins are all enthusiastic about you. They love mutations. They have this false hope that nature will provide the right combination of DNA to improve our race. But if you want to know the truth, you are just an abnormality, a random chance. If you think about it, it's like squirting paint on a canvas, hoping it will become the *Mona Lisa*." He twitched. "Do you understand?"

Did I just get insulted?

Broak clasped his hands behind his back and looked into the pond below. He sniffed the air and sneered, then brushed a bit of dust from his chest. The grimmets rustled nervously, never taking their eyes off him.

"Whether you know it or not," he said without turning, "you are somewhere in between, dear Socket."

"In between what?"

"This world and the one you came from, where the regular people live." He looked over his shoulder. "I sincerely doubt you can go back. In case you haven't noticed, they don't know we exist."

Whether South Carolina was my home or not, I knew right then and there I didn't want to end up wearing a onesy in jungle colors. And the *dear* thing was really stepping on my nerves.

Broak walked along the rocky ledge. The grimmets stirred a cloud of dust getting out of his way. Broak glared at them crawling along the branches. He brushed his chest off again.

"You don't like this place," I said.

"I am not a fan of the Preserve," he said, wiping each arm dutifully. "It is absolutely filthy. It is unorganized. Unpredictable. Pivot belongs here, not me. After all, the Paladins built it for him."

"They built what? That tree?"

"The entire Preserve."

Five point two square miles of tropical jungle, all for one person? "That's impossible."

He brushed both arms, both legs, licked the back of his hand and rubbed it off. Clean as a cat. Broak squatted next to Pivot and brushed the hair from his eyes. Pivot did not move.

"He is a mutant. Like you. Although you had the benefit of your father's association with the Paladin Nation, Pivot came from the general population. He was an accident. I suppose we found a *Mona Lisa*, after all." He looked at me. "What do you suppose the odds are of finding two?"

"Let's get something out in the open." My gut lit up. "Are you looking for a fight? Because it feels like you are, and I just met you."

The rehearsed smile creased his porcelain cheeks. "It's a great moment in history, dear Socket." He raised his hands in celebration. "I'm the perfect breeding. Pivot's the lucky mutt. And you... well, we're not sure what you are, just yet. Let's just say you show promise."

"Not that this matters, but I don't give two shits what you think. I don't care if I ever read another thought or stop another moment in time. You can drop me off back home, if you like. I was happy with my old life."

Then it hit me. *Happy with my old life?* Every day of my life felt like pushing a boulder up a hill, waiting for something to happen. It was always that way, like I was missing what I was supposed to be doing. Now that I was with the Paladins, I didn't feel like a freak.

Broak pulled Pivot up and put his arms around us both. "Pivot's special. And I don't mean the he-can't-see kind of special, either. The Paladin Nation needs him. They need me. And, from what we've seen so far from your preliminary tests, you just might be special, too. Whether you like it or not, we have been chosen by a higher power to serve. All we can do is celebrate, dear Socket." He leaned close, his breath odorless. "Long live the Paladin Nation."

He shook us once, twice and let go.

"Now if you will please excuse me," he said, "I have to get out of this place. When you get some free time, join me on the tagghet field, won't you? I'll teach you the sport in no time. It will be worldwide within a couple years; you should know the rules, at the very least. And I must warn you, I'm quite good and I don't go easy on beginners." He smirked, the first sign of real emotion. "I'll give you quite a thrashing, but you will thank me for it later."

"When am I done testing?"

"They evaluated me in three days." He looked at Pivot. "They gave up on Pivot. You? Like I told you, you are somewhere in between." He winked. "Come see me when you can."

He walked down the slab. The grimmets hovered over me, watching. A red one landed on my shoulder. We looked at each other, both surprised at the sudden intimacy.

"By the way, you will have to clean yourself up," Broak called. "The white hair is odd, but I like it, I really do. But you're going to have to clean it up. Better yet, cut it." He stopped at the edge of the trees. "And for God's sake, don't let those things sit on you, dear Socket. They live in the trees."

Broak walked into the forest.

PIVOT WAS GONE. So was Sighter. Hot, sticky fingers clung to my skin. The red grimmet walked to my other shoulder and wrapped his long tail around my neck. His gold eyes glittered. Blinked. The rest of the grimmets sat on the branches. Watching. Blinking. They started climbing into the holes, one after another, disappearing into the tree.

The red grimmet leaped off, flying after them. He marched down the branch, one of the last to go inside. One thought rang inside my head. It was a single word coming from the little red one.

[Rudder.]

The red grimmet's name was Rudder.

10

Orphans

THREE DAYS, my ass.

I had the feeling dear Broak was lying about his testing because mine was endless. Weeks went by and every morning I woke up hoping it would be over, only to be trotted to another tester and another boring day. I eventually turned my room into an exact replica of my bedroom back in South Carolina. My messy desk was in the corner and, next to that, an open door that led to the bathroom. If I didn't know any better, I would've gone to the kitchen to grab something to drink, but there wasn't a kitchen through that door. Just another short hallway with a leaper at the end.

"Himalayas."

The white space swirled inside a huge frame until wispy clouds hung on the icy capped mountain in the distance. It reminded me of the Rime. That's where it all started. What if I didn't go there that day? Would the shadow have found me? Would I be lying around the house, watching TV on a three-day suspension?

"Good morning." Mom walked in and looked around, ignoring

my obvious plea to go home. *This is your home, Socket.* She put on a smile, a courageous attempt to mask the exhaustion, but her facial muscles just couldn't keep up. Did she even sleep anymore?

"I've got good news," she said. "I received clearance for you to meet Streeter and Chute on the Internet. You can virtualmode to a secure location and they'll meet you."

"You did?" I jolted out of bed.

"I did." She smiled back. "I know it's not the same as seeing them in the skin, but it's the best I could do. I'm not sure when it can be arranged, but soon."

There was hope after all.

"I want you dressed," she said. "Some testers arrived late last night to see you this morning and they need to leave by lunch."

BREAKFAST WAS anything I could think of. *Anything.* Eggs, slightly runny, a bowl of grits with two pats of butter, and two and a half strips of bacon. I added a side of poached salmon just to screw with them. Two minutes later, a servy carried a piping hot tray that stunk up the room. I sent it back. *Okay, you win.*

I went to the test, this one with a man and a woman. I inserted my hands into special gloves and put on dark glasses. They gave me different scenarios and asked me to respond. "You find yourself in a room with three strangers. One of them is a murderer. The lights go out. Respond."

What am I supposed to say to that? If I leave the room, I'm a coward. If I kill them all, I'm the murderer.

"Am I the killer?" Tiny lights flashed, I saw some data roll through the dark glasses and heard some *mmmmm-mmm.* That meant my answer was very interesting. Not necessarily right, but interesting.

I was starved for lunch. I sat in an ordinary white room at a long table, watching the news reports on a three-dimensional TV. I ordered peanut butter and jelly with a thick layer of spicy potato chips and sliced pickles. Spindle sat at the other end, with his hands splayed out on the table. I continued eating. He continued watching.

"Tell me about Pivot," I said.

"I can only give the general background. You are not cleared to access his entire database."

Mmmmmmm... interesting.

"Master Pivot was found in a children's home. His parents were never seen."

"Has he always been blind?"

"Yes. According to the director of the home, he just showed up one day. The other kids named him Pivot because of the way he turned around without lifting one of his feet. Much of his time, according to the director, he spent sitting in a chair, as if observing. The other kids did not care to play with him. Some of the older kids assaulted him. After that, the director called the authorities."

"He called the Paladins?"

"No. The Paladin Nation monitors the world for suspicious activities. Once they secretly learned of Pivot, they took him without notice."

"Was he hurt?"

"There were screams from other children. When the director arrived in the bunk room, five teenagers were unconscious at Master Pivot's feet. The other children told the director that the boys were teasing him. They wanted him to take off his clothes. When they attacked, they began to spasm like they had touched an electrical wire. They convulsed for a minute before they went unconscious."

I was holding a half-eaten pickle. "He killed them?"

"No," Spindle said. "They recovered fully."

If they got a dose of what Pike had given me on day one, then, hell yeah, they were screaming. "What happened after that?"

"Master Pivot went through much of the same tests you are now experiencing."

"And he lives in the Preserve?"

"He does. At one time, he had living quarters much like yours, but he experienced extreme agitation. Since coming to the Preserve, he has stabilized."

"You know, Broak told me they built the Preserve just for Pivot." I wagged the pickle at him. "That's crazy talk, right?"

"Master Pivot is a very powerful cadet and, I might add, one of the most unique. He expresses minder potential yet is not a pure minder. He is quite possibly the most powerful cadet alive, but it is not known how well he controls his abilities. The Paladin Nation is very patient with his development. They want him to be comfortable."

"What's so important about him?"

His faceplate became a mess of gray specks. "That information is classified."

I licked the peanut butter off my thumb and took another bite, remembering that, even though Pivot had dead fisheyes, there was a magnificent depth to them. It only took one look to know he was something special. And not the he-can't-see kind.

"What about Broak?" I asked. "What's he all about?"

Spindle's head dimmed, a deep scarlet line jagged on the lower half. "Master Broak's story is much different. He is the result of careful breeding, artificially conceived. He has been very promising, expressing his skills at an age earlier than anticipated. He is also very important."

"Believe me, he thinks he's important, too," I said. "He doesn't have parents?"

"He was raised by trainers."

Trainers, huh? There's a new concept. What could be worse than training the day you came out of the womb... or slid out of a test tube or hatched from an egg? He was built.

"So what he said is true?" I said. "He's the Paladins' darling."

"If test results are any indication, he will be a very potent Paladin. The Paladin Nation is currently cloning his gene sequence for future generations. Earth will be very secure under his leadership."

Spindle's faceplate turned pale for just a second. *Under his leadership.* That was the company line. I didn't think Spindle was on board with that.

"So what exactly are the Paladins protecting us from? Monsters? Aliens? Killer tomatoes?"

"I am afraid that information is classified."

"I'll bet it's terrorists. Right?"

"I cannot confirm nor deny that statement."

"What's the big secret? Terrorists are blowing stuff up every day. Why do we need a secret police agency? I mean, they aren't keeping secrets. They just attacked some building the other day and told the whole world about it."

Spindle remained still for several seconds, perhaps contemplating what was classified. His faceplate brightened when he had the answer. "It is best that humanity does not know what danger it is in. They would be very unhappy. There would be mass chaos. Financial stability would collapse worldwide. No, Master Socket, it is better that we serve humanity without their knowledge. Keeping them safe is most important."

We keep the world safe, Socket, that's all you need to know. Mom always said that. *Secrecy leads to corruption.* That's what my Global Politics teacher always said. Of course, Paladins weren't ordinary people. That's what Spindle would say.

A servy fetched my empty cup. I was full.

11

THE TESTS CONTINUED. I had yet to see Streeter and Chute. Mom said she was working on it. But every day, no Chute or Streeter. Just tests. She promised it would work out, and I believed her. There was only so much she could do.

They let me into the Preserve. Occasionally I'd hear shouts and whistles coming from the tagghet field, but I stayed away from that end. Broak could do whatever, as long as it didn't include me. I was more interested in finding Pivot, but he was nowhere to be found. Spindle said that was pretty normal, said he often went missing. He wouldn't explain what *missing* meant. That, he said with a smattering of gray, was classified. Sometimes I thought I'd catch a glimpse of Pivot through the trees, but then it'd turn out to be nothing.

There was no more getting lost. The main trails were the easiest and the lesser-known ones were good for avoiding the scientists who lurked around doing research. Sometimes I made my own trail and fought dogtooth vines and razor-sharp elephant grass. I'd lose some skin and blood, but it beat being in the box. Although, once my arm went numb after getting scratched by some toxic-laced branch and I ended up in the infirmary, getting lectured by Spindle to be more careful.

"You are not invincible," he said. "You must understand your environment."

ONE AFTERNOON, after a morning of exhausting tests, Spindle went with me to the Preserve. He insisted on going first. With him in the lead, I made it to the stream without a scratch then raced ahead to the grimmet tree.

I slipped on mossy stones, crashed through the trees and skidded onto the slab. The grimmet tree was empty, but this time there was one waiting. A red grimmet sat on the lowest branch, his feet going *tom-tom-tom* on the wood. He was the only grimmet there, staring right at me. I started for him.

"Grimmets are not receptive to strangers," Spindle said. "You should let him come to you."

Rudder had given me his name. That meant something. I stopped several feet away, offering my hand. Rudder dropped off, flapped over and snagged my fingers with his tail, hanging like a possum.

"Where've you been?" I said.

He was breathing rapidly and loudly; purring shook my hand. I poked his round belly, tight and scaly, and the purring went right into my arm.

"You have a friend," Spindle said.

Rudder jumped onto my face and pinched my cheeks; his forehead pushed against mine, and he tickled my chin with his tail. Then he flew to the tree and pointed down. I went to the ledge. There they were, swimming and floating, some on the sandy shore. Pivot was at the far end with water up to his waist, washing dirt off his arms and face. His clothes were spread out on a rock. He looked skyward. Smiled. Why did it feel like I'd known him all my life?

"*If you don't mind,*" Sighter said, fluttering in my face, "*Pivot would like to dress without you watching. He might live in the trees, but he still has a sense of modesty."*

A few minutes later, Pivot climbed up the tree, wearing nothing but shorts. He moved effortlessly, muscles rippling down his back, along his arms and calves. Wet strands of hair hung over his face. He moved his head side to side, listening. Energy radiated from his skin that seemed to bend the light in a holy, aura sort of way. He continued to turn his head. Mild psychic pressure wrapped around me.

[Follow me.] His thoughts were big and loud in my mind and sounded much older than they should have. He pushed his hair back, exposing his milky pupils. Energy, sweet and filling, bubbled in my chest. *[I will show you things.]*

In one fluid motion, Pivot leaped off the rock, splashing into the deep part of the pond.

"Call when it's time to eat!" I shouted.

"But, Master Socket..." Spindle's voice trailed away.

I jumped without looking. My stomach lurched. I went several feet under and never touched bottom. I broke the surface, trying to breathe, pulling in all the air I could to scream, "COLD!"

Pivot was in the trees, with the grimmets swirling behind him. Insects fled for their lives. I swam to shore, with Rudder hanging onto my hair. I ignored the branches and vines and followed. Pivot bounded over obstacles, swinging around tree trunks or running up them one foot over the other. Nothing slowed him. Few things cut him. I couldn't do what he was doing. If it weren't for the grimmets, I would've lost him. At one point, he was high in the canopy, running along the limbs, crashing through the leaves like a parachutist falling to his death only to grab vines at the last moment.

When I couldn't even hear the grimmets, I stopped at a small pool to catch my breath. Was that the game? Catch me if you can? Well, I lost. And I doubted the lookits could even find me. Maybe that was how he went missing.

A tight, piercing whistle cut the jungle. A family of yellow, long-beaked birds stared back. I heard it again. Directly ahead, the trees were full of color. Pivot crouched behind a tree and put his finger to his lips. I stepped carefully and quietly next to him. The grimmets were just as stealthy, silently crawling along the limbs. Their bright colors became muted and natural, blending into their surroundings.

Broak was on the other side of the trees, coasting over the tagghet field on a jetter at midfield with something like a red stick on his shoulders that was curved at the end and held a yellow discus. *The tag.* Five bulbous servys drifted at the far end around a large shimmering blue dome. A brilliant green cube was suspended a few feet off the ground inside.

Broak sped up and banked toward the dome. The servys gathered in front. Broak juked left, spun right and sprinted wide. The servys reacted and changed their defensive arrangement. The stick flexed with the momentum of Broak's swing and the tag flung off the end, splitting a tiny gap between the servys, through the dome and into the green cube.

Goal. I guess.

Broak set up another play. The servys changed formation. Broak scored again, this time from thirty yards out. This happened over and over. Different formation, different attack. Same result. Each move was more difficult than the one before. Each shot more precise.

Why are we watching tagghet?

The servys formed a defensive wedge. Broak hunkered down like a bowling ball, looking for the pocket. He spun left, then right, and just before he made contact, bounced wide left. The servys were set for a collision and unable to respond quickly enough to stop him. Broak was all alone, except for the one servy that intercepted his shot. Broak followed it with the stick over his head and chopped with both hands.

"I ORDERED YOU TO FOLLOW DEFENSIVE FORMATION 2B WEDGE!"

The servy retreated. Broak pummeled it again. And again. The club sank deeper with each blow, blobs spurting with each hack. It tried to evade every swing, but lost navigational direction and went in circles. Broak speared it through the center and twisted. The servy split open, spilling goo all over. Broak stomped the remains.

The remaining servys gathered in front of the dome, their eyelights bright red. Broak dropped the club and waved them off. They quickly dispersed into the trees.

A small hovercraft emerged from a path. A man in uniform handed Broak a towel. Broak held out his hands and the man in uniform sprayed them with a small bottle. Broak wiped his hands on the towel. The man gave him a second towel and Broak wiped his face. They spoke. The man stood rigid while Broak replied forcefully, banging his fist on his own leg. The man listened and said something back. Broak looked around, scanning the trees. He wiped his face and looked again. *He knows we're watching.* He nodded to the man. They got onto the hovercraft and left.

We waited a long time and no one moved. Pivot finally walked onto the field. The grimmets followed in a flurry. The gray material was melting like snow in August. Pivot scooped up the remains. He took my hand, dropping it in my palm. It was sticky. Cold.

Dead.

It was only a machine. There was no life to mourn. But Pivot sat there on his knees, head bowed. Maybe it wasn't the death he lamented. Maybe it was the killer. He didn't bring me to see tagghet, after all. *Understand your environment.*

He took the gray substance from me and placed it on the ground. By the time we stood, it was gone. Pivot looked at me, his face warm. I heard no thoughts. He spoke no words. He just looked at me with cloudy eyes. He was warning me, but more than that, teaching me. Respect life, was that it? Respect it in all forms. Those servys were afraid while they watched Broak gut one of their own. They raced off the field when they were released.

When Pivot seemed satisfied, he walked away.

12

ORPHANS, **Take II**

"I CAN'T RIDE THAT," I said.

Three jetters lay on the ground. One hummed to life when Pivot stepped on it, hovering several inches off the ground. He drifted across the field.

"*Why not?*" Sighter asked.

"Because I don't know how."

"*Lame excuse.*"

"Why can't we just go on foot?" I said. "It seems stupid to ride these things. Besides, we'll have to stay on the paths, and what's the use—"

"*Just step on it.*" Sighter flew over me. "*And stop whining.*"

Pivot was already on the other side of the field. I stepped on the jetter. It bobbed under my weight, shifting back and forth to keep me upright. My feet magnetically locked onto the surface.

"All right, I'm on it," I said. "Now what?"

"*You know how to virtualmode, correct? It's simple thought projection. Focus on a command and the jetter will respond.*"

I closed my eyes, visualizing going forward.

"And don't close your eyes. You want to see."

He wanted to add *dumbass* to the end of that sentence. I tried it again and this time I floated up. The jetter teetered side to side. I held my hands out like a beginner, but already I felt more connected to it. I opened my mind, like reading thoughts, and mentally merged with the jetter. I kept my arms out, just in case, and crept over the field. By the time I reached the trees, I sped up and came skidding to a stop.

"Oh, man. This is easy."

"Your head is growing by the second," Sighter said.

I WAS GOING FAST ENOUGH to die. The jetter was magnetically rooted to my feet. Pivot was ahead of me. I followed in his leafy wake. We stayed on the main paths then took the narrow ones. Pivot carved the turns like breaking waves. The grimmets filtered through the trees. There was one close encounter with a low-reaching branch, but other than that it was balls-out blazing.

When we reached the far edge of the Preserve, we dismounted and climbed a narrow path up the rocky face, above the canopy. The ledge angled up and twice switched back. We were several stories up and kept going. I didn't think much about falling. Somehow, I felt safe and in control near Pivot, like he could do something if I did.

The path ended at an alcove several feet deep and sheltered from above. From our vantage point, we were well above the Preserve. White birds glided over the treetops. A blanket of fog that looked like clouds lay in some of the low areas. Miles away was the entrance to the Garrison.

The grimmets perched on nooks and crannies jutting from the rock. We sat on the ledge, dangling our feet. Pebbles chipped off and took flight to the bottom, glancing off the cliff along the way. The sun was behind us, changing the color of the sky from blue to purple and red. Pivot's face was turned up, his cheeks rosy orange. I could stay here forever and watch the shadows grow, feel the sun go down and wait for it to come back up. I don't know how long we were up there. We didn't speak. We just shared the moment in seamless silence until the sky was no longer glowing.

There was gentle pressure on my head; then I saw an image in my mind. The face of a woman. Her hair was bound at the back of her head, strands of gray poking out. Wrinkles cut her face. Her smile was much like his, quiet and undemanding.

"Your mother?" I asked.

He looked directly at me. The pupils engulfed the faded blue irises. It was like looking into his soul, a pathway through the solar system, deep and black and limitless. He reached out and closed my eyes. A dream appeared as clearly as if I were there. The woman was with a man. They were sitting on a beach around a smoldering fire. The water lapped near their feet and the fire hissed. A boy with blond hair, barely old enough to be out of diapers, slapped a stick twice his size in the water, wading out deeper and deeper.

The boy ran, but the dad scooped him up and slung him over his shoulder like a duffel bag. The woman wrapped him in a blanket. The family watched the sun paint the sky.

What happened to them?

The scene dissolved. The mom's and dad's faces turned gray and lifeless. They died, but how and why I couldn't tell. Did it matter? I mean, they were dead and he was alone. That's how I felt. My father died, didn't matter how, just that he was gone. And Mom? Part of her died, too. At least I had a mother. A broken one was better than none at all.

Another vision began.

I saw my mom standing in my bedroom. I was five years old and fast asleep. Mom knelt next to me and dropped her head. She was sobbing. I never saw her cry, not once. Not at the funeral and never after. The dead zone took care of that. But in the vision she cried so hard my bed shook. She took my little hand and held it to her cheek.

I opened my eyes. "How do you know all that?"

He looked up, humming a song in his throat. It sounded familiar. Felt soothing, like a lullaby. He didn't answer my question. Somehow, it seemed he knew me better than I knew myself. Maybe he didn't know what happened, he simply showed me a memory that was buried in my mind. He uncovered it for me to see.

How many other things were buried inside me?

13

I woke the next morning in a bed. No trees. No sky. Just a white ceiling. The visions from the Preserve were still fresh. I revisited the memories, over and over. It only made me long for escape, but I couldn't stop recalling. I could still envision the vast treetops and settling fog and the sun casting strange colors in the sky. Mother crying.

"Room?" I called.

"Yes?" a woman's voice answered.

"Are there any records of my father?"

"Yes. Most are classified."

"Show me what you got."

A faint magnetic field passed through the room. A hologram appeared next to me, a man six feet tall. His goatee was sprinkled with gray, his white hairline receding. I stood on my toes and looked into my father's eyes. I reached for his hand to see if it was callused, but I passed through the illusion. The image shrank in scale to reveal him standing in a workshop.

"Trey Greeny was an exceptional student in circuit mapping and gel intelligence," the room said. "He was promoted to advanced standing and level four security clearance by the age of twenty-two. He was awarded the Medal of Commendation for his bravery in the sector five space attacks."

Space attack?

Dad shut a panel and ran a welding pen over the seam. A servy retrieved the tools on the floor. There was no sound from the image. He looked like he laughed and waved someone over.

"Trey Greeny completed 204 deep-space missions while employed at the Garrison. He was married to Kay Greeny and had a son named Socket."

Another man entered the scene. He could've been a Paladin, but the hair was down to his shoulders. I walked around to get a better view.

Pivot.

Dad showed him something on the workbench. The room continued with details about his everyday life, stuff my mom told me over the years. Stuff everyone knew. But all the good stuff was classified. Space missions. Inventions.

Spindle entered the room.

"Pivot knew him," I said. "Why didn't you tell me?"

"You did not ask."

"Didn't you think I'd want to know?"

"I do not see thoughts, Master Socket."

"Well, you can use logic, can't you?" I said. "It doesn't take a genius to calculate that I'd want to know about my father!"

I get tested for this and that, and no one explained anything. Bullshit.

"There is not much to know." Spindle's face was blue. "Pivot has always been withdrawn, but he responded to your father. The Paladin Nation encouraged their relationship in hopes Pivot would fully develop."

"Develop? What's that mean?"

"Pivot emits an extraordinary level of psychic energy. He is a minder of another breed. His energy has a profound impact on other Paladins. His presence increases other Paladins' powers."

"So they're using him. They're leeching off him, is that it? They're taking from him, does he know that?

Spindle's face turned many colors. "Pivot provides the Paladin Nation with precognition."

"He can see the future?"

"It is not so much the future, but a deduction of events to come."

"Deduction of events..." I shook my head. "That's the *future*, Spindle. He's helping them see the future."

"The odds of future events," Spindle said proudly.

No wonder they built him a jungle. He gave them the ability to see what would happen. There was no limit to that. They were rich: building a jungle for the future was a wise investment no matter how many trillions of dollars it took.

"So that's why they keep him," I said. "They're using him to watch the future."

"They are not using him like a tool, if that is what you mean. Pivot is a remarkable and highly valued cadet..."

He blabbered the company line again. Instead of *remarkable and highly valued* he should've just said Pivot was a great commodity. Getting a real answer from Spindle was impossible. He was programmed, after all. He said what the programmers wanted him to say. He couldn't say what they forbid him to say. He had to follow the script. Every meaningful question just led to another standard answer, never a real one in sight.

He had the answers I wanted, but he wasn't programmed to give them to me. I didn't have security clearance. If I could bypass the programming, I could get to them. Or I could just take them. The Paladins taught me how to read thoughts. *What about machine thoughts?*

I opened my mind to the present moment. Let things present themselves. My consciousness expanded in a way it never had in the presence of a tester. I was growing. My personal energy filled the room. I touched everything. Knew it intimately. Inside. Out. My mind touched Spindle, wrapping around him. He experienced pressure. Spindle remained still, his face a curious color. There would be no time to get all the answers; he would surely shut down before I could. I had to make time.

The timeslicing spark twinkled. I didn't know what I was doing, but if I was going to do this, it had to be now.

I entered the spark.

My fists clenched. My body ignited from the inside. Spindle was still. Time, for me, had stopped.

I closed my eyes and expanded more. I left my skin like virtualmode discs pulled me out, but I didn't go to the in-between. I was my own captain. I floated from my skin like a ghost and entered Spindle's psyche. His thoughts were different from people thoughts. They were lined up, all connected in a purposeful directive, like an assembly line, destined for execution. But there was so much of it, I couldn't comprehend it. It wasn't like walking into a room and looking around; the mind was another dimension. I *felt* the thoughts, *tasted* them. They merged with my awareness. One or two thoughts were easy to absorb and comprehend, but Spindle was filled with a massive amount of data. There was no telling which thoughts allowed him to walk and which ones were top secret.

So I absorbed them all.

An avalanche of data filled me. My mind swelled. I heard things popping inside me. I teetered off balance and fell over, holding myself up against the wall. It was a paralyzing brain freeze that immediately started to thaw as the new information, the new experience of another's mind, trickled into my mind and found some sort of order. I stayed open for anything about my dad, but I stumbled onto something so much bigger. The information floated before my mental eye like a juicy nugget of gossip.

I saw what the Paladins were protecting the human race from.

The Paladin Nation has had many enemies throughout history, but they were usually human. And if the enemy wasn't human, it was at the very least living. For the first time, Paladins were faced with an enemy that imitated life.

I returned to my skin, releasing my grip on time. "Du..." My mind was coming back from the overload, reconnecting with basic functions, like standing and talking. I grabbed a chair to keep from falling. It took a second for my tongue to work. "Duplications are in the *skin*?"

"Master Socket," Spindle said softly, "you breached my database... that is against—"

"The Paladin Nation is protecting the world against... FAKE HUMANS?"

"I cannot—"

"How the hell does a duplicated identity get out of virtualmode and WHERE THE HELL DOES IT GET A FREAKING BODY!"

"There is much humans do not know about their own world."

Three servys emerged from the wall and surrounded Spindle. His head and shoulders slumped.

"Get out of here!" I waved at them like flies. "We don't need assistance, leave!"

Spindle turned to exit, a servy on each side.

"Wait! Where're you going?"

He stopped. The servys came to an abrupt halt. "I will need to be reprogrammed."

"Reprogrammed?"

"My database has been breached. It will need to be reinforced to prevent that from happening again." His eyelight looked to the floor, his faceplate dark blue. "You are more powerful than estimated, Master Socket."

I grabbed his arm. "You're coming back, right?"

"I will come back." He patted my hand, like Mom did when something bad had happened. Or was about to.

I looked around the room, hoping I was making eye contact with whoever was watching. "I swear I won't do that again." An arm grew from one of the servys and took Spindle's hand. I refused to let go. "I'm not letting go unless you promise to bring him back."

We played tug of war. Spindle jerked back and forth. Two more servys entered. I shifted my weight, prepared to kick them across the room. Spindle's eyelight was bright. He gently took my hand and removed it from his arm.

"I will return, Master Socket."

His eyelight rotated away. The servys escorted him from the room. I would've done anything to take back what I did. I wanted to know why I was here. I wanted to know what they were doing with me. I wanted to know about my father and Pivot. Instead, I discovered a titanic war.

I WAS USHERED to a secure room, maybe it was an infirmary, I don't know. I don't remember. Once the adrenaline wore off, I was spinning in thoughts, not knowing which ones were mine and which were Spindle's. All I knew was that I was lying down, staring at the ceiling like a mental patient. Eventually, Spindle's knowledge settled like grains of sand in a jar of water.

And then I understood. I understood it all.

When duplication first started however many years ago, the duped identities were set loose in virtualmode environments. People didn't think much of it; it was kind of cool knowing there was an exact duplicate of you that lived a separate life, even though it was digital. They were virtual clones and they were perfectly linked to whoever cloned them. The creator knew exactly where they were and what they were up to.

But anomalies in code developed, the human equivalent of genetic recombination, which allowed the dupes to break the link and roam free. They started living their own lives and their identities began to drift away from that of their creator. Dupes knew they were reproductions. They knew they weren't real and neither was their world. They wanted more than a virtual environment, a reflection of the physical world. They wanted to see what real life was. They didn't want to be told how the ocean breeze smelled or what love felt like, they wanted to know and not be told what an apple tastes like. They wanted the direct experience. They wanted to *exist*.

Dupes sought out their creators and attempted to download into their skin bodies, not to merge with them but to hijack their creator's skin. That's when the deaths spiked. People were dying at the hands of their own creations, their own selves. Their dupes were killing them.

Paladins discovered the new threat and secretly made the general population aware of it, but before duplication was eliminated and banned, the existing ones went into hiding. Virtualmode was a seemingly endless universe, but the Paladins were tracking them down. Dupes were being snuffed out. If they wanted to exist, they would have to escape virtualmode.

They found their way into factory networks that specialized in experimental textiles, specifically nanotechnology-based textiles, the very stuff that made up the moldable servys and Garrison rooms. Dupes, speaking the same language as computers, were able to download into the moldable material and secretly form human bodies without the factory operators being aware of it. They assumed bodies that grew hair, sloughed skin cells, sweat, shit and spit; they were indistinguishable from real humans, the organic soul-filled bodies, that were operating the factories, and they walked out into the real world with a real sense of smell, taste, touch and sight. They escaped into the physical world. They were alive, and they were among us.

The Paladins caught on but too late. So many had escaped and blended into the population. The manhunt continued. The dupes remained fugitives and dispersed, disappearing into the human population like a cup of water dumped into the ocean. The only way for them to survive was to eliminate their enemy. *Humans.* With computer-like intelligence, they knew they could not win an all-out war. Brutality would be the weakest approach. Real power was of the mind. They surmised the key to defeating the human plague, as they saw it, was from the inside.

Win their heart, then destroy their mind.

Dupes used subversive methods to multiply their numbers. They created their own duplicates, and duplicates of those duplicates.

They found ways into government, universities and major companies. Eventually, they would become a political party. Paladins had done the analysis, they consulted the future through Pivot, and discovered that dupes would take control of the world's most powerful nations within a decade and embark on the genocide of the human race. There would be no gas chambers, no firing lines or gallows. The dupe race would become the doctors that treated us and the cops that protected us. They would be our teachers and lawyers, our neighbors and friends. We would die of untreatable diseases and unstoppable terrorism. It would appear that some people were immune to the new age plagues, but in actuality, those that were immune weren't human at all. Eventually, there would be no humans left.

The human population wouldn't even see it coming. Dupes would be a master predator. Humans would not even know they had been hunted. As the Paladin Nation saw it, the human race would be extinct in twenty-seven years.

Without the Paladins, the human race would already be extinct.

Spindle was right. It was better they don't know.

14

RECYCLING **Death**

I WAS GETTING TWICE AS many tests after I hijacked Spindle. I refused to cooperate. I was not allowed in the Preserve, not allowed to see Pivot and not one mention of Chute and Streeter, either. And, of course, no news about Spindle. Mom was more distant than ever.

They were punishing me, I thought. But there was something else. Something had changed. When I felt angry, I saw something in their eyes. Something well-disguised, well-hidden, and controlled, but something nonetheless. They wouldn't admit to it, but it was there. I saw it. *Fear.*

I penetrated Spindle's database and that shouldn't have happened. They feared something about me. Maybe it was my potential. Maybe it was my unpredictability. Was I their obedient servant? Or a time bomb?

I would get a few hours of sleep and then they had me up again. I refused to cooperate. If they wanted me to play their Paladin games, then they needed to meet me halfway. First, bring back Spindle. And he better be unharmed. But every day there was no Spindle. And every day I told them to go screw. My anger sometimes exploded in waves of heat. They could feel that. I know they could.

Eventually, they turned to their best weapon, Mom. She sat me down and gave me the cold facts: They'd keep testing whether I cooperated or not. They'd keep testing and testing. I wasn't going anywhere. I would become an old man inside this box and she wasn't bullshitting. But, she said, they would consider releasing Spindle if, and only if, I cooperated.

I held out some more, but in the end they won. Mom was right. I had no leverage. No matter how powerful I thought I was, all they needed to do was send in a guy like Pike and I'd be pissing in my pants again. And I had a feeling they had a lot of Pikes. That night I answered their questions. I read their thoughts, sliced time and did whatever they asked, just like a good boy. Whatever they wanted, I did it for what seemed weeks. I'd been inside so long I had no idea if it was Christmas or summer vacation. When I was tired, I slept. When I was hungry, I ate.

In between, they tested the hell out of me.

SPINDLE WOKE ME ONE MORNING. He just walked into the room and the light came up. "Good morning, Master Socket!"

I rolled over, squinting.

"It is time to wake. I have wonderful news for you!"

Spindle opened a drawer embedded in the wall and brought pants, a shirt, underwear and socks to the bed. Neatly folded and neatly stacked.

"Spindle?" I said, shaking the sleep out of my head.

He turned his head, cocking it curiously. "There were adjustments made to my programming to account for your extraordinary skills, but I have been cleared to interact with you again. Is that not wonderful?"

He pulled the sheet off the bed and helped me up. He brushed lint off my arms and held me by the shoulders. "I have come to inform you that your test results are complete. The commander will meet with you tomorrow."

You're mad, Socket Greeny. You think you can stop time and believe human duplications are taking over the world. We'll need to chop your head off.

"According to my records, you have been sequestered inside the Garrison for twenty-five days. I thought you should come with me to the Graveyard this morning. It is our mechanical maintenance and manufacturing center. One of my duties is quality assurance. I can show you where your father worked. I think you will find it very interesting."

I think I sat there with the covers on my lap, trying to decide if this was a dream. But there he was, the faceless one, all happy and glowing. He seemed more human than most people I'd met in the real world, but he was just a machine. He would hold no grudges for what happened. In fact, he was probably just happy to be back in the game. And I was, too. "I'll shower."

"Great!" He pumped his fist. "I will have breakfast waiting. Eggs, grits, bacon and poached salmon."

———

SPINDLE handed me a pair of earplugs before the leaper opened, and strongly recommended I "insert them into my ear canals." We stepped into the Graveyard and the noise shook me. The plugs blotted out most of the sound. My hearing would be gone without the plugs.

Discarded machinery formed precarious walls on each side, loosely forming corridors. The ceiling was too high to see. The air was clogged with hovering platforms carrying parts and tools and equipment. Green servys rode on the platforms, steering them in every direction, giving the atmosphere the look of a well-organized hive.

Spindle waved for me to follow.

The corridors went in several directions. Openings in the spare-part walls revealed rooms without ceilings so platforms could drop in, deliver a broken something or haul a refurbished something away.

When we entered a room, the noise from outside stopped like there was a sound barrier. Each room was filled with fastidious green servys repairing, building or delivering. The first room manufactured cell-sized nanomechs, spewing them like molten clay on conveyor belts. They were packaged in boxes, barrels and vats and hauled off by an endless string of hovering platforms. A person supervised the room, standing behind a network of consoles, monitors and switches. Spindle walked along the conveyor belt, stopping to assess the products. He touched the clay. His face turned colors. He seemed satisfied and waved to the supervisor. The supervisor waved back.

"Did my father work here?" I asked before I fastened my earplugs.

"Your father was director of operations."

"He never got his hands dirty?"

"On most days, he did not. However, he serviced one servy quite frequently." Spindle stood taller, his face brighter.

The claylike nanomech stuff was shipped to the next room, where it was piled onto a shiny platform. Some sort of current was infused into the blob that made it quake, then shimmer. It began to shape itself into a round oval, and then long jointed legs grew from it, four on each side, lifting the body off the ground like a giant daddy longlegs spider with a glowing eyelight. It was ushered off to the side to make room for another blob.

"What's that?" I asked.

"That is a crawler. They monitor the Garrison outside the cliffs and accompany Paladins on certain missions."

Servys floated around the newborn crawler, working with the ends of its legs. "Spiders are tremendous hunters," Spindle said. "They have the ability to move fluidly through any environment. They are excellent protectors."

Spindle visited the supervisor situated in the corner behind a wall of equipment. The supervisor guided us through the room, pointing out the various functions they tested: weapons, surveillance and the ability to rip most living things apart. The supervisor constantly looked at me, then looked away when I looked back. *Is that the Greeny kid?* I didn't hear him think that, it was written on his face.

AT SOME POINT, we got to the weapons room. The supervisor sat at an island podium. She couldn't keep her eyes off me, and not in a good way. Spindle climbed onto the podium and I walked to the back of the room. At that point, I'd been looked over by every single supervisor. It was good to see that Paladins weren't immune to gossip. They were still human.

The servys weren't bothered by me. Most of the stuff was inner mechanisms and didn't resemble anything too dangerous. Although, once assembled, they looked plenty lethal. It was the club-like handles in the back corner that got my attention. They were like the handle of a samurai sword missing the blade. They looked familiar, like the evolvers I used in virtualmode battles.

The servy gripped a white one. The handle unfolded inside-out, reshaped and fused to its arm. An iridescent dagger emerged. The servy diced a metal cube. There was no smoke, just thin slices of metal. The evolver dagger split in two, re-forming into pinchers. The servy picked up a sliver of steel and squeezed it into a neat metal bowtie.

Evolvers were for real. After everything I'd seen, I still wouldn't have guessed that.

A bright light flashed somewhere far across the Graveyard. The floor shook. The flow of hovering traffic shifted, turning in the direction of the accident. Even Spindle and the floor advisor looked.

"There's been a change of plans, dear Socket." Broak was behind me, arms folded behind his back.

The air tightened. Automatically, I was on the balls of my feet, knees slightly bent. Broak strolled toward me, dragging his fingers over the bench. The servys backed away.

"What're you doing here?" I said.

"Regretfully, I have come to deliver a message."

The mental pressure tightened, spilling warmth into my chest. Broak manipulated my psyche, but he was no Pike. I tightened my mind, blocking his efforts.

"You see, dear Socket, I haven't had the opportunity to educate you. Allow me a moment, will you?"

"What?"

Perfect smile. "The Paladin Nation protects this world. We are the good guys who fight the bad, but we are more than that. You see, our aim is not just protecting the human race. Our primary business is perfecting it." He stopped, looking up. "Does this make sense?"

Of course not. "Sure," I said. "We're better than them, I get it. How about we discuss our global dominance on the tagghet field?" *Where I'll never go.*

"I know it is difficult to comprehend, but I am trying to help you understand the message, dear Socket. We're not better than ordinary humans, we're more evolved. We want the human race to become advanced, like us. Nature does the same, you see. Inferior species die off. Stronger, more adapted ones live on and multiply. We're helping the human race become stronger and more adapted for life in the universe."

"I get it."

"But every once in a while, even nature takes a wrong turn. It churns out the retarded and disfigured. And if their DNA is allowed to remain in the human gene pool, the race becomes less equipped to survive. That is logical, wouldn't you agree?"

He rolled an evolver back and forth across the bench. His tone changed, words sharpened.

"The Paladin Nation has to be diligent, dear Socket. Sometimes we have to come to Nature's aid, to weed out her mistakes."

Most of the hovering traffic moved toward the thundering flashes that continued to shake the floor. The timeslicing spark glittered in my gut, moving on its own, trying to get my attention.

"Great, Broak," I said. "You're making total sense, I'm in total

agreement with you, but I'm done with science class and not interested in taking it again. I'll catch you later."

"Pivot is a mistake," Broak said. He was a horrible listener. "But he
is useful. You are also a mistake, dear Socket. We clearly don't know
what you are, but you were not designed by gene scientists. You were
a fluke of your father's tinkering. In other words, you are a mutation.
There's a name for mutated DNA." He took another step. "It's called
cancer."

"Step away, Broak." I clenched my fists.

"You see, you threaten me without understanding the message.
You are unpredictable and unreasonable." He turned his head
daringly. "Do you think you can fight me and win? I was designed to
fight. I know fourteen styles of hand-to-hand combat. I know every
weapon in this room, intimately. It would be foolish to attack me."

"I can stop time. That's all I need."

His jaw muscles tensed and the pressure intensified, dumping
adrenaline into my bloodstream. He could beat me in a straight-up
fight, I'll give him that, but what good was that if he couldn't stop
time?

Broak walked down the bench while my emotions boiled. He was
getting inside me. I tried to fight the pressure, even opened my mind
to read his, but it made things worse. I didn't know how to close
myself from this mental attack. He was manipulating my emotions.
He wanted me pissed off.

Spindle was in the tower with the supervisor, still looking at
whatever was flashing and rumbling. The tower elevated high above
to get a better view.

I backed away from the bench and touched my cheek. "Spindle,
come for me."

But he did not hear me. I took another step, every instinct telling
me to run. I would *walk* away, not run. It was the smart thing. I
turned—

"They murdered him, you realize," he said. "Your father."

My throat tightened.

"His workmanship was ghastly. Mechs leaked fluid, weapons

jammed, cars whined. I'm sorry to report that your father was quite pathetic. So the Paladin Nation ordered his death."

Now I just couldn't walk away from that. If he wanted an ass beating, then all right. Let's talk.

"Murder seems quite drastic, I know," he said. "But do you know why they did such a thing?" He faked concern, drawing his eyebrows up like he cared. "His incompetence would eventually cost a Paladin his life, dear Socket. It sounds reprehensible to you, I realize, but if you weigh the balance of your father's life with that of a Paladin's, it was an easy decision, really. We had to weed out the weak and incompetent. For the good of the human race."

I was going to break his perfect freaking nose. "You're lying."

"You may check the records," he said. "It's all there."

I stopped inches from him. The timeslice spark crackled. "I don't know what your game is, *dear* Broak, but I'll give you one last chance to end it. Then I'm breaking your teeth."

"I told you, I'm simply here to deliver a message." He did not flinch. "I just want you to understand."

"I understand, all right. You don't have parents and you got some unconscious ax to grind, but you don't know who to blame. So you pick me, the one with no dad, and open that wound to make yourself feel better. You're coping with subconscious pain. You're projecting it onto me. However the therapist wants to explain it to you, you need help. I suggest you get it before something goes wrong. Before you get dirty."

Broak was expressionless. He worked his lips but stopped the words. I was on the verge of timeslicing. He could feel it. The spark burned, tendrils of energy pulsing through my nervous system. My fingers dug deep into my palm.

He stepped back. The tension between us eased. He knew his limits. Whether he could kung fu or not, it wasn't going to do him any good when I froze his ass in time. He parted his lips and bit down, his teeth clicking together. Something shot between his lips and stung my neck. A pinprick. I rubbed the left side of my neck, the spot already numb.

"What the hell did you just do?"

"I am sorry, dear Socket. The message has been delivered."

Something wiggled inside, bumping against my throat. I turned, pressing harder. My entire neck was numb.

Broak backed further away. I swung wildly and fell to one knee. The wiggling went to the back of my neck and pierced my spine. I tried to scream, but my throat was dead. My lips worked silently. I tapped my cheek, activating the nojakk, and attempted to call Spindle. I couldn't make a sound. I crawled on my knees, reaching for the tower, but Spindle was thirty feet above the ground.

Broak watched. I drooled a long string onto the floor. The wiggling sensation penetrated deeper. Numbness traveled down my spine. It reached the bottom and exploded. Fire erupted.

On my back. Colors bright. *Timeslicing.*

And I wasn't controlling it.

15

Lullaby

IN TIMESLICED SILENCE, I lay still. I could see the ceiling now that the hovering platforms had thinned. It was a hundred feet above. It was blue. Like the sky. I could not feel the hard floor beneath me or the wiggling sensation in my neck. I couldn't move and I was alone. I'd die like that.

Just wish I could say goodbye to someone.

Unconsciousness came like a black fog, rolling in from above, eating up the remaining hovering platforms and gobbling up the walls. It came for me, creeping over my face. But something was moving within it. There was sound.

Pivot crawled over me and the black cloud scattered. He slid his fingers behind my head, probing a spot burning on my neck. I trembled, hoping he would get the message TO STOP DOING THAT!

He picked me up. The room spun.

In several blurry moves, we dropped into a dark, musty tunnel, where the light was gray and the ceiling smooth. He put me down and his hair fell over his face. He listened like a morning bird, pressing his fingers on the back of my neck again, this time harder and deeper. Like driving nails. Pain burned into my skull and down my spine. I was helpless to stop him. Unable to scream.

The source of pain was in my neck, branching like lightning, searing me from the inside, until Pivot pulled something out. I fell limp and relieved, taking tiny gulps of air. Pivot leaned against the wall, his knees pulled up. Something squirmed in his hand like a long crystalline horsehair.

[An accelerator.] His face was slick with sweat. *[Your energy centers are now attempting to prematurely bind.]*

"Broak did that." My teeth chattered.

[Yes.]

"Why?"

[Your awakening is failing.]

I pushed off the floor and winced. Small sparks shot down my back, crackling just under the skin. "I can still feel... things happening."

Pivot gently pushed me back down, placed his hand on my chest, turned his head and listened. He touched several spots. The Adam's apple in his throat bobbed up and down, and a low hum vibrated through his hand. The humming was soft and numbing, but the sparking pain fought back. I closed my eyes while Pivot moved his hand across my chest and hummed in different pitches. Sometimes loud. Sometimes soft. It tried to carry me off to a dreamy place, but jagged rips of pain yanked me back. He hummed louder to soften the blows. And then I would drift again.

Mmmmmmm. The sound travelled into my bones.

Warmth oozed inside and the pain receded.

Mmmmmmmmmmmm.

I floated away and left the hurt in my skin. I saw Pivot hunched over my body, with his hand on my chest and humming. I continued to float upwards and away. I tried to swim back, but I was helpless. Despite the pain and agony back there, I wasn't ready to leave. Not yet. Please.

I went through the ceiling and into the ground above. I rose through the compacted soil and red streaks of iron. Roots appeared, branching out with little white tendrils, tiny hairs sucking moisture from the pore space. Higher still, there were more roots and insects feeding on them. I passed through it all and emerged above ground, into the sunlight.

A breeze rustled fallen leaves across the slab. Pivot was against the grimmet tree. Grimmets crawled down his arms and hung from his fingers. He lifted his head. A man walked up the stone slab with a bundle of blankets. He wore the uniform of a Paladin, but his hair was long and face unshaven. *Father.*

He knelt next to Pivot and pulled the blankets open. A baby struggled in the light, his eyes clenched. He opened his toothless mouth and let loose a cry that woke every last grimmet hiding inside the tree's hollows. They shot from the branches and stormed overhead, casting an ominous shadow over the child.

Pivot turned his face up and grinned, his sightless eyes searching. While my father looked young, Pivot looked exactly the same. He touched the baby's chin, stroked his cheeks and touched his nose. The child stopped crying and wrapped his whole hand around Pivot's finger. Pivot's laugh came out like a hoarse bark.

The grimmets shifted and laughed, too. The child's gaze moved through the colorful cloud and the grimmets wrestled to get in front, sticking out their tongues, thumbing their noses for attention. Fights broke out. They whipped each other with their tails and pulled each other's ears. The baby squealed with delight. The grimmets crowded closer, making goo-goo and gaga sounds. Pivot waved them off.

"He's got my eyes," my father said. "And his chin's square, too. He's going to be strong. And independent."

That was me in the blankets. I was hoping this was a dream and I wasn't watching my life pass before me.

My father placed the bundle in Pivot's arms. Suddenly, I was swaddled in the blankets. I'd become the baby. I could feel Pivot rocking me side to side. I felt his chest heave when he barked out laughter, and the grimmets' wings beat the wind onto my face. I reached up for his face and caught a handful of hair. I pulled his face closer, feeling his breath stream onto my cheeks. I felt so safe.

Pivot rubbed his nose against mine and cooed a lullaby, a sound humming deep inside his throat. It started with a single note, vibrating long and low, and then drifted up and down. He closed his eyes, moving his head to the rhythm of his wordless song. The grimmets joined in, their little voices humming a higher pitch.

Mmmmmmmmmmmmm.

There was nowhere to go. Nothing to do.

MmmmmmMMMMMM.

The world was perfect in that moment.

Mmmmmmm.

Mmmm.

The ground quaked. I jerked into the rock and resurfaced. The tree was empty. Pivot was gone. My father was, too. A dust cloud swept over the rock, carrying fallen leaves.

I went down again, hard this time. Past the insects, roots and rocks, and slammed into my skin like brick on brick. My teeth clamped. Something hardened like an iron fist in my groin. I convulsed. Another knot tightened in my stomach. My chest knotted. My throat constricted. Electricity ripped through me. Pivot's touch faded in the gloom.

The awakening had arrived.

I COULDN'T REMEMBER Pivot picking me up or how long he'd been carrying me. I could only see the tunnel fall away behind us. His legs were blurred below, moving inhumanly fast. The walls were flying by. My hair was plastered to my face, but I no longer felt fiery pain. I was just numb.

Where are you taking me?

[You must awaken.]

The tunnels were endless and all the same. Sometimes we took a left turn, sometimes a right. We passed through an archway outlined on the wall and dropped; then we went through another archway and dropped again. Vertigo churned my stomach. With each drop, the air turned colder and heavier. Pivot slowed, turned the last corner, and put me on my feet. He held me up so I wouldn't fall.

I faced an archway at the end of a tunnel. The last stop.

Somewhere deep inside, I felt a quiver. Something I couldn't ignore. It was time to face my demons. "I'm scared, Pivot." My lips were fat. "I admit it."

He held me firmly. *[Even heroes experience fear.]*

"I'm no hero."

The archway buzzed. I pushed back into Pivot. He held me tighter, then let go. The doorway drew me closer. My feet scuffed over the gritty floor. I reached back for Pivot, but I was sucked through to the other side.

Agony returned.

———

THE ROOM WAS small and the walls etched with symbols. Blue light pulsed at the other end. *BOOM-boom. BOOM-boom.* Voices came from the light. They wanted me to come closer. I locked my knees, but my right foot slid forward. I tightened up and leaned back, but the voices pulled. My left foot moved. Left, right, left, I shuffled toward the light against my will. The voices were a jumbled crowd, talking among themselves, but the closer I got, the clearer they became.

[Who is it? This is unexpected. He is young... so young. This isn't right. Should he awaken? It's too late for him to turn back.]

They argued in circles, no voice sounding the same. Meanwhile, the room was volcanic. I was afraid to look down. *Is that my skin dripping?*

There were hundreds of voices now. Unseen fingers probed my body, feeling and studying. Deciding. Their minds penetrated me, looking through all the dark corners of my past. Memories opened, flipping too fast to recognize. They consumed the entire catalog of my life and all the intimate details, the ones I'd forgotten and the ones I wanted secret. I was completely exposed. Naked.

The voices stopped. The probing halted. In unison, they spoke one last word.

[Awaken.]

The blue light freed me from my skin. There were no walls. No ceiling or floor. I was somewhere in between. The light was a ball the size of my head. Or maybe it was the size of a planet. There was nothing to compare. Maybe *I* was as big as a planet. The surface swirled blue and white. Liquidy. It pulsed, alive. I'd seen this before.

A virtualmode portal!

I reached for it. I don't know what I reached with, I didn't have hands, and I don't know why I did it. Something urged me to. I reached and reached, through endless space.

The voices chanted far away. They buzzed inside me, building tension until it felt more like humming than buzzing. The more I reached, the louder it felt and the tighter I became. The thinner I was until I felt so thin I didn't even exist.

There was a warm sensation when I merged with the portal. It filled me. Then I knew that I was not breaking, I was not thin, but I was full. I was everything, as if I was dissolving into the universe.

Blip.

There was nothing. I think I screamed, but there was no pain. There was just nothing. I continued to dissolve into deep darkness until, for once, I felt complete peace. For once, I understood what this life was all about, yet I couldn't say what it was. I could only be there. I could only experience it. *I understand.*

I faded into a dreamless sleep. Part of me hoped I would never have to go back to the skin, but I knew that wouldn't be. There was still so much to do. And so many people I couldn't leave behind.

16

Unforgiven

It was sometime later, I woke. A dim light radiated under the bed. All kinds of things came out of the dark. Lookits hovered over me. Long mechanical arms extended from the walls, tending to a thick band wrapped around my left arm, where tubes came out, one filled with blood, the other blue. I licked my lips. A lookit pressed against my mouth and squirted something.

They did their jobs like a surreal nightmare. Maybe it was the blue fluid pumping into my arm, or I was just too tired to make sense. Or maybe the abnormal just seemed normal.

One of the mechanical arms touched my forehead and I was sleepy again. I woke a few times, but no one was there. I dreamed that little creepy things crawled inside my head and went through my memories, putting everything back in place before I woke.

Then one day, I woke fresh and clear. The room was bright. I threw my legs over the bed and sat up. I touched my nojakk and asked for the date. Thursday. Three days had passed.

Broak tried to kill me.

I didn't ache or burn, and none of my skin melted. I felt light and strong, my spine solid as a hundred-year oak. Hot spots hummed along my back from my tailbone to the top of my head. And there were smells. Lots of them. The air was filled with thousands of distinctive scents. There were traces of people, servys, and food in the air and places they touched along the wall. There was a distinct tangy, steely scent. *Spindle.* And another scent mingled with it, another person was in the room with him. She smelled like jasmine. I sensed her on my wrist, the back of my hand, my shoulder. Mom was here.

I've awakened.

A tray extended from the wall, with neatly folded clothes. I pulled the shirt off the pile, holding it by the sleeves. It was dark, dark purple. The pants, too. I got dressed and the tray folded into the wall.

"You are feeling well?" Spindle came into the room.

I just looked at him, not knowing what to say. He had to know what happened, but you wouldn't know it by the way he walked in like any other morning. He put his hand on my chest, put his fingers to my neck. His face flashed multiple colors.

"Your vitals are perfect. You may follow me."

"Wait." My voice sounded different. Deeper, maybe. Richer. "Where are we going?"

"Your preliminary judgment." The colors on his face muted. "The Paladin Nation will decide your immediate future."

His skin was cooler than usual. His voice wasn't really Spindle-like, either. It was more businesslike. More robot-like.

"What did they do to you?"

"Information classified."

"What?"

"I am not classified to discuss the case."

"What case?" I pulled him from the door. "Listen, Broak attacked me. He said some crazy shit about delivering a message, and then he shot this accelerator into my neck with his teeth..." Spindle's face contained no color. "Are you listening?"

He pulled his arm away. "We cannot be late."

The lights in the room dimmed. Spindle waited in the leaper, his shoulders thrown back and his head high. The leaper wobbled the moment I stepped inside. They did something to him again. They stripped the Spindle out of him. Now he was just another servy. I started to say something, but he stepped through the door.

———

THE ROOM WAS ENORMOUS. Everyone in it wore the same color clothes as me. Mom was on the right next to the minty man, Walter Diggs. *Commander* Walter Diggs. His eyes were harder than the last time I met him, what seemed like a lifetime ago. Pike and two other minders with black wraparound glasses were several yards in front of me. They were skinny waifs that were at least a foot taller than Pike and stood just off his shoulder, a half-step behind him.

To the left, standing all alone, was Broak.

I clutched my fists and warm spots whirred along my spine. Time warped as the metaphorical spark glittered in my belly and I started after him. I had a message to deliver.

Spindle clutched my arm. "Control your actions, Master Socket. An act of violence will be dealt with severely." His face darkened. "Crawler guards are on alert."

I yanked my arm, but his grip tightened. Broak stared ahead, unblinking. He didn't plan on me surviving. The minders went through my memories; they would see what he said. They would see him spitting the accelerator. He would get what he deserved.

"Please step forward." Spindle pointed at a circle glowing on the floor.

The spongy floor squeezed between my toes. Mom and the commander stood with their arms locked behind their backs. Her lips were thin and her eyes red. The commander had a soldier's unmoving expression.

The room rumbled and sections of the floor rose up behind the minders, forming a horseshoe wall encircling us all. The room turned brown, the floor hard marble, and the ceiling sky blue. Men and women appeared at the top of the wall, like a panel of judges, from the chest up. Soldiers' expressions.

"Hearing 24489 of Socket Pablo Greeny"—a woman's voice rang through the room—"is now in session. Evidence mined from Socket Pablo Greeny's memory has been presented to the committee. Witnesses and the accused are present."

A big man with slumping shoulders sat directly above the minders at the top of the wall. He looked around the committee and cleared his throat. "Socket Greeny." His voice boomed. "Do you know why you are here?"

I shook my head.

"I see." He looked down at notes or something. The rest of the committee kept hard looks coming. "You have accessed an awakening portal without authorization."

I moved my mouth, searching for words, then found them. "Um, Your... Honor?"

"You may address me as Authority." His deep-set eyes hid under the shadow of his protruding eyebrows.

"Your Authority, I don't know what this is all about. Broak approached me and initiated my awakening with an accelerator, which was like this squiggly wire he shot out of his mouth and went right in my neck." They stared, no one saying a thing. "Look, I know this sounds crazy, your star pupil over there attacking me out of jealousy and all, but it happened. Just check my memories, it's all there."

The Authority held up his hand. "Broak is not on trial. It is you, Socket Greeny, that we are here to judge. I'll confirm that you understand why you are here and we can continue."

"Wait, he's not on trial? How can... are you kidding? He tried to kill me!"

He held up his hand again and I stiffened under his psychic pressure. He looked around the circle, and each member of the committee returned his knowing glance.

"Each of these members is projecting from around the world, so let me get on without further interruption. Your preliminary results are exceptional, demonstrating the highest potential the Paladin

Nation has ever recorded, including the young man to your left." He nodded to Broak. "You have very promising timeslicing skills and have demonstrated superb psychic aptitude. For a cadet, that is quite impressive, especially at your age. And while you might claim cadet Broak attacked you out of jealousy, the minders have probed both your minds sufficiently and found no evidence to support your claims."

"Impossible."

The Authority grimaced, on the verge of emotion. "We're not here to play games, Socket Greeny. The memories mined from you were distorted by your premature awakening. Many of them were indecipherable, colored with hallucinations. Broak's memories were clear and accurate and have been confirmed by security. You two had an argument. Broak instigated the altercation and has been reprimanded for his behavior. However, the fact remains the argument incited your awakening. Provoked or not, this is of concern. All of this has been confirmed by the minders."

"Him?" I pointed at Pike.

"The minders monitor each other. There was no deception on the part of Pike, I can assure you. There is enough psychic power in this room to keep him from concealing anything from us."

"This isn't fair!" I looked around for support, but there were only soldiers looking ahead, letting me dangle. Mom quivered, her jaws grinding, but she held still. "That isn't what happened, Authority! He attacked me! Check the records. He spit an accelerator through his teeth—"

"Enough!"

I slammed my fists into my legs, careful not to step out of the circle. This couldn't be happening. He's getting away with it. I glared at Broak standing at attention. I reached with my mind. Invisible psychic tentacles wrapped around his head. I squeezed. Broak shook, his face twitching in pain, until an icy lance of psychic energy cut through me. I almost fell. The minders hadn't moved, but had immobilized me physically and mentally. One last cold wave squeezed my brain and I could breathe again.

"Authority?" Pike said.

"Continue."

"I'm willing to excuse cadet Socket's insolence due to his ignorance and youth." Pike's left eyebrow twitched.

"Noted." The Authority leaned forward, furrowing his wild eyebrows. "No more interruptions. The real issue, Socket Greeny, isn't the unauthorized awakening or the intrusion. It is your stability."

The atmosphere tightened. The air moved in waves. I stood straight, drawing air to purge the scraping discomfort of Pike's mind against mine.

"Your father was feral, which means he developed Paladin powers outside the breeding program. Therefore, you will face greater scrutiny because of your potential instability. The fact is, there are many Paladins that do not want you awakened, regardless of your potential, because you were not bred. Do you understand what I am saying?"

I nodded, efficiently.

This pleased the Authority. His lower lip plumped out and he looked to his notes once again. "Let me officially recognize that Socket Greeny prematurely entered the awakening phase. While this does not prove instability, it is suspect. He infiltrated the awakening portal, a most sacred source of power hidden deep within the Garrison, to complete the awakening—"

"He could've died!" Mom finally broke, storming in front of me. "He did what any Paladin should do! He assessed the situation and responded accordingly! And you ignore the evidence that cadet Broak incited this premature awakening and you condemn my son for saving his own life!"

The Authority stuck out his chin, his brows setting his eyes deeper in their pockets. The commander stepped to Mom's side, put his arms around her, nodded to the Authority, and ushered her back. Her cheeks flamed.

"I WILL NOT TOLERATE ONE MORE EPISODE OF IMPUDENCE!" the Authority said with a booming voice, shaking the walls on which he sat. "The next outburst will be dealt with severely, Commander Diggs. Is that understood?"

The commander nodded once. Mom resumed the pose, hands behind her back and head down, quaking. Pike's expression softened with a curl at the corner of his mouth.

The Authority took a deep breath. "This matter is not an easy decision. The committee understands that cadet Broak was involved in a confrontation. We also know that Socket Greeny was *taken* from the Graveyard. This person who took you there will be held responsible, just as you are."

"Pivot?" I said, barely above a whisper.

"He will be judged when found."

Found?

"However, the committee has voted, eight to seven, for a continuance to further investigate the matter," the Authority said. "In the meantime, your abilities will be clamped. You will not be able to timeslice or exercise psychic ability. You will reenter society. The clamp will prevent you from discussing Paladin matters and will remain in place until final judgment is rendered. Do you understand this, Socket Greeny?"

"You're going to make me normal?"

"For a time."

Like normal was punishment.

"Very well," the Authority said. "If there is no more from the committee?" He looked around and got cold stares in return. "Then hearing 24489 will conclude. You will be summoned for final judgment in four weeks. Please be escorted to receive the clamp." The Authority nodded to me. "Good day."

THE WALL COLLAPSED into the floor, taking the images of the Authority and his companions with it. Pike and Broak quickly went to a leaper on the other side of the room. Not until they were gone did the glowing circle disappear and I could move. I tried to speak, but nothing intelligible came out. Mom put her arm around me. I tensed.

The commander still had his hands behind his back. "You have a lot of questions, but for now there is business at hand. While you were recovering, we lobbied for a continuance to further investigate Broak. If what you believe is true, there is much to understand."

What I *believe*. Even he thought I was cracked.

He patted my shoulder, but not so much like everything would be all right. More like *hang in there, kid.*

"But—"

"Socket, you truly don't understand the impact you're having on the Paladin Nation," he said. "When you display your kind of potential, you make enemies as fast as allies. Penetrating Spindle's database caused a lot of concern, but this awakening..." He paused. "I want you clamped so there are no problems while we sort some things out. It's the only way."

Mom squeezed me again. "I'll be with you very soon."

I could feel her emotionally disconnect. I had always felt that hollow craving for her, the missing element of a mother, but now that I was awakened, it was painfully present. No escaping the dull pang of watching her leave with the commander.

Or just leaving.

Spindle guided me to the leaper. He was stiffer, consciously picking each leg up and putting it down. There was no sway at the hips. His eyelight was fixed on the destination. He stepped in the leaper and did an about-face fresh out of boot camp.

"Where're we going?" I said.

"We will go to the infirmary to have the clamp installed. Your mother will meet you there to take you home."

"Home?"

"Yes."

"They're letting me go home?"

He didn't answer because he was a program and my question didn't make sense to a program. Spindle would've answered, but not this hollow shell. I could sense his optical gear viewing me as another human, just a task to complete. Once he was done, he would move on to the next thing on his list. And that was to put a clamp inside me.

17

CLAMPDOWN

WE ENTERED an infirmary with a sterile table in the center. A hood of lamps hovered over it. Three rotund servys waited. The one in the center was red and larger than the others.

"Lie face down on the platform," Spindle said.

I swore I wouldn't do it again, but I *reached out* to read him. It got him reprogrammed the last time, but what was there to lose? That wasn't him standing there.

When I moved my mind this time, it seemed as effortless as lifting my arm. I could take his memories like plucking apples. The circuit fluid flowed with a steady rhythm, not the *BUM-bum* of a heart but the mechanical efficiency of a pump. I sensed a fresh set of criterion burned into his procedural code. He had recently been reprogrammed, but this time there was a dimness surrounding his circuits. They shut down his heart processor, the thing that made him Spindle. It was what made him curious.

Spindle shut down my psychic intrusion, kicking me back to my own skin. "Lie on the table."

"What're they going to do?"

"The medical mech will install a suppression clamp."

An appendage grew from the center of the red servy. It looked more like a talon than it did a hand. It held a C-shaped ring.

"The suppression clamp," Spindle said, "will fit between the third and fourth vertebra."

"You're going to put that thing inside me?"

"You will not feel it. The servys will render you unconscious for the nine-minute surgery."

The servy's fingers were sharp as scalpels. My fingers twitched. The awakening stripped away the mystery of timeslicing. I saw inside myself, how it all worked. I clenched my hands to timeslice, but that's not really what did it. The fingers were just a crutch; what really triggered the timeslice was a signal from my brain, altering the metabolism throughout my body. I could turn it on or off with a thought.

And the clamp would take that away.

I needed a minute. I had to talk with the commander; there had to be another way. I would stay in the Preserve if that's what they wanted. Maybe I could find Pivot. I didn't have to go home, as long as they didn't put that thing in my neck.

The surface of the red servy glittered like a magical orb. A halo engulfed all three of them as I timesliced. Spindle had his hand raised. Maybe he anticipated what I was about to do. I just wanted out of the room. I could figure out how to operate that leaper. All I had to do was *reach* inside its circuit panel.

Legs emerged from the leaper door, multi-jointed with sharpened tips. A crawler stepped into the room, bright and glistening in the timesliced light. A red eyelight burned on the front, directed at me.

They're watching.

I let go of time and the crawler vanished, returning to its post, waiting to see if I was foolish enough to try it again. Spindle stood at the corner of the table.

I scanned the room for a weapon. Fighting was a ridiculous

thought, sure, but I had to exhaust every possibility before I gave in to what was about to go down.

"Lie down."

"You're going to have to make me," I said.

Spindle did not move. Instead, ten more servys entered the room. There was barely space to move, but I would stomp them until I couldn't stomp anymore if that's what it took. But it didn't take the servys to disarm me. It was a scent. *Jasmine.* I could sense her before she entered the room.

"I know it's hard," Mom said, touching my arm. "But there is no choice. Without the clamp, the Authority and his committee will not agree to a continuance. They want to send you home to keep you out of the Garrison. They want you disarmed and far away. It is the only way, Socket. It is the only choice we have."

She pushed the hair behind her ear. Despite the pale look, she was strong. I would fight every Paladin before doing what they wanted, but it only took a look from her and a gentle touch to change my mind and to fill the empty ache.

The table reformed to fit my body. My face fit in the opening and it didn't restrict my breathing.

"The medical servy is going to place nighter gear on the back of your head," Spindle said. "It will only take a moment."

Mom held my hand. The medical servy pushed my hair around and slid something cold against my scalp.

Her hand was warm.

The nighter gear whined.

My head vibrated. My teeth, lips, and tongue became numb. And then, like a switch, it was night.

I WAS SITTING UP, I thought.

"I'm going to stay with Socket tomorrow," Mom was saying. "I'll make the meetings by projection. I've already forwarded apologies that I can't return in person, but I think they'll understand. If all goes well, I'll be back the next day."

She was right in front of me, digging through her briefcase. Spindle was next to her, standing at full attention. His face was dull.

My blood was like syrup. I was afraid to turn my head. It might fall off.

On a floating chair.

In a hallway.

Mom wasn't standing, she was walking.

We were just in a room. Now we were going through a doorway. We entered the dank stalactite parking garage. Mom's car was at the bottom of the steps. Servys stood at the open doors. One of them took Mom's briefcase and loaded it into the backseat. Appendages grew from the ones next to me and took my arms. Their fingers were soft and tacky. They helped me inside the car and shut the door. When I looked out, Spindle was already gone.

The car banked sharply to the left and we flew through the wall and over the boulder-strewn field. A crescent moon was fading in the sky as the sun was about an hour from rising. The dashboard was illuminated with instruments, casting an orange glow on Mom's face, accentuating the lines pulling her eyes. We drove without lights.

"Spindle had to be washed out." Mom pretended to steer. "The Authority wanted him deactivated for his involvement in the incident. They suspect he somehow helped you escape the Graveyard through an unmarked exit. They think he had something to do with Pivot's disappearance, too. The commander had to compromise with the Authority. Spindle's personality was deactivated."

I rubbed my neck, feeling the raised line where the clamp was surgically implanted. The seat sensed my discomfort, wrapped tightly against my neck, and applied heat. Live oaks blotted the moon from view in a black sky. We were already in South Carolina. I couldn't remember going through the wormhole.

"I don't like this." I touched my lips. They didn't feel right. "My voice sounds weird. This doesn't feel like my skin."

"Your body is adjusting. It'll take a few hours for your nervous system to accept the limitations of the clamp. Soon enough, you'll feel just like you did before all this started."

"Why'd you let them do this to me?"

"Many Paladins aren't in favor of your awakening. The clamp bought us time to change some minds."

"You *want* me to be a Paladin?"

She sighed. "If they vote to permanently disable your awakening, you won't be the same. You'll be alive." She wouldn't look at me. "Just not the same."

Just like Spindle.

She took her hand from the steering wheel and plunged her thumb into the moody. I was tempted to pull it away from her and make room for my thumb. I'd try anything to take this deadness away. If the moody helped, then a big fat thank you goes out to the drug companies. The Paladins had me. *Check.*

"That's illegal," I said. "They can't operate on people against their will. There are human rights that protect people from that."

"No one even knows we exist."

She said 'we.' She's one of them.

"You have to understand, they can't let someone with the ability to timeslice back into the general public. If a cadet is considered unsuitable, unstable, or incapable, they will alter the nervous system to squelch his or her abilities."

"I didn't ask for this."

"No one does."

"You're one of them." I said it like a right hook.

Mom took a moment to dig her thumb in deeper. Her next breath trembled.

"You have no idea what lurks in the world, what kinds of danger threaten our very existence every single second. As reprehensible as the Paladins seem, they're our only hope. I don't expect you to understand."

We passed an exit that connected to a northbound interstate, lights flashing. The road was open and long. If we went north without stopping, we could be a thousand miles away by daybreak.

"We can't run," Mom said. "They'd find us within the hour."

And checkmate.

We turned onto the highway heading home. Few cars were in the way. It was close to the middle of the night. Mom let go of the wheel and let the car drive in autopilot.

"Broak said they assassinated Dad."

"Your father was respected in the Paladin Nation. If there was even a hint of foul play, the commander would've investigated the accident until the day he died. Your father was in an accident. Broak was merely taunting you."

I tried to *reach* out to see if she was telling the truth. The clamp slammed against the bottom of my brain. I moaned.

"Don't try that," she said, taking my hand. "Any attempt to do *something* will hurt."

I was normal now. I had no *power*. It was what I wanted, to be normal, but now that I had a taste of the awakening, normal didn't seem all that normal. I wasn't sensing Mom's jasmine-flavored energy anymore.

Off the interstate, Mom took the car out of autopilot. We turned left, waited at a stoplight, then made the last right home. Almost eight months had passed. The azaleas were in full bloom in front of our house. Our porch was lit. We silently coasted up to the driveway. Someone was on our front steps. I threw the door open before the car stopped, ran across the grass and crashed into Chute. She crushed me in her embrace, weeping into my shoulder, her chest heaving against mine.

"I didn't think you were coming back." I could barely understand her. "I didn't think I'd see you again."

My heart was clutching. Suddenly, I realized just how much I missed her.

"Glad you're back," Streeter said. He didn't hug me. He sort of punched my shoulder while Chute squeezed me until I couldn't breathe. "It hasn't been the same without you."

"Come inside," Mom said on her way to the door. "It's too late to stay out here."

CHUTE AND STREETER stayed the night. We talked until three o'clock that morning. Never once did they ask where I'd been. Maybe Mom prepped them; those questions were off-limits. Or maybe they didn't care, they were just glad to see me. Maybe both.

Chute slept in my bed. Streeter and I crashed on the couches. For once, Mom slept in her room. It didn't take long to fall asleep. I was glad to be home.

PART III

Every self-aware intelligence eventually asks the question: Who am I? There is a yearning to know the answer, to find out what we are and where we fit in. Do we matter?

18

Bleed

THERE WAS some discussion whether I should go back to school. Truth be told, Mom didn't care either way. In fact, I thought she wanted me to stay home. In my entire life, there had never been a morning I woke up excited about going to school. Not one. I didn't care about what field trips we were taking or movies we were watching, I'd just rather do something else. But when I was home alone and everyone else was at school, what else was I going to do?

I slacked off around the house for a week. It took that long just to feel halfway normal with the thing in my neck. I could feel it when I turned a certain way or thought about something that had to do with Paladins. Once, I imagined telling Streeter and Chute everything and the damn thing about knocked me out. Most of the time it just wiggled and vibrated like something crawling under my skin. I couldn't stop thinking about it, so I had to get out of the house. I packed my book bag and caught the bus in late April.

Two freshmen were whispering in front of me. Occasionally, they looked around the cafeteria, pretending to search for a friend as an excuse to look at me. I pretended not to notice. They went back to whispering. The line moved forward. One of them grabbed a lunch tray first; the other had to run to catch up. They looked back, one last time, not bothering to whisper anymore.

There are rumors about where you went, Streeter had told me. Yeah, I heard the rumors, too, whispered behind hands when I walked down the hall, and in the locker room when they didn't know I was there. I was under CIA investigation and got locked up in juvenile detention. I lost my mind in the virtualmode journey and had a nice long stay in a psych ward. I joined a secret cult worshipping technology and was building a spacecraft in a secret hideaway. That wasn't too far off, really.

Streeter waited for me to say something about the freshmen. When I didn't, he stared at the menu with an unspoken question left on his tongue. Every day he wanted to ask the question, but he didn't. Where *have* you been? He never asked, but every day he came a little closer.

I stepped up to the window. "Um, give me a three, eleven and a twenty-two."

A metal tray rolled out. Applesauce, cheesecake and chicken spilled over the sides and mixed together. The servys would never let that happen. I followed Streeter into the cafeteria. Chute was at a table by herself, wearing a purple jersey. An *athletic* jersey.

"Nice shirt," I said.

"Thanks," she said. "You were on vacation when I got it."

Vacation. That was what she called it. I went on vacation for eight months, just didn't bring back any pictures.

Chute smoothed the front of her jersey, showing off the holographic lightning bolt across the front, illuminating our mascot: a fox stomping through the swamp. In the time I was gone, tagghet had moved into the high school system and teams were formed and a stadium built. Spindle wasn't kidding; the sport was exploding. Chute told me how her dad nearly knocked over a light when she made the team. The more she talked, the more her freckles crunched in her dimples. If I could feel her energy, it would be vibrant and tingly. I imagined it smelled orangey. But the clamp stopped all that. It was an ever-vigilant fairy that stole the words from my mouth when I even thought about saying something that might reveal the existence of Paladins or dupes. Instead of sitting on my shoulder, this fairy was buried in my neck and turned me into a robot. *Follow orders, Socket. Or else.*

"I wish I could see you more," Chute said. "We've been doing two-a-day practices for the last week with the game so close. They're talking about a huge crowd, too." She took a deep breath. "I'm getting nervous."

I cut another piece of chicken and looked away. When she talked about tagghet, the memory of Broak bludgeoning a servy popped up. He was smiling when he did it, cold and perfect. If I let the memory linger, the clamp throbbed.

I rubbed my neck.

"They'll stop whispering, Socket," she said. "Just give it some time."

She thought I was bothered by the rumors. People seated near us were talking and I hadn't even noticed. I grunted, chewing my food. Honestly, I didn't give a rat's ass what they thought, but I let Chute believe it bothered me. It kept her from asking what was really on my mind. Streeter was too busy eating to notice anything.

"You coming to my practice tonight?" she asked.

"I want to. Really, I do. But there're so many people there. I'm not really into crowds right now."

"You're going to have to get used to it, sooner or later."

"I vote for later."

"I'll save a seat for you in the stands, have the coach post lookits around to keep people away."

"Oh, that'll work," Streeter mumbled, food spilling out of his mouth. "No one will wonder who the royal prince is with the king's guard. The lookits will just point at him."

"What if I give you guys tagger uniforms?" she said. "You can stand on the sidelines, blend right in."

"Or you can dig us a hole at center pitch, cover it with a trapdoor," I said. "We can watch you with a periscope."

We laughed. Streeter pounded the table. Everyone looked at us again, wondering what was so funny this time. *Look, the freak is laughing.* It didn't stop me. I pictured a bunker with a manhole cover over the top. I could push it up and look with one eye over the edge. Were they thinking the same thing? Before I could stop myself, I *reached* for their thoughts to see. The clamp slammed against my spine.

I held my neck and moaned. They asked if I was all right. I said yeah, it was just a migraine. Streeter wondered how a migraine gets in your neck. Chute pried my fingers away to see what I was hiding. I wanted her to stop, but didn't want to put up too much of a fight.

"Where'd you get that?" she asked, touching the thin red line on my neck.

"It's nothing."

Streeter stood up. "It looks like you got operated on."

"It's nothing." I spooned some applesauce off the tray to look normal, but my hand shook.

Chute traced the line with her finger. It felt good. I wanted to tell them everything, but I couldn't go there. I couldn't even tell them I couldn't tell them. I wanted them to know what I really was. I wanted them to know there were Paladins hiding in mountains with amazing technology and a bona fide jungle. I wanted to tell Chute about the grimmets and Streeter about nanotechnology. And Spindle! They would love him (if he were back to normal). And what if Streeter knew about the dupes? *Dupes? In the skin?* He'd piss all over himself.

Streeter and Chute knew everything about me. Now, my entire life was a lie. I wanted to be closer to them, but the secrets built a wall around me. They could feel it, too. They knew I was keeping something from them. I was even more alone than ever and I never thought that was possible. If only I could tell them—*pppssslllptttt.*

A wad of pizza splattered on my forehead.

"Bull's-eye!"

Several tables over an uber-punk group of bleeders—boys and girls, all with black eyeliner—stood to get a look. They were a bunch of freaking wannabe vampires. The only thing that separated them from the goths was two spots of fake blood on their necks. Plus, they were giant assholes. The biggest of the bunch weighed nearly three hundred pounds and had a freshly shaved head that shined under the cafeteria lights. He used to play football in middle school, but he got kicked off the team for beating up one of the assistant coaches.

"Freak," he said deeply.

The table shook in my grip. The clamp quivered, grinding against my spine, and not because I wanted to read his mind. No. I fought the urge to show the fat-ass bleeder just how freaky I was. The clamp made sure I didn't.

The entire cafeteria watched, not even trying to hide it. The bleeders were after someone. Better yet, they were going after the freak! It was a main event! Fat bleeder drew his lips back, exposing tobacco-stained teeth, and blew imaginary smoke from his imaginary finger-gun. *Bull's-eye.* But he wasn't finished. The crowd was behind him now. They all wanted to see it go to the next level, but I was just sitting there with a two-handed grip on the table. He reached for another chunk of pizza. If I was going to be a willing target, then he didn't need an invitation to take another shot.

The table legs chattered on the floor.

Chute snatched up her water bottle. Her wind-up was tight, the release quick. The plastic bottle flew on a straight line, end over end, and hit that fat makeup-wearing dickweed so square in the forehead that it bounced straight back. He shuffled sort of cross-eyed.

The laughter paused.

Silence drifted from table to table. Laughing at me was one thing, but laughing at this guy could shorten your life. But the laughter started again, this time with the bleeders around him. They laughed right at him. And then the cafeteria followed right along. The dumb bastard rubbed his head and looked at his fingers to see if he was bleeding. Then he swatted the bottle off the table and kicked a chair.

The crowd cleared a path between us. Round one was going to be a bloodbath.

I still couldn't let go. The timeslicing spark flitted in my belly, aching to be clutched. But if I took the spark, the clamp knocked me out. The table quaked so violently that the trays were moving over the surface. All I could do was watch him stomp toward us, fists at his sides. He was going to roll me like a garbage truck.

Chute stood in front of me. Streeter slid his chair out and stood up, too. He was a half-step behind Chute, but he was up. He wouldn't be anything more than a stepping-stone in fatty's march to mutilation, but he might slow him down half a second. I closed my eyes, breathing deeply and calmly, hoping to get the clamp under control. At the very least, I could stand up with Chute. I'd fight the guy straight up, no Paladin powers needed; I just needed the clamp to SHUT THE HELL UP!

Chairs slid behind us. Fat bleeder stopped. Lacrosse players and tagghet players, united, surrounded our table. The 'crossers were bigger, stronger and meaner than the taggers, but there were enough of both to stall lardass and his troupe of fake bloodsuckers. Chute was out in front.

Streeter leaned over. "You want to get up?"

Fat bleeder wasn't a fan of a fair fight, as long as he was on the winning side. I could sense the simple math burning in his brain as he calculated the odds. They were outnumbered five to one. There wasn't a chance in hell, but there was also a lot of snickering going on behind him. Either anger got the best of him or he was really shitty at math because he came at us, fists up. His crew was behind him, coming like a band of theatre misfits, climbing over tables and chairs, stepping on food. The 'crossers stiffened. The taggers crouched.

"BACK TO YOUR SEATS!" Lookits dropped in like hornets, their eyelights spinning. "Go back to your seats before authorities are called."

The bleeders stopped a few feet away. Their hate shimmered like summer heat.

"An assault will be treated as a criminal offense." A lookit went to eye level with the fat one. "You have a previous record. Do not make this mistake."

The moments ticked long, the crowd silently hoping he'd do it anyway, knowing security would be there any second. He finally opened his hands and surrendered. If he could breathe fire, he would've roasted that shiny ball. He swatted at it, instead. The lookit dodged effortlessly, repositioning near the ceiling.

"Another day," he said to no one in particular.

He went back to his table, his crew in tow. He slapped one of them in the mouth. The others stayed out of reach, still snickering. Security arrived. They walked through the crowd and had a little chat with the bleeders. The cafeteria went back to the daily chatter and whispering and staring.

"Oh, man, that was close." Streeter collapsed in his chair. "I thought we were dead meat."

"You didn't have to do that, Chute." I wiped the pizza off with a napkin. "I can take care of myself."

"You expect me to sit there and watch?"

"That guy is twice your size. What were you going to do, chew on his kneecap?"

"If that's what it takes."

The 'crossers and taggers went back to their seats. Some of them slapped Chute on the back. They weren't standing up for me.

"You're one of them," I said. "Congratulations."

"No, Socket, I'm just me. I play tagghet, but I'm just me." She grabbed her tray and stood. "You know, a simple thanks would be enough."

She walked off. The bleeders watched, whispering.

"Why are you complaining?" Streeter said. "She just saved our lives, man."

I finished cleaning my forehead and dropped the napkin. I let out a long sigh. Things were so messed up.

"You need to say you're sorry," Streeter said.

He was right. I needed to apologize. I'm sorry the shadow turned me into a freak. I'm sorry there are Paladins out there and dupes threatening to kill every last one of us. I'm sorry my mom doesn't come home. I'm sorry there's a clamp in my neck that beats the shit out of me whenever I want to say something real.

I'm sorry that nothing will ever be the same.

AFTER SCHOOL, I made my way down a shortcut past the lacrosse field, where they practiced in shorts and helmets, past the empty baseball field to the brand new tagghet field. It was oval and green with three sides hemmed in by live oaks. Large bleachers flanked each side, with a smattering of fans.

I hid in the trees close enough to watch. The team flew around the field, flipping the tag back and forth, bouncing it off the ground or throwing it across the field. The coach barked plays from the sideline. I couldn't see their faces, but I could see the player with red braids swinging from under her helmet. She soared across center field on the jetter faster than anyone and caught a long pass in full stride, faking the defender with a backhand and spinning around to sling it into the scoring cube. The fans stomped the bleachers, cheering.

I tapped my nojakk. "Nice shot."

Chute looked around while her teammates patted her on the back. She tapped her nojakk, asking where I was. I told her. She looked in my direction. I stayed in the trees and watched the entire practice, chiming in with a comment whenever she did something outstanding just to let her know I was there. Whenever she scored, she looked my way.

When I got home, there were several messages. I didn't answer them. Streeter was sure to be calling, wondering why I didn't meet him in Buxbee's virtualmode lab after school. That night, I was on my bed, tossing a roll of socks at the ceiling when Mom called. *I'll be home late, but I will be home. You'll have to order out.* I told her not to stay too late.

A delivery man dropped off an order of Chinese food. I ate it on my bed and fell asleep without brushing my teeth and a half-box of fried rice on my bed. When I woke in the morning, there was a message on my nojakk. Mom's room was empty. She never made it home. Her message was an apology.

Something unexpected came up.

19

IN THE PIT

MOM CAME HOME TWICE that week. Both nights she collapsed on the couch and fell asleep. I made dinner and cleaned up. By morning, her bed was made. She was gone.

She was back to her old ways. She rarely came home. She checked in on the nojakk every evening, telling me to order out. Sometimes I didn't take her calls. We were having the same conversation, so what was the point? And we were back to the mother-son relationship with few words and no feelings. I stayed up as late as I wanted and watched movies. I stopped brushing my teeth altogether.

THE DAYS at school went by uneventfully. I seemed to be smarter than before. I never forgot a thing my teachers said. While everyone was taking mad notes, I just listened and nailed the exams. Sometimes, I thought I understood the subjects better than the teachers. Everything was just so logical. I supposed the clamp couldn't stop me from thinking.

I blended back into the normal crowd at school. People stopped staring. Even the bleeders forgot about me, throwing food at other people. Everything was back to the old days. I went to my hiding spot every day after school to watch Chute practice. I wanted to see her, sure, but more than that, I had to stay out of the house. The longer I sat around by myself, the more I started thinking. The slightest Paladin-related thought turned into a headache that could last for hours. But if there was a distraction, it was easier not to think, but then after a while I would wonder why I wasn't thinking and remember the clamp.

Headache.

The nights were the worst. Sleep came in small chunks. The clamp even monitored what few dreams I had, and anything that crossed the line pounded my ass. I spent hours going through meditative breathing exercises to empty my mind. I couldn't even think about when the Authority was going to rule. It should've happened weeks ago. All I could do was stay in the moment. But the moments were getting longer.

Streeter slept over every other night, and that helped. We stayed up late watching movies. I was careful not to catch any news reports. It was hard enough to keep from wondering who may or may not be a duplicate at school; I didn't need to be reminded about it on the TV. I caught the news once by accident and watched it long enough to see protesters fighting for the right of virtualmode duplication. There had to be a few in that crowd, or maybe all of them. One was a frizzy-headed dude that got plowed by the cops when he threw something. Did it hurt when the cops planted his face in the street and cuffed his hands behind his back? Could they control pain? Were they like computers?

The clamp taught me not to think about that.

I wanted it out. If that meant moving my shit into the mountain and never seeing Streeter and Chute again, I'd do it. This was no way to live. But even when I asked Mom when they would decide, she wouldn't tell me what was taking so long.

But the whole world was about to find out.

———

IT WAS the week before finals. There was a pep rally for the inaugural tagghet season at the end of school, but no one seemed to care except for the taggers wearing their jerseys to class. There was more talk about football and that was five months away. The tagghet season was only going to be two months long and go through the summer so it wouldn't interfere with more important sports, like lacrosse, baseball, basketball, football, soccer, tennis and softball. Tagghet seemed to rank just above tetherball for the time being.

It was the period just before the rally. I went to virtualmode studies in the Pit, a steep, circular auditorium with a domed ceiling. Buxbee was down at the center table. I made my way to the front, where Streeter was waiting with his transplanters in hand. I left the seat empty between us. Chute's seat. She wasn't in class very often. She'd been doing the assignments in the evening when she had time. I sat in her seat once before and Streeter insisted I move over. I thought maybe he thought it was gay if we sat too close. Maybe he did, but I thought he missed her. He wouldn't admit it.

Buxbee was a round man with a bald head and a horseshoe of hair around the outside. He tended to plump his bottom lip when he thought. He had a finger in one ear, talking on his nojakk, his brows pinched together.

"You promised you'd launch today." Streeter handed me a pair of transporters.

I had gone virtualmode only once since I got back and it was weird. Just as my awareness was pulled from my skin, there was some back and forth chatter between the transporters and the clamp like they were telling secrets about me. It didn't get any better once I was in my sim. I started skipping virtualmode lab after that. Headaches, I said. Then I'd go to the nurse and she'd let me lie in a dark room until my migraine settled. Turned out that wasn't much better because I'd start thinking and end up with a real migraine.

Streeter watched me trace the edges of the transporters. He sighed super loud. Twice. He already had one empty seat next to him. He didn't want two. He once grumbled that I'd changed, that he wanted it to be like it was before I went on my vacation. *Ditto that, brother.*

"All right, all right," I said. "I'm going, like I said."

Class was running ten minutes late. Buxbee was still chatting on the nojakk, with fingers in both ears to hear over the class. We tried to launch into virtualmode, but the transporters weren't active. Streeter was already being accused of crashing the school's portal.

"Attention!" Buxbee held up both hands. "I have an announcement. Everyone, I have an announcement." He walked around the center with his arms up like he was signaling a touchdown. After one trip around, he dropped his tired arms. His bottom lip plumped out and tension tightened his forehead. "Virtualmode is down for the day."

He didn't bother talking over the moans and groans and Streeter getting blamed for it. This was the last week of school, when everyone had a free pass to virtualmode anywhere and the school had one of the best portals in South Carolina. The experience was ten times richer than any home connection or any commercial connection in the tri-county area. Now Buxbee was telling them it was a no-go. "Don't do this to us, Mr. Buxbee," someone wailed.

When it was quiet enough for someone to ask why things were shut down and it was quiet enough for Buxbee to speak, he explained, "This is not a local blackout," he said. "Virtualmode has been shut down *globally*."

Another uproar, this time with a trace of curiosity mixed in. People were looking back and forth like they just heard the front end of a juicy rumor. Buxbee held out his hands, calming the class.

"I've uploaded the final assignment to your accounts. You can complete it when it's back up."

When, why and what happened? All those questions were met by

Buxbee's plumped lip and a shake of the head. When it was clear he didn't have the answers or wasn't willing to part with them, everyone broke out the laptops and tablets to look at the Internet on a screen. Buxbee was back on his nojakk, with a finger in his ear. Everyone was getting updates and I didn't want to hear it. The clamp was beginning to throb.

Streeter pulled out a collapsible touchpad and stretched it open on his lap. Three-dimensional images projected on the surface. He activated the sound on our nojakks. A global virtualmode blackout was the same as closing all the airports. It didn't take but a second to find the news. The reports claimed that a third of users were unable to launch into virtualmode that morning at approximately 6:32. At first, it was a minor inconvenience. Connections were typically reestablished within minutes. Typically, a portal facility experienced a small anomaly, something like a sunspot that was easily corrected. But then complaints started coming in from all over the world, threatening transportation and financial trading. At 7:29, the entire virtualmode grid went dark.

"That's never happened before," Streeter said.

I was rubbing the ache in my neck. I should've looked away. Knowing more wasn't going to help, it was only going to make the banging between my vertebrae louder. But I couldn't look away. And I couldn't help thinking. I let the thoughts come. *A third of virtualmode users? Did the Paladins block the world from virtualmode? And if they did, why? It had to have something to do with the dupes. Maybe they were beginning to distinguish the difference between people launching onto virtualmode from the... dupes? But why shut down virtualmode?*

The clamp slammed into that thought. I clenched my teeth. But I kept watching.

At 9:55 that morning, there were reports of federal testing of employees at a portal facility. Agents would not comment on what they were testing for since drug and euphoria-gear tests were made public. The testing was not met kindly by the employees, and arrests were made at an independent portal facility, where riot police were called. They charged through the doors into a warehouse of glowing portals.

The scientists and laborers didn't look surprised. In fact, they looked ready for them. They had weapons. Forty-two police were killed. There were a lot of dead workers, too, but the footage was censored even though police were required to fully disclose all public news footage. However, the report claimed all lookits stopped operating in the warehouse like they'd been shut off.

I was holding the back of my neck with both hands. I needed to get some air, needed to get out and clear out the thoughts, but the last scene caught my attention. I had to grit my teeth just a little longer. I had to make sure what I saw was right.

"Rewind that," I said.

Streeter wasn't sure what I was looking for. I turned the view on his lap and expanded a close-up on a white-coated scientist at the very back of the facility when the riot police made their entrance, before the bullets started flying. We both leaned closer to make sure what we were seeing. It was low resolution and pixilated. But I was right.

"That's impossible," Streeter said. "That's instant death."

Yeah, it is impossible. For real humans.

The scientist had his sleeves rolled up. His arms were plunged up to the elbows inside an open portal. That amount of energy was enough to vaporize flesh from a human being, but that wasn't a human doing it. The dupe in the white coat was glowing blue. *What the hell is going on?*

I ran up the steps. I don't remember getting to the doors. Everything was blotted out by the bright light of pain.

20

VACATION

I COULDN'T STOP the thoughts. They needed to be assembled before I could forget them. I needed to make some sense out of what had come up at the Paladin Nation, what kept Mom from coming home, what kept the Authority's decision in limbo, while I held my neck with both hands to keep it from exploding.

The Paladins are raiding portal facilities to test for duplicates. The Paladin Nation must've made police forces around the world aware that something was up, somehow tricked them to help flush out the enemy without them knowing what they were really looking for. But why did that guy in the warehouse have his arms plugging into the portal? Do the dupes need access to virtualmode to survive?

"Socket?" Streeter said. "Are you all right?"

I must've slid down the wall. I was sitting on the floor in the hallway, with my knees against my chest. I held out my hand and told him to give me a minute. I managed to turn the mind-scrambling pain into a dull reminder with several deep breaths. The thoughts clamored for attention, but I didn't give them a place in my mind to cling and felt them dissolve.

Streeter helped me up. "Let's get out of here," he said. "I've been helping Buxbee install security updates on the school's virtualmode portal. Let's go down to his lab."

The empty hall was much less stuffy. A slight breeze cooled my sweaty face. I concentrated on walking, breathing and holding the clamp down.

"Are you sure you're all right?" he asked.

I muttered something and kept moving. I was seeing spots, but things were clearer. I couldn't manage a conversation. But Streeter filled the awkward silence with a question that started the avalanche all over.

"What d'ya think they're testing for?"

The clamp thumped a warning. *Don't go there.* "I can't talk about it," I spit out.

"Can't talk about what?"

"Never mind," I said. "I can't talk about it."

"But why can't you—"

"Goddamnit!" I grabbed the back of my neck. "Just stop, will you?"

"All right, all right," he said. A teacher looked up from his desk as we passed his class. A lookit showed up a minute later. Streeter flashed a pass to Buxbee's lab and it buzzed away. We went down the hall quietly.

"So what's wrong with your neck?"

"Stop asking questions!"

"What the hell is wrong with you, man? I'm sick of you snapping at me all the time. Ever since you got back from your *vacation*, you hardly talk and you never do a goddamn thing. You half-baked on some euphoria gear or something?"

"Do I look like I'm having a good time?"

"You look sick. In the head."

"I'm going home."

"That's great." Streeter stopped in the middle of the hall. "Go home, then; forget about me."

"It's not like that."

"Then what?"

I couldn't let go of my neck. The lookits returned and told us to shut up or we were going to the office instead of Buxbee's lab.

"Just forget it," Streeter finally said. "Go home and do whatever you do. Clearly, you got more important things to do."

"I can't talk about some things, but that's just the way it is, Streeter. There are things you just can't know about." *Jesus Christ, who does that sound like?*

He looked at my neck. I still hadn't let go. He tapped his teeth together; the question he'd been holding back for weeks filled his mouth. He could hold it no longer.

"Where'd you go on vacation, Socket?"

"Streeter... don't."

The floor sloshed up and down like a one-winged airplane. I started toward the exit, pulling my head down to steady the bucking clamp.

"Your mom told us to let you work it out on your own, but all I see you do is go home." He stopped me before I reached the exit. "Where'd you go, Socket?"

My brain was going to hemorrhage. *Bump, bump, bump.* "I can't do this."

He called after me. Said he was sorry, I thought. He didn't mean it.

I GOT on a bus and lay on the back seat. It wasn't the right bus, but it went toward town. I got off downtown, caught a taxi home, and lay down on that seat, too.

The pain shot down my spine with each thump. It wasn't letting up this time. I pushed too far. Something was wrong. The cabby adjusted the rearview mirror; his eyes flickered from the road to me. *You okay, kid?* Somehow, I convinced him I was.

I ran in the house and went through breathing exercises. I concentrated on each breath and cleared my mind. No thoughts. Just this moment. But the clamp still rattled. The thoughts still came.

They're torturing me.

I tapped my cheek. "Mom."

The nojakk ticked. She wasn't answering.

"Mom," I said again, tapping my cheek. "Mom. Mom. MOM!"

"*Socket,*" she said, "*I'm in a meeting.*"

"I can't do this. This thing in my neck has gone off. It's killing me. You got to get it out, I can't take it."

I sniffed back tears. There was a long silence. I thought we lost connection. Maybe she was leaving the meeting.

"*There's nothing I can do, Socket,*" she said. "*Go through some breathing—*"

"WHAT GOOD ARE YOU?" The pain took control. "You let them do this to me then tell me to just do some breathing exercises! What kind of mom does that, huh? What kind of mom leaves their son like that? WHAT'S WRONG WITH YOU?"

The room looked blurry; I couldn't wipe the tears fast enough. Snot was dripping.

"*Why don't you get the moody out of my top drawer; it'll take off the emotional edge.*"

"I don't want a goddamn moody! I want this... this thing out of me. I want all of this to go away. I don't want to be one of you people! Let Broak... the rest of those... *freaks*... let them save the world. I want out. I want to be normal, AND THIS ISN'T NORMAL!"

The words jumbled together in a muddy string of confusion. I collapsed on the couch, muttering into the cushion. I thought we had lost connection again. I figured I was alone. Again.

"*I know this is hard.*" Her voice was soft, but firm enough to make me listen. "*It takes a strong person to do it, Socket. You* are *that person. I know you want to quit, but sometimes life doesn't ask for your permission to act. Life demands. And when that demand falls on you, it does so for a reason.*"

I bit my lip.

"I can't say any more than that, Socket, because quite honestly I don't know any more. I only know the world is lucky to have you. I see so much strength in you. I know you can't see it, but I can. You have to trust me. Trust what I see in you. One day, you will see it, too."

She didn't sound like she was on a mission this time. She sounded more like someone helping me with an impossible task the only way she could. Like a mother.

"Get some rest. The clamp will be out soon. I promise."

Somehow, the pain receded. It still hurt, but it was washed in sorrow. I fell asleep on the couch. The clamp thumped in the distance, keeping me from dreaming. I went in and out of sleep, fighting to stay under. I pulled a blanket over me, hid my head, and took my sweat-soaked shirt off. I managed to sleep until a hand gently touched my shoulder.

"Have you eaten?" Mom asked.

My eyes were puffy. "No."

"Go take a shower. I'll make dinner."

The pots and pans rattled in the kitchen. The hot water washed down my neck, the heat seeping through, dissolving the pressure. By the time I dressed, food was on the table. Mom sat across from me. We didn't talk much, but we ate together. She cleaned up. By the end of the night, the clamp's presence was a whisper.

MOM STAYED HOME the next day. It was weird, seeing her play mother. She was probably good at it once upon a time. It took her a while to find the utensils and food. She made eggs for breakfast. By mid-morning, she did breathing exercises with me. She talked me through them and helped me focus. She talked a lot about the present moment and one breath at a time. The clamp became tolerable.

I slept through the afternoon. Mom took a meeting in her bedroom by projection. The house looked orderly. That night she made dinner. We ate quietly, then cleaned up together. She washed dishes by hand. I dried and put them away.

"How'd you become one of them?" I asked.

"Your father and I studied genetic engineering in college. We took jobs with an engineering firm that turned out to be a recruiting agency for the Paladin Nation." She rinsed a plate and handed it to me. "If I knew what I was getting into..."

I flinched, expecting the clamp to react to the word *Paladin*, but it lay quiet. We washed some more; then I chanced a reply. "You wouldn't do it?"

She mulled that question over. She started cleaning the sink and left the question alone. She didn't know the answer.

"How'd Dad become one of them if he wasn't in the breeding program?"

"Your father was a genetic engineer. He worked on splicing Paladin abilities into adults."

"He did it on himself?"

She pinched her lips together on the bitter memory. She nodded, then said, "The method didn't work, though. The ability wouldn't fully awaken and after a while the powers faded. His program showed great potential but was discontinued until further notice."

"And that's why I'm like this?"

"We think so."

"So it worked."

She started wiping the refrigerator. Decided not to answer that one, too.

After cleanup, the clamp reminded me it was there, again. Maybe it realized, in retrospect, that the conversation about my dad was really about the Paladins.

Mom sat with me. We breathed in.

Breathed out.

I made it through another night. By morning, she was gone. *There is an urgent meeting,* her message said. *I'll call you later.*

Life resumed, a little less painfully.

A little less empty.

21

WATCHDOGS

THE SUN WAS SETTING at the first ever South Carolina game of tagghet. I wore a dark hoodie because the weather was cooler than usual. Everyone at that game would remember what they were wearing. Small details, like what you're wearing and where you were, were easy to remember at life-altering events.

The parking lot was mostly full. Must've been more people than the school expected because there was only one security guard and he was busy with an eighteen-wheeler that was obviously lost and now plugging up the parking lot.

I found a spot at the top of the visitors' bleachers, upper left-hand corner, right where Streeter was going to meet me. We talked the night before through nojakk. We didn't say much. I couldn't tell if he was pissed or sorry.

The benches were firm but slightly molded. This sport had money. The scoreboards had video screens bigger than they needed to be. The disposable programs had imbedded videos that explained the rules of tagghet and how they could get started on their own tagghet career. *You-know-who* had to be funding this through various businesses. They seemed to be fond of the sport. Or maybe it was their way of introducing technological advancements to the rest of us.

The oval field was empty. The seats were filling up and the anticipation to see flying discs was in everyone's conversation. The little kids started jumping up and down on their seats when the scoreboard lit up. The first tagger rode onto the field to cheers from both sides of the field. He banked left and the person behind him went right. They alternated until the entire home team was on the field, the grass swooshing in their wake. Everyone was on their feet.

They formed a circle, riding clockwise, and slung a red tag back and forth. The lightweight sticks flexed with each one-handed toss, expertly fired across the rotating circle. The curved end of the stick had some sort of magnetic impulse that grabbed the tag. I couldn't recognize anyone, except for the one with red braids dangling from under the tear-shaped helmet. Chute caught a pass on the short hop and tossed it to the far side of the circle with a sharp backhanded flip.

If I could *reach* out, I could feel her nervous energy. *Taste* its jagged frequency. Maybe I could help soothe her nerves, she was always nervous... but I couldn't think that way.

THE VISITING team rode onto their end of the field and the people around me cheered. That's when I noticed Streeter lumbering up the steps. He turned sideways and excused himself down to the empty space next to me. People were still standing around us.

He pulled a bag of popcorn from his jacket and filled his mouth. "Been here long?"

"Not long."

He stuffed two more handfuls in his mouth, chewing loudly. We sat there and watched the field, but since everyone was standing, there wasn't much to see.

"So what've you been up to?" I asked.

"Been helping Buxbee with the security updates. Global

virtualmode is back online, but authorities aren't letting independent portals open until updates are operational. They must be serious.

"The updates are taking longer than I thought, but we're almost done." More popcorn fell on his lap than went in his mouth. "I'd ask what you've been doing," he said, "but that didn't work out so well last time."

"Right," I said. "Nothing personal."

"Why would I take it personal? You wanted to punch me in the face."

"I wish I could explain..."

"But you can't." He picked at a kernel stuck between his front teeth. "You know, I've been thinking. If you can't tell me what's going on, then it must be a big deal."

I grunted. Half-laughed.

"And that one of these days, you'll tell me everything."

I'd tell him everything right there, on the spot. He would never know how much it was killing me to withhold from him. He was always the first to know my secrets. Streeter and Chute were the only ones that kept me from feeling all alone in the world. Sitting next to him with all those secrets, I didn't want it that way. *But when life demands, you answer.*

I held out my hand. "You'll be the first one I tell."

He smiled, his lips glistening with butter, and slapped my hand. Then I reached into the bag and grabbed a handful. Then we watched us some tagghet.

THE TEAMS HUDDLED along the sidelines. They had their hands in the middle, chanting and jumping. Captains from each team met at center pitch. The coaches went with them. "Welcome to the soon-to-be-most-popular sport in the world... *TAGGHET!*" a voice rang across the field. "Where your Charleston Rapid Foxes take on the Columbia Bolters. Now, introducing the inaugural season, please welcome Coach King!"

Coach King was the lacrosse coach, too. He walked onto the field, wearing his purple shorts and socks pulled up. He held up both hands and our players slapped them as he made his way to center pitch. He said something like: Great sport, some of the best talent you'll ever see, we were going to win the state championship like we do in every other sport. And if anyone wanted to learn how to tag, training sessions were available.

"And now!" he shouted. "Your Rapid Foxes!"

The scoreboard projected an image of each tagger, live from the field, as he called their names. Some kept the yellow visor down, others retracted it into the helmet.

"And starting at left lancer, and the only female tagger to start varsity... Chute!"

Only he said *Shhhoooooooooot*.

It could've been my imagination, but it sounded like she got more cheers than anyone else. She was the only girl out there. Chute cruised in a small circle near center pitch, mumbling. I couldn't see her lips, but that's what she does when she gets nervous.

"She almost quit, you know," Streeter said.

"Quit what?"

"Tagghet. She was so worried after you left she couldn't focus. Your mom told us you were all right, you were just having some medical tests, but after a month, Chute wasn't herself. Your mom wasn't coming home and we weren't hearing anything at all. She was a wreck, said she was quitting."

"Why would she quit?"

"She didn't feel right having fun while you were..." He glanced at me. "While you were probably *not* having fun."

I watched her floating in a tight circle with the stick yoked over her shoulders, muttering. I knew she was glad to see me come back, but we didn't talk much about the time in between.

"How was that going to help, I told her," Streeter said. "I mean, you weren't coming home any sooner if she sat at home and twisted her hair." He fished the unpopped kernels from the bag. "You know what I mean?"

"So you talked her into staying?"

"She loves the game, Socket. It was just stupid to quit. Besides, she needed something to keep her mind off of you."

"She never told me that."

"Mmmm, imagine that, someone keeping a secret."

I could see her taking deep breaths. Something was delaying the start. I wanted so badly to take away her discomfort, but all I could do was watch.

Finally, a lookit dangled the tag over center pitch. A player from each team squared off under it and shook hands. Not one person was sitting. It got loud. Numbers counted down on the scoreboard to zero.

The tag dropped.

The centers chopped at it. The Bolters pulled the tag away and set up an offensive formation on their side of the field while our team retreated. Chute hovered near their cube. The Bolters attacked and the Rapid Foxes looked confused, running into each other. The Bolters threaded a pass between the two defenders. Two passes later, one of them rode up the dome, caught a pass and rifled a shot into the scoring cube.

GOAL!

"That was easy," I said.

Streeter didn't hear me. I didn't even hear me because the kid who scored was related to the lady in front of us. She curled her fingers and screamed his name like she'd been stabbed.

"The team is breaking up," Streeter said.

"They just started, give them a chance."

"I mean us." He patted his chest. "You, me and Chute. *Our* team. We're falling apart."

I shook my head and watched the teams regroup. I didn't know what he meant.

"We used to do everything together," he said. "Now Chute's out there and you're... doing whatever you're doing."

"It's not a vacation, Streeter. Believe me, I wish I never left."

It was the closest I came to telling him something. The clamp didn't budge.

The teams squared off at center pitch again. This time the lookit dropped the tag to our team. Our center took it behind three blockers and set up a play. Chute flared out to the left.

Streeter wasn't watching. He was thinking. I gently elbowed him and reminded him that he was the most popular virtualmoder at school. Reminded him he was globally ranked. I mean, the school trusted him to patch the security codes into the portal. I reminded him that he would never be alone, if that's what he was thinking.

He nodded, but he wasn't listening.

Our team lost the tag. The visiting crowd cheered.

"Remember when we were kids and you and Chute would come over?" Streeter said. "We'd enter Level V tournaments when we were Level I. Remember what we named our team?"

"Watchdogs," I said. "And we got slaughtered."

"You would spend the night, and once my grandparents were asleep, we'd virtualmode to another tournament."

"And get slaughtered again."

"Remember the time we planted a data bomb in the principal's account and froze it for a week?"

"*You* planted it."

He looked up at the moon hanging just above the school. "I'm going to miss all that."

The Bolters looked to score again but lost control of the tag. The visiting fans groaned.

"You'll invent something and become filthy rich," I said. "Maybe Chute will become a professional tagger. It doesn't matter, none of that changes the team, Streeter. We're the original Watchdogs."

"What about you?" he asked. "What're you going to be doing?"

"I'm sure I'll be around." *I might disappear, but I'll be around.*

Now I had the distant look. What if the clamp got removed and I returned to the Garrison for good. What would Mom tell them then? *He went on vacation. Forever.*

"She's open." Streeter jerked my sweatshirt.

Chute slipped past the defensive line. Her teammate had the tag.

He got around a defender, darted to the sideline and zipped a sharp pass across the center pitch. Chute caught it fully extended.

We stood on our seats.

Chute lost her balance for a moment and a defender intercepted her on the way to the dome. Chute leaned heavily to the left, pulling the jetter almost on its side to stop. She juked left. Right. The defender lunged after the tag dangling from the end of her stick. Chute spun, getting behind him. Her stick flexed to the limit and the tag came off like a bullet, just a blur that straight-lined into the center of the green cube.

GOAL!

The home bleachers were about to come crashing down under the cheering stomps. Streeter and I were the only ones cheering on our side of the field. Chute's face appeared on the scoreboard, strands of red hair plastered to her cheeks. She was mauled by her teammates.

For a moment, I forgot about the clamp. I forgot about the Paladins and the uncertainties and all the unanswered questions. I wanted to run down there and hug her. I wanted to drag Streeter with me and we'd squeeze her until her head popped off. I wanted it to be just another night in our lives, just like it was when we were Watchdogs.

"Socket?" Streeter said.

He tugged at the back of my sweatshirt. I was busy screaming Chute's name through my hand-megaphone, hoping she'd hear me. I thought about nojakking her, but there was no way she had it turned on.

"Socket!"

I shrugged my shoulder. It felt like he had his arm around me. "Dude, what are you doing?"

"What the hell is that?"

"What's what?"

He looked at my opposite shoulder. He didn't have his arm around me. A long red tail curled under my chin. Rudder poked his head around my hood, his golden eyes looking into mine. I quickly stuffed him inside my hoodie. No one but Streeter seemed to notice.

I looked around, completely suspicious, then pulled the collar out and whispered, "What're you doing here?"

Rudder purred against my chest. Warmth radiated deep inside.

"Did I just see that?" Streeter said.

I sneaked a few glances around, then opened my sweatshirt for Streeter to look inside. It might've looked creepy, but no one was watching. I started to introduce them, but knew the clamp would start thumping. "Ummm... this is... one of the things I can't talk about."

Streeter stared. Rudder stared back. Blinked. Waved his little fingers. Streeter waved back. He looked like he was waving to a... well, waving to a little dragon in my sweatshirt. The lady in front of us turned around. I smiled back until she was uncomfortable enough to look away. Rudder crawled around my side, tickling my ribs up to my neck. I tried to grab him.

"What's it doing?" Streeter said.

"I don't know."

I reached into my hood to pull him off, but he scampered up to the back of my neck, lay flat against the thin red line, and purred louder. The vibrations sank into the clamp. The ever-present ache, low and dull, faded. I almost drooled. I bent over and hid my face. I thought Streeter said something. The vibrations got stronger, warmer and deeper. Rudder suctioned tightly to my skin.

There was a sharp energy beside me. Clear and clean. *Streeter. I'm feeling Streeter!* I braced myself for the clamp to buck, but it lay still beneath Rudder. I opened my mind to the ebb and flow of the crowd's collective energy. The joy and frustration, cheer and anger. The essence of hundreds of people mingled through me.

A scene unfolded in my mind. Mom went to the grimmet tree. Rudder came to her, as if he was waiting for her. The other grimmets sat on the branches and watched her walk off with him on her shoulder. She took him outside the Garrison. At the base of the cliff, she held him up.

"Free him," she said.

Rudder shot from her hands, smudging the air red like a streaking star.

I opened my eyes. The game was still on. The air was thick. There was a charge in it, an unnatural tension, like the moments before lightning strikes.

[Pivot came to her.] Rudder's thought was as clear as if he'd spoken it. *[He told her to release you from the clamp.]*

Pivot's back? Is he all right? Do the Paladins know?

[He told her They are coming.]

Who?

[You must get your friend.]

Streeter?

[The girl.]

Who are They?!

He returned to working on the clamp. *[You must hurry.]*

It was nearly halftime. Chute was flying across the center pitch, her stick up high, calling for the tag.

They were coming. That could mean only one thing. The duplicates were going to fight back.

No one would forget this night.

22

Arachnophobic

I COULD FEEL THEM. The duplicates were here, at the game. I stood up and looked over the crowd. I sniffed the air like a bloodhound. There was a scent, a feeling, but I couldn't locate it. The clamp wasn't completely deactivated; Rudder was still working. *Faster. Go faster, Rudder.*

"Sit down, clown," someone said behind me.

Streeter stood next to me. "What's going on?"

There were hundreds of people here. I sensed all their individual essences intermingle, how their emotions ebbed and flowed, what kind of thoughts they were having. Somewhere out there was a different flavor. Something that tasted plastic-like, something fake. *Duplicated.*

"Hey, the both of you," someone shouted. "We can't see the game."

The lady in front of us turned around. It wasn't her. I could feel her pulse quicken when I looked at, looked *into* her. I could taste her essence. The same for the people around us. Even the guy that was standing up and reaching over a row to snatch my hood to get my attention. He was real.

I pushed Streeter to the side and we forced our way to the aisle without waiting for people to move. One guy told us to get some goddamn manners. I stopped on the steps. The fake feeling was stronger. Streeter was apologizing behind me when I saw it. The eighteen-wheel truck was still in the parking lot. It was rocking side to side. Something was getting ready to escape.

I took the steps three at a time. "STOP! GET EVERYONE OUT OF THE BLEACHERS!"

No one could hear me except the people around me that figured another high school kid lost the battle with drugs. I leaped off the bottom step and crashed on the track that circled the field; then I jumped the fence onto the soft grass. I sprinted onto the field, waving my arms. "CLEAR OUT THE BLEACHERS!" I screamed at the home crowd.

Whistles were blowing. Assistant coaches were already after me. The taggers slowed down to watch the madman sprint over center field. I kept ahead of my pursuit and made it to the other sideline, leaping over the other fence. I could hear them laughing. The security guard was nowhere to be found. Every lookit was on my tail, beaming their eyelight at me, but they weren't going to do shit.

I made it around the home bleachers and no one was listening, but people got out of my way. There were half a dozen men after me, some of them fans just trying to keep the crazy off the field.

"EVACUATE THE BLEACHERS!"

The parking lot was fifty yards away. The truck was going side to side so violently that the tires were lifting off the ground. People were taking notice and I felt a shift in mood. Some already were moving in the other direction. But I couldn't stop. I had to let them all see where I was going. They all had to see that something was about to happen.

A man appeared in front of me. Just appeared. His clothes snug and dark blue. Another two men blipped into existence next to him, their hair cut tight. Their expressions hard. *Paladins.*

I stopped. My pursuit stopped, too. They saw the Paladins materialize from a timeslice. I understood they had temporarily stopped time, but the others didn't. They were trying to process how these hard men just appeared and what they were doing with the spikes in their hands. Why were they sticking them into the ground, and why was a yellow laser beaming straight into the dark sky?

"CLEAR THE AREA!" I pushed past the gathering crowd and their blank stares. I clenched my hand, searching for a grip on a timeslice but couldn't get there. "SOMETHING'S IN THE TRU—"

The explosion was bright.

Then it was dark.

It sounded like a high pitch.

I couldn't remember what I was going to do. It was something. Something urgent.

The darkness took form. First it was just that some blobs were darker than others. Then there were lighter colors flapping through the darkness. It looked like snow drifting out of the sky. I had that feeling like I needed to wake up for school or something. A blurry face popped up like a puppet.

"We got to go!" Streeter's voice was far away.

I could taste the tang of blood. The fluttering white things, they were debris: paper and cups and popcorn bags. Panic crawled over me. The atmosphere tensed. Streeter pulled me up. "Are you all right?"

I touched my head. The bleachers were partially shattered. People were running. They were screaming. I saw people pulling limp bodies from the wreckage. I saw some bodies that were just lying there.

"We got to go, get up." Streeter pulled some more. "Get up, man. WE GOT TO GO!"

I got up and the world was wobbling. The Paladins were setting more spikes that looked like yellow bars circling the flaming truck. Beyond that, the school walls had crumbled. Half of the dome over the Pit was missing. With each spike and yellow bar, the heat from the roaring fire cooled. They were sealing off the site, protecting the civilians. They only had six up when the thing blew again. I could hardly feel the second explosion except through the ground. What would the place look like if they had got here a minute late? Would there be anything left?

Maybe they weren't protecting the public. Maybe they were here to catch something.

Streeter led me onto the field. I stumbled after him. People ran past. Half a dozen taggers lay in the grass. Chute was one of them. I pushed Streeter off and ran, sliding into her on my knees, wrapping her in my arms. A blue knot was on her forehead, blood trickling between her eyes.

She touched my lip. "You're hurt, Socket."

"We have to get out of here," I said. "Can you stand?"

She saw Streeter behind me. "What's happening?"

The ground shook from a muted explosion, this one not as intense. The yellow bars had contained most of the sound as well as the impact. "Socket." Streeter pawed at my arm. "Socket, Socket... you got to... you got to see this."

The dome had completely collapsed, and fire erupted from it, licking the sky. Something was poking out of the burning trailer. It looked like a tree branch, but it wasn't burning. It was growing out of the flames, red-hot and pointing up, and then it bent on a hinge as it cooled. It grew longer and bent at another hinge several feet below the first. More of them emerged, bending at angles until they were long enough to reach the ground and lift an oval body from the carnage. The giant daddy longlegs spider stepped out of the flames, its glowing body cooling.

The crawlers had come with the Paladins. They would save us. But something wasn't right. Why were they coming from the truck?

The Paladins locked the last of the spikes in the ground, sealing off the heat and sound from our side of the parking lot. Their evolver weapons unfolded around their hands, glowing blue, then engulfed them in protective bubbles just as the crawler reared back. The bottom of the crawler's body opened. I could hear it through the ground; the sound the thing let loose was shrill and deafening. It vibrated through the bottom of my feet. The Paladins faltered, but the shields held.

Chute latched onto my sleeve. "Who are those people?"

I wanted to tell her they were the good guys, but I was watching them spread out while a second set of legs emerged from the flames. The crawler backed up like a mother protecting her newborn in a burning nest as the Paladins set to attack. I thought Streeter or Chute might've asked what those things were. I thought I knew what they were, but the Paladins were attacking them. They were sent by an enemy.

The duplicates are coming.

23

Pillars

IT WAS A SCENE FROM A MOVIE. People were running. Screams and cries and hysteria soaked the air. Bodies were all around. Some were dead. Sirens could be heard in the distance and the first of many emergency vehicles started down the road. And there were still only three Paladins. Three! Where were the rest of them?

That's what didn't make sense. A disaster like this and the entire Paladin Nation should be here treating people. Instead, there were three of them and they were barely holding their own against the duplicated crawlers oozing nonstop from the burning wreckage. The fire flickered red, yellow and blue as it burped out one spider after another. The agents sliced and diced them, but some escaped and made for the giant hole in the Pit.

The spot on my neck warmed. I touched Rudder still working on the clamp. As he deactivated it, knowledge seeped from him as our minds intermingled. It came to me not as thoughts but more like a stream of memories that imbedded themselves in me, as if he were melting into me. I saw what he saw, knew what he knew. And then I understood.

The duplicates were attacking worldwide.

While the duplicates had dissolved into the general population, Paladins discovered they needed to stay in touch with virtualmode as if it was some sort of life force. They didn't know exactly how or why they needed to periodically get back into virtualmode, they just knew that if they cut them off, they would die like weeds without roots. Paladins installed worldwide code that kept duplicates from logging in to virtualmode. After that, the Paladin Nation went about flushing the duplicates out of hiding, even alerting public authorities about illegal virtualmode activity. It was only a matter of time before they starved. And the duplicates knew this. They were cornered.

It was fight or die. They chose to fight.

The crawlers were doing the duplicates' dirty work. They'd sent them to seek out access to virtualmode. Schools, cafes and businesses across the planet were being attacked simultaneously, hoping one of them could circumvent the security patches, get to the inside of virtualmode and unlock it for the rest of them. The duplicates were waiting for the life-giving taste of virtualmode. They held their last breath, hoping.

Paladins didn't see the wide-scale attack coming. Of course not. They didn't have their fortuneteller anymore. Pivot was still missing. But Pivot saw. And that's why he sent Rudder to free me. He needed me for a reason. He needed me in the fight.

"They're after the portal," I muttered.

Streeter and Chute were staring at me with mouths open. I forgot to tell them all the details, but what was I going to tell them? They were witness to it all. I just pointed over my shoulder and said, "That's what I couldn't talk about."

Streeter was sort of nodding, watching the ongoing fight, the sounds muffled by the pillars. Chute was staring at me, though. I could feel her fear, taste it like a bitterness at the back of my throat, a rotten energy eating at her stomach. She was freaked by the death and destruction, and she was wondering what I was. She felt guilty for fearing I would leave her again despite the misery all around. I took her hand. Her energy flowed down inside me and I opened to let it flow back into her, mingling with the fear that rolled inside her. *[It's all right.]*

I didn't force the thought into her mind. I didn't make her believe it. I just laid it out for her to see. She blinked. The smile of relief didn't show on her face, but I felt it rise inside her.

"Why are those things climbing into the Pit?" Streeter said.

"I think they're accessing the portal."

"But... that's like twenty feet below ground and encased in hardened steel. They can't..."

His thoughts trailed off. Maybe he realized he was watching spiders climb the wall and that reality was doing a 180 on him.

For some reason, those things were going after the portal. And the Paladins desperately wanted to stop them. "Is there any way to access the security patch?" I asked Streeter. He looked at me, but his glassy eyes were unfocused. "Streeter, how can I get to the portal security?"

His lips quivered, but his thoughts were a mess. I needed answers quicker than that. I started for the pillars.

"You're not going in there." Chute's voice was firm.

Maybe if she hadn't said anything, I would've tried to slip between the pillar beams. But what was I going to do once I was in there? I had no weapon, no training. I couldn't even slice time yet. I was just going to get in the way. So I stood there looking at the endless parade of crawlers flow from the fire and the Paladins' tireless efforts to control them. But they were starting to tire. They weren't blinking into timeslices anymore. They were conserving their energy, fighting them in real time.

"I'm not going to lose you again." Chute stepped next to me. Her cheeks were glowing in the yellow aura. "I don't care who you think you are or what you can do, you'll die if you go in there."

Panic was clenching my chest. What could I do, then? What? If the duplicates got through the portal, what was next? Something in Rudder's knowledge told me the Paladins didn't have a backup plan. They had gambled on their move to end the existence of the duplicates and now the whole world was on the table. Winner takes all.

"We can get to Buxbee's lab." Streeter felt lucid. The slack in his face had taken up.

"What do I need to do?" I asked.

"The security shells need to be completed."

"How do I do that?"

He looked at me. "You want me to tell you now?"

"Just... just think it." I closed my eyes, focusing on his mind. I could absorb what he knew the instant it came up, but it was a murky cloud of thoughts.

"What the hell are you talking about?" Streeter said.

"I got to know how to finish that security shell or those things could get into virtualmode." I stepped toward him. "They're dupes, Streeter."

Like that was all I needed to say, he would figure out the rest. But he was staring at me like there was a tiny dragon attached to my neck.

"I've got to finish the security updates," I said.

"No, you're not," Chute said. "You see what's going on back there? You're not going anywhere near that school. Neither of you."

"Buxbee's gear is only coded for me," Streeter said. "It'll reject you. You can't get on."

That was a problem, but I'd figure it out later. If Rudder would get the clamp completely deactivated, I could slice time and have plenty of time. *Come on, Rudder. Faster.* I felt him twitch impatiently.

"Look, there's no danger if I go," Streeter said. "Buxbee's lab is all the way on the other side of the school. Those yellow beams got that truck barricaded around the Pit. Whatever's on the inside isn't getting out. We can go log in and get it done, in and out. If you're helping, I can finish in like five or ten minutes."

"I'm going," Chute said.

"No, you're not," I snapped.

"Yes. I am."

"Look." I gently gripped her bicep. "This is—"

She yanked her arm out. "I'm going with you. Try to stop me."

"I will."

Sometimes she hit me in the arm when I acted like an asshole. Sometimes she just set her feet. Always, she got her way because she usually made more sense than me, thought clearer. This time, I was right. But this time, she didn't swing and didn't dig in to get her way. I felt her energy soften.

"Don't make me stay out here," she said. "I can't just wait."

"It's too dangerous."

"I can help."

"I wouldn't forgive myself if something happened to you."

"Neither would I."

I took a breath and looked around. Truth be told, I didn't want to leave her. I didn't want to be away from her, not when this was going on. Maybe it was selfish to let her come along, but was she any safer out here? I would never know the answer to that.

We started for Buxbee's lab.

24

WALKING on Shells

LIGHTS WERE on in a portion of the hall, but beyond that it faded to black. Dust drizzled down like mist. Buxbee's door was partly open. The classroom was so dark the desks and chairs looked like lumps waiting to jump us.

"What now?" I said.

"We virtualmode," Streeter said. "It's the only way to finish the upgrade."

"I thought virtualmode was shut down."

"Yeah, unless you've got high-security access. That would be me."

"You can't just call it up on a monitor?"

"Maybe." He sounded thoughtful. "But I'm not sure."

"Can you do it or not?"

I could see him turn to me but couldn't see his expression. It felt hot.

"Look, we can't afford to leave the skin," I said. "I don't care if those things are trapped out there or not, we need to call it up on a monitor."

"Well, now's a perfect time to experiment, wouldn't you say?" he snapped. "I'll boot up the monitors and break out the manual so we can work in the skin. Got a light?"

I didn't like it, either. Streeter was staring at me, waiting for an answer. *Which is it?* Somehow, I had become the leader and he was waiting for my blessing. I just couldn't bring myself to say it. They shouldn't be here. They should be at home or out there with the cops and EMTs. This was a bad idea to bring them along, but I had to be honest, I couldn't do it alone.

Chute's touch broke the tension. Her fingers slid down my arm and laced with mine. "How long will it take if we virtualmode?" she asked.

"Five minutes," Streeter said. "Maybe ten."

"What d'ya mean 'we'?" I said. "You're not going."

"I'll stay and watch things, make sure it's all right. You and Streeter go, get it done. We're wasting time."

Her smile was forced. Streeter said, "Then make that twenty minutes if she's not coming."

"Why?" I asked.

"Look, you want to sit here and debate every possible scenario? Jesus Christ, we'd be done if we jumped on as soon as we got here."

"All right! Let's get on." I dropped into a soft seat. "But you're staying, Chute."

She gave me that same smile.

STREETER GRUMBLED as he sat down and stuck the transporters behind his ears. As soon as I applied them, I was in my sim. The gray space around us went on forever. Streeter's giant sim stood next to a hovering bluish ball.

"This is a replica of the portal," he said. "There are shells around it that monitor access. The only way to virtualmode is through it. Anyone, or any*thing*, that tries to access it illegally will not get through. If those things reach the portal below the Pit, they'll have to come through this in order to virtualmode onto the worldwide Internet. If they don't get through this, then they're just stuck in a hole with nowhere to go."

A black figure flickered between us, and then Chute was standing there. She pushed the dark cowl from her head. "Hey."

I just shook my head. She knew how to play me. Now it was either argue with her about getting off while the clock ran or shut up. "Let's just get this over with," I said.

The portal was enclosed in several translucent shells, the last one partially complete. "We need to finish the final shell to make the portal impenetrable," he said. "Then we get off. Done."

Streeter reached into the empty space beside him, his hairy fingers grasping something invisible. He took several breaths, closed his eyes and muttered something as though he were wishing for something. Then, between his dirty fingernails, a curved puzzle piece appeared. He hunched over and slid it into a gap in the unfinished shell.

"Anything we can do?" Chute said.

Streeter twitched. The piece dissolved. He let out a deep breath and bowed his head. "Yeah, how about not scaring the shit out of me?"

"Do you really need the giant sim with the fat fingers?" she said. "There's no one here to fight, you know."

"Oh, sure. Give me an hour and I'll build another sim."

"Don't give me that, you've got generic sims in reserve. I've seen them."

"You don't know what I—"

"Can we get on with this?" I said.

Streeter blew a curly lock of hair from his eyes and stared at Chute. "I have to recall the pieces and fit them into the shell. You can hold each one in place for about ten seconds or until the piece stitches while I retrieve the others."

He held up his hand and, again, a piece appeared between his fingers five seconds later. He bent over, carefully placing it. Chute put her finger on it and he created another piece, put it in place and I held it. He did it again. Now Chute held two of them. I let go of my piece to grab the next and it disappeared.

"Longer, Socket," Streeter said. "You got to give the stitching code time to lock it in place."

"You said ten seconds."

"I said *about* ten seconds," he said, bringing another piece to where the first one just evaporated.

I kept my finger on this one as long as I could. Streeter pulled them down faster, sliding each one in place and barking at us to hold them tighter and longer. We had no more fingers left. Streeter paused to give the pieces extra time to stitch. When they were a shade darker, we let go and he started after more.

"Halfway there," he said.

We took deep breaths and began again. It was getting stuffy. Buxbee's lab must've been overheating. Streeter had most of our fingers occupied when the gray space trembled and two pieces crumbled from the shell.

"They're coming," Streeter said.

"What do you mean *they're coming?*" I said.

Streeter moved faster, with both hands, and brought two pieces down. "As soon as those things make contact with the portal, they could come through this ball right here." He clicked the pieces in place. "We have to have this final shell done to keep them inside."

Distant thunder shook somewhere. "Why does it sound like they're out there?" I said.

"Focus, Socket!"

Streeter hauled the pieces out faster than we could hold them. Chute used her chin on one of them. Three crumbled. Streeter had to stop adding pieces and help hold them until they stitched.

"What'll they do if they get here?" Chute said.

He took the time to put two more pieces in place before answering. "Well, seeing as this isn't finished, they'll shatter the security shells, blow by us and roam free in virtualmode." He flicked his eyes at me. "You'll have to ask Mr. Secret Agent what they'll do after that."

I pretended not to notice, like we needed to be focusing and not talking. But I didn't know what they were going to do if they got free. I had one of those feelings there was a lot riding on getting this shell completed because the Paladins were out there fighting like it was life or death.

"Will they come after us?" Chute asked.

When I didn't answer, Streeter said, "Probably not."

"Probably? What's that mean?"

"I don't know, it means probably. Maybe those things don't care about us, they just want inside. Or..." He took a second to place a piece. "Or maybe they'll be pissed off that we were trying to stop them and... you know."

"You know?" Chute's fingers wiggled enough to shatter two pieces. Streeter started to say something, but Chute cut him off. "No, I don't know!"

Streeter took a deep breath and went back to concentrating. He should've been doing what I was doing, but now it was too late. The side of his head was getting a full-bore stare from Chute.

"Chute," I said, "maybe you should get off; we're almost done."

She turned the heat on me. "No. And don't ask me that again."

Another disturbance rattled close by. We held the pieces tighter.

"Hurry," Chute whispered.

"*As fast as I can*," Streeter sang, grabbing two more pieces.

"Why weren't you grabbing two pieces to begin with?" she said.

"This isn't easy!" He shoved them in place. "I got to concentrate."

"But they're coming," she urged.

"I KNOW THAT!" He stopped for a second to refocus, then retrieved two more pieces.

The next disturbance vibrated through my sim. I felt that one. Maybe it was because the clamp was shutting down and I was getting back to normal, but the timeslice spark still wasn't ready. Rudder wasn't done. The look on Streeter's and Chute's faces meant they felt it, too.

"Ten more," Streeter said, huffing.

"You can do it," I said.

Two more pieces locked in. The shell darkened. We had our fingers splayed out over as many pieces as we could hold.

Kaaabooooom!

The portal shuddered under our hands. We lost a piece.

"Three more!" Streeter shouted. "Hold them!"

The gray space transformed, swirling like fog, dense and grainy. Footsteps echoed under the distant thunder. Someone was out there, shoes clicking on a hard floor. I looked around, listening. There it was again! Footsteps echoed, closer this time. Was Streeter wrong? Were they coming in from somewhere else? Did they already get through another portal somewhere in the world and now they were coming to open this one?

"WILL YOU CONCENTRATE?" Streeter shouted. "Only two more, just focus on these next two, all right?"

"Chute, get off, now," I said. "I can hold the rest. Get off."

"You can't hold all the pieces. He'll be done in a second and we can all get off."

Streeter pulled the final piece down and held it delicately over the last hole. Our fingers filled the gap, holding the last pieces in place. He waited with the last one, his chest heaving.

"All right," he said quietly, "let them go."

We took our fingers out, holding our breath. The pieces trembled, but held. The shell went two shades darker. Streeter so carefully laid the last one over the gap and touched it with the tip of his finger, pushing it into place. The shell clicked and turned black.

"There." He exhaled so long his shoulders deflated. "The portal is locked."

KAAABOOOOOOM!

The floor tilted.

Chute dropped to her knees; Streeter teetered forward on the tips of his toes, windmilling his arms to keep his balance. I couldn't stop the virtual giant from falling on top of the portal. He didn't just graze it: he pushed it all the way to the floor, bounced on it and flopped on his back. The portal bounced back to its original position. It bobbed between us. We stood extra still, not even breathing, while the portal jiggled in place.

A hairline fracture slithered across the black shell. Piece by piece, it crumbled until every single shell lay at Streeter's feet. The portal glittered blue and white, bright as ever.

A mechanical screech called from inside the portal, like a crystal ball playing the near future.

EeeeeeeeeeeeieiiiiiIIIIIIIIIII!

"They're in," Streeter said.

"What now?" I said.

"You've got powers, right?" Streeter said. "Fight them."

"FIGHT THEM?"

"Aren't you stronger or something?"

"Do you see a cape on my back?"

"Those guys up there in the parking lot, they were disappearing and reappearing and slinging some badass weapons. You telling me you can't do that?"

"I'm not like that." *I don't know what I am.*

"Streeter," Chute said, "can we hide the portal somewhere else?"

Streeter's mouth contorted, about to shout his frustration, then stopped. "That just might..." He placed both hands over the portal, his lips moving, eyes closed. His muttering grew louder, like an enchantment, and a clear shell wrapped around the portal, snapping shut.

"That's a basic security shell," he said. "But it will buy us some time. I can set up transportation coordinates to an obscure website and take the portal with us. It'll confuse them. They'll find us, eventually, but it'll give us a few minutes."

"How much time do we have?" I said.

He shrugged. "It's hard to say."

"Guess."

"They'll be looking for us in ten minutes, maybe twelve."

"Well, do it," I said.

He took the portal in his hands and closed his eyes, whispering new coordinates. The echoing footsteps started again. I circled Streeter, searching for the source. They grew louder.

"Hurry, Streeter."

He muttered louder, not hearing me. Hands clenched in concentration, his fingertips dented the shell. Someone whispered my name. *Socket.* I jumped next to Streeter, hands up, knees bent. Chute beside me.

A white, generic sim appeared out of the fog, its hands folded behind its back. It had no eyes, ears or nose. A slit opened where a mouth would've been, imitating a smile.

It said, "Salutations."

25

FALSE PROPHET

"BROAK?"

"Indeed, it is." His voice was distorted, hardly recognizable.

"How'd he get here?" Streeter hid the portal, deftly concealing it behind his back.

"My dear ogre friend, I'm sure you're well aware of what would happen if the duplicates' crawlers get through this portal. We want to be sure no one, or *thing*, has tampered with the security shells." He kicked at shattered pieces and they rang on the end of his foot. "It appears I'm a tad late."

"They put you in charge?" I said.

"They are a bit busy, as I'm sure you have noticed. The entire world is under attack, my dear Socket. The duplicates have launched a full-scale attack and I'm afraid we were caught, as you might say, with our trousers down." His face twitched where eyebrows would normally be. "We are using every last resource to stave them off. It is the last stand, my friend. It just so happens I have come to help you protect this compromised portal security shell." He looked down at the pieces again and held out his hand. "If you had completed your assignment, you wouldn't be in this mess, dear ogre. You have failed. I suggest you turn the security over to one more suitable."

"I don't think so," Streeter said.

Broak tilted his head toward me. "Can you talk some sense into your friend? The world is at stake, you know."

"You tried to kill me, you piece of shit." I rammed my hand around his neck, wedging my finger and thumb under his jawbone. He did not resist. "I'd be dead if it wasn't for Pivot."

"Can we put that aside for now, dear Socket? There are greater issues before us than a street fight."

I threw him so far into the gray fog he almost disappeared. I wanted to break him in half, somehow reach through that sim and choke him, make his throat burn like mine did. Maybe I couldn't beat his ass in a straight-up fight, at least not until I got control of time again.

"I can explain my actions." Broak righted himself and folded his arms behind his back as he walked back. "It is difficult to understand my motivation, but if you give me a moment, I will do so. However, do be reasonable, dear Socket. We do not have a moment to spare. If you grant me the portal, there will soon be time to explain everything. I beg of you."

Mechanical screeching called from inside the portal.

"I am capable of a two-hundred-cube security shell within five minutes," he said. "I have the programming loaded in this sim and can secure it before it's too late."

He took a step closer. Gray fog whooshed around our ankles, muffling his footsteps.

"We have the technology. You have seen it yourself. Do the right thing and put our conflict aside. Can you do that?"

The slit-mouth did not smile. The generic face had no expression. The world couldn't afford for us to fail. They needed us. They needed the Paladins. They needed *him*. I had to admit it: Broak was more qualified than me. And that way, Chute and Streeter could get back to their skins.

"There's no time to debate this; I want the portal." Broak took another step and our sims shifted into battle garb. Weapons unfolded on my hip. A battle stave materialized in Chute's hand.

"What're you doing, Streeter?" Chute said. "We don't need this stuff."

He looked at the nicked battleaxe dangling from the barbarian belt crisscrossing his chest, the studded war boots and spiked battle gloves. "The battle alert just triggered. There's a threat nearby."

"I'm not going to ask again." The slit-smile creased Broak's face.

"Streeter!" Chute cried.

Broak unfolded his arms from behind his back. His fingers fused together like spears. He lunged like a swordsman, his arm plunging through Streeter's stomach, the axe clattering away. Broak's arm-sword slid all the way through Streeter, wrapping around the portal. In the next instant, he yanked it halfway through Streeter's body.

"Cut it!" Streeter grabbed Broak's arm with both hands. "Cut his arm off!"

I grabbed the evolver clubs from my belt. They unfolded and fused around my hands and forearms, and I tried to focus on a weapon. So many of them jumbled in my head; I couldn't concentrate. It happened too fast. I couldn't take my eyes off the gaping wound in Streeter's stomach spewing molten gray goo. Chute jabbed her battle stave at Broak's face, but he caught it with his free hand.

"Don't make this mistake," Broak hissed. "The world needs me to have this!"

He yanked again and pulled Streeter toward him, but the virtual mass of the giant sim could not be taken down. Streeter resisted and they played tug-of-war, the portal half buried in Streeter's spleen.

"CUT THE GODDAMN ARM OFF!" Streeter yelled.

I shook my head, closed my eyes and held my breath. An image formed and twin curved sabers emerged from my hands. Broak kicked my knee, breaking it backwards. Bones cracked and I went flying, but the tip of a saber caught his arm, severing it from Streeter. Broak tumbled, ripping the battle stave from Chute's grip. His slit turned upside down. His arms flattened into edged blades.

"I will clear the chaff," he cried, getting to his feet and criss-crossing his executioner's arms above his head, "before reaping the harvest!"

He was too powerful. Too skilled. I managed to stand on one leg, but it was all I could do. He would cut me in half, send me back to the skin. The gleaming arms rose higher. I envisioned an evolver shield, but there was Chute. I would not leave her, even if it meant leaving the portal in his charge.

A fat hand gripped my arm.

The fog thickened, turning gray to black.

I left.

To the in-between.

WALLS BUILT from out of the dark and surrounded us in a wood-paneled room. Stuffed heads of an antelope and a grizzly bear formed on the walls. A fireplace blazed. Broak was gone.

"What happened?" Chute pushed the cowl off her face.

Streeter lay sprawled on the floor, his head wedged against the couch. The glowing portal peeked from a gap in his stomach and lit up his chest. Broak's limp, white arm lay across him, fingers stuck in the portal's shell.

"I got news for you," Streeter said. "Broak sucks ass."

I grabbed his arm and tried to pull him to his feet.

"Don't bother. He destroyed my spine. I don't have time to rebuild it." He pulled the portal out of his sucking guts, pushing back his intestines. He plucked Broak's hand from the portal shell and tossed it against the wall, where it smacked like a piece of wet liver. He handed the portal to me. "You're going to have to take it."

Several more pieces of the basic shell fell away, exposing the bare portal beneath.

"Make sure you don't touch the portal directly," Streeter said. "Buxbee always warned if the shells failed, to never, ever touch it. He didn't say why, he just warned us. But he also said the shells would never fail, so maybe he doesn't know what he's talking about."

Chute looked out the cabin's frosty window. "Is this the Rime?"

"It was the first place I could find in my virtualmode history. I didn't have a lot of time to evaluate locations. There was an arm in me at the time."

"But the Rime?" Chute turned on him. "They're going to know we're in here and then what?"

"Hey, let me stick my fist through you and see how clearly you think."

"You've been back here, haven't you? You've been hacking back into—" Chute ducked just as one of Streeter's battle hatchets helicoptered over her head. It buried in the wall. I stopped her before she staked his head into the floor. She walked off, counting out loud.

"That guy wasn't planning on protecting the portal, Socket," Streeter said. "I don't care what you say."

I didn't know what Broak was doing. He was the Paladins' darling, so maybe he had orders to protect it at all costs. After all, it wasn't like he was trying to kill *us*, just our sims. But Streeter was right, there was something off, no need for superpowers to see that. The guy was a head case, but he was up to something. I cradled the portal carefully, holding it up to my ear. The screeches echoed far away.

"It might take them five minutes or so to figure out the portal is in the Rime," Streeter said. "Virtually, this is a large world and that means it contains a lot of data. They'll have to sort through it all to locate the portal, especially if you hide it somewhere. Find a waterfall —something with massive dataflow."

"What're you going to do?" I asked.

"Stay here, what else? You couldn't carry me with a tank."

"I don't like leaving you." Chute was across the room, arms folded and fingers tapping. Poking him with her stave was one thing, but leaving him with those things was another.

"It's just a sim," Streeter said. "I'll build a new one."

"Yeah, but you said they might be able to hurt us."

He smashed his elbow through the wood floor, sending splinters up to the ceiling. "I'll hide under the cabin if that makes you feel better."

I dropped to my working knee and helped him pull up the floor. "You sure about this?"

"We don't have a choice. You got to keep that portal safe as long as you can. Whatever you do, don't let Whitey get it." Streeter rolled from the floor onto the frozen ground beneath. "Head west, along the ridge. There's a network of caves at the foot of the hills. Don't ask how I know. Get lost and maybe they'll never locate the portal."

The floorboards rebuilt themselves, dirty and scuffed, as though they'd been there the whole time. "GO!" Streeter's muffled voice shouted through the floor.

CHUTE WATCHED me limp onto the porch. She took the portal from me and tucked it into a bag. We stopped at the edge of the weathered steps and looked up at the gray sky and blowing snow. *Seems like just yesterday.*

"Maybe one of us should get back to the skin," I said. "Maybe—"

"Forget it," Chute said. "I'm not leaving."

I clenched my fist, hoping I could timeslice, but the spark wasn't bright enough. Face it, I was more like her than I was a Paladin. She tossed her lookits and they zipped into the trees. She loped down the hill like a deer, hit the trickling stream at the bottom and started up the other side, the pregnant sack bouncing off her leg. I followed, half-stepping with my left leg, the knee still not working. She slowed down just so I could catch up.

The trees all looked the same and soon the path ended. We slowly picked our way through the forest until we reached the next ridge. We stopped on a stone outcropping that overlooked ten thousand acres of white treetops. Walnut-sized snowflakes blotted out the sun.

Streeter was right, the Rime was huge. With all the dataflow needed to keep it running, we would be like grains of sand on a long beach. A lookit spy returned from the trees and warbled in her ear.

"There's a small cave a quarter mile down this side."

The hill was steep. I couldn't slow down, not with the gimpy leg, and ended up rolling half the way. I bounced off trees and tumbled from rocky ledges. Chute hooked an arm around my waist, hauling me to level ground. We splashed through a stream. My leg was hardly working by then.

The water weaved between snow-covered boulders and fell over a cliff. We stopped at the edge of the waterfall, the water dropping twenty feet into a pool of rising steam.

"It's over there," she said. The opening to the cave was partially obscured by heavy spruce branches. "Let's follow it into the mountain. Streeter said the more we get lost, the harder it will be to find us."

We leaped together, arm in arm, torpedoing down the waterfall to the bottom of the pool. Our battle gear was too heavy for swimming, so we climbed out. Chute wrung out her cape, throwing it over her shoulder. We were well protected by ancient conifers and cliffs. The wind howled high above, but at the mouth of the cave it was as still as dawn.

"Come on." Chute moved ahead, dotting the virgin snow. "Let's get inside before we freeze solid."

Ice crystals formed on my nose. My pants crunched. Chute held the branches out of the way and I hobbled into the dreary darkness. The portal glowed through Chute's pouch, silent ever since we left the cabin.

"Got a light?" I said.

"Hold on." She felt around. "It's in here somewhere."

Just pull out the portal. Or forget it; we'll walk in the dark. I never said either of those things. A snaky sensation rolled in my guts and seized my mind. Something was in there—with us.

"Will this do?" A dim light flickered in someone's palm, glowing brighter, illuminating his white face and body. "Dear Socket?"

26

We ran from the cave, but I fell headfirst into the snow. Chute stooped to help me to my feet. "Go!" I yanked away. "Take the portal and go!"

Chute pulled me through the snow. Behind us, Broak watched with his hands on his hips, both arms intact, slit-mouth turned up.

"What d'ya want?" she shouted. "You want this?" She tore away the pouch. "You want to save the world by yourself, is that what you came for? Well, here, go save the world, hero!"

"No!" I caught the corner of the pouch and it landed at my feet. "Don't give it to him."

"He's going to shred our sims, so what?" She squatted down, put her arms around my chest, and sat me up.

"I'm going to be saving the world, indeed," he said, "though perhaps not as you envision."

Broak eased the portal out of the pouch. His generic face radiated pale blue. He turned it around, admiring the swirling colors. He snapped off a piece of the shell and sank his fingers into the portal. It jiggled like a gooey mass and jumped away, at first, then oozed up his wrist. The opaque whiteness of his skin darkened. Blue flames ignited from inside the portal, creeping up his arm. Veins pulsed up his shoulder, bulging like slithering purple snakes. The flames wrapped around his shoulders then engulfed his entire body, the whiteness giving way to fleshy color. The details of his skin-body took form and absorbed the flames, and then he was there, the real Broak. Black eyes, black hair and perfect teeth.

He stretched, admiring his hand, front and back. Smiled. "Welcome to a new era, dear friends."

"What just happened?" Chute's voice quivered.

The portal was the same colors as the wormhole Mom drove through. The same as the sacred portal deep below the Garrison that ripped me from my skin and took me somewhere through space and time. The portal was a transporter, too, transporting our awareness from skin to sim. But he was, in a sense, making direct contact with it. Did it transport *him*? Was that really Broak? Did he bring his skin into virtualmode?

He twirled around, head back and arms extended, catching snowflakes on his tongue. Snow crunched under his feet as he giggled. He didn't want to save the portal, he wanted to use it. Broak had nothing to do with the Paladins. And if he wasn't a Paladin...

"You're a duplicate."

He bent down next to me. "That is very astute, dear Socket, but incorrect. I am not a duplicate, but it is true I am no longer associated with the Paladin Nation. They will find my skin in the Garrison connected to a portal, but it is of no use to me now. That heart need beat no longer."

"You never had a heart. You're a traitor."

"Of course I had a heart. I am flesh and blood, but never was my heart with the Paladins. I find them to be soiled and imperfect." He tilted his head, looking for the right word. "Too *human*."

"They created you. How could you betray them?"

"They *created* me." He chuckled. "Do you hear yourself? They *created me*. Does that sound human to you?" His lip quivered. "They *built* me, *manufactured* me, put breath in my lungs, and told me what to do. Does that sound human to you? Mmmm?" He nudged me with his boot. "Mmmm, tell me, does it?"

Chute slid back, pulling me with her. Broak planted the tip of his boot into my shattered knee. My leg flopped like a rag, crackling like a bag of rocks.

"DOES THAT SOUND HUMAN TO YOU?" he bellowed.

His smooth cheeks flushed with rage, he went to the cave and stared into the darkness, collecting his thoughts. He was feeling something and needed to get it under control.

When he turned back to us, his smile was a perfect mask. "The duplicates showed me the way. If life is good, why waste it with imperfection? Duplicates make decisions based on fact, not feelings. You will see, dear Socket. The world will be a better place when the duplications make decisions. There will be no more corruption, only perfection."

"They're imitations. Not real."

"Who says they're not real? They think, they laugh, they feel. I believe those are the characteristics that define you and me as human, isn't that so? Mmmm?"

"Who said we're supposed to be perfect?"

He tilted his head, looking all too much like Spindle. "Who says we shouldn't?"

Screeches called from the portal. Broak held it to his ear, swaying back and forth. His eyes fluttered and closed. "Let's get on with the task at hand, shall we?"

He yanked me toward him with effortless strength—so quickly that Chute fell over my shoulder. She boxed him in the middle of the face, pulling me away with her other arm. Broak grabbed my hand. He casually wiped the blood trickling out his nose and looked disgusted.

"They wanted to kill you, dear Socket. The duplicates wanted their crawlers to unlock the virtualmode and kill you at the same time." He shook his head, tsking. "Those darn imitations are so efficient. Always multitasking."

"Why do they want virtualmode?"

"Why, to get back to the source, of course. They share the same desire as humans, you see. They crave to be connected with the source of their creation just as humans seek peace in their so-called soul. They were born of the virtualmode universe; they cannot survive without it. Paladins sought to cut them off from their life source, but they did not foresee the size of the snake they were taunting. The duplicates cannot be stopped. There are just too many of them. Too bad they didn't have that dirty rat Pivot to tell the Paladins this truth." He leaned in and whispered, "The world is ours now."

I struck with my rigid fingers, aiming to split his face in half. He caught my wrist and broke it, my fingers went limp, and then in one smooth motion he plunged my hand into the portal. Blue flames crept up my arm to my shoulder. My teeth tingled. I struggled, but Broak held me firm. Chute swatted at the flames walking around my neck, encircling my chest. Veins swelled on the back of my hand. White hair fell over my face.

My sim doesn't have white hair.

The flames stalled and flickered, then rushed around me and Chute like we were bales of dry straw. My hand burned. My smashed knee ached.

Cold nipped at my cheeks.

Frozen fabric pressed against my skin.

Chute screamed.

The pain came all at once. Shattered bones and broken nerves radiated like nails into my knee. Chute squeezed tighter.

"Baaill... bail..." My lips were stiff and numb. "Code... bailll out code bail."

"Welcome, dear friends, to your new skin!" Broak raised his arms. "Sometimes you feel pleasure, sometimes you feel... *pain*."

I blacked out.

CHUTE WAS ROCKING me back and forth when I came to. "What's going on, Socket?"

Her teeth chattered. That's when I noticed her hands wrapped over my chest. They were fleshy. She was shaking.

"I did not bring you here to murder, dear Socket." Broak paced restlessly toward the cave. "I will admit I tried to end your life in the Graveyard, yes. Forgive me for that, will you, dear friend? Because since then, I have had an epiphany. I cannot take credit for this brilliant idea. It was my mentor that understood your true potential. This was all his idea, yes."

The portal swelled to twice its size in his hands. It was screeching.

"If you will excuse me a moment."

He dug his fingers in and pulled it open. The remains of the shell twinkled onto his feet. He smiled, at first, then grunted. His arms bulged as the portal attempted to close, forcing Broak to one knee for leverage. He stretched it open again and this time a jointed stick poked through, feeling around. Another poked out and then another until there were eight. The jointed sticks helped hold the portal open until it gave birth to a putty-colored glob.

The crawler fell into the snow, then rose up like a newborn calf, its body pulsing. Two more plopped next to it, all three shaking on new legs, growing with each pulsation.

"I will admit, your death seemed to be the only solution." Broak tossed the portal aside. "The duplicates already find Paladins a formidable opponent; they couldn't have you making the Nation stronger, faster and smarter. They wanted you dead. But then my mentor came up with an idea, not just a way to eliminate you but a way to steal you from them."

The crawlers were already double their original size, spiking their legs into the ground. Broak stroked their backs.

"You see, my friends are going to pull you apart and integrate your genetic code into our database. Your DNA will be the blueprint for new and improved duplications. You will help us, dear Socket. You will become one of us." He smiled wide and whispered, "Is that not wonderful?"

27

SAVIOR

CHUTE TRIED TO LIFT ME, but I screamed at the effort. She slid me to the water, panting. Her foot plunked into the pool. The crawlers' bodies beat like hearts, watching us struggle with their brightening eyelights. Broak edged closer.

"Don't fret, dear Socket." He wiped the water from my cheek. "You're going on to a better life."

Chute slapped his hand. "Don't touch him!"

He only smiled and went back to his pets, now shoulder tall, bobbing and weaving. He rubbed their bodies. They nuzzled back.

"As you can see, we have everything the Paladins have. Technology is our specialty."

"You're not a duplicate," I said.

"Not yet." He held out his arms. "But soon, I will download into a fabricated body of my choice. I will determine my fate. I will be the captain of my life." His energy darkened, casting a shadow over his face. "Do you think I want to be victimized by those Paladins any longer? Slave to the human race, mmm? I am my own god now, dear

Socket. I can become whatever I want in the real world. What's not real about that, mmm? Why would humans resist their heart's desire? They are far too selfish not to follow. And here's the big surprise, my dear one. Are you ready for it?" He stood straight and his expression brightened. "You're coming with me."

Chute whimpered, pulling me deeper into the water. I was struggling just to keep from screaming. "There's... nothing real... about you."

"Well, if I'm no longer real..." He kicked my broken knee. The pain radiated like electricity. "Maybe that will change your mind."

I could hold the scream in no longer.

"Rejoice!" Broak shouted with his back to us, his voice echoing into the cave. "Mankind will no longer toil in incompetence."

My teeth clattered. Chute's breath was warm on my ear.

"Humanity's suffering will come to an end! We will put the world in order. The human race will evolve into a super species of choice and freedom!"

The timeslicing spark flashed inside me. Brighter. Firmer. I wrapped my mind around it and colors swirled. Snowflakes staggered. Broak lifted his arms, palms to the sky, surrounded by a halo of light.

I sliced time.

Energy filled me, pouring into every muscle and every broken bone. In the dead silence, I closed my eyes and searched out the source of my agony. I traveled through my own veins, penetrating tissues and nerves. I knew the ways of my body intimately and commanded it to heal. Cartilage reconnected in my knees; bones fused together in my wrist. Pain was arrested.

But the spark slipped like a greased rat, squirming from my grip. Nerve lines screamed again. A crawler lifted Broak onto its back. Broak squeezed it between his knees, his face lifted to the heavens.

"Do that again," Chute said. "Whatever you just did, do it again. You felt stronger."

"I... can't." The spark was dim. It was too soon. "I'm sorry I got you into this."

"Don't say sorry." She squeezed tighter. "Don't you say that!"

"Flawless." Broak almost sang the word, the hard line of his brow darkening his eyes. "That is what we'll bring them, dear Socket. Unadulterated perfection."

His choppy laughter echoed over the trees. I chased the spark again, squeezed it in every direction I could, but it avoided me. *Rudder! Please, bring it back.*

The crawlers reared up on their hind legs like wild stallions and unleashed a screech, blowing the hair away from my face. Blood rushed past my throbbing eardrums. Chute scrambled deeper, dragging me with her. Water crept above my waist.

"We are saviors." He raised the portal with both hands. "Rejoice... for it is at hand, dear Socket... rejoice, for I WILL LEAD THEM TO THE PROMISELAND!!"

The crawlers reared again, their jointed legs aimed at us. They would pull me apart, study every cell and every strand of DNA. They would become stronger because of me. They would become faster because of me. People would suffer. The world, the real world, would end. It would end because of me. I didn't want this. Pivot was wrong. I was no hero, I was a curse. The world would pay, because of me.

"*LOOK OUT!*" Streeter's voice vibrated in my skull.

CccrrraaaaaAAAACCCKKKKKKKKKK!

A flash, then blindness. Deafness. The percussion stopped my heart and the world spun.

Colder. And wetter.

FRIGIDNESS STOLE the feeling from my skin and the air from my lungs. I opened my mouth and sucked a mouthful of water. My wet clothes pulled me down. I couldn't tell which way was up until I hit the rocky bottom. I tried to kick upward, but my leg would not work. I heaved myself up, but the surface was too far away. I wouldn't get there. My lungs blazed and unconsciousness settled around me like a warm blanket. My hand slipped and I fell. I scrambled again, but felt myself drifting.

Something grabbed my wrist and yanked me up. Once. Twice. Three times, someone pulled at me with frantic desperation. Darkness had settled on my wide-open eyes.

SOMETHING soft and warm pressed on my lips, blowing air into my chest. It happened again. And then I puked warm water.

"Oh, god," I blubbered, rolling over.

"Socket." Chute grabbed my tunic and shook me. "Oh, thank God you're all right! I thought you were gone."

The world was bleached and bleary. Water dripped off Chute's chattering chin. Her eyes were red and misty. Her hair smelled sulfuric. We lay on muddy ground; the snow was gone.

"What happened?" I asked.

She sat back on her knees. "Lightning."

I turned my head. A blackened crater sizzled at the mouth of the cave, smoke rising from the center. The crawlers' misshapen bodies were scattered around, their legs twisted and bent.

Chute helped me stand, our water-soaked clothes already stiffening in the arctic air, but it kept me numb. I hobbled with her help to the smoking crater. Broak lay in the bottom. The left half of his chest was missing, as was his left arm. His hair and clothes had evaporated to his waist, revealing skin blistered like tar. Perfect teeth gleamed through holes in his cheeks. The portal, blue and glittering, lay wedged under his arm.

"*Holy shit.*" Streeter's voice echoed in my skull. "*I just fried those assholes like butter. I'm sorry it took so long, I don't have the control panels in this crawl space and I wanted to build a lightning bolt with enough voltage to melt them like plastic.*" He chuckled. "*They won't virtualmode for months. Not in those sims.*"

Chute couldn't look away. She began to shake, pushing me away and staring at the bottom of the crater. She tried to speak. I held her close, but she pushed again. "This isn't happening... this isn't..."

I turned her from the scene, holding her closer. Tense and shaking, she tried to fight me off. I held her until she went limp. She laid her head on my shoulder and wept. We stayed that way, swaying back and forth while she cried.

"*Socket?*" Streeter said. "*Chute? Can you hear me?*"

I told Streeter what happened. I told him about the awareness transference, and how our sims had become skin. We couldn't log off. We could smell things. We could *feel*.

"*Impossible.*"

"The portal, Streeter... there's something about the portal being a transporter. When I touched it, our sims became skin. We're here, Streeter. We're not back in the lab, we're actually here."

He babbled on, argued and shouted, "I told you not to touch—"

"Listen!" I cut him off. "None of that's important. It's done! Now, how do we get out of here? There has to be a way to get back to our skin."

"*The portal. If you destroy the portal, it'll send you back. It pulled you out of your skin, you should return if it's destroyed.*"

"Can you redress us?" Chute let go, her teeth clicking together. "We need dry clothes, Streeter. Warm, dry ones."

"*Yeah, yeah... I can do that.*"

The hard frozen clothes faded, simultaneously replaced with identical garb and a hot, soft coat. Cold still penetrated my bones. I went back to the crater. The portal was there. Steam hissed from cracks along Broak's blackened body.

"*I didn't mean to kill him, Socket,*" Streeter said softly. "*I thought... I didn't know he was real.*"

"I know."

"*Maybe he's not dead. Maybe he bolted back to his skin and I fried his sim. That's all I was trying to do, you know.*"

But Broak didn't return to his skin. He was at the bottom of a burned-out hole. The look on his face said he hadn't even seen it coming. I doubted he'd felt a thing.

"*I'm sorry,*" Streeter said. "*I didn't mean to do it. I didn't kill him, did I? I'm not—*"

"He probably escaped, Streeter," I lied. "Now tell me, how do I destroy that thing?"

There was a long pause. "*Use your evolver,*" he said uneasily. "*Just cut the thing in half.*"

Chute stood next to me, wrinkling her nose. The unmistakable smell of fried skin wafted up from the pit, clinging to the back of my throat. I breathed through my mouth without pinching my nose and sat on the crater's edge. I slid down the side a few feet and avoided touching the body. I fumbled for the portal, coaxing it with my fingertips. It was stuck. I slid closer and hooked my hand around it. It broke away with a wet snap. Chute stepped into the crater and held out her hand. Something yanked me back.

"Socket!" Chute screamed.

Broak had my arm. Bones protruded from his crispy fingertips. His head turned and crackled, and flakes of blackened skin fell away. His eye sockets were empty, and his tongue darted out, licking what remained of his lips. He pulled me closer.

"Dear Socket..."

His hand trembled. The tongue fell back into his mouth.

No. Broak did not make it back to the skin.

28

BURIED

WE LAID the portal on the ground. I pulled the evolver from my waist and let it unfold around my arm, piercing my nerve lines. Never before had I felt an evolver tap into my nervous system. I imagined a weapon: A long, arching saber emerged from my hand. I curled my damaged hand against my chest and raised the weapon with my other arm. Heat radiated from the blade. Chute stepped back.

The blade sank in. The portal swelled. It turned purple. Red. Blue-green-violet-yelloworangeblue. The saber spat back, blasting the evolver from my arm. I landed hard on the frozen ground, jolting the loose bones in my leg. It took several tries to breathe again. The evolver half-folded back into a handle, coughing electrical arcs.

Chute helped me sit up. When I was breathing normally, she asked, "What now?"

Long pause. *"I can, uh, well... I can build another lightning bolt with twice the voltage. The portal won't survive that, but the website might crash."*

"If you crash this website," I said, "won't that release us?"

"*Not necessarily. If for some reason it doesn't destroy the portal and crashes the website, you could end up in-between.*" Another long pause. "*I need to think about this.*"

A fire grew from the ground, courtesy of Streeter. Flames crackled off the dry wood, sending up sparks like glowing bugs, which dissolved in the bitter air. Snow began to fall again, dusting the frozen mud.

Chute had that look. Her forehead was tight. Her lips pinched.

"You all right?" I said.

She nodded, rubbing her hands together. We listened to the water fall. "Are we going to get out of here?" she finally asked.

"We'll get out of here."

She spread her hands out toward the flames. She silently debated whether to believe me. There was no reason she should.

"Why do you think he did it?" Chute gestured at the crater.

I thought hard about Broak, with his perfect breeding and his perfect smile. He was a perfect specimen of a human being. But that was the rub: he was still human. He might've had perfect genes, but he'd been raised like a servy. He became just like a mech, following the rules. He was *supposed* to be perfect. But he could not *be* perfect. He was human. Somewhere in his teenage brain he was letting Mom and Dad down. A mom he never had. A dad that never existed.

How could the Paladins be so short-sighted? They were a greater race of humans and they couldn't figure out they'd raised a monster?

"He was a little messed up in the head," I said. "He was just a kid."

"I don't care, he wasn't good."

"No." I pushed a stick into the fire. "He wasn't."

The fire blazed. The heat stayed right there by the flames, not dispersing into the wintry air. Steam no longer rose from the crater as it slowly filled with snow. It was cold out there. I shook the snow off my head and limped toward Broak.

At the edge of the crater, I held my breath and ignited the evolver. It refused to completely unfold. I squeezed it harder and it finally fused to my arm, shooting sparks in protest. I formed a spade and jabbed at the frozen ground, the blade thumping through it a chunk at a time. Each time I opened the earth with another swing, I cursed the Paladins for creating Broak. I cursed them for their ignorance. Cursed them for what they did to him.

"What're you doing?" Chute said.

"He should be buried."

"I don't think he deserves it. Not after what he did."

I turned to breathe clean air, wiping my eyes. "Maybe."

I didn't know what to think. Broak might've been the leader of the dupes, for all I knew. He might've single-handedly led the human race into extinction had Streeter not roasted him. The Paladins dealt him an impossible life, but where was he supposed to take responsibility? At what point was it his fault and not theirs? In the end, he was just a stupid kid, believing he was the center of the universe, that he was indestructible like all the rest of us.

I mean, it's not like we're born with the manual on how to live life. No one gives us a clue how this is supposed to be done, so can any of us be blamed when it all goes wrong? Think about it, we grow up being told there's a fat man dressed in red that lives at the North Pole that gives us presents for free, and if we question the absurdity of it, they tell us we just have to believe and it'll be true. *Are you freaking kidding me?* Reindeer don't fly and jolly fat men don't shove presents down the chimney. But just believe and it'll be true. NO, IT WON'T!

Maybe Broak had the manual to life. He just read it wrong, took it too literally. He wanted life to be perfect and that wasn't possible. Life was perfectly imperfect.

I took another chunk of ground from the shallow grave. No sense deciding on blame. The boy needed a proper burial. Fair or not. The ground thumped again. Chute pried up another piece of the ground with her battle stave. We tossed frozen earth into the crater. The dirt clods were like bricks. We buried him, along with the crawlers, as best we could, then shoveled snow on top when we ran out of earth.

We stood at the lip of the crater, our heads bowed. "God help us all," I said.

Chute laid her head on my shoulder and wrapped her arm

around my waist. We let the snow pile on our heads and shoulders until the cold seeped inside.

"Come on," she said. "Let's get back to the fire."

———————

WE STAYED warm in front of the endless fire, waiting for Streeter to come up with an answer. We didn't talk much. I wished there was something to say so that I could stop thinking about Broak, the way he bubbled in the bottom of the pit. The way he said my name at the end, almost with an edge of final regret. It was so complicated, I just wanted to stop thinking about it, but there wasn't much to say, either. So we sat in silence until a dirt clod rolled off the grave.

I didn't think much of it. It wasn't a big deal. Surprised I even noticed it with the wind howling above the trees, but when the second one tumbled off, I tensed up. I limped around the crater's edge. A jointed stick poked from the fresh snow, feeling the grave like a blind man's cane.

"Streeter!" I hobbled back to Chute.

"What's wrong?" she said.

"Streeter!" I tapped my cheek. "Streeter! Get us out of here!"

All the frozen clods rumbled. A seven-legged crawler stood, legs kinked and wobbly. It fell to one side and tried to stand again. Its scarred body undulated. The burn wounds and deep gashes sealed. It was healing.

"The crawlers, Streeter! They survived!"

29

SNOWDEAF

A SECOND CRAWLER rose up from the grave, its body pulsing. The evolver unfolded onto my arm, but it was sputtering. I summoned hot whips, I'd lash the things to pieces, but a weak flame only flickered in my hand.

"*You guys need to run,*" Streeter said.

"Are you out of your freaking mind?" I shouted. "My leg doesn't work! You need to build us something... a transporter, a cruiser, anything!"

"*I'm busy with the lightning. I can't do it all!*"

"If we don't get out of here, LIGHTNING WON'T MATTER!"

A third crawler squirmed, running in a circle like a fly with one wing.

Chute shoved the portal into her pouch and slid her arm around me. "We have to try."

We headed past the cave and into the trees. Each step throbbed with agony, and I was panting after only a few yards. There was a narrow trail winding uphill. The going was easier, but the pain worse.

Behind us, the crawlers screeched, weaker than before the lightning strike, but at just the right pitch to twist my nerves.

"I can't." I covered my face. "I can't... I can't do this..."

"STREETER! GET US SOMETHING NOW!" Chute shouted at him like he was a god looking over a forsaken world.

"Come on, you can do this," she urged me in a softer voice.

"I can't, Chute." I turned so she wouldn't see my face. "It just... it hurts too much."

"You don't have a choice."

"I'm only going to slow you down."

"I'm not leaving you here, Socket Greeny!" She placed both hands on my face and forced me to look at her. "I'm never leaving you, so if you want to save me, you got to save yourself."

Her cheeks flamed red. The *look* was gone—the worried look— replaced by steely courage. I couldn't move and deadly spiders screeched behind us, but all I wanted at that moment was to kiss her on the lips.

She held out her hand and hoisted me up, hip to hip, and together we started up the path. I closed my eyes, searching for strength to match what I'd seen in her eyes. The spark grew brighter, the power centers of my awakening whirring along my spine. If it would work, if I could stop time, I could save us.

Metal clashed as the space in front of us twisted and warped. If a crawler was materializing before us, there was no use running. We watched something assemble from empty space. Pieces sprang from the air, clinging together as more pieces emerged, rolling, turning, and clicking into place until a round platform hovered inches off the ground.

"*It's all I can do,*" Streeter said. "*Take the jetter and go. They're on the move.*"

"It's enough," Chute said. "I can get us miles away before they get this far."

She helped me onto the back edge of the jetter and climbed onto the front. I wrapped my good arm around her waist and laid my chin on her shoulder. The jetter sagged under our weight.

"*Go to the tundra,*" Streeter said. "*There's a power dome that will protect you. It's indestructible. Once you're in, nothing can touch you.*"

"Tundra?" I said. "Build it right here, Streeter, right in front of us! We don't have time to get to the—"

"*JUST GET TO THE GODDAMN TUNDRA! I can't build it right in front of you. It's complex code; I don't have time to build it from scratch!*"

The jetter hummed loudly, lifted and surged forward. Chute tossed her lookits and followed them. The sharp wind blurred my sight. My inner ears ached, but Streeter's voice, calmer, sounded clear in my head.

"*The power dome is remnant code from an earlier battle on the tundra, that's the best I can do.*" Screeches blasted from all around. "*So please... just get to the tundra.*"

CHUTE LEANED FORWARD and pushed the jetter at top speed. How could she see? Her hair whipped my face and I clung to her tightly. We reached the top of the ridge and followed a sloping path to the left, gently slaloming left and right.

A lookit returned. "We're going into the trees," she shouted back. "It's the quickest way!"

The forest was dark and dense. The going got slow. We painfully bumped trees, stumps and logs. I squeezed tighter. The forest rumbled. Tremors traveled deep underground.

They were coming.

I didn't need to say it. She heard it, too. *Go faster.* If we hit a tree and damaged the jetter, it was over. Streeter didn't have time to build another. *But still, go faster.*

Up ahead, the shadows gave way. Light poked through the impenetrable forest. "We're almost there!" she shouted.

We leaned into a tight turn and ducked beneath a low branch. The crude path widened beyond the last turn. Chute took the corner tight and caught a twisting vine hidden in a snowdrift. The jetter turned a full circle, tipped back, and couldn't right itself.

A bell rang.

It was ringing in the darkness.

Something picked me up. Shook me.

"Get up, Socket!" a voice said. "Don't quit on me! It's right there... It's—"

It wasn't so bad where I was. I didn't know where that was, but it wasn't so bad. Maybe a little chilly. I couldn't see in the pitch black, but at least it didn't hurt.

Where was I? Wasn't I supposed to be doing something? We were trying to get... something... or somewhere. *We?*

A light twittered, like a lighthouse beacon going round and round. It was sparkly. I urged myself closer to it. It was curious and bright. It wanted something. The next time it came around, it glared like the sun. I tried to look away before it burned out my eyes, but it was impossible. I had no eyelids. The light was every-where. I wanted to run and hide, to sleep. The light refused to let me.

It rushed into me. Filled me.

Power centers burst to life and energy surged. I had a body, but I wasn't in it. It was broken. I saw my shattered knee and, with a thought, healed it. The bones and cartilage fused together as good as new. The wrist was damaged, too. I commanded it to reassemble. Nerves repaired. Muscles healed.

I am awake.

In a single thought, I returned to my renewed body. Cold tight-ened my skin and took my breath. Time was not moving. Motionless snowflakes glittered like diamonds in the air. The waning sun cast an iridescent shine on the snowdrifts, like ocean waves in moonlight. Chute was crouched over me—stuck in time—her face turned to the sky, mouth open, about to cry for help or curse our fate. Jagged energy enveloped her.

A yellow dome, like a vibrant igloo, squatted in the snowdrifts on the far side of the tundra a thousand feet away. I wouldn't be able to timeslice forever; weakness had already entered my legs as the times-licing metabolism devoured me. I had to get to the power dome, had to squeeze every second out of the spark that I could. The crawlers weren't far behind.

I picked up Chute and started over the white desert, carving through the waist-deep drifts, hopping when the snow was over my knees. Snowflakes bounced off my face. Snot ran over my lips. Chute got heavier.

Halfway there, I began to quiver. How far could I push it before my body was sucked dry? *As far as I could.* I plowed onward, going around the deepest drifts. Exhausted and numb, Chute slipped. I tumbled over her.

The dying sun brightened. Snowflakes jolted sideways. A breeze washed over me.

The dome was fifty yards away. I could do it. I picked her up and started up the deepest drift yet. My breath streamed out in a long cloud. I blinked several times to focus. The drift ended abruptly and we went down again. So numb, my legs were nothing. Gravity intensified. I tried to lift her, but couldn't get her past my knees. The world quaked.

Can't do it.

The timeslicing spark slipped from my grip. The wind sheared the feeling from my face. Snowflakes struck like rocks. Chute sat up, dazed. I took her hand and tried to lift her. "The dome... we're almost there."

She understood and helped me up. I pretended to run but could barely throw one leg in front of the other. We fell again. She shouted, but the wind blasted her words away. I started to crawl. She tried to pick me up.

Trees exploded on the far side and crawlers blasted onto the tundra like galloping creatures from another planet on twitching legs, their stride distorted by missing limbs. The pitch of their screeching was perfect. It made the gale-force wind seem like a summer breeze, slamming our nervous systems, cutting away any strength we had left. We dropped like the dead.

The sky swirled darkly over us. Lightning crackled in the clouds but did not come down.

Scccreeeeeeeeeeeee!

The portal slipped from Chute's pouch. I took it and crawled. Chute was next to me, her ragged hair hanging over her face.

A shadow passed over us.

Snow exploded around my forearm and the portal rolled out of my hand.

The crawlers stepped over me. I pushed up and collapsed again. A gash from my elbow to my wrist flapped open, exposing bones and spilling blood. The snow was sprayed red.

This is the Internet. This is not the skin. THIS IS NOT REAL!

I tried to run, but my legs only kicked. Tried to roll. Tried to scream. It was too much, too much. TOO MUCH!

A crawler hovered inches from my face, stinking of burning circuits and baked clay. Its faceless body pressed its sticky body against my cheek and quivered like it was sniffing. Another one wobbled over Chute while a third one bobbed between us, waiting its turn.

It lifted off me, undulating like a thinking brain. A hole opened on its belly, black and bottomless. It screeched, but I didn't hear it. My eardrums immediately burst. In silence, I convulsed.

In darkness, I screamed.

MY SIGHT RETURNED. The crawler limped away, swaying in the silent wind towards Chute to have a turn with her. The third one stooped over me and pressed against my cheek.

My eyes wanted to close, but I refused to let them. Chute was limp. I reached for her. I couldn't let them kill her. I could not let this happen. I forced myself to move, but the crawler corralled my hand, placing it gently on my chest. It pressed against my severed arm and came up with a splotch of blood on its belly, absorbing the stain. It turned pale and looked to the others. Undulated. They abandoned Chute. She remained still.

They gathered around me, lifting me with their twiggy legs. They spread my arms and held my legs together. They'd found me. I was the one to pull apart. I was the one they would decode. They would integrate me into their database and I would become one of them. They would put me inside the duplications. I would become the living dead.

Mission accomplished.

Two crawlers held me while the third one, slightly larger, pressed against me. It wrapped its round body around me, warm and sticky. My cells began to dissolve, liquefying as the world faded.

Gray became darkness.

Would I go to the in-between, or would I just go to sleep, never to wake? Would I awaken as one of them—see the iron rule of duplicated humans for centuries to come? Would I experience every cry, every plea, to make them stop? Or would I see the human race follow them like lemmings?

The time spark beat somewhere inside. It was the only thing I could feel, thumping in my awareness. There was little left of me now. If I took the spark, I would empty my body. The timeslice would suck out the last drop of life.

I clenched my hands and sliced it anyway.

I would slice time to the end.

30

RIPPED

I SLID out of the crawler's snotty grip and stared into its maw. What was left of my clothes was covered in slime. The thick mucus kept me from freezing.

The portal had rolled inside the dome. My grip on time was already slipping. I didn't have much left. Life was fading. I would die in the timeslice and disappear from the world. I would die so the crawler wouldn't absorb me. Die before they could integrate me.

Chute. I couldn't leave her. I rolled for her, just to touch her. There had to be something I could do. There had to be an answer. I held her head firmly against my chest and wrapped my legs around her waist, trying to crawl to the safety of the dome. But I didn't have the strength to even do that.

I need help! I cried. The words drifted silently from me. No one would hear my plea. Not even me.

I convulsed again. The ground trembled.

Time stood still, but the world shook. The sky tore open,

revealing a bright red slice through the dreary clouds. I felt the ripping in my chest.

The website was crashing. A crevasse opened at the far end of the tundra, swallowing snow into a deadly void of random data. It traveled across the tundra slowly, widening and inhaling the environment. Snow rushed across the plain. The forest bordering the wide tundra bent under its force. Sticks, leaves, rocks, rabbits... all of it was sucked into the rip.

It would reach us and suck us in as it split the tundra. My evolver belched but unfolded around my good arm. I summoned a whip that fell short of the dome. I cursed, pulling it back. I closed my eyes, imagining the longest whip possible, then let it fly. It lashed out, slightly brighter, slightly thinner, and long enough to wrap around the base of an ancient spruce.

My grip on time slipped before I passed out. Snowflakes jittered and danced. The wind returned, driving snow over the tundra that curved like breaking waves under the voracious appetite of the rip. The tundra had split open, the rip halfway to us. The horizon was nearly gone. The details of trees and mountains had dissolved.

The website was going down and nothing would stop it. In deafness, the destruction was eerily silent. The forest began to shake as the rip widened. The portal bounced against the dome, trapped inside its protective barrier. The evolver whip grew taut as I was drawn toward the approaching chasm. The crawler stood tall, scanning the environment. It took only seconds to analyze the situation. Seconds they didn't have. The rip gained speed, raced past us and into the trees, sucking up branches and snow. The two smaller crawlers leaped, but the rip vacuumed them down. They hit the ground, their spindly legs scratching the frozen ground as they bounced over the edge. Down they went. Forever.

The third crawler anchored into the ground, fighting the rip's force. The first of the large branches bounced past. The evolver whip stretched. The force was too great. We slid toward the encroaching abyss.

The crawler slid, too, etching tracks in the permafrost. I grabbed the lash with my other arm, the wind blowing the wound open, the skin flapping. The crawler jabbed at me with one leg, impaling the ground inches from my ribs. It lost its hold and slid faster, flopping over the edge, desperately hanging on.

I clutched Chute between my legs. I could feel nothing. The evolver lash stretched thinner. The rip was closer and the vacuum stronger. My legs fell over the edge. Chute dangled inside. Below, the void was colorless, depthless, and dimensionless. She was slipping. I hooked my wounded arm around her.

The entire horizon was fuzzy gray static. The data was gone. The ground near us rushed overhead, curling like carpet on its way to chaos and randomness. My knees had slipped under Chute's armpits as we twisted on the end of the line. The crawler's red eyelight rolled around its body and focused on me. It teetered on the very edge.

The lash flickered. The evolver started unfolding. I grabbed for the slippery ledge, slipping deeper. Chute's legs faded in the void's depth. The evolver fell off my arm and rolled past me, dissolving below into millions of specks.

We didn't fall.

Something was latched onto my wrist.

There, bent over the edge, was a shadowy arm, its fingers locked around my arm. A head and torso looked down at us. The shadow returned.

Pivot! You came for us!

Another shadowy arm clung to Chute, her body turning in the wind. He held us there. He didn't pull us up, he just held us.

[I have you, Master Socket.]

Spindle?

Trees vaporized in the void's depth. The crawler slashed at us one last time, slipped off the ledge and dissolved into nothingness.

We twisted helplessly as the rip crept beneath the dome that slid down like electrical gel. The portal stuck to the side of the wall, oozing like molasses. It picked up speed, the colors bright and glowing. It broke free and shot down into the ravenous void.

The explosion was silent. Bright, like that of a dying star.

The light consumed us.

No cold. No pain.

IN-BETWEEN.

I was in the dark in-between. Bodiless. Pure awareness.

There was something different, this time. Another awareness floated with me. A familiar presence.

Spindle?

There was movement.

[Yes, Master Socket.]

Spindle! I thought you were Pivot! I thought this whole time Pivot was the shadow!

[I am the one that assumed the form of a shadow. Not Master Pivot.]

It was you... My thoughts rang like words. *Am I... am I dead?*

[You are not dead. You will return to your body when it is ready.]

Which body?

[Your skin, of course. The portal was destroyed, releasing you from the sim.]

The darkness moved again. It hummed. I felt it at my core.

You saved me, Spindle.

[Your father saved you.]

My father?

[He imbedded a secret code in my processor. When the time was right, I came to you as the shadow and activated your powers. And when you needed me, I came to your aid.]

He told me on the day I first arrived at the Garrison that he was programmed to assist me. And that's why the shadow felt so familiar, why he felt like my father. Even in death, my father was there.

Why did you wait so long?

[Despite what you believe, you did not need me.]

The darkness hummed stronger and deeper. I was moving.

The Paladins will know what you did, Spindle. They'll shut you down completely this time. I won't see you when I return, will I?

[Master Pivot seems to think they will not shut me down.]

Pivot came back?

[He never left.]

But... the Paladins will imprison him this time. They can't see the future; they'll never let him leave again.

[The Paladins could never stop Master Pivot from leaving. They have always known that. He stayed in the Preserve of his own volition. After taking you to awaken, he decided it was time to leave.]

Where did he go?

[Missing, Master Socket. He went missing. They will not find him. But he can always be found if you need him.]

The darkness swirled this time. The hum was closer. It hurt nowhere specific. It just hurt.

Pivot loved my father.

[Indeed, he did. Without him, I could not have come for you.]

Pain lanced through me, up and down and side to side. Something thumped in rhythm. Pain focalized in several spots throughout the darkness.

I was returning.

Chute and Streeter. I almost forgot! *Are they all right?*

I moved faster. Noise was coming.

Spindle! Where are you? Tell me, are they all right? ARE THEY ALL RIGHT?

The pain returned in full force.

MUFFLED SOUNDS. Chairs and tables were turned over and shoved aside. Muted voices shouted.

"Three kids, two boys and one girl. About sixteen years old."

"Sir, this one's the Greeny boy. Alert the commander."

"Get the EMT here immediately. Set up a secure perimeter. I don't want to see lookits within a hundred yards. Clear the room!"

There were tables. A ceiling. It was a room. A *real* one.

"I need three reconstitution IVs on the Greeny kid immediately," a woman shouted. Her fingers pressed on my neck. "Weak pulse."

"How's he alive?" someone else muttered.

I was on my back. The lights were dim. People were now everywhere, looking down at me. Three of them were dressed in black. The Paladins. They were right there in plain sight of everyone.

"The girl's in shock," the woman said.

"Get the minders in here to stabilize her." One of the Paladins squatted next to me. The emergency worker stared at him.

"Who the hell are you?" she said.

The Paladin didn't acknowledge her. He put his hand over my head and a healing warmth oozed through me. He slapped a patch on my neck and strength leached into my body.

"What did you just do to him?" The emergency worker was about to call for assistance, but then the Paladin looked at her, *thought* at her, and she stopped.

More EMTs burst into the room, called more orders and hovered over me. A warm, soft presence crawled from the back of my neck and slithered down the front of my shirt. Rudder hid inside my sweatshirt from the EMTs' poking and prodding. I could feel his purring against my stomach and how it radiated through me.

"You did it, Socket." Streeter grabbed my shoulder; his voice seemed so far away.

His face was slack, but he was smiling. My arm was skinny, like the muscle had been sucked out. My cheeks hung. Big hands pulled Streeter away and rolled him onto his back, but he was still smiling. His mouth moved. *You did it.*

There must've been ten people over me. I could barely see the ceiling anymore. They strapped gear around my arms and attached things to my neck and chest, holding up bags, squeezing fluid into my veins. The Paladin put another patch on the other side of my neck. I couldn't feel my left arm, but it was there. No bone, no blood. I wiggled my fingers. A woman shoved my arm back down.

"Where's Chute?" My voice echoed in my head. I had the feeling I was shouting, but I could barely hear it. "Streeter, where's Chute?"

"I need a heart regulator," some guy said. "Presets will work for now, but activate the nervous relay, we need to decompress their nervous systems immediately."

"Where is she?" I tried to shove them out of the way. "Where's Chute?"

The lady put my arms down again. I didn't have the strength to break her grip. I looked side to side. There were too many of them. I couldn't even see Streeter anymore.

"I need that regulator over here, now!" the guy shouted again, to my left.

I tried to look between their legs. I arched my back and shouted, "CHUTE! WHERE ARE YOU?"

"Relax, son." The lady put her hand on my forehead. "We're going to get you out of here—"

"No, no, no..." I shook her off. "I'm not going, not until you show me where she is..."

A thin finger hooked around my finger, squeezing softly. A woman squatted to my right, wrapping a band around my elbow. She stood, shouted to others coming into the room, moved out of the way, and revealed Chute's exhausted face and her arm reaching out to me. Her finger hooked around mine.

"I'm right here, Socket." Chute smiled weakly. Blinked heavily.

We got out.

Chute didn't let go, her arm sticking through a gap between boots. They lifted the stretcher. More shouts. More commands. A woman's face hovered over mine. She put something on my forehead and I was suddenly sleepy. They moved me from the room. I couldn't remember letting go of Chute.

31

FISHING

I WAS ON A BEACH. The sand was hot and dry and pushed between my toes. I dug my feet down to cooler, damper sand below. The beach appeared to extend for miles in both directions. A ship sailed on the horizon, with shrimp nets hanging from the sides. The orange sun reflected off the small waves. Dolphins looped on the surface, blowing showers near the beach, where fiddler crabs raced foamy waves.

In reality, I was in a small room. If I tried to dip my toes in the water, I'd kick the wall. Just another illusion. Those tricky Paladins.

They put me to sleep after I was evacuated from the school. They kept me like that for a month. They filled me with medicine and liquid food. I had the puncture wounds in my arm to prove it. Their gear decompressed my nervous system so I could hear again, so I would believe my arm wasn't actually split open by an artificial spider on a snowy tundra. They kept me on that cot and servys tended my injuries while Paladins stood over my comatose body, tapping their chins, murmuring about my future. Their future. Humanity's future.

Mostly they thought to each other so I wouldn't hear them, but I heard their thoughts when I came close to waking.

Sometimes I heard them come in and out of the room. I could smell them. I smelled jasmine most often. *Mom.* Quite often, she would sit on the edge of my bed and push back my hair. Then I'd fade again, back to the painless void of sleep. That's when the minders would come, penetrating me when I was least present, picking through my memories like looters, piecing together the events of the Rime. When they had everything they wanted, that's when they let me wake.

They wouldn't let me out of the room, for observational purposes. But after a day, it was suffocating, so they started up the simulated environment scenery. One morning I'd wake up in the desert, the next I was at the top of Niagara Falls. This morning, good ole Charleston, South Carolina. All I could do was stand there and watch, smell and listen. "What scene would you like tomorrow?" a servy asked.

"I want out of here."

"I am sorry, please repeat your request. What scene would you like?" Like it couldn't understand why I'd want to leave the Garrison.

This morning, the third morning, a leaper shuddered. Mom walked into the room. Her steps landed slowly. She watched the waves wash ashore. The shrimp boat cast its nets. Her expression was stoic, but her energy jittered between waves of hardness and softness. She was not accustomed to feeling what she was feeling right then. It wasn't often she experienced the depth of fear like she had in the past month, not since my father had died. Nor had she experienced this kind of relief when she saw me standing there, alive and well. "My son," she whispered.

She didn't hug me or weep, but the energy around her was soaked with salty flavors. Her hands were quivering. *[Allow me a moment of weakness,]* she thought to me or whoever was tuning in.

She dropped her head and walked closer to the water. The crabs scattered like she might step on them. We watched the sun get closer to the horizon and the shrimp boats sailed out of view. When she was composed, she said, "When your father died, they wanted me to quit."

She tucked her hair behind her ear.

"They said it would be too difficult for me to stay and watch you awaken. It would be too difficult to make sound decisions instead of emotional ones. They said I would only interfere and, in the end, I would harm you. I had to choose." Her voice faltered. "To be a mother or a leader."

She wiped her nose and folded her arms. No moody, this time.

"The best way to help you, to be whatever mother I could be, was to stay. To be here when you awakened. I knew you would hate me for it, but life demanded it."

Her emotions flailed around her. It took all her strength to allow them to thrash without overwhelming her into another moment of weakness. But she was losing that battle.

"It has been harder... to watch you suffer... than I ever could've imagined."

My heart thumped in time with hers. I stepped next to her. Like a magnet grabbing a metal rod, she put her arms around me. When was the last time she'd hugged me? It had been too long.

"Forgive me," she said.

Her eyes were wet, but not a single tear fell. My senses heightened. I smelled her fragrance, heard the leapers creep above and below us, felt the minders in nearby rooms watching our thoughts. I had awakened. Somehow, her embrace awakened me even further and her saltiness seeped into my awareness. It settled in my throat and swelled behind my eyes. All that anger I reserved for her had vanished.

"Your father..."

"Would be proud," I said.

She smiled, half laughing. She was shaking.

"Thank you," I said.

She pressed the back of my hands to her eyes and let go. She stepped back and calmed her breathing. Her emotions, once white-capped waves, settled glassy and calm. Her Paladin nature was back in control, although I could now see Mother there, too.

"As you may have guessed," she said, "the Paladin Nation is no longer covert. The past month has forced us into the public eye. The world now knows of our existence."

"So the world survived?" I said.

"The war is over. The duplication population has been eliminated."

"What about Streeter and Chute?"

"Their parents are with them, here in the Garrison."

"When can I see them?"

"They're still recovering."

"Still recovering?" I fidgeted. "What's that mean?"

"It's nothing to worry about. Streeter is undergoing precautionary mental decompression. Chute sustained more serious injuries."

"She's going to be all right." My chest fluttered. "Right?"

"She's going to be fine; it's just taking longer than anticipated. The doctors don't want to rush her recovery; they're allowing her nervous system time to reconnect to her body. The awareness transference she experienced was quite traumatic. Her physical brain activity had stopped for over an hour."

"I recovered just fine."

She squeezed my forearm. "You're not like her."

Not anymore.

"Is Broak dead?" I asked.

"You're not responsible for his death. Neither is Streeter. Broak had been corrupted."

Like a computer. "The Paladins are just as much at fault," I said. "They manufactured him like a weapon."

"Broak was responsible for his own actions. He chose to betray the Paladin Nation. To betray the human race."

"They raised him like a machine. No wonder he went to them."

Her upper lip tightened. "Broak will not receive my pity."

She was not taking any more questions on that topic. That was that. Broak was dead. Life was such.

"What about Pivot?" I asked.

"It was time for him to go missing. The Paladins were going to take him inside and set every minder in the Nation on him, although I'm not convinced that would've worked. But I don't think that's why he left. He watched out for you while you were here. Somehow, I think that was his mission."

"Tell me what it means when he's missing?"

"He has the ability to make others... not see him. He could be right in front of you, yet convince you not to see him. His powers are beyond comprehension. I don't think I need to convince you of that."

"He's got to come back."

I almost said *I need him.* It was what I meant. Mom thought for a moment and softly touched my cheek. She let her Paladin mode slip to show me the sadness that rested in her soul, the sadness of my father's death and how she carried that with her every day. She let me know that I, too, carried that sadness, whether I knew it or not. My father was gone. So was Pivot.

Life is such.

A door appeared to open in midair between two swaying palm trees. She was done. No more about Pivot or my father or Broak. She was leaving. But I wanted more. I wrapped my mind around her to uncover her thoughts, to spill what she knew against her will.

"Stop." Her mind tightened, guarding her thoughts that, seconds earlier, she allowed me to see. She didn't have the strength to hold me out, but bristled like a cat that wouldn't go down without a fight. "Don't look inside me, Socket. Stealing thoughts is not something you can do whenever you want."

I pulled back.

She smoothed nonexistent wrinkles on her jacket. "You have a lot to learn about the mental realm."

She left the room. Her fragrance lingered. Another shrimp boat sailed in from the right.

32

The Pebble

I WAS STILL KEPT in the room, promised that it would be soon when they let me get out. I spent a lot of time contemplating what had happened, and what would happen, but I was getting tired of thinking. And I was tired of shrimpers throwing their nets into the sea.

I called for news reports in the Charleston area. A holographic man and woman appeared at a desk with sea foam swirling around their feet.

"More information is being released about the Paladin Nation," the woman said with a reporter's dramatic flair. "A representative is scheduled to speak to the public. How long have they been in existence? How are they funded? Why are they secret? These are just some of the questions global leaders want answered."

"It's the classic movie *Men in Black*," the man said.

"It certainly is." She smiled at him. "And the public is responding."

The reporters disappeared, replaced by an angry mob, smaller in scale. Hundreds waved signs, shouting things like *Justice* and *Freedom of Information.* Several spoke to an interviewer.

"The Paladins need to be accountable." A balding man stood before me with his arms stiffly at his sides. "They are not above the law. The secrecy is an outrage. I don't care if they're fighting aliens, man-eating tigers or the wicked witch—we demand full disclosure!" He pounded his fist into his other hand. "A society that keeps secrets has something to hide!"

"While the initial reaction is mostly outrage"—the woman spoke as protesters continued to march—"Paladins are reluctant to disclose much. The question everyone is asking is whether we would know anything at all if multiple attacks had not taken place around the world, one of which occurred at a local high school."

"That's right," the male reporter chipped in. "Little information has been released since it was left in ruins."

An aerial view of the school appeared. The dome roof of the Pit was gone, so were the seats and the floor. The tagghet field was littered with the bleachers.

"We're not even sure who or what attacked," the man said. "There appears to be some sort of machinery that emerged from an explosion, and local authorities want to know who is responsible. It is thought the attackers were targeting the school's virtualmode portal, one of the most powerful in the state, that also lacked sufficient security, but what they would do with it is unknown."

The grainy footage hovered around the parking lot, but the thick smoke obscured much of the view. Occasionally, jointed legs poked out as the Paladins' weapons flared blue from the ground, leaving remains of the crawlers twitching on the asphalt.

"What you may not know is that some believe children had something to do with stopping the attack. Emergency workers reported three teenagers were found in a remote virtualmode lab. They were in very poor condition, but they were not able to explain why since the Paladins on site quickly took them away."

The view switched to Buxbee's lab. The Paladins hustled three stretchers into a large black vehicle. The emergency workers were swarming around them but not able to do anything about it.

"However, the Paladins refuse to identify the youths or reveal what they were doing during the attack."

The images dissolved into the sand. "The Authority requests your presence," the room said. "Formal attire is required. A leaper will arrive in five minutes."

WITH THE ILLUSION GONE, the room was white and ordinary again and claustrophobia was quickly falling around me like a straightjacket.

A suit emerged from the wall, hanging on a hook, plum colored with mustard trim. The pants were loose-fitting, the overcoat hung nicely, although the shoulders were a bit square. The shoes were square and clunky. I stripped down, dressed and waited for the leaper to open, leaving the shoes on the bed.

There was no escort. I tried not to think where Spindle was. I stepped inside and was transported to the same room I met the Authority the last time. Mom and Commander Diggs were on my right. Pike and his minder assistants were in front of me. Broak, of course, was not there.

The room flowed with unseen currents. It was thicker than electricity, more like cream. The mental realm. Psychic energy emanated from the commander, shining like an organic power plant, and Mom, less so. Thoughts and energy beamed in from around the world, from all those watching this event, peeping in through unseen lookits embedded in the moldable walls.

The minders, however, did not shine. They were dark vortices sucking energy back, holding their thoughts at guard against probing minds. They were impenetrable psychic giants, the ability to pry a mind in half like a walnut or close theirs like a two-hundred-cube encrypted vault. They stood motionless, staring ahead through black wrapped glasses. Their nostrils flared, smelling me. Their dimness lightened like they were tempted to open for a look into my mind, although there was nothing new for them to see.

I walked to a bright spot on the floor. The circular wall rose fiercely. The figureheads were seated and staring. New energy swarmed around the large room of subtle pinks, reds and violets. Each color exuded a different flavor. I let my mind experience the silky flow of their essence. Some were coarse, some fine. All of it luminescent, except for the minders. Their essence was forbidding, dark and gritty. Not like sandpaper, but like a rock in my shoe or something stuck between my teeth. Something like a pebble they held, a fine grain of sand, solid and dense. Something they held secret from the rest of us.

"Hearing 24489 of Socket Pablo Greeny," a bodiless woman said, "is now in session."

"Right." The Authority, with his beefy jowls and tired eyes, looked down on me. "No need to make this lengthy. You have been accepted into the Paladin Nation, Socket Greeny."

Mom released a long-held breath. I was not surprised. Was anyone? But I surprised myself, and everyone else, when a question emerged. "What if I don't want to be one?"

Tense emotions rippled amongst the council and the luminescence dimmed. Had no one ever asked that question? He wasn't asking me, he was telling me I was accepted. Now I wasn't so sure I wanted in this club. The Authority laughed like a coughing dog, his cheeks jiggling. The mounting tension broke.

"Every man and woman has a choice, of course! We are not captors, Socket Greeny. We fight for freedom so that every person has the opportunity to answer a question like that for themselves. It is a great opportunity to see what you are, but, more so, have the courage to be it. There are many people that see the tremendous potential inside you, but I cannot tell you what that is. Nor can your mother or anyone else. *You* have to see it for yourself. Only *you* can become it."

I could refuse to be one of them, just like he said. Walk out of that room and leave it all behind. Go back to the house, call on the television and kick back with a plate full of nachos. But life couldn't go back, not like it was before. No matter what he said, there was no going back no matter how much I wanted to, no matter how much I tried. I had awakened. There was no changing that any more than I could become a baby sucking my thumb. I had seen my true nature. How could I be anything else?

Sometimes life doesn't ask for it to happen. It demands.

The Authority nodded, sensing the resolution and acceptance of my thoughts. He had my answer. I saw. *I am a Paladin.* He looked down at his notes.

"You are untrained, Socket Greeny," he said. "You have recently awakened with little more than instinct to guide you. I can only imagine what kind of Paladin you will be once fully developed. The world will be a better place, a safer place, once you have."

His big belly pushed out beneath his hanging robe when he stood. He began to clap his thick hands. The walloping sound shook the room.

"Congratulations." A tiny smile broke across his droopy face. "And bravo."

One after another, the members stood at the top of the wall and clapped like thunder. Not all of them, though. Several remained seated, their hands planted firmly on their laps. The minders didn't move. They didn't frown, scowl or glare. And the annoying pebble was more noticeable.

I opened my mind to the room, absorbed all the energy, all the thoughts, colors and essence. I opened to the happiness and bitterness and the full range of emotions. I had nothing to hide; they could look into my mind all they wanted. I was fully open, fully aware and fully present. My awareness washed over everything, including the pebble. It took shape. I experienced its size, texture and hardness. It was a distinct object, a substantial container of thoughts. It contained information. And it had a location. The minders weren't holding the pebble. It was Pike.

The Authority held his arms out and silenced the applause. The ones standing remained standing. He paused, allowing silence to settle. The Authority tipped his head. "Your duty is to serve, Socket Greeny," he said, "to your utmost."

I have to be quick for all to see.

The walls trembled and began to sink. The images of the Authority and his cohorts shriveled. Their essence became chaotic, drawing back through their projected, shrinking images as their awareness sought to return to their skin somewhere in the world.

I summoned all my psychic energy and gathered it like an arrow with an indestructible tip. I pulled back the string, filled the arrow with tension and fired it, with every thought, every bit of strength I had. All my essence drained into that shot. I was depleted, fell on my knees, and almost passed out. It took the minders by surprise, boring through their mental walls before they could throw themselves against it. The arrow spiked Pike's mind like an icy sliver. Pierced the hidden pebble.

Penetrated it.

It burst with a million colors. Endless thoughts sprang from the pebble and filled the room for all to see. The thoughts he hid from his assistant minders. The thoughts he carefully tucked inside the pebble to make himself forget so that none would know he was hiding them. The thoughts he couldn't dare let anyone know. The ones that would break his mission. Crush his existence.

He had sabotaged Broak's lessons, exposed his human pain, convinced him there was a better way. The Paladins could not be trusted; look what they were doing to him. They were dirty. Imperfect. Mortal. There was a better way, Broak. One you were meant for. Join me. To make a better world. A perfect world.

Pike was still human, but he was a spy. *He was Broak's mentor.*

A second did not pass in normal time. I barely raised my head to see the wall spit back out of the floor. The Authority and his minions' eyes bulged with surprise. They heard the hidden thoughts. They understood. A SPY? IN OUR SANCTUARY?

The assistant minders comprehended immediately. They turned on Pike and corralled his poisonous thoughts before he counterattacked with a psychic arrow of his own, one that would turn my brain into grits. They saved me from his mind, but could not hold him. It took a tenth of a second for Pike to disappear into a timeslice, like slipping through a fissure in the fabric of space-time.

He reappeared, in that same instant, a step in front of me, his lethal fingers aimed for my windpipe. His strike—centimeters from my neck—was stopped short by three crawler guards. They popped out of a timeslice and loomed over us, their jointed legs anchored like steel bars. Silky strands wrapped around his legs and arms. They were watching, slicing time when Pike sliced. This time, the spiders saved me.

The room sizzled with essence. Warnings flew. Alerts commanded. The crawlers wrapped Pike tighter. The minders strained to control his mind. His thoughts seeped through their containment like fibrous roots, crackling after me. He pried through my weakened psychic defense. I leaned back, but space was no match for the cold tips of his sharp mind that squeezed inside. He slithered behind my eyeballs. I couldn't stop him.

More minders entered the room. They circled him like blind men, giving support to the struggling assistants. The icy tentacles slowly pulled out of me. They sealed him inside their psychic prison. Pike struggled, spit bubbling on his lips. He cursed, tossing his head around to break the containment.

There were shouts. ORDER! ORDER! More crawlers entered, poking their legs between us, hovering over us, their eyelights ominously directed at Pike. The commander directed traffic. Doors opened along the walls. Mom rushed me to an open leaper. The crawlers had Pike cocooned, knocking his glasses from his face. His white eyeballs looked in my direction. Blood vessels branched like lightning across them in one last effort. Minders stepped between us.

The leaper closed.

I would've crumpled on the floor had Mom not held me. "They continue to underestimate you," she said.

33

Spiderwebs

THE GARRISON WAS STRUCTURED and suffocating. A tomb. They sent Pike to a remote prison for debriefing somewhere in the world where few people knew. It might've been a thousand feet below ground, might've been in space. No one was going to get to him and he wasn't getting to anyone. A team of minders were assigned to him around the clock, scouring his mind for every memory, every thought, that would expose every instance of deception. He was not a duplicate, he was human. *But is the battle really over?*

What did I get in return for exposing the world's most dangerous spy? Tests, that's what I got. No reward. No vacation. I got tests. Five days later, they sent a guy to my room. "Would you like to go to the Preserve?"

Um. Yes.

LONG-NECKED BIRDS GLIDED over the treetops, finding bare branches to rest. I stood inside the entrance and breathed deep the flow of Mother Earth. Weeds sprouted along the trail leading to the banyan tree. Swards of grass and tropical palms lined the shrinking path. Great big leaves hung in the way, dripping condensation. Banana spiders built intricate, dewy webs across the path and perched in the center, awaiting the next victim. I wandered down the slope and knelt in front of the first web. The enormous spider, white and yellow, walked in circles and dropped her abdomen on each strand to repair holes from an earlier kill. Her long legs navigated the death trap with ease, pulling the web tighter and deadlier. Only she could walk the web without getting tangled.

I scooped up a handful of soil and let it trickle between my fingers. I could stay in the Preserve as long as I liked, the guy said. Just let us know when you're ready to come back inside. But that would never happen and they knew that. They wanted another Pivot. They were betting on me.

A zebra butterfly hit the outside of the web. The spider stopped, feeling the vibrations. I plucked the butterfly from the web. It perched on my finger, wagged its black-and-white-striped wings and lifted off in a safer direction.

The leaper vibrated back at the entrance. I sifted another handful of soil. Footsteps softly approached from behind. Bare feet stopped next to my pile of dirt. Mechanical tendons stretched under the supple, silver skin. I looked up at the wavering plum overcoat and the faceplate that reflected the forest greens and orange sunrise.

Spindle. *He's alive.*

I held my excitement in check, not wanting to spoil the moment. He was there, giving pause to the morning. I smiled to myself, knocking the dirt off my hands. "Where have you been?"

"They have been testing me, Master Socket," he said. "Much like you."

"What'd they find?"

"They discovered your father's programming. They looked for more but did not find any."

His chest expanded as if he took a deep breath. I squeezed his bulging bicep and smacked his back. I wanted to hug him, but that would've been stupid, hugging an android. Right?

"I'm really glad to see you, Spindle."

"And I am happy to see you, Master Socket." He bowed slightly. "You have been a joy to serve."

"Happy? Joy? You're feeling now?"

He cocked his head, the colors tangled on his face. "I do not know if they are emotions, but when I interact with you, my tactile sensors are more... excitable."

"You saved my life."

"I was merely following your father's orders."

"Those weren't orders. You *wanted* to save me."

He stood taller, his face muddier. "Wanted?"

Spindle was more than an android assistant. He was artificially intelligent, just like the duplicates. But the Paladins rationalized his existence, said he was closely monitored and encoded to never think freely. That was the difference, they said. Duplicates, they were like viruses, spreading throughout the world for their own purposes. Their number one priority was to survive. *They* were self-centered, not Spindle. He existed to serve us. That, they said, was the difference.

The first time Spindle came to me as the shadow, he followed my father's orders. It was a onetime shot. The Paladins would figure that out and see my father had set up Spindle to activate my Paladin potential.

The second time he came as the shadow to save us in the Rime, that wasn't so easy. My father knew encrypted orders weren't going to survive after the first time. And he knew they wouldn't destroy Spindle. So he took a chance. He instilled the ability for Spindle to choose. Spindle could've turned into a self-serving duplicate. Maybe he took the chance because Pivot was watching, or maybe my father installed some safety precautions. No idea. Either way, when it came time, Spindle *chose* to override his Paladin-installed programming and save me.

I didn't tell Spindle that. Maybe he already knew. Maybe nobody knew. I saw it all when I absorbed his intelligence long ago, but it didn't make sense until now. I held out my hand and he took it. His was warm and soft. I took it with both hands and shook gently. Really, all I wanted to say was, "Thank you, Spindle."

His face was rosy red, swirling with darker, bubbly shades. "You are quite welcome, Master Socket."

A RACCOON STEPPED into a spider's web. It sat on its haunches and rubbed its face, staring at us with bandit eyes.

"No one comes out here anymore?" I asked.

"It has been quite some time since someone walked this path."

"Pivot's gone," I said. "He's not coming back."

"I am afraid not, Master Socket."

A rogue breeze rushed through the limbs. A band of leaves swirled off the ground and danced overhead. The wind held them high, circling tighter, falling, then rising again. A wave passed through my body, starting at my head and ending in the pit of my stomach, expanding until I felt like I was glowing. I put my hand over my gut and smiled.

"Funny," I said. "I don't know who Pivot is, but I feel like I've known him all my life." Spindle's face was radiant like never before. "You know? Even thinking about him... it fills me."

"He has that effect, I am told."

The leaves pulled together in a tighter, shifting bunch as the wind twisted. Then, all at once, it evaporated and the leaves fluttered down like crinkly snowflakes. I pulled one from my hair. The breeze whipped through the banyan tree, disturbing none of the trees around it. The limbs shook. For a moment, I could see him standing on a branch. Bronze skin. Bleached hair over his eyes.

And then the breeze fell silent. The apparition gone.

"I will miss them," Spindle said.

"Them?"

"Master Pivot, of course." His face darkened. "And the late Master Broak. I will miss them both."

"Your programming skipped a beat, Spindle. You'll miss Broak?"

"Why, yes. He was a promising young man. Very bright. Full of life. The world is a sadder place without him."

"You do know he tried to kill me, right? Twice."

"Yes."

"And you think the world will be sad? Check your logic, Spindle. I'm not sure the world misses him."

"He was a beautiful person. I knew him from the time he was born. I cared for him." The sun reflected on his face, dimming when a cloud passed over. "He warned us there was something wrong with him, and we did not listen."

"What're you talking about? Broak didn't warn anyone; he fooled us all. He was supposed to start the next generation of Paladins that protected humanity and he turned on us. Where was the warning?"

"He told us all, Master Socket." Spindle tilted his head. *Is it not obvious?* "He told us he was broken."

Broken. He was broke. He was *Broak.*

He changed his own name.

Was he calling out, telling the world he was hurt? That Pike controlled him like a puppet? Someone come save me. I'm broken. Or was the name just a joke, a chance to laugh right in our faces? He didn't want to be human because humans were imperfect. *They* were broken. And since he was human, he was broke. He wanted something better. Something perfect. Until then, he was Broak.

"What was his real name?" I asked.

"Master Vestal was his birth name."

"Well, then, let's pause for the memory of Master Vestal."

Spindle thought for a moment, then brightened. "Yes, I would like that very much."

"Should we pause at the tagghet field?"

"He would like that, Master Socket, but I believe right here and now is appropriate."

We turned to the sunrise. I closed my eyes, feeling the warmth on my face. Birds called. Insects buzzed. Dew dripped from the leaves, splattering on the ones below.

Master Vestal. A much better name.

A CHANGE in the air pressure. "Are you expecting someone?" I asked.

"Perhaps."

A leaper stopped at the wall. A servy glided out, the eyelight pointed at us. Two people followed. Streeter stopped immediately. His mouth hung open. It was his first time in the Preserve. He didn't notice us down the sloped path under the palms. Chute stepped out of the leaper and didn't see the wondrous jungle. She headed directly for us. I sprinted toward her. We stopped a few feet apart. My chest melted like chocolate, dripping inside. Her freckled complexion was so smooth.

"Are you all right?" I asked.

"Yeah." Her shins, knees to ankles, were wrapped in violet leg warmers. "Circulation enhancers are helping."

"Are they going to be all right?"

"They're fine."

"So they're... they're all right?"

She nodded. Smiled. *Yeah. They're all right.*

When I saw her last, her legs had disappeared in the rip, but now she was in front of me. *She's all right.*

The awkward space between us evaporated. We fell forward like we'd been pushing on a wall and now it was suddenly gone. She threw her arms around my neck. I squeezed back, breathing her essence. Satisfying the ache.

"I'm so happy to see you," she whispered.

Energy beamed from my core, enveloping us. Nothing separated us, not even our flesh. Our emotions flowed from one body to the next. I could've held her like that for days.

Streeter's mouth gaped open. "Take it easy until you get a room, why don't you."

Streeter was plump as ever. Clearly he'd found the all-you-can-eat kitchen was no joke. He tried to look disgusted by the hug, but he couldn't stop smiling. He put out his hand, but I put him in a headlock. He punched me back and shoved me off the path into the small trees. I fell in the leaves drenched in dew. He held out his hand and pulled me out.

"Man, I'm glad to see you, Socket." We shook hands a long time, even came close to hugging.

"I want you guys to meet one of my best friends," I said. "This is Spindle."

"Really?" Streeter feigned surprise. "Because we met him a month ago."

"You did?"

"He's been taking care of us. He took us to breakfast, walked us to the infirmary, and rode the leapers with us. Can you believe this place?"

Streeter rambled on about servys, holographic imagers and bottomless kitchens. Spindle's face lit up. Streeter, in mid-sentence, held up his hand for a high-five, but Spindle buried his fist in it. Streeter shook it.

"You taught them the *stick-it* handshake?" I said to Spindle. He cocked his head slightly, his face lit up. "Really? You taught them... I can't believe you taught them—"

"It's cute," Chute said.

"It's not *cute*," Streeter added. "It's just the way he shakes hands. Right, Spindle?"

"Do you know where he got that handshake?" I asked.

"It is my way." Spindle's eyelight blinked. *Don't ruin the moment, Master Socket.*

I looked back and forth between their faces. Streeter waited for my revelation. *Don't ruin it.* "You're right. That's the way they do it," I said.

"This is a new world, Socket," Streeter said. "They do things differently around here."

"You have no idea."

The trees shook and showered us with dew. The leaves fell like autumn arrived. We jumped back to get out of the rain. Hiding in the dark canopies, tiny golden lights blinked at us by the hundreds.

"What is this place?" Chute asked.

"The Preserve is a man-made, enclosed environment supporting the growth of over ten thousand botanical species..."

Spindle spouted the introductory speech. Chute and Streeter scanned the vast jungle. They wouldn't be here long. They would go back home soon. They were normal people; they needed to live normal lives. I wasn't going home. I would stay. I would train. I would become a Paladin. Between us, things would change. Streeter was right: this was the last day for the Watchdogs. It was officially over. But for today, we were still Watchdogs.

The leaves rustled again. A red bat darted out. I held up my hand and Rudder hit it like a rubber toy, curling his long tail through my fingers and nuzzling against me. His essence burst down my arm.

Chute squealed.

"This is Rudder." I held my hand out like a small platform. He stood. Bowed.

After introductions and Rudder doing a little show, Chute held her hand flat. He walked onto it and rolled over, twining his tail between her fingers. "He's so soft." She pushed him against her neck and he purred louder.

"Does he bite?" Streeter asked.

"Not that I know of," I said.

Streeter stepped back. Chute dangled him by the tail. "You hold him."

"Don't force him on me, Chute! What's your problem?"

"He's just an innocent creature, Streeter. Like a kitty."

He shook his hands and backed up another step. "Yeah, well, I don't know where that kitty's been. I mean, that thing could have rabies or Ebola. You don't know, Chute."

Rudder's eyes opened wide. *[Ebola?]*

[Never mind him,] I thought back.

"There are a lot more." I pointed to the golden lights. "One of every color."

"Can we see them?" Chute asked.

"Oh, you're going to see them. I'm going to show you everything."

The sun rose above low-lying clouds. We shaded our eyes against the glare. A monkey howled. A bobcat cried. Something slithered nearby. We paused in the new morning without a word. The pause just happened, and they didn't even know it. We just stood there. Listening. Seeing. *Being.*

"What's going to happen to you, Socket?" Chute whispered.

"I'm staying here."

"What about us?"

"You're going home."

She hooked her finger around mine. "You're not coming?"

"There're some things to sort out first, but I'll be home to see you. I'd like to see them stop me. Right now, I'm sure there's a test or two they want to run. Right, Spindle?"

Spindle was still pausing. Or maybe he didn't want to get involved. He stared ahead.

Rudder crawled down her arm and wrapped his tail around our hands, squeezing them tighter. Hanging upside down. "Rudder will keep you company," she said, "while I'm gone."

"Yeah. He'll watch out for me."

Chute smiled and shook my hand. Rudder scrambled up my arm and lay on my shoulder, nuzzling against my neck with a deep groan. He sensed Chute's sadness and batted his eyes at her, trying to make her laugh. She just smiled. It was all she could do. I wasn't coming home, at least not yet.

She looked at the sunrise. The light flashed in her eyes. "I went to the Grand Canyon when I was little, but this place... this is beautiful."

"It is quite grand," I said.

"Quite grand?" Streeter scowled. "Are you freaking kidding me? When the hell do you say quite grand?"

"I just... I don't know. It just seemed like the thing to say."

"Quite grand." He waved a stick through the spiderweb and peeled it to the side, muttering, "He's lost his freaking mind."

"Shall we?" Spindle said, extending his arm. "There is a lot to see and little time."

Around the banyan tree and into the jungle we went. I didn't know what the next day would bring. Or the day after that. I just knew it was a great day. A perfect day.

Just as it is.

BOOK 2

THE TRAINING OF SOCKET GREENY

For the lost

PART IV

When the student is ready, the teacher will appear.
Buddhist proverb

Weapons are forged in fire.
The hotter the flame, the sharper the edge.
Pon

34

KILLING **Mother**

THE NARROW ALLEY was filled with cups and newspapers, empty cans and bottles. It was sandwiched between two-story buildings with grimy windows glowing with yellowish light. One window was open on the second story, where curtains occasionally waved from an oscillating fan while I hid behind the lone dumpster.

I should've finished this mission by now.

Get to the window and save the victim, that was all it was. I was good at that. But nothing was that simple. Not anymore.

I was through the window on my first attempt and saw my mother tied to a chair with a faceless enemy behind her. I hesitated, only 0.04 of a second, plenty of time to watch him drag the sharp edge of his hand over her throat. You lose, Socket. Try again.

Control your emotions, Pon always preached. *Action must be decisive and pure. Never hesitate.*

Pon, the mentor of all mentors. With him, there's always a lesson. Even when you've watched your own mother choke on her blood a hundred times, there was a lesson.

Pon taught me how to think, how to move. And when the situation demanded it, he taught me how to kill. He designed my daily missions. In the beginning, they were simple, but now there were subtle traps, and traps within traps. Mind games. The solution wasn't straightforward. Not anymore.

Brute force is always the weakest response. Another lesson.

This mission wasn't about outmuscling an opponent, even though it looked like it on the surface. It was more about performing regardless of the situation. It was about focusing and seeing the course of action. It was about serving *life*. It was easy saving someone I didn't know. Saving my mother, that was like walking a tightrope. One wrong thought, and it was a thousand feet down.

Still, I should've been done hours ago.

The back of my arm was sticky and hot. A sharp slit ran down the back of my sleeve. I felt my skin flap open. A deep gash went through the muscle. One of the duplicates caught me on the last attempt. I disposed of the thing quickly—its generic head toppled down the steps—but it slashed on the way down and got me. *Bastard.*

Duplicates were human imitations. They did everything a human did—eat, sleep, shit, whatever—only they weren't human. At one time, they blended into society, intent on killing every last one of us. Now they were gone. But for some reason, I was still fighting duplicate mock-ups in training sessions; only now they were faceless.

They can look like you, me, or your mother, Pon would tell me. *The enemy has many faces.*

I pulled the wound open, probing for poison tips that sometimes broke off and slowly shut down the nervous system. I'd be laid up for weeks if that was the case, but the wound was clean. I put a medical patch over it, sealing the skin shut. The patch dispensed microscopic nanomechs that mimicked white blood cells. They would reattach muscles, rebuild skin cells and dull nerve endings. Basically a high-tech Band-Aid. In most cases, an imbedded device at the back of my neck would directly release nanomech cells, but I couldn't take the chance on it being slow. The patch was insurance I'd be good for tonight. If I ever finished.

Chute and Streeter were expecting me. I wondered if Chute would have her hair pulled back this time. The last time she had her hair down and wavy and even had on a little makeup.

I shook my head. Focus. My enemy was getting smarter. They learned from every attempt. They knew my tendencies, strengths and weaknesses. If my last attempt almost worked, it was guaranteed not to come close the next time. I was running out of options.

I pulled my aching legs under me. Another breath. Focus. Allow thoughts to fall away. Distractions to dissolve. The solution was in the moment. All that was needed was the space to allow it to be present.

Allow the unbroken circle, Pon would say. I wasn't sure what the hell that meant, but visualizing a circle calmed my mind. When there was nothing but the city sounds of distant traffic, I opened my eyes.

The moon was brighter.

The air was stiller.

I flicked open my gloved hand. A three-dimensional image of the alley illuminated in my palm. I hardly needed mapgear to know what was behind me, but preparation required vigilance and discipline. *Battles are won or lost before the first strike.* If I could note one more detail, it could make the difference.

A rat scurried from one building to the next. The enemies were on the roof, in the shadows and doorways. It wasn't realistic, duplicates weren't into guerilla warfare. When they existed, they were more about infiltration and deception, but Pon designed these missions. Don't question the master.

I stared at the mapgear image. Nothing new. I closed my eyes. Breathe in. Out.

Less is more. Pon repeated that one like a goddamn mantra. *The solution is always simple.*

Look at it from another angle. See all the possible solutions. If brute force is not the answer…

I reached for the evolver clubs on my belt. They unfolded—inside out—and wrapped around my hands and forearms like thin transparent gloves, fusing with my nervous system like a thousand needles, awaiting thought-command.

The enemy didn't know I was behind the dumpster, but they knew I was coming. They'd be expecting me to approach engulfed in a bubble shield, because that was what I'd done all day. If I didn't, they'd just shoot me on sight. With the shield, they had to engage me hand-to-hand. If they couldn't beat me that way, they'd just execute the captive.

I needed to be faster. Unpredictable.

Less is more.

With a thought, a translucent strand emerged from my fingertip. It snaked between the wall and dumpster, slithering to the far end of the alley, where the shadows were darkest in a broken doorway. Sweat stung my eyes. The evolver was stretched to its limits and shifted on my hand. Hundreds of nerve fusions broke away. I strained to maintain the thought-transmission.

I imagined a lanky form. Short and wiry. Bristly hair. Suspicious eyes. The tendril plumped in the doorway, taking a human shape. It occurred to me I was building Pon's body. Would it strike extra fear in the enemy's heart? Or did that just happen to me?

Weakness poured down my back like icy water. Indecipherable voices warbled in my head. I strained against the distraction. *Is that the enemy's thoughts, sending them out like static to distract me?* Of course, they were learning. They knew the distraction was as much a weapon as a dagger. I braced against the intrusion until the random thoughts subsided.

I redoubled my efforts, grinding my teeth. I focused on the end of the strand, holding the image in my mind until a body stood at the far end of the alley.

I took a moment to focus. I had to be quick. If this didn't work, it was going to hurt.

Breathe in.

Out.

A tranquil moment settled inside me, the silence a warrior experiences before certain death; the complete acceptance of the present moment filled me. *Live or die,* Pon says, *it does not matter when you serve the present moment. Embrace life* and *death.*

I was never quite sure if I could actually die during training. It could hurt like hell, but death? They wouldn't let me die, would they?

I focused some more.

In that silence, the evolver ripped from my arm and snapped down the alley toward the figure. Trash scattered in its path. The alley stirred to life. The enemy emerged from hiding, climbing from the roof and out of the shadows, strategically hemming the possible attacker into the corner.

My timing had to be perfect. I waited behind the dumpster, gripping my lone evolver-wrapped hand. I waited for the precise moment.

The figure in the doorway picked up the evolver club that slid to its feet. It glowed softly, illuminating the figure's aggressive posture. The enemy was careful. They stayed near the ground and climbed down the smooth walls like insects, watching. The figure would not escape, but they had to confirm its identity. My attack would be useless the moment they discovered it was a decoy. The figure slumped against the doorway, sliding to the ground like a drunk. The enemy reached for its face—

A bright whip blasted from my evolver-wrapped hand like a serpent's tongue and smacked around the railing outside the second-story window. It yanked me off the ground. Wind rushed into my face.

I twisted to avoid colliding with the railing and swung through the window, ripping through the curtains and careening over my mother's head with her captor's hand to her throat. I smashed into the far wall.

The whip released the railing and returned to my outstretched hand, immediately recoiling like a stiff-pointed lance. The sharpened tip pierced the enemy's forehead with a dull *ffthmp*. His head kicked back.

The enemy was colorless. Blue circuit fluid drained from the hole in its forehead. Its body crumpled like an empty sack. A red line appeared across my mother's throat.

But she didn't fall.

The line didn't gush, didn't drain her life. They had opened her throat a hundred times that day, but this time it didn't cut deep enough. Finally, she lived.

I fell over, couldn't breathe. A shifting in my back meant cracked ribs. Mother put her hands on me. Her expression of concern was accurate and realistic, but her touch was cold. In the distance, a wailing police siren faded.

A single curtain blew in the open window, then fell on the floor and melted. The walls turned white. The image of my mother melted like wax into the floor, followed by the walls. In seconds, I lay in the center of an ordinary white room.

"Mission complete," the room reported.

35

HOME ACHES

THE FLOOR WAS spongy and sterile, but the smell of the rotting dumpster was still hanging around. Pain spread across my ribs like claws. *Not tonight. I can't be laid up tonight.*

The room was empty, except for the faceless enemy lying next to me, a gaping hole between the eyes. I touched the thing's forehead. I could mentally scan the thing, but direct touch would allow me to experience its thoughts while I drained its life force. It wasn't real, so it wasn't murder.

Those things were just fabrications of the training room, designed to be exactly like a duplicated human. A duplicate of a duplicate. I always touched them when a mission ended to get insight into their motivation. Why did they want to live? Because they were copies of humans? Because they were self-centered? But each time I drained one, all I saw was programming to destroy humans and multiply. Was there anything else? Did they just want to feel real?

A SIX-FOOT SILVER humanoid walked into the room, his plum-colored overcoat waving around his knees, his physique chiseled. He was similar to a duplicate, thinking with artificial intelligence, but he served the Paladin Nation. It contradicted our mission, but I wasn't going to argue. If humans were more like Spindle, the world would be a better place.

"Congratulations, Master Socket!" Spindle had no face, just a textured surface with a single eyelight. "You have completed the mission with near perfection. The diversion was effective and your elimination of the abductor flawless. Trainer Pon will be very pleased."

Spindle's naked foot was a perfect replication of a human foot dipped in molten silver. He slid his hand over my ribs, his fingertips emitting healing vibrations. Warmth seeped beneath my skin.

"You have fractured two ribs. I will stimulate healing to assuage your discomfort, but I recommend we go to the infirmary for deep penetration—"

A pair of boots stepped quietly next to Spindle. Pon was no taller than me, slightly lanky. His skin was brown, his hair a shore of stubble. A thin scar curved beneath his jaw, starting at his left ear and curling under his chin. Some Paladins say he destroyed twenty enemies in hand-to-hand, that he cheated death by holding his throat together while he finished the last one. But no one knew for sure. No one knew anything about Pon.

I struggled to my hands and knees, stifling a groan.

"It is highly recommended you rest before standing," Spindle said.

My vision blurred, but I stood anyway. Pon watched Spindle press his hand against my ribs. The spot was already feeling better. The bright eyelight that rotated on his featureless faceplate focused on the medical patch oozing on my arm. Dark blue sparkled on his face.

"That needs medical attention," Spindle said.

"It can wait," I replied.

I felt like I'd survived a stampede. I stopped breathing to avoid wincing, but hiding pain from Pon was pointless. I could pretend like it didn't hurt all I wanted, smile like I was top-notch, but he would know just by looking at me. I let my breath rattle out, grimaced, and stopped pretending.

Pon paced around me while Spindle's hands radiated warmth. I wanted to shake him off, but it felt too good. I needed it. Pon intentionally let his almond-shaped eyes fall on my bandaged arm, a slight curl on the corner of his lips.

"Well done, cadet," he said. "You saved your mother on the one hundred thirty-fifth attempt." He stopped in front of me and let the smile spread to the other side of his mouth. "Well done, indeed."

"Trainer Pon," Spindle said, raising his hand, "the exercise was completed faster than any previously recorded attempt—"

It only took a look and Spindle stepped back. Pon's presence spoke clearly.

"I want a fully detailed synopsis of each attempt," Pon said. "All one hundred thirty-five of them. Have it done in full animated reenactment with an analysis of each failure. You will walk me through each one."

"I have a break tonight. I'm going home."

Home? He didn't have to say it, the expression did it clearly enough. It was the tension along his jaws. But I was going home whether he liked it or not. I hadn't been there in months. He could put a stop to it, could make me stay, require me to analyze every goddamn failed attempt so I could learn, learn, learn and train until my ass was chapped. But if he made me stay, he'd have to deal with my mother. An assassin like Pon knew how to pick his battles.

He looked to the floor and began to pace again. "Would your father failed to have saved your mother?" he asked. "Would he have failed *134 times*?"

"I'm not my father."

"That doesn't answer the question."

I met his stare as he came around. "I am who I am."

"You don't know who you are, cadet."

He locked his hands behind his back, awaiting a response. I gave him a response, but not in words. I was fully present, centering my awareness in the core of my stomach. I could not make myself be anything but what I was. But who was I? I showed him. *I am now.*

He narrowed his eyes. The atmosphere intensified. He sucked his breath between his teeth. Perhaps he was considering a discussion with Mother after all; have me train another three months before going home. Hell, if he got his way, I'd never see home again. The guy lived for this shit. Not me. I still had a life and a home I wanted to see. I had Chute.

He stopped in front of me. "The synopsis is due in forty-eight hours."

I nodded. He nodded back, just a slight tip of his chin. A slow blink. He paced behind me and then his quiet footsteps fell silent. The tension in the air suddenly evaporated. I turned. Pon was gone, leaving as mysteriously as he appeared.

I PULLED at the bottom of my shirt and felt my ribs shift. "Help me with my shirt, will you, Spindle?"

"It is advisable to cool down." He put his hand on my forehead. "Your energy levels are near exhaustion. You have been in this mission for over seven hours and you have not eaten nor rested."

"I'll grab a snack on the way."

"You cannot maintain this schedule, Master Socket."

"So far, so good." I tugged on my shirt. "A little help?"

Spindle pulled the shirt over my head. I wiped my sweaty face with the shirt, threw it over my shoulder and started for the dim archway on the wall. While Pon got around through some mysterious network of hidden tunnels, the rest of us still used the leapers.

"If I may ask," Spindle said, marching with me, "what are your plans for tonight?"

"I don't know." I stopped at the archway. "You coming?"

"Home?" Spindle's face lit up. "Out in public?"

"I was referring to the locker room but, sure, if you can get permission." *He won't.*

THE SHOWER RAINED from the ceiling, running over my shoulders, over the bruises and scars and cuts. Spindle stood around the corner, still talking. He used to stand in the shower with me, but that had to stop. He wasn't human, but still.

"Trainer Pon wants to remind you that your Realization Trial is only a month away." His voice was muffled. "He would like you to take your training more seriously."

I stuck my head out. "I'm sorry, what'd you just say?"

"Your Realization Trial is only a month away."

"No, the other part."

"To take your training more seriously?"

I stepped out. Water puddled around my feet. Spindle's eyelight spun away. I was about to say something. Take my training seriously was Pon's little jab to remind me that I wasn't done training. He just wanted to see if I'd react to the criticism, a lesson for the road. *Don't react. Always respond.*

I went back to the shower and rinsed my hair. "Tell him I'll be here in the morning."

"Very well."

Spindle continued with his list of things-to-do while steam filled the shower room and water trickled into the drain. I imagined I was in a cloud where no one could find me. Inside the Garrison training facility, someone was always watching. Always judging. Sometimes I just wanted to be normal. Nothing about living inside a mountainous facility was normal. I didn't choose this life, it chose me. Still, I needed to get away from it or I'd go insane. If Pon didn't kill me first.

I called the water off. Warm air filtered through the room. Spindle's arm appeared from around the corner with a towel. I wrapped it around my waist.

"May I ask what your plans are tonight?" he asked.

"The Charleston Squall tagghet season is opening tonight."

"They have already established a professional team?"

"It's minor league."

"And will you be meeting Master Streeter?"

"Yep."

"Your girlfriend, Master Chute, she will be present, as well?"

Girlfriend. I sat in front of my closet and wrapped my hair back. My stomach fluttered. Spindle asked about them every day. Wasn't sure if he missed them or he just sympathized. He knew how much they meant to me. It wasn't easy being in the present moment when she was so far away.

I pulled on my shorts and reached into the closet. Black pants, white shirt and a tie were on a hanger.

"What's this?"

"I assumed you would like to look nice for your friends, so I took the liberty of having dress clothes sent up."

I ran my fingers down the tie and couldn't remember if I had ever worn one. Wouldn't even know how to knot one. There was no way I was going to blend into the crowd. And in public, the number one rule was to blend in, don't draw attention. *Be invisible.*

"Thanks, Spindle," I said. "You have great taste, but could you have a servy bring up jeans and a black T-shirt?"

"Certainly, Master Socket."

I let go of the tie, noticing the scars crisscrossing my arms. "Could you also have a long-sleeve button-down shirt sent up, too?"

"It is eighty-five degrees in Charleston, South Carolina."

"I'll leave it unbuttoned."

A large, spherical servy floated into the room, holding a stack of clothes in elastic arms emerging from its otherwise generic body. Its eyelight rotated around its cue-ball form and fixed on me.

The clothes felt good. *Normal.* It had been a long time since I felt cotton. Most of the time, it was sweat-wicking armorcloth that resisted impact like metal. I saw myself in the mirror and pulled my hair back then brushed the front of my shirt and tugged the sleeves down. I was more nervous about going home than facing a faceless flame-throwing agent of death.

"You look wonderful." Spindle fussed with my collar, smoothing out wrinkles and pushing stray hair off my face. He stepped back, looking at my left side then my right. He tugged on my shirt, wiped my sleeve—

"I'm not going to prom, Spindle."

"Yes, well, you want to look your best." He stepped back for one last look; his faceplate was very bright. "You are due for a short meeting with the commander before you leave."

"Ooooh, that." I actually thought maybe he'd forget that, not that he ever forgot anything.

"It will not take long." Spindle clasped his hands together. "And before you go to South Carolina, may I remind you of public policy?"

"Blend in, I know."

"As a cadet, you are not allowed to use your abilities in public."

"Unless I have to."

Spindle's face appeared muddled with color. "I do not believe that is part of the policy, Master Socket."

"It should be."

"Also be aware that you may contact me for assistance at any time."

Assistance? Spindle was virtually connected with my vital signs. At all times, he knew my pulse, my blood pressure, if I was asleep or if I was taking a shit. It was a lifeline. If the signal faded, he would assume there was trouble and come for me, so there was no need to call for assistance. He knew all this, but he still wanted me to know I could call.

He followed me to the leaper. "You are driving?" he asked.

"I am."

"May I remind you of the driving policy?"

"You may not." I stepped into the leaper and left him in the locker room. Spindle's voice faded quickly.

36

CHILLED

I STOPPED by my mother's office just to see her. The thoughts of her gagging on her spurting jugular were still vivid. Even though it was just an image composed of clayey, cellular nanomechs, it wasn't easy to forget. So I looked in on her, confirmed she was alive and breathing, even looked at her neck. I'd sleep better.

I went to the platform, a half circle that jutted out from a cliff wall without a railing. It was high above the tropical forest of the manmade Preserve, a private jungle carved from the isolated mountains of the Garrison. We weren't on any map, nor were we accessible to the public by automobile, helicopter or mountain climber. I knew we were nowhere near a tropical climate, that was why the Preserve was enclosed with an invisible ceiling that covered the entire 5.2 square miles. From the platform's vantage point, I could see to the other side, where it was enclosed with a similar cliff, and in between it was all trees. And below the trees there were trails and streams and creatures from all over the world and, in some cases, other planets.

An enormous tree stood out in the middle, different from all the rest because it was barren of leaves. Its monstrous limbs were like arthritic fingers reaching for the sky, and on those limbs were the off-world grimmets: small bat-like dragony creatures no bigger than a sparrow with tails as long as a possum's. It would be impossible to see them from the platform, but the grimmets pulsated with color. Some were burnt orange, others were sunshine yellow or plum purple or jet black. Like a living rainbow.

Maybe I wouldn't notice them on the tree if I couldn't feel them. The grimmets were playful; they would laugh at anything. They were also powerful, and we shared a special bond. Our energies gyrated like time and space didn't exist. They knew when I was sad, tired, or bored, similar to the lifeline I had with Spindle.

That tree was where I met Pivot for the first time. It had been over a year since I'd seen him sitting at the base of the grimmet tree, but it seemed like yesterday. Long sandy hair, native tan, and dead eyes. He was physically blind, but he saw better with his mind than anyone saw with eyes. Sometimes, I wondered if he was even human. If it wasn't for him, I wouldn't be here. He saved me when I first arrived at the Garrison. He showed me a purpose to the Paladin life that, quite frankly, I wasn't all jazzed up about. It wasn't anything he said, it was just the way he felt. His presence. No words needed.

But Pivot wasn't around anymore. He left, and no one knew where. Sometimes I felt his presence, that sense of security, like a warm blanket. Occasionally, I'd turn around and catch a glimpse of something and swear it was him, but it never materialized into anything real. Pivot was such a psychic master that he could be right in front of you and make you believe he wasn't there. Suppose he was doing the same thing to me. Maybe he was from another planet like the grimmets.

***

"Ah, there he is." Commander Diggs, a hard-faced man with short-clipped gray hair, stepped onto the platform.

I turned at attention. Another high-ranking official walked with the commander, along with two escorts. They wore similar uniforms with a horizontal red stripe above the right breast that signified their training facility. I hated all the military bullshit, the saluting and ranking and arrogance that sometimes came with it, but I went with the flow. To run a society this powerful, there had to be order.

The commander squeezed my shoulder, his smile creasing his leathery complexion. "Cadet Socket," he said gruffly, "this is Chief Commander."

"Chief Com," I said.

He nodded slowly, as if to say *at ease* but not really. His hair was short and his nose flat. His eyes were especially relaxed. His mind tingled around me, feeling my psychic structure like a dog sniffing another dog's ass. I tensed, but remained open. Closing down to someone of his status was considered an insult. But to remain fully open wasn't good, either. *Always be ready.*

Chief Com stepped slowly forward while the others remained still. His escorts looked more like assassins, their eyes barely slits and their mouths equally grim. Chief Com closed in on my personal space. My heels caught the edge of the platform and a magnetic field pushed back.

"How are you, cadet?" His voice was hypnotic, pleasantly reverberant.

"Doing well, Chief Com."

"You may address me as Com."

"Com." I nodded respectfully.

"Are you familiar with me?"

Com, overseer of the Paladin Nation's most successful training facility. More cadets graduated under his tutelage than all the other facilities combined. If the math was done right, he was responsible for nearly a third of the Paladins' population today. Without Com, duplicated humans would be crawling all over the planet like cockroaches.

He stayed close to me and applied a bit more psychic pressure. I stiffened this time. He was testing me now, seeing how I'd react to standing at the edge of the platform while being prodded. He'd heard about me, now he just wanted a taste of what I was made of. A cold chill that poured down my neck during training started again. *Shit!*

This time I saw things. Images appeared.

I saw weapons flash.

Pon's sweaty face, bruised and bloody. His body lying still.

A drip of sweat ran down my cheek. I clenched my fists, fingernails digging into my palms, and beat back the chilly sensation and the images it brought. And then it was gone.

Com didn't seem to notice I checked out for a second. He stepped back, satisfied, and cupped his hands behind his back. "Your preliminary training scores are exceptional, cadet. I was touring your facilities and, while I haven't had a chance to speak with your trainer, you appear more than ready for your Realization Trial."

I hesitated. "I feel prepared."

It was my standard answer. Look confident. Sound it, too. But it wasn't an honest answer. *Prepared for what?*

Com turned his shoulders slightly, sensing tension ripple around me. "What is your question, cadet?"

No hiding it now. It was nearly impossible to hide any thought from a guy like that. *So how'd he miss those chilly images?*

"I would be able to answer your question with greater confidence," I said, "if I knew what the Realization Trial was about. Pon hasn't given me any objectives. I don't know if I'm swimming across an ocean or jumping out of a spaceship. Tell me what exactly I'm training to do and I believe I can answer you more truthfully."

Com laughed heartily, and the commander smiled. The two assassins had yet to blink. "Yes," Com said, "the Realization Trial is frustrating. Let's just say Pon will have you ready for whatever comes your way, yes?"

I nodded, frustration clenching inside me.

"Another question?" he said.

I was doing a horrible job of controlling my thoughts. I minced them quietly, considering if I was pushing too much. My frustration was too visible. He would only tolerate it so long. *Enough is enough, control your mind, cadet.* But these were my thoughts and, to be honest,

I already knew the answers. In fact, the question was ludicrous. I didn't want to say it out loud, so I just allowed the thoughts to crystallize for him to see my doubts.

[Why are we training so hard? We haven't seen or heard of a duplicate in a year. They've been conquered. Shouldn't we be doing something besides preparing for a nonexistent war?]

Like I said, I already knew the answers. Intelligence suggested that duplicates would have a backup plan, that they would blend into the population until they were ready to strike. After all, they were undetectable. One could be standing right in front of you and you wouldn't know the difference, even if you cut its head off. It's the predator you don't see that you should worry about.

Thank you, Pon.

Com saw my question. He also saw the answer in my mind. There was no reason, but instead he said, "Keep your enemies closer than your allies, cadet. That way you always know what they're doing."

"Yes, sir."

He stared a bit longer, judging my stance, my psychic arrangement, my physical conditioning. No need for conversation when you could look directly at one's soul. It cut out all the words and personal agenda.

"I am anticipating record attendance at your Realization Trial." He leaned closer. His breath puffed in my eyes. "I will be present along with every commander in the Paladin Nation."

"I look forward to it."

"I have commended your commander for bringing a prodigy such as you to the great Paladin Nation. It is efforts like his that will make this world a better place." A subtle tension vibrated in the air like electrical currents. He was hiding something. Perhaps it was bitterness or contempt. After all, he wasn't accustomed to travelling outside his facility to see star pupils. They came to him, not the commander. This was a first.

But the energy around us felt tight, almost menacing. I did not adjust my stance, did not want to appear aggressive or tip them off, but instead took notice of the space between us, estimating the range of motion and possible responses to an attack.

"I would argue that you could not find a better commander," I said.

"High praise, indeed." Half-smile for me. Half-smile for the commander. "Very well, then. I will not take up more of your time. I understand you have been given leave for the evening and I sense you're anxious." He nodded and said in a lower tone, "We expect great things from you, cadet."

"Yes, sir."

My heels were still on the edge; I shifted my balance to the front of my feet.

Com started for the exit, the commander beside him. The escorts turned, their motions fluid. The one on the left, his eyes were down, but they cheated a glance back at me. Their momentum kept them turning, their arms falling toward their belts and in tandem they unleashed their evolvers. They spun on their inside heels, pushing their weapon hands at me. Bluish spikes shot forth and space crackled as they sliced time.

But I was ready. I gripped the metaphorical time spark I felt in my belly and stopped time along with them, leaving Com and the commander standing still in normal time. I ignited the evolvers around my hands and deftly parried the tips of their blunt spikes that would knock the wind out of me for a week. Fortunately, they did not counterattack. I was at a woeful disadvantage with my back to the ledge. They retracted their weapons and stood back at attention.

We returned to normal time, where Com and the commander took another step and turned. I deactivated the weapons and placed them on my belt.

"Well done, Commander," Com said. *Half-smile.* "Yes."

The assassins followed them through the exit.

I took a minute to allow my heartbeat to return to normal before doing the same.

37

NORMAL NIGHT Out

THE SERVYS WATCHED me idle the black sedan across the garage and through the illusion of a solid wall into the outside world.

The sun was falling below the trees on the far side of the boulder-strewn field. Behind me, the Garrison's rusty cliffs soared hundreds of feet like a sentinel watching over the world. I stopped the car and let the remains of daylight fall on my face. The breeze rushed through the open windows with scents of bending grass and fallen leaves.

The wheels thumped on the underside of the chassis, folding into the wheel wells, and the antigravity boosters whined into action, keeping the car afloat. The car bobbed slightly off the ground. I twisted the steering wheel, then stomped the accelerator.

The car shot forward and the force threw my head into the seat. The rocky terrain raced under the car. I tapped the stereo and selected Bongo Monday's latest hit, "Parade on Me." The bass thumped in my chest. The Garrison cliffs receded in the rearview screen.

"To review public policy," the car's feminine voice said, "there is no use of antigravity boosters off the Garrison's premises. There is no—"

I turned the music up until my eardrums throbbed and turned the wheel until the car tilted on its side, carving the air in a deep right turn. Lookits, the small silver balls used worldwide for surveillance, tried to keep up, their eyelights watching, reporting back to the Garrison. I yanked the car left and soared to the other side. I'd flown these cars hundreds of times in the simulated training rooms, but there was nothing like the real thing. Besides, simulations didn't have music systems.

I reached the end of the field and slowed onto a barren road that entered the dense forest. I tapped the music down.

"To repeat," the car said, "you will drive responsibly while in public. Obey all laws. Do not engage any automobile functions that are not available to the public. You are due back by sunrise. It is recommended that you get back to your house by two a.m. at the very latest."

"Yessss, ma'am."

A large wormhole bubble warped the space at the end of the road, swirling with blue colors. The wheels touched on the ground and the road bounced below. The first time through a wormhole was like walking through Niagara Falls. Now it was more like getting steamrolled. Still not pleasant.

I came out the other side thousands of miles away from the Garrison. The exit was on a deserted road in the country. Dusky light filtered through the South Carolina oaks, where the air was humid and the rules changed.

Be normal.

CHUTE AND I never lost touch when training started. I went home a lot in the beginning. When I couldn't go home, we met in virtualmode. And when that didn't work, we talked on the nojakk, sometimes until the sun came up.

But then training got for real and those opportunities got scarce. After a while, I barely had time to sleep. At first, days would go by before I could nojakk her. Then weeks. Now it had been months. It was my fault, really. I was too exhausted to return her calls. If I was awake, I was training. I trained so much that I dreamed I was training. I couldn't escape it.

Sometimes, I wasn't so sure if we'd called it quits. The whole long-distance relationship thing was hard enough for two normal people. She had to be having the same thoughts. *Is this worth it? Are we just wasting time?*

I was nervous to see her. Nervous that spark in her eyes would be gone when she saw me. Or maybe I was nervous of what she saw when she looked at me. Sometimes, I didn't feel all that human. I was an outsider. I didn't want her to see me like that. I didn't want to be on the outside while she was inside.

I'm going to puke.

COOPER RIVER BRIDGE was gridlocked and the game had already started. All the major sports were taking a backseat to tagghet. Paladin-sponsored manufacturers rolled out the flying jetter discs to anyone who wanted one. People were learning thought-projection skills at unheard of rates. Virtualmode Internet accounts reached new levels every day. The technology wave was turning into a tsunami. Clearly, the Charleston roads weren't prepared for the madness of a semiprofessional tagghet team.

Chute called while I looked for every possible route around the bridge. She promised to save me a seat. *I can't wait to see you,* she said. That was a good start, but then traffic completely stopped and that took care of the good feelings. Now I was about to rip the steering wheel out of the dashboard.

I considered leaving the car in autopilot and abandoning it, but unattended autopilot was against the law. The car would rat me out. They'd call my ass back across the world if I tried.

There was nothing to do but watch the ships pass and smell the low tide. The car slogged along and I counted my breath. In and out. I settled into the present moment and the tension inside me, recognizing all the expectations attached to it. They were stupid thoughts like: Would she really be happy to see me?

That was pretty much it.

"LEFT TURN IN ONE HUNDRED YARDS," the car finally said.

I came off the bridge and took the shoulder to catch my turn. I hit the back roads, hugging corners between abandoned warehouses.

"Obey the speed limit," the car said.

"I've been driving two miles per hour for the last hour! This will average out!"

The shortcut didn't last long. The stadium was still four blocks away when I hit traffic again. I wasn't waiting this one out. I yanked the car to the side of the road and parked in front of a row of broken houses. I sprinted down the sidewalk and turned the corner, and there, two blocks straight ahead, was Blackbaud Stadium.

I hardly recognized it. The last time I was at Blackbaud was for a soccer game just two years earlier. They'd added on, since. It was twice as tall. I couldn't see past the imposing wall at the main entrance, but could hear the crowd roaring inside. Lightners floated high above the stadium, illuminating the field and surrounding area.

The parking lot was stuffed. People were hanging around grills and tailgates, raising their drinks when I passed. A red discus tag whizzed over my head, hovering to the other end of the lot, where a kid ran it down and caught it with the curved end of a long stick. He slung it back a few hundred yards to someone on the other side. A bumper sticker read *Just like lacrosse. Only better.*

I stopped outside the main entrance. The line was out to the curb. My nojakk cheek vibrated. Chute's voice bubbled inside my head.

"Where are you?"

I told her where and what I was looking at: a long, unmoving line. The crowd erupted inside the stadium.

"Well, just hurry up!"

A guy pushed out of the line, throwing his tickets over his head like confetti. A three-dimensional hologram glittered on the stub, a picture of a storm flashing over the ocean. The seats were good ones, center pitch, third row. A kid in front of me sucked Coke from a straw, wearing a plastic tagghet helmet with a retractable yellow-tinted visor. The Charleston Squall logo flashed on the sides. He held the cup with both hands, staring at me.

"What's going on?" I asked the kid.

He yanked his dad's sleeve. His father continued shouting obscenities through his hands. The kid yanked again. The father finally looked down. The kid pointed at me.

"They oversold the goddamn game," the father said.

"But you got tickets."

"There's a bunch of counterfeit tickets floating around. The fire marshal closed the gates. Guess who got screwed?"

"But they're your seats, just have them check the stubs."

"What the hell you think I'm trying to do here, kid?"

He turned back to shouting. People started throwing things. Soda cans bounced off the wall over the gates. Not long after that, the metal gates clanged shut. More trash went flying. A cold sensation drained down my neck, followed by garbled sounds, voices that didn't make sense. It quickly turned into a brain-freeze. Suddenly, I was cold again.

Haagloppllls-sssaaaa-sssss-HHHEESGAWTTA!

"You all right?" The little kid slurped his drink.

I was on my knee, head cradled in my hands. The sensation went from cold to hot. And I couldn't remember stepping back and getting on one knee.

Why is this happening?

"You want a drink?" the kid asked.

"How about an ice cube?"

The kid popped the lid off and fished out a handful.

"Thanks," I said. My hands were shaking.

The crowd dispersed, but only to the parking lot, where they threw more trash at the gates. Security pushed them farther out. Sweeper mechs hovered out of holes in the stadium walls like mechanical mice, sucking debris into their snouts.

"*Where are you?*" Chute's voice chimed on my nojakk.

I got far away from the entrance and explained the deal.

"*I'm coming out.*"

"You should stay," I said halfheartedly. "You don't need to miss the game."

"*We'll be out in a few minutes.*"

She was coming out. Streeter, too. They would miss the game for me. That was what I wanted to hear.

I WENT over to the grassy park area to the right of the main entrance and sat at one of the picnic tables, massaging the cold sensation that lingered in my neck. The cold fits were getting worse, and now there were voices talking through a watery veil. It wasn't like I was picking up thoughts from bystanders, it was more like energy swelling up inside me. Something wanted out.

Pon can't know about this.

Unexplained experiences weren't good. It meant instability. The Paladin Nation did not look kindly on the unpredictable and unreliable. I already had Pon breathing up my ass, I didn't need to tell him I was broken. It had to be the tension. The night off would help. Seeing Chute, too.

A cup rattled. The kid was standing next to me, holding out the cup of ice. I took it. *Thanks.*

His father called him over. The kid stood there, staring at me. I motioned to his father standing out on the curb. "You better go."

The kid ran and took his father's hand, looking back as they headed out to the parking lot. He waved and staggered along, trying to keep up with his father's long steps, trying to see what was behind him. The world was so big and fast at that age, it was hard to see everything. My father always walked fast, too.

I sucked on the ice. Didn't care how grubby that kid's hands were or how many boogers he had caked under his fingernails; the cold felt good. I tapped out the last cube stuck to the bottom, crumpled the empty cup and tossed it to a passing sweeper. The blinds were drawn on the ticket windows.

I was about to tap my cheek to nojakk Chute when a gate opened and a group of kids stumbled out. One had a red ponytail bouncing on her shoulders. *Chute.* The other four were guys and one of them had his arm across her shoulders. It wasn't Streeter.

My stomach didn't exactly flip with excitement. It hardened like a fist.

38

PALPERBOY

I REMEMBERED those guys from school, a bunch of virtualmode addicts. They were still ugly, but now they sported tagghet jerseys and strutted through the gates like big shit. Jenson had a huge nose, Perry had no chin, and Lee's eyes were too close. The fourth one was Sheldon. He had blond hair. He was the one with his arm over Chute's shoulders.

They bookended Chute—two on each side—and walked close to her. She held a game program and they pretended to be interested in what she was pointing at, but they were slobbering wolves pretending to be sheep. I didn't need to see their thoughts, I could feel their hunger.

My lip was twitching.

Chute ran for me when she saw me. I held out my arms and caught her leaping, spinning her round and round. I buried my face on her neck, inhaled her fragrance. Her energy tingled through my senses.

Her hair was longer. *Were her boobs bigger?*

"Oh, it's so good to see you," she said. "It feels like forever."

The tension in my chest melted.

She squeezed my shoulders. "You're like a machine. What're they feeding you at that place?"

"The same as you, I guess. Look at those guns."

She pulled her short sleeve back and flexed her chiseled biceps. We had a laugh and I was lost staring at her, like I was drinking through my eyes. I'd never forget what she looked like, but time tends to erode the details. It was the brightness of her smile and the wrinkles at the corners of her eyes I'd forgotten.

She introduced her teammates. It had only been a year, but everyone was forgetting me.

"This is Shelly."

"Shelly?"

He uncrossed his skinny arms. "Sheldon."

We shook hands like arm wrestlers, squeezing a little too tight. A little too long. "What kind of name is Socket? You related to Craftsman?"

The others snorted and sort of hid their smarmy grins.

"Shelly!" Chute said, shoving him.

"What? That was funny, come on. You ever heard of anyone named Socket?"

"He's my best friend, so be nice," Chute interrupted before blondie had a chance to say something else. Or maybe he did say something and I didn't hear it. I was still reeling. *Friend?*

We were just friends? And who the hell is Shelly? My mouth hung open and twitched. I hated giving away emotions.

"Where's Streeter?" I asked.

"He's busy, couldn't make it tonight."

"Busy? I get one night off and he's *busy*?"

"You need to call him."

"I will." I reached for my cheek. "I'll call him right now."

"Hey, man. If you got somewhere to go," Shelly said, "we can take Chute off your hands. We got some tagghet business to talk about anyway, so you go call your *little* friend and we got this."

Little friend. That was a crack on Streeter's height. He wanted me to know he and Chute were tight, that they were hanging out and talking when Streeter and I weren't around. He wanted me to think they might even be doing things.

"No," I said. "It's good, I got it."

I tapped my cheek and activated the nojakk, mumbling Streeter's name. The call ticked along, trying to connect. Meanwhile, Shelly put a piece of gum in his mouth and stared at me like he was some badass. Christ, tagghet was making him delusional. The other morons were busy with Chute and her program, but Shelly was itching for trouble. Why couldn't he just play nice? Was he trying to be big dick in charge and I was on his turf?

I could play nice if they didn't come off like possessive jocks. And they weren't even jocks, they were goddamn computer dorks wearing uniforms. The only reason they tagged was because jetters required thought-projection and virtualmoders were prime candidates. Most of them had horrible coordination.

He dropped the wrapper on the ground. "You ever tag?"

"Huh?"

"Tag. You know, *tagghet*. The game we were watching until you couldn't get a ticket."

"Uh, yeah." My call went to Streeter's voicemail. I didn't leave a message. I considered calling again.

"So where do you go to school?"

"Uh, nowhere. I'm homeschooled."

"Homeschooled? You got a homeschool team, is that it? What do you call yourselves, the Homeschool Hippies?" He hit Lee in the chest and the three of them laughed on command. "Homeschool Hippos?"

He smacked the shit out of that gum while he laughed with his mouth wide open. Chute scolded him for being an asshole. But he had the other three rolling.

"You're lucky you don't play us," he said, catching his breath. "I'd beat your ass so wicked your goddamn hair would turn white."

They let loose this time, half-turning, falling over each other.

There was no stopping him, laughing right in my face. He was taking me out of the picture. Chute drilled him in the shoulder this time. Called him a jerk-off.

"Oh, come on, now that was funny." He regained his balance. "He's already got white hair, get it? I'm so good that his hair is already white. Before I even play him, his hair is white. Get it? That shit's funny. Come on now."

"What position you play?" I asked.

"Second lance." He shadowboxed at me and shuffled his feet, throwing an awkward right hook. "The best you'll ever see."

"Lancer, huh?" I picked up the gum wrapper. "You must be quick."

"Dude, I'll make you dizzy."

I was still nodding thoughtfully. He juked around his boys, play-faking moves. When he was done pretend-scoring, he held his hands up like a heavyweight and bounced on his toes.

I folded the wrapper and held it between two fingers. "You dropped this."

He smiled at his boys and swiped at the wrapper without looking but came up empty. He swatted again and missed. I'd barely moved my fingers and he'd whiffed twice.

He stopped torturing the innocent stick of gum and finally looked at me. I turned my hand over, palm up, and the balled-up wrapper rolled into my hand.

"I learned that in homeschool."

He pecked at the silver ball to catch me off guard, but I bumped the wrapper off his wrist and caught it low with my other hand. He swung with his left, just trying to knock it away, and I batted the wrapper back to my right. Now he was swinging wild while the wrapper went back and forth between his hands. His cheeks were flush, but he was chasing the bouncing ball like it was a phantom housefly.

Finally, I popped it high above our heads. He watched it come down, but before he could grab it, I flicked it like a pebble shot out of a slingshot; hit him right between the eyes. His head snapped back in surprise.

It took a second for him to get his wits back. A red dot was glowing between his eyebrows. I had my empty hands up and parted my lips, the silver ball between my teeth.

Shelly tried to smile, but I'd crossed that friendly line. His boys weren't smiling, either. He thought about taking it to another level, but he couldn't fight. He wished he could fight, but he was over his head. All bark, no bite.

Instead of taking a swing, he wrapped his arms around Chute and interlocked his fingers over her stomach, pulling her against him tight. Smiling, sort of. "Let's get out of here, guys."

He thought he had the upper hand, that teammates meant more than friendship, that Chute would choose them over me and that was the best way to strike back, but Chute was about a half second from planting an elbow in his left ear. He crossed her line.

I should've let her do it, but when he touched her like that, I didn't respond. I reacted.

I reached my mind around him like a net and dragged through him like fingernails. Pon had put the brain-freeze on me a hundred times. It was the quickest way to confuse an opponent.

Shelly turned pale and wobbled backwards. She helped him along with a stiff shove. Shelly's knees gave out and his boys caught him before he face-planted in the grass.

Chute stomped off, cursing at all of us. Me included. Shelly might've been a jerk-off, but I was a bully. She knew I did something. I was quickly after her. Shelly, he was drooling.

Maybe she was right.

39

A Slice of Time

I was braced for a nojakk call from the Garrison to return for an unauthorized mind read, but I didn't read his thoughts. It was a bare minimum movement of the mind that could be considered an assessment of a situation, nothing they'd censure me for doing.

"I'm sorry, Chute. I just kind of, you know, lost my mind when he—"

"They don't usually act like that."

Maybe she's not mad at me. "They're jealous, that's all."

"They're just friends. They don't have anything to be jealous about."

I sort of half-laughed, half-coughed, and looked away with a loud *eh-hem.*

"What?" she asked.

"Have you seen yourself lately?"

"What's that supposed to mean?"

"I just mean, duh, they're guys."

"And I'm a girl, so what? That doesn't mean we can't be friends."

"No. But they're *guys*. They don't know how to be friends with a girl, especially one that looks like you. Unless they're gay. Are they gay? Because, you know, I was getting a vibe from Lee and I wasn't sure—"

"Listen, we're just *friends*."

Friends. Okay. But a friend could mean anything. Could be someone you call to get something off your chest. Someone that shared notes in class or loaned you money. Could be a friend with benefits. I started to ask the question, to get a little clarification, but I didn't. I had to stop reacting. Besides, the night would go up in flames if I asked something like that. Call it a hunch. I wasn't sure I wanted the answer to that, anyway.

We waited for traffic before running across the street. My car was another four blocks up, all alone beneath a streetlight. We walked in step, the old houses crowded against the sidewalk. Even shared a laugh. After a couple of blocks, she reached over and hooked her finger around mine, and just like that it felt like I'd left just yesterday. Our hands were sweaty, but I wasn't letting go. And Chute was still squeezing.

"Do you want to go downtown?" I asked.

"It's late."

"We can sit at the market café and make fun of tourists, what do you say? Just like old times."

She had a curfew, but a quick call would push it back, especially when her older sister knew she was with me. She tapped her cheek and talked with her dad. It took a little conversation, but when she tapped off, she turned and smiled. "I've got until midnight."

"Who says I'm taking you home?"

She socked me in the arm. Not hard, but directly on the triceps wound. It startled me, felt like she put a blowtorch on my arm. The pain shot across my back and through my other arm. I had to put my hands on my knees for a breather.

"Oh, are you all right?" She bent over, rubbing my back. "I'm so sorry. I didn't realize training had turned you into such a wuss."

"Oh, you're going to get it."

She attempted to outrun me. I caught her four houses down, hoisted her on my hip and carried her like luggage. She laughed and screamed. There was no one around to hear her fake cries for help.

"Oh, you've got such big Paladin muscles," she said, giggling. "Are you taking me to headquarters?"

"Yeah, I am. Then it's right to the dungeon for some old-fashioned torture."

"I'm calling the police!"

"They won't get here in time, but what I'm about to do to you could be considered a crime. My car's right up there."

"I thought maybe you parked in Myrtle Beach. You should've picked me up at the stadium."

"And leave you with Shelly?" I set her down. "Not without Streeter."

She didn't laugh so much at that. It felt like something just happened between us. She was quiet, then said, "When's the last time you talked to him?"

"Last time I saw Streeter? It was like three and a half months ago. Actually, I didn't see him, we met in virtualmode. He took me to this new world he's been working on—"

"I think he's in trouble." She looked at the sidewalk, following the cracks with her eyes. "He's been avoiding me. I call him all the time and he never answers. He's hardly at school anymore. I'm a little worried." She looked up. "You know, that's not like him."

Two people came out the front door a few houses ahead. I followed behind Chute to let them pass and tried to think of anything Streeter might've said or done that seemed out of character. He'd said something about a statewide award he won for codebreaking. What if he went codebreaking somewhere he shouldn't have, like national security? Or worse, a Paladin database? They don't have a sense of humor about that shit.

The two men approached. They weren't well dressed, but they had a bunch of gold chains and bathed in cologne. I accidentally bumped the stocky one.

"I'm sorry about that," I said, over my shoulder. "Chute, did Streeter say anything about—"

Warning.

The men were turning.

No vehicles on the road. Twelve houses have lights on, only nine have a view of us. No visible residents.

Their muscles tightened. I smelled adrenaline surging through them.

Two men. One short, stocky, visible scars. The other is muscular with tattoos. Both twenty years of age. Cologne masking smell of perspiration.

I shifted my weight.

Chute is 4.2 feet away. The curb is 3.5 feet. Sidewalk uneven from a live oak growing 5.1 feet behind me. House is 2.8 feet to the right.

The stocky one was driving his fist at the back of my head. He was fully committed to the swing. I easily moved out of the way and rammed my finger and thumb under his chin, lifting him onto his toes. The jolt to his jugular lit him up. His eyes rolled and, before he became dead weight, I tossed him at the other guy.

I grabbed Chute's arm and started around the live oak. The car was only a half block away. If the taller one gave chase, I'd knock him out, too.

"SOCKET!" Chute screamed. "HE'S GOT A—"

Flash.

The night lit up.

There was no choice.

I triggered a timeslice.

My metabolism went through warp speed, dumping enzymes and adrenaline into my system. Synapses twittered at light speed and I saw, thought and moved at a velocity unknown to ordinary humans. For me, time stopped.

The 9mm bullet was out of the barrel, suspended in space. I shook my head. *The night is over.*

Why would they do it? Was it money? Is that what they wanted? If they'd asked, I would've given them everything just to keep this from happening. But now this? The Garrison wouldn't understand. There would be no forgiveness. I should've assessed the environment, known I was putting us at risk in this neighborhood at night. There was no excuse. *Battles are won or lost before they begin.*

Chute's mouth was open, halfway through warning me that he had a gun. I brushed the hair from her face and touched her freckled cheek. My only night and I blew it. When would be the next? *Never.*

I held her hand and gently moved her out of harm's way. My steps echoed in the silent slice of time. No insects. No wind. Just dead silence. The glittering streetlight reflected off the bullet's metal casing. I slapped it into the road; it tinkled down the storm sewer.

I took the gun from his hands, careful not to touch the flaming barrel, and placed it on the sidewalk where the police would find it. The bruised spots behind his ears were fresh. I pulled the scumbag down and looked into his dark eyes. The pupils were abnormally dilated, the beginning stages of gear addiction. Gear junkies like him forced high levels of endorphins from their bodies with emotional gear manipulators. It was a natural high, but there was nothing natural about it. They turned their bodies into poppy fields, producing their own narcotics.

His breath stank and slimy pockets of spit stuck in the corners of his mouth. Just touching him made the back of my throat tight. I held my breath, penetrating his mind. His foul energy clung to him like smoke. His mind was corrupt like a scratched hard drive, the nervous system twitching beyond his control. His thoughts intermingled with delusions and childhood memories and sour thoughts of crimes he'd committed, some very recent. He was human, but seemed more like a duplication of a human. A copy. A program that followed the orders of his addictions and warped egotism. I was tempted to look inside him with a direct touch just to see how similar he was to a duplicate, but that would be too dangerous, could suck the life out of him. Even if he deserved it.

I let go of time, feeling my body tingle back to the ordinary march of the world. Distant cars honked.

"An unauthorized expression of abilities has been recorded," a voice called on my nojakk. *"Return to the Garrison immediately."*

His eyes darted back and forth. His senses tried to reconnect, unsure if he was dreaming or just high. Then he lost it, slapping at me like a kid trying to escape his father's clutches. I squeezed his mind, overloading his consciousness, and his body surrendered, falling weightless. I laid him on the sidewalk next to his partner and folded their arms over their stomachs. I made a call, giving my coordinates. The police would be here soon.

"What happened?" Chute said.

I took her down the sidewalk, but couldn't get her to look away. I held her close. Her breathing was quick and shallow. She was trying to assimilate the impossible. There was a gun. A bullet. And then what?

Chute knew what I was. She knew what I could do. Still, her mind was ordinary. Those were the sort of things that happened in movies. I hated that she was trembling.

A black car pulled up to the curb. It was from the Garrison, slicing time the moment I broke the rules and coming for us. The driver got out and opened the back door. I helped Chute inside. She was still looking at the bodies, wondering if they were dead. She looked back to me, struggling.

"Where am I going? Are you in trouble? Are they..." She looked at the gun. "Are you hurt?"

"I'm fine. And so are you. The driver will take you home now. You're safe. We're all safe."

She was sorting it out now, grabbing my hand. "You're going back?"

I hooked my finger around hers. I didn't have the words to tell her what I was feeling. She didn't need me to say it, but it would've been nice. The driver fidgeted. Chute's lips quivered, but the words wouldn't form.

The sirens were near.

I watched the black car drive away. Everything I wanted was in the backseat.

I walked down the middle of the road. Blue lights turned the corner a few blocks back and the sirens wailed. People parted the curtains and looked out their windows, but no one came outside. No one would remember seeing black cars. No one would remember seeing the boy with white hair drive away.

40

Pets

"REPORT TO THE DEBRIEFING ROOM," was the message I got when I arrived at the Garrison.

I went to the Preserve instead. The order repeated on my nojakk and I marched through the heart of the jungle. The order finally stopped. Someone would come get me. Eventually.

A few miles later, I stepped out of the trees onto a wide open stone slab with an ancient, barren tree at the far end. The grimmets' vivid colors squabbled along the limbs. They stared at me approaching, their golden eyes blinking. Their somber mood reflected what they sensed inside me.

They knew me so well.

The slab dropped off like a small cliff into a pond below, where the tree was rooted. I sat on its ledge and stared at the sparkling water. A red grimmet came over, wrapping his long tail around my neck.

"It was a disaster, Rudder," I said. "A freaking disaster."

I lay back. Rudder reclined on my chest and imitated my posture with his hands behind his head. The moon was nearly full, casting the tree's shadow over me, but the sky was beginning to lighten where the sun was close to rising in this part of the world. The universe was so vast that light travelled 2,500 years just to reach the nearest galaxy. There were a billion galaxies beyond that with billions of stars in each one. It was all so limitless.

Why do I feel so trapped?

I had the power to do things normal people wished for. I knew more about the mind than psychological experts, but I was the one wearing a leash.

Steps quietly shuffled up behind me. Spindle's eyelight softly turned the tree trunk red. He waited quietly while I counted stars, following the Big Dipper to Orion's Belt. Was there someone out there staring back, wondering why life was so unfair, too?

"We must report for debriefing, Master Socket," Spindle said softly.

The grimmets stirred, their golden eyes sparkling like the stars beyond. "Do you know why the grimmets are here?" I asked.

"They aid the Paladin Nation."

"I've been here a year and I don't see them aiding the Paladins. They don't go anywhere; they're not involved in training or explorations. So how, exactly, do they *aid* them, Spindle?"

"Grimmets are masters of psychic technology. They aid cadet awakenings. You have seen them do these things, Master Socket..."

I nodded while he read me the information in his database. He was a company man. Rudder walked to my hand and curled up, closing his eyes, gently purring. I held my evolver up, the one that was damaged during the exercise. It only took a series of thoughts and the grimmets somehow read the technological problems inside and told it to repair itself. It warmed in my hand and I replaced it on my belt. It was fixed. I never had to check their work.

"I have a theory," I interrupted Spindle's spiel. "When the Paladin Nation punched a wormhole through the Milky Way, they found a habitable planet on the far side of the galaxy with these intelligent creatures." I held Rudder up by the tail. "And they said, 'Hey, let's take them home and add them to our collection.'"

"But, my data suggests—"

"They brought them *against* their will, Spindle. Dragged them light-years from their home into this manufactured forest carved out of a mountain and said here's your new home, boys and girls. Enjoy. They brought them here to *serve*. Not to aid, but to serve. Against their will." I stood up and punched each word with emphasis. "Now, do you think that's fair, Spindle?"

"I am afraid your hypothesis is incorrect."

"Yeah? Well, where do you get your information?"

"I am kept up to date with all Paladin records. They are current and accurate."

"You get your information from the Paladins. *They* tell you what *they* want you to know. You don't *know*."

Truth was, I didn't know either. I knew what Spindle told me was the standard answer, but I always had a feeling there was another one. The grimmets never told me anything, but I sensed the flock was restless, like they were waiting for something. It was how I felt, too: like something was supposed to happen and we were just waiting until it did.

Only that something never came.

"You ever get the feeling you're a pet, Spindle?" I pondered the sky. "That you're just some specimen in a collection?"

"I do not understand, Master Socket. The grimmets are a valuable asset to the Paladin Nation. As are you."

Valuable asset. My point exactly.

The grimmets were wise. They accepted their imprisonment. Here they were, trapped millions of miles from home, and they still found peace and happiness. They still found comfort on a distant planet in a dead tree. I was too stubborn or stupid to do the same.

"We must report for debriefing," Spindle said.

I placed Rudder in a hole in the trunk. I could see his glowing eyes watch us as we entered the trees.

41

The Dance of Colors

Paladins took notes on my side of the story. I opened my mind to show them the event recorded through my senses, as I experienced it. I did these things because I was a good soldier. I didn't like it, but I put those feelings aside. *Good boy.*

After that, I went back to training. I went back to forgetting what happened with Chute, ignoring how I felt, and I completed my assignments and missions. Pon was busy with Paladin business and didn't have a chance to meet with me, to pick my analysis of training apart. He relayed commands through Spindle. And I completed them.

In my spare time, what little there was, I went to the moldable training rooms and built isolated environments to help forget about home. Sometimes it was a desert, a tundra or other habitat of equal desolation.

Pon returned weeks later.

I was sitting on top of Mount Everest. Snow was piled over my lap like a winter quilt, but the seat carved out of ice was otherwise comfortable. Clouds were strewn below like a cotton bedspread. The air was crisp, rustling my hair. I could not feel the temperature that should've been peeling the skin from my face. It was a balmy breeze, despite the altitude and the deadly ice storm approaching on the horizon.

Ten feet in front of me, a doorway opened in space. Spindle walked up the mountainside, buried up to his waist in snow. A gale-force wind cut between us, pushing him sideways. It whistled in my ears, holding my hair sideways. Spindle's faceplate lit up, but his words were sheared away. He crawled through the snow until he was at my feet. "Perhaps you could return the room to normal, Master Socket?" he shouted.

I flicked my fingers. The clouds and ice dissolved back into an empty white room.

"Are you feeling well?" Spindle asked.

"I don't want to talk about it."

Spindle's face scrambled with colors, but he wasn't able to formulate a response. He looked in one direction, then another. Then, as he often did, returned to the task at hand. "Would you like to consult the evaluation of your training and status now?"

It wasn't a question, really.

"I think it will cheer you up immensely." His face was brighter. "Let me show you the data."

Bright colored bars grew several feet from the floor and rotated, pulsed and spiked. Green, blue, and yellow lines circled the bars like electrical arcs, jumping from one bar to the next. All the colors in the spectrum danced around the room, reflecting in Spindle's faceplate.

"It is my pleasure to translate the analysis, Master Socket." In Spindle's words I was superior, magnificent, and grand. My evaluations were on par with fully realized Paladins. Spindle started with the spiking red bar on his right that represented my raw instincts, citing specific examples in training exercises, even calling up replay videos to point out highlights. Then he moved on to the next bar:

timeslicing ability. The next one was speed and agility, then evolver manipulation, tacking aptitude, combat readiness, and so on and so forth.

They were all *stupendous.*

Spindle didn't seem to notice I didn't give two shits. It struck me I was sitting in a white room, wearing a one-piece battle garb. I plucked it off my skin, rubbed the silky texture between my fingers, and poked it with my thumb, feeling the armorcloth threads stiffen to resist impact. It was white, matching the room. If I walked into the jungle, it would turn green. I swore a long time ago I wouldn't wear something like that, but there I was, listening to an android dance around the room while I sat there in a stupid onesy.

"There is some concern with this bit of data," Spindle announced.

He was behind a translucent pyramidal bar that dwarfed all the others. Its base was as wide as Spindle's shoulders and the tip twinkled near his knees. The surface was pearly, encasing sparkling lights within.

"It appears to be an undefined hidden potential that you have just recently begun to express. However, we do not know what the ability is. It has never been detected before." Spindle stepped through the pyramid. "Are you experiencing anything unusual?"

He was talking about the cold sensation that washed down my neck, and the garbled voices that came with it, the weird visions I had with Com. *Was Pon dead?*

There was something definitely unusual and if my raw instincts were as good as the data suggested, I wasn't telling him. I needed time to sort through it, but I had a feeling I already knew what was happening.

Haagloppllls-sssaaaa-sssss-HHHEESGAWTTA! I heard that nonsense trickle down my neck when I was waiting in line for the tagghet game, when the kid gave me an ice cube. And then I heard it again when Chute said it, just before the gun fired. She was warning me: *Socket! He's got a—Hhheesgawtta... He's got a...*

He's got a gun.

I heard her warn me an hour before it happened. The future was coming to me as a cold, paralyzing sensation, speaking through a thick barrier of time. And I wasn't controlling it.

I looked Spindle square in his eyelight.

"No, nothing unusual."

Spindle waited for me to elaborate, or to perhaps finish my thoughts. I didn't.

He waved his arms and the colored bars, spikes and lines vanished. "Let us move to the training room to prepare for the pre-Trial, shall we?"

"Pre-Trial? That's not scheduled for two weeks."

"There has been a change in the schedule. Pon will soon be temporarily reassigned to assist in Pike's relocation."

"Pike is being relocated? Again?"

"There is evidence he has contacted someone outside his imprisonment. His location is crucial to his isolation. Only trusted Paladins can relocate him."

Pike, the greatest Paladin traitor of all time, had been secretly imprisoned for an entire year, ever since I exposed him. He carried more knowledge about the duplicate population than everyone thought, but it came with a price. Pike was already a superior minder, a Paladin with exceptional psychic skills, including the ability to read thoughts, to see without eyes and to heal minds. Or destroy them.

But his abilities were appearing to grow when they should have been diminishing under the pressure of Paladin minders. In fact, he recently gained control of a minder, drained his personality and will, and turned him into his own personal puppet. The minder turned on his companions, killing one and injuring two more. He was stopped, but was a zombie by then.

"Trainer Pon would like for you to complete the pre-Trial exercise this morning," Spindle said. "This is the second of three pre-Trial exercises required to be completed before the Realization Trial. According to the data, you are ready."

Off to training we went. I was one of the best Paladins of the future. *Why don't I feel like one of them?*

42

RIDDLED

I WAS ALONE in the training room. Fresh air filtered through microscopic pores in the walls, carrying a subtle undercurrent of purification.

It was early in the morning, not that there was a clock. Spindle left at 5:55 a.m., as he did every morning, and let me stand ready in the center of the room, hands behind my back. Pon would arrive precisely five minutes later. He was never late. Never early.

I never knew where he was going to enter the room. It was always a surprise. He could enter anywhere along the walls or through a trapdoor. Once he dropped from the ceiling. Sometimes he strolled into the room. Sometimes he attacked. *Always be ready.*

And he always pointed out something I fucked up. Just once, it'd be cool if he walked in, clapped his hands, and said, "Oh, you've outdone yourself this time, Socket! That's my boy! MY MAIN MAN!"

Instead, he'd drop from the ceiling because he knew secrets. He claimed to know every secret tunnel in the Garrison. Claimed he knew them better than the commander himself. Maybe he dug those tunnels himself because he was *sooo* goddamn important—

"Control your thoughts, cadet." Pon emerged from a solid wall.

I tightened my mind.

He pursed his lips, taking a moment to observe. Then, with his hands behind his back, he paced around me. His footsteps fell like a predator's. I mindfully followed his presence without turning as he walked out of eyeshot. I followed his energy, followed his movements and searched his intentions. He stopped directly behind me and took a balanced stance. His mind reached around, searching for weakness. If I was not vigilant, he would squeeze me unconscious. He'd done it before. That sort of thing was not easy to forget, especially when you piss your pants.

"Tell me, cadet, that I haven't wasted a year training you?"

He probed my mind some more, giving me an opportunity to respond. I wasn't answering that.

He circled around, looking thoughtfully at the ground. The psychic pressure intensified, threatening to push through my barriers and creep inside. If he got in, I would suffer major brain-freeze and, politely put, *go night-night*.

I closed my eyes to steel my mind, whittling my focus down to a tiny point. Weak minds were clay in Pon's hands. He was an artisan who could mold the mind's fabric or squish it between his fingers.

He made a complete circle and stopped in front of me. I remained resolute. Knees flexed, ready to timeslice if he attacked... for the purposes of training, of course.

"You can never go home, cadet. It does not exist for you anymore."

"It was just a visit."

"That life has passed."

"They're friends, like family. I'm not turning my back on them."

"Understand the conflict, cadet. Understand what you wanted your trip to be. You want a girlfriend to hold your hand. You want to do things ordinary people do. You want to be what you once were." He tapped his head. "Those are your thoughts, and therein lies your suffering."

I'll tell you what suffering is. It's training nonstop. Suffering is going a week without sleep. It's breaking bones and gashing skin. It's getting your brain squeezed like a fucking lemon.

"This present moment is vital, cadet. This moment is all there is. The present moment does not care what you think or how you feel, it exists regardless. You exist in it, not separate from it. The present moment is the beginning and the end." He made a circle with his finger and thumb. "Your feelings about it are irrelevant."

What if I don't care?

His eyes were light blue. A psychic storm rushed through his small, sharp pupils and absorbed my thoughts and emotions. I let him see the doubt rumbling inside.

"It feels suffocating, mmm?" he asked. "Emptiness? Uselessness? Is that how you feel?"

"How about uncertainty."

"I see," he said. "And these feelings of apathy suck the life from your focus, mmm?"

"Something like that."

He stood still. Only the room seemed to breathe.

"Cadet, we serve this world, that is our purpose. Our sole directive. Do you think your loneliness is a fair price for that service, mmm? We save the world from itself, not because we *feel* like it. Because it is our duty."

"Not all of them want to be saved."

"They are lost. We are their shepherds."

"And they still don't give a shit."

"We don't ask for gratitude." He lowered his eyebrows. "When the universe cries, cadet, you answer. Do you think life will understand your failure because you don't *feel* like serving?" The words imprinted on my mind, burning like a hot iron. "Growth is difficult, cadet, that is a fact."

He moved very close. His breath streamed through his nostrils. I did not look away. I reached out to him with my mind and pushed back. The room crackled with our energy. My backbone vibrated. His eyes were open and empty. There was never anything to see inside

Pon, but I always looked for a hint of weakness, a clue of motivation. But there was never anyone inside; he was seamless. Pure, like water.

I was rooted to the floor, ready to strike. I was in the room. *In the moment.*

He stepped back. Satisfied. "The Realization Trial is in twenty-two days. If it was today, you would fail."

"I still don't know the objective."

"The objective is simple: You must see."

"I see just fine."

"Says the blind man. The urgency to see clearly, to act directly, is upon you. It is now, cadet. Your preparation is not just physical and mental, it is your entire being. You prepare to be everyone. And to be no one."

"That doesn't make any sense."

"Precisely. The true enemy is within you. But first you must see the enemy. Do you see him, blind man? Do you see the enemy, mmm?"

My body tightened.

Precisely.

Pon stepped backwards. The room transformed with each step. The putty walls turned brown and tan. The floor became sandy and the ceiling an endless blue sky. Boulders grew around me, tall, sharp and dusty. By the time Pon reached where the wall had been, it looked as if the Sonora Desert ran for miles beyond.

"This is a pre-Trial exercise," Pon said. "Defeat your enemy, cadet."

The sun was high above, stinging my cheeks. Spindle looked down from one of the boulders. He was not wearing his plum-colored overcoat. Steam rose from his silver body, the scalding heat bending the air around him.

"That's an image," I said. "That's not actually Spindle, right?"

"Do not hesitate to do what life requires. When you know the truth, action is immediate, decisive and complete."

"I can't destroy Spindle, Pon."

A smile touched his lips. "Spindle is not his body."

"But that's not right."

"Do not fear death, cadet. Embrace it." Pon took one last step, vanishing through the invisible wall space. His voice remained. "For in death, there is rebirth."

Spindle's faceplate was blank. His red eyelight darkened. He had no weapons. He didn't need them. He bent at the knees and touched his fingers on the ground, crouching like a tiger. I touched the evolvers at my belt.

Do not let feelings obscure the truth.

See clearly.

See what is, not what you want.

Why does that fucker speak in riddles?

Spindle sprang to the other wall, puncturing the stone with his fingers, gripping it like a cat on a tree. Pebbles trickled down. Pressure was inside my skull. Defeat my friend.

"*It is not your enemy you fight, but your thoughts.*" Pon's voice was in my head. "*That is the training.*"

Dust obscured my vision. Spindle's dark eyelight pierced the cloud. Pressure built within me, culminating in my chest. I clutched my weapons, bracing for impact.

Spindle would have to die.

43

DEAD BATTERY

"YOU WANT A DRINK?" The kid holds his father's hand and sucks on the straw.

They walk across the parking lot, leaving me on the curb. When the kid turns around, his face is blank. It has a black eyelight.

My chest is tight.

The parking lot is gone. The kid and his father, too. I am pinned against a rock, sand grinding into my shoulder. Spindle is over me, his eyelight black. His fingertips are slowly piercing the bubble shield surrounding me, aiming at my chest.

"Where's Chute?" The kid is back, holding his father's hand. They're behind Spindle.

"I don't know," I say. "Um, where am I?"

"You want a drink?"

He points the straw at me.

Spindle hovers over me, pushing his fingers closer. Slowly, slowly they creep toward my heart. *This is a test. It is only a test. Fail and you die.*

The eyelight is dark.

Pressure.

Ice rattles in a cup. The kid and his father are halfway across the desert now. He's sucking on the straw. I hear him as if he's three feet away. *You want a drink?*

I just, ah... where're you going?

Spindle's face flashes, his fingers an inch away. My chest inflates. Something wants out.

The kid tugs on his father's hand and tries to pull him back, reaching the cup toward me. His father looks down. *It'll be all right, son.*

But he wants a drink.

The father turns. But it's not the kid's father holding his hand. It's *my* father. *It'll be all right.*

I reach, but they are too far. *Wait, wait! Don't go. I... I need a drink.*

Black eyelight.

An eruption. Something gets out.

Spindle is crumpled against a boulder, its surface indented with the force of his body. The boulders, sand and sky disappear into the ground. I'm in a white room. Spindle is sprawled on the floor.

Eyelight out.

I SCREAMED.

"You're dreaming, Socket." Mother placed her hand on my arm.

I was in a bed. The room was warm and spacious. The only furniture was the bed I was sitting on and the chair Mother stood by. Several monitors blipped near the bed. A wide window, across the room, covered the entire wall and overlooked green mountains in the distance. The view cast a glow through the dimly lit room.

"Where am I?" I asked.

"You're in the infirmary."

My left arm tingled where skin was scuffed away. There was a fight. Spindle's fingers. Sand. *Was that yesterday?*

"You were in the pre-Trial exercise two days ago," she said. "But you exhausted your energy levels and slipped into a short coma."

"I don't remember timeslicing. How could I exhaust myself?"

"There were some... unexpected reactions."

"What happened?"

"I don't want to say until we get a full analysis. It's nothing to worry about."

"Did I pass?"

She nodded, then took a note tablet and some recording gear off the nightstand and put them in her briefcase.

"Why am I dressed in street clothes?" I asked.

"We're going home."

"Home? I was just... wait." I looked around. "Where's Spindle?"

She finished packing, stood straight and pushed her hair behind her ear. She blew out her breath, as if it was stale and tired. She tried that fake reassuring smile but didn't even have the strength to do that. "He's being attended to."

"Is he all right? I didn't... he's not hurt, is he?"

"He'll be good as new, Socket, but he'll need some maintenance before he's activated again."

He was slumped against the boulder. There was an indention in the stone, as if he'd been shot from a cannon. No eyelight. He had me beat. He was inches from ending the exercise, but somehow I threw him off. That part was blank. But I saw him, motionless. Lifeless.

"Pon made me do it."

"It's part of training. Spindle will be fine, trust me." She stroked my arm reassuringly. "Now, can you swing your legs off the bed? I don't want you to stand just yet, just let your feet touch the floor."

I just woke up and she was rushing me out the door. Why didn't they just wheel me out to the car while I was comatose? *Maybe that's what she was getting ready to do.*

My feet were cold, tingling with pins and needles. The floor hurt. Mother clutched my arm to slow me down, making sure I didn't try to stand. My weight ached in my shins. I was already breathing hard. The room was getting darker.

"Sit there a second." She touched her nojakk cheek. "I need three servys in infirmary 204 with a floater as soon as possible." Then she muttered to herself, "Where the hell are they?"

"He cannot leave the premises." Pon stood against the wall. *Was he there the entire time?*

"I don't need your permission," Mother said.

"He is my cadet. He will stay."

"He's depleted, Pon! You can read the diagnosis yourself. He needs rest."

Pon stood resolute, hands clamped behind his back. "He needs to focus."

"HE NEEDS REST, GODDAMNIT!" Mother slammed the nightstand, knocking a cup to the floor. "He has barely slept in the past month. He has logged more training hours than any other cadet. He cannot continue at this rate, and I think the result of the last exercise is proof enough!"

"The Realization Trial is too close. He must not lose focus. I insist he remain under my tutelage."

"Your tutelage? You have destroyed more cadets than any trainer in the Paladin Nation. You have wasted so much talent with your relentless antics. You cannot grind them down, Pon. They have to recoup."

They were the same height—Mother was twice as fiery—but Pon could break her with a thought. I eased more weight onto my feet, but even the slightest movement made my head spin.

"Cadets that survive my training are the best the Nation has to offer," Pon said, simply and softly.

"Survive?" Mother said. "The lucky ones survive. Socket isn't going to become one of your *unlucky* ones; he's coming home. Step aside."

Pon considered her demand, then slowly walked over to the window.

Mother tapped her cheek. "Where are my goddamn servys?"

"These circumstances are quite unusual," Pon said. "A cadet's mother making demands of his trainer."

"I'm acting as a responsible member of the Paladin Nation, whether he's my son or not. Set your ego aside and look at the cadet sitting on the bed. He cannot stand. He is of no use to the Nation if he's broken."

"Home will not help him."

"Well, then consider it a vacation."

"I will not tolerate these demands!" Pon shook the walls with a psychic burst. "You will not interfere with my training. *He will remain.*"

The lights dimmed, but it wasn't my clouded perception. Pon sucked the energy from the room. The atmosphere became dense and grainy. I never saw a single loose thought in Pon's mind, but I could tell that he hated dealing with Mother. He didn't like her interfering with his student. And he *never* spoke with his teeth grinding.

[*Always respond, Pon. Never react.*]

He flicked his eyes at me, seeing the thought I projected. Calm settled around him. Deadly, but calm.

Mother shook her head, pushed her short hair behind her ear, and stood in front of me. Pon would have to go through her. But we weren't leaving, either. They stared, daring the other to blink. Mother would eventually wear down under Pon's gaze, but until then, stalemate.

I bowed my head to ease the nausea swirling in my empty stomach. The pins and needles had faded from my feet, but my knees were too weak to hold me. I was going to puke if the room kept circling. I didn't have time for their game of chicken. I needed to feel better, and I didn't care where. Just sitting up was sapping what little strength I had.

The air lightened. A heavy, callused hand squeezed my shoulder. "How are you feeling, son?"

Son. The word chilled inside me, but it was the commander's hand. His eyes were decisive, but gentle. He tousled my hair, then read the monitors, taking his time at each one. He wasn't seeing anything new, but studied them nonetheless.

"Your vitals are good," he said. "You're in fine shape, although I'm sure you feel otherwise."

"I've never felt this weak."

"You were very close to complete depletion."

Depletion was like a dead battery. Emphasis on dead. "I don't remember much."

"Your mind is coping with stress. The memories will come back, although for now it's important that you rest."

"But what happened?"

The commander turned to my mother. She returned his knowing look. Pon had not moved. The secret passed between them, unspoken. The commander rubbed the corners of his mouth. "We're not sure."

Did the icy voice come back? I was careful to hide that thought from them, but one day I would slip. One day, they would see my doubts. My imperfection. I couldn't hide forever.

The commander walked to the window and watched clouds cast shadows over the green mountains. Pon stood soldier-still next to him, eyes ahead.

"Your Realization Trial is near." The commander spoke while gazing out the window. "However, recent events have cast doubt on the exact date. Pike will be relocated in the next few days, and his whereabouts need to remain undisclosed. I will need Pon's service during this time."

Pon did not respond.

"There is also the matter of analyzing this pre-Trial exercise. We need time to fully understand the events before moving ahead with your training. More importantly, I need you to be fully recovered. I would rather sacrifice a week of training than to have you less than one hundred percent. The Realization Trial is too important. While you have so much potential, I have my doubts the Paladin Nation will show leniency if you do not pass. There are still those that doubt your stability."

Shit.

The commander's gaze followed a hawk circling the trees. It

folded its wings and dove out of sight, returning to the sky with something flailing in its talons.

He was not one of those doubters. If he was, I wouldn't be here, count on that. He was a fair man, but not a fool. If he suspected instability, I'd be done. He knew there were Paladins that doubted my father because he altered his own genetic code to give himself Paladin abilities. But his powers failed to stabilize. *And like father, like son.*

The commander faced the room.

"I'm sending you home, Socket. A week in your own house will facilitate your recuperation, after which you can return to the Garrison. There will be no more discussion on this matter."

Mother slung her briefcase over her shoulder, lifting her chin. *Game over.* Three servys floated into the room with a hovering chair. They parked next to my bed. Pon's expression did not change, but I could feel his agitation. *I don't care how you feel, Pon.*

"I expect you back in a week," the commander said. "You mean so much to the Paladin Nation's future, we cannot afford to fail."

The commander paused. I nodded back, not sure if I should thank him.

"Kay, I'd like to see you before you depart," he said. "Pon, if you'll follow me to my office."

The commander exited the room. Pon was rigid. He aimed a glare at Mother. She sensed it and returned one of her own, but it was her cheeks that paled, not his.

I jumped from the bed. The room wobbled. The timeslicing spark ached to be clutched, but was barely able to glitter in my belly. My knees gave way and I collapsed onto the floater chair. The servys' rubbery arms helped me sit up. I panted and could hardly lift my hand.

Pon pursed his lips and blinked slowly. He accepted the decision. And with a slight nod, a warm wave of energy surged through me, vibrating through the pain, easing the aches. I stopped quivering.

Before I could nod back, before I could acknowledge his healing gift, Pon followed the commander. Mother took a moment to compose herself. I floated out of the room on the chair, following the servys. Mother was behind me.

I waited in the car, looking through the clear roof at the parking garage cave and the natural stalactites pointing down like accusing fingers. *You are the chosen.*

Pon was right. I couldn't go home. At least not the home I wanted. There was a house in South Carolina. There was a bed in that house I slept in and a backyard I played in, but that wasn't home anymore. Home didn't exist, not one where I returned from school and lounged in front of the television. A home where I stayed up all night in virtualmode battles and we sat around talking about what we were going to do when we grew up. A time and a place where anything was possible. I was searching for that sort of home.

It didn't exist. Not anymore.

Mother cruised out of the garage into the boulder-strewn field. I rolled my head against the seat to catch the breeze. The air was dry but non-filtered, carrying the scent of nature emerging from the ground. Of growth and decay. *Do not fear death, for it brings rebirth.*

Garrison Mountain was in the rearview mirror, casting a long shadow over the field. It sped into the distance, further into the past. We drove out of the shadow, into the sun. The windows darkened against the glare. I would be back in a week.

The wheels unfolded beneath the car as we approached the tree line, touching the uneven ground, jostling me in the seat. We pulled into the shade of the canopies. The wormhole glittered ahead. We passed through the compressed space and came out the other side, where the air was humid and thick, laced with the fetid aroma of pluff mud and the siren-song of tree frogs. I closed my eyes and let South Carolina in. Mother's instinct was right; I needed to be home.

Or at least a place I could call home, for just a little while.

PART V

For now we see through a glass, darkly.
Bible, 1 Corinthians 13:12

Without pawns, there can be no king.
Pon

44

CROSSROADS

THEY WEREN'T FAR BEHIND.

I squeezed through a narrow tunnel barely wide enough for my hips. It was pitch black, but the shift in air pressure indicated I'd stumbled into a cavern. I flicked open my evolver-wrapped hand, ignited an infrared flame and adjusted my goggles. It was a mineral-rich cavern. Water trickled down the walls, pooling in the center. In infrared, it looked like blood.

I cupped a cold handful of water to my mouth. There were seven openings in the cavern that led in different directions. I needed one to get me to the surface before the enemy found my trail.

My arm was red. That wasn't infrared water; that was blood. I only had about ten minutes before they zeroed in on it. If I moved quickly, I could buy a few more minutes.

I waded into the icy pool and washed my arm, the blood clouding the clear water. The temperature penetrated like death. I came up and pushed my hair away. Six caves were near the ceiling. Most were small. They had a slight glow. Could've been fluorescent algae, or maybe sunlight. The seventh one was behind me. It slanted downward and went deeper. It was dark. Water trickled across the sandy floor, finding its way into the bottomless depths of the dark cave. If I wanted to get to the surface, that was a loser.

I closed my eyes, allowed the moment to unfold, and listened to what it had to say. My frigid skin felt shrink-wrapped. I took a deep breath and let it out. The enemy was still far away, but their movements echoed distantly, like rodents scratching their way toward food.

Another deep breath.

The air was moving. It wasn't a breeze, just a gentle sway, not enough to even nudge grass seeds on lofty stalks. My breath was shallow; my chest hardly moved. I followed the slightest motion, letting my awareness drift with it like vapor.

Go deeper.

I had to trust my instincts and follow my assessment. I eased out of the pool and dropped to my knees, felt along the gritty opening, then plunged into the darkness of the cave behind—

"No training!" Mother's voice echoed throughout the network of caves.

I slammed my head on the ceiling, cutting my scalp wide open. Blood streamed down my cheek like sweat, dripping off my chin. The enemy was scrambling toward me.

An hour, wasted.

"Log off, Socket. I need to see you."

I closed my eyes and let my awareness drift out of my sim, through the bodiless in-between, until I felt the flesh and blood of my body. Back in my skin.

I looked around my bedroom while my awareness returned from virtualmode. The posters were curling at the corners, a signpost of life before the Paladins. I couldn't care less about Nine Inch Nails or Dismal anymore. A Jackson Pollock print, the only nonmusical poster, was pinned above the bed. Now that I could still dig. His work was a free-slinging montage of paint splatters, unstructured and just I-don't-give-two-shits what you think. I felt something different every time I looked at it. Some considered Pollock a genius, but he was just as fucked up as the rest of us.

I wiggled my fingers and toes, and ran my tongue over my gums. The transporter imbedded in the back of my neck tingled. It allowed me to transfer my awareness into virtualmode Internet no matter where I was, and in full sensory perception. It just took a little longer reconnecting to skin than usual.

My scalp hurt. There was no cut or blood. It was just a memory. I opened the door. Mother was at the kitchen table, dumping things into her briefcase.

"How'd you know I was training?" I asked, rubbing my head.

"Your imbed was active."

"I had a silencer running. Didn't you think I was sleeping?"

"There's only one reason to run a silencer."

"Maybe I was hooking up with someone. You know, in a social world or something."

She paused to sip her coffee and flicked her eyes in my direction. *Please.*

"You're going back to the Garrison?" I asked.

"There're some urgent meetings."

"When aren't they urgent?"

She grunted, tilting her head in agreement.

"When can I go back?"

"You've only been home two days, Socket. Besides, Pon is still on assignment. There's no point, so just relax."

It felt like two years. The weakness I left the Garrison with was already gone. Well, mostly gone, but I'd been through worse. Sitting around the house wasn't as glamorous as I imagined. The normal world went about their daily lives while I sat around scratching my balls.

I shuffled to the refrigerator and grabbed some orange juice, then fell in a chair at the table. My frizzy hair fell in the cup.

"Why don't you do something today, like get together with Chute and Streeter?" Mom asked.

"Chute's coming over tonight."

"Well, there you go. Get out and enjoy your time off. Go watch one of her games or hang out with Streeter. I'm sure he'd love to have you in the virtualmode lab."

"If I could find him."

She mumbled about forgetting something and rushed to her bedroom. "That reminds me," she called. "He left a message."

Why didn't he just call my nojakk?

"Yes?" Mother said, apparently answering a call. "Yes, I'll be there within a half hour. Make sure the ambassador has a projection pad..." She closed the door.

I finished the juice, spilling some on my shirt next to a jelly stain. "Play messages," I called.

The television square lit on the wall in the adjoining family room. Streeter appeared inside it. Well, it wasn't exactly *him,* it was his animated sim. The details were so good that someone might think it was a real person; that is, if they believed a bloodstained barbarian lived in this world.

"Socket, hey." His bushy mustache shook over his lips. "Just returning your message."

Which one?

"I've been, uh, kind of busy, you know. Things have been weird... not that you'd know." He looked like he wanted to spit. *What's that all about?* "Anyway, I, uh, I'll get back to you later on, you know. Maybe I'll see you at Chute's game tomorrow night."

Message over. No goodbye, no later on, no see you some other time. Just out. He wanted me to see him make that face, see that something was on his mind. *But why the sim?*

"What's wrong?" Mother stood at her bedroom door, fixing her collar.

"Something's up with Streeter."

"What?"

"Don't know. I called him half a dozen times yesterday and then he just sends a message instead of calling back."

"That doesn't sound like him." She checked her face in the mirror next to the front door, then finished her coffee in one gulp. "I'll be back tonight."

"Something going on?"

"Some complications with Pike's relocation." She tipped her cup again, even though it was empty. "There was a slipup in the preliminary move. Pike overwhelmed another minder and nearly escaped."

"You call that a *slipup?* Is he all right?"

"No."

Minders weren't child's play; they were masters of the psychic realm. They could strip a human of all his memories, erase his mind like a hard drive, spin his consciousness around until he vomited. They could will a man's heart to stop with a single thought. They were the most valued of all Paladins. The most trusted. Still, none of them could compare to Pike. In the past, two of them could subdue him. Now he broke them like toys.

"Pon was only supposed to be secondary support," she said. "He's in charge of the move now. I doubt he'll be back to the Garrison until next week, so, you see, there's no point in you coming back. Your trainer's busy."

"When are they going to just kill Pike?"

"That's not Paladin policy."

"How many people have to die to change it? Three minders are dead, you know; and they wouldn't be if we just got rid of him. Three lives for one, the math doesn't work."

She rinsed the cup and placed it upside down in the sink. She stared out the window. "Sometimes it's hard to know the right thing."

"Yeah, well, the right thing is to get rid of his ass. It might stink, but that doesn't make it wrong."

She dried her hands, then pushed my hair off my face and looked at me. She'd been doing that more often lately. Like she knew something. If she did, she didn't let on. Or maybe that was what happiness looked like on her.

"You'll be home for dinner?" I asked.

"I'll be later than that. Why don't you make dinner for Chute?"

"Believe it or not, I was kind of thinking that. But, you know."

"You know what? Don't be wishy-washy, make some food. She's not going to care what it tastes like. I'm leaving the car, so go to the store."

I walked her to the door. A black sedan stopped at the curb. The driver's door opened. There was no one inside, having driven from the Garrison on autopilot. She dropped her briefcase in and waved goodbye.

I WENT to the front porch and propped my feet on the banister. Fragrant tea olives were in early bloom. I noticed things like that now, like the density of humidity, the clarity of the sky, the taste of fresh juice. Since training began, my senses continued to open. New experiences presented themselves everywhere; even the simple things like subtle scents or textures were exciting. It seemed lame to say it like that, but the world was everywhere. I just needed to see.

A school bus squealed around the corner. The passengers stared through the dirty windows like zombies. Some days I wished I could be sitting on a school bus again, mindlessly carted off to school, where I could whittle the day away. At least boredom didn't kill you. But then again, sometimes it felt like it.

Streeter wasn't on the bus. Maybe I didn't see him, or maybe he drove his grandparents' car. I had a feeling it was none of the above.

"Locate Streeter," I said, touching my cheek. My nojakk linked up with Streeter's and calculated his location.

"Streeter is currently at 724 West Market, Charleston, South Carolina."

A house call was in order.

45

GATES **of the Dead**

THE WHITE HOUSE was thirty feet from the road. The shades were drawn. The driveway was empty. Streeter's grandparents never parked in the garage because there wasn't room. It was strictly storage. They never threw anything away and I'd dug through that mess with Streeter a thousand times looking for a plate or lamp his grandmother just knew she'd put in there.

I stepped onto the front porch, past the wicker chairs and potted ficus trees, stopped at the door and listened. Nothing stirred inside. Maybe my nojakk was wrong and he wasn't there, or maybe he was just late for school and missed the bus. Maybe his grandparents took him. *So why am I tiptoeing?* Because the energy around the house was foreboding, like a ghost was in the attic.

I knocked. It echoed inside. Knocked again.

There was a key under the ficus. It had been there since I was five. I could use it, but it would be hard to explain if his grandma came home and, on the chance Streeter wasn't home, I was wandering around inside.

The small surveillance eye, about the size of a marble, was still above the door. The surface swirled. It was still working. Something wasn't right. The house just felt... dark.

I hopped the privacy fence and crept up to the first window. The shade was drawn on Streeter's room. I cupped my hands against the window and peered through a gap below the shade. The desk and dresser were covered with clothes, and the floor wasn't visible under books, papers and Internet gear. Nothing had changed.

The bed was in the corner with a mess of covers. I thought about going around back and looking through the kitchen window, when the bed twitched. A hand was sticking out, fingers twiddling on the mattress. A cable stuck out from under the pillow.

Virtualmoding.

He was on the Internet, virtualmoding in his giant sim. He knew I was at the front door, that surveillance eye would've reported the view to him. In fact, there was another eye somewhere outside his window, watching me watching him.

"Streeter!" I tapped the window. "I need to talk to you, get up!"

His fingers stopped twitching.

"I see you, I know you're in there."

It wasn't enough.

"I'll get the key," I said. "I'll let myself in and drag your ass out of bed."

He still wasn't moving. Maybe the key wasn't there anymore. Slowly, the mound came to life. Streeter sat up.

No way.

He was still short, but thirty pounds lighter. His face was dark. He rubbed his eyes and stretched, pulling the oversized transporters from behind his ears. He sat on the bed, slumped over. Thinking. Maybe I was going to have to get the key after all. But then he stood. He used to be built like a hot air balloon. He'd sprung a leak.

The door was open when I got to the front porch. Streeter was walking away.

"You all right?" I followed him to his bedroom.

"I'm not feeling well."

I touched the lamp on his desk, lighting his room. Dark energy pulsed around him. His breath was shallow, as if it didn't matter whether he stopped breathing altogether.

"What's wrong with you?"

"I got the flu or something?"

"Flu? Dude, you're half gone!"

"Yeah," was all he said. He wouldn't look at me. "I've been puking a lot."

"Have you been to the doctor?"

"It'll pass."

"But you've lost all that weight. Something's not right, you got to get it checked out."

"Maybe I'm on a diet."

"Why didn't you tell me you were sick?" I said. "I haven't seen you in three months—"

"Look, I'm sick!" He bristled with hot energy now. "What d'ya want me to say?"

I pulled the shade and flooded the room with light. His color was all wrong. He blinked at the bright light and sat back down on the bed. I grabbed his face with both hands, forcing him to look directly at me. His pupils were dilated; the rims of the irises were blurry.

"How long have you been virtualmoding?"

"I'm not gear-addicted." He knocked my hands away.

"You didn't answer the question."

"I know what I look like; I'm not addicted!"

"Look at the signs, man! Your eyes are the first to go! You look like a freaking withered-up gearhead."

"Yeah, and what do you know?"

"Face facts! Do you want to feel better or what?"

"Don't pull that Paladin shit on me! I know more about virtualmoding than you'll ever know!"

"What?"

He struggled to stay still. He pulled the shade down and sat at his desk, shaking his leg. He wanted me out of there in the worst way, but knew asking wasn't going to do it. It wouldn't be hard to pick a few thoughts from his mind; they were scattered like fallen leaves. It would be as easy as dragging a net through a school of minnows. My mind reached around him, gently applying pressure. I didn't want to get inside him, just see a loose thought or two.

"Don't pull that bullshit on me!" he said.

"What're you hiding?"

"I got a life, so just stay out! You wouldn't know about it. You and Chute."

"What're you talking about?"

He sat there drumming his fingers on the desk, grinding his teeth, and finally said, "You're not around, Socket, so it doesn't matter. Neither is Chute. It's just me. Just me, bro. So why don't you leave me the fuck alone."

"I'm here to see you, not somewhere halfway around the world, you nut."

"Where you going to be next week?"

His eyes were larger than ever. He was sensitive to thoughts, even though he couldn't control them. That was how he felt me looking inside him. And that was another sign of gear addiction. He needed help.

"You got to stay off virtualmode, man," I said. "It's killing you."

"I'll do what I got to do."

I looked at the box on his dresser. "I'll take your transporters."

"You don't think I have backups?"

"Streeter, this isn't right. I'll bring Chute here, if that's what it takes. She'll make you do it."

"Give me a break, she doesn't have time." He held his belly and burped. "I got to puke now. You know the way out."

He crossed the hall and slammed the door on the bathroom.

He was always vigilant about gear addiction. In fact, he always made sure Chute and I had safeguards on all our gear before we went virtualmode. He checked records to maintain proper hours. In fact, the only way to abuse virtualmode was to disable the safeguards. Virtualmode would shut down if it sensed addictive symptoms. What was he doing? Better yet, *where* was he doing it?

It sounded like a dry heave in the bathroom. How long would he fake that until he thought I was gone? I grabbed the disc-shaped transporters wired to the black box off his dresser. It was cheap-ass gear. Nothing was wired these days, but Streeter could make anything work. This was crap he got down at a gear swap for next to nothing. It was probably easier to disable the safeguards so he could virtualmode endlessly.

I slid the transporters behind my ears, felt them suck against the skin and search for my nervous system. My awareness left my skin sitting on the bed, floating through the bodiless in-between until I landed in a giant sim.

I was ten feet tall in a small white room with no furniture or monitors. Streeter's gear didn't even recognize I wasn't him. The enormous body felt sluggish and powerful. The environment was cartoonish and senseless: no feeling, no smell.

"Take me to the last destination," I called in a deep, gravelly voice.

The walls jiggled, searching the coordinates for the last place Streeter was at. The walls weakened, then crumbled. An imposing metal gate appeared before me. It was thirty feet high with sharp staves on top of the bars, hinged to ivy-covered brick columns. Beyond was solid darkness. The night sky was covered with clouds, but a full moon peeked through an opening, illuminating the weedy path in front of me.

"State your target," a creepy voice said from the other side.

"Where am I?"

"The Gates of Death."

"What's that?"

Pause. "If you need orientation to navigate this world, please enter the room on the right." There was a mausoleum buried in overgrown vines. "Otherwise, state your target."

"Just tell me what this place does."

Another long pause. "Gates of Death is a database of all those deceased. You may visit celebrities, historical figures, family or friends."

Family. "As long as they're dead?"

"State your target."

This wasn't Streeter's style. He was a smash and bash guy. He went to battleworlds, not historical. He didn't look back, he looked forward.

"Take me to my last target."

The gates opened slowly. The dark beyond took form. Colors and shapes emerged from the darkness. Water sloshed in an ocean. Trees sprouted—

Click.

The world disappeared.

I was yanked through the in-between like a fish snagged on a hook and slammed back into my skin. I tumbled off Streeter's bed. My stomach churned. Streeter's dirty socks hung off the ends of his feet near my face. He held the transporters in his hand.

"What were you doing?" he said.

"You can't rip those off like that. My nervous system—"

"What were you doing?"

I leaned against his bed, taking a moment to catch my breath. "I saw the gates. Is that what this is all about?"

"You have no right—"

"I'm your friend, Streeter. I'm not trying to take anything from you or... or... listen, you're a goddamn mess, man! You can't keep doing this."

He turned his back on me, facing the corner like he was in time-out.

And then I knew.

"You're looking for your parents."

He twiddled the transporters in his fingers. "This is none of your business."

I didn't budge. Instead, I emitted a soothing energy, filling the room with a calming, loving, embracing essence that permeated his radical aura. The energy settled around him. He started to say something, but the sweetness of the essence felt too good, penetrating his jagged mind. Calming it. Relaxing. Opening.

When his posture released the tension, his shoulders dropped and his fists opened. He fell into the chair at his desk and slumped over, dropping his face in his hands, rubbing his tired eyes.

"I was doing research for history class and stumbled onto the gates," he said. "I talked to Einstein about the atomic bomb and his theory of relativity, pretty standard shit. He didn't tell me anything new, really, but the details were good. I was about to leave and just had a thought. I didn't really think they'd be there..."

He didn't finish. Streeter never talked about his parents, even when we were little. They died when he was five, about the time my dad died, but he said he didn't remember much. Always figured he felt the same way I did about my father, really. It happened a long time ago, so what was the point of bringing up memories? That was then. Now is now.

"That's all?" I said.

Energy spiked off him. "THAT'S ALL?"

"No, I just mean—"

"Imagine your dead fucking dad walking into the room, right now. You think you'd be a little freaked out? You think you'd be like, oh, hey, Pop, how's it hanging? YOU THINK THAT'S HOW IT'D GO?"

"What I mean is the gates is just a game world, it's not real. Those weren't your parents, it was just an image. You're talking to data."

He twisted in the chair and stared a long time. "You think you're better than me, is that it? Or do you just not have feelings anymore? Which is it, Socket? Huh? Are you just a robot programmed to save the world now, is that it?"

He shoved me against the bed.

"I'm no superhero, Socket, I can't control my thoughts and feelings or, or... stop time or any of that horseshit. I'm like everyone else, just trying to get by. So, yeah, it's just a game, I'm sorry. I can't handle my feelings, boo hoo. But I didn't ask you to come in here. I didn't ask you to give a fuck. I GET IT!"

"I'm sorry, I'm sorry... I just thought..."

"You thought it shouldn't matter, seeing my parents? You don't understand, that virtualmode world is as close to being real as this right here." He thumped his chest. "I thought you might get it, but clearly you're not human anymore. It matters to me, superboy. It matters to me."

The front door opened. Bags rattled somewhere in the house.

"You need to leave," Streeter said.

"Hang on a second—"

"Granny?" Streeter called.

His grandma looked into the room. "Are you feeling all right, darling—oh, you have a friend. Good."

"He was just leaving."

"Hi, Granny," I said.

"Hello, darling." She looked confused and held out her frail hand. "What's your name?"

I'd been coming over to the house all my life and she'd forgotten me after a year with the Paladins. I shook her hand gently.

"I'm not feeling good," Streeter said. "Could you take him to the door?"

"Certainly, sweetheart."

He stood in the corner and watched me leave. His grandpa was in the kitchen, putting away the groceries. He waved as I passed. What else do you do to a stranger but wave?

Granny stopped on the porch. "Please come back," she said. "He needs company."

I should've told her to unplug the transporters, but Streeter would find a way to fire them back up. We spent many nights in virtualmode without them knowing. And what was I going to tell her? Your grandson is visiting your dead daughter? Oh, and I think he's gear-addicted.

I should've.

46

The Fade

I PULLED the glass dish from the stove. The baked salmon flaked apart with a fork, just like the directions said it would. It seemed like if I was going to screw up dinner, it shouldn't be fish, but the guy at the market recommended it, said all I needed to do was throw some butter and brown sugar on it and bake. Even a dope can't mess that up, he said.

I turned the stove off and slid the dish back in to keep it warm. What was I going to tell Chute about Streeter? I couldn't lie, but she'd want to know. She'd been calling him, even knocking on his door. She just wasn't willing to peek through his window like I was. He was lucky she didn't see him; she would've dragged his ass to the hospital, no mercy.

So, if I told her the truth—how he looked, the thing with his parents—she wasn't going to stay for baked salmon no matter how it tasted.

I'd tell her after dinner.

A CAR DOOR SLAMMED.

I checked the sweet potatoes, making myself look busy. I didn't want to look like I'd been looking out the window for the last forty-five minutes. My heart thumped when she knocked. *Get a hold of yourself, man!*

"Come in!"

I was bent over the stove, pulling the dish out when she came in. Then I stood there like I forgot where I was, staring at her. She didn't need to dress up or do the makeup thing. Just the way she was, right then, it was perfect.

"I came right from practice." Her braids were frayed like she came over on a motorcycle. "I'm sorry, but Coach worked in some new plays."

I was still standing. Still staring.

"I'll go clean up," she said.

"Yeah, yeah," I said. "Use my mother's bathroom. I've got a few things left to do. Um, it's over…"

"There." She pointed. "Yeah, I've been here before."

I ARRANGED each filet on a plate, then spritzed them with lemon. I split two sweet potatoes and hit them with butter and reached for the spinach salad, hitting that with cherry tomatoes, sunflower seeds and parmesan cheese.

"We're expecting a record crowd at the game tomorrow night," she called from the bathroom. "They're saying more people will be there than football. They're talking about two or three *thousand* people showing up. Can you believe it?"

I lit the candles on the table. I called the television on and a fire crackled on the screen.

"I'm getting a little nervous, thinking about it," she said. "The expectations…"

She stepped into the living room. Her face was radiant. Not in the way someone steps out of the shower or returns from the beach, but bubbling with this essence of pure joy, like one of those paintings of patron saints with the halos. I was staring, again.

"You expecting someone special?" she asked.

"Not anymore." I pulled out a chair. "*Madam.*"

She curtsied and danced to the table. "Why thank you, kind sir."

I went back to work on the salad, focusing on cutting cherry tomatoes and onions.

"It smells good," she said. "Who cooked?"

"The chef is in the house, my lady."

"Are the Paladins training you for housework?"

"Cooker, cleaner, and slayer of evildoers." I slid a plate in front of her. "They leave no stone unturned."

She closed her eyes and hovered over it, letting the steam drift against her face. She forked a small piece of salmon in her mouth. "Oh, my." She moaned. "Oooooooh, my."

She dug into the food. Her lips glistened with butter and the fire popped on the wall. I watched her eat half of it then tried some. That market guy was right on the mark. It was freaking awesome. Chute hardly opened her eyes, and when she did, they were brilliant.

The whole scene was like a romance novel. Pon would shit. If he could see me sitting around like some star-crossed, zit-popping teenager, his head would explode.

"Did you see Streeter?" she asked.

"Yeah, I saw him earlier. You know, this morning."

"He's not right."

"Yeah, well, no... he's not well."

"What do you think's wrong?"

I chewed slowly, watching the flames dance on the candles. There were so many ways to answer that question, none of which were lies. Most of which weren't exactly truths, either.

"I didn't get a chance to talk to him all that much," I said. "His granny wanted him to rest. So, you know."

"Maybe we should go over there."

"He's coming to your game tomorrow night," I said quickly. "We're planning on getting together afterwards. The three of us, you know. Just like old times."

Now that, the second part... yeah, that was a lie. I'm pretty sure the first part was, too. Even though Streeter *said* he was going to her game in the message, I knew he was lying, so in a way I was lying. *Just go with it, stop thinking about it.*

Things were just too good. Streeter could wait until the morning, right? What were we going to do if we went over, anyway? It wasn't like he was going to let us in, and his grandma wouldn't know who I was, so nothing was going to change. I just wanted this night, that was all. Not too much to ask.

"He misses you," she said. "He won't tell you that, but I think that's what's going on."

"It's more than that, I think."

"He's just having a hard time since you left and I think some things are coming up. He doesn't feel like he's got anyone."

"Don't we all."

"He's got it worse."

I clutched my fork. "He's got great grandparents, he's one of the smartest guys around, and he's not starving. Is it really all that bad?"

"He's got no one, Socket, that's all I mean. Making friends is hard for him."

"Well, maybe he needs a new skill."

Chute looked at me strangely, not sure what to say. Even I was a little surprised by the tough love I was spewing.

"Look, I'm sorry," I said. "Sometimes I forget what it's like to be normal. I know it's all relative, but we can't save Streeter. Only Streeter can do that."

"We need to be there for him."

"I know, I know," I said. Desperation was creeping through me. "You're right. We'll get with him tomorrow night at the game. Who knows, maybe everything will sort itself out by then."

"You sure he's coming?"

"He said he was." *That's what he said, swear to God.*

She pushed her food around, contemplating. I turned my attention to my own plate, avoiding the temptation to *look* at her thoughts. Soon, she was eating again. Eating until everything was gone.

THE EVENING WAS COOL, but humid. The sun was down, but the sky was still lit. Chute hooked her arm through mine and laid her head on my shoulder. I couldn't have scripted it better. We walked down the sidewalk, stepping in time, occasionally tangling our feet and laughing.

An old woman was at her mailbox, sifting through a wad of magazines.

"Hi, Mrs. Higgins," I said.

She looked up from her cache and squinted. "Hello."

Chute looked back. Mrs. Higgins was already on her front steps. "She acted like you were a stranger."

Yeah, the lady I lived next to most of my life. I watched her dog when she was away. She brought cookies over at Christmas and always sent a birthday card with money and a note that read, *Don't spend it all in one place.* And now she just said hello to me, a little nervous about the longhaired teenager walking past her house.

"She doesn't remember me."

"Oh no." Chute squeezed me tight. "She has Alzheimer's?"

"No, she's all right, as far as I know."

"Then what's her problem?"

"It's a Paladin thing," I said. "They call it fading."

"You're turning invisible?"

"Yeah, that's it," I said. "No, it's just that anonymity is important to Paladin service. People forget us easily. We naturally emit energy that loosens memories to fall away from the mind. Now you see me." I waved my hands in front of my face. "Now you forget."

"Why?"

"It makes things less complicated. We can function with less attachment to relationships. At least that's what they say."

"I don't like that."

I didn't want to tell her I didn't mind it. I wasn't big on conversation anyway. Now that people forgot me, it wasn't rude for me to just avoid them.

AZALEA PARK WAS DENSELY WOODED with stalwart pines and light-hogging magnolias. Cars were parked in the narrow slots between the trees. We walked through leafy corridors on the mulched paths. Chute slid her hand down my arm, her fingers twining with mine.

We crossed over a footbridge and found a bench at the koi pond. An enormous sculpture of a swan spread its wings in the center among water lilies and cattails. Another couple was tossing bread crumbs on the water and the greedy fish fought for them. We watched them giggle and snuggle. It was sickening, but I was doing the same thing, so I needed to shut up.

Several ducks hopped into the water, swimming after the bread crumbs that landed on the lily pads. They squawked at each other, nipping at each other's wings to get the food first. Everybody wanted a piece. The couple threw the rest of the bag into the water to let the ducks and fish work it out before leaving.

"I'm about to fall asleep." Chute rested her head on my shoulder again.

"It's still daylight."

"It's a school night," she said. "I've got practice in the morning."

"You know, we used to goof on the jocks, and now you're one of them."

I expected her to slug me one, maybe even walk away. I revealed what was on my mind. Maybe I was trying to get rid of some guilt, trying to blame her for Streeter. The way she said it at the table made it sound like his situation was my fault. I was a Paladin; I didn't have a choice to leave him. But Chute didn't *have* to play tagghet. She left because she wanted to.

"I've followed you and Streeter all my life," she said, "did all that virtualmode fighting and camping out when we were little because y'all wanted to, but I never really cared all that much, you know? I just needed something that was mine. Tagghet's mine, it's not yours. It's not Streeter's. It's mine."

She watched the ducks spread out on the water.

"Listen, I didn't plan on playing tagghet, but I'm good at it and I want to share it with both of you. I want you at my games, to cheer me on. It's not the same when you're not there."

I bit my lip. I was having some stupid thoughts that didn't need to become words. Maybe I was jealous she had something besides me. Jealous she *loved* something besides me. I wanted to be the center of her universe, not tagghet or anything else. I wanted to be her everything. *Stupid*. She was no sheep. And that was why I was so into her.

The magic was slipping away from the evening. It was going to end as horribly as the last time. Last time, someone shot at us. This could be worse. Panic clenched my chest.

Chute wandered to an old bubble-gum machine and inserted a coin. When she turned the handle, the ducks raced toward her. She caught the fish food falling out of the dispenser and flung the kernels at the foot of the sculpture. The ducks went after it.

"I know I'm not saving the world," she said. "It's just a stupid game, I know, but it's what I do, Socket. We all can't be heroes."

"I'm no hero."

"Yes, you are." She tossed more food in the water. "You stop time. You do things with thoughts. I'm not even sure how human that is, to be honest. That's a lot for us to live up to. Streeter feels the pressure, too."

"I didn't do that to Streeter. He's got his own life."

She poked at the remaining food in her palm. "Did you forget what it's like to be ordinary?"

Something like that should've hurt like a poke in the eye, but she wasn't saying it like an accusation. She wished, at some level, things were the same as before, I thought. That the world's problems didn't get in the way. It was so easy when we were kids. Dreams were anything we wanted them to be, but now reality was here and it was so complicated. It wasn't always what we wanted it to be.

She gazed in her hand like the answer was in the fish food. I walked over and took it from her and scattered it over the pond. I took her hands. She looked into my eyes with an intensity that could've matched Pon. She grazed her fingertips over my face like it was Braille.

"They won't make me forget you, will they?" she asked.

"That's not possible."

We embraced for an eternal minute while the insects sang. She turned her head. I pressed my lips against hers. They were warm and wet and we melted together. Our energy mingled, open and defenseless. Her vibe was sweet and filling. I squeezed her tighter, closing my eyes and swimming through a swirling tide of emotions.

Pon said I couldn't come home. He was right. This was someplace entirely new.

Chute jumped away and I was left empty-handed, still in mid-kiss. The ducks waddled after her, snapping at her hands.

"They want more!" I said.

"I don't have any!" She scampered backwards and the ducks gave chase. She squealed with delight, yelping each time they snapped. It was the best sound in the world.

"Make them go away!" she shouted.

"Just throw at the water!"

She faked a throw and the ducks went after the imaginary food. We made our escape down the dark path.

The emotions were intoxicating, but each step took us closer to my house and the moment got farther away. The kiss was already a memory; it would stay at the koi pond. It wouldn't last. It wasn't meant to. Maybe that was where Streeter was stuck, coming back to the cold empty present moment when he'd rather be in a world with his parents.

Truth was, reality could suck.

We stopped at her car, holding hands. She bumped her forehead into my chin and I kissed it. No need to go any farther. And then she left.

I stood in the street, watching the taillights turn at the corner. I stayed there, attempting to hold the moment, but it slipped away. There was no choice but to let it pass. I went into the house, wondering when I'd have another moment like that. Reality was already starting to ache. Just another sacrifice a Paladin makes.

Do you think reality cares how you feel?

I DIDN'T SLEEP much that night.

I stared at the Pollock poster, sorting through my thoughts. My emotions were like a boiling cauldron. One second they were sweet and dewy. The next, black smoke.

Did you forget what it's like to be ordinary?

Mother came home after midnight. She cracked my door and I closed my eyes, pretending like I was sleeping. My emotions finally settled. And it was then that I gave way to sleep. It was fast and deep. Restful, until I dreamed.

I dreamed I had fallen through thin ice. I flailed for safety, but the ice kept breaking. I sank into the cold black depths, too heavy to swim. Someone called to me. A voice gurgled through the water. It was far away and distorted.

"*Help,*" it said.

I awoke, startled. Light sliced through the blinds. A chilly sensation was still on my neck.

The voice was mine.

47

Old Friend, New Body

Next morning, there were messages from Mother. I'd be returning to the Garrison at the end of the week. There was no time to waste; I went to Streeter's house. I couldn't live with myself if I didn't, not after the half-truths I told Chute.

There was no car in the driveway. I didn't bother knocking, just went around the house. His window shade was up, his bed made and the virtualmode transporters on the dresser. Turns out, he wasn't home. GPS located him on the Interstate, heading for Charleston. Maybe his grandparents opened their eyes and saw him wasting away. There were plenty of good doctors in town, ones that specialized in gear addiction.

I nojakked him and got his voicemail.

"Streeter, hey, it's Socket. Listen, I'm sorry about barging in on you yesterday and snooping around, but you should've seen yourself, man. You needed an intervention in a bad way. My only hope is that you're getting help. Listen, I'm sitting on your front porch right now. I'm going to hang out for a couple hours in case you get home. I'm probably leaving at the end of the week and don't know when I'll be back.

"I want to see you before I go. I'm sorry about the mess you're in. I miss hanging out with you and Chute. I wish it wasn't like this, I really do. If I don't see you today, I hope you can make it to her game tonight. Just ring me when you get there. Maybe afterwards, you and Chute and me can stop for a bite and live some old times. You know, like we used to. Anyways, hope to see you soon, buddy. Take care."

I stayed on the front porch the entire two hours, just like I said I would, occasionally checking the time, but for the most part I watched traffic. When two hours were up, Streeter was still downtown. Seemed like going to a tagghet game that night was not likely. I'd have to come back to his house the next day. This time, I'd bring Chute.

At least Granny would remember her.

THAT AFTERNOON, I got more updates from the Garrison, this time an encrypted message through a secure connection. The message was narrated by a standard animated voice, announcing the planned funeral for one of Pike's victims. The other two victims were undergoing psychic decompression, but they were expected to make full recoveries. The Garrison would be back to standard operation within three days. Just in time for my return.

Pon was in transit, probably still occupied with Pike's secure imprisonment. I didn't expect to hear from him until I was back. For some reason, I wanted to hear his voice again. *I must be losing my mind.*

I was in the kitchen when the imbed planted in my neck began to tingle, spreading around my scalp like electric fingers. I hadn't triggered it to activate. It blurred my vision as it connected with my nervous system. Suddenly, someone was in the room.

Pon faced me, hands locked behind his back. I was seeing him, but he wasn't really there. No one else would see him, though. He was transporting his image directly into my eyes.

Pon looked around, left and right, and smirked: A guttural acknowledgement of my home. *Not a recording.*

He looked back at me. "Good morning, cadet."

I nodded.

"You'll be reporting to the Garrison in three days. I expect you to be fully prepared to continue training. I will not accept any reduction in your physical stamina. You will present a full synopsis and demonstrate a true understanding of your last exercise."

He outlined the physical exercises to be completed before returning and also explained that a virtualmode environment would be uploaded to my link along with a mission statement to be completed, which also had to be analyzed. I wasn't sure if my mom approved, but I wasn't going to ask. Sooner or later, I'd be back in the training room and she wouldn't be around.

"Is Pike secured?" I asked.

"Do not concern yourself with such matters." He paced to the right, stepping over a crumpled shirt. *Is this really a projection?* "I want you to remain focused on your training. Other matters will unfold as needed." He stopped, lifting his chin with a slight nod. "Engage only in the present moment."

The electric fingers released my scalp and my eyes stung as the imbed disconnected. Pon disappeared. I touched the back of my neck. No one said the imbed could do something like that, but then maybe Pon was the only one that knew how.

THAT EVENING, I was in the backyard, doing pull-ups on a maple tree, when a car pulled into the driveway. Two doors slammed, but I couldn't see who it was. They went inside the house, through the front door, so I snuck in through the back. It was Mother, all right. She was in the kitchen, talking with someone dressed in a long, black overcoat with the hood pulled up. His long boots were cinched tight over baggy pants. He took a plate from her. His hand was silver.

"Spindle?"

Spindle pushed the hood back and the red eyelight spun on his smooth faceplate. "Master Socket!"

"You're alive!"

"I am, Master Socket! I am alive!"

"But... the last time I saw you... you were..."

"Oh, this is not my original bodyshell, Master Socket. I have been uploaded to a new one."

The body didn't survive, but Spindle did. "It's not the body that makes the man..."

"But the heart," he finished.

Even though Spindle was a database, technically he didn't *exist,* I still hated it when he broke a body, especially when I did it to him. But he could cheat death by downloading into another body.

"What happened?" I asked.

"I cannot discuss the exercise. The analysis, however, is complete. Pon will discuss the results upon your return."

Bright colors rippled on the surface of his faceplate.

"It's good to see you," I said.

"Thank you for inviting me."

"Inviting you?"

"You invited me to come home," he said. "Do you not remember?"

"Spindle has come along for observation," Mother said. "He wants to experience a public event."

The world was different than it was a year ago. Ever since the Paladins became known, their technology was finding its way into the public like never before. In hindsight, Paladins were behind every major discovery for the last decade. Most people thought Steve Jobs and Bill Gates were Paladins. (They're not.) These days, humanoid mechs, like Spindle, weren't impossible to see in public, it just meant you were sloppy rich. But even the wealthy didn't have humanoid mechs of Spindle's caliber. Spindle could pass for a man. If he had a face.

"Where are you going?" I asked.

"To the tagghet game with you." His eyelight focused on my mother; darker colors stormed his faceplate. "Have you not told him?"

"I wanted it to be a surprise," she said, on her way to the bedroom.

"Are you disappointed, Master Socket?"

"Am I... no! No, I'd love for you to come. I just... uh..."

"What is it?"

"I just was wondering why you're dressed like a commando."

He pulled the hood over his face. The eyelight dimmed until it was difficult to see the featureless aspect of his faceplate. He showed his hand, front then back. The silver tinge sparkled, then darkened to a healthy tan.

"It will lessen the burden of attention. We can enjoy some privacy in the crowd."

He was wearing pants and a shirt, boots and coat in South Carolina. People would avoid us, all right. The cops, however, might want to ask some questions.

"You look psycho," I said.

"Wonderful! I am so looking forward to experiencing a public school tagghet event in South Carolina. I have heard so much about the fans' fervor, and Master Chute is quite good. Currently, she holds the national record for female taggers in assists and single-game goals."

She does?

"She is currently ranked in South Carolina's top ten taggers. It will be quite a joy to see her play tonight, and I know her!" He tilted his head. "I would expect you to know these details about her. She is your girlfriend, after all."

"You're probably right."

"Will Master Streeter be joining us?"

"Ummm... yeah, maybe."

He pumped his fist. "That is great news, also!"

Any other day, Streeter would love sitting next to a humanoid mech. In fact, he'd pull off Spindle's hood and show him off. Now, I don't think he'd give a rat's ass.

"I can prepare dinner," Spindle said. "You may relax, Master Kay."

Mother grinned. "That's all right, Spindle. I'd enjoy doing it myself. I think Socket would like to spend some time with you."

EVEN THOUGH SPINDLE was anatomically neutral, I still preferred he wear something when we sparred, so he stripped down to his shorts. His new body was quicker and stronger. By the time we were done wrestling, my clothes were soaked with sweat and I was aching. It only took three days to lose my edge.

"I like this new bodyshell." Spindle admired his hands. "It seems more capable."

He started doing tai chi in the center of the lawn, where we wore out the grass. His faceplate was frosty, with subtle hints of green. Perhaps the bodyshell was an upgrade, one that knew tai chi. Could I best him in the desert exercise with this one? Would he be crushed against a boulder this time?

"I had a dream after the pre-Trial exercise," I said.

"Oh, really?" he said, striking a pose. "What was it?"

"You had me pinned against the rock, pushing your hand through my shield. You were about to best me."

"That was not a dream."

"Yeah, well, then I saw something else. I saw this kid with his dad. I'd seen them a few days earlier when I went home to see Chute; they were at the tagghet game. But then I dreamed they were there, in the pre-Trial, standing right behind you. He kept asking if I was thirsty."

Spindle turned slowly. "That is very interesting."

"And then the kid's dad turned into my dad."

"Why do you think that is?"

"I don't know. I mean, I only saw the kid for like a second outside the tagghet game. You know what was even crazier? *I was thirsty.* The more I thought about it, the more I wanted a drink."

"And then you saw your father." Spindle stopped the meditative dance. "Perhaps you should investigate how you feel about this dream."

"I would, if I knew what really happened. You were about to beat me, the next thing I saw you smashed against a boulder." I pulled my shirt off and wiped my face. Spindle stood very still. "Maybe you can fill in the blanks."

"I cannot discuss this, Master Socket. Trainer Pon will address the occurrence when you return."

"Occurrence? So something happened."

He tipped his head. He'd already said too much. "I believe it is time to eat."

Spindle was through the door, helping Mom set the table.

Conversation over.

48

Back in the **Game**

I HADN'T SEEN the high school since it was destroyed by the duplicates' last stand a year ago. Some of the old live oaks had burned and the reconstruction was expansive. The building was wide, not tall, with green and tan colors that matched the countryside. The walls were made of triple-paned insulated fiberglass that could change colors and opacity, letting in more or less sunlight depending on the season and time of day. The Paladins paid for it all.

I parked far up the road and avoided the traffic. The last thing I needed was the Garrison getting a traffic summons. Besides, Spindle would annoy me all night if I parked illegally. I wanted him to enjoy the game. *I* wanted to enjoy the game.

All Spindle needed was a death sickle to complete the whole grim reaper look, but no one seemed to notice. There were already enough high school freaks to make him look normal. He couldn't get enough of them. *So much culture!*

"This is where you went to school?" Spindle asked.

"That's the place," I said. "I like to think of it as my *prison years.*"

"You were incarcerated?"

"No, it's just what it felt like."

Spotlights beamed up ahead into the low-lying cloud cover, bright enough to illuminate the dusky sky. I avoided walking through the parking lot, where we were sure to find problems. Rednecks, burners, and every other sort of troublemaker would be there. Lookits constantly cruised over the area and reported fights or any other suspicious activity, bringing security as needed, which was at every game. Years ago, it was a prime spot to score weed, speed or meth, but those were the drug days. Now specialized gear could induce a similar high, and no one would know the difference.

The school stadium was on par with Blackbaud. While the color scheme matched the school, it was two stories tall. The outside walls were open scaffolding, and spiraling ramps circled up each corner where people walked to the top.

The crowd funneled toward the main entrance. An arch curved over the gate, swirling with greens and tans and an animated fox mascot clenching his fists at the crowd. A bunch of guys ran past us, bumping into Spindle.

"My apologies," Spindle called.

A couple of them turned around, then turned again. They grabbed their buddies. Thankfully, the rest were too distracted by the girls ahead of them.

"Come on," I said. "We should get inside."

In front of the gates was a low, concrete pond with fountains, where little kids threw coins. A concrete pillar rose from the center of the water with the inscription, *In Memory*. The inscription left out what it was remembering, but everyone knew, they didn't need the words to know all this new stuff was in memory of *those lost in the attack,* when the duplicates launched their first and only public attack.

The fox mascot high-fived the fans. Teachers handed out programs and directed traffic. I didn't bother saying hi. None of the teachers remembered me. As we got closer to the gates, the crowd got tighter. *Look at that* and *it's a humanoid* murmured from those around us, but the line kept moving. We got to the gate without incident, but then a girl tugged on Spindle's hood.

"Hello." His eyelight spun around. "How are you?"

"What are you?"

"I am a—"

I grabbed his sleeve and yanked him onto the pedestrian ramp. "We're going to draw a crowd."

"I just want to be polite."

The girls followed. "Is he yours? What's his name? Hey! Don't be a jag, we just want to see him."

We got up the ramp before they slowed us down. I just wanted to be invisible, which usually wasn't a problem. I should've known this was going to happen.

"He's a prototype," I said. "No big deal."

"Who are you?" the girl said.

"Nobody."

"You don't go to school here, I can tell you that," she said, looking at my white hair.

"You're right."

"I like your coat." One of the girls had a hold of Spindle's sleeve.

"Do you really?" Spindle said. "It came recommended from a website on popular culture..."

"Spindle!" I stood on my toes and tried to whisper. "What're you doing?"

"Your name is Spindle?"

The girls were waving more people over. This needed to be addressed. I flooded their collective awareness with thoughts of boys and cars and food and homework. Their expressions emptied into the storm of pressing thoughts and the emotions that followed. Two seconds later, they were fixated on some boys and forgot they ever saw a one-eyed humanoid.

"From now on," I said, "let's be a little less polite and more invisible."

"I do not want to be rude."

"Just because you don't say hi, that doesn't mean you're rude."

We walked to the top of the ramp and through a short corridor. The stadium seats surrounded the entire field and enclosed skyboxes with black windows looking down from the top. The bleacher seats were steep and filling quickly.

A lookit floated down. *"Do not block corridor."*

I pulled Spindle along like a six-foot kid with attention deficit disorder. The crowd was less rowdy in the seats at the ends of the field, where green scoring cubes hovered off the ground inside bluish domes. We found seats near the top with people that looked like grandparents. Old people couldn't care less about humanoid mechs, and even less about freakishly dressed students. *Perfect.*

I nestled into the soft, moldable seat—no expense spared—and placed a program on the seat next to me, just in case Streeter showed up. A couple had their interactive program open in front of me, watching imbedded vid of their grandson scoring a cube from last season. Spindle's eyelight was bright again, scanning the crowd.

"Explain to me," he said, having to lean his head against mine to be heard over the crowd, "the various subcultures."

I described high school students and how like-minded personalities were attracted to each other and formed group mentalities. There were the gearheads, the bombers, crossers, and brainers, to name a few. I avoided explaining the burners and droppers since they were in the parking lot because then he'd want to know why they weren't supporting the team. I pointed to people I remembered, told him who used to hook up with who and who was popular and who wasn't. And why.

"What about those kids?" Spindle stood and pointed at the band of misfits walking down the aisle, all dressed in black. I yanked him down before they came over and made a scene.

"Those are bleeders," I said.

"They appear to have neck wounds." His eyelight brightened. "If they are not treated, they could become infected."

"Those aren't wounds, just fake tattoos on their necks to look like puncture wounds. It's a whole vampire thing."

"Vampires do not exist."

"Yeah, well, tell them." I stopped him before he did.

"I do not understand. If, in fact, vampires did exist, why would those boys and girls want to walk the earth as the undead?"

"Beats the hell out of me." I smacked his leg. "Kids these days, huh?"

"Which group did you belong to?" he asked.

"None of the above."

"You know what group I believe is right for you?" Spindle crossed his arms, surveying me with his red eyelight. "The potters."

"The what?"

"The potters." His eyelight dimmed, as if squinting. "Surely, there must be a gang of kids that follow the story of Harry Potter, the famous wizard of Hogwarts. It was a worldwide phenomenon."

"And you think I'd be in that group?"

"Why not, Master Socket? I can see it now, you and your friends dressed in your long, flowing robes and knobby wands at your sides, practicing spells between classes..."

"You lost your mind."

I looked over the edge of the stadium while Spindle continued on with his favorite Harry Potter book. I recalled the day when the duplicates attacked the world. I was wearing a dark hoodie, watching Chute in her very first tagghet game.

"You see that over there?" I interrupted Spindle's analysis of Professor Snape. "That's where the truck erupted."

His faceplate sparkled, recalling the incident from his database. He probably had a fully detailed account of the incident from lookit vids that captured the entire ordeal, but he listened to my firsthand account. How the eighteen-wheeled truck caught on fire. How the explosion destroyed the old bleachers and killed people. How the crawlers spewed from the flames like a volcano of freakish spiders, tossing parked vehicles to get to the school's portal underground to let the duplicates have access to virtualmode before they died.

Now, instead of the domed roof, there was a tower encircled with dark windows, like the school was looking in all directions. It was the

Paladins' clever design to remind the public we kept them safe. That we were always watching.

THE CROWD STOOD AND CHEERED. The Hilton Head Hightide rode onto the field on hovering jetter discs, swinging sticks curved at the end over their heads. The self-balancing jetters whizzed at dangerous speeds and the team circled the entire field before huddling at the opposite end.

"*Socket!*" Chute's voice rang in my head. "*Where are you?*"

"On the home team end, behind the goal at the top."

Whatever she said next was blotted out by the roar of the crowd. The Charleston Rapid Foxes blazed onto the field, sticks in the air. Their heads were projected as a hovering three-dimensional image as they hit the field. The players pumped their fists. They were twice as nimble as the last time I'd seen them.

Chute was the last one out and the crowd announced her arrival with an explosion of cheers and the signature *shhhhooooooooooot*. Her projected head looked in our direction with a bright smile. I stood on the seat and pulled Spindle up. *Wave, wave*, I told him, and Spindle raised his arms, bright colors dancing inside the hood. She saw us and pointed, but her teammates pulled her into the huddle. I was still standing when the crowd sat. And Spindle was still waving. I pulled his arms down.

They started pregame, doing a double figure-eight and passing three tags. They formed a large line at center pitch and, one at a time, flew toward the goal. Each person cut back and forth with their own display of evasion skills, taking a pass from the sideline and throwing it at the green cube inside the electromagnetized dome. The tag went through the dome and stuck in the cube. Some rode to the top of the dome and fired the tag through it.

Chute worked the jetter like it was an extension of her feet, cutting turns sharply, quickly and precisely. She executed a double-spin move, took the pass blindly with her stick behind her and bounced a shot off the ground that stuck in the center of the cube. *Sweet.*

The crowd was on its feet again.

"Should I wave?" Spindle asked.

"No!" I stood on the seat. "Just shout!"

Fans cupped their hands around their mouths. Spindle put his hands inside the hood and let out a baritone roar that shook the seats, sounding like a goddamn cargo ship. The entire section looked at us.

The energy was exhilarating. I called Streeter and got his voicemail, again.

"Locate." My nojakk reported he was there, at the school, *at the game!* "Where are you?" I said on his voicemail. "Spindle and I are sitting behind the home goal at the top! Get here before the tag drops!"

But as announcements were called and the teams took the field, Streeter's seat was still empty. The announcer's voice was barely audible over the crowd. A lookit hovered over the center pitch with the tag. A player from each team squared off underneath. Holographic numbers counted down over them. On zero, the tag dropped. The stadium shook. Another tagghet season was underway.

I called Streeter again without luck. I wasn't going to leave another message. There was little chance he'd find us in the madness. I called to locate him and get a closer look on his location. I could go get him while Spindle held the seats. He was so fixated on the game, he might not even notice I was gone.

"Locate Streeter." The noise was drowning out the volume in my head. I sat down and covered my ears, calling the command again.

"The recipient's GPS is blocked," it replied.

Streeter shut off his GPS since I left a message. He didn't want me to know where he was.

My neck was beginning to chill.

49

Void

STREETER WAS DEFINITELY LOSING his mind if he thought he could hide from me. Did he forget what Paladins can do?

I activated the imbed and felt it connect with my eyes. I was encouraged not to use it in public because my eyes would be brighter than normal, sometimes even sparkle if it was dark enough.

[Locate Streeter,] I thought.

A virtualmap platform of gridlines stacked in the air, then curved and formed a sphere. Blue oceans and terra firma developed and planet Earth was now rotating in front of me. The Paladin's version of Google Earth was finely detailed, but unlike Google, it was a live feed. The view zoomed into the United States, South Carolina, Charleston, and finally the stadium. A tiny figure was highlighted on the far end of the parking lot.

"Come on."

I pulled Spindle out of his seat and we pushed through the crowd. The imbed locked onto people as we passed and automatically downloaded their history, identifying objects with glowing outlines. Spindle didn't ask questions. He sensed the urgency in my step.

WHEN WE ENTERED the parking lot, the burners stared at us; their hair was no longer than mine, but it was knotty, unwashed and hanging in their eyes. One of them blew a long cloud of smoke at us. The distinctive smell of burning skin lingered in the smell of cigarettes, the sort of smell that would emanate from slow-roasting meat. That was the gear cooking their brains, ever so slowly. Most people wouldn't smell that, but most people didn't see what I could see. Or smell.

I didn't recognize any of these people from school, but the imbed immediately downloaded their histories along with names, whereabouts and criminal records. They were mostly small-time punks with dim futures, although some of them were good kids hanging around bad people. Small discs were tucked behind their ears that emitted a low drone and convinced their brains they were happy and good. They were burning on mood gear, cooking their brains like a meth lab.

We were heading for the low-riding black pickup truck parked in the grass with the tailgate down. Streeter had his back to us, talking to a guy with artificially tanned skin. His face was sort of shrink-wrapped over his cheekbones like he'd sucked on the end of a vacuum cleaner.

"This won't take long," I told Spindle.

He slowed his pace and let me approach the truck that reeked of cologne. I reached for Streeter as he put something in the tanned guy's hand.

"What're you doing over here?" I asked.

Streeter jumped back when I touched him and yanked his arm away, breathing heavily. There was another guy sitting on the tailgate that looked lean and dangerous with veins bulging down his forearms. He closed in on me, his muscles tensing. The imbed reported he was a mixed martial artist and a registered bodyguard.

"It's all right, Edward." Vacuumface put his hand up and karateman stopped; then he stared at me for several long seconds, keeping his hand up like he was holding back an attack dog but might change his mind. My reflection looked back from the black sunglasses. Most people wouldn't be able to see with lenses that dark, but he wore them to protect his eyes from light, not to look cool. Even moonlight was too bright for him.

His birth name was Patrick Black and he was a virtualmode dealer, a guy that pushed mood gear to the loitering burners. He was also called a void merchant because he helped people avoid their lives, to get rid of pain and seek pleasure. In reality, he helped them empty their lives until they were void of realness, but his victims wouldn't know what hit them. By the time they were strung out, they wouldn't know the difference between dream and reality. And Streeter was making a deal with him.

Vampires do exist, Spindle.

"My friend," Patrick said, flashing a pearly-white smile, "I'm afraid I only work by appointment. My assistant gets a little nervous when people barge in, you see. You'll have to wait your turn."

"I'm not here to see you. I only need a word with my friend."

"Well, then you and I are mutual friends. Mr. Street and I have spent a lot of time together as of late."

Streeter sort of cringed and turned away.

"My name is Mr. Black." Patrick extended his hand. I didn't shake it. Edward the watchdog twitched. Patrick only smiled.

"No offense, Mr. Black, but I only need a second and I'll be out of your way soon enough."

"No problem. I see you have urgent business and I wouldn't want to be a burden, but you see we're in the middle of an exchange." He held up the item that Streeter had placed in his hand. "Mr. Street has given me something that I desire and I wish to reimburse him for it."

My imbed deciphered the marble as he rolled it up and down his fingers like a magician. What looked like a child's plaything was actually a complex piece of gear that would allow someone to codebreak encryptions. Mr. Black was not likely to use such a device for the betterment of mankind. And Streeter would know that. *Why would he do that?*

"If you'll allow me just a moment to verify the contents," Mr. Black said, "I'll be done before you can lick your lips."

He stared a moment longer. I had the feeling he was staring at my eyes and I was suddenly aware of my imbed's effect on them. Patrick held the marble out to Edward without looking away. Edward took it around to the cab of the truck.

Patrick's cologne stung my nostrils, but it still wasn't strong enough to mask the smell of his burning skin that emanated from tiny discs buzzing behind his ears. His stink was worse than any of the other burners because he'd been doing it for so long. A real veteran of gear addiction, he smelled like summer roadkill.

I turned to Streeter. "You all right?"

He wouldn't look directly at me, but I could see his enlarged pupils and the inflamed ring around his irises. He wasn't in Charleston the other day seeking help. He was with Patrick, but for what? Streeter had everything he needed at home, why would he go to a void merchant? He knew this guy was a new-age heroin dealer, giving his clients free mood discs until they were hooked. Maybe this was more about addiction than his dead parents.

"Mr. Street is quite a talented codebreaker, wouldn't you agree?" Patrick said.

"What're you doing here?"

I didn't mean here in the parking lot or dealing gear. I wanted to know why he bothered leaving virtualmode to come back to his rotting skin. He knew exactly what I meant, but it didn't faze his fake smile. Only made it grow.

"I like to get back to the skin every once in a while," he said. "Mix it up a bit."

More burners were near us, most of them staring at Spindle. They were all teenagers.

"Why don't you go somewhere else, recruit your own kind, not these people," I said. "They're just kids."

"My friend, I don't need to recruit; they line up for my services. Like children at an ice-cream truck. They need what I have."

"You're making them that way."

He frowned. "I haven't done anything. I've only extended my hand; they simply take what's in it."

"You know exactly what you're doing."

"Yes, I do. I'm giving them what they want. Tell me, where is the crime in that? How am I responsible?"

"They don't know what they want."

He gestured to the crowd that seemed to be waiting for us to be done, to have their turn. The smell of smoldering flesh grew stronger.

"Clearly, they do," Patrick said.

Edward came back around and nodded, then fixed his stare on me. Patrick took a red disc from his pocket and held it between his finger and thumb. Streeter reached for it, but Patrick snatched it back.

"We had a deal," Streeter muttered through thin lips.

"I'm curious." He gestured to Spindle. "Tell me about the mech, first."

"He's not for sale," I said.

"I see." He nodded for a while, studying Spindle while he rolled the disc in his fingers, purposely tempting Streeter until he started to fidget. Patrick pushed off the tailgate and circled around Spindle, tugging at the ridiculous overcoat.

I scanned the security lookits through my imbed. Normally, they would've made a few passes through this area by now, but I hadn't seen one since leaving the stadium. It appeared they had been reprogrammed to avoid Patrick while he did business. No doubt, he had the gear to do that sort of thing, so I reset the security paths. One would be around within minutes.

"Very impressive." Patrick peeked into Spindle's hood. "Where do you get one like this?"

"My parents are rich."

"Oh, I've got money, my friend. Surely, you have a price. Everyone has a price."

"I've got everything I need."

"Perhaps your friend has a price?" He went to Streeter and looked down on him. "Mr. Street seems to need something?"

"Listen, there's a lookit coming this way in another minute," I said. "We're done here."

Streeter wasn't about to leave until he got what he came for. And Patrick didn't seem concerned about the incoming lookit, and even less concerned how I knew it was coming.

"You promised," Streeter growled. "I did what you asked, now give it to me."

"Of course, my friend, I will give you what you want. First, I need you to give me what I want."

"I did."

He put his arm around Streeter and stroked his cheek, whispering, "My wants have changed."

I closed in on Patrick. Edward met me there and the four of us stood uncomfortably close like we were about to dance. I pulled Streeter to the side. "We're finished, Mr. Black."

Patrick held up the glittering red disc like a valuable jewel. Streeter was visibly shaking.

"I offer access to dreams," Patrick said.

"Not interested," I said.

"Mr. Street is terribly interested, I'm afraid to say. You see, he wants what I have, what everyone wants." He took Streeter's hand and placed the item in his palm, gently closing his fingers around it. "He wants his heart's desire."

The lookit arrived and did a slow loop overhead, its eyelight pointed at us. Patrick watched it but spoke to me. "You see, I'm doing nothing illegal, my friend. I'm giving people their dreams. Can you do that? Can you make their dreams come true?"

Streeter pushed through the crowd and ran through the parking lot. Patrick pulled his glasses down his nose. His enlarged pupils had nearly swallowed the whites of his eyes, reflecting the headlights behind me. If I could take this guy out, there would just be another one to take his place. How could I argue with him? What people wanted was to fulfill their emotional and physical desires, to get happy and get rid of weakness. To not be afraid. There would always be someone like him to sell that to them, even if the price was steeper than they could ever imagine.

"Maybe we'll meet again, my friend." He flicked his hand at me, as if he'd given me permission to leave.

Spindle and I left the crowd without incident. The scent of charred skin faded behind us. The only way I'd see that cockroach again was if Streeter came back. And I intended to put a stop to that.

50

THE KEY

HOLOGRAPHIC FIREWORKS EXPLODED above the stadium, followed by the announcer shouting above the roar of the crowd.

CHHHUUUUUUUUTTE!

"Wait, Streeter." I caught up to him just as he was leaving the parking lot.

"Go away."

"What're you doing? This isn't like you." I stepped in front of him, but he cut around. "Where are you going?"

"Home."

His lips were tight, and there were too many lines around his eyes. He was lying.

I caught up again. Spindle was trailing behind. "I want to know where you think you're going."

"You deaf? I'm going home."

"No bullshit, Streeter," I said flatly. "Where you going?"

He shut down, marching toward the front of the school with a distant stare.

"What'd Mr. Black give you?"

"Candy. Chocolate-covered candy. Now, can I go home and eat it, or do you want me to share?"

He was squeezing the object in his hand like he was hanging on for his life. I chopped his hand as his arm swung back and the disc dropped in the grass. I picked it up. The center was ruby red, glittering with depth. My imbed read the contents, drawing its data inside and deciphering the code. It was an access key to a moody den in downtown Charleston.

"Give it back."

"Just tell me what's going on." I tossed it back. "I want to help."

"You want to help? Then get out of my way."

"Seriously, just tell me why you're going there." I put my hand on his chest and he finally stopped. "That's all I want to know."

He rubbed the ruby center with his thumb and sighed, looking off in the distance. Maybe it was my touch, or just someone finally caring about where he was at and what he was going through.

"It's just a gear booster, that's all," he said. *Lie.* "My home gear is junking, I need more dataflow to, you know, go to that one... place."

"Back to the gates?"

He nodded.

"I thought you were going to get help?"

"I will," he said. "After."

"I don't think you should go."

"Yeah, well, it's my life."

"That's a key, Streeter. It's not a gear booster."

"Then why'd you ask? Look, if you want to stop me, fine; go ahead and stop me. I don't give a fuck because in another week you'll be gone and I'll go get another one." He threw the thing at me. "Keep that for a souvenir."

"How can you do this? That guy's a void merchant. You'll be hooked."

"I'll take the chance."

"You want to be one of them?"

He rubbed his eyes with the heel of his hand. "I got to do what I got to do."

I dropped my hand and he didn't run. He just stared down.

"You don't know what that's like," he said. "I got to see my parents and I'll do whatever I got to do."

The key twinkled, like it agreed.

"Your parents are gone, Streeter. You're still alive; don't do this to yourself. You got to let it go."

He looked off to the side and sort of laughed. "Man, I at least thought *you'd* understand."

"My old man is gone, Streeter. I know that. I don't need to spend time on a memory. You got to face the facts, you're addicted to gear. Don't let a memory ruin your life."

He was nodding and, for a moment, looked like he was considering what I said. He was trying to go somewhere that didn't exist anymore. He was trying to go back home, back to a time when he was a little boy and his mom and dad were still around. But that was a memory and he was here and now. He couldn't throw his life away for something that didn't exist.

"Give me the key, I'll use it now or I'll get one for later. Either way, I'm going and you can't stop me. It's my life. Go live your own."

"Forget it." I clenched my fist. "I'll assign a Paladin sentry wherever that key leads. I'll send doctors to your house, if that's what it takes. I'm not letting you do it."

I couldn't do any of those things. He knew it.

His energy swirled darkly around him with waves of blue and violet, saturated with grief. His chest heaved.

"I don't have anyone," he whispered. "You know that? I'm all alone. I just got some things to say to my folks, that's all. I know that doesn't make sense to you, you don't have to feel, but I... I do. I just think, maybe, things will be easier if I see them one last time. That's all I'm asking."

"This is wrong; you need help. I know it stinks, but sometimes the right thing smells like shit."

"If it smells like shit," he said, "it's shit, Socket."

Halftime had arrived and it seemed like half the crowd was walking past us, laughing and having a good time, but whispering after they passed. They recognized Streeter, the school's virtualmode king, the number one codebreaker, slumped over on the front steps with some white-haired stranger and a goofy trench-coat man. *Stranger.* Is that what I'd become? A cold-blooded asshole?

He wiped his nose and eyes.

The facts were this: He was going. Now or later. I'd rather be with him if he was going to do this. I could protect him if I was there, but if he went alone, there was no telling what would happen.

"Promise you'll get help after this?" I held up the key.

He nodded.

"I mean real help. Like a family counselor and gear-addiction therapy. I mean it, I'll tell my mother to send the best doctors."

"Yeah," he said, nodding, looking up. "Yeah, I'll do it."

I sent Spindle to fetch the car.

Streeter sat on the step, deflating with relief. I stood in front of him, warding off stares of curiosity, until the black sedan pulled up.

51

JUDGMENT DAY

THERE WASN'T a lot of talking.

Streeter sat in the passenger seat. His fingers twittered on his leg like his hand was trying to run away. In the window's reflection, his eyes didn't look at anything in particular.

It was stop-and-go traffic until we reached downtown's historic marketplace, a long narrow building that extended for blocks, where vendors peddled T-shirts, fragrance and sweetgrass baskets to cash-heavy tourists. I found parking halfway down the market in front of an outdoor café, the exact one Chute and I were destined for a week earlier. Streeter sat quietly. Fingers running.

"You sure you want to do this?" I asked.

He nodded and got out.

"Stay here." I turned to Spindle in the backseat. "Pull the hood tight and don't move. Stay vigilant. I'll be back as soon as possible."

"Yes, Master Socket."

I locked the car. Streeter was fidgeting on the curb. "You know where we're going?"

"There's a moody club around the corner. The virtualmode den is in the back."

"We're not old enough."

He held the disc between his fingers. "We are now."

Streeter led the way. We worked our way around tourists gawking through windows and licking gigantic ice cream cones. We got to the end of the market and turned the corner, where bars and restaurants lined the street, the doors open to the sidewalk.

A five-star hotel was on the corner. Nothing but suits and dresses sat in the first-floor restaurant with padded menus that didn't have prices. Next door, techno music thumped where singles got their freak on. Sandwiched in-between the five-star restaurant and techno bar was a door with peeling red paint. A barrel-shaped man sat on a stool in front of this door.

Streeter held out the disc. It took the man a moment to even see him. He scrunched his face like he was about to tell him to beat it until he saw the disc. He looked twice, thought about smacking Streeter for the hell of it, then pressed the disc into the palm of his glove. He handed it back and simply nodded.

Above the red door, in small, old-school neon lights, was a sign. *Judgment Day.* Behind the door was a flight of stairs. Streeter took a hesitant step inside and I followed. The door slammed behind us, sealing out the traffic and music like a tomb. The stairwell smelled like five hundred years of mold and made my head light as if memories of the building tried to get inside me. A single light bulb hung at the top of the steps. Someone had gouged *Stairway to Heaven* into the first step.

The walls were smeared with graffiti. Most were names immortalized with the tip of a knife or a Sharpie, or just statements of who loved who forever and ever. Then there was one that hit me. *Paladins Feed on the World.* And if that wasn't clear enough, *Paladins Suck Ass.*

I wanted to put my fist through the wall. Without the Paladin Nation, the world would be dead. And they embraced the enemy? Pon's voice echoed from somewhere deep in my brain.

We don't ask for permission to serve.

At the top of the steps, another man on another stool. Not as round, but just as big. He stared at us all the way to the top. Streeter held out the disc. He pressed it to his glove without taking his eyes off Streeter.

He nodded, then held the disc up like a communion wafer. Streeter, unsure, plucked it from his fingers. The guy didn't move. The door behind him was old and peeling, too, but this one had a crystal doorknob. Streeter put his hand on it, turning it slowly. *Heaven's inside.*

The room inside was reddish, long and narrow. A bar was along the left wall. A bartender leaned on the polished surface; another guy was on a barstool. His tie was loose. He had no drink.

Booths were along the right, filled with people. Most were young, some were locals. They had their fingers dipped in a black saucer in the center of each table. Some had their heads back, some slumped over, their eyes glassy and aimless. *Moody bowls.* Unlike the moody discs Patrick was dealing, moody bowls were legal mood enhancers. *The body's natural opiate. Make life feel better, dip into a moody bowl today.*

The government ruled years ago that moodies were no more dangerous or addictive than a cup of coffee. "It's just a little escape," the woman in the commercial used to say, with her frizzy hair and crying baby. "Who doesn't need a vacation now and then?" She looked back at the baby, then put her thumb in a small moody bowl. Her eyes closed. "I know I do."

The booths had teenagers and adults, some with clothes that needed washing, and others looked like lawyers or doctors. They could've been my next-door neighbors. Escape had them mesmerized, escaping whatever they were running from. They tricked the brain to boot out good feelings, that the world was all right, just like it was when they were kids watching their favorite show. *I love you, you love me...*

The crowd in the middle of the room was more sophisticated. They belonged in a five-star restaurant instead of the moody den. They sat at elevated tables or stood in groups, swaying to the soft notes of a piano playing somewhere in the back. They smiled and laughed, speaking in hushed tones. They all looked around every few seconds, like they were waiting for something.

We politely worked our way around the tables and between the well-to-do people that ignored us like kitchen help. One lady grabbed my hair and let it fall between her fingers. "Nice hair," she said. Her pupils were enlarged, but she still had irises. Not yet a void, but on her way.

There was a doorway on the back wall and a silver podium facing it. A woman walked out of the doorway as if the archway was a solid outline on the wall. *Like Garrison technology.* A gentleman and his date shoved past us without an apology. He placed a disc similar to Streeter's on the podium. The silver surface absorbed it and the doorway started glowing. The couple rushed through it.

Streeter approached the podium next. There was no one stopping him. He did like the guy before him and the doorway responded. He took a deep breath and looked back, then walked through it like a curtain of water. Gone.

I went through the cold archway and stepped next to Streeter into a tiny elevator room. There was slight nausea in my belly and the atmosphere became slightly more humid and cooler. The wall lit again.

This is a leaper! They have access to Paladin technology!

Streeter took another long breath, but I stepped through the lit wall first.

THIS ROOM WAS gray and damp, mold in the corners, big enough for a bunk bed and two chairs. The stench shot up my nose, like something rotten hovered just below a heavy dose of sterilizing solution. The mattresses were bare with large yellowish stains. Stains layered upon stains. Empty life-support jacks on the wall were options for long-term virtualmode living, lines that would pump nutrition into veins for weeks, months or however long a client's bank account held up.

Putrid memories haunted the room. No joy ever remained, yet the promise of such was always present.

"I know what you're thinking," Streeter said, his voice wavering. "But I'm not here for a long trip." He sat in a chair, sinking in as the ultra-molding pads reformed to his body.

"You're not using their transporters, are you?"

"I have to." He took two discs off the table between the chairs and slid a transparent film over them. "But this will sterilize them."

He was lucid enough, not too desperate, to realize that transporters in a void-ridden place like this would have leacher technology that gave the user a *taste* of that connection and left him wanting more. People thought heroin was addictive? Try leacher gear that left an imprint on your brain, like a permanent brand with instructions to come back for more. No cure for that and guaranteed repeat customers. Ask those that pissed on the mattresses.

"I've got extra sterilizers for you," he said.

"No, thanks." I tapped the back of my neck. "I've got an imbed."

Under normal circumstances, he'd want to know everything about imbed technology. He'd heard of it, so what was it like? When could he get it? But he didn't flinch. He pressed the transporters behind his ears and lay back. Unlike the moody discs that the burners placed behind their ears, the transporter discs pulled Streeter's awareness from his skin into virtualmode. I sat in the chair —the remnant energy of all the addicts that sat in it before me crawled over my skin like ants—and activated my imbedded portal.

I LEFT my skin and arrived at the Gates of the Dead. Streeter was already there. For the first time ever, he was in a sim that looked like his actual skin body, back when it was plump and healthy. I felt hopeful.

Leaves crunched under my feet. I stepped next to him, looking into the black depths between the bars.

"I didn't plan on this happening." His gaze was blank. "But when I saw them..." He swallowed.

"I understand." I didn't understand, but he needed to hear that.

"When I saw them, something snapped inside me." Focus returned to his eyes. "You ever seen your dad?"

I shook my head.

"You should try it," he said. "It'll fuck you up, bro."

The gates opened. The blackness behind them swirled and details took shape. Streeter took one deep breath and marched through them. Grass sprouted under our feet. Live oaks from before the time of the Civil War lined the large expanse of turf. Traffic cruised outside of that. Tourists were looking over the wall at crashing waves, and a barge loaded with containers slowly cruised into the harbor. We were standing at Battery Park, right downtown, where tourists could see Fort Sumter across the harbor.

Streeter was stoic, eyes fixed straight ahead. The park was filled with the usual crowd. A couple college guys were tossing a Frisbee and some kids were throwing food to the seagulls. Streeter watched it like a movie.

"This world is addictive." He held out his hands, turning them over. "The details are better than anything I've ever seen. I can smell the ocean and feel the breeze, like I'm really here. You start to forget what's real."

"The Battery is just three blocks away in the skin. Let's get out of here and go."

He pointed. "They won't be there."

On the far side of the park, a couple was holding hands. They walked at a leisurely pace. I recognized them from a picture in Streeter's house; it sat on a shelf in the den, right above his grandfather's desk. Streeter was two years old, sitting on the beach with the tide rushing in. His dad had curly hair and a big round face, what his grandfather called swarthy. His mother had blond hair and her lips were red; she smiled big and there was lipstick smudged on her teeth.

Streeter always said that was his favorite picture. I never knew why, it wasn't all that flattering, but then after a while I got it: It was real. Nothing pretend about it; those were real people with their son at the beach. The same two people walking across the park.

"You see, this is where the trip always ends," Streeter said. "I see them across the park." His father, still a hundred yards out, waved at us. "They wave. Then it ends, the world goes black and I end up back at the gates, starting all over. You know what it would cost for me to get closer?"

"By the look of that crowd in the lobby, I'd say half a million."

"Close." His lower lip started to tremble. "The security of this world is tight, I couldn't hack my way past that point without paying, and I ain't got half a mil cooling in my pocket. And once I got a taste, I couldn't stop. I went night after night, trying to codebreak the security, just so I could get a little closer, but I couldn't pull it off. I stripped the safety features off my gear. I know it's dangerous—that I've started gear addiction. I stopped going to school because if Mr. Buxbee saw me, he'd lock me up. I'll go to detox, Socket, I swear I will. But not until after."

They were fifty yards out. His mother waved this time. Streeter made an odd sound, like he got punched in the stomach, started to reach for his face, and seemed unsure about what to do.

"I made a deal with the devil, Socket. I wrote some difficult code to get this key and Mr. Black is going to use it to rob some innocent people with it. But I had to, you understand?" His eyes were wet. "I just had to."

I squeezed his shoulder. *I understand.*

He took a step, slow and frightened that the trip would end. When the ground was still under his feet, he took another. On the third, he was running. His parents put their arms out. Streeter crashed into them. He buried his face between them, his body convulsing. They hugged him tight, held him an arm's distance away like long-lost ones trying to see what their boy had become. Streeter was trying to talk, but just made weird sounds. He was in a full-on meltdown.

I was feeling it, too. I felt guilt mixed with relief. Guilt for not understanding. Relief he found what he needed. Guess there was a lot more buried in him than I thought.

Flicker.

The world crinkled.

I grabbed a bench for support. Streeter was still there. His parents, too. But the traffic was gone, so was the water.

Flick, fiililckkkk.

I lost contact with my sim, floating in the in-between. I pulled my awareness back into my skin and sat up. My nostrils had soured in the room's rancid odor. Streeter was still in virtualmode, tears streaming down his face. The doorway to the leaper was glowing.

"Socket?"

"Chute!" I touched my nojakk cheek.

"Is Streeter all right?"

His lips were moving, tears still flowing. "Yeah," I said. "He's going to be all right."

A cold chill leaked down my neck, voices gurgling. My body was alight with tension, the timeslicing spark dancing in my belly. I shook my head to clear the confusion. I couldn't leave Streeter, but I was pulled in forty directions. I bent over, closed my eyes and held my head together. Chute was saying something.

"...glad Streeter's with you. Where are you?"

I was going to answer. I was thinking of meeting her down at the market, at the outdoor café. Streeter, maybe he would be up for telling her about it. We could reconnect, all three of us.

The chill froze my neck, harder than ever.

The voices.

Heeee's in there is what it said. Or maybe Chute said it.

"What?" I answered.

Chute said something, but I couldn't hear through the voices. I needed to hear what that cold chill was telling me. It was Streeter's voice; was he speaking on the nojakk? No, it was... from somewhere else, some time else...

CRACK-flash.

It was a blunt object. A club.

The back of my head.

I sensed it, at the last second, and tried to slow time. But the world spun.

My face numb.

I had face-planted into the floor. Blood gushed through my lips to the back of my throat. There were people in the room, like a dozen, swimming back and forth. I couldn't count them all. Maybe three. I just couldn't... focus. I flopped over; Streeter was in the chair, oblivious to what was going on. I squeezed time to stop it, but couldn't get a grip. There was little feeling in my body.

A tanned face hovered over me. "Hello, friend," he said, his voice far away. "You didn't think I could smell a fucking Paladin?"

I tried to sit up, but the bottom of a boot knocked me down. The back of my head exploded on the floor.

Time?

There was only a brown face in front of me. No details. No room. Just a smudgy face. Someone spat. Something wet splattered on my cheek. "We don't fear the Paladin Nation."

My lips were too fat, but they tried, quaking and bubbling. Couldn't get them to work. I couldn't utter a single word, couldn't send a single lucid thought to Spindle sitting safely in the car. Couldn't do anything but let the dead silence of my confusion flounder. I managed a sound, but it was nothing.

"Call all you want." The face receded. "We've isolated your communications. No nojakk, no thoughts, no nothing. It's just you, now. Deep underground. You're in our world, friend. And you're not going home. Not tonight."

My lips, fat and bloated, split as I smiled. *They cut my communications.*

Commotion in the room.

My communication is my lifeline. If there's no lifeline...

Something crashed on the wall. A body fell over me.

Screams.

He hears my heartbeat.

Silence.

When he can't hear it...

A silver face hovered over me.

...he comes.

"We are leaving, Master Socket."

52

Drown

IT WAS like a throbbing metal rod had been rammed up my nose. Pain and pressure rhythmically spread over my face.

The bridge of my nose, broken. My cheek, fractured. They had to secure two of my front teeth and reattach nerves along with bone mending. I was told that was what happened on the first day. I only remembered half of the second. On the third day, I woke to the brutal reality of a broken face.

"You have been denied pain control," they told me. "Orders from Trainer Pon."

Pon still hadn't returned from Pike's relocation, but he was giving orders. There was no explanation with them, but then again there didn't need to be. *Deal with pain.* Oh, and that was what you get for being a fuckup. You get pain. *I told you that you can't go home. Should've listened.*

I SAT up in bed and my sinuses swelled. I paused before my face exploded. Mother could override this order to keep me in pain if she took it high enough, but then what? I had to deal with it on my own, that was what Pon was teaching me. I started to grind my teeth, resisting Pon's apparent wisdom, but this only sent a spike through my brain. I don't know what I hated more: When Pon was right, or when it hurt this much. *Both.*

I took a cup of water from the nightstand without leaning over. I wasn't sure if I had the balance to keep myself upright if my momentum started in any one direction. My throat was parched from breathing through my mouth. I chugged the water in three gulps.

What a joke.

I was nearly destroyed by a goddamn void merchant, a piece of shit that rarely came back to the skin. Face it, if Spindle wasn't there, they never would've found me. And Pon was training me to go into the world to save it? *I can't even save myself.*

No matter how much I wanted to deny it, I was still human. I still had emotions and I was still fucked up. Maybe I was too hard on Streeter. I mean, I got every expert in the world, maybe the universe, to help me deal with daily problems, and look at me: I'm racked up in the infirmary. Streeter was on his own, dealing with emotions that didn't make sense the only way he knew how. And not just Streeter, all those burners in the parking lot and those people dipping into a moody bowl, they just wanted to ease the pain and emptiness of life, that was all. What chance did those people have if I was still an idiot with a more evolved race of humans at my disposal?

Pain is part of life, Pon would say. *There's much to learn from it.*

Once my head found peace with the upright position, I touched my feet on the floor and eased my weight forward. The pulsing pain diminished. It was getting from horizontal to vertical that hurt.

I was in a one-bed infirmary with a single window. The view was projected from the side of the Garrison's sheer-face wall that faced the wormhole that led back to South Carolina. The sun was high and the grass shivered in the breeze. I asked Mother for the view. I needed something that would remind me of the way home because I was pretty sure I'd never see it again.

"The commander is very disappointed," she told me.

She had paced at the foot of my bed. I'd let the commander down. Let the Paladin Nation down. Worst of all, I let her down. She trusted me.

"You went into a known duplicate-sympathizing club *with Streeter!*" she said. "How irresponsible!"

The graffiti. The leaper. And the bouncer at the top of the steps was running an imbedded portal. And Patrick? Those weren't headlights I saw reflecting in his pupil-engorged eyes, that was a sparkling imbed. He knew exactly who I was and where I came from the second I arrived.

I should've aborted the whole thing, but no one was going to understand. Streeter was going in there and I wasn't stopping him. I took a chance and failed. Streeter's life was not worth the life of a Paladin cadet, my superiors might believe. Ordinary people were as common as raindrops. A Paladin was rare. Do the math, Socket. You made the wrong choice.

"Streeter?" I had asked. "He's okay, right?"

Mother had stopped her pacing. "Yes."

"Can I talk to him?"

"You are not allowed communication with Streeter. Or Chute."

The emptiness of her expression spoke volumes. Pon had total control now. She once had the advantage, but that was long gone now. *You're too emotionally involved, Kay. You will be allowed to check on Socket, but Pon now has complete authority to squash him like a mosquito. Sorry about that, but it's his fault.*

Pon's first order: a heaping dose of pain. Let Socket reap the harvest of his mistake and feel each nerve cry. And forget about home. Not even pictures. All he gets is training, starting now. Welcome home to that.

Spindle entered the room. "How are you feeling?"

"Fantastic."

He was back to wearing the purple overcoat swishing around his ankles. He held my face gently with both hands. "Let me take a look," he said.

His eyelight cruised over my face. He touched the back of my head and let his fingertips softly brush over my cheeks. A few colors danced in his faceplate while he evaluated my recovery. I could see my reflection. Purples and blacks darkened my eyes and my nose had doubled in size. I looked like I'd kissed a train.

"Have you heard from Chute and Streeter?" I asked.

"Mmmm." He continued examining. "They have sent messages."

"Will I see them?"

"Pon will not release them."

"What'd they say?"

"Streeter is getting help for his gear addiction. He thanked you a dozen times, Master Socket, and apologized for getting you in trouble another dozen." His eyelight focused on my eyes. "He is truly grateful for your friendship."

Then the facelift was worth it.

"Chute is thankful, as well," he said. "She cannot wait to see you."

Maybe Pon should let her know that'll never happen. I doubt Spindle should've summarized the messages, but maybe Pon wasn't specific about not telling me what the message was.

"She set a state record that night," Spindle said. "She scored a single game high for scores. I believe that should make you proud. She is quite an athlete."

Maybe Pon was right, it was better I didn't hear these things. It hurt worse than my face.

"Well, then." Spindle stepped to the doorway. "Your healing is coming along nicely, although a bit painful, I believe."

"The understatement of the year," I said, trying not to move my lips.

"Trainer Pon would like to see you in the training room."

"Now?"

"Time is scarce. The Realization Trial will not be rescheduled. You have fifteen days."

If it wasn't apparent no one was doing me favors yet, it was now. Train, no matter how swollen your face.

I WAS in the middle of the training room, again, waiting for the teacher to appear. This time with my nerve endings on fire.

It hurt to have my hair pulled back in a ponytail, so I let it hang over my face. Forget awareness and the present moment, I just wanted the pain to go away. Standing at attention was not helping.

Maybe Pon would understand. I was helping someone in need. Okay, so I fucked things up, but I'm still a cadet. We could put the scenario back together; it would give me a chance to analyze it.

I paced around, trying to stay one step ahead of my thoughts, but they trailed behind like cans tied to strings. I focused on breathing, letting the thoughts rise and drift, but there were so many of them. Thoughts about Streeter and Chute, Pon and this godforsaken place. The weight of the mountain felt like it was sitting squarely on my chest. I took a deep breath, but the pressure wouldn't let up.

Pon popped out of the floor and startled me. I went back to the center, where I should've been. I blew at my hair hanging over my eyes.

He was rigid. His hands were not behind his back but crossed over his chest. And his posture was slightly askew, his shoulders thrown back a few degrees. I expected utter disappointment on his face, perhaps disgust. But he was void of any of that. He was expressionless.

He gazed at my midsection. Pon rarely looked anywhere but my eyes. They revealed more than any word or movement. His gaze was unfocused, slightly hazy. Deep in thought.

"When I was twelve," he said, "I watched three boys drown."

What?

He swung his foot to the side, took three paces, turned, and paced back.

"Perhaps they swam too far out into the ocean or a riptide carried them, it did not matter. Their heads were barely above the water and they were waving for help. I imagine they were calling, but I could not hear their voices over the surf. One second I could see them, the next they would disappear behind a wave and then they were back."

He stopped at the end of his pacing and bounced the tips of his splayed fingers in front of his chest.

"I calculated how far out they were, the weight of their bodies and the energy I would need to bring them back. I knew I was not capable of saving them, and had I gone, I would have drowned as well. So I watched them bob in the ocean until they did not reappear."

The pain receded in my focus. Something wasn't right.

"There was quite a commotion after their deaths. The community was saddened and I felt disgusted with my inaction. But as the days passed, I realized guilt was a useless emotion. I could not save those boys. My death would not have justified their deaths anymore than standing there. And how I felt about it, how anyone *felt* about it, was pointless."

"You could've tried."

He stopped mid-stride. "You cannot save everyone, cadet."

"I'm saving the ones that want to be saved."

He nodded, but still looked at the floor. He resumed his one-man parade.

"The Paladin Nation has asked that I terminate your training. Your failure to act responsibly and capably was reprehensible. You are not fit to be a Paladin, regardless of your aptitude."

"Fine."

"You believe it is that simple, mmm? That you can return to your former life? You would prefer that?"

I didn't answer.

The room shifted, forming objects and colors and bodies. A long bar took shape to my left and booths on the right. Men and women emerged at elevated tables around us, all frozen in a lifeless moment.

The Judgment Day club had been resurrected to the very moment I had entered it with Streeter. Pon stood in front of a woman and touched her face. She was the one that touched my hair.

"This woman identified you as a Paladin cadet and confirmed your identity. A year of training and you could not assess this simple action? You cannot perform a simple task on your own?" He brushed the wrinkles from her shoulders carefully. "You will not waste any more of my time."

"Then be done with me."

"Even now, you react. You let your emotions guide you."

"Maybe those kids wouldn't have drowned if you did the same."

"If I did the same, I wouldn't be here today to save you."

"Maybe one of them would."

He looked at me for a second. His eyes were glassy. He looked away, pacing between the still-formed crowds; the reddish light from the bar cast strange color onto his cheeks.

"You cannot act upon what feels good or bad, cadet. Emotions will betray you."

"I should be a calculator, is that it?" I said. "Add up the numbers and see what lives are worth saving and which ones aren't. How much is a Paladin life worth, Pon? Ten ordinary people? Twenty? You need to give me that formula so I'll know when it's worth swimming out."

"There's no formula. As I have trained you for the past year, the present moment contains all existence. Just listen. Learn to listen to the present moment, do not tell it how you feel about it."

I slammed my fist on a round table, spilling a drink. "I DID WHAT THE MOMENT REQUIRED!"

"Your friend is responsible for his own life."

"He needed help."

"You failed," Pon said simply.

"I saved a life, isn't that what we're trained to do?"

He picked up the fallen glass and gently placed it on the table. "Your friends will forget you."

"They won't."

"You will become a ghost in their memories. They will recall a childhood friend, but they will not remember your face. They will not remember the sound of your voice or the touch of your hand."

"She won't forget."

"You are slipping from the memories of all that knew you, shedding your old life, preparing for a new one. Your loved ones will be the last to hold onto that memory, but even they will forget. In the end, you will be alone."

Pressure gripped my chest. I forced myself to breathe.

"You cannot have attachments. Would you have saved your friend if you did not know him?"

No, I wouldn't walk a stranger up to that room. But what if they were all strangers? What if no one remembered me, who did I save then? How did I decide?

The energy in the room shifted. Pon walked past me with his hands at his sides. His gait changed. The steps became shorter, his balance lowered. Tension rippled up his arms, over his shoulders. I brushed the evolvers on my belt, turned my hips toward him and analyzed the room and the contents for position. Pressure clamped my chest; my breath wheezed in my throat. *Is this an exercise?*

"Do you know what it feels like to drown?" Pon paused at the bar. "There is panic, at first, when you realize that death is imminent. Thoughts seize the muscles. You fight to stay above the water until exhaustion sets in. You sink a few times and come up for air, perhaps take in water, until you no longer have the strength to stay above the surface."

He walked along the bar; each step was purposeful, his fingers curved like claws. I turned so he would not see my back.

A man leaped from the booth behind me. I shifted my weight, caught his arm and tossed him across the room.

"You hold your breath, at first, try to make the air in your lungs last, fighting the water that pushes on your lips. But your lungs contract."

The bartender pulled a gun from below. The evolver unfolded around my arm and a burst of blue energy shot from my open hand, melting the barrel and half his arm.

"A fire burns the hungry cells in your lungs."

I kicked the tables away, clearing space. With both evolvers, I crouched in the center of the room.

"Your head swells painfully."

All the glassy-eyed patrons with their fingers stuck in the moody bowls attacked. I cut away their knees with a long stroke of a blue saber. Blood splashed the walls.

"Water, the very substance that gives you life, now takes it."

One man eluded my counterattack and got close enough to bring a glowing dagger down on me. I activated a shield and inserted a knife between his ribs. *Why am I slaughtering these people?*

"The useless air is expelled from your lungs and you choke soundlessly. You thrash helplessly. You sink." Pon walked behind a small group of men in tuxedoes. "Inevitably."

He did not emerge on the other side. Instead, Streeter appeared. His hands were glowing with evolvers. His eyes were dark and angry. Vengeful.

"Save me, Socket," he said.

He took a step, then another, and then leapt, hands above his head, a long spear aimed for my chest. My heart thumped inside, aching to be released from the building pressure. It needed space. It wanted out.

I dodged to the left, using an impact pulse to launch Streeter across the room. His frail body cracked into the wall, falling over the back of a booth at a broken angle.

I couldn't get enough air. My chest squeezed my lungs smaller and tighter. *I'm suffocating.*

"Sometimes you have to let them drown." Pon was behind me.

I spun. He was gone again.

"You have to surrender."

I screamed, shoving tables and bodies away, blasting them against the walls until I was the only thing standing.

Pon's bodiless voice spoke. "You have to *die!*"

I rolled sideways, ignited a shield from my left hand and sprayed bursting projectiles blindly behind me. Pon moved deftly, his motions animal-like, lanky and graceful, blocking my shots and advancing. I jumped onto the booths and swiped at him with a three-headed whip, a sweeping line that he bent his body around. The whips carved through the floorboards.

Our shields clashed and our weapon hands locked together. I had the advantage from above, careful not to overcompensate that he might shift and toss me. He was stuck in the corner. Maybe it was the weight of my chest or the adrenaline or his exhaustion, but I overpowered him. I forced him into a compromised position. His neck was prone.

I would best him.

Spit shot from his lips and he pulled me closer, the tip of my weapon closing in on his neck. He wanted me to win. I smelled his breath and looked into his eyes.

His eyes.

The depth, the steel, was gone. This was not the man that had trained me. There was something else in his eyes, someone familiar. From another time. It was the eyes of another man. An enemy I once knew. That was not Pon inside.

It felt like... *impossible.*

I pressed the tip of my weapon closer, touching the throbbing artery on his neck. His eyes were wide open, as if begging me to look inside.

Pon is the greatest trainer of all time.

He leaned forward, my dagger sizzling on his skin with no regard for life or death. He wanted me to see.

My mentor.

The smell of burnt flesh wafted up. I pulled the dagger back. Leaned closer.

Closer to see.

It wasn't Pon inside. It was a predator. A deceiver. I saw inside... PIKE.

Pon is a pawn!

Pon/Pike hooked his leg around mine, twisted his hips and turned me on my back. I was flung hard into the wall.

White light exploded in the back of my already thumping head. I squeezed the shield to full strength with both hands.

Pon's face was inches from mine, but Pike's eyes bore down. The tip of a dagger pushed through my shield and touched my throat. Now it was my jugular throbbing against a deadly edge. His eyes were tunnels that reached deep into a shell of a man that guided me through my training, that had been with me through my development, the man that prodded me to grow, to realize. At the very end was a vengeful puppeteer. A master of psychic manipulation. Pike had defeated Pon. Through him, he would defeat me.

"No." I shifted my weight, squeezed the shield tighter, pushed the dagger back, but he found renewed strength to force the weapon closer to my neck. His lips pulled back over his teeth. I could not stop him.

"NO!" My chest resisted the pressure inside. There was nowhere to go. Nothing I could do to stop him.

"Your father was a pig." His voice was hardly recognizable, beaten and hoarse. "Pigs do not go to battle. Pigs go to slaughter."

I expected the killing blow to be cold and quick like a shank that would slice through my throat. But instead, there was an explosion from deep in my chest. My heart had been set free, destroying the steel cage that imprisoned it. I heard nothing. Saw nothing.

And there was great relief.

Tremendous freedom.

I fell onto the floor, exhausted. Full surrender. Complete liberation.

Everything was broken. Across the room, slumped against the wall, was the body of Pon, buried into a depression like he'd been driven into it. It was limp and lifeless. It didn't match the vision that I had when I was with Com, but the details were irrelevant.

That is not Pon.

Newfound life crackled through me, fueled by bitterness and hatred. I snapped open my hands; blue flames flickered in my palms. I would smite this traitor from the world, take this unholy affliction from the face of the earth. No more people would drown because of him. No more death. *NO MORE!*

I pushed off the wall, soaring across the room. Hands together, above my head. Long, broad swords emerged to impale the heart of evil. Anger shook my body, thirsting for the salty tang of his blood. The death this world deserved.

I was hit with a detainment wire. Another line wrapped around my midsection like a thin snake and another around my arms and legs. I crashed into the manufactured bodies piled against the wall and carelessly cut the lashes from my skin with the evolver, searing deep wounds in my calves and elbows.

"*NO!*" I cried.

My evolvers yelped with power, drawing from the depths of my rage. Fireballs melted the first spidery crawler guard that appeared. I destroyed a second one preparing to fire another detainment line, but more entered the room. I slashed and burned them, but they overwhelmed me with numbers. The cool, silky lines encased me.

"Master Socket." Spindle knelt next to me.

"He's a traitor, Spindle! That's not Pon, that's Pike! Look in his eyes! PIKE IS CONTROLLING HIM! KILL HIM NOW!"

Spindle took my head with both hands, but I thrashed him away. He took my head again and again until the healing vibrations from his palms sank deeply. I strained against the constraints, hissing through my teeth. Several crawlers huddled around.

I let myself fall limp. Breathing came easier. The traitor was only five feet away. I could do nothing. But when I looked between the crawlers' spindly legs, there was only an indention.

Pon's body was missing.

"He's gone," I muttered. "You let him get away."

"Pon has been transported to the infirmary. The impact has caused him great harm."

Impact?

The commander's voice resonated inside the room. Others were with him. Spindle had both hands on my chest, sending healing warmth inside me. My body was so empty and depleted. The colors on his faceplate ran wild. I grabbed his wrist, unable to squeeze, suddenly aware of the complete exhaustion. Barely able to whisper, I asked, "What happened?"

"Master Socket," he said, his eyelight looking at me, "you are telekinetic."

53

THE EDGE

THEY SUBDUED me after the attack. I slept for days. I woke with my legs bandaged where I tried to cut away the crawler guards' detainment lines. When they released me from the infirmary, it wasn't without a fight. I rebelled by trashing the room, demanding to see Pon, or Pike, or whoever the fuck he was. I blamed the meds they gave me for that freak-out, some stuff that was supposed to keep me calm and relaxed and open to understanding. I understood, all right. Understood I wanted to wreck something and everything in that room was the winner.

I didn't see a live person that day, only servys. The next day, I settled down. Minders came in to do some tests, penetrate my mind and body, see how I was holding up. They did their job like usual, with confidence that bordered on arrogance, but they were hiding a quiver of fear. They saw what happened to Pon/Pike. If I could do that to him... so they tread lightly, like a bomb squad.

Spindle was the only one acting normal. He refused to talk about the incident, citing the commander's orders. This went on for days and it only pissed me off. I think I trashed the room again. But then it was clear they were going to keep me until I got a hold of myself. It took some effort and a couple of days of meditation, but I disengaged from the frantic emotions and returned to the present moment.

That was when the commander finally showed up and told me the details of what had happened and what I was becoming. He gave me another day in the infirmary and when he was satisfied, he allowed me free range of the Garrison. *Get out, stretch your legs, son.*

I requested the leaper to go to the highest point in the Garrison. I didn't want illusions anymore, I wanted something real. I wanted to feel the wind and sun.

No more tricks. Please.

I STOOD in an alcove five hundred feet up the Garrison's cliff. I had never seen it from that vantage point. Bitter wind circled into the opening. I put my toe over the edge. No rail up here, just me and the elements and five hundred feet to the ground. I was cold and alone.

Pretty much how it was on the inside.

If I took a five-hundred-foot step off the ledge and somehow survived, maybe I could run to the wormhole, get as far away from the Garrison as possible. But even if I could survive such a fall, even if I could outrun the long leash of the Paladin Nation, there was nothing on the other side. No home out there. A butterfly cannot transform back into a caterpillar any more than I could become normal again.

There was no stopping growth. If it would bring back Pon, I would gladly lay my Paladin membership down. They needed him more than me. It was a great loss to the Paladin Nation. A great loss to the world. But there was no bringing him back. Would he even want me to?

He said they were going to terminate my training and send me home. That was a lie. They were never going to terminate my training, never let me return, because I was special. Even among Paladins, I was one of a kind.

I am telekinetic.

I wasn't unstable after all. It was all part of the development, and that was the big mystery. I was hearing future events, too. The cold wash preceded the insights. The precognition was enough to make me special, to send me to the top of the Paladins' power list, but it was the telekinesis that put me over the top. No Paladin had ever moved objects with his or her mind. I not only moved them, I blew them across the room. I crushed their bodies. That was what happened in the pre-Trial exercise. Stress levels built up and I exploded. Spindle was destroyed. They weren't expecting it. Spindle had me beat, and then he went flying. It was like fishing for trout and hooking a goddamn pot of gold.

They weren't sure what happened, so they sent me home. According to the commander, they cooked up a scheme to put me under stress to replicate the outcome. They couldn't make me aware of the plan because it might skew the results, so they concocted a confrontation. And lucky them, I set them up with my colossal failure at the Judgment Day club. Pon behaved like Pike, pretending to be a traitor. He attacked. And I responded.

According to the commander.

Then let me see Pon, I told them. *Bring him here and I'll tell you if he was pretending.* I saw it, the eyes don't lie. Pike was in there. He held the dagger to my throat. He had every intention of killing me.

Pigs go to slaughter.

But they didn't bring Pon to me. *Trust us*, they said. *Pon is no traitor.* But they were hiding something, I could feel it, sensed it in their minds. Even the commander. And trust? They exhausted that privilege long ago. But I had nowhere else to go. No one else to believe. My own mother withheld information from me. Who was I going to trust now?

Another gust of wind whipped my hair across my face, like the world was asking a question: *Sure you don't want to try jumping? You never know, you might survive.*

I kicked pebbles over the edge and watched them bang against the cliff until they disappeared. I took a knife from my belt and unfolded it, touching the reflective steel and razor edge.

I'm one of them. I can be nothing else.

With one long stroke, I cut my hair at the scalp and held a handful before me.

Socket Greeny had long white hair. It had always set me apart, identified me in every crowd. Pon hated my long hair because it had no purpose, no function. But Pon was gone. No matter what the commander said, I would never see him again, even if they produced a person that walked and talked like him. *The teacher is gone.*

With my toes over the edge, looking straight down, I let go of the hair. It fluttered in a thousand directions, swirling and separating like strands of silk.

I cut away another chunk, and another, the hair sucked out and dispersed to the world. The world took. What choice did I have but to give them all of me? To surrender. To accept what I was, whatever that might be. To accept whatever this moment contained. However ugly. However cruel.

Life, as it is, the only teacher.

"I have come for you, Master Socket." Spindle approached from behind. "The commander would like to see you."

I cut away the last lock of hair and replaced the knife.

"You look very different," Spindle said.

"You know what used to be out there?" I pointed across the field. "Home."

"It still is."

"No, Spindle. It's where I was born. That's all. Nothing more." I caressed the rough stubble on my scalp. "I no longer matter to that world."

"Pardon my opinion," Spindle said, "but the world is very lucky to have you."

I held up the last lock of hair. The strands slipped between my fingers, flaying in the wind then yanked from my grip like the world was hungry. There was nothing left to give. I wasn't a boyfriend, not a best friend, nor a son. I was empty.

"The world can have all of me."

With my toes perched over the edge, another gust of wind asked, *Last chance, Socket.* I turned to Spindle standing patiently at the leaper entrance, with my heels over the edge. Spindle tilted his head, his faceplate void of color. He did not lunge after me. The end was a mere shuffle away, but he gave me the opportunity to choose. He was an android—a machine—not capable of emotion, created only to calculate. Maybe he knew I wasn't going to make that step. He knew I was only resisting my fate; there was no chance I would step back-wards. Or perhaps he was watching me swim in the ocean and could not save me. No man or machine could save me from myself. They could only watch.

I will serve the world.

I stepped away from the ledge. Spindle's faceplate swirled with a myriad of blues and greens.

But not embrace it.

We went to see the commander and to chart a new course for the Paladin Nation. One that included a cadet that sensed the future. A cadet that moved things with his mind.

A new age was upon us.

PART VI

The teacher opens the door. The student enters alone.
Buddhist proverb

Your past is an anchor that cannot be cut away. Ignore it, and it will drag behind you, snagging coral and rock in your wake. Your only choice is to pull it aboard to sail freely in all directions.
Trey Greeny

54

Flawed

A BEAD of sweat tracked the side of my face and dangled from my chin.

Breathe in.

My feet were on opposite thighs, my legs folded in a tight lotus position.

Breathe out.

I closed my eyes; the stagnant air wrapped around me, pulling sweat down both cheeks. Drip, drip, drip.

Breathe in.

My awareness expanded to the four walls.

Breathe out.

Every tissue attuned to the infinitesimal swirl of electrons and the pulsing essence within.

Breathe in.

Empty of thoughts.

Breathe out.

Just the room.

Breathe in.

Here.

Breathe out.

The walls spit faceless warriors, their deadly fingers aiming for my throat. The evolvers ignited onto my arms. I twisted. Long, blue whips flailed from my hands. Fiery energy burst from the quiet core of my being, waves of telekinetic power hitting the assailants.

Swipe. Roll.

The whips cut through them. Dismembered arms thumped on the floor. Claylike substance spattered the walls.

Feint.

They counterattacked. Fingers extended.

RrrrrrrrrrrrrrraghараRRRRRRRRRG!

Another subsonic wave burst from my chest. The warm substance of their bodies splashed over me. I dropped to one knee, chest heaving. I felt the last twitches of their lifeless torsos around me.

Except one.

The last assassin was legless, but lifted itself onto its hands. It craned its neck and circled around the room.

The evolvers unfolded from my arms. The enemy moved carefully over the body parts. I closed my eyes and centered my awareness. Sensing the room, I located the enemy's energy and felt it stalking me.

It bent at the elbows, braced itself against the wall and sprang like a lion.

I felt the space close between us. I deflected its arms open and plunged my hands deep into its chest. The torso flailed, the muscles contracting as I brought it closer, leveraging my grip, my arms bulging until it ripped apart. The body split open with a wet, sucking sound, spewing warm fluid.

My bicep was cut open. White and meaty. Blood beaded on the edges, then began to ooze over my slime-caked skin.

"*Mission complete,*" the room reported.

The room was still.

"AGAIN!" I shouted.

The floor quivered. The slimy substance absorbed into the floor like a sponge until the room was white and pristine. The smell of wet clay lingered. Filtered air wafted through the walls, clearing the atmosphere.

I took my place at the center and pulled my feet into lotus position.

Breathe in.

"Master Socket." Spindle entered. "I must insist you rest."

"When I am finished."

"You have completed this exercise twenty times this morning."

I looked at the gaping wound. "And I have failed as many."

"I cannot allow you to continue. You do not have safety precautions activated. Failure could result in great harm."

"How else am I going to learn?"

"Trainer Pon would not condone your methods."

"Don't patronize me."

Pon was gone, but the Paladins and Spindle still pretended like he had simply been reassigned. He wouldn't be available but would instead send orders. And trust us, Socket, do you really think Pike could overcome a Paladin like Pon? *Then let me see him, just one look.*

You'll see him again, the commander promised. *For the moment, focus.*

But Pon never came. Instead his orders were relayed through Spindle, supplying daily exercises. Not for a second did I believe Pon was actually sending them, so I silently became the teacher and learned how to swim. I looked inside myself for guidance, driving myself far beyond the menial exercises "Pon" was sending. I didn't want to achieve the goals, I wanted to crush them. I wanted to obliterate everything set in front of me. I wanted nothing less than the flawless achievement of total annihilation.

"I beg you to rest, Master Socket. You have not slept in three days." He reached for my forehead to read my vitals. I pulled away. He didn't need to tell me how I felt. I had infinite energy, as if something had been released inside. This energy came out hot and angry. Undeniable.

I had never moved more freely. I had to keep moving forward, don't look back. Home was back there. Chute. The rest. *Just don't look.* I found solace in the pureness of action, when I immersed myself in missions, banishing all thoughts. I annihilated the enemies sometimes wondering who or what I was actually fighting.

"There are many exercises remaining." Spindle stepped back, sensing my agitation. "The Realization Trial is near and I am afraid you will not be prepared if you do not complete them."

"I'll get to them."

"Could I send for food and drink? I believe you are running low on sustenance."

"You can leave." I pointed away. "I'll call when I need you."

Colors scattered across Spindle's faceplate as he contemplated what to do. He was watching me burn out, but, just as on the ledge, he did not attempt to save me. He bowed slightly and left the room.

I didn't need Spindle anymore. I didn't need anyone.

I returned to breathing, calming my mind, letting thoughts fall away. Soon the room opened to me and, once again, I expanded into its spaciousness. Silence washed over me, carrying away the heat of anger. Patiently, I awaited the essential flow of life to open in my awareness.

Instead, cold drained down the back of my neck.

It spread through my shoulders, down my back. Voices warbled distantly. Inaudibly, at first. I braced tighter, pushing the sounds away, but they would not be denied. It wasn't what they said that caused the cold anger to flame brighter. It was laughter.

From somewhere across the planet Pike was laughing. He would have me in the future was what it meant. Surrender was inevitable.

"NO!"

I activated the evolvers, lashing whips from my hands, tearing at the air, gashing deep tracks into the walls. I spun, twisted and attacked the laughter that rang all around, thrashing at the invisible voice.

My lungs suddenly deflated, unable to hold air. My balance swirled inside my head; I couldn't hold myself up.

The room dimmed.

Spindle picked me up. The furnace of hate was still burning.

And laughter trailed in my head.

55

A Paladin is Born

"To the Preserve, Spindle."

For some reason, he listened. We loaded onto a floating cart and sped down the dark paths of the Preserve. The clouds spun overhead and cold laughter trickled down my spine. I clamped my hands over my ears like I could stop it.

As we came out of the trees, the vehicle slowed, creeping up a wide slab of stone. We approached the muscled branches of the grimmet tree. They crawled from their holes and perched on the limbs, turning the barren tree bright with color. As we neared, the cold sensation began to warm. The laughter faded.

Spindle walked around to my side and lifted me from my seat. He ignored my order to leave me alone. When he attempted to put me on my feet, my legs buckled.

"You will recuperate here, Master Socket." He laid me gently between the gnarly flares in the tree trunk. "Rest here."

Warmth vibrated from the tree as if the core were alive. The grimmets gazed down, the trunk flares holding me like my mother's arms.

Rudder crawled down and nestled onto my neck, purring intensely. His breath rattled through my chest. Soon our breathing synchronized into long, deep draws.

WHEN I OPENED my eyes again, it was dark. The sky was filled with stars. The grimmets were still out, staring down at me. Then I realized it wasn't stars, it was the grimmets' eyes, sparkling with points of light. Warmth rose up from inside once again, hanging heavy on my eyelids. I sank into the oblivion of sleep.

I didn't dream. Sometimes, I could hear the night sounds around me, mosquito wings buzzing in my ear, and feel their piercing bites, but I never opened my eyes. My body felt heavy, like mercury bubbled up from a wellspring deep inside, filling my veins, weighing on my heart, encasing it like a suit of armor.

THE PRESERVE WAS alive with birds welcoming the morning when I woke. The branches of the grimmet tree were empty, their purrs vibrating inside. A thick layer of dew sparkled on the trees. My face was damp, the tip of my nose cold and numb. Rudder rolled off my shoulder onto a coarse blanket covering my legs. I sensed the floral essence of my mother's touch.

The Realization Trial was days away, but no one was urging me to get up. No servys floating up the slab with breakfast. Spindle wasn't there with the morning's schedule. It was just the birds singing. The sun rising.

I tapped my cheek for messages. Thirty of them. Most were from Streeter and Chute. They were weeks old. Spindle must've released them. Pon would've destroyed them, if he was around.

The messages played while I crawled down from the slab to the pond below. *Hey, Socket, it's Chute. I hope you're getting these messages. Can you call back, or send a reply through your mother? I know you have some big test coming up and I just want to talk to you. I just want to know you're okay, that's all. And, well, you know, I, uh... just call. Okay.*

I splashed water on my face and stripped off my shirt. My skin contracted in the brisk air. I dipped my shirt in the pond and squeezed out the excess, rubbing it over my shoulders.

Socket, it's Streeter. Hey, where are you? Did they send you off planet? Call me soon; I got to tell you about gear-addiction therapy. Seriously, call. Or have Spindle call or something.

My knees dented the sandy mud. A foggy cloud of emotion filled my head. My face got heavy.

I'm checking messages, Chute said. *Why haven't you called? I'm a little worried because, you know, the way things went the last time you were here. Your mother says you're all right and I believe her and everything, but I want to talk to you. I really want to hear your voice.*

Sadness hardened in my throat.

I wish you would call, Chute's message said. *I just want to hear you're okay.*

I convulsed.

Socket, Streeter's message said, *you all right?*

I squeezed the muddy sand between my fingers.

I think about you every day, Chute said.

I dropped my chin to my chest, heaving like the oxygen had been sucked out of the air, suffocating like I was on another planet. The atmosphere was crushing me.

My hands plunked into the water, sinking into the mud below. My reflection stared back. My hair stabbed in all directions. My cheeks were stretched against the bones, my ribs poking out.

Who is looking back?

"Delete!" I slapped my cheek, again and again. "DELETE IT ALL!"

The nojakk voicemail reported: *Messages deleted.*

I was no longer that person! That was yesterday! *Another life!*

I marched into the pond. The cold seeped through me, numbing the heaviness.

I can't look back, you understand? I just... I just can't.

The water was at my throat. It took the feeling from my skin. Another step, the water crept over my lips.

I'm sorry, Chute.

The chilly water grabbed my scalp. I floated off the bottom, drifting beneath the surface. The water buoyed me in limbo. Life above. Peace below.

My cheeks expanded with my last breath.

Fighting the water that pushes on your lips...

Sunlight shimmered down, flickering around me. Water leaked into my mouth, pooling under my tongue. Tiny bubbles streamed out, finding their way to the world above.

Water, the very substance that gives you life.

My toes touched bottom. The sun was a distant ball blurred on the surface, its light dim and distorted, barely reaching the cold depths where I lingered.

When life calls for you, Mother once said, *you must find the strength to answer.*

My lungs burned.

Let's hope you are stronger than I am, she said.

The watery sun dimmed in a darkening tunnel.

You can't see what I see in you, she said.

My heart thudded.

But trust me, she said. *Trust what I see in you.*

Shrinking. Smaller. And smaller.

Trust.

Disappearing from this world.

What I see in you.

My body, my cells, my being stopped struggling. The dying light was replaced by images of my past. Memories. I saw my father. My mother. I saw Streeter. And Chute. The cold had reached my core. *Are you sure?*

The world was so heavy. I was so small. So imperfect.

Their faces flicked through my inner vision, spinning further and further back, nearing my earliest days. *Are you sure?*

Maybe they were just memories, but there was something indestructible. Something of infinite value. Something that said, *Yes, the world is lucky to have you.* Something that reminded me that no matter what the struggle, there was nowhere to go. There was no place else. There was only now.

Are you sure?

I had to answer. Yes or no.

In the last moments, I pushed off the bottom.

Water gushed into my mouth as I broke the surface.

I inhaled hungrily at life. Hacking and choking, I struggled to the shore and collapsed. The grimmets watched me struggle to breathe. To live.

Were they watching me on the bottom, too? Where was everyone? Mother was never around. Pivot left. Pon, too. And my father, he was the first of all of them to leave. They all checked out. All of them, letting me drown.

I slapped at the water. Cursing no one. Cursing everyone.

Everything.

My chest contracted. Pressure building. Stiffening.

The pressure wound inside my chest, locked and loaded. I smashed my fists into the water and telekinetic waves erupted through my body. Water exploded in a geyser of foam and spray, thumping with supersonic depth, reaching the top of the grimmet tree and raining down. I screamed their names, cursing them for abandoning me. I pounded the water until my knees gave out.

My strength was sapped, but a resolution had settled in its place. I did not choose death.

Live, I would, but not for joy.

I would mourn the death of Socket Greeny, for he was still on the bottom of that pond.

Water dripped from my face, distorting the water's reflection. I recognized the face looking back. It was hard and empty. It had no name. But I knew it.

A Paladin had been born.

56

ICE SHATTERS

THE DAYS WENT by in a timeless blur.

Not many people spoke to me, leaving Spindle to pass along instructions. He didn't lecture me on the importance of rest; he gave up on that.

He announced when my day of Realization had arrived. He walked to the grimmet tree. I was sitting beneath it, my legs folded under me, in meditation. He waited until I emerged from my stillness and gently requested that I follow him. Energy rustled in my wake.

WE WENT TO A ROOM. He left me there, perhaps expecting me to meditate once again. Instead, I called for it to build an environment. The white walls formed an exact replica of the alcove perched high on the Garrison cliff. I sat on the ledge and let my feet dangle.

It was an important day, that day. Invisible cars had been approaching the Garrison since morning, masked by back-reflection,

making the space appear warped around the car. Crawler guards
crept along the perimeter, running their own back-reflecting gear,
distorting the tree trunks as they passed, following each car that
swayed in the grass.

A very important day.

A revolutionary cadet would be tested in the Realization Trial
today. One that moved objects with his mind. One that might see the
future.

Rain fell from the gray sky and the room mimicked the drops
with exact precision. It soaked my hair.

Another car approached, this one evident as the rain was repelled
by the warped space cruising over the boulders. Crawler guards
followed right out in the open this time, their spidery legs gracefully
covering the open land, their glowing eyelights scanning the environment. The clandestine vehicle breezed quickly over the field, slowing
as it approached the sheer face of the cliff wall. I leaned over and
watched it merge inside.

So important.

Mother emerged from empty air several feet in front of me. She
called for a personal bubble to resist the rain. Her breath staggered at
first. I could only assume it was the way I looked. I'd lost weight, sure,
but it was more than that. My energy was darker than ever, like a
storm cloud. She composed herself, then appeared to walk on air to
sit next to me. Together, we watched the invisible cars float over the
field. Some fast, some slow.

She placed her hand on mine. Her touch was hot. Perhaps she
was not any warmer than normal. She had attempted to eat meals
with me in my final days of training, but I didn't take the time to stop,
preferring to get my nourishment from lifepatches and hydration
paste. I slept beneath the grimmet tree. When I woke, I trained. No
one came to get me. No one bothered me. Alone, I completed my
training. All exercises perfected.

I executed every move, every thought, with exact precision. I
learned new information by absorbing it. I merged with the enemy,
merged with the environment, melted into the intelligence innate in

all forms. I became the enemy, knowing it from the inside. I was empty of obstacles.

I am the weapon.

"Ice shatters." My mother took her hand away. "Water flows."

I narrowed my eyes and watched the field. An emotion twisted in my belly, threatening to manifest.

"It's what your father said after he failed his Realization Trial." She was lost in a memory. "It's what he said when he emerged from a three-day coma. At one point, they didn't expect him to awaken, but then he muttered those words and opened his eyes. He doesn't remember saying them."

Oddly, I couldn't recall my father's face.

"This is a lonesome journey, Socket. In the end, you are on your own. But when you complete your realization, you'll know you were never alone."

"You mean *if* I make it."

"No, I mean *when.*"

"Father failed."

"You are not your father."

The rain came down harder. It was difficult to see across the field. The putty taste of the imitation raindrops was on my lips.

Mother placed her hand on top of my head. The bubble around her hand encompassed my head, repelling the rain. She ran her fingers over my face, wiping my brows.

I resisted the rising tide of warmth threatening to move my heart. She kept her hand on my neck so the rain would not fall on me.

Spindle entered the room. "It is time, Master Socket."

My mother's essence mingled through my mind, leaving fragrant traces of scintillating energy. She paused before she left, but there was nothing left to say.

The alcove faded. Even the moisture evaporated from my hair. I stood in a plain white room. "We will go to a preparatory room for half an hour," Spindle said. "Then you will enter the Realization Trial."

I nodded.

His faceplate bristled with texture and color. "Your father once told me the Realization Trial is quite simple. He said there is nowhere to go. You are already here."

"Then why'd he fail?"

"He said it was simple." Spindle paused before exiting the room. "He did not say it was easy."

THE ANTEROOM WAS LARGER than it needed to be. Ten servys hovered along the back and I faced a blank wall with Spindle by my side, waiting for the signal to enter. I could barely feel my body. No longer cold, I hummed. No emotions, no feeling, just *hummmmmm*. I did not fear, did not want. Whatever was beyond the wall, I would face it without prejudice or preconception.

Hummmmmm.

Nobody entered the room to wish me luck. No one called or sent a message of goodwill. For that, I was grateful.

The room was entirely motionless for thirty minutes. I breathed in, out. Did not move to scratch or ask for the time. It was just in. Out. And on the thirtieth minute, Spindle placed his hand on my shoulder.

"You have been summoned to enter the Realization Trial."

His hand slid from me. I took a deep breath and let it out slowly.

"I will be waiting for you, upon your return," Spindle said. "*Master Socket.*"

He emphasized my name, as if to remind me of something I forgot. I took another deep breath. When I was clear and focused, razor-sharp and deadly rapt, I stepped through the wall to the other side.

No going back now.

57

HUNTING the Predator

AN ARENA.

The center was flat and bare. Circus-like. Seats so steep a man would tumble to the bottom if he fell forward.

There was no roof, but the illusion of the sky. It smelled like a transformable room. The staleness of filtered air confirmed it.

The seats were filled with hundreds of Paladins. And not just Paladins, but the elite, highest commanders; the most powerful men and women in the world sat expressionless, wearing dark uniforms cleanly pressed and snugly fit with various bands of color depicting the origin of their facility.

None were projecting their presence; they were all there in the skin. All humans emitted an energy—an unmistakable essence—that many called an aura, but now I was seeing it around the Paladins like never before, blazing around them.

The floor was spongy, but the silence was so dense that my footsteps echoed. The closer I got to the center, the hotter the room became. Not a cough or a fidget, the silence was pristine.

My commander was in the front row next to Chief Com, but there was no way to recognize his rank since they were all impeccably dressed the same, their expressions identical. Their thoughts were like the desert sun, pricking my cheeks. Sweat popped up along my forehead. I remained resolute. Still.

What do you want?

It was psychic heat. They were frying me like a bug. I closed my mind to deflect the pressure. I wouldn't survive long if I didn't. If they wanted to see how many punches I could take, then they had their man. I could take a beating.

My mind clanged like sheets of metal, warding off the psychic pressure that drilled through my pores. But the heat continued. I took a chance, closing my eyes for just a moment to refocus, but my mind felt like an eggshell, fissures appearing like spiderwebs. *Ice shatters.*

Suddenly, a cold sensation washed over me, providing an instant of relief until I realized it was running down my back. *Hahahahahahaha.* Pike's laughter rumbled like thunder.

The floor shimmered. I took the chance of closing my eyes again, to draw on every bit of strength to solidify my mind, to build a wall. The laughter receded.

WHEN I OPEN MY EYES, the Paladins are glowing like beacons. Energy beams from most of them in waves. But others almost look pale and lack the pulsing quality, almost like they are lifeless projections. Maybe they aren't here in the skin.

Distractions.

A fleeting motion disrupts my focus. The already fraying fabric of my mind quickly begins to tear. The icy wave returns, along with Pike's laughter. It echoes around the arena. And then another voice joins it. Chute's calling.

Socket! Please, don't go, she says. *You said I wouldn't forget you!*

I'm sinking to my knees but my feet are still on the floor. The voices are still there. Pleading, calling, and laughing.

These are just hallucinations, I'm not really hearing anything. These aren't real. Just focus.

"You will fail, Socket Greeny!"

I spin on my heels, sweat flicking off my face. Someone stands and shouts for real, then ducks out of sight. It's a brown-skinned man, but now he's gone, like he evaporated. All is still again. I wipe my chin with my sleeve. The fabric is searing.

Socket, don't fight, Chute's voice calls. *Why do you always fight?*

Yeah, Streeter chimes in. *Just relax.*

Chatter, chatter, chatter. Laughter. More voices. Two. Then ten. Mother. Pon. Spindle. Teachers, strangers, neighbors—

Socket, are you listening? Chute says above them all. *I need you! Just come withmedon'tleavejust—*

"SHUT UP!" I shout.

Something scurries under the seats, Paladins shift like it's tunneling beneath them. I run after it and point. "I see you! I see you up there!"

The Paladins don't change their expressions. Some of them are still glowing in waves and others are dimmer. Darker.

I finger the evolvers on my belt and follow the gopher around the arena. I'm about to climb over the front row and into the seats to catch the bastard—

"Father?"

I wipe my eyes and look again. My father, he's there, in the crowd, arms folded, staring with the rest of them. It's him, but I'm sweating sheets. It's hard to see, but now he looks like just another face in the crowd, just another Paladin.

"FAIL, SOCKET!"

The heckler is on the other side of the arena. I blink heavily, nearly tripping over my own feet. Someone stands up and slowly reveals his face. His skin is brown. Eyes almond-shaped.

Pon.

I'm trying to talk, but my lips are quivering. I manage to say something like, "I thought you…" And that's it. Sweat is stinging my eyes and Pon is gone. I unleash the evolver and snap a handful of whips into the crowd, their bodies exploding in a cloud of white dust that settles like gravel.

"FAIL, SOCKET!"

Something thumps off my shoulder. A stone rolls across the floor. I activate an evolver shield.

"FAIL!"

Now they stand and shout, one at a time, chucking rocks. Each one utters the single word. *FAIL*. All with hatred, pulling stones from their pockets and hurling them. I drop to my knees to increase the shield's power, but the stones are relentless, thudding like granite hail.

They're all on their feet. All of them except the two in the front row.

I stand.

Walk to the edge. "Father?"

The arena falls silent. The last of the stones trickles past my feet. He's sitting solemnly next to my mother. Arms crossed. His graying hair hangs over his ears and he has a week's worth of whiskers. His eyes are set in wrinkled pockets.

"Do you see the predator?" he asks.

"I don't understand." My hand reaches slowly, like it doesn't belong to me. I just want to touch his face, feel the leathery cheek, make sure it's really him. I'll know if I touch him. If I sense his musky essence, feel his security, then I'll know for sure.

My hand moves through an eternity of space, and as my fingers brush his chin, he dissolves. The seat's empty.

"WHERE ARE YOU?"

I stumble back to the center, stones rolling under my heels. I fall, catching the jagged edge of a rock with my mouth. Blood spots the floor. I pull myself up. I pull myself.

Up.

Pon is standing there. His eyes are black and empty.

Pike's laughter roars.

It's the predator you don't see...

I reach for an evolver, but the atmosphere is too thick. I watch Pon lift his hand.

I cannot move. I cannot—

It's Pon. It feels like my father. But it's Pon. His hand swings in slow motion.

My father. He was my Paladin.

Pon's finger lightly touches my forehead with the smacking metal-on-metal sound of a three-pound hammer on a steel plate.

"Journey deeper," he says, "into the night."

And night comes.

Night stays.

58

REFLECTIONS

DOWNTOWN.

I don't know how I got here. I don't care.

The market is vacant. Even the vendors' tables are gone. Not a person anywhere.

The streetlights cast a yellowish glow on the littered streets. My breath is thick and white, but I don't feel cold. I don't feel anything.

A stoplight clicks from red to green. My footsteps echo. Inside the five-star corner restaurant, menus are propped on the tables, the napkins neatly folded, but no one is sitting at them. A television above the bar flashes highlights of a tagghet game.

Around the corner, a neon sign splashes electric red light on a fat man on a bar stool. He's staring at me. I go over, the sign going *bzzz-zzzz.*

"He's up there." The fat man points at the door below the flickering sign.

"Who?"

"You know."

"Pon?"

He doesn't answer, just thumbs at the door. I check the evolvers on my belt. Fat man doesn't seem concerned that I'm armed. I stop at the peeling red door.

Bzzz-zzzz. Bz.

The door opens on its own. I walk up the creaking steps; the walls are covered with graffiti. *Ice shatters,* one blurb reads. Seems like I've heard that before.

Another behemoth at the top of the steps, the heels of his boots wedged on the bar stool. He jerks his head at the crystal-knobbed door behind him. The door thumps rhythmically.

"In there," he says.

"Who?" The word puffs out of my mouth.

He does the same jerky motion with his head.

A black fog rolls in through the door at the bottom of the steps. It stops, but continues to swirl, the tendrils twisting and curling and waiting like it's just cleaning up behind me. *No hurry, take your time.*

The man sees the cloud, too. "Too late now."

I wrap my hand around the angular doorknob. It jiggles with a pounding bass, vibrating in my palm, sending a tickling line through the tendons in my wrist.

Music bursts from inside in loud synthesized dance beats, vibrating deep in my chest. *Dssssszth-dssssszth-boom.* Over and over. The black cloud roils on the top step behind me.

The club looks the same, but the crowd is different. They're younger, packed together with their hands in the air, hopping to the mad, driving beat. The bartender stands with his arms crossed, the vivid red light illuminating his white shirt. He jerks his head towards the crowd and mouths the words *over there.* I don't hear anything over the drowning beat.

The crowd notices me, one at a time, as the rumor of my arrival spreads. They're expecting me. It doesn't slow them down, but they're looking. I know them. A girl leans over and shouts, "Come on!" It's Carmen, from my eighth grade history class. I had a crush on her, but she moved to California. She's waving at me, like she wants me to join the party.

Dssssszth-dsssssszth-boom.

One person isn't dancing. I see the top of the brown head ducking behind the ocean waves of the dance floor. Without breaking stride, the crowd parts. Pon has his arms locked behind his back. His expression is hard. So many times I'd seen that look push me harder, challenge me, tell me time was precious and it was running out. But this time the look mingles with something else, something that shouldn't be there. It's a smirk, one that belongs to someone else. It belongs to a traitor. *Pike.*

He mingles into the crowd behind him, getting lost in the hard bouncing bodies. Hands in the air.

Dsssssszth-dsssssszth-boom.

I follow.

The crowd cheers my first step, reaching for me, the roar of their approval rising above the music. Slaton, a lanky kid that was in one of my gym classes, scruffs the top of my head. Then there's Jane, my old babysitter, rubbing my shoulders and celebrating with a *wooo-hooo!* Next to her is Albert, a quiet kid that was my bunkmate at summer camp. He never said more than ten words a day and picked his nose when he lay in bed. But he was making plenty of noise now, smacking me on the back.

The black cloud gobbles up the bartender and crystal-knobbed door.

Up and down the crowd goes, sloshing back and forth. They gently tug at me, congratulating me, hugging me. There's Shelly right in front, his blond hair bouncing in his face. He reaches into the crowd and pulls a girl out by her wrist, spins her around and grinds his hips into her. She turns her head. *Chute.* She doesn't look happy, doesn't look sad. Shelly's hands crawl up her belly, over her breasts—

I blast him.

It's effortless, just a thought exploding from my gut, hitting him like a telephone pole, driving him through an endless corridor of dancing bodies, arms flailing, until the crowd swallows him up. Chute is gone.

Deeper I go.

I reach the end. It's the silver podium where Streeter inserted the key. An arching outline is on the wall. The party rages on behind me.

"He's in there." Streeter's on my left. *I've heard him say that before.*

"Who?"

"Your teacher. He went through the doorway."

"What're you doing here?"

"We're all here." Chute's on my right. "You have to follow him," she says.

"I don't want to."

"Too late for that now," Streeter answers.

The thumping fades. My ears ring as the music stops. The sea of people have solemn expressions. The black cloud roils at the far end of the room. *Any day now.*

"You have to follow," Chute says again.

"Why?"

"It's the only way."

She's sad. But it isn't her. Not really. None of this is really here. Right?

I step to the podium. The surface is cold and smooth on my fingers. The podium connects with my nervous system, recognizing me. The archway on the wall begins to glow.

Whatever is on the other side seems more frightening than anything I've ever faced. I don't want to go, but the black cloud is losing patience. It furls over the crowd, obscuring their faces as it advances. I slide my hand off the pedestal.

"Goodbye, Socket." Chute doesn't wave. Part of me wants to run back and hold her. But that's not Chute. The black cloud is going to take her from me.

I have to go through that door.

It's too late for anything else.

I PASS THROUGH THE DOORWAY. It's not a leaper this time. It's a bright, circular room. The walls are reflective, like hazy mirrors. My reflections look back with fuzzy edges. Doors are evenly spaced around the perimeter.

I walk along the room; the doorways won't open. Pon's not here. Maybe he went through one of the doors, but I'm not going to make this into a game of hide-and-seek. Those doors could go anywhere. I turn to go back to the club, but the archway is gone. In its place is a blank space.

I slam my fists on the wall. "Where are you, goddamnit?"

There's a silver podium now in the center of the room. It wasn't there when I entered, as if it magically appeared, identical to the one in the lobby. My reflection is perfectly clear on its surface. I dip my fingers in it; my image ripples. The taste of aluminum tings in my mouth.

And then the podium opens to my awareness.

The room spins like a carnival ride. Data courses through my fingers, ticking through my nerves like grains of sand, expanding my awareness, filling me with thoughts and images. My mind grows out of the top of my head like tentacles. The air whistles as they swing around. More emerge from the back of my head, then along my neck and back.

I wrap them around the podium and smash it into the ceiling. Now *this* is telekinesis. My True Nature. This is what the Trial is about. I've been released from my body. I am pure power. And Pon thinks he can hide from me?

ME?

The podium crashes, its post spiking into the floor, fragments twinkling around the room. I plunge my slithery mind into the podium. The surface splashes. Currents of information surge through me. I let my awareness absorb it. *Become it.*

I'm everywhere, like the multifaceted vision of an insect. There are thousands of virtualmode rooms throughout the underground of Charleston and they're all connected to the room of mirrors. It all starts here.

It all starts with me.

I am the room. I am the conduit. *I am everything.*

The rooms are filthy little prison cells with patrons lying on piss-stained mattresses. Their bodies are wasting away and forgotten. Maybe I know these people like I knew the ones in the lobby, but I don't pay attention. I don't care. None of them taste like Pon.

I go room to room, sniffing with my mind, searching for the one soul I came for, the one that will quench my thirst. I need to find Pon. I can bring him back, I can send Pike away. If he would just stop hiding.

PON! My thought shakes the walls. *DON'T RUN FROM ME!*

The corridors are networked like an ant colony. My awareness spreads throughout. I can taste the foul flesh of the gear-addicted voids. I plunge deeper. It's colder and the rooms are smaller. The voids are shriveled and weak, but I storm past them. Room after room, life after life, I taste them all. And when there are no more rooms, when there's nowhere left to look, nothing left to taste, it's clear to me. He's gone.

POOOOOONNNNN!

The gear-addicts quiver, twitching to life. They moan like babies pulled off their mommy's tit. I feel their cries inside me, but ignore them. They want to go back to their virtualmode life of dreams and fantasy, and I don't give a fuck what they want. I hate them. They're the ones filling me with rage. It's them. It's their fault.

"Come, you shitbags." The walls crackle. "Come and see what you've become."

I absorb their essence, interweave through their minds and bodies until I'm one with them. They'll come with a simple wish. A single thought.

I open my eyes back in the circular room. The podium is shattered at my feet. The reflections on the walls and doors are crystal clear, the hazy fog lifted from the polished mirrors. My face looks back in every direction.

Come.

They cling to their beds. But I have no mercy. If I'm going to drown, they can join me.

Come to the light.

The first body falls through a door on my right. I feel him smack on the floor like wet meat. His skin is gray. What's left of his long white hair is frayed and matted over his face.

"Please," he moans. "Leave me."

He tastes old and neglected. Forgotten. He's wasted, near death, but somehow he won't die. He paws at my feet.

"Please..."

I've got every intention of wasting him, but there's something so familiar about him. His heart patters and I feel it in my chest, fluttering with fear. I feel the cold floor beneath his palms, the sting of air on his oozing wounds. When he moves, it stirs inside my gut like a spear twisting and breaking.

Who is this?

I hook my finger under his chin. The hair falls from his face.

I fall back a step.

Me.

He reaches a clawed hand. It's my voice. "Please..." The word slips from his cracked lips, but I feel it rattle in my throat. I feel his pain and loneliness.

Another body falls into the room and there's stabbing pain in my knees. He sits up, throws his hair back, and I look directly at my face again. Three more tumble in like the living dead and they're all me. I feel each of them, all their pains and fears swirling in my stomach.

I thought they were just voids hiding from life, but they're me. And now I can see them and feel them. I've become them. And now I want them to go back. I want to forget.

"Go." I flick my hand like that would make them disappear. "NEVER SHOW YOUR FACE AGAIN!"

But they keep coming. Some older. Some have longer hair, others missing teeth. They climb over each other, cling to me, tear at my shirt. They wail and cry, each moan vibrating in my throat until I don't know if it's them or me. I don't know which ones are reflections and which ones are real.

Who am I?

I try to disconnect, try to wish them dead, but they won't die. Their hearts thump in my chest.

"GET AWAY!"

A burst of telekinetic energy slams them against the walls. The mirrors crack. I push with all my will and the cracks run beneath my feet.

I push harder.

They have to go back. I close my eyes, mumbling incoherently, listening to them scream, feeling their bodies squirm. One of them steps out of the crowd, impervious to my will. He comes closer. I open my eyes.

Pon.

He's motionless, hands behind his back. Eyes placid. There's no trace of Pike's menace inside. But he's unconcerned about the hell I've uncovered. Hopelessness howls inside me, and everyone in the room moans like they feel it, too. Collectively, we stare at our mentor. We wait for him to speak. Wait for him to save us, to lead us out of this forsaken place. But he does nothing.

And it's all so hopeless.

I hate him.

He's going to leave me again. He's going to watch me drown.

I wrap my hands around his neck, pressing my thumbs into his windpipe. I squeeze until the tendons ridge from my wrists. Pon's face quickly darkens. His eyes bulge, but he doesn't resist. He gives himself to me.

And I squeeze the life from him.

I pull him close to look deep inside his eyes, to watch him die. The pupils are bottomless. Soulless. I feel him with my mind, taste his waning essence. It's not the essence of Pon I taste. Nor is it Pike. It's something so much more familiar. Something I'd forgotten. And then I see the reflection in his black eyes, the reflection of my own face.

I hold him out at arm's length. Pon's face has become my own. I'm strangling me.

I am my own master.

"Don't." The strength drains from my hands. "Don't do this."

The floor crumbles beneath me and I fall. I hold onto the edge but can't climb out. Below my dangling feet is a mine shaft. Its bottom disappears in the darkness.

Pon is back, standing over me. He doesn't offer a hand as I slide from the edge. He doesn't reach for me as I fall into the darkness. And as I slide down the ever-tightening shaft, the light above becomes smaller. I descend ever deeper. Ever colder. And before the opening above disappears from sight, people are watching. It's not the voids. It's Mother. It's Chute and Streeter. They watch. The walls cave in around me.

The earth crushes me. And before the last gasp of air leaves my lungs, I can utter only a word. It's the single word that I heard myself mutter in a cold dream weeks earlier. A word that seems stuck inside.

Help.

59

Reborn

THE HOLE IS A FUNNEL. The deeper I sink, the tighter it becomes. There is no hope. Only sinking.

And pain.

Slimy mud shoots up my nostrils and packs my sinuses. It courses down my throat and fills my mouth. There's no space to gag, no way to puke the fluid forced into my stomach, into my ears.

Things snap. Muscles tear. If there was space to wish for death, for unconsciousness, I would've called for it, cried for it, begged for it, but I know only agony. There's no escape. No way out.

Falling. Forever. And ever.

Open, a voice calls.

No. I won't open, not to this torment. I won't allow this misery. I fought all my life. I'll resist to the end.

But what if there is no end?

I have to get out, back to the top. Mother's up there; she saw me slip into this trap. She has to be digging after me. I just need to give her space to find me, to pull me out, to take me back to where I was. The way I was.

I pull my awareness inward. What's left of my flesh I could pull to the surface, we could still save it, we could rebuild it just like it was. I just need space. I focus inward and find the timeslicing spark glittering brightly. It's smaller and brighter than ever. I wrap my awareness around it and call on its power. When every bit of me is pulled inside, I pull it tighter still. I'll blow the earth away. I will escape.

Allow, the voice says.

NO! There is no space for allowing! I need to escape the pain!

I release the pressure of telekinetic energy quaking inside the timeslicing spark, and sonic waves rumble through the planet. They'd feel it in Australia, at the bottom of the ocean and the top of Everest. The force will trigger landslides and tsunamis, the universe will feel my wrath. I'll destroy in the name of freedom.

But light doesn't shine from above.

In one cascading moment of utter annihilation, my body is completely crushed. My organs spew. My cries are lost in the silence of obliteration.

And yet, death does not come.

I remain fully aware, buried alive. My body couldn't be functioning, yet I feel every nerve. I feel the burning suffocation of my lungs and the crushing pain. Utter devastation. There are no boundaries to my body anymore, yet I can't escape it. Every thought of struggle, each movement of resistance flares with fiery agony. And every thought of escape brings more pain.

More weight.

More hurt.

(Sob.)

My cries echo throughout eternity, throughout all that has been and all that ever will be. It brings impressions and memories, flavors of my past; fleeting images of my youth scroll past. Each episode carries its own flavor. Some bitter, others sweet. As I experience each one, they release their energy, revealing their essence.

The mirrors are clear.

I am complete.

I see clearly.

Listen, the voice says.

I listen. I open.

I allow.

I begin to thaw, percolating through the earth's pore space, trickling deeper, filtered of impurities, finding the resting aquifer of my True Nature.

Water flows. The essence of bitter sadness transforms into sweetness. I expand, no longer my body because I no longer exist. *Being* is my body. *Existence* my True Nature.

I expand until thoughts are no longer. There is just being.

I just am.

Humming in the great, endless void of space.

Galaxies emerge in spinning wheels. Planets, stars, black holes and light spread out before me. I'm not separate from them, I am them. I can traverse the entire plane of existence simultaneously because I'm not separate from anything.

All the possible pasts and all possible future events exist in the present moment. The future paths spread out like endless veins on the fabric of existence. I could return to any path of my choosing.

Come.

The voice calls from everywhere. Calling me back from another dimension. Yet, if I want to stay in this blissful moment, I can remain for eternity. But something draws me to follow.

I answer. *Yes.*

My answer rings through the heavens. The stars sparkle with renewed life, like points poked through a dark cloth. I recede from the endless expansion of knowing, focusing into a point in space and time.

There is earth below my feet.

A coyote calls.

I raise my hand.

A fire burns within a ring of stones, illuminating cacti and desert.

Beyond the light, in the fringe of darkness, is a man. His hair is long. I can't see his face, but I know his presence. *Pivot.*

It was his voice guiding me, willing me to open and allow. To come.

Another figure emerges next to him. His silhouette is unfamiliar, but not his essence. I know this man, too. I have known him all my life. This man steps into the light. His face is unshaven and a familiar smile lights his face. It's a smile that's not on his lips, but in his eyes.

"Hello, son," my father says.

60

THE LAST RESOLVE

THE FIRE POPPED BETWEEN US. Orange light danced across my father's face, casting deep lines at the corners of his mouth. He pushed his hand through his hair and let the gray locks filter between his fingers. Something swelled inside me.

He stretched out his arms. His nostrils flared as he drew in the cool, dry air. He paced away with a familiar hitch in his left leg and gazed at the full moon. I can't see his face, but he was studying the craters on its surface. I suddenly remembered how we were in the backyard and he told me how the moon rotated around the planet and the same side always faced us, that we never saw the dark side.

"I know what you're thinking," he said, his voice scratchy. "Where the hell are we?"

The fire was getting hot. I sat down on a boulder, suddenly weak. He remained at dark's edge, breathing like he missed the simple act of breathing.

"Do you know what happened?" he asked.

It felt like a dream, but if it was a dream, then I was totally awake.

Would that still be a dream? I rested my elbows on my knees and recalled for him the sequence of events, as much for me as for him.

He came back to the fire. "So where are you now?"

I felt the soft rub of my fingertips and the desert night on the back of my neck. "This isn't my skin."

"That's right."

"Your physical body is on the floor of the arena," he said. "They forced you into a timeslice, and while it seems like you were buried in that hole for eternity, about an hour has passed. But the clock is ticking, son."

He rubbed his whiskers and it sounded like a steel brush.

"They've been watching you journey through this insanity. They've looked inside your mind and observed your struggle, your resistance. In most cases, the Trial would be over by now, but Pivot brought you here."

"But why?"

"You've got one last resolve."

He scratched at the whiskers again and gazed into the fire, allowing the moment to stretch out. Pivot was still out in the dark.

"You're not real," I said. "You died. I'm dreaming you like all the rest of this trial. You're a hallucination."

"Correct."

"Then what's to resolve?"

He grunted, which was part laugh, part acknowledgement. The firelight flickered in his eyes.

"Most of what we assume is reality is our own thoughts, our unresolved emotions, our lack of understanding. That's what the Realization Trial is about, purging your depths, exposing your soul. There can be no preconceived notions about what it's about. You cannot prepare for it, you can only be open. You arrive naked and journey into the mind."

"Into the night," I muttered.

"For some, the depth of the soul is very dark."

My thoughts became real. I couldn't escape them. The more I fought the hole, the deeper I sank, the more I was lost. I was crushed under my own delusions and forced to understand. To die. *To be reborn*.

"You see clearly now," he said. "And it comes with immense power, strength and fearlessness."

"I wasn't afraid to begin with."

His laughter echoed deep into the canyon. "Fear has many faces, my son! Anger is just one. The Paladins held up a mirror for you to see."

"Is that what you are? A reflection?"

"I'm a bit more than that."

"Then what?"

He half turned to Pivot. His expression softened, sadness taking the edges off his wrinkles. "You see, Pivot absorbed all my memories when I died, I suppose for this very event to take place. I walk, I talk, I act just like your father, but basically I'm a program." He rubbed his thick, callused hands in front of the fire. "So no, I'm not real. I'm more like a ghost."

"You're data."

"That's another way of putting it."

"You remember Streeter?"

"Your best friend? He was about as tall as a stump and just as wide." He chuckled to himself. "How is good ole Streeter?"

"Never mind." I didn't want to talk about Streeter and the virtualmode trip to see his parents. This was getting way too real for me. Data or not.

"Before you return to physical reality, you have one last obstacle to resolve. Not all cadets survive the Trial, son. Many of us weren't capable of letting go of our beliefs and thoughts." The fire tossed out a streaking ember. "You have one last attachment."

The swelling hiccupped in my chest, spreading outward. "I've seen the ugly, rotting images of myself. I faced them and reclaimed them. There's nothing left."

"Ah, yes. There's still one more." A smile and a sparkle told me it was standing in front of me. "Pivot felt you needed this last one to be special. It's a tough one."

"But you're not real, and you know that. I went through hell back in that hole and, to be honest, I'm not feeling like there's anything left. I mean, you died and that's that."

He dipped his head. The authenticity of the expression was chilling, but my chest was warm. Something was growing. The experience of omnipresence was missing.

"I'm as real to you as I need to be."

"I barely remember you." Something twisted in my stomach and I resisted letting it in, but the instinct to open to it, to be with it, took over and I felt it ache. The swelling entered my chest.

My father looked at the stars, searching the constellations. When the right thought hit him, he said, "You still got that scar behind your ear?"

I touched the raised line behind my right ear.

"I pushed you too high on a swing set when you were three, cut you open on the chain. You bled like a water hose. I caught ten degrees of hell from your mother for that."

The memory crossed my mind. I was telling him to push me higher. Nothing could hurt me. His powerful hands were on my back and sent a fluttering buzz through me each time he shoved. I soared to the peak of the swing set, gripping the chains tight enough to dent my palms, and for a second, I was weightless. I laughed and screamed, *Higher, go higher, Dad.* My father would say, *Oh, higher still, huh?* And then I felt it again, his hands on my back and a sudden surge of power.

The swelling flooded my throat.

"You want my favorite memory?" He shook his head and looked up. "They had this ride at the fair that shot five hundred feet off the ground. You were too young to go, but you went anyway. You were so scared I thought you were going to squeeze my kidneys out." He watched the fire, his expression still. "I liked being there for you, son. It wasn't the ride or the other stuff, it was just being there. That's my favorite part."

Suddenly, I was losing track of what was real again. I knew I was in front of a fire and my skin was somewhere on Earth, but now I was watching my father laugh. I remembered his face when I was young. He was always unshaven. Mother liked that about him, always a little rough and unpredictable. So did I.

I remembered him at the fair. We were eating fried food and my father was holding my mother's hand like they were teenagers, their hands swinging between them. She was laughing. He was, too. But then the memory transformed into a rainy day and he was lying in a coffin and Paladins were lowering him into the ground. Drizzle beaded on the casket lid.

All I could muster was a whisper.

"Why'd you die?"

The fire was just embers glowing in a ring of stones, just enough light to keep his face out of the dark.

"I didn't leave you, son."

"That's not the question. *Why did you die?*"

He looked into the fire.

"Answer the question." The swelling was heavy; it took my strength and blurred my vision. The glowing embers smudged in streaks of light as my eyes got wet.

"You left us..."

The swelling sprang a leak in my throat. Emotion gushed out. But I had more words. I swallowed back the leak.

"You left Mother... and she never smiled again. How could you do that to her? How could you... just leave us? If you loved us..."

I sniffed back the snot and blotted my blurry eyes with my sleeve. The swelling was like an overfilled water balloon. It was about to pop, but I just wanted to know...

"If you loved us..." *I've always wanted to know.* "Why did you have to die?"

The balloon broke.

A flood of emotion, warm and deep, coursed through me, releasing the hidden sadness and deep longing lodged somewhere deep. It filled. It gave.

I shook, holding back the sobs, but they weren't to be denied.

Once again, instinct took over and I opened to the essence coming forth, allowing it to flow within me. I was completely helpless.

Completely vulnerable.

The last resolve.

"You see clearly now, son." My father's arm gently draped across my shoulders and pulled me tight. For a moment, just a split second, the essence of my father—his smell and tone—transformed and I sensed Pon sitting next to me. And then it passed in the unfolding of my emotions because I understood Pon had been filling that hole inside me. The hole missing a father.

THE FIRE IS GONE, but the warmth remains.

I'm nowhere again. I have no eyes, yet I see. No ears, yet I hear. I bathe in the deep, pervading love that has been inside me my entire life.

I have no thoughts of returning to my skin withering on the floor of the arena. I could allow it to pass on, and those I cared about would mourn. I envision their faces, but one stands out in more detail than the others. *Chute.* She'd find happiness after my body died. Eventually.

All the possible pasts and futures lie before my mind's eye once again. I allow one path to choose me. I don't follow its future to see where it leads, where it will end and how. I don't ask if Chute is in it or if the world is safe; I only allow it to take me.

Somewhere in the flow of time, I feel my limp body. My awareness contracts, rushing past pulsars, through galaxies and solar systems, racing with the solar winds. Back to my skin.

AN OCEAN CRASHED SOMEWHERE.

Feeling returned to my extremities, vibrating like I'd been sitting on my legs too long. My fingers trembled on the quaking floor. The ocean grew louder as if a wave would soon fall on me.

You see clearly.

My eyelids fluttered. The putty floor was below. The arena.

No salty air blew in from an ocean. No waves crashed. It was applause shaking the foundations of the enormous room.

I couldn't lift my head, but I could see the blurry Paladins standing in their seats. They were clapping, shouting my name, roaring with approval. No Paladin had ever sustained a timeslice of that length without life support.

Be the path.

Servys blocked my view, their rubbery arms slapping lifepatches to my neck that pierced my arteries and dumped emergency carbohydrates and electrolytes and other life-giving components. The sustenance rushed inside like a cool drink, tingling my nervous system. They hovered around me like satellites, tending to my weak pulse, cradling it lightly, bringing it back so that I could reside in the skin once again.

And the cheers went on.

The Paladins were congratulating each other, shaking hands and patting backs. The Paladin Nation took a leap in evolution that day. What new skills did I bring back from the brink of annihilation? How many more Socket Greenys could they create and how soon? Oh, the possibilities! It was a time to rejoice, indeed. Long live the Paladin Nation!

But I brought back so much more than any of them realized. I returned to serve life, not the Paladin Nation. And as my vision cleared and focus returned, I saw the path before me. I saw the light pulsing around some of the Paladins and the dim deadness around the others. It was the same differences I witnessed when the Trial began, but now I saw it so much more clearly.

And understood what it meant.

"Spindle." I managed barely a whisper, but it would be enough. "*Protect.*"

Spindle crackled from a timeslice, appearing over my helpless body. With his legs on each side of me, he was poised for battle.

The most powerful people in the world were gathered in that room celebrating a new era. But they did not see the path. They could not see what was right in front of them.

I will show them.

"Come now, Spindle." The commander's voice resonated above the noise. "Let the boy breathe. The battle is over."

No, Commander. The battle is just beginning.

61

THE TURN

THE PALADINS CAME DOWN from the seats, still clapping. It was a historic moment. The commander would forever be known as the one that mentored Socket Greeny. He didn't notice Spindle still crouched over me, eyelight scanning. When the commander gave an order, it was followed, especially when it was given to a mech.

But Spindle overrode the direct command to step away. He was assigned to protect my life and to abort commands when the situation demanded it. Spindle didn't ask why I gave the protect command. He only heeded.

The servys had formed a circle around me, like a crime scene, and took turns administering lifepatches wherever they could find an artery.

I needed strength. Every lifepatch was sucked dry. Servys scrambled to change them, but I drained them faster than they could get them primed and replaced. My blood pressure picked up. I slid my hand across the floor. I'd be able to sit up soon.

[I'm vulnerable to psychic attack,] I thought to Spindle. *[Quietly call the servys into tighter positions and be prepared to erect a psychic shield.]*

Spindle didn't reply or ask for clarification. His eyelight brightened with acknowledgment.

[Lock the arena down on my signal. Allow crawler guards entry, but no exits. No one in this room is allowed to leave. Also, give the order to lockdown timeslicing so that nothing is allowed outside the standard procession of time. Everything inside has to remain in regular time—]

"Spindle!" The commander's expression was mildly agitated. "Step down from the cadet."

He would've come across the room, but another contingent of Paladins approached with hands to shake and backs to pat. The commander glanced at me and doubt crept over his face. Why was Spindle on protective alert?

He wouldn't figure it out. He couldn't see, not yet. He couldn't see what I was seeing. He could see the energy around the Paladins, of course, but not the variations between these subtle differences in energy, how some vibrated in waves and others were dim imitations.

The commander couldn't see that he was surrounded by the enemy.

Perhaps the commander sensed something was wrong—Spindle's unexplained behavior and the insatiable rate at which I was consuming lifepatches—but he was distracted. Even if he wasn't, he wouldn't see what was coming. And I couldn't warn him.

The vision would be revealed to all of them soon enough, just a few more lifepatches, a bit more sustenance, enough that I could survive the revelation. After that, my life was in Spindle's hands. *Will that be enough?*

The servys blinked with confusion and began to send out the warning that I was overconsuming the lifepatches. The ground was littered with them. Something was wrong. Spindle overrode their calls and ordered them to continue and maintain tighter formation.

A curious energy buzzed in the room. Paladins were beginning to notice the servys' agitation. They had witnessed hundreds of Realization Trials and probably stood around while the cadet recovered until he or she could stand and be congratulated. They knew how long it took, they were aware of what it was like to recover, and they were becoming aware something was abnormal.

They looked more often, their glances lingering. But it wasn't the Paladins' stares I sensed. The enemy's True Nature was about to be revealed and, somehow, they felt it coming. Perhaps they sensed the room locked down. Their minds quietly scanned for possible escapes, preparing for the worst. They could handle betrayal, but not in this setting. They were sheep disguised as lions.

Footsteps pounded. "This is unacceptable, Spindle," the commander said. "Step down before you are forcibly removed."

Just another minute. I just need a little extra to survive.

"Is this understood?" The commander spoke his last warning deeply.

Paladins now gathered. Spindle's eyelight spun around his head, calculating position. His body posture readjusted as they surrounded us. The enemy, however, broke away unnoticed and gathered in small groups. *Something's coming.*

"What's the meaning of this, Commander?" a Paladin said. "Your servant mech is taking an aggressive stance. I suggest an immediate power down before—"

"Thank you, Captain Dushawn," the commander snapped.

Just a bit more.

The commander's lips curled, about to utter his last order, when Spindle's eyelight focused on him. "You must prepare, Commander."

The commander's hand moved near his evolver. He sensed it now. The room rippled with tension. The enemies had fully positioned themselves in one large group. The Paladins sensed the tension without knowing where an attack was coming.

Or who.

I needed more life force, but there was no time. I couldn't let them strike first. It had to be—

SSSSSSSSSSSSSSSSSSSSSDDOOOOOOOOOHPPBM.

The subsonic wave detonated from my core, rattling the floor. It went through them like gamma rays, stripping away their subtle delusions, revealing the enemy's true nature. The telekinetic wave imparted a sixth sense for all to see that the enemies among them hummed with duplicated tissues and blood and organs. They thought with processors. Followed programming. They were imitations of life.

A third of the Paladins are duplicated humans.

The last thing I heard was the sizzle of weapons.

———

HOW COULD THIS HAPPEN? The greatest race of humans infiltrated by the very falseness they sought to extinguish. A third of them were duplicated. Were we too busy looking to save the weaker human race, so consumed by protecting what we perceived as the less worthy, that we didn't see what was in our own house?

———

HALF THE SERVYS were gone when I awoke covered in lifepatches. We were overshadowed by the long legs of crawler guards, their legs anchored around us like a prison cell. Outside the circle, the war raged on.

It was a slur of bodies and weapons. I blinked away the moisture building in my eyes just enough to see a dismembered arm beyond the crawler legs, the fingers still twitching like they were trying to grasp the evolver club just out of reach.

I blinked again.

———

MORE BODIES WERE PILED up and there were fewer servys. I was covered in sticky fluid that tasted a bit like clay. And there was one less crawler. I felt pressure trying to pierce the psychic shield the crawlers had erected. Where were they finding the strength to still attack? *And where's Spindle?*

Another blink.

———————

THE SERVYS WERE GONE.

One crawler remained. And the pressure felt like someone standing on my skull. The bodies were stacked higher. The arm was joined by a boot with a bone sticking from the top.

The crawlers had joined the battle, spearing men with their legs or swiping them in half. My eyes were heavy, ready for another blink. The crawlers were battling each other like titans, behemoths piercing each other with deadly legs.

Why would they be battling each other?

One man moved swiftly through the mob, his weapon blazing as he cut, pounded and bullied his way in my direction, unconcerned with the battle around him, only where he was going.

Spindle... watch...

Spindle was somewhere; I could feel him in the room. He would heed my call, but I couldn't get the thoughts clearly formed. There was too much psychic force leaking through the barrier, shredding whatever thoughts I could form. I reached for a lifepatch, but most were spent. A stack of them was near my waist. My fingers crawled over the slick floor.

The mysterious Paladin was still slashing his way toward me. His weapons clashed with others and shields collapsed under his blows. The crawler guard did nothing. His translucent shield obscured what he looked like, but I could see his brown skin was bloody. I didn't need to see the almond-shaped eyes to know it was Pon.

He crawled low to the ground, elbows and knees up, like a leopard about to pounce, and engulfed me in his shield, relieving the psychic pressure. Sweat streaked his face. His scar twisted beneath his chin like a snake. He wouldn't look at me.

Pon spied the war outside the security of the shield. A small group of warriors was being methodically torn apart. The battle would soon be over, but I couldn't distinguish who was who in the melee. Their energy was too intertwined, impossible to distinguish one from the other. They all looked physically identical, brother fighting brother. Pon remained crouched, watching. He smelled like fear.

The floor quaked. The center of the room began spewing clay. A roar knocked everyone off their feet. The crawlers staggered. A shadow passed over us like a tidal wave.

Pon looked down. And then we were sinking.

62

The Predator

PON CRADLED ME LIKE A CHILD. The space around us was black and cool; the war faded away. I felt weightless, like we were floating. I couldn't see walls or a ceiling, couldn't even feel the wind against my face, just the humidity gathering on my exposed cheeks and tickling the end of my nose.

Pon's heart beat against my ear, his chest drawing long, deep breaths like he was working hard. His essence burned hot. It was not the same energy when Pike was in his eyes. Pon was back.

Did he ever leave?

I didn't think to ask him where he was taking me. Or why. I wasn't sure I even had my eyes open.

SOMETHING HARD PUSHED against my back. Tiny points of light coalesced in strange patterns swirling with darkness; then I realized there were knobby branches that looked black and the points of light were stars. The smell of the Preserve was unmistakable.

I had no strength to wipe the drops of moisture off my face. My head was against the trunk of the grimmet tree. Pon stood on the edge of the stone slab, looking into the pond below. The moon cast its glow through the tree, draping jagged shadows across his face, making it appear he was wearing a mask. He looked tired and hungry.

Grimmets scurried out of the tree, observing us below. Rudder landed gently on my chest. I was much number than I thought. It wasn't just strength I was lacking; I could barely feel the soft padding of Rudder's feet. He lay against my neck without a word or a thought and shared his warmth.

"They infiltrated long ago," Pon said, without turning.

I moved my lips but only grunted. Pon didn't glance over, only gazed up at the moon. I waited a moment, gathering the momentum to push out a single word. "How?"

He nodded ever so slightly, acknowledging my question, perhaps editing his thoughts down to the fewest words possible.

"When I relocated Pike, I discovered something no other minder had seen. Perhaps he wanted me to see, or maybe he just couldn't hide it any longer. The duplicates wanted us to have him, they wanted him to betray them, to give up their secrets so the Paladin Nation would win the public war, but in reality we won nothing. They were a thousand moves ahead of us."

I wanted to ask *why*. Why would they want to be exposed? Why would they want their secret agent to give them up? But the answer was now obvious: *The game of war and politics requires a chess master.*

"We thought we defeated them." He lifted his chin, exposing the edge of his jawbone. "All along, they were part of us like a virus, silently spreading the disease of falseness."

He appeared lost in thought. I started to form another question, but Pon held up his hand so I would conserve my strength. It felt like he still refused to believe what happened, too. How could they spread throughout a population? It wasn't like we could become one of them. They were more like artificial intelligence that assumed a moldable body that appeared human. They weren't born and fed; they didn't grow up like humans. They were just duplications.

"They," he said slowly, "were converting us, cadet."

He took a moment to let me process this. He tapped the back of his neck.

"The imbeds in our necks were being programmed to produce nanomechs like a mechanized tumor. Over time, the nanomechs would replace our blood cells and organs until our bodies were completely transformed into something that resembled a human. Until we became *duplications!* In the end, we would become the enemy."

It's the predator you don't see.

Our imbeds were nanomech factories that could produce synthetic white blood cells and repair nerve damage with manufactured connections. We had duplicating technology inside us! *Am I still completely human? Would I know if I wasn't?*

"Why didn't the commander do anything?"

"I didn't tell him," he said. "I didn't tell anyone."

"Why would you do that?"

"It wouldn't have mattered. They needed to see the truth for themselves."

"They would've listened."

"The Garrison is lost, cadet. The Paladin Nation is on the brink of collapse. We are the only thing that stands between the human species and the duplications. If we perish, all is lost."

He exposed his eyes for the first time. He could hide from me no longer. I saw humility. Weakness. Vulnerability. He was imperfect after all. He was human.

"The Paladins needed to see," he said, "what they were becoming. No one could tell them."

He breathed deep again, closing his eyes. Rudder stirred on my neck. I could feel my toes and fingers.

"When I learned this from Pike, I returned to force your telekinetic response the only way possible," Pon said, speaking to the moon again. "I put you under duress, destroyed your identity, and exposed your true nature. I had to bring your powers forth, for it was you that would give them the sight. You weren't ready for such knowledge, but time was not on our side. I betrayed you."

"I saw Pike in you."

"You saw my knowledge." He looked at me. "You mistook it for Pike. But the commander secretly believed I betrayed you. He believed I was sent to assassinate you, that I was a traitor. He sent minders to bore through my mind, seeking information about the enemy. I would've done the same, but he was not aware that the very minders he sent to harvest my thoughts were the exact enemies he sought to expose."

Muscles flexed along his jaw. His eyes revealed the psychic agony he'd endured. His essence was faint, like color bleached from the sun. There wasn't much left of him. They had drained him to find out what he knew. Only a shadow of a great warrior remained.

"The enemy has been waiting for you, cadet."

"Why me?"

"You are the telekinetic one. They would replicate your DNA and quietly infuse Paladins with self-replicating code by stamping it into the imbeds."

He rubbed the back of his neck. I would've done the same.

"But they did not expect you to bring forth the vision."

I shut my eyes. What good was I, lying catatonic on the rock? All the power in the world couldn't save us now; what good was the ability to see clearly? I had nothing left to give.

"How did they win?" I asked. "They were outnumbered in the arena, how could they possibly have won?"

"They are duplicates, cadet. They are manufactured beings that speak the language of technology. What is a crawler, mmm?" He paused. "What is the room?"

They were all nanotechnology; they were scripted programs made up of cellular-sized machines that followed orders. The duplicates managed to reprogram the crawlers and turn them against their creators. And the transforming room! The Paladins were in the belly of the enemy at the end. The floor exploded and a tidal wave was falling on us when we escaped. We were being swallowed by the room.

"We created our enemies, cadet. We didn't see what was in front of us. Who do we have to blame?"

The duplicates wouldn't stop with us when there were millions of humans in the world. Why not give them all an imbed and start the conversion until no one got sick, no one felt pain, and everyone got what their hearts desired?

Thoughts of hopelessness seized my insides. I put them to rest, let them fall away like useless chaff and returned to the present moment. I pushed myself up an inch or two.

"We need to gather the surviving Paladins," I commanded. "Call forth a transporter and get us to a hiding place. Get us somewhere remote; send out a beacon to all surviving Paladins. All is not lost, Pon." I scanned the surrounding trees. We were in the open without weapons or protection. "This is the last place we need to be."

Sensation returned to my legs. I pushed against the tree trunk until I was sitting up. Pon gazed back at the moon, breathing deep, like my father had, relishing the moment and not the least concerned our tactical position was horrible.

Rudder urged me to be still. I consumed whatever strength I had just to sit up. My pulse had weakened rapidly. If I had some lifepatches, I'd be in better shape.

"Pivot trained me." Pon was still looking heavenward, ignoring my struggle. "He opened me to my potential. The Paladin Nation thought I would become his successor." He turned to me and, for the first time ever, a faint smile broke the corner of his mouth. "I was only meant to guide you."

How else would he know the underground tunnels?

"Pivot is older than our planet." His tone was louder and stronger. "I don't know who he is or where he came from, cadet, I only know him. And for that, I am eternally grateful."

Pon bowed his head and his lips moved silently, as if giving thanks. The grimmets squabbled. Pon glanced at them. He shuffled away from the edge and walked down the slab.

"Why did he leave? Why not stay and fight? He could've defeated them himself."

"Pivot didn't need to stay." He took the evolvers from his belt and they unfolded quietly around his arms. The palms of his hands were glowing blue, awaiting command.

"You," he said. "He gave us you."

Pon's eyes remained open and soft, allowing me complete access to his admiration and love. Without him, where would I be?

And then the glare returned. The look of steel ridged his brows and creased his forehead. His lips pulled back, thin and grim. He nodded to me, slowly, deliberately, and turned his back. He flicked his wrists and three long whips slithered from each hand, the glow illuminating the surrounding forest. The whips crawled along the stone like snakes.

Several figures emerged from the trees, all dressed in Paladin uniforms. The central figure was tall with broad shoulders, his hair short, nose flat. It was the Chief Commander. Com. The most successful commander in the Paladin Nation. *Keep your enemies closer than your allies, cadet. That way you always know what they're doing.*

Com stopped at the bottom of the slab. His six assassins continued forward, activating evolvers. Pon did not activate a shield. He stood between the enemy and me, completely vulnerable.

Brute force is the weakest response. But sometimes, it is the only option.

63

THE CALL

IT WAS A BEAUTIFUL BATTLE.

They surrounded him, each engulfed in a glowing shield. There was no need to slice time; they were all capable of matching each other's skill. They fought in ordinary time, as if the showdown was merely a ritual. Six to one, the fight was a formality. The ending wouldn't be a surprise. Pon took the center.

They raised their weapon hands like a firing squad. Blue pulses blazed from their palms and converged in the center. Pon danced inside a furious storm of electrical whips, deflecting the impossible. The enemy stopped firing in order to power up their shields to block the energy Pon was deflecting back, and in that moment he clapped his hands together. A lance emerged and spiked one of them between the eyes, the two-handed weapon too much for his shield.

The remaining enemies repositioned, allowing Pon to return to the center in ceremonial fashion. They aborted firing pulsars, instead charging with a variety of weapons. They came at him with staves and swords and scorching whips. He couldn't guard against them all, but Pon parried and spun, simultaneously defending and attacking. The air churned and crackled. Shields buzzed and the enemies pressed on until another fell, this one cut in half. Pon wiped his face as he returned to the center.

Com watched as his men fell.

———

PERHAPS PON DIDN'T SEE the crawler emerge from the trees, did not sense it creeping close to the ground. It stopped near Com, swaying hypnotically like a praying mantis sighting its prey. Pon drove the enemies backward, but his back was to Com and his crawler. An enemy stumbled. Pon raised his hands to end the fifth assassin.

Com nodded.

One of the crawler's legs darted; its needle tip blurred through Pon's chest.

Pon stopped, mid-strike. The enemies lowered their weapons. In reverence, they watched this warrior slide off the crawler's leg. The evolvers unfolded from his arms. He lay face up, eyes on the glowing moon. His last breath gurgled, but he held it. Blinked. And then it leaked from his lungs. His eyes remained open.

All I could do was watch.

My vision had been fulfilled. I saw Pon's death when I first met Com. If I understood what it was, could I have stopped it? Could I have changed the future, or were we all destined to our end?

I did not experience anger's burn, nor the tension of hatred. I only felt the warm release of affection for a man that guided me to realization, a man that served life and had given his own. For that man, lying breathless and alone, I was filled with love. Pon would not ask that one ounce of energy be expended in regret.

But it was impossible not to want revenge.

Pon is dead.

———

Com approached Pon's body. The two remaining assassins stood at attention while he looked over it. The crawler jerked me to my feet. My head snapped back.

"Gently," Com called. "We prefer him alive."

The crawler's grip eased, the leg still warm from Pon's blood. Its spherical body pulsed like a beating heart. I wanted to destroy it for blindly following orders, but I could barely keep my head up.

Com kept his distance as the enemies approached. One limped badly; the other's face was half-blackened from a near fatal strike. The crawler rose up and allowed them to walk underneath. Rudder stayed tightly wrapped around my neck.

The enemies looked hard, but their stares softened as they neared. They looked into my eyes, trancelike. Their last steps were mechanical and aimless. They leaned in, their lips moving silently.

"Beautiful," the blackened one muttered.

They were mesmerized not by what they saw, but what they felt. It was everything they dreamed of. When all their orders had been completed and every command followed, the duplicates were still left void of life. They could learn to act like a human, to feel and do everything like a human, but they could never *be*. They would always imitate life. What they felt, when they gazed inside me, was the pure moment of presence.

"Step away," Com said.

The two hesitated, but moved to the side. Com was wiping dust from his hands, staring at Pon's body. "I would rather your trainer was alive, but I don't think he would've cared for becoming one of us. He would've been very problematic, yes." He looked at me. "I believe it's better it ended this way."

"How could you do this?" I said.

"How? Why do you think I'm the most productive commander in the entire Paladin Nation? I make Paladins, young man. Then I turn them into duplicates. They're much more successful that way, I think you would agree."

"You're mistaken if you think you've found another one," I whispered. "Lay me next to Pon."

"You haven't heard my offer."

"I've heard enough."

"We've been misrepresented." Com lifted his hands in an offer of innocence. "It is true we've become synthetic beings, but we think and feel exactly as we were when we were organic, yes. We're still very humanlike. In fact, we're better." He shrugged. *And that's a fact.*

But he said humanlike. Even he knew there was a difference, even if he thought it was better.

"I was once human, very much like you. I was born into the Paladin Nation and trained. In fact, I was very successful in my Realization Trial, so much so that I rose to commander in a very short time. I had a great aptitude. I had vision, young man. It should not surprise you that I decided to convert. You see, the duplicates have been part of the Paladin Nation a long time. You'd be surprised just how high up the betrayal goes. They knew I would be a good candidate because I know what works." He glanced at Pon with a hint of a smile. "And what doesn't."

He walked a bit closer to me. The grimmets squabbled overhead, their movements squirming inside my chest.

"Duplicated humans are more intelligent than their originals, young man. They calculate on levels never even conceived of by mankind. They have the next thousand years planned, and it starts with taking over the Paladin Nation. Do you think any of this has been an accident? The Paladins are a formidable foe, and to beat them meant to become them. Duplicates are the superior breed, young man, like it or not. So when I was invited to join them, I simply chose to be superior."

He stood quiet and very still. Strength trickled through my body as Rudder hummed against my neck, but it only made me more aware of the pain.

"I resisted at first," he said. "I mean, the thought of giving up my humanity..." He nodded, looking away. "That's a big one, yes. But I understood that, ultimately, we *can* control our destiny. Why should we leave it up to chance? Why should we let nature decide what we'll become when we can program our own DNA? We can decide what we'll be, what we'll look like. Cancer? Not anymore. Memory loss? Not possible. I can *tell* my body what I want it to do, what to feel. I am an impeccable representation of the human species, young man. *Impeccable.*"

He jabbed at the ground like he was presenting evidence to a jury.

"You see, even Albert Einstein once said that God does not roll dice. God has laws. Laws? Mmm? Does that not sound like programming to you? And in the end, aren't we all made in the image of our Father, if you want to quote the Bible? Humans are self-centered; they are imperfect programs. What kind of honor is that for God to be proud of, I ask you? If we are truly made in his image, then we need to be impeccable. We were given the intelligence to fix the broken human species."

"You're a machine."

"And who says God isn't manufactured?" He smirked. "He could very well be a machine, too. Yes?"

"I've seen the beauty of existence; there's nothing to accomplish." The two assassins still hadn't looked away. "Ask them."

"Yes, well, you've displayed quite a vision, and we hope to integrate that into the mainframe database. We'll all be uploaded with your existential experience. But indulge me for another moment. What are all humans afraid of?"

He lifted his chin, allowing tension to build.

"Death, wouldn't you say? They're all afraid that one day it's all coming to an end, and no one wants that. They want what they have, what they've worked so hard for. They want to keep that." He clenched his fists. "They want to hold onto what's theirs, don't you think that's fair? They've worked so very hard for their life, why should they have to give it all away simply because their bodies can't go on? Wouldn't it be wonderful to possess your life forever, yes? But you can't do that if you remain organic, young man."

He held up his finger, head lowered, holding the final, clinching answer.

"Nothing has to die. We can all live and live and live. Just think, we can manufacture a likeness of your father and upload his memories. He can be standing here, right in front of us tomorrow! He'll walk and talk and remember you, what's the difference?" He tipped his head back and looked down his nose. "If you're one of us, you never die. You live, young man. Forever."

"Delusion," I said, "is not living. You're not real, and you don't even know it."

"You cannot stop the inevitable. Humans are the past. We are the future."

"But you're not here."

He locked his hands behind his back and took a deep breath.

"It doesn't matter what you decide to do," he said quietly. "The human race will all convert in the end, young man. And, trust me, there won't be a problem. They're already programs, yes? The human race behaves from psychological experiences, blindly acting out suppressed memories and fears. Few ever try to understand themselves. They're not interested in discovering what's real, young man, they're only concerned with what makes them happy. They only *want*, they're not interested in *being*. They're infants searching for a breast." He extended his empty hand, palm up, and said gently, "With us, they get what they want."

"And what do they want?"

He smiled for the first time. "Whatever their hearts desire."

I'd heard the argument before, in a parking lot at the high school with Mr. Black. Was he a duplicate? Com was right. They'd be lining up to convert.

The trees rustled at the bottom of the slope. Two crawlers approached with a single duplicate between them, his suit torn and bloody. Com left his hand extended toward me, the invitation still on the table with his eyes locked on mine. The messenger stopped a few steps behind him and waited at attention, his gaze locking on my face. Com finally stood upright and dropped his hand. He nodded to me. My answer was final.

"Very well, then."

"The Garrison is secure, Com," the messenger said. "Civilians and remaining Paladins are trapped in a sublevel sector without escape.

All communications are contained. Air supply has been cut off. Estimated time of surrender is two hours. The other ten training facilities are currently under siege. Seven have already been secured by our forces and the expected surrender of the remaining three facilities is within seven hours."

"Escapees?" Com asked.

"Twenty-one percent have escaped."

"Twenty-one percent?"

"Trackers are hunting. We expect to find locations of refuge within fourteen days."

Com paced thoughtfully. The crawlers stepped out of his way. The corner of his mouth twitched. He touched his cheek, looking around. He looked at me.

I was supporting my own weight, but the crawler's grip was killing the nerves in my arms. Any effort to overwhelm it, mentally or telekinetically, would drain me entirely. Not even Rudder would bring me back after that.

"I want him taken to an infirmary immediately." Com turned his back on me. "Get a preliminary coding of his DNA; then take him for full infusion. Do not hold back, I believe he is capable of handling pain, yes? I expect the full conversion of Socket Greeny in twenty-four hours. Pass the report to others."

Com's head jerked again, as if a thought hit him like an arrow. He looked at the grimmets. He swung around to me.

"You will become one of us." He stepped closer. "It will all make sense when you are converted. You will understand, yes." Closer. "We all understand, young man."

His expression softened, as did the others', as he gazed into my eyes.

If I had the strength, I would vaporize his ass with a thought, but there were more of him. If this many could deceive the Paladins, how many were still walking the streets in ordinary life? How many Chief Coms were there waiting to take his place? How many assassins on the assembly line?

And Com was right, people were willing to become like them. Ask

Mr. Black. They were all out there, wanting what they wanted. I couldn't destroy them without destroying their freedom to choose. How did I change them if they weren't willing to change? Destroying this duplicate would not bring peace. They were self-centered programs. Of course they were self-centered; they were reflections of their creators: *HUMANS!* The duplicates were perversions of our selfish desires; they were self-perpetuating, a more efficient version of the deficient human.

"Com?" the messenger asked. "Would you like me to—"

He held up his hand for silence. *Twitch.* He had the faraway look again, like he was distracted by an idea. He glanced at the grimmets then to me. His gaze turned from unfocused distraction to yearning. He was caught by what he saw. Suddenly, it was too tempting to keep his distance. He needed a closer look.

Com stopped a few feet away. A child's joy lit up his face. He shook his head like he was trying to break away. He began to lean closer. He shuffled like he didn't want to, but he couldn't stop himself. The experience was right there, in my eyes, he could sense it.

He gently touched my shoulders and continued to lean closer. His breath was hot and humid. His eyes were light blue with streaks of darker blue radiating from the pupils. His sweaty forehead touched mine. Eye to eye.

He wanted to *know* the essence he craved like a hungry ghost. He wanted to grab it, to make it his own. So he raised his hand. He wanted more than to just see it. He wanted more than to just feel it. Have it.

He touched my forehead to take it from me.

A LIGHT BURST behind my eyes.

Com's fingers burned, his mind spreading like a fungus inside me, chasing the experience to make it his. He tried to take what was ungraspable, and the more it eluded him, the deeper he plunged. His mind penetrated through me until we were impossibly tangled.

Shapes took form in the white light. I wasn't seeing with my eyes, though; I was seeing like a minder.

Com was convulsing.

The messenger tried to pull him away, but his fingers were welded to my forehead. He shook like an electrocution was taking place. I felt my life force being pulled through his fingers. He didn't mean to kill me, but he couldn't stop.

The density of my physical body lightened. My heartbeat faded and blood pooled quietly in the chambers. My arteries and veins relaxed. I didn't know where I was, but it wasn't my body. I could see it, though, like I was sitting in the tree. I saw Com still convulsing. My body was limp.

All was silent.

There was a graceful solitude to the event below, moving in an odd, slow cinematic way. Nothing was out of place. Everything as it should be.

The grimmets stirred on the branches. I felt their movements. They shuffled again. Rudder clung to my neck and the rest watched from the tree, blinking their golden eyes. I could feel each of them as individual life forces, their essence a fountain of youth that flowed through my body.

Com fell away. The grimmets watched him. He shook his head. He looked at my body like he was coming back from a dream. Then he looked at the grimmets.

"Destroy him." He reached for the evolver on his belt but fumbled it.

"Com?" The messenger stepped forward. "But, sir..."

He had glimpsed what was about to happen.

Grimmets began to leave the branches, circling above, emitting vibrations, a call not heard by ears, but felt by all. More grimmets lifted off and the call gathered momentum.

Com stripped the evolver from the messenger's belt. It began to unfold but fell from his quaking hands. Com crawled after the unwieldy weapon. He clamped his hands over his ears.

The grimmets called to the duplicates.

"Kill him!" Com cried.

They were calling them...

"KILL SOCKET GREENY!"

...to deactivate.

The crawlers cocked their legs. Stopped.

The crawler holding my body gently laid it beneath the tree and heeled like a dog, answering the grimmets' call.

My vision illuminated in my mind's eye in full detail. I sensed my lifeless body calmly resting beneath the storm of grimmets circling above. The call pulsed through my flesh, through the tree, stone and earth. It was a sound beyond the plane of thought and emotion. It was much more fundamental, much simpler. It was the call of existence, spanning the globe as if there were no separation. As if they were one with the universe.

The grimmets were pure presence.

And I was their conduit.

They swarmed down upon my body, crawling beneath it. Rudder gently cradled my head. The beating of their wings stirred dust and debris, fanning life force and heating my flesh. They held me up for the world to see.

The One that Sees Clearly.

The assassins laid their weapons at the tree and bowed. Com and the messenger joined them, placing their foreheads on the stone. They sought to possess the majestic beauty of presence, but the grimmets' call gave them clarity.

They realized they would never have the being of presence. Humans had the ability to understand their psychological programs; they could realize their true nature. Humans had the potential to transform. The duplicates understood, in that very moment, that they would always be a program. They understood that when they gave up their humanity, they lost the ability to truly transform. They would stagnate in their programming for eternity.

The wisdom of the grimmets' call released them from their obsessive chase of something they could never have, to abandon their futile efforts. Regardless of how perfect their programming seemed, no matter what it promised, their search was pointless. They could never be human again. They could never *Be*. And for that wisdom, they bowed.

My vision expanded and I began to rise. I saw the grimmet tree from high above. I saw Garrison Mountain and the endless miles of uninhabitable land around it. I saw the ocean. I continued to rise until I saw the continents. I rose above the planet and saw Earth suspended in black space. I felt life pulse within it and heard the duplicates answer. One by one, millions laid down their weapons across the planet and bowed. They rose above their programming. They understood. They changed at a fundamental level and heeded the call. Perhaps, in the end, they were as close to human as possible.

My vision continued to recede further into outer space. The moon orbited nearby. And as I sped away from Earth, my vision expanding outward, the moon passed in front of me.

And, for the first time, I saw the dark side.

64

Railroad Tracks

Where did we go when we died?

I knew people had lots of ideas, but they didn't really *know*. Even if you died and came back, that wasn't the same as being put in a box and buried. Did we go to heaven? Hell? Nirvana? Were there virgins waiting for us?

I didn't get any answers. I knew my body was lifeless. And I knew I could see it from above like the grimmets carried my awareness and I shared their vision, but where did I go after that? Wherever it was, no one greeted me. No old man with a white beard or dead dad. No virgins.

There was dark and light. No shapes, just the sensation of dark and light intermingled and dancing some eternal dance. And I was in the middle of it. Dark and light.

Dark and light.

But then there was more light than dark. It shrank down and took shape. Sometimes it became a square, and then it would fade and reappear sometime later.

But then the square of light returned and never left. I felt the confines of my body. And the wheel of time, once again, began to turn.

I opened my eyes.

A SQUARE LIGHT was on the ceiling with cobwebs blowing in an air-conditioner vent. I was lying in a bed with the unmistakable presence of my boyhood around me. The essence of my past saturated the sheets and the carpet, the posters on the walls.

I was in South Carolina. While the Garrison was capable of replicating it perfectly (even the cobwebs), I knew reality. There was no way to explain how I knew, other than a lack of separation between me and my surroundings. I just *knew*.

But how long I'd been there, and how I got there, I didn't know. My nojakk didn't respond when I asked for the date and neither did the imbed. Both were dead.

Sunlight streaked between the blinds. I put my feet on the floor. A red ball was snoring next to me. I held Rudder by his long tail like a possum, his tongue rolling in and out. I laid him on my pillow.

My body ached like I'd run a hundred marathons. I stretched and twisted to loosen the stiffness in my neck and back, and just doing that much made me tired.

I sensed a lot of people in the house. They could sense me waking and stretching. I couldn't tell who was out there. Probably Paladins. Whoever they were, there were a lot of them in the next room. Mother was there, too. Her scent lingered in my bedroom. She'd been in to check on me.

I scratched and stretched, and then did my morning business in the bathroom. I stopped at the mirror. I'd lost so much weight and my hair was a few inches longer.

I leaned closer and scratched whiskers on my chin. My skin had aged like a sun-baked cowboy. I was an old-looking seventeen-year-old. My eyes had changed, too. It wasn't so much the appearance, they were still blue, but now there was something in them that reminded me of what I saw in Pon's eyes. There were no distractions inside.

I'd put up and taken down enough posters in my bedroom to wallpaper the entire house. Where there wasn't a poster there was grimy tape where one had been. My ancient iPod with the cracked screen was on my desk. A skateboard stuck out from under the bed, a Toy Machine sticker scratched on the bottom.

There was a photo above my desk of train tracks, long and straight, disappearing on the horizon. I was thirteen years old when I put that up. I'd ripped it out of a National Geographic at the library. At the time, I wasn't sure what was so compelling about it, I just wanted it. It represented somewhere else to me. One day I would follow those tracks and get away from the conflict in my head, the anger and sadness that twisted inside me. Those tracks were my yellow brick road to someplace else, something better.

But there was no *over there,* there was just here. I wasn't any more special now than when I was thirteen. But now I understood that. I didn't need train tracks to get there.

Mother stood in the doorway. She had lost weight, too. She approached and, after a long pause, put her hand through my hair. She worked her fingers around my head, not looking in my eyes. Not yet. She eased into the moment, like she was making sure it wasn't a dream. She clamped her lips tight, brushing my hair around like she was getting me ready for school pictures.

I took her hand. *I'm alive.*

In that moment, just being near her, touching her hand, I knew her. In the clarity of my awareness, where nothing was separate, I knew her thoughts, felt her emotions, and saw her experiences. It wasn't like taking her thoughts; it was just a passive knowing, like her memories were as much mine as they were hers.

She had watched my Realization Trial, and while she could not see the torture I experienced in my mind, she watched my body collapse. She watched it convulse and shrink while I experienced rapid degradation in a prolonged timeslice. She didn't move from her seat, ignoring Spindle's pleas to get some rest. She saw the end nearing for me and felt the devastating pain a mother feels for her dying son.

The servys ushered her to a safe haven when the war broke. And when the duplicates converted the entire Garrison into their command, the servys turned on them. They escaped deep underground. She sat in the darkness while the duplicates were outside the door. She didn't know if I survived. Didn't know if she would.

And when it was over, the doors opened. The Garrison was in chaos. She ran from room to room, where servys lay deactivated. The arena was covered with bodies. The surviving Paladins were covering the lifeless. Mother pulled the sheets off, going to each and every one, but not finding me. In the center lay Spindle's body, his eyelight snuffed. He deactivated himself before he was converted to serve the army of duplicates like the rest of the servys. Mother knelt next to him, brushing her fingers over his textured faceplate, staring at the blank space next to him where Pon activated a trapdoor for our escape.

The commander, bleeding but alive, put a hand on her shoulder. "We need you, Kay," he said.

She was brought to the Preserve. Paladins lined both sides of the wide stone leading to the grimmet tree. My body lay beneath it. Rudder sat on my chest. The grimmets filled the branches, watching her approach. They would not let anyone near me, guarding my body like a sacred treasure. But they didn't stop her.

She knelt next to me, felt the weak pulse in my wrist and knew my heart was not beating on its own. Rudder did not have to tell her that he was keeping me alive. It was his essence that beat in my chest and pumped my blood. Without him, all would be still.

"Please," she said to those within earshot, "bring help."

The Paladins set up a life-support station under the grimmet tree. For three days and nights, she sat next to me. Rudder did not leave and Mother refused to move. They waited until I returned from beyond, where the dark and light danced. They waited until my heart, on its own, beat again.

Those were the things she did. And there was joy in her heart to touch me, to see me standing and smiling back. That was what I knew about her.

"IT's BEEN SIX WEEKS," she said. "The Garrison is undergoing a purging; nearly all technology has been shut down while we search for dormant code that might reawaken duplications. We have to expect they were prepared for this sort of thing."

"That's why the nojakk and imbed aren't working?"

"Yes. And as you can imagine, the public is outraged; they want explanations. The Paladin Nation is keeping silent until they clean up their own house. First, we need to develop testing to assure Paladins are human before appearing in public again."

I pried the blinds apart. No cars were moving. People were walking down the middle of the road. Two houses down, three boys leaped off their porch and hid in the bushes with squirt guns and water balloons. If duplicates reawakened, like Mother said, what would stop them?

"Why am I here?"

"Right now, this is the safest place in the world."

I imagined crawler guards perched on the roof like pigeons, but that was impossible. They'd be deactivated along with the servys. *Along with Spindle.*

"Pon?" I asked.

She paused, but didn't need to answer. She never saw his body at the grimmet tree; it had been removed before she got there. She didn't see him like I did.

"He wasn't a traitor," I said.

"We know that now."

"He saved us."

"He shouldn't have kept his knowledge secret."

She'd spent the last year watching him grind me down, and despised the brutal tactics. I could tell her Pivot had put Pon in charge of me; that he was responsible for my development and protection. That he gave me the ability to become what I am. That he kept his secrets and endured endless torture because that was what life demanded. He did those things so the Paladins would see the truth for themselves. But forgiveness did not come easy to her.

"How did he even escape to come for me?" I asked.

"We don't know much about what happened during that period. The minders that were guarding him were duplicates, but we have reason to believe he somehow overcame them before the battle."

The boys' father walked on the porch and casually down the steps. The boys ambushed him. Balloons exploded on his back. He retreated and they pursued until they ran out of balloons and resorted to squirt guns. He chased them and they screamed and laughed.

"I saw Father." I touched the scar behind my ear. She didn't say anything, but I felt her breathing stall. I explained how Pivot had set up the scenario, that it was some other dimension and that it wasn't really him I was talking to, but it may as well have been. "He looked exactly the same, like he hadn't shaved in a couple days. He even did that thing where he smiles with his eyes."

She hummed in response, that was it.

"You know, I always thought I was okay with his death. We sat around this fire and talked about stuff, and then..." I recalled the emotional swelling in my chest. I let go of the blinds. "I miss him."

Mother was looking at the floor, all too familiar with that feeling.

"What do you miss most?"

"When he came home at night." She leaned against the wall and folded her arms. She was still looking at the floor without seeing it. "Every time I heard the door open, I knew he was safe and we'd have another day together."

"Did you know he was going to die?"

"This is a dangerous business. I never took anything for granted."

"So you weren't surprised?"

She imitated a short laugh. "You can't prepare for that, Socket."

Sadness rumbled through her. I let her experience those traumatic memories, how long ago they shook her like earthquakes. Now they were just tremors, but they were still there.

I gently took her hand. She put her hand over mine. We stayed like that for a while.

SLAP. A red sticky grimmet hit me square in the face and latched onto my cheeks. I backed into the wall while Rudder hugged my nose. He pulled his head back and stared into my left eye then hugged me again, squeezing my cheeks with his hands and feet, then gnawing on my nose. I grabbed him by the tail. He squirmed and wriggled.

"You sleep a lot, you know that?" I said.

Rudder giggled that rapid-fire laughter, so infectious even Mother couldn't help but laugh.

"Are the rest here?" I asked.

She pushed the door open to the front room.

They were everywhere. Sleeping under the coffee table, hanging from the lamp, drinking from full-sized cups, ripping apart magazines and tossing wadded pages around like volleyballs. The rest were wrestling on the floor and kitchen table, climbing across the ceiling and flying around. It looked like the zoo for the really weird.

When they saw me, it was immediate silence, like someone shouted *freeze* and meant it. They looked back and forth, not sure if they were in trouble, waiting for my reaction.

"All I want to know," I said, "is where you're pooping?"

Long pause.

Laughter.

Like the funniest thing they ever heard. They fell off the lamps and rolled off the tables, bouncing on their bellies while the walls shook.

They took wing and stormed around the room like a school of fish and out the back door, torn paper and empty cups rattling behind them. We followed them into the backyard. Hundreds of grimmets flocked into the maple tree, hiding behind the broad leaves.

They couldn't stay quiet any more than those kids down the street. We sat on the back steps and watched an enormous free-for-all on the lawn.

Our neighbor looked over the privacy fence. Mother waved to him. He waved back, mouth open, then went back to fertilizing his lawn. The grimmets made him forget what he just saw. The most powerful creatures on this planet—psychic giants, technological wizards, mental titans—playing like children.

"The answer was right in front of us," I said. "The grimmets were waiting for the truth to unlock them, only needed someone to channel their power. They needed someone to see clearly. All this time, no one knew."

She shook her head. For once, she didn't have an answer. "Why didn't they use Pivot?" she asked.

Yeah, why not Pivot? But I knew the answer was beyond my comprehension. There was a plan out there, and I was part of it. That plan needed me to unlock the grimmets. Pivot was just there to guide me. *Where did the plan go from here?*

"I don't know," was all I could say.

We sat quietly, for some time. There was nowhere to go, nothing to do. Mother wouldn't return to the Garrison for weeks. Neither would I. So we watched the grimmets slug it out. Eventually, I chased after them and they cheered and clapped and wrapped their tails around my legs and tripped me and mauled me. They gnawed on every part of my body like needle-toothed puppies until I grabbed them, one at a time, and threw them high into the air. You'd think that was the greatest thing in the world, to be thrown up like that. When they came back down, they said, *Higher, go higher.*

"Oh, you want to go higher?" And I'd throw them again. They laughed and laughed, their bellies filled with joy.

Mine, too.

65

Ice Cubes

THE WEEKS WENT by at home. The first couple days I slept like an old dog, but after that it was time for business. Mother was taking meetings in her room. Then we'd both take meetings in the living room with Paladins projected in front of us. The tone was somber; we lost a lot of good men and women in the battle. A lot of families were disrupted; children were going to grow up without a mother or father, some both. My heart ached for the experiences that lay ahead of them, like coming home to an empty house or a single parent struggling with loss. Some would grow stronger because of it; others would struggle with the emotional holes left behind.

The grimmets made a mess of the house until I called a meeting and set them straight. They were cooped up, accustomed to a forest to romp around, not this stuffy little room and the backyard. They sat quietly while I lectured them, occasionally swinging their tails or kicking their legs. They listened to my impassioned speech about keeping the house in order. I couldn't believe the words coming out of my mouth. A year ago, I was stacking empty pizza boxes as high as the dirty laundry. But the grimmets, led by Rudder, turned their restless energy to housekeeping and our home became immaculate.

The time neared to return to the Garrison. The Paladin Nation needed every single person available. More than that, I think they needed my presence for morale. And I was ready to go back. There was so much to do. But before I left, there were still a few things left to attend.

I was not leaving my life behind. It was as much a part of me as those galactic experiences of spiritual oneness.

I SHOWED up at Streeter's house unannounced. It wasn't like he and Chute weren't calling every day, wanting to come over. I wasn't physically ready to leave the house. I got winded just taking a shower. Death takes a lot out of you, even with a grimmet breathing life back in.

Streeter's backyard was a lush garden with crape myrtles, bamboo, roses and such. His grandfather taught horticulture and spent most weekends tending to his private paradise. Streeter rarely helped. He rarely went outside even though they had a swimming pool with a deck and a pergola covered with jasmine. We used to swim all day when we were little, even before we could touch the bottom, but then we got older and virtualmode came along and the pool became nothing but an expensive chore.

But when I got there, Streeter was sitting in the sun on one of the lounge chairs, sucking on an ice cube and hunching over a small table. He'd gained a few pounds, but was still a skinnier version of his plump self. And, he was tan for once.

I unlatched the back gate and came up the side steps to the deck. He was muttering to a small gear box on his lap, poking it with a tool, slurping the ice cube.

"That's illegal, you know," I said.

"Ho!" He jumped back in the chair. The gear box and tool skittered to the edge of the pool. "You need a bell around your neck."

I picked up the gear and put it on his lap. We took a moment, looking each other over, adjusting to the new looks. *Had that much time gone by?* He was there when my dad died. He was at every after-school fight, sometimes the only one on my side. But now here we were, remembering what it used to be like.

Streeter shoved the chair back and held out his hand. We latched with hands up, then he pulled me close and sort of hugged. It was the first time we'd ever done that.

"Shit, man," he said, "it's good to see you."

I knew his thoughts the way I had with my mother. I knew how he'd suffered gear addiction withdrawal, how his eyes ached for weeks, how his entire nervous system hurt while he adjusted to being back in his skin full-time. I knew how he carried a guilty weight for the incident at the Judgment Day club, that what happened to me was all his fault. I also knew the loneliness inside him, like a block of ice in his stomach. I knew that ice block, too. Streeter hated it, fought against it, but now he was finally acknowledging it.

He was back. Good old Streeter.

"You look different," he said.

I grabbed my short hair. "It's the shampoo."

"Well, there's that. But there's something else." He moved his hand in front of him like a magic trick was coming. "It's the whole package; you feel different."

"Look who's talking. What, you weigh a hundred pounds now?"

"I've never weighed a hundred."

"You did when you were a baby."

"True." He laughed the old Streeter laugh and nodded thought-fully like he was looking through me. Chute must've taught him how to do that.

"So, how's things?" I asked.

"Some good, some bad." He tapped his nojakk cheek. "I'm guessing this technology blackout is your fault."

"Sort of. But not really."

Streeter lay back in the lounge chair. "I want details."

"You don't want to know." I pulled up a chair. "It's boring, really."

"Yeah, you're right. Fighting death matches with assassins with flaming swords and laser cannons is boring shit. That's the last thing I want to hear."

"Besides, what're you doing with a gear box? I thought you were in therapy. You shouldn't be virtualmoding yet."

"What, this?" He turned the black box over. "This is just a nojakk generator. You know, there's a huge reward for the first pirate generator to override the blackout. It's like ten thousand dollars or something."

I took the box and sensed the circuitry, could feel the basic structure was correct, but his coding was too primitive. He'd probably make it work.

"I know what you're thinking," he said, taking the box back. "But the therapist wants me to do things outside as long as it isn't virtualmode. I can use the nojakk and Internet. I even helped with the garden, pulling weeds. Believe that?"

"You can't do virtualmode ever again?"

"Eventually. Right now, the therapist wants me to talk about feelings and other bullshit. Mainly about my parents, but there's other things." He rotated the box around and around, like it might tell him the future. "We've been talking about you a lot."

That wasn't easy for him to say. Tension wrapped around him. He didn't expect to go there with his feelings with me sitting right in front of him; it took him by surprise. But he stayed with it.

I said, "Hey, well what can I say? I'm honored."

Over and over the gear box went. He shook his head, looking at the clouds. "You know what it is?" he said, his throat tightening. "It's just, you're not afraid of anything, Socket. And I am. I'm afraid of everything. You fought my fights, were always there, and now I got to do this shit on my own and I'm hating it, man. Freaking hating it."

He twisted his fingers like pretzels.

"Streeter, I can walk through the worst neighborhood in the world and nothing can touch me. Nobody and nothing can hurt me. But I still experience fear. I'm no different than you."

"*Right.* You walk on water and I'm crying in the therapist's office because I miss my mom and dad." He looked away, didn't mean to say that, either. "Yeah, we're *exactly* the same."

"What I mean is just work with what you have. That's all you got, just be there with it. Don't be comparing yourself to me or Chute or the president of the United States."

"Yeah, well, don't quit your day job. You're no therapist."

"Never said I was."

"I'm not so sure about your day job, either. What happened at the Judgment Day club? I wake up, you're gone, and then I hear you got thumped. What gives?"

"Yeah, well, I got distracted."

"You're a freaking Paladin!"

I laughed loudly. "You'd be surprised just how human we are."

He fished an ice cube from his cup. Long pause. "I know you didn't understand my obsession, you know, of having to go see my parents. You being a Paladin and everything, I'm sure you got that all figured out, but us mere mortals got to do things the hard way."

Oh, I understand, Streeter.

"Why, Socket Greeny!" Granny walked onto the deck. "Where have you been hiding all this time, young man? I thought you moved away."

"He's in disguise, Granny," Streeter said.

"I can see that." She rustled my hair. "You mustn't do that, you're like family here." She handed me a tall glass of sweet tea. "Are you going to spend the night?"

"No, ma'am. I've got to be home tonight. My mother's expecting me."

"Well, if your mother's home, by all means." She looked at Streeter. "Are you all right, dear? Do you need another drink?"

Streeter said no. Granny said it was nice to see me and went inside. There was no more fade; people knew me once again, like I reclaimed my former life. Now it was a part of me, not something I left behind. I was fully aware of my entire being, had completely integrated all facets of my Self, and I chose not to fade. I'm not sure all

Paladins reached that level of understanding and were able to do that.

"You going back to the Garrison?" Streeter asked.

"Not for a while, it's getting renovated."

He asked about Spindle. About Mother. About all the cool things I'd been doing. I answered in generic truths, avoiding the details that mattered the most. Someone once told me the public doesn't really want to know the truth around us. They just want to feel safe.

"Any new powers?"

I shrugged.

"Come on." He dipped his finger in the cup and flicked tea at me. "Who am I going to tell?"

I gathered a bit of strength around the core in my chest, focusing it in Streeter's direction. He was about to dip his fingers again when the cup dumped in his lap. He leaped off the chair, brushing icy sweet tea off.

"Did you just do that?" he asked. "Seriously?"

Later, I did it again. Streeter set up targets for me to hit. Maybe I shouldn't have done that, but it was Streeter. Who was he going to tell? I ended up eating dinner with them. We didn't hug on the front porch. We didn't even shake hands, that wasn't something we usually did. We just nodded and said goodbye.

"You coming back?" he asked.

"Yeah."

"When?"

I got in the car and rolled the window down. "As soon as I can."

I wouldn't leave my best friend behind.

66

THERE WAS MORE Paladin business that night, but I couldn't concentrate. I'd been thinking about going to the park for weeks. And when the day finally arrived, I couldn't think of anything else.

The shade beneath the magnolia tree was deep and cool. The koi pond shimmered in the noon sun, where dragonflies hovered over the lilies. I picked at the kernels of fish food in my hand, tossing one on the water. The surface swirled yellow, orange and white and the kernel disappeared in the chaos of hungry mouths. I waited until it was calm again and threw another.

Chute was late.

I talked to her on the phone the night before (phones were working, still no nojakks). *I've got a surprise,* I told her. She said just seeing me was enough, she didn't need a gift. I wanted to jump through the phone when she said that, but held myself in check. We'd meet at the koi pond at noon. So I sat in the muggy shade, tossing fish food with a mess of emotions in my stomach.

A young couple walked around the pond, holding hands. I only needed a few minutes with Chute and I wanted this place to be empty. The trees rustled like a wind funnel dropped out of the sky, debris whipping around the swan sculpture then pelting the couple with leaves. They covered their heads and jogged off.

Freak weather we're having, wouldn't you say?

I sensed her before I saw her. Felt her park the car by the road. Sensed her beam with exuberance. Her essence pervaded the entire park; I felt it vibrate in my guts! She was a beacon, a lighthouse of essence that buzzed inside me. I closed my eyes and inhaled.

She appeared at the small bridge, emerging from the path enclosed by trees. She stopped in the sunlight like she stepped onto a stage and looked around. Luminescent and beautiful, her essence tasted sweet. She didn't see me and I sensed the fall of disappointment. I didn't want to torture her, but I wanted just to savor the moment.

I tossed a kernel into the pond. She stepped to the water and watched the fish scramble for it. I stepped out of the shade and she saw me there on the other side. Chills danced on my skin.

There wasn't another moment to waste.

I stepped onto the concrete ledge and into the pond, the water up to my thighs. I splashed through the lilies. The water slowed my steps and the lilies wrapped around my ankles. Chute leaped in from the other side, and beside the swan sculpture, wings spread and soaring, we embraced. Her essence permeated my senses, overwhelming me. We squeezed and shook. No separation.

Just wonder.

I could see future moments. In my moment of Realization when all the possible futures were laid out before me, I allowed the path to choose me, allowed life to be present. I didn't look to see if Chute was in the path. Maybe it was better I didn't know.

"I had a dream you died," she said.

"It was just a dream."

The trees rustled. Leaves fell like a snowstorm.

"Don't go away like that, Socket Greeny. Never again." She grabbed my face with both hands. "Can you quit your job?"

"My resignation's in the mail."

Another storm of foliage fell.

No words followed. None needed. I had loved Chute all my life. Just like the grimmets, it was an immense power and joy waiting to be released, waiting to be expressed. And there it was in her face. In her smile.

And then we kissed. Long and hard. Our warm bodies pressed together, our hearts exchanging beats, our essence intermingling. Time seemed to stop and I basked in the moment, standing in the muddy water.

Wondrous.

Something squirmed between our bellies like a fish had leaped from the water. Chute jumped back. The squirming thing stopped on my shoulder and blinked its oversized golden eyes.

"I remember you."

Rudder wiggled with excitement. I held him by the tail and he continued to shake. "He's a bit excited," I said.

Chute cupped her hands. Rudder rolled on his back, hands and feet up and tail curled around her wrist. "*Aaahhhh,*" she said and stroked his stomach. "He's so soft and warm."

She pressed him to her cheek and he purred louder, his tail pushing through her hair. Rudder's essence was part of me; he kept me alive when Com absorbed me. He kept my heart pumping until I could live on my own and even though I was back, a bit of him was left inside me. Our lives were intertwined, inseparable. We felt the same things, sensed the same things and loved the same things. Chute was now as much a part of his life as mine.

"Is this my surprise?" she asked.

"Part of it." I looked up into the trees and saw the glittering eyes looking back.

Then nodded.

The trees exploded, leaves and sticks everywhere. The flock of grimmets corkscrewed and circled the pond, whizzing between us and around us, diving in the water and skimming the surface with dragonflies between their lips. The fallen leaves whisked off the ground.

Chute threw her head back, smiling and laughing, her voice lost in the exuberant chatter. They brushed against her and tousled her hair. One of them hit her square on the face with a fat kiss, pinching her cheeks until I snatched him off. She spun around and around, letting them, one after another, drop into her outstretched hands. They dive-bombed and circled her, coming together for a group hug.

I could've stood there for eternity listening to her laugh.

"Hey! You're not supposed to be in the pond!" The park superintendent stomped onto the path. He was set to snatch us up by our earlobes. That is, until he saw something he'd never seen before. Still pointing, he was mesmerized by the impossible creatures fluttering overhead. Making him forget what he came to do. Making him forget what he was seeing. He dropped his hand, mouth open.

Chute and I didn't wait for him to leave; we chugged out of the pond, lifting our legs high. The grimmets disappeared into the trees, scratching along the branches and staying out of sight. Rudder curled up into the palm of my hand, twining his tail between my fingers. We stopped on the second bridge and caught our breath. I hooked my finger with hers and Rudder wrapped his tail around our hands.

She watched the water run beneath the bridge. "Are you going to leave me, again?"

I didn't want to know the details of our future. It just seemed like a bad idea because if she wasn't there, could I live with that? But when a future glimpse presented itself, I couldn't resist. I saw the future of our path and knew that Chute would be with me the rest of my life. I saw us together. We were old. I saw us walking with wrinkled fingers hooked together.

No, I will never leave you.

67

Comet

IT WAS months before the world got their nojakks back. Virtualmode's return, however, had yet to be determined. A Paladin spokesperson made an announcement to boos, but public officials didn't condemn them. They didn't say anything. The Paladins were pretty convincing, it appeared, to make them see it that way. I doubted they told them what *really* happened, but who knows, maybe they were changing public relations policy.

The Garrison had limited functionality. The training rooms were just white rooms and servys didn't greet us in the parking garage. We carried our own bags, served ourselves lunch and sat on plain chairs, just like everyone else.

We lost over half the Paladin Nation in the battle and most of the commanding tier. The void of leadership was filled with inexperience, and decisions were slow and heavily debated. Mother was needed more than ever. She spent her time travelling around the world and I spoke to her through projection more often than in the skin, but I could feel her no matter how far away she was. I could feel her pulse inside me like an organic lifeline, and knew when she was well and when she was stressed.

I spent most of my time in the Preserve. Before, when I was just a cadet, no one paid much attention to me. I was a promising cadet, but I was still a cadet. In the eyes of accomplished Paladins, I was a kid. Nothing more. I still had to prove something.

But that was then.

I changed the world; maybe even saved the human race. So now Paladins looked at me with reverence. Sometimes, fear. I stayed hidden, most of the time. I didn't want to cause fear; I wanted them to adjust to the new era. One day, when I was dead, the stories would make me larger than life. But I was still alive; there was nothing to fear.

I would not become another Pivot, segregated from society in my own jungle, reverting to a modern-day Tarzan. I would embrace the Paladin Nation, and, if possible, guide it. For the path called me to lead, and that would require knowing those around me. But until things settled, it was just me and the grimmets.

"ALL CADETS ARE RECOGNIZED for their Realizations." The commander had come out to the grimmet tree alone. "More than ever, we need to recognize this one."

We need you, Socket Greeny.

When the day came, I reported. It wasn't so much for recognition or fame or to prove all those doubters wrong. The Paladin Nation needed to believe in something. Even though these were highly evolved humans, the degree of betrayal had destroyed their trust. Existing without hope was difficult. They needed something to rally around. Even though I understood there was nothing to hope for, that the present moment was perfect, the Paladin Nation needed something to believe until they could see that for themselves.

I WENT to the Preserve deck where I had first met Com. If I knew what he was then, could all that death have been avoided? I still had a lot to learn about seeing the future and what I could do about it.

I stood at the edge, watching dusk settle over the Preserve. The jungle inhabitants greeted the rising moon. Far away, I saw the barren branches of the grimmet tree. Colors swirled around it as the grimmets chased insects.

If only Pon could be here. I didn't want him at the ceremony, although his expression would be entertaining. *No need for frivolity!* No, I just wanted him to see the fruits of his labor. There were so many that paved the path on which I stood, I could only hope that on some other plane of existence, they could see where it led, that their efforts had not been wasted. That I was grateful to have walked with them.

Spindle stepped next to me. He was the only mech to be activated, my special request. His data was backed up and uploaded to another bodyshell.

"How many times are you going to save my life?" I asked.

"As long as it is required."

We paused a bit longer and listened to the jungle

"It is time," he said. "The ceremony has begun."

"Has Mother made arrangements?"

"All those you requested are in attendance, awaiting your arrival."

Yes, Pon would frown on such frivolity, but I would not waste his efforts. Let's celebrate the moment. Nothing frivolous about that. I looked across the Preserve, to the grimmet tree.

[Come,] I thought.

The colorful mass spiraled towards us. Spindle and I went to the door and, before it opened, Rudder smacked into my palm. Hundreds of wings batted the wind behind us. We walked down a long corridor, side by side, and entered the only functional moldable room in the Garrison.

It was a floor and nothing else, like it was floating in silent space with the stars and planets above and below. A half circle of Paladin leaders stood in the middle. In front of them were the people that mattered most. My mother was there. And, upon my request, Chute and Streeter. The three of them stood at attention.

It was good to see Streeter distracted by the technological wonder. I could see his mind already spinning with all the things he could do with technology like this. Chute, though, she was smiling. Her hair was down around her face and her energy was brighter than all those in attendance, pulling me toward the center.

The grimmets erupted from the tunnel and, for a moment, buried us in the furious patter of leathery wings. They circled the platform several times until they were all present, then filled the empty space on the floor, leaving a path for us to follow. Spindle took a step back and a spot glowed in the center. Rudder swung from my fingers as I made the walk.

There was no echo of my footsteps, not even the rustle of wings. All was silent. The commander acknowledged my presence with a slight nod and then looked skyward. While only a few Paladins were in actual attendance, the rest were surely watching the event from around the world.

"It is with great pleasure," he said, his voice booming, "to recognize the accomplishment of Socket Pablo Greeny. The one who sees clearly is truly a gem beyond value, for he is one that lays the path for us to follow."

He made eye contact with everyone on the platform before continuing.

"If there are any in attendance that wish to speak against the induction and Realization of Socket Pablo Greeny, this is your moment." After a long, silent pause, he bowed his head. "It is an honor, Paladin."

A raucous shuffle resounded as the grimmets bowed in unison, all well-behaved. Their eyes were to the ground, tails curled around their bodies. Mother stepped forward and put both hands on my shoulders. She gently turned me around so that my back was to the congregation. Chute and Streeter stepped to each side.

"There is nothing we can give you to equal what you have given us," the commander said. "For the understanding you embody is priceless. But, sadly, it does not come without a cost."

Mother's hands tightened.

"In honor of all those that lost their lives," he said, "a memorial is launched." A bright light emerged from below the lip of the platform and seemed to be far out in space, a long tail trailing behind it. "May its glory blaze throughout the universe until the end of time, so that they may never be forgotten."

The comet slowly streaked away and we watched it shrink into the distance. Nothing was said. Nothing stirred. The ceremony was for all of us. For the world. For all existence. And then I realized where home was. It wasn't in the Preserve or a house in South Carolina. It was here, in existence. It was right this moment.

I put my arms around Chute and Streeter. Chute laid her head on my shoulder and we watched the comet until it was a tiny point of light glittering through the constellation of the Big Dipper. We watched it with wonder.

We watched it right here and now.

BOOK 3

THE LEGEND OF SOCKET GREENY

For the truth

PART VII

Life won't take you where you want to be;
It will take you where you're needed.
Like it or not.
Pike

To love deeply is to risk grandly.
One cannot be without the other.
Chute

Those who know, don't tell.
And those who tell, don't know.
Buddhist proverb

68

CHILD'S PLAY

DREAMS RARELY CAME to me when I slept. Visions were a different story. I could see them and feel them. Smell them. They were a glimpse of things to come.

This night while I slept, I saw a man walking down a crowded sidewalk, a man that hadn't seen daylight in years. A man destined to never see it again. But in the vision he was there, walking among people with the sun on his face. I wouldn't believe such a story any more than Jack climbing a beanstalk. But this was a vision.

My visions were rarely wrong.

I sat up in a massive chair, my forehead numb from the desk, but it was nothing compared to the cold tingling sensation in my neck, a side effect of visions, a dense uncomfortable numbness that took hours to fade. I rubbed my neck.

I rarely made it to bed. My desk served as a poor substitute. My office was oversized, to say the least. A hundred feet long, maybe fifty wide. The walls, floor and ceiling were made from microscopic nanomechs the size of skin cells and equipped to mold any object, create any environment or situation. It was also buried under a billion tons of granite beneath Garrison Mountain, home of the Paladin Nation.

Currently, the room was glowing blue from the intricate web of lines that represented naturally occurring wormholes throughout the universe. It was the soft glow and pulsating stars that made me drowsy, but now I was awake with the image of a free man branded on my brain. A man that, if I had a choice, would no longer be breathing. No going back to sleep now.

[Off,] I thought to the room.

The blue threads and twinkling stars disappeared, leaving me alone in the darkness. I called for the room to connect me with the man in my vision.

The walls bled brown from beneath the surface. I walked around the desk. The ceiling turned a deep shade of violet and a chair grew from a blackened floor. It was solid with stout armrests, immovable and empty. I paced to the end of the room with my hands locked behind my back and stared at the blank wall. The vision remained sharp and detailed, like a lighthouse illuminating deadly shores. And the dull sensation hung over my neck like a blanket of chains.

"Can't sleep?" a voice sang.

The chair was now occupied with a frail, bald man. His glasses were black, meant only to cover the white sightless eyes beneath, for the benefit of others.

"You should try warm milk," he said. "Dip some cookies in it, the ones with the creamy filling. They'll hit your stomach like a bomb, blow you into the next morning." He folded his legs. "At least, that's what they tell me."

Three hairless men appeared behind the chair, wearing black glasses. They were blind minders, as well, seeing with psychic vision instead of eyes, but they were no friends of the one in the chair. They stared at the man now pretending to dip cookies into a glass on his lap.

"You're dismissed." I waved at the three minders. "This exchange will be private."

The one in the middle said, "Request denied. Pike is to be kept under continual surveillance."

Constant surveillance? Pike was hardly a threat. After years of imprisonment and minder pressure, the fabric of his mind had been stretched and frayed, his thoughts and motivations splayed open like a butchered pig. His brain struggled to function, and what few thoughts he had were hardly coherent. There was no need for three minders to contain his mind, hardly a need for one.

But he'd fooled us all before.

They resumed their focus on the man now double-dipping imaginary cookies, shoving them in his mouth. "Uu unt sum?"

"At least back up," I said. "Give us some space."

The minders considered my request. Ignored it. Pike cowered under the intensified psychic heat that restricted the expansion of his mind. He looked over his shoulder like he just got slapped with a ruler.

"I call them Mo, Larry and Curly, you know. Larry's on the left and Mo's in the middle because he's the boss. And that's Curly there." Right shoulder. "I used to call him Shemp because he's not funny." A very serious look stretched over his face. "But Curly's my favorite. So, you know."

His favorite episode was "The Three Stooges Meet Frankenstein." I knew that because he told me. And now he was going through it, scene by scene, and quickly seemed oblivious to me, as if telling the story to himself.

I walked closer to Pike's image and began to sit slowly, allowing the room to form a chair below me. It was wider than the one that confined Pike. I sat forward, resting my chin on my knuckles, allowing my mind to surround and penetrate Pike's mind. Even though he was just an image in front of me, something constructed by the room, it was projecting his presence from a secure location. It was no different than if he was sitting right there in front of me, laughing about the way Mo hammered Larry and Curly. His essence still flowed through the image, much like a voice travels through a phone. I could follow it with my mind, all the way back to the prison cell he shared with a rotation of minder guards.

Is there something the minders aren't seeing? It would be impossible for him to hide anything, but he'd done it before. He couldn't escape one of these minders. And three? Impossible.

I needed to see for myself, just to see if there was something they were missing. While he ranted about Mo's comic genius, I penetrated his mind like vapor. His thoughts were so disjointed, randomly appearing in a mix of memories and delusions, separated by basic impulses of hunger and sleep, that if he could escape, he wouldn't know what to do in the free world.

His energy was jagged and broken, no longer the cohesive mind-field that he once was, no longer resembling the treacherous mind he used to deceive the Paladin Nation. A mind that could kill with a thought or hide secrets of betrayal. A mind that once tried to kill me. In his prime, it took a dozen minders to contain him. Now, he drooled on himself. But predators often lured their victims with deceit. *Good traps never look like traps.*

"What are you looking for?" Pike asked.

He caught me peeking, distracted by my own thoughts.

"No need to search far and wide for my thoughts. No need to be sneaky, it's open season on Pike; everyone's taking a turn. Why shouldn't you?" He pointed to the crown of his head. "You can look, but I'm afraid you're a little late, the cupboards are bare."

There were no dark corners left in Pike. No thought left unearthed and analyzed. I retracted my mind and sat back.

"Don't like what you see, then? You're all powerful, the next coming of the world's savior. Right? Right? What are you doing, wonderboy, looking inside old Pike? Do you think there's a single thought these savages haven't raped? There's something left of me? I assure you there is not. I'm sure you already knew that." He turned his head slightly, awareness returning sharply, not so childlike. "So what are you looking for, wonderboy? Really."

"Tell me something," I said, "why did you betray the Paladin Nation?"

"*Booooring.*" He rattled off a long raspberry. "Whatever your real inquiry is, just look inside again, will you? Take a peek and see why I despise humanity. Go on, wonderboy, have a look. Have-have a look, won't you?" He punched the side of his head. "HAVE A GODDAMN LOOK!"

Spittle drooled over his lower lip. He leaned forward and the heat of the minders filled the room. Pike was yanked back into the chair by invisible restraints. His chest heaved, laughter gurgling in his throat, coming out in short bursts. He threw his mouth open, laughing silently.

To see a mind unravel was dreadful, but Pike was not worthy of pity. He betrayed humanity, tried to sell us to the artificially intelligent race of duplicated humans. He betrayed all those that trusted him and almost destroyed us. And for that, his mind deserved to be unwound and dissected. For that, he could not be allowed to go free.

The vision returned to me, the lighthouse swinging its beam around, projecting the details for all minds to see. I clamped my mind down, snuffing it out, but not before Pike caught a glimpse.

He took a sharp breath. "You had a vision? Oh, you are a bad boy. A bad, bad boy, wonderboy. A bad wonderboy you are, coming here to tell old Pike about a vision. The bosses are going to be pissed that you came here, yes they are."

Sloppy work, Socket.

"You had a vision about old Pike, didn't you, wonderboy. Didn't you? Oh, yes, I believe, I believe you did. You did, you saw me and you come here to see what old Pike would think about it." He twisted around and winked at Larry, then Curly, and gave Mo the okeydokey. "He had a vision about me, boys, you hear that? Good old Pike, gone but not forgotten."

Pike's location was undisclosed. Only a few knew where he was imprisoned. He could be in a cell a thousand feet below ground, or in a satellite circling the planet. With constant minder presence creating psychic static, I couldn't ascertain his location but, whatever the circumstances, no one could escape the Paladin Nation. Not even Pike on his best day. Still, I needed to know... *is he hiding anything?*

Pike bounced in the chair. "Let's play a game. A game, a game. A guessing game, what d'ya say, wonderboy? A game, shall we?"

He looked at the ceiling, thinking hard, really trying to find the answer floating somewhere above him. Would it matter if I told him? No vision was guaranteed; there were so many variables.

"You saw something in the future," Pike said, "about me, I think. Do I get fat, is that it? I hardly get exercise in this chair. I complained to the warden, but no one listens to old Pike, say that's what you get for betraying your species, or something like that, I don't know. Or I get relocated again, to another cell. You know, I like this one. I think it's the color. Brown just works. They turned it pink once and I didn't like that one bit, wonderboy. I started shitting myself and Mo don't like cleaning grown-man underwear, so they changed it back. You don't mess with old Pike's cell—wait, I know." His smile was wide, the gums bright red. "*I kill your girlfriend.*"

He projected a thought, and had I not been open and looking through his mind while he rambled, it never would've reached me. His thought was harmless, but clear to see. It was Chute, her sweaty hair stuck to her forehead. Pike had a knife to her neck. I squashed the thought.

Pike drummed his fingers across his pouting lip. "It'll hurt when I kill her, wonderboy. It'll hurt-hurt pretty bad, I think. And just imagine how your heart will feel after I strangle her, you know. How I lean over and suck the last breath from her lips." He inhaled deeply and closed his eyes. "It'll probably taste like cherry lip gloss. Your hearts will hhhhrr... it'll hurrrr..." He licked his lips. The smile died. "Hurt forever. Wonderboy."

I punched out with telekinetic force and his image rippled in the gale force of raw energy as it travelled through the image and found his body somewhere in the universe. I slid my mind inside him like a cold shank. He clenched his teeth like 120 volts shot up his ass.

"HOOO! What a grip!" He shook his head like a wet dog. Pain was better than nothing at all. "But tell me something, won-wonderboy? How am I going to kill your girlfriend if I'm in here—" He covered his mouth with both hands. Held his breath. "Don't tell me..."

I only blinked, but it was enough. He saw more of the vision than I thought. He was fucking with me.

"Are you joking? You're here to tell me..." He was bouncing again. "That I'm going to... escape?" He sang the last word like a little girl, the last syllable squeaky. "*ESCAPE?*"

I didn't budge, move or think. I wouldn't give him the satisfaction of seeing the details, wouldn't let him see more of the vision that revealed him wearing street clothes and smiling at the sun. I didn't want him to see that no one paid attention to the curious man until they got near him and his dangerous mind; how he projected a mere thought to tear a little girl from her parents. How he shoved her into traffic. Tires screeched. Someone screamed.

"Tell me, how do I do it?" he asked. "Oh, please. Tell me."

"It won't happen, Pike."

"You saw it, huh? Show me, right? Show me how it happens." He clapped his hands. "Please, pretty p-p-pleeeeeeease. I got to know, I just got to know."

I stood. The chair collapsed into the floor. "I'll alert the commander of what I've seen. I promise, you'll not escape."

"Yes, but you could tell me just one thing?" He looked around the ceiling again, entertaining the possibilities. "Do you know about *wheeeen* it might happen? I mean, I'm not saying it *wiiiiill*, but just in case. You know, I need to clear my calendar."

"Be advised." I projected the vision to the minders. Mo nodded. *Received.*

"Do I kill you, wonderboy? When I get out, do I kill you? That's not too much to ask, is it?"

"As long as I live, you will not walk free."

"Perhaps you should ask good master Pivot about that." He cocked his head. "Or is he still AWOL?"

Pivot. The greatest Paladin to ever live. My personal mentor. One that could see the future. One that disappeared over a year ago. I could still sense his presence; some days it was stronger than others. He was always around. I could feel him watching. I never thought much about the fact that he never showed himself, just secure that he hadn't disappeared entirely.

"Good old Papa Pivot doesn't talk much these days, would you say?" Pike said. "Tell me, what's it like to be abandoned by someone you love? I'll bet it stings, like maybe it was your fault." He leaned forward and sniffed. "Maybe it's, you know... you."

"He's around."

"He is?" He looked in both directions. "Is he in the room right now? This second? Like an imaginary friend?" His laughter was high-pitched and much too loud, cutting right through me. "Poor wonder-boy. All alone in the world. That's why he comes to see good ole Pike, he does. Lonely." He tipped his head back to the minders. "That's why he's here, boys."

"You're broken, Pike. You deserve worse."

"Do you trust him, wonderboy? Do you trust Papa Pivot?"

"He's the reason you're here."

"Yes, well, all good things come to a screeching halt, they say. Just ask your vision, wonderboy." His tongue pushed through a smile. "Listen, you come to old Pike when you have your next vision." He dipped his head, letting me glimpse the white eyeballs behind the black glasses. "I'm here to help, wonderboy."

He said it sincerely. He was a master of keeping an opponent off-balance. Nothing he said could be trusted.

The color faded from the walls. The images of the minders shrank. Pike melted into the floor. "Be sure to call my secretary," he said, his voice fading. "She can squeeze you in..."

I left the dark room, more disturbed than ever.

69

Discards

I sᴀᴛ cross-legged in a field of manicured turf, breathing rhythmically in meditation. It had been weeks since the vision of Pike's escape and, still, it was with me. Most visions faded with time, but this one remained in full detail. Like a siren that refused to stop. I noticed my thoughts about it and returned to the present moment, listening to the birds sing.

Six kids sat cross-legged in front of me on firm, round pillows. Their eyes were closed and hands gently folded in front of their bellies. They tried to ignore the pain in their knees, sitting like concrete figures, holding steady, their breath coming and going. But they heard the birds. Dawn was near.

Sitting was almost over.

Their minds were in various states, some open, some scattered. The girls—Madeline, Aleshia and Grace—were mostly calm, but the boys were somewhere else. Joseph was dreaming, Dylan half-asleep, and then there was Ben hating everything. His eyelids were cracked open, watching me.

They could leave the Garrison any time they wanted. But if they stayed, they had to commit to the daily schedule, and that included food and a warm, dry place to sleep and a tropical forest. But there was also meditation practice, physical training and emotional therapy. The price for all these pleasures was but a gift itself: *Understanding.* I wanted to show them what they already possessed: essential wonder and unlimited freedom.

"I want you to return to this moment." I unfolded my legs, letting the aches fade from my knees. "Allow the moment to be present. Allow space for your entire experience, whether it's excitement, resistance, love or hate. Allow space for whatever is in this very moment and be with it. Recognize thoughts about it. Notice if you want it to be different."

The dewy grass slid between my toes. I stepped quietly behind them, gently straightening their sagging backs.

"Just notice what you think and return to your bodily sensations. Allow the present moment to unfold."

Excitement vibrated around them. The best part of meditation was the end. They listened, remaining sitting and present, but there was more exuberance than usual. Even Ben was grinning. They all cracked open their eyes, looking behind me.

The trees were far away, their canopies dense and dark. But even so, I could see the bright-colored grimmets crawling along the branches, scurrying to get away without being seen. The little dragony creatures—no bigger than hummingbirds—were probably hovering behind me, making faces or holding their tails up behind my head like horns to make the kids laugh. My frustration shot like sparks, rustling the leaves like a rogue gust of wind.

Grimmets.

They were psychic titans, each one of them with more mental strength than the entire human population. They defeated the duplicates, the entire population, several months ago without any hint of resurrection. I was the conduit for their power, for I understood. I saw life clearly. *The One Who Sees Clearly,* they called me. Through me, the grimmets called to all duplicated life forms on the planet, instructed them to deactivate, and they did.

And now the grimmets were bored. And when the kids were around, they were insufferable.

"Socket?" Ben asked. "Ummm…"

Sigh. "Dismissed."

They jumped and ran, pulling at each other as they raced for the opposite end of the oval, grassy field. I let loose an earsplitting whistle. They turned while running. I pointed at the meditation cushions tumbled in disarray. They fought, laughing along the way, and swept up the cushions to put them away. Every part of the schedule was their responsibility.

Ben fell down and rubbed his numb leg. Feeling came back slowly to his calf, and when it did, pins and needles tortured his nerves. "Why do we have to sit so damn long?"

No one gave Ben much of a chance. His father died when he was little and his mother was addicted to prescription drugs and mood-altering gear, anything that would make her feel good, escape the emptiness inside, until she mixed too many pills and never woke up. Ben landed in a children's home, like the rest of them, only he ran away. He was resistant, a fighter, but I saw something in him. And he trusted what I saw. That was all I asked.

When the pain ebbed, he hobbled after the others. They were already leaping onto the jetter discs nestled in the grass at the opposite end of the field. They hovered off the ground once their feet locked in place. They scooped up sticks that were curved at the ends and flew across the field, the jetters tilting a few inches off the ground, responding to their thoughts for direction and speed.

The tagghet field was in the middle of the Preserve, a tropical jungle carved out of the mountain and protected from the elements by an invisible force field overhead. It was like a 5.2-square-mile conservatory and the kids' very own playground. A place I thought of as home.

I walked to the edge of the field, where the trees met the turf, where a silver android awaited. His long plum-colored overcoat hung to his ankles. Colors flashed across his featureless faceplate, a bright red eyelight following the kids across the tagghet field. He held out a breakfast bar and a bottle of water.

"How was your morning meditation?" he asked.

I chewed the breakfast bar and observed the kids weaving expertly around each other. "Aleshia is ready to begin sitting every morning. I'd like to keep the others sitting twice a week, at least for another month."

"You should be aware that Grace is stealing food from the others."

Of course Grace was stealing. I knew her memories, experiencing them when we sat. Like the others, she was considered *damaged*. She ran from her memories, distracting herself with thoughts and desires and fears. Most normal people did that sort of thing, but no one could blame Grace. Her foster parents did unconscionable things to her. Mostly it was beatings, but some were sexual, the sorts of things that destroyed people and left gaping emotional holes that could never be filled.

But Grace was resilient. She had a lot of work to do. I wouldn't recommend meditation for a person like that, especially not that young. But she was different. All these kids were different. They didn't just endure; they were highly evolved, possessing an innate, genetic disposition for learning and transformation. I know, because I handpicked them.

After the duplicates were defeated, the Paladin Nation needed direction. I launched the Orphan program. Ironic, I suppose, that the whole existence of the Paladins was to defeat an enemy that were like orphans. Duplicates had no maternal parents and considered themselves free and independent of the psychological problems that hampered humans. But the duplicates were programs; no matter how efficient they were, they could not *be,* could not transform and grow. Unlike the duplicates, the children could rise above their handicap.

I wanted to reach out to the human race, integrate the Paladin Nation into society, and help people understand themselves. Understanding wasn't just a right of the Paladins, it was a human right. So why not start with society's most underprivileged. That didn't mean people would want the understanding we offered. Many people possessed a lot of psychological difficulties. Could they overcome them? We couldn't make them. So I selected the ones I sensed would.

"I would like Grace to join group therapy on Wednesday," I said. "I don't want to separate her from her peers, though. She needs additional support from some like-minded children with similar experiences. Empathy will go a long way for her. I'll be leading the group session. I also want to schedule Ben for individual counseling." I took a swallow of water. "I'll be leading that, too."

"But you are not approved to counsel the children, Master Socket."

They were on the other side of the field, but Ben spun around and looked at us, as if to make sure we were still there.

"He needs trust, Spindle. He trusts me."

"Do you have a suggestion on how to get permission?"

"Don't call it counseling. Just schedule him to chat with me for an hour. Let's start a week from now, on Friday."

"But you are leaving that morning."

The trip. I conveniently forgot. One of those things I was told I would be doing. All Paladins must make at least one trip through the intergalactic wormhole network. For the experience, I guess. My work was here, right now. I didn't need to see what sort of research was being done on planet Krypton or what alternative fuel was being mined from an asteroid.

Sorry, I'm busy, I wanted to say. But I already knew the commander's answer. *No, you're not.*

Sunlight had crossed the sky, stretching long shadows over the field. Some of the grimmets emerged from hiding, fluttering over the kids, swarming so thickly they nearly buried them. Aleshia bounced the discus-shaped tag off the ground and the grimmets chased after it, then mauled Joseph when he snagged it with the magnetic curved end of his stick.

A red grimmet was in the trees behind me. *Rudder.* I could *see* all around me with my mind, feel the negative space between objects and *know* the essential spirit of all things, building an image of what things *looked* like in my mind. But I didn't need all that to see Rudder, he was different. I felt him, like a part of me that moved separately in the world. We had bonded when he brought me back from death and a part of me stayed with him. And part of him with me. He dropped onto my shoulder and wrapped his whiplike tail around my neck, purring.

[I told them not to do it,] he thought to me. *[I knew you'd be angry.]*

"I see. And you weren't with them?" I peered over at him, his golden eyes blinking. "That wasn't you, the red grimmet out front, sticking your tongue out to get the biggest laugh? That wasn't you?"

His eyes darted back and forth. A thought began to form in my head in response to what I said, and then he shot off to join his pack in a chase for the tag.

"You need to do something about the grimmets, Spindle," I said. "They were very disruptive this morning."

"Me?" Spindle put his hand to his chest. "They will not listen to me, Master Socket. They only listen to you."

"Well, then, we're screwed."

The kids zoomed around the perimeter and came up our side. They held out their hands as they passed and I slapped them. Around the field they went again, a colorful cloud of grimmets nipping at their butts.

"Has my mother called?" I asked.

"She left a message that she will call in two days. She is very busy with Congress today and tomorrow." A smattering of dark colors blotted Spindle's faceplate. "The commander is not pleased you met with Pike this morning without prior consent."

"I figured he wouldn't be thrilled."

"He would like to remind you that premonitory visions are to be immediately reported."

"He has a full report."

"He would like to emphasize *immediately*. He also forbids future meetings with Pike without his foreknowledge. The commander is very reluctant—"

"I know how the commander feels, Spindle. Trust me, there's no danger. Pike can no longer hurt me any more than you."

Fact is, could anyone? I was the only telekinetic alive. I was almost seventeen, but I was not a child. I didn't like being treated like one.

The kids were coming around again, this time with an empty jetter in tow. They pulled Spindle onto the field. The grimmets hovered over, cheering, casting a dark shadow over us, blotting out the rising sun. They helped shove Spindle on the empty jetter. Spindle's eyelight circled around his head. I nodded. He was off with the kids, tossing the tag back and forth.

I turned my back on the tagghet field to go inside Garrison Mountain, back to my office, wishing I had two lives. That way, I might make a difference.

70

JUST ANOTHER TOURIST

IT WAS two days before I got back to the tagghet field. I was in the office the entire time, building mock scenarios, analyzing programs, having meetings by projection. My meals were brought to me and I'd experienced forty different countries through the office's magical transformations when, in reality, I never left the room.

The kids were begging me to come watch them; even Spindle suggested I take some time to come out, they were much improved. So I got outside and immediately felt the difference between fresh air and filtered air. Besides, the molding office had a certain taste, something that was fake and empty that penetrated every object and hung beneath every fragrance. I watched and clapped and slapped their hands as they showed off their best tagghet skills.

I took the long way back to the office, inside the mountain and down a wide hallway that curved left. Tall, rectangular windows were along the right, spotting the floor with stretched boxes of sunlight. All of this stuff was new, an attempt to transform Garrison Mountain from a dreary tomb to something open and inviting.

I gazed at the wide boulder field below that separated the mountain and the transportation wormhole on the far side, connecting our remote existence to the rest of the world. It used to be impossible terrain to cross, unless you had something that could hover. But now there was a road that dipped and curved through the giant rubble.

Girls in school uniforms, chattering in Japanese, came around the hallway bend. Their teachers tried to keep them together like shepherds. John Tackleton, their tour guide, was trying to keep up. He was a civilian, recruited a few months earlier to lead public tours through the Garrison.

Not only did the public have access to the Paladin facilities, they used the wormhole to transport back and forth from around the world. In fact, there were discussions about opening wormholes for public transportation, but that wasn't easy. To tear a hole in space-time required an enormous amount of psychic energy. Much of the Paladins' efforts went to just maintaining our own network. It would be decades before something could be done for the public. But the talks were in the works, and that had never even been considered before. Much like field trips.

The children ran to the windows, their shiny black hair bouncing. They ran around me like I was nothing more than a pillar. They pointed across the field and shouted about the wormhole. That was their favorite part of the trip, so far: one second they were in Tokyo and the next they were here. And the weird feeling in their stomachs when they crossed over was like the world's tallest roller coaster ride that lasted all of a second. Wormhole transportation was never that fun, but we changed that, too. They said this in Japanese, but I understood. The words might be different, but thoughts and emotions were universal.

They ran for the steps and out of sight, on their way to the Preserve, where they would forget all about the wormhole. The tour guide would tell them about all the great research the Paladin Nation was conducting in the Preserve and all the species of plants and animals it supported. Those kids wouldn't hear a thing once the grimmets arrived.

Word about the grimmets had spread across the world. The tours came to learn about the inner workings of the Paladin Nation, but it was the grimmets they came to see. Monkeys and otters couldn't compete with grimmets on their best day. In public, they'd already manufactured stuffed grimmets with wiry tails that kids hung from their book bags. They came in all different colors and people lined up to buy the newest release. *Collect them all!*

MY FOOTSTEPS DENTED the pliable floor of my office and the walls swirled with color, shifting and molding shapes from the floor and ceiling. A bed developed at my right and an entertainment center to the left. A large patio formed with folding doors thrown wide open. A cool, salty breeze blew inside.

My mother lay on the lounger on the balcony overlooking the Pacific Ocean. Her snores came in mild waves. I gently touched the railing. The resort was built right on the northern California cliffs, overhanging the tide that crashed on ship-eating rocks.

"Socket." Mother wiped the corner of her mouth. "I didn't know you'd arrived."

"Nice place."

She pushed her cropped hair behind her ear, where it didn't stay. The same haircut she always had, but now with kinky strands of gray. She took a deep breath and stretched. "The view is fantastic."

We remained quiet, listening to the ocean speak. We did that often, just sitting together without speaking.

"I see you're taking leave in a few days," she said.

"Chute's award ceremony." I looked over my shoulder. "She's Tagghet's Most Valuable Player, you know."

"Streeter going to be there?"

"He better be. Chute will skin him if he's not."

"I just thought with his new girlfriend, he might get... distracted."

Streeter found new love, a girl just as smart but twice as pretty. He should just propose now.

"You're coming back to the Garrison tomorrow?" I asked.

"No." She slowly got up and stood next to me at the railing. She was thousands of miles away, but I sensed her exhaustion as if she were right next to me. "California is aggressively pursuing a Paladin-sponsored education/conference center, but they need funding. It would be a great outreach for our integration program, but there's a lot of opposition from the government. Lots of suspicion."

"Who can blame them?"

"Yes, well, I need to convince them our policy of secrecy is a thing of the past and we're genuinely interested in sharing our knowledge."

"They're not buying it?"

"They haven't seen what we have to offer. Our advancements in health care alone will convince them." She drank from a water bottle and patted my hand. Her palm was warm and soft. "By the way, your Orphan program is doing quite well."

I hated that name, but the *Displaced Youth Program* wasn't catching on.

We talked about how many more kids we were planning to take on, how we could expand the program to the rest of the training facilities and, of course, get the word to the public on what a great job we were doing. I hated public relations; that was Mother's job. Everything we did, she had to find a way to tell the public. Television even started carrying the Paladin Network, a twenty-four-hour news station that exclusively covered us. She was a weekly regular.

"I'm scheduled for my wormhole trip in about a week."

"Everyone does it," she said. "You nervous?"

"I'm not doing jumping jacks." I drummed a short rhythm on the railing, watching waves crash below.

"I can't do anything to get you out of it, if that's what you're thinking," Mother said.

"No, that's not it at all. I'm just wondering why I need to go. Clearly there's a million things here I can be doing. I can't imagine why I'd ever be sent off-planet, so what's the point?"

"You sound nervous."

I glanced at her. She was serious. Then I realized, she was right. I was resisting some nervous tension inside me. Why was I being like this? It was just a trip, get it over with and be done with it and move on. Stop being a baby. But even acknowledging that feeling didn't make it go away.

"Look, I'm not nervous," I said, laughing nervously. "Okay, I'm nervous."

She laughed, too. I told her what I was feeling and she listened without responding. Maybe there was a good reason I was hesitant, I just didn't understand it yet. My gut feelings were often on the mark.

"I don't know." I spit over the railing and watched it disappear in the swirling wind. "Maybe it's as simple as not wanting to go through that wormhole."

"It's not comfortable."

"It feels like your spleen is getting squeezed out your ass, I'm told."

She grunted, pushing her short brown hair behind her ear. She'd never been off-planet, but she'd heard the stories. No one enjoyed the ride. No one.

A cruise ship moved from the left, the deck dotted with brightly dressed vacationers. I wondered if the partygoers were looking back at the shore.

"I read your report about the vision," she said. "About Pike."

"Not a happy ending, huh."

"What's your feeling? Does it have merit?"

I squeezed the railing. The quality of visions sometimes indicated their likelihood. When they were hazy, it was suspect, probably due to unforeseen variables. Even the weather could alter a vision, make someone stay at home instead of walk across the street and get hit by a truck. But when they were fully detailed, well, the odds were good.

"The vision was... solid." I swallowed hard. I hated to say that.

"Hmm." She nodded, thinking. "His security will be reexamined. Relocation may be considered."

"And maybe that's when he escapes."

The future was tricky. Perhaps if I never had the vision, he'd sit in his cell until the end of time. But then I have a vision and there's a relocation because of it and that's when he escapes. Self-fulfilling prophecy. It was much easier when I didn't know these things.

"Have you opened to related visions?" she asked. "Something that might clarify the event?"

Opening to visions meant trying to have one, but that never worked. They came on their own. I wasn't controlling them. But why did I have them at all? Was there some intelligent force deciding what to show me?

"There's nothing," I answered.

"Report any new visions, no matter how trivial." She watched the ship head for deeper waters, her thoughts coming in all directions.

"I better go."

"Yes." She took a deep breath. "I have a dinner meeting tonight."

"A date?"

"No." She laughed. Anything personal like that was funny to her. "All business. Work never ends."

"It could, you know."

"And then what?"

Work was just a word, she once told me. What she did was her life. Why would she attend to anything else?

Her eyes were green. She looked at mine, like she often did. Like she couldn't believe how big her boy had gotten, as if she wanted to tell me to buckle my seat belt and make sure I looked both ways before I crossed the street. That mother-essence was strong in her, but sometimes it disappeared and she felt like a stranger staring at me, just an employee of the Paladin Nation, like she suddenly remembered something that chased the mother-essence away and I was all alone in this world. A stranger to everyone. Just like Pike said. Like he knew.

The ship was small on the horizon.

"I'll call when I get back from my trip," I said. "Tell you how they stuffed my spleen back inside me."

She smiled and patted my hand. Fatigue bunched in her shoulders, and then it faded. The details of the room washed away. I dropped my arms. The darkness of my office was cold. I hurried to the leaper and urged it to take me to the tagghet field, where I could see real sunlight and breathe real air.

71

PINK SHIRTS

THE DAYS WENT by in a blur of commitments, but it still felt like my day off would never arrive. I was counting the minutes and there just always seemed to be more. But, finally, the week ended. Finally, I'd see Chute.

The parking garage was still a dank, stalactite-riddled cave. The dampness was in stark contrast to the rest of the Garrison, where the air was filtered and eighty-five degrees. A black car was waiting for me with the door open. I started to get in—

I HEAR rain battering the roof. In front of me there's an angry ocean, the waves white-capped and the water black in between snaps of lightning.

"EVERYTHING ALL RIGHT?" Someone grabbed my elbow.

I was holding onto the car door. My entire body was quivering with the numbing sensation of a vision that normally only trickled down my neck. My gums felt dead; I tapped my teeth together to get the feeling back.

"Yeah," I said. "Just... I was, uh, just remembering something."

It took a second, then I recognized the someone that grabbed my elbow was a Paladin named Jaret. He helped me lean against the car. I sensed he was about to call for assistance, maybe bring a few servys down to check me out. I had enough strength and sense to convince him I was fine. I stood up, barely able to keep from swaying. He watched me get in the car. I waved him off.

"I'm fine," I said. "Training caught up to me. I didn't hydrate enough, that's all."

He waited, until I said, "No, seriously. I'm fine." I left with a glance back to make sure.

What the hell was that all about? A vision only a few days after that last one? And during the daytime with a full-body numb out? The details were so vivid. I felt transported to another space and time, like I was standing on a sandy beach. I should've reported it, but that was sure to screw up the whole evening. I'd do it when I got back. They could lock me up in the infirmary if they wanted. *Just not before tonight.*

"Are you ready?" The car spoke in a calm, feminine voice.

I took the wheel. "I'll drive."

"Very well. It is currently sixty degrees in Charleston, South Carolina. The wormhole transport is cleared for entry. After exiting, you are approximately thirty-four minutes from your destination. Please obey the laws and drive carefully."

An image of the boulder field materialized on the dashboard. I eased the car over the slick floor and through the apparition of the cave wall into the field. The face of Garrison Mountain went up several hundred feet behind me, like a wall of resistance that the world needed to respect. It was the first thing tourists saw when they approached. It let them know we were big and strong. That they were safe.

I crossed the field and entered the dense trees on the other side to the swirling mass of the wormhole. I left Garrison Mountain behind. But the vision of the beach came along.

CARS WERE PARKED alongside the road leading to the high school. Dozens of shuttles picked people up and carted them to the tagghet stadium. I continued down the road, people staring.

"There's no parking up there, dumbass," someone shouted.

Shuttle drivers directed me to turn around, but I eased down the road until I reached the turnabout that looped in front of the massive high school steps leading to the front doors. I gave the car instructions to park somewhere far away; I'd call for it when I was ready. She said, "Certainly."

No one stared at me once I was out of the car. It wasn't like they couldn't see me. I wasn't invisible. It was a simple mind trick, that was all. I convinced people that the space I occupied was not interesting. They saw me. They just didn't care.

The car waited while I stared at my reflection in the window. My hair, still white, was long again, but not like a few years back. I'd gotten in the habit of pushing it straight back over my head, but it didn't stay there long, much like Mother's behind-the-ear habit. Most of all, I noticed what Chute called *the serious look*. My eyes were piercing; my jaw muscles flexed and my lips were a thin line.

"Smile a little," Chute would say, and squeeze my cheeks.

So I practiced in the driver-side window. It looked like something from school pictures. Third grade. I tried again and it just got worse. "Go," I said, waving the car off.

I'll wing it.

I FOLLOWED the crowd toward the tagghet stadium, one of the most expensive venues ever constructed at a high school, all funded by the Paladin Nation as an apology for the duplicates' deadly assault a few years earlier. The team went undefeated in the inaugural season, became nationally ranked, and had South Carolina's MVP. A girl with red hair.

The extravagant entrance was crowded. Little kids dipped their hands in the rectangular pond and high school teachers handed out brochures about the evening's events. A fox mascot tickled kids with oversized cushy hands.

The concession stand was inside the main gate, selling popcorn and drinks and souvenirs to a packed crowd. Three girls passed by with green and tan shirts, *33–0* plastered on the front. On the back was Chute's face, a game photo of her holding her helmet with one hand and the curved tagghet stick in the other.

Most Valuable Player.

A vendor pushed through the crowd, holding up hats and towels. "You got any shirts?" I shouted.

He looked around and noticed I was standing right next to him. He reached in the box strapped over his shoulders. "I got three kinds, which one you want?" I nodded at the girls. "You want the girl shirt? All I got left are pink. You want the pink?"

"I'll take it."

He sold it to me and moved on. I pulled it over my head. Pink. No one saw me anyway.

I walked past the pedestrian ramp that led to the upper deck. The corridor was filled with displays hosted by student clubs and local charities. The awards night was as much for civic awareness as it was for jocks. I remained unnoticed until I saw the crowded display ahead.

It was the Student Virtualmode Club. They were future programmers that built elaborate virtual worlds and constructed complex gear to transport a person's mind out of their skin and into a sim where they could experience the Internet in virtualmode. Holographic monsters walked across the top of their banner. A hulking rock monster thumped its chest and an armored knight broke his sword over its head. The kids laughed, then watched a dragon waddle over and incinerate the rock monster.

The virtualmode students were talking to adults, explaining what the club did, extravagant membership fees and field trips. They touted the highest graduation rate among the student body and the highest grade point average. And scholarships, too. There were more scholarships available in virtualmode world-building than any career field out there.

The bulk of the crowd was gathered in front of a short, plump kid explaining a gadget in his right hand. I leaned against the wall, near enough that I could hear what Streeter was saying.

"It will revolutionize the way we communicate," he said. "Our minds are as unique as our fingerprints. We can find anyone after we meet them by using this to capture their *mindprint.* You'll never lose track of family, friends or even pets. We can call them, link up with their mind, and then virtually *see* them as if they're in front of us. Virtually touch them. Space will become irrelevant."

"Not only that, once calibrated with your mind," Janette said, "it will record every thought and emotion you experience. It will record your *entire* life." Janette was by Streeter's side. She was short, too. "The government has already asked for a demonstration. He's flying to Washington next week. NASA wants to buy the rights."

Streeter looked at her and smiled. He may as well have batted his eyes.

"What do you mean *virtually* see them?" a dad asked.

"This gear," Streeter said, holding up the half-globe, "will link your mind with, say, your grandmother living in California. Your eyes will see her in front of you. You'll see what she's doing right this second, like she's in the room."

"Let's see it work," someone said.

"All right." Streeter scanned the crowd. Little kids raised their hands, jumping up and down, shouting *me, me, me.* He swung his finger around like a spinning wheel to pick the winners. He placed the gear against their foreheads, one at a time, and asked them to think of a friend or relative. And when they did, a holographic image of planet Earth materialized with a glowing dot on it, signifying where the person they were thinking of was located. And he was right, every time.

"Big deal," a kid said. "You said we'd see them."

Streeter smiled. "Oh, you're going to see them. I'm going to pick someone at random and dial up whoever that person thinks of." He circled the spinning finger. "You ready? Huh? Who's going to be the lucky one?"

Me! Me, me, me!

The finger spun around. Parents were even raising their hands. The crowd grew larger. Streeter worked them like a street performer, waving his hand around and around. It started to come down to pick a winner—

THUNDER RUMBLES through the sand under my feet. The next flash of lightning illuminates the silhouette of a figure in front of me. The heavy rain blurs the details, but I notice the knife in the right hand.

"YOU THERE, IN THE PINK SHIRT." Streeter was pointing at me. People were staring. "Yeah, you. I'm talking to you. Wake up. What d'ya say?"

I was still leaning against the wall but couldn't feel my legs. I don't know how I managed to keep from sliding down to the ground. My entire head was ringing like a bell. I was moving my mouth, but nothing was coming out. Now the kids watching the holographic battle turned around and looked.

"Hey there, stranger." Streeter came over. He laughed nervously, looked back at the crowd and pulled on my shirt. "That's a nice shirt. Isn't that a nice shirt, folks?"

They laughed nervously, too.

I managed a single step and it reverberated to the top of my skull. It hurt, but it brought me back, flushing away the heavy dullness.

"What's your name, stranger?" Streeter asked.

"Um. Socket."

"Boy, you nervous or just excited?" The crowd laughed, going along with the joke.

"Just, um, a little nervous, I guess."

"Nothing to be nervous about, my friend." He held up the gear. "Now I'm going to ask Socket to visualize someone in his family. That person is going to materialize in front of us. Now, normally, only Socket would see this person, but I've calibrated the gear to project it for all of us to see. But first"—he put the gear in my hands, slightly heavier than a paperweight—"we need the locator to find Socket in time and space. Once it finds him, standing right here, it'll seek out his mystery guest."

Others joined the crowd to watch the pink-shirted, funny-name kid holding a paperweight. All I could think about was the thunder and the lightning and the knife, how the figure felt familiar. And how I'd never had two visions in one day. Panic began to rise, along with a thought: *Not again.* Something was changing in me and I didn't understand it. Things like that made me nervous.

"Close your eyes, Socket," Streeter said. "Let the locator connect with your being, much like a virtualmode transporter pulls you from your skin."

I took a deep breath and relaxed. I was already feeling normal again. The last thing I wanted to do was freak a whole bunch of people out. I closed my eyes and gripped the locator tightly. I could feel it travelling through my arms like filaments, searching through my nerve lines for all my organs and the awareness of my being. It was a good prototype, but now I understood why Streeter chose me. It wasn't ready to fully connect with a normal person. He needed extra-perception, someone like me to assist its communication. So I fully engaged with the gear, letting it merge with my awareness.

"There we go," Streeter said.

I opened my eyes. A hologram of Earth materialized in front of us, turning on the axis, like it had done with the others.

"So the locator is finding Socket, it'll show us where he is, and then we'll ask him to..."

The crowd began laughing. A dot was glowing in the United States, but not in Charleston, South Carolina. It was in the middle of Illinois.

"You're only off by eight hundred miles, kid," someone said.

Several people walked off, someone tossing in, "Good luck in Washington. Loser."

"No, just a second." Streeter took it from me. "I forgot to reset the... it'll still work..."

But he lost them. They were heading for their seats. The ceremony was going to begin in ten minutes anyway.

"Man, why'd you have to go and do that?" He scowled.

"I didn't do anything," I said.

"Because I made fun of your pink shirt?" He stared at it. "Why are you wearing a pink shirt?"

I showed him Chute's face on the back.

"They have those in other colors, you know."

"I didn't buy it for the color."

"Yeah, well, it doesn't work on you. And what's with the look of shock? You knew I was going to call you and then you looked like you were going to start drooling. You having a seizure?"

"Yeah, well, I just was... thinking of something. You caught me by surprise."

"More like I kicked you in the balls."

"Hi, Socket." Janette bobbed on her toes, holding Streeter's hand.

Janette and I talked while Streeter went over to the display. She liked my shirt and asked how I was doing and said how excited she was for Chute. "Are you two going inside?" I asked.

"We got to break down the display," Streeter said. "And recalibrate this, apparently."

"You're close, Streeter. The code was correct and most of the internal structure. It must be holding some data from previous reads."

"We could take it back to the lab," Janette said, "run another test drive to realign the synapse relays."

"I suppose." He had that look again, as if she was speaking the language of love and only he could hear it. Then she blushed.

"I'm going to leave you two alone," I said.

"Well, come by later." He grabbed me before I could get away. "And don't tell Chute we're not in there. We'll watch it on relay, but I can't get in there to see it live."

"So you want me to lie?"

"No, just tell her you saw me and that I saw her, that's not a lie. If she gets suspicious, just run. That's what I do."

He looked at Janette for support, but she didn't know Chute all that well, yet. Chute wouldn't miss something like this for either of us and she expected the same in return.

"When are you bringing me out to the Garrison? You've had Chute out there like twelve times. Me? I've been there once." He put one finger in my face to make his point. "You like her better than me or something?"

"Infinitely."

"My feelings are hurt."

I pushed his hand away. "Every time I ask you to come out you got something planned." I stared at Janette for a long second. "Whose fault is that?"

She nodded in agreement.

Streeter said, "All right, well, I got a life. Sue me."

"Maybe I could schedule you to come out in a few days, before I leave on a trip."

"Two days?" He rubbed his chin and glanced at Janette. "Yeaaaaah, I can't do that."

"You're hilarious, you know that?"

"How about this? I project into your office through virtualmode, you can show me how the whole molding technology works. You don't need permission for that."

"I'll see."

Virtualmode club members grabbed Streeter and Janette followed. He pointed at me as if to say *do it*. I nodded, but they were already discussing the next meeting, taking down the banner and boxing up the gear while the kids screamed for more action from the monsters. By the time I reached an entrance to the stadium, the corridor was mostly empty. Two minutes before the ceremony began.

72

RAINING Roses

EIGHT THOUSAND SEATS in that stadium. All filled.

Lightners floated above the stadium, spotlighting the crowd that cheered when their images appeared over the field in three-dimensional detail. Holographic fireworks streaked harmlessly from one side to the other, like a battle of green, blue and red fizzling missiles. Hundreds of shiny lookit orbs hovered around, their red eyelights circling their shiny softball-sized bodies, scanning and directing the crowd. I made my way near the front and stood along the railing just above the field.

Security guards were along the perimeter. There were some real important people on the stage in center field, including the governor, mayor and all the members of the county school board. The rest of the stage was occupied by coaches and parents. There in front, sitting with a blanket over his lap in a wheelchair, was Chute's father, Mr. Thomas, who was paralyzed in the car accident that took his wife's life. Behind him was Chute's older sister, Angela, her hands on his shoulders.

A bone-rattling explosion shook the seats, and then the sky lit up. Fog oozed from the tunnel at the end of the field, smoky tendrils crawling over the grass. Synthesized music hammered out a beat. The head coach emerged from the thick cloud and the crowd erupted.

He reached center stage and shook hands. And then the first player stepped from the smoke, hands in the air, dancing in a circle, whooping the crowd to another level of fanatical frenzy. Another tagger emerged, hopping up and down, swinging his arms. The announcer's voice barely registered above the excitement. The third player out broke rank and raced for the wall where fans leaned over with outstretched hands. The next one out followed until several of them were running along the perimeter, shaking hands and signing shirts and programs. The crowd rushed down the aisles to get a piece of the action.

Two students pushed by me, booing. They threw poppers at the players, laughing with the squeal of gear-induced euphoria. Their energy tasted sulfuric, their synapses burning from the small patches they hid behind their ears that kept the dopamine production on high. They started to throw another round of poppers.

"Turn yourselves in to security." I barely spoke above the noise, but they didn't need to hear the words. They felt them. "Report you are using illegal gear and need help."

Their complexions became pasty. They were frozen in mid-throw, absorbing what I just imprinted on their minds. They accepted my thoughts as their own, feeling the compulsion to turn themselves over to the authorities. The command wouldn't last long, soon it would fade and they would resume control of their being, but it would last long enough to get them out of the way.

"AND, FINALLY!" the announcer shouted. "SOUTH CAROLINA'S MOST VALUABLE PLAYER..."

The crowd drowned his final word out, shouting a name that had been called hundreds of times during the tagghet season.

CHHHHUUUUUUUUUUUTTTTTE!

Chute stepped out of the tunnel. My chest melted, seeing her step into the spotlight. The crowd began throwing stuff onto the field. My instinct was to stop them, but then I realized... roses. They were throwing roses. Some had stems, others threw just the flowers that perished in a flutter of petals that looked like a pink cloud falling onto the green grass. She raised her hands to catch them.

We would be together for the rest of our lives, that much I knew because, from time to time, I had a vision. We're old. My hair is thin, but still white. Streeter is short, round and bald. Wrinkles soften Chute's face and her red hair is more of a rust color and sprayed with strands of gray. I'm holding her right hand. In her left, she holds a rose. We're in a wasteland of dead trees, their silvery-gray branches barren. Weeds brush against our knees until we reach an enormous stump worn and chiseled by the weather. Chute kneels and places the rose on the stump. We stand in silence. She lays her head on my shoulder.

It feels like we're paying tribute to someone, but I don't know who. All I know is that it's a solid vision. As solid as they get.

We'll be together, to the end.

Chute reached the steps leading up to the stage and the coach handed her a long-stemmed rose. It was the students that started the rose ritual, throwing them like hockey fans threw hats on the ice after a hat trick. It started with any old flower, but when Chute was quoted on the news that roses were her favorite, it was roses the rest of the season. Whenever she scored, it rained red.

Her teammates pulled her onstage. Together, the whole team raised their arms. The crowd went berserk. It was several minutes before there was any control. In fact, no one could hear what the coach was saying. When he was finished, he turned it over to the other very special people. They handed out awards to various players. They each got to say something, shouting out to their friends and families and pretty much whatever came to mind. I could barely hear them.

Chute was the last up, blushing as the crowd ramped up again, tossing more roses, turning the field more red than green. She held her father's hand and tried to speak but choked on her emotions, which only riled up the crowd more. When she finally spoke, and the crowd settled, she sincerely thanked everyone for coming, it meant so much. She held up the MVP award—a glittering globe—and the crowd responded.

"I hope this empowers girls everywhere. NOTHING IS IMPOSSIBLE!"

She wiped her face and kissed her father's cheek and hugged her sister. She thanked her mother and wished she could see her now.

Best ceremony ever.

It WAS ALMOST MIDNIGHT.

I waited at the back entrance, watching the team leave. Chute was the last out. She was escorted by a security guard to my car in front of the school. I opened her door, thanked the man and went around to my side, and when I got in, we met in the middle, hugging tight. I loved the way she smelled. "I knew you were there," she said. "It was like I could feel you, you know."

I know.

The last of the crowd was being ushered out of the parking lot by security. I took the wheel and drove down the empty road littered with programs and cups.

"Can you believe it?" Chute pounded the dash, shaking her head and screaming. "I'm going home with this! *Can you freaking believe it?*" She displayed the globe award on the tips of her fingers. The surface was clear and polished, but it was milky and opaque in the center, like it contained a galaxy. "Socket, I don't know if you know this." She eyeballed me, deadpan. "But I could be the best tagger of all time."

I laughed. "Where was that humility at the ceremony? I mean, all you did was thank everyone and hope to inspire every girl to wear a sportsbra."

"Let's see if I go pro." She waved her hand around the globe. "Oh, mighty award that looks like a crystal ball, please tell me where I'll be in ten years."

Asking for the future made me cringe. I'd had enough of that. She chanted some mumbo-jumbo, fogged the glass with her breath and rubbed it on her shirt. She pressed it against her ear like a seashell.

"Socket! Guess what?"

"You win every tagghet award known to mankind?"

"No." She leaned close. "You're going to stop at a red light."

I eased up to the stoplight, already red. "Wow. That thing really does work."

"And now you're going to turn left."

"Um, your house is straight."

Her hand crawled across my chest. "But the park is that way."

"It's midnight, Chute."

"Oh my." She feigned surprise. "That means... we're going to turn into pumpkins any second. Promise me, Socket, they won't make me into a pie? Promise me!"

"But your dad is expecting us."

She nibbled on my earlobe, her breath in my ear. "I told him we were stopping at a party."

"He trusts me to get you home."

"Oh, you'll get me home."

The light turned green.

"Your dad," I said. "He has a baseball bat, you know."

"I just want to see the park," she whispered. "Is that so bad?"

"But you've seen the park."

Her tongue was hot. Shivers ran down my spine. "Not tonight."

The blinker flashed on the dashboard. I turned left.

73

PROOF

IT WAS 12:50 when we got to Chute's neighborhood. She was looking in the mirror on the sun visor, fixing her hair. Her house was in a cul-de-sac, a single-story ranch with white siding. The lights were bright in the bay window to the right of the door. Her father was at the kitchen table. He looked up when my headlights flashed across the house. I turned the lights off.

"We're here."

"I look like I've been wrestling."

"It'd be good if you didn't."

"Give me a second, then."

"Your dad's watching."

"Let him watch. We're not doing anything."

Mr. Thomas sipped from a can, staring out the window. I tapped on the steering wheel, counting the seconds. Chute flipped the visor back. "All done. How do I look?"

The dashboard glow softly lit her face. Sometimes I forgot time when I looked at her. She was beautiful. Most would agree, but it was different for me. Her face moved me, deeply. Her smile. The way her eyes crinkled in the corners. Her energy swirled sweetly, vibrating somewhere inside me.

"What?" she said. "Do I still look like the Hulk?"

"No." I turned the car off. "Let's go in."

The doors slammed in the quiet night. We hooked our fingers as we walked up the concrete ramp. Chute pushed open the front door.

"There she is!" Mr. Thomas's voice boomed from inside the house. "There's my Annie-darling!"

Chute ran through the house. Her dad wheeled in from the kitchen. She kissed him on the cheek, then walked behind him and wrapped her arms around his neck. Anna was her birth name, but her father was the only one that called her that.

"You letting the mosquitoes inside to breed, boy?" Mr. Thomas shouted. "Get in here and shut the door!"

I closed the door and came inside. Mr. Thomas held out his thick hand and shook mine and then Angela came running into the front room, screaming. Chute laced her fingers with her sister and they both screeched. Mr. Thomas covered his ears, muttering, "Jesus Christ's holy shit," and went to the kitchen for another beer. Can, not bottle. Mr. Thomas always said bottles were for girls.

The girls embraced, still screaming like ten-year-olds, bouncing up and down. He took a swig of Budweiser and watched his daughters celebrate. He flinched when they hit the high notes, but it never wiped the smile off his face. Angela was a cheerleader in high school, doing one of her old cheers, kicking her leg up high and shaking her hands. "A-W-E-S-O-M-E! Awesome. Awesome. Totally!"

Chute imitated her, but was laughing too hard to keep up. Mr. Thomas's laugh boomed over the top of them. "You see that, Socket? They're taunting me with their perfectly working legs."

"Oh, stop it, Daddy," Angela said, not breaking stride.

Mr. Thomas put his beer on the table and wheeled over to the girls. He expertly leaned back and pulled a wheelie, moving in time to the dance. The girls kicked out like Russian dancers while Mr.

Thomas wheeled back and forth. The cheer broke down when the girls fell down laughing.

"Let's see that award, girl!" Mr. Thomas shouted.

The girls lay on the floor, catching their breath. Mr. Thomas waited at the table. The globe was by the front door, so I fetched it. He muttered thank you. And then the energy changed.

He gazed into the globe like there was something inside, oblivious to the ruckus on the other side of the kitchen. His eyes glassed up. Mr. Thomas was not the type to get misty, but the water in his eyes reflected the kitchen light. He held the globe close to his nose. His breath was choppy.

Angela leaped up when she saw the award, leaning over her father, hands on his shoulders, looking into it much the same way. Chute sat next to them. Suddenly, the house was very still. Mr. Thomas's lips started to move, but they didn't say anything. Angela felt him quiver and hooked her arm around his neck.

"Mom would be so proud, Chute," she said.

Mr. Thomas took Chute's hand. She laid her head on his shoulder. Angela wrapped her arms around them. Their energy intermingled, merging with deep sweet hues, connecting at a very real, essential level. All barriers stripped away.

Angela nodded at me. I hesitated. Mr. Thomas cleared his throat. "Get over here, boy."

Chute held out her hand. I took it, joining them at the table, and felt the family essence weave into my being, their hearts beating through my arm next to my own pulse. I was five the last time I felt something like that, just before my father died.

We gripped each other tightly, staring at the globe. But it wasn't the award we were looking at. We weren't admiring its beauty or fame. It was a symbol of Mr. Thomas's family, representing how grown up they were. There was a time he was convinced he would never live to see it, but there he was. There they all were, wrapped tightly at the table.

Chute was a young woman. And here was something to hold, something to prove it.

Something her mother would be proud of.

"Don't close the door!" Angela shouted. "Dad said he'd get his bat."

Chute fell back on her bed, arms out. "Listen to her," she said. "She used to sneak out of the house all the time, and now she's telling me when I can close my door."

"You sneak out all the time," I said.

She rolled on her side, buried her face in the pillow, and said something about the greatest day of her life. She used to have posters of celebrities and bands on her wall. They were replaced by a shelf full of trophies. She'd have to clear some space for the globe.

The only thing that remained the same was the picture over her headboard of the three of us. We were on the curb in front of Streeter's house. It was our first day taking the school bus. We were seven and had our bookbags strapped on our shoulders. Chute was in the middle, arms around us.

"I can't sleep," she said into the pillow. "Will you stay the night?"

"Right."

"You can sleep on the couch."

"I told you your father had a bat. If he finds me on the couch in the morning, he'll use it."

She lifted her head. "You can hide, then knock on the door like you came over for breakfast."

She's serious. "Look, I'd love to see you all day and night, but I can't. Not tonight."

"The world can wait." *Still serious.*

"I've got some things to do, and there's a trip."

"Where are you going?"

I grabbed a tagghet puck from her dresser and inspected the scuff marks. "Somewhere far away, but it won't take long."

"Well, I guess I'll have to get used to you being on the road, once

I'm Mrs. Greeny." Her laughter muffled into the pillow. "It's not easy being the wife of a superhero, you know."

"I'll bring you to the Preserve when I get back. I've got some kids that would love you to teach them some tagghet moves."

"Really, really?"

"Promise, promise."

She rolled over, closed her eyes and hummed. Her sleepy imagination flashed with images of trees and grimmets. "Could you do that energy thing?" She tapped her forehead. "I'm not tired."

I sat on the bed and touched her forehead. My essence mingled with hers and our experiences merged. A closeness. Oneness. Something that reminded us we were never alone.

She was softly snoring within a minute. I stopped at her doorway and glanced at the picture of the three of us again. It seemed like just the other day. I leaned closer. The details were smudged in the background, like there was a figure using back-reflecting gear to appear invisible. Then again, it could just be the printer smudging up.

I had a gut feeling that wasn't it.

74

To Reign

THE ROADS WERE empty and slick from a light rain, reflecting the streetlights. I turned the music off and cruised down the interstate. I didn't miss leaving South Carolina, but I hated leaving Chute. Someday, I could bring her with me. But then what? Were we going to play house inside Garrison Mountain? I was still so torn about my two lives. Somehow they were going to merge. Maybe one day I could retire and find peace and quiet and a normal life when the world was saved.

I took my exit after crossing the Cooper River bridge, the blinker flashing—

THE FIGURE STEPS FORWARD, revealing the strands of wet hair over her face. Red hair. Chute lifts the knife, her face twisted with anger. Then she leaps, swinging the weapon down at me, lightning flashing off its edge.

.   .   .

"A̶ᴜᴛᴏᴘɪʟᴏᴛ ᴇɴɢᴀɢᴇᴅ," the car reported.

The tires hit the gravel on the shoulder as the wheels turned the car back onto the pavement.

I was slumped in the seat. My lips were fat and rubbery. The moon passed between branches. The car found its way to the secure location of the wormhole while I tried to get the feeling back. Only when we entered the blue swirl could I take the wheel. I wasn't thinking clearly, but I knew enough that these weren't normal visions. If they got any stronger, I'd be dead. I had to get some answers.

I flew across the boulder field toward the vertical wall of the Garrison. The commander would get my reports soon enough, but not before I made one last stop. Call it compulsion or gut instinct. Or insanity.

If I have any more visions, Pike said. *As if he knew I would.*

I ᴄᴀʟʟᴇᴅ ᴀʜᴇᴀᴅ to my office. When I arrived, Pike waited with his legs folded beneath him. A string of spit jiggled from his mouth. The minders appeared behind him.

"Wha' dewyew wan?" Pike lifted his heavy head, his dark glasses askew, revealing the white eyeballs filled with rooty veins. "So soon?" He smacked his lips and sat up. "To what do I owe the pleasure of—"

"What do you know?"

"I know, I know... what do I know? What do *you* know?"

"You know something, Pike. Something about the things I'm seeing. You tell me WHAT YOU KNOW!"

His mind was scrambled, thoughts floating like weeds in the ocean. Perhaps that was the idea, make things chaotic, hide the secrets in plain sight. Like a shredded document thrown into the wind. It would take centuries to put it back together. And the minders just kept blowing.

"Play a game with me, wonderboy, shall we?" Pike smiled.

"You think this is a game, Pike? You've lost your mind."

"Quite right, you are. But if you want me to tell you things, ole Pike will tell you things. Let's play a game."

I snatched his neck, the knobby Adam's apple pumping up and down in my palm. "You tell what you're hiding, you filthy traitor. You know something about these... these *visions*."

He slid his glasses back up his nose with a single finger and waggled his eyebrows. I threw him against the seat and paced to the back of the room. This just didn't make sense, these experiences were unlike any others, but now they were bringing images of nonsense. In what universe would Chute attack me?

I crossed my arms, staring at the back wall. Had I made a mistake coming here? No, Pike knew something. He was very specific about *if I had any more visions*. He knew.

Eh-hem. He tapped his foot.

I looked over my shoulder. "This is all just a game to you."

"It wouldn't be any fun if it wasn't. Indulge me." He waved his arms and the floor shifted between us. A checkerboard formed with globular shapes, each taking a space. "And I'll tell you everything."

The globular shapes were black and white, each of equal number. Outwardly, each piece looked exactly the same, but each was as unique from each other as a dog is from a cat. Another checkerboard formed several inches above that one, this one smaller with fewer squares. And above that, another smaller one and another, until there was a total of seven boards forming a pyramid, the top level a single square at eye level.

Reign. He wanted to play Reign, where the rules and moves were beyond the comprehension of ordinary people. The object: get the king piece to the top. First, one had to see the king piece, but not with your eyes. It required opening your mind, to see the pieces differently, to feel them, sense them with extrasensory perception.

I sat down in a chair forming below me.

"Ill-advised, Paladin Greeny." The middle minder stepped forth. "Opening your mind to a convicted—"

"THERE IS NO THREAT!" The walls shook. The minders felt the infinite power of my mind peel through their advanced minds. They faltered, then resumed their dutiful focus. My outrage would be reported to the commander. Hell, I was surprised the room didn't just shut down. But it didn't.

Pike looked over his shoulder. "You're talking to wonderboy here, Mo. Better watch yo'self before you wreck yo'self." He threw his head back and howled.

What was becoming of me? I didn't like the mystery. Why did it seem the answer was right in front of me? It just countered any logic, but still, there was something here. I was losing control of the visions; why were they changing?

I scratched my chin and considered the multilayered game and innocuous pieces. Pike waited patiently. And then I opened. He sat up, tasting the availability of my mind, its essence wafting toward him. His feeble mind crept forward like arthritic fingers. Pike clapped. *Pitter-patter.* "You-you go first, my guest. Guests go first."

I allowed my awareness to penetrate the game. The generic pieces exposed their true shapes as my psychic vision opened, forming rooks, animals, weapons and warriors. Pike's pieces flickered, changing identities as he integrated with them. This was a game of deception. Of hiding. And exposing. It required strategy and trickery, the ability to hide deception within deception within deception. To lay traps within traps.

Pike's mind entered my space. It was ragged and frayed, but still capable. It observed how I moved, how I planned. How I reacted. In turn, I reached out for his mind, to see what he was planning. Looking into your opponent's intentions was the equivalent of looking at one's cards in a game of poker. But Reign was psychic deception.

Sometimes you wanted them to look.

"I see, I see," he said. "You have dreams."

My pieces flickered back to ordinary shapes, away from the powerful warriors that defended my regal king piece. His gallant knight pieces crossed the bottom board to trap me.

"Not exactly dreams," I said.

"Who do you think gets the rose?"

"The what?" Pike's monkey-beast pieces advanced to the second board, pulling his king piece with it while his knights kept the majority of my pieces trapped. He was talking about the vision where Chute places the rose on the stump. "I'm not talking about that one."

"Because you like it, do you?"

"Because it makes sense! None of the others..." I stopped short. He didn't need to know anything else, but it left me wondering how he knew about the rose and the stump.

"Who says that is you?" His laughter was almost a growl. "In the vision, it looks like you, but who says that-that is you with her, huh?"

"What?"

"Your dream." He coughed. "You think that is you in your dream, in your vision. You... with your..." He coughed again. "You think that's you with your wife?"

"Who else would it be?"

"Well-well, now. Looks can be a tangled web we weave, if we seek to deceive." He gazed back at the battle. "Or something like that."

My pieces transformed into nimble swordsmen slashing his pathetic soldiers into pieces before advancing to the second level. Only a strong ring of rooks formed around his king piece kept me from destroying everything.

"Who is sending these... vi-vi-visions to you?" he sang.

"No one *sends* them."

"Oh? So you, you think them up, huh? You think up the future, wonderboy? Is that how it works?"

"Insights are an extension of my being, a connection with presence. The moment contains all past, present and future."

"Oh, you are such a treat, wonderboy." He laid his head back, savoring the moment like it was melting on his tongue, then spoke softly. "If they are an ex-extension of you, then why don't you stop them, huh?"

"They have something to show me."

"You? You have something to... to show you?"

My pieces transformed into brutes with oversized axes and began chopping at the protective rooks; bricks and mortar scattered across the second level, trickling to the bottom board. My king advanced to the third level while his cowered behind the crumbling walls.

"Don't patronize me."

"NOR ME, WONDERBOY."

The force of a once-great minder punched the unguarded fabric of my mind, but it was mild, nothing more than a slap, and I took advantage of the distraction by wiping out the entire second level. His king piece leaped to the fourth level, but without protection it was doomed.

"*Who* is sending you visions is irrelevant." He looked over the game while his king drew a sword. "A better question is *why* he is sending them."

"Why is it a he?"

"He, she... whatever. God is a he, no? Yes?"

My three warrior pieces, the only remaining besides my king, surrounded his king piece. I would walk to victory.

He laughed *at* me. "Where is someone taking you, wonderboy, huh? Steering you like a ship to where, huh? That is the question you should investigate. That question you should be asking and answering. Wrong questions beget wrong answers."

My warrior pieces transformed into enormous serpents with impenetrable scales and dagger teeth. My king piece slowly moved up behind them.

"I control my own destiny. I am responsible for my own actions. Are you having difficulty accepting your own fate, Pike? *You* betrayed us. No one else is at fault for that."

"Don't lecture me." He spat on his lap. "I despise this flesh and everyone like it. You like it there in your skin, wonderboy?"

I took a moment to gather my composure. Pike was controlling the conversation. He could plant suggestions in a victim's mind with a seemingly innocent conversation. Great minds did not need to overwhelm victims to beat them. Victims of great minds never even knew they were beat. They never even heard the swooshing of the guillotine; only felt the pinch of its blade.

Pike sang a song while my king piece climbed to the sixth level. "Why do you come to see me?" he asked, unconcerned he would lose.

"I come," I said slowly, "because I cannot accept a world where you live."

"Oh, that." He raised a finger and cleared his throat. His king piece spiked the long sword, its only weapon, into the board, clearly giving up with no options to get past the vicious serpents. "I particularly enjoy that vision, wonderboy. It gives me reason to live, if you want to know the absolute truth. That one day, I may be free to murder and pillage and raze this planet, that-that-that gives me hope there is a god." He raised his arms up and gave thanks to the ceiling. "There must be a god, don't you think?"

"No god would allow you life."

"The world needs the devil."

"Love is the reason the world exists."

"And evil is its soul mate."

"I could end you, Pike." He felt the power of my mind slither coldly inside him. With a thought, I could will his heart to stop. My king paused.

"That would be... suicide." He struggled to breathe. "Death to me... there-there would be no reason for you."

"It would be justice."

"Are you God?"

"No," I said. "I'm the judge and jury."

"Then I want a new trial."

I removed my mind from him. He only got pleasure from it, anyway. Any feeling was better than the numb imprisonment he endlessly experienced. I had all I needed from him. The game was over; there was no need to finish. Sometimes gut feelings led to dead ends. The details of the room began to shrink as I got up.

"Have a safe trip," Pike said.

I stopped. The room remained in full detail. I recalled my last interaction with Pike and found no reason that he should know about the trip. When I turned, he smiled mischievously, like a child that sprang a secret.

"How do you know about that?" I penetrated his mind again, but there were only random thoughts. Pike offered no resistance to the invasion, relishing the uncomfortable sensations of his stretching mind. "Tell me, Pike. How do you know anything?"

"You think-think old Pike is useless, huh? There are things that... leak in the air, you know." He waved his hands like a magician pulling something from space. "Perhaps I know you better than you know you, wonderboy?"

You never even hear the swooshing of the guillotine.

"You know, it's funny," he said. "If you think about it, we don't control anything, really. The universe tosses us about like an ocean of water. Really, we're just driftwood. If you think about it, really. That-that-that's what I think."

"You're a plague."

"We remember pain, wonderboy. *Remember that.* Pain makes us feel *human.* Do you understand? It is not love that reminds us of who we are, it is pain, it is loss, *it is death.* Humans relish suffering, holding it close to their heart. They define themselves by the hurt, do you understand, wonderboy? Do you? We are vulnerable. Pain reminds us of that, that we exist. It is not love that we remember."

He lifted his chin, as if to offer his neck. Pike was repulsed by his own flesh, yet he craved the satisfaction of his being, his own essence. To feel. To be. He wanted to escape the misery of his ghostly existence, the separation of his own self, divided into psychotic elements. He did not see clearly. And for that, he would always suffer.

"Remembering is not a prerequisite to humanity," I said. "It is our presence."

"But it helps. Otherwise, you are a goldfish."

"Without presence, we are computers."

"Oooo, touché. Memories and presence. Like milk and cookies, would you say?"

His king had taken a knee with hands folded atop the jeweled hilt of the long sword. My king reached for the top square and the serpents opened their daggered mouths to devour his king. And as they bit down, as my king neared the top, a long steel tip slid from the top square through my king's head, impaling him moments from victory. Somehow, Pike's king stood victorious at the top, the serpents left squirming on the ground.

You only feel the pinch of its blade.

"You come with questions," he said. "I give you answers."

He was no longer smiling like the insane, but for once appeared quite lucid.

"You give me nothing."

We stared for several moments until a smile finally broke his face. I called the room to break the connection and flopped into my chair, no clearer than I was before this senseless meeting.

"If you see Papa Pivot, pass along a message for me," Pike said, as the details of his image began to shrink. I heard him shout one last word from a long ways away, could feel him smiling when he said, "SHOWTIME!"

Perhaps the commander was right. He was not one to toy with.

75

Knotted

MY OFFICE WAS FILLED, once again, with the intricate web of worm-holes that infiltrated the universe, illuminating the blank walls with an electric blue haze. It was a map to the universe's roadway system and I was supposed to know it by now. I sat with my feet propped on the desk.

I just couldn't concentrate. I couldn't even remember how many hours had passed since I left Pike, and that was the first time I could remember ever losing track of time. I always knew everything, down to the very second, like my mind was a ticking clock. Now I felt like some insomniac consumed with work.

Sound familiar?

Back in my old life, before I was aware of my Paladin nature, I spent countless nights waiting for my mother to come home, only to answer her calls that something came up, she was stuck at work. Sometimes I'd stare at her image when she video-called, noticing the dark rings under her eyes, wondering when the last time she'd slept was. Now it was me.

It wasn't some trivial distraction that had me wide awake. I wasn't even thinking of the wormhole trip or the strange visions. It was Pike. The guy was a mental master and here I went and underestimated him. Even in his decrepit state, he knew how to hit me. He had me so consumed with him, I couldn't think straight. Or sleep.

He had answers to something, I could feel it. But I wasn't asking the right questions, that was what he wanted me to know. I think. Had he become some brat smirking behind his hand while he watched me step into an obvious trap, milking every second of joy from my immediate future? Was I walking into it? Was he leading me there? Was this part of it?

Get a hold of yourself!

I dropped my feet and rubbed my tired face. I really needed sleep; this was no way to deal with problems. But I'd just end up staring at the ceiling. And I couldn't let this go. *If I'm going to obsess, may as well stop half-assing it.*

"Show me Pike," I said.

The maze of wormholes evaporated, leaving a wide open blank space between my desk and the opposite wall. An image flickered a few feet in front of me, then materialized into a solid projection of a figure slumped in a chair. This was simply a projection of what Pike was doing at that moment. He couldn't see me. Didn't know I was watching.

I paced around the desk. The three minders solidified in front of me, like immovable objects, staring at the back of Pike's bald head. Pike was hunched over with his legs folded under him, swaying back and forth like a mental patient. The ever-present string of drool jiggled off his lip while he mumbled. His glasses had fallen off, lying in his lap, exposing the sightless eyeballs that were filled with red veins.

I knelt in front of him. This was how he spent his endless days. There was no sleep. No exercise. Just second after second of the minders frying his mind like a microwave.

Showtime. What'd he mean by that? Out of everything he said, that stuck with me, like he knew something was coming. Something to do with Pivot. Or was he just clever enough to make me think he did, because there was no way this secluded madman could know anything.

I paced around the empty office, leisurely throwing each foot in front of the other while I stared at the black floor. It was dark at the far end, barely lit by the image of Pike muttering near my desk.

What makes you believe that's you?

The space brightened around me as I called up the vision. Weeds sprouted from the floor between rising boulders. The rose in Chute's wrinkled hand. I walked around to look into our faces. The traces of white hair, thinner and receding, covered most of my head. How could that not be me? But now he had me wondering. I looked back at the image of Pike still wavering. Still mumbling.

That's me. End of story. My visions weren't wrong.

So does Pike escape?

I waved the image away just as Chute placed the rose on the enormous charred stump. I was standing in darkness again, hands clamped behind my back, no more at ease than I was ten minutes earlier. And Pike still chattered.

"See Chute."

Chute's bed materialized in front of me. It was a live feed from her bedroom. She'd let me tap into her home's security months ago. We started to project images back and forth like I did when I met my mother, but it was just too impermanent. We didn't use it much anymore because we decided if we were going to talk, it had to be in person. But sometimes, I would call it up just so I could watch her sleep.

Her head lay softly on the pillow, eyes shut. Her lower lip fluttered with each exhale. Sometimes I'd watch her long enough to hear her sleep talk, but there were never words, just moaning and turning.

I sat on the floor, wishing I could stroke her hair. All I could do was watch. It was better than nothing. At least I knew she was safe. I recalled the vision of her attacking me, more impossible than Pike escaping, even in the most bizarre alternate reality. She wasn't capable of that, not with me. Not with anyone.

So maybe my visions were going off the rails after all.

"Your visitation rights with Pike have been revoked." Spindle was standing by my desk, his red eyelight glowing in the dark. "The commander has put a moratorium on your contact with him until further notice."

A lock of hair fell over Chute's face and was puffing out with each breath. I wanted to move it, all too aware Spindle was patiently waiting for me. I stood and turned my back, my steps shuffling a bit. Fatigue filled me like sand. I felt so heavy.

"I believe it would be prudent for you to get some rest, Master Socket."

I was nodding. He was right. I wanted to tell him I was heading to my bedroom, but stopped in front of Pike, mesmerized by his repeated movements.

"Why are you watching him?" Spindle asked. "He should not be of interest."

I was still nodding like I was stuck in a trance, transfixed by Pike's suffering. I could feel Spindle's eyelight on me. Finally, I muttered, "Because I don't know if I can trust my visions."

"Are you referring to Pike as a free man?"

Pike jerked in his chair like he heard his name. His head rolled around and settled. "There's that," I said. I told him about the black-outs and the intensity of the visions that were nonsensical and unsettling.

"You have not reported these visions, Master Socket. The commander will be displeased."

Pike was back into his moaning rhythm again.

"I'll report them," I said. "It's just... these visions are different. They keep drawing me back to him." I gestured to Pike. "Somehow, he knows I'm having them. Like he knows what they mean."

"That is impossible. He has no means of contact outside his

confinement, and that is precisely why the commander forbids you further contact."

"He knows something, Spindle." I looked directly at his eyelight. "I can feel it."

"Would you like me to schedule an appointment with the minder psychologist? Perhaps he can unblock subconscious thoughts that will allow you some understanding of your situation."

I looked across the room. Chute rolled over and settled back into sleep. Maybe he was right, I should get things checked out. Maybe someone could help me get some clarity. Or maybe, for once, my future was cloudy. I'd known about things that were about to happen for too long and now it was bothering me that I didn't. Maybe it would be good to be in the present moment without knowing the future.

I shook my head. Spindle's eyelight brightened. He waited for me to respond. I called for the room to kill the projections. Chute's and Pike's images faded out and the walls began glowing to keep us out of the dark.

"Perhaps we should begin a review of your wormhole travel." Spindle took a step. "Your trip is in two days and you still have to complete the orientation."

"Tomorrow. Right now I need to sit."

"If I may suggest—"

I held up my hand. "Thank you, Spindle. But we can go over this later."

"Very well."

The office transformed into the darkened forest, a live feed from the middle of the Preserve. The floor sprouted the green turf of the tagghet field with trees all around. I went to a meditation cushion nestled in the lush grass. The sky was dark, but sunrise wasn't far off.

"Spindle." He stopped before exiting. "Send the kids up here when it's time for them to rise. We'll sit in my office this morning."

He nodded and left. I folded my legs and straightened my back, taking a deep breath. The present moment felt so fragile. I didn't like that, but being present had little to do with how I felt.

76

Lost **in Space**

I STEPPED out of the shower room and pressed my face into a towel. It'd been over fifty hours. Still no sleep. I was feeling it in my face, but my eyes refused to shut. The exhaustion wore on me like a suit of armor. I wasn't fighting it anymore; I just let the heaviness be there. Still, no sleep.

I'd finished a long game of tagghet with the kids earlier that day, and told them about Chute's visit when I returned. Playing tagghet with me and Spindle was one thing, but testing their skills against one of the best high school players would let them know where they were. The boys weren't half as excited as the girls until I showed them an image of her. She was talented *and* hot.

I got dressed and sat on the bench, leaned against the wall and closed my eyes. Maybe I could catch some sleep, but when I took the leaper to my office, it was filled with the electric blue lines of the wormhole network. Miniature galaxies were suspended throughout the web.

"This can wait no longer, Master Socket." Spindle was standing next to my desk. His tone was stern. His eyelight glowed intensely, lighting the surface of my desk like it was on fire. "Your launch is scheduled twenty hours from this moment. It is critical that you understand your journey."

He said it like he meant more than just the trip.

I stepped through a disc-shaped galaxy and put my hands up like the web had snagged me. "You caught me."

"If you kindly step next to me, I can begin."

"I'm joking, Spindle. Come on, you wake up on the wrong side of bed this morning?"

"I do not sleep, Master Socket."

"I know."

He didn't reply, but simply waited until I stepped through the dazzling blue lines crisscrossing my path. I finished putting on my shirt. "You have my undivided attention."

"Thank you."

So Spindle started off with the history of wormhole development, how the Paladin Nation began space exploration before the Wright brothers were even born. It was information I already knew, but I wasn't about to interrupt. That eyelight was as bright as I'd ever seen it.

Natural wormholes existed in space. In fact, most planets were connected to one, and once the Paladins learned to access the one flowing through Earth, they had access to the universal wormhole web. Paladins developed special equipment to travel through them and began mapping the universe. My office was filled with every known avenue that existed. If a traveler was skilled enough, he could jump from one galaxy to the next. Most Paladin space travelers never returned, spending their lives somewhere in the galaxy, jumping planet to planet, mapping and sending back their data as they went.

"Your ship will be programmed to take you to your destination," Spindle said. "But it is critical that you make a psychic connection with your ship for accurate projection. You will experience an instantaneous relocation to your destination. It is quite unpleasant."

"I know what a wormhole feels like."

"Traveling from the Garrison to Charleston is not the same as traversing the universe!" His words were sharp. "If you lose a psychic connection with the ship, you could lose your way, Master Socket. One errant thought and you could be lost in space."

His eyelight was reaching laser-beam intensity. I nodded slowly.

"You need to be rested before you depart. You must be able to focus."

"Noted. I'll knock out a nap as soon as we're done."

His eyelight relaxed, dimming down to a subtle glow. He appeared to tower over me, examining my true intentions. Finally, he stepped into the web of wormholes, tracing one particular line with his finger that sparkled as he followed it into a massive tangle of intersecting lines. The web began to shift. The wormhole led to a galaxy, which appeared to be the Milky Way. Spindle was halfway across the room—

"Danger, Will Robinson. Danger."

Spindle stopped. His eyelight circled around to the back of his head. Streeter's projected image was standing next to me.

"Get it?" he asked. "*Lost in Space*? Will Robinson?" He looked back and forth between Spindle and me. "You mean you guys never heard of that ancient TV show with the robot? They did the remake." He did robot-arms. "*Danger.*"

"Why is Master Streeter projecting into our meeting?" Spindle asked.

"I'm sorry," I said, trying to stop Streeter from doing the robot. "I forgot I scheduled him to come over."

Actually, I forgot completely. A small wave of panic swept through me. Spindle was right, I was losing focus.

"Did I drop in on something top secret?" he asked.

The wormhole network was public knowledge, but I still thought Spindle might shoot that eye-laser. I calmed Streeter down and asked Spindle to keep going. I should've told Streeter to leave, but he was making me laugh. Maybe I was delirious. It just felt good to smile.

"Do you think this is a joke, Master Socket?"

"No, Spindle."

Streeter waited quietly, like listening to parents fight. I knew this stuff was important, but I needed a break. Streeter was exactly what I needed. Just seeing his image lifted the fatigue. I think Spindle picked up on that. There were still important matters at hand, but he could feel the tension relax inside me.

"Can we cover the destination?" I asked. "I'll work with the ship-integration focus later today."

He agreed. He followed the wormhole to a planet on the outskirts of the Milky Way. It was not a long trip, not by intergalactic standards.

When Spindle touched a planet that swirled red, white and blue, the wormholes vanished, leaving us in the dark for a moment. Then the room projected the planet's atmosphere, like we were standing right there on the surface.

It was a bleak environment. The sky was steely. The distant mountains were red and the surface gritty. The few trees that sprouted here and there on the flat plain were enormous, but they had no leaves. Instead, their bright green bark was photosynthetic.

"Your destination is the Grimmet Outpost." Spindle pointed to the enormous dome-shaped structure that appeared between us and the mountains; the white surface looked pink with red dust. "Your ship will land directly inside the outpost and you will be greeted by the Paladin crew that resides there. You will not be venturing out of the outpost since that would require further training and fitted gear. You will be tested for signs of fatigue and given a tour of the facility before returning home."

"I thought you were going away for a month?" Streeter asked.

"Time does not operate that way, Master Streeter. Since Master Socket will be traveling at the speed of light for a short period, time will slow down for him. While his trip may only seem brief, weeks will pass for us."

Spindle charged into the rest of the visit, who I would be meeting, what we would be doing and what I could expect. Now I was getting sleepy.

A distant flutter echoed from one of the leafless trees. Then a cloud of brightly colored grimmets appeared to be heading for us. When they were close enough to hear their wings, my office projected their images around us. They were as playful as the ones in the Preserve. Maybe the trip wouldn't be so bad.

Streeter walked into the mob with his hands up. It was hard not to join them when they were near, even if it was just a projection. Spindle gave up. He left the office without saying another word. I'd apologize later. In the meantime, Streeter and I would have some fun.

An hour.

I'd been asleep for an hour before waking up with a cold shiver running down my back. No memory of a vision or a dream, just the remnants of one. Maybe it knocked me out again, only this time I was already sleeping. I laid there staring at the ceiling but couldn't remember having a vision, but there was no doubt one had happened. *Now I'm not remembering them?* I was buzzing with adrenaline.

I had transformed my office to replicate the tagghet field again. I hated that I was getting accustomed to the convenience of it—the sounds and smells were dead-on—because I much preferred the real thing, but I let myself be lazy. I told myself there wasn't time to get out there, but that was bullshit. I just wanted to sit. Now.

I had been sitting for almost an hour, sweat running down my face as the room replicated the humidity. Even though I hadn't eaten in almost a day, I felt full. The longer I sat, the fuller I became. Not full, really. *Dense.*

An hour and a half into sitting, the kids quietly walked in with their cushions and sat with me. A certain joy vibrated between us without a word. I couldn't help but smile as they folded their legs and settled their minds. Soon, our breathing was synchronized and we blended with the surrounding sounds and scents.

The silence was shattered by an earthshaking tremor. Despite the unnatural interruption, none of us broke from our sitting. We remained motionless, but I could feel the thoughts of concern rumble through the office. Finally, Spindle stepped inside. He paused at the entrance and folded his hands in front of his belly. He waited until I looked his way.

"Your escort has arrived, Master Socket."

We sat a few moments longer. The kids didn't move until I gave a short bow. I was sluggish to get off the ground, loosening my joints like my blood had turned to syrup. I gave the kids encouragement to keep up the schedule, and told them Spindle would be taking care of them and I'd see them soon. The girls gave me hugs. I held my hand out to shake Ben's hand, but he pulled me in for a hug, patting my back.

"Hugging ain't just for chicks," he said.

I had to laugh and hugged the rest of them. I'd gone on trips before. This felt like a long goodbye. Did they sense the heaviness weighing inside me, sharing my agitation while we sat?

"Tagghet when you get back," Aleshia said. "Don't turn rusty on me, old man."

I was five years older than them, and I was the old man. I was certainly walking like one. I informed Spindle to take them to the tagghet field and I'd meet him down at the launch.

I put on my official space travel outfit. It was dark blue and fitted with numerous pockets and built-in communication modules, thermal-conditioning adjustments to keep my body temperature adequate under extreme conditions, and armor-imbedded material to resist impact. Even had a back door to drop a load. I doubled-checked the backpack that contained everything needed for surviving extended periods in the middle of nowhere.

When the office was quiet, I called for the walls to dim the tagghet-field projection so I could rest in the darkness for a while. There was just enough light to see the desk. I straightened up some papers, activated messages for anyone contacting me while I was gone, and checked over my schedule one more time.

It was too dark to see to the other side of the office. Like my future. I was tempted to call Chute and Streeter one last time, but I'd already said my goodbyes. Instead, I called up Chute's room. Her bed appeared. The covers were thrown back and the pillow dented. She was already about her day.

I needed to do the same.

77

SHOWTIME

PALADINS WERE LINED up in the parking garage. Most just nodded as I passed, some shook my hand and patted me on the shoulder. Servys were hovering in lines behind them. All seemed present and accounted for. The floor was vibrating with the hum of something powerful, pulsing through the bottom of my feet; I could feel it in my teeth. I stepped through the wall to the other side, where the ship would be waiting in the boulder field.

I stopped immediately. I'd seen images of these deep space cruisers in my studies, knew what they looked like, but in person it was just... daunting. It was black, oval and smooth, like a skipping stone. And it took up the entire field, almost three hundred yards across. There were no windows, none visible at least. The air around it trembled like it was fiercely hot, but it seemed to have more to do with the color, a black totally void of light. The ship seemed to be eating the space around it.

The commander was standing to the side, letting me take it all in. He nodded at me as if to say *take your time.*

The vibrations I felt inside the parking garage emanated from the ship, quivering through the ground with a low frequency that penetrated solid granite. They intensified for a moment, like it sensed I was staring. Like it was saying, *yeah, this shit's for real, son.*

"I had no idea it would be this..." I trailed off. I didn't know what I meant. I just had no idea. Period. "This is just for me?"

"You'll be travelling alone," the commander said.

"Seems a bit much. Couldn't you send something a little..." Again, I wasn't sure if smaller was what I was thinking. *Maybe something a little less badass?*

"It takes a lot to travel through space," he said.

"That thing will fit through the wormhole?"

He smiled, but instead of answering, he adjusted the straps on my backpack. It weighed over seventy pounds, but my body felt so dense that the backpack felt like a box of tissues. The ship contained everything I needed. The pack was just an insurance policy.

"In case you're wondering, I don't personally see every Paladin off on their first trip." The commander smacked my back like he was sending off a horse. "But your mother insisted."

"I appreciate that, sir."

He grabbed both shoulders. "This is a routine trip, son. No need to be nervous. You've been through things plenty worse than this." He winked.

He sensed my nervousness. Was that what it was, nervousness? I was feeling as rigid as a flagpole and heavy as a tank. I trusted my gut feelings, and this one was saying stay right here, this was not the trip I wanted to take. But something also told me this trip was inevitable. It was now or later. But why did something so routine feel so imminent?

The ship's humming intensified again. A doorway was glowing on the black surface. The commander patted me again, one more wink. "Godspeed, son."

"Thank you, sir."

I started the slow march toward the doorway, the wind whistling in my ears. Each step was heavy, vibrating every time the bottom of my foot touched the ground like it was a vibratory plate, compacting my insides. The air was becoming dense, like the ship was pushing back the closer I got. Each step took more and more effort.

I thought about turning around and asking the commander what he thought, but it wasn't the ship pushing against me. It was me, like rigor mortis setting in. Maybe it was those vibrations just whacking me out, getting me ready for the super-squeeze of the wormhole. Like Spindle said, we were going to the other side of the galaxy, not Charleston. Was this prepping me for the ride?

I could feel the cold wave emanating from the ship's surface like it was sucking the energy out of the atmosphere. I had to push my last step through the doorway. First, it was bright and so cold it squeezed out my last breath. But then I was through and the ship was gone. Gone, as in gone-gone.

I was standing in the boulder field. No ship around me. Everything, completely silent.

There was a table in front of me, round and black like the ship. The surface was smooth. The field silent. The trees moved, but the wind didn't gust in my ears. Birds flew over, their beaks jerking open while their heads searched below. But no caw. I scratched my face and heard my fingertips rub against my skin.

The commander was still where I left him, hands clasped behind his back. I started to walk back, but an invisible force pushed back. I must be inside the ship, the walls projecting the view from the outside so they appeared invisible to me. The commander would still be seeing the black ship. *Spindle must've missed this detail. Or maybe I wasn't listening.*

I expanded my mind, feeling the smooth surface of the invisible walls and the circuitry within them. I merged with the ship's intelligence, sensing its directive to serve. It felt cold and alien. And massive. I opened to the ship's database, allowing it to connect with me and read my intentions. The experience of its artificial intelligence stung with a slight metallic ring. Soon, we were intertwined with a single goal in mind. *The Grimmet Outpost.*

The trees shook violently, whipping leaves into the sky, the grass jerking back and forth. The ground slowly dropped away beneath my feet. I lifted magically into the air. Vertigo swirled in my stomach.

Higher and faster I went. And closer to the cliff. I soared over the top to see tree-covered mountains far in the distance and drifted near a great chasm that was filled with the Preserve. Nothing stirred as I cruised over it, the jungle separated from me by its invisible force field. In the middle of the trees was a dark green oval dotted with six children and a silver humanoid, looking up. They were waving.

I drifted further until they blended with the scenery. A lightning bolt, absent of thunder, licked the sky. I was moving near the center of an electrical storm that swirled ahead. It began to open, the center black, swallowing the bands of lightning like it was hungry for our world, growing larger and wider. I felt like plankton being inhaled by a whale. I gripped the table, cold and smooth and solid. Maybe that's why it was there, to keep me from falling over.

The black opening suddenly ripped open, exposing a blue throat. I was swallowed with no time to brace for impact. No time to scream. It was like being sucked through a straw. But just as suddenly as my body felt steamrolled, there was no sense of motion. There was no sight or smell. For a long moment, I was bodiless. There was no pressure. No pain. There was nothing.

Getting past the first part was nothing short of being blown to bits. After that, it was the greatest peace I'd ever known. No body, no thoughts. No sense of going anywhere. Maybe this was what death felt like.

But I was moving. Towards destiny.

There was no stopping that. We all arrive where we're going. And as my body began to exit the other end of the wormhole, preceded by the siren scream of my nervous system reminding me that it was working again, I had the nagging thought my destiny was near.

Showtime.

PART VIII

Serving life is not always beautiful.
Pivot

A perfect trap is one the prey readily accepts,
even when he already knows the outcome.
Pike

Ye shall know the truth, and the truth shall make you free.
John 8:32

78

Outpost

THE EXIT WAS as quick as the entrance. For a second, I sensed my body had already arrived at the destination before I did. But I was catching up, arriving in time to feel the wormhole shit me out the other end of that intergalactic straw.

My extremities were cold and my fingers tingling. I blinked several times to focus the blurry details of men, more than one, somewhere in front of me. There was a hollow pain burning inside my chest. I wasn't breathing.

I pulled in my first breath like I was drowning, gasping for air. I bent over and, with my hands on my knees, was ready to puke. It passed, but when I stood up, my mouth was filling with spit. I blinked away the tears. Now I could see three men. Maybe they were smiling.

I walked toward them, each step tentative. I couldn't feel the ship's walls anymore, but then again I couldn't feel much of anything. Five feet away from them, I passed through the ship's cold doorway and was bombarded with an earthy smell and the sound of the ship's hissing. And that's when my stomach revolted.

I blew chunks all over. It was mostly green liquid, but I was hands on my knees again, wrenching until it was all over my shoes, the floor and whatever else was below.

Someone slapped my shoulder. "That first trip's a bitch, ain't it?" The others chimed in with laughter.

The man in the middle was the commanding officer. His name was Samuel. He handed me a bottle of water to rinse out my mouth.

"Spit it on the floor," he said, when I looked around with a mouthful. Evidently not their first time greeting a first-timer.

I WAS EXPECTING the inside of the outpost to look industrial. Where the ship had landed, that was exactly what it was: all gray walls and concrete floor. The translucent ceiling of the dome was far above, letting pale light through.

The other two guys with the commanding officer introduced themselves as Pepper and Fadden. They showed me the rest of the outpost. It was a small city, complete with streets lined with elms and maples and houses and warehouses. Mosquitoes buzzed and squirrels chirped. They farmed crops and raised animals while they researched the planet outside the dome.

We walked for hours and never reached the perimeter of the dome. We stopped at the central cafeteria, a gathering place for the settlers. They ate. I didn't.

We sat around for a good hour. People dropped into the conversation until there was a couple dozen. They asked the questions, mostly about life back home. Most of the residents were on extended stay in the outpost, some had been there half their life. Some even born there. While most of them said they didn't miss it, they were still curious. No one forgets home.

My celebrity status among Paladins was missing on a planet millions of miles away. Some had heard of me—the Paladin that defeated the duplicates, *The One Who Sees Clearly*, as the grimmets once named me—but it hardly seemed to matter. That was another planet. This was the outpost.

The sun was a gray disk as seen through the dome when I was escorted outside Samuel's office, a set of steel doors tightly closed. A few minutes later, they slid open. I ascended a short flight of stairs to an enormous room at the edge of the dome. A large desk was alone in the middle of the empty floor, and beyond that was a panoramic view of the vast plain.

Samuel was at the desk, looking busy and more officer-like than he did when he was laughing at my pukefest. Military tension set my body rigid, waiting to approach. This was the president of the Grimmet Outpost.

"Have a look," he finally said. "I'll be done in a moment."

I relaxed and let my gaze wander. My footsteps echoed in the silence, but the outside world was a dry, whirling windstorm. Dust devils dropped to the ground, picking up debris and sending it airborne before disappearing as quickly as they formed. There were ancient, leafless trees sparsely populating the flat, baked ground, like the ones I saw in my office, and red mountains in the distance. I went up to the dome, putting my fingers on the surface. It was warm.

There were no signs of life. A beaten planet. Only a clear barrier that separated life on the inside from death on the outside.

"Quite a view, isn't it?" Samuel stepped next to me.

I nodded, but not convincingly. Captivating, yes. But I failed to see the beauty in a lifeless landscape.

"This is where the grimmets live?" I asked.

He nodded.

"Up in the mountains?"

"Mostly, yes. They occasionally visit the plains and flock to the outpost out of curiosity, but we don't see them much. Mostly when we venture out."

The planet didn't look diverse, but it was rich in elements valuable to Earth. Why else be here? The outpost was just one of many settlements on the planet. Mines were set up all over. They weren't here just to live on another planet. There was profit involved.

"This planet wasn't always dead," Samuel said, gazing out. "There is some water and the atmosphere can support life, but when we discovered it, there was none to be found. There is evidence that beings once lived here, the remnants of houses and roads, cities and farming. Signs of advanced civilization. One can only imagine what it looked like when it was still vital."

He was looking at a plume of smoke in the distant mountains.

"I'm sure you're well aware of our mining industry, but our primary objective for being here is research. This is an expensive operation and the mining of energy-rich minerals helps fund our exploration. Those trees you see are some of our first successes. Instead of leaves, the bark is photosynthetic, tolerating the harsh conditions. This is one of the first links in planet-building. Our goal is that one day this planet will be habitable once again, that many generations from now, the human population can call it a home."

"I don't understand. How could the entire planet be void of life if the atmosphere is habitable? I mean, asteroids or pestilence or war couldn't wipe out *all* life."

"We're not sure." He was still curiously eyeing the mountains. The cloud was dispersing, growing larger and nearer. It didn't appear to be smoke. "All our research indicates that life just vanished. As if a heart just stopped beating. What could do some-thing like that is, currently, beyond our understanding. And that's another reason we're here." He flicked a glance toward me before resuming his watch on the cloud. "If it can happen here, can it happen on Earth?"

I wondered if he was holding back information. We knew so much, how could there be so much mystery about a dead planet?

"What made the grimmets immune?" I asked.

"Tenacious beings. Unlike anything in the universe. They're similar to cold-blooded organisms, going extended periods of time without food. They seem to have some ability to photosynthesize as well as utilize minerals and nutrients from soil, rocks and trees. Somehow, they resisted whatever wiped everything else out. Of course, I don't need to tell you about their psychic ability."

All right, so he was aware of my connection with them. Of course he would know I shared a special bond with grimmets back on Earth.

"But even as tough as they are, their populations are dwindling. We tried to incorporate them into our environment," Samuel said, "inside the outpost, but it just didn't work. They weren't acclimated to the friendly climate and didn't care to be separated from the flock."

He stared to the distant plume, letting his thoughts drift for a moment.

"One day," he said, "this planet will be revitalized. The grimmets will reclaim its wonder. And, hopefully, we'll be able to share that with them."

Long ago, I accused the Paladin Nation of kidnapping grimmets, bringing them back to Earth for selfish reasons, convinced they intended to make a weapon of them or simply display them like zoo animals. Even when the grimmets defeated the duplicates, I assumed that to be a fluke. But now it seemed like an act of compassion, an attempt to preserve their kind until their home was saved.

Perhaps my trip was not just for the wormhole, but to see some of the truly humane aspects of the Paladin Nation.

Samuel dismissed me to return to my escorts with a firm handshake and a warm smile. "You're welcome to return any time you wish. Trust me, the wormhole ride gets easier."

I thanked him and left, but not before noticing that he was still watching the growing cloud. I could feel a slight tug in my gut, like something familiar was coming.

MY GOODBYES WERE SHORT. Everyone waved in passing, but life resumed in the outpost. We walked through the large docking doors into the hangar, the gray room that housed the black wormhole ship, where it was cold and sterile.

"In case you're wondering, the trip back is even worse," Pepper said, patting my shoulder. Fadden laughed and mentioned the room still smelled like puke.

I knew what he meant. Now that I knew what to expect, my thoughts were making the anticipation of the trip worse. Even so, there was a pleasant sensation tugging inside my belly and it was getting stronger. I was sure someone would be waiting for me at the ship. Someone I knew.

My backpack was sitting on the floor in front of the doorway glowing on the ship. It was a little fuller than when I arrived, filled with items from the outpost to take back.

"Come back if you're bored." Pepper extended his hand as the sky seemed to dim. "You don't get a waiting party on your next visit, so you'll have to clean up your own barf."

"Thanks," I said, shaking his hand. "You're an excellent host," I said sarcastically.

"What can I say? By the way, you know when you get back everyone will be about two weeks older. Time's going a little faster for them."

I sensed a bit of sadness. Did he leave anyone behind? No one was immune to homesickness.

"Well, I better get back before they forget me," I said.

Fadden slapped Pepper with the back of his hand. He was looking up, mouth open. The top of the dome was a couple hundred yards above us. Dark lumps could be seen squirming on the opaque surface.

Fadden and Pepper shaded their eyes like that could somehow clarify what they were seeing, but it was just getting darker as more things dropped out of the sky, scratching and clawing along the surface. The dome was too thick and far away to hear anything, but the commotion was frenzied.

"Yeah?" Pepper touched his ear, listening to a nojakk call. "Seriously? No, no. We see it over here, too."

"Check this out." Fadden was squatting on his haunches in front of a thin silver sheet spread out on the floor, projecting a three-dimensional image.

It was an aerial image of the outpost from far up. Thousands of brightly colored things were crawling over it. *Grimmets.* And more were coming. Floating lights kicked on. I looked up at the thick layer of grimmets obscuring every bit of sunlight.

Pepper and Fadden looked at me. They'd never seen anything like it. No one had. Every grimmet within range of the outpost was coming. *They can feel me.* And I could feel them tugging at my insides, connecting with their energy, their unlimited essence, bonding to me like the grimmets back on Earth.

Strangely, though, I felt they were connecting with something else, like I carried something inside me, something dense. Maybe they came because of that.

What's inside me?

THE SHIP WELCOMED me with its impatient hum. I could see through its invisible walls once again. Pepper and Fadden waited far away from the ship. They didn't bother waving. Didn't seem concerned about the white-blue light that crackled behind me, illuminating their faces. They'd seen the wormhole open inside the outpost too many times to be amazed. I stayed still, not wanting to see it swallow me. Braced for impact.

My teeth snapped together, just missing clipping my tongue. I was pulled into oblivion, once again, with my mind focused on home, guiding the ship back to the warm life that waited with familiar surroundings and loving friends and family.

The black nothingness of the moment was peaceful. It didn't feel like I was moving, but I sensed home was near. My destination began to pull me back into existence, like my body had been evaporated and was being reconstructed inside Earth's atmosphere somewhere over the Preserve. I sensed oncoming pain.

I was jerked in another direction like a fish snagged with a treble hook.

I went back into the black peaceful oblivion, but home felt like it was far behind. But then I felt my body again, reassembling somewhere near the planet. And then there was the excruciating agony as my awareness squeezed back into it.

My eyes were clenched as tightly as my jaw. I was mostly numb again, but felt water slosh around me.

I moved my arms in a swimming motion, unaware if I was below water or not. My lungs burned. I opened my eyes, the salty water stinging. Panic propelled me upward, but I was too heavy. My arms were like useless poles. I desperately kicked and barely broke the surface, inhaling just enough air to relieve the fire in my chest. But I sank again.

There was no chance of getting back up, but fortunately I hit the sandy bottom. I pushed upward, this time clearing my entire chest above the water. One deep gulp of air and I let myself sink again. I pushed off at an angle but found the water getting deeper, so I turned around, jumping again and again.

Finally, I stood on my toes and gulped air. My heart was slamming. I took feeble steps and slowly walked into shallower water.

A sandy beach was ahead. The full moon was bright in a clear night sky. I missed my landing. But I had no idea by how much.

79

Silent Forest

SOMETHING FLUSHED OUT of my body, like a plug had been pulled and drained molten metal weighing in my veins. I was light as driftwood. The water around me turned cloudy. I rubbed my eyes and looked again. The milky cloud drifted deeper and spread out like an oil slick.

When I reached dry sand, I dropped to my knees. Exhausted. I was catching my breath, the air cool and humid. Seawater dripped off my nose, over my lips. It tasted odd. It was salty, but there was something else, something familiar. Something that usually wasn't associated with ocean water, but I couldn't place it.

There was no sign of civilization. Just endless water, sand and tropical trees. This was bad. It could've been worse. The north pole. Or the sun.

I tapped my cheek, but got no response from my nojakk. Not even a *tick, tick, tick*. I dug through my backpack and activated a handheld phone, but it was nonresponsive, too. The same with a homing beacon. Everything, dead.

Maybe an electromagnetic pulse killed everything upon entry.

Something went wrong right before I got home; I'd felt it jerk me around. Maybe the ship malfunctioned and dumped me in the ocean. At least it didn't drop another twenty feet out to sea or I'd be stuck to the bottom like an anchor.

My suit had already dried. I sat down in the sand and leaned back against a tree. *What now? Surely, the Paladins knew I was coming back. They would eventually search for me. But if I didn't have power to signal them, how would they find me?*

The waves were small, sloshing onto the beach in a steady rhythm. I closed my eyes, listening to the ocean go in and out. In and out.

It lulled me to relax, but something was missing. Everything felt so... so empty. Like an environment in my office where nothing was real. But I couldn't sense any walls. I considered, for a second, that I was in my office. But I could always sense the confines of a moldable environment, sense the walls of a room even though it looked endless. The beach had no such limitation. It just felt empty.

Maybe I imagined it. I was tired.

THE WAVES GREETED ME GENTLY. I imagined I was floating in the water, warm and cozy. But then I opened my eyes and stared at coconuts. My survival suit was warm, but the cool air was nipping at my ears and the tip of my nose. I sat up and rubbed my face. My eyes were heavy with sleep. I couldn't remember lying down. The moon hung just above the horizon. It felt like I'd been asleep for hours, but everything looked the same. And not a single bug bite.

It was quiet in the trees. Too quiet. The only thing that broke the silence was the ocean, but everything else was as still as a museum. No breeze from above, no drifting leaves or scuttle of a crab. Absolute stillness.

The backpack contained small packets of food. If that ran out, there was a supply of lifepatches that could sustain me for another six months. If I hunted and gathered, I could survive for much longer.

The forest looked dense and dark. It would take a long, sharp machete to cut through it. Since there was no such thing in the backpack, I walked along the beach, looking for a path. But after a few miles, everything still looked exactly the same. In fact, even the trees appeared in some sort of pattern. Up ahead was a palm that leaned and curved skyward. I turned back, swearing I'd passed one like that a few miles back.

Just beyond that was a small opening that gave way to a narrow path. That wasn't there before. I looked out over the water one last time. The night sky looked black and smudged just above the horizon, like ink was leeching up from the water.

I HAD PULLED a small box from the backpack and let it unfold into a tent. I lay inside it, staring through the dome-shaped ceiling. I couldn't see the sky through the trees. The moonlight filtered through the leaves like pale sunlight. I had walked for what seemed a full day and expected the sun to come up, but I was exhausted and couldn't wait for it any longer.

The forest was endless and repetitive. The path continued to wind through it like something or someone walked it often enough to beat down the vegetation, but there was no sign of life. Nothing. No spider webs or mosquitoes or stinging ants.

It was still cool, but humid as ever. I sweated through much of my water reserves and there wasn't much left in the backpack. I needed to find some before long.

I WOKE when a single drop of water struck the tent.

The raindrop jiggled, then slowly made its way down the side, racing to the bottom. Something about that was strange, then I realized that was the first sound in a day that I hadn't directly caused.

It was darker outside. Maybe clouds had dimmed the moonlight. *Wait. Did I sleep through another day?*

I felt rested, like I'd gotten another eight hours of sleep, but it was still night. Was I sleeping right through the daylight?

Maybe it was for the best. I didn't need to be moving around in the heat of the day. I was already parched.

ANOTHER DAY OF HIKING. Still no sunlight.

I don't know how far I got. Thirty miles, maybe. The last ten miles were like wearing concrete blocks. Raindrops continued to find a way through the thick canopy. My lips were cracking and I'd stopped sweating. I finished the rest of my water.

I sat against a tree.

THUNDER CLAPPED.

I woke in a thick mass of groundcover. No tent. I must've fallen over asleep.

Rain dripped through a fern leaf, splashing on my forehead. I stuck out my tongue and caught the next drop. And the next.

They were plopping throughout the forest with a regular beat. I scrambled on my hands and knees and found a large leaf holding a pool of water. Carefully, I cupped it and tilted it toward my mouth. It was wet, tasteless. Just like water was supposed to taste. If this was some sort of moldable environment, I wouldn't be able to drink it.

The lifepatches kept me from dehydrating, but water was a better alternative, so I spent the next couple hours going leaf to leaf, scavenging what I could.

The path continued to curve through the otherwise impenetrable forest. It seemed endless and pointless, but it had to lead somewhere. Something made this path. Maybe I should've stayed on the beach. At least a search party would see me there. Nothing would spot me through the trees. Too late now. I just had to keep going until I got out or found someone that could help.

I only managed an hour on the trail before I had to rest. I was drained. And sleepy. These were tough conditions, but this was unusual. I shouldn't be gassing out this quick. It was like something was sucking the energy out of me, reminding me of the Grimmet Outpost. *Like something just sucked the life out of it.*

I slapped another lifepatch on my neck and felt it pump essential nutrients into my jugular. Thunder rumbled somewhere in the distance. I remembered something my grandma used to tell me about storms. She said when it thundered, the angels were wrestling.

The ground began to tremble like they'd fallen out of the sky.

MAYBE IT WAS the third night that I saw the end.

The winding path straightened out and widened. There was an opening in the trees. I quickened my pace, eager to find something. The trees ended abruptly, like a wall, and the path dropped down a steep slope. I stood just inside the canopy, mesmerized by the view. Hills rolled off into the distance, covered in tufts of grass. Mountains were farther out.

The air was cooler and drier. The moon was still full, but the sky seemed hazy. On the horizon, the ink stain was still visible. It was deep and dark, blotting out the stars as it bled further into the night sky.

Below me, a couple hundred yards out, the grass gave way to rows of fruit trees. Something moved among them. It was a woman. Her clothes were white, her hair blonde. She was picking fruit and putting them into a basket.

Finally, a way home. I screamed through my hands, but she didn't hear me. I didn't bother shouting again; instead I started down the path. Adrenaline filled me with excitement and burst with renewed energy. I'd catch up to her in minutes. Maybe I could find home by sunrise. The thought of sleeping in my office boosted my stride down the slope. I ignored the thought lurking in my head, the nagging concern that had been with me ever since I walked out of the water. Something I tried to reason away because help was finally within reach.

Why does everything still feel so empty?

80

EMPTY ANGEL

STILL RAINING, maybe a bit harder.

I wasn't about to let the woman out of my sight. I left the winding path and took the grassy hill full speed, leaping over boulders. I lost sight of her as I dipped into the valley, cresting the hill to once again see the magnificent view.

The forest behind me seemed further away than it should've been. I'd only been running a few minutes and it was hundreds of yards back.

A subtle breeze, the first I could remember since arriving, caught my attention. It carried the fragrance of tea olive blossoms and the salty spray of an ocean. And the scent of a woman, soft and loving. She was there, I could see her on the next hill in the orchard, still hundreds of yards away. I hadn't gotten any closer.

Her white gown fluttered while she stopped to reach into a tree, pulling fruit from a branch and putting it in her basket. She was glowing, like a beam of moonlight found its way through the rain to touch only her. I cupped my hands and shouted again. "HELLO!"

Still she couldn't hear me.

I started down the next grassy hill into the orchard. The trees were taller than I thought. My perspective seemed off. The trunks were gnarly and the muscled branches held plump apples the size of softballs. I lost sight of the woman as she walked over the next hill. But I was gaining on her. I dipped my head, pushing harder. I reached the next hilltop, expecting to maybe catch her while she went searching in another tree, maybe only a few yards away. At the very least she'd be within shouting distance, but then I saw her still hundreds of yards out.

I stopped, putting my hands on my knees. How did she get that far out?

My heart pounded. The adrenaline was already wearing off and I was sweating out precious water that mixed with the rain dripping down my face, leaving a salty tang on my lips.

This isn't logical. Where am I?

When I looked up, as if answering my questions, the view had somehow changed. Had I not noticed it when I emerged from the forest? Was it just hidden from my vantage point? Because now, beyond the rolling hills, was a vast black ocean. The lines of orchard trees followed the undulating hills, ending short of a massive house built right on the shore, surrounded by sand dunes and sea oats.

The woman was gone.

The sterile forest and the perfect temperature, short of the rain this is paradise. This exists nowhere in nature. Nowhere on Earth. I looked at my hands, turning them over and studying them like the truth was written somewhere on my skin. I'm not dreaming or virtualmode. I'm here, in the skin.

I turned back and saw what I expected. The trees were gone. Nothing but rising and falling mounds as far as I could see. This entire environment was transforming, manipulating me toward the house on the beach. Something changed when it started to rain, like it let me out of the forest. Once again, I opened my mind to connect with the environment, searching for something substantial, something real, but everything felt empty. So beautiful, but so empty.

The house already seemed bigger. More inviting.

Why does it feel like no matter what direction I walk, I'll end up at the house?

The wicker basket was nestled in the grass at the base of a tree. I picked one of the fruits out. It was deep red, almost purple. The skin was soft but not fuzzy. I press my thumb into it, juice squirting out. Saliva filled my mouth. It was clear liquid, not milky.

I tossed it on the ground. First, I needed to find the woman. She was in the house.

THE HOUSE GREW as I approached, building onto itself, forming walls and floors and windows until it was a monstrosity blocking out the ocean. Wide steps led to thick double doors, both open and waiting. Sand ground beneath my boots as I crossed over the marble threshold and passed through the doors.

It was one enormous room filled with credenzas, sofas and antique furniture. The walls were covered with art from various eras, from Victorian to modern, realistic to abstract. Expensive vases, candelabras, and sculptures were set about. All in all, a stunning display, but nothing compared to the back wall made entirely of glass, offering a full view of the scenic ocean and the darkening sky. A single fruit tree grew behind the house, its limbs heavy with fruit.

Multi-folding doors were pushed all the way open, leaving wide open access to the beach. I stopped just short of the beach that extended right up to the house. The breeze came off the water, moist and ragged, blowing my hair off my shoulders. *I've seen this place.*

Sand. Rain.

A blackened sky.

The realization rang inside me like I'd been struck by a two-handed mallet. It was where I'd seen Chute attack, slashing down with a knife. *The vision is taking shape.*

I went outside. The rain was colder, pelting my cheeks. I tensed, looking in both directions for Chute and her knife, but it was empty. I walked further out until the foamy water wrapped around my ankles. And then I saw the woman, far down on my left.

She was standing with her feet in the water, a faint figure blurred by the rain. Her arms were crossed and she was staring out to sea like she was waiting. I could feel her yearning. It was the first thing I'd felt since arriving. Just to experience something real, a quiver of reality, jolted me with excitement.

I started after her, but with each step, she got no closer. The ground moved under my feet, but the back of the house was still exactly where I exited, like the beach was a treadmill.

Thunder clapped without any sign of lightning. The woman was still there, yearning for what was out on the empty water, where waves were beginning to swell. Or maybe her gaze was settled on the ink-stained sky.

I walked in the other direction and watched the house. Same thing: it didn't move even though my tracks continued far behind me.

Enough. I'm not entertainment.

Understand your environment, one of the first lessons I learned as a Paladin. Without understanding your Self or your surroundings, you are a ship sailing without a compass.

I tracked puddles into the house. The pillows on the nearest couch were soft velvet, but firm. I centered the largest one near the opening in the back wall and folded my legs.

My breathing quickly became rhythmic while I settled into the present moment. Soon, thoughts faded away. I was aware of the objects around me, the emptiness of the house and angry sea. Occasionally, the sky cracked with thunder.

I would sit in the moment until something, or someone, revealed the truth.

Where am I?

HOURS WENT BY.

There was nothing but the steady rhythm of the rain, the rise and fall of my chest and the occasional bump of the tree banging its fruit-laden branch against the glass wall. The waves had taken on foamy white crests. I had no expectations and made no effort to escape where I was. I just remained open.

And the world remained empty and mysterious.

I sensed a faint presence of another being somewhere in this world, likely the woman, but I couldn't feel exactly where she was. It was like she was everywhere. And out there, somewhere, was somebody besides the woman. It was a man, his presence somewhere on the horizon.

My back ached and my legs became numb. Thirst burned my throat. I considered finding water, but there would be none. The fruit hung tantalizingly.

I sat. The rain continued.

And the fruit continued to knock on the glass like a stranger wanting to come inside. The metaphor was all too obvious.

Paradise.

The Tree of Knowledge.

Thump. Thump-thump. The fruit said yes.

* * *

THE SPLINTER of glass woke me.

I'd fallen off the cushion. My tongue was like a piece of meat stuck in my mouth. I tried to swallow. I couldn't remember passing out.

I glimpsed the woman standing in front of me, holding out the fruit. I blinked and she wasn't there. I was hallucinating, but now my mouth was full of saliva. I could smell the fruit, its tangy citrus scent penetrating the humid breeze blowing off the storm-ridden coast.

My head was on the floor, pain pulsing through my ear. I scratched at the floorboards. Waves were punishing the beach, pushing closer to the house. The window was cracked where the tree branches smacked the house, swinging the heavy fruit like a wrecking ball.

She wants me to eat the fruit. I'll die right here on the floor like a dog, shrivel up like a salted slug, before I eat it.

But I didn't die.

I kept on living.

The agony wiped out any thoughts of home. Of Chute, the kids, my mother. I was just writhing on the floor, doubled over as dehydration cramps pulled me into a fetal position. Sometimes I heard the rain and thunder and the constant banging. I could feel the hardness of the floor.

I could also hear voices. The woman was calling. I sensed the man out there, too. He was just watching.

And I imagined the taste of the fruit.

This seemed to go on forever.

And then it was there, on the floor in front of me. The fruit was as red as a shined apple. I was dreaming of reaching for it. I didn't have that kind of strength, the kind to even slide my hand across the floor, but then I felt it in my palm and sensed the promise of life inside it. I punctured the skin with my fingertips, watching the sweet juice dribble onto the floorboards. My throat contracted.

I touched my tongue to the fleshy skin of the fruit; the sweetness ignited the taste buds in my mouth. Inside me, rapture exploded.

I devoured it like a starving beast, juice flowing down my chin, the meaty pulp sliding down my throat, filling me, scintillating my nerves. I sucked at my fingers and licked the drippings off the floor. I could smell the ocean wafting into the house along with a loving presence. I heard soft laughter.

It was no dream.

She tricked me. I couldn't resist it any longer. In the end, I willfully took it. But now I was thinking clearly. I knew where I was because eating the fruit had connected me with this world. It was no longer empty. It was real. It made sense.

This isn't Earth.

81

A Happy Family

THE TRUTH.

I was pulled from the wormhole just before arriving home, redirected to another part of the universe and absorbed into an alien world. I didn't know how or why it happened, but I knew this much: *this world is artificial.*

The entire planet was composed of cellular nanomechs that formed everything I saw and touched, heard and tasted. That wasn't the sky above. Not sand or water or rain. Not even a tree. It was just the generic stuff made to look like those things. It was my office on a global scale. How this was even possible I did not understand. All I knew was that I was somewhere inside it.

I knew these things because I had eaten the fruit, partaken of this world, and now I was merging with it. That was how I knew these things. My being—my essence, *my soul*—was interweaving with this artificial world. I was becoming one with it.

This was no ordinary automated world, either. It was not like my office that only responded to my commands. There was an intelligence that was inseparable from it, a feminine being fused into every single nanomech, as if she was this world. It was her will that formed the ocean and grew the trees, her will that sent the moon across the sky. She was everywhere.

That feminine energy was in the room. The woman in white was standing just inside the house, facing the torrential storm. Her arms were crossed, her fingers drumming her biceps.

"Manumit is making quite a mess," she said, without turning.

Manumit. I knew who she was talking about. There was another presence in this world that was separate from her. He was the reason the sky was black. Why it was raining in paradise. She called him Manumit, but now I recognized this presence. I'd known him all my life. *Pivot.*

"Who are you?" I asked.

"You know who I am."

I knew this world, how it worked, that it was artificial. But I didn't know her. Didn't know her thoughts, where she came from. Why she was part of it.

"You don't know everything?" She smirked.

She knew my thoughts, taunting me with her secret. I didn't even know her name.

"Fetter," she said. "Manumit called me Fetter. And he calls you Socket. You call him Pivot." She looked at me over her shoulder. Her eyes were blue like the deep part of the ocean. "Aren't we one big happy family?"

I pushed off the floor. There were no aches or numbness. I felt in total control of my nervous system. In fact, I felt like I could move the environment with a thought like fingers and toes. I looked at a footstool and willed it to slide near me. It came to a stop in front of me. I contracted my awareness, trying to disconnect from the environment.

I'm becoming this world. Like her.

"I'm not staying here." I said it like that would make it true, like I would wake up if I heard myself say it.

She smirked again. "Have a seat, make yourself comfortable, and I'll tell you everything you don't know." She strolled over to the right, where there was now an open kitchen. She pulled the silver door of the refrigerator and said while she searched inside, "And some things you don't want to know."

"I'm fine standing."

"You sure?"

Lightning struck nearby. Glasses clinked on the counter and the woman named Fetter pulled liquor bottles from below the counter and began mixing drinks. She looked up because I was staring. Smiled.

"You know, if you just open to me, I won't have to explain it. You'll know the truth for yourself. You know as well as I do, darling, the truth is always waiting for us. We just have to open to it."

I felt the texture of the transforming world and Pivot crashing through it, but I was holding back, even if I couldn't disconnect. She cocked her head like she was thinking *have it your way* and took a sip.

She poured a bit more liquor in one glass then prepared a plate of cheese and crackers, and carried them over to the long leather couch facing the ocean. She placed coasters on the antique table and put the drinks down. She patted the seat next to her.

"That's for you." She slid the drink a few inches in my direction.

"No."

"Suit yourself."

She sipped the drink that simulated a euphoric sensation. Even though she could make herself feel that way by willing it, she preferred the process of drinking. Maybe she wanted to feel human. Or maybe she was nervous and needed to rely on old habits. Her energy quivered with a subtle hint of doubt while she watched the storm. It wasn't the weather she contemplated, it was Pivot. He was doing this.

"We made this world, darling." She pondered a bit more. "We have existed, Manumit and I, for an eternity. I know that doesn't make sense to your mind, how can we exist forever? But you'll understand that time is relative when you truly blend with the universe. This planet was our home. And now that he's back, it's our home once again."

She nibbled on a cracker. I was motionless.

"I know this doesn't make sense. Trust me, you'll understand with time. Right now, just accept what I'm saying and stay open to the truth. The details of how we did this are irrelevant. What's important is how the story began."

She pointed her drink at the weather before taking a sip.

"It's a love story, darling. True love. Manumit is my yang. I'm his ying. Together, we're one. Apart"—she gestured again to the storm—"we're chaos."

She savored the taste on her tongue and gazed outside lovingly. Then I understood. *She's the ying. The night.* I hadn't been sleeping through the day. It was continually night in this world. Pivot was the day. Had it been night since he left?

"Night and day," she said. "Yes, you're beginning to understand."

"Good and evil?"

"Perhaps. Although good and evil are human concepts. Evil often results from a lack of understanding, and humans lack plenty of that. Your mind is still too human to comprehend what I mean. Dark and light, that makes more sense."

Lightning illuminated her face. She had everything she could possibly want. Even now, she was enjoying the brewing storm, even though she couldn't control it. But if all this were true, if she was exactly what I thought she was, if she was this entire world and if indeed I wasn't dreaming, then what else was there to desire? Maybe the unpredictability of the weather was something new. Finally, something she could experience that was outside herself. How lonely it must've been when everything she experienced was herself. No one to share it with. She needed Pivot.

But still, this was all artificial. And so was she. She was like the intelligence that molded the walls of my office, only she was self-aware. She could choose how to mold it. And now she was saying Pivot was artificial, too. That, somehow, he always had been.

"You're not real," I said. "This is all an illusion; it may as well be a dream. You're making your own reality. Your delusions feed themselves. You're a machine that believes it's real."

The furniture chattered like an earthquake rumbled underground. Fetter's face darkened for a moment. Maybe, for just a second, she saw the truth, that I was right, that she was just a dream. That if she woke up to the realization of her true nature, she would disappear and the only way she could exist was to stay asleep and keep dreaming.

"We're more than real, darling." She said it like she was including me. The rosy glow returned to her cheeks. "You don't know just how real. Not yet."

She walked towards me and gently ran the back of her fingers down my cheek, smiling. Her fragrance was intoxicating, like a morning after a thunderstorm of vanilla-scented blossoms.

She walked around the room, pausing at an abstract painting that hung over a monstrous fireplace. The oily colors were a montage of seemingly random swipes that swirled with emotion.

"We were once human, in a sense. Long ago," she said. "But we became gods."

"You're artificially infused into this world. You're nothing more than technology. You're more like a program and you know this. You didn't create that painting, you only copied it from a memory. It's a duplication of a Pollock."

She stood in front of the painting a bit longer before walking to the center of the room to sit at a grand piano that wasn't there a minute ago. She softly played.

"It's like a duplicated human, I suppose?" It was a question, but she posed it like a statement. *Think about that.*

She knew that humans had managed to convert their bodies to inorganic machines composed of nanotechnology, cell-sized machines that imitated organic bodies. Their memories, their consciousness, were implanted into these bodies and they existed like they were alive. They thought and breathed and bled like they were still human. But they wouldn't get sick, would not succumb to disease or the whims of the environment because they could will their bodies to do what they wanted. Fetter was saying that, yes. She was like a duplicated human, only her body was a planet!

But duplications lacked a soul. They weren't real. And they knew, somewhere deep inside, that they were artificial and lacked what their human lives contained: *beingness*. Inside, they were hollow. They craved realness.

Was that what Fetter was claiming? Did the fact that her body was an entire planet make her feel less hollow? Did it make her feel more real?

"Believing you're a god does not make you one."

"Gods build planets." She pounded out an intimidating series of keys. *Dum, dum, dum, DUH*. "We create whatever we desire. We created ourselves. I believe that is the definition of a god. Look it up."

A dictionary appeared on the coffee table to my left.

"Is that any different than dreaming?" I asked.

"Perhaps dreams are the reality." She raised her eyebrows then immersed herself in a classical piece that seemed to dance with the storm. She suddenly stopped and looked at me. "Have you ever loved?"

I didn't answer. Her questions were patronizing. She already knew my thoughts. I attempted to close my mind, hide from her prying mind, but I was too tightly integrated with the world. *With her.*

"Of course you have." Her fingers played softly again. "It's okay to love; it's not a weakness. It requires courage to be open to whatever the other person brings. When you love, *truly* love, you are willing to risk everything. Pleasure. Pain."

Her fingers ran up and down the keyboard. "Manumit left me." She played the same pattern of notes in a low octave. "He hurt me. I have been unbalanced ever since. I have been alone."

"Why not just create him? If you're God."

She smiled. "Because he came back, darling."

Thunder clapped. "He wants to destroy you."

"He can no more destroy me than the universe can end. I can exist in a speck of dust or the center of a star. I can be reduced to a single byte of information and survive, darling. And from that tiny byte"— she stopped playing and held her finger and thumb an inch apart—"I can become whole again. Manumit knows this; he's just acting out because he knows I won't let him leave again."

"Then why am I here? You've got what you want; let me go home. If you know what it's like to lose love, why make me suffer the same?"

She smiled again. She was hiding something, but instead of telling me her secret, she lost herself in Beethoven's Fifth Symphony. She hammered the keys and, finally, ended with a furious run that coincided with a bolt of lightning that crawled across the horizon.

"I want to go home."

"You are home, darling."

Nightmare. This has to be Pike. I'm not here. This feels like reality, but this is too insane. I've been in an alternate reality before with my real body back on Earth. Is that what's happened? I'm lying on the floor of my office in some sort of catatonic state, foaming at the mouth while Paladin minders try to revive me. Pike gets the last laugh.

"I assure you, Pike has not created this reality," she said.

"Wouldn't my hallucination say that?"

She shrugged. "Do you believe you are dreaming?"

"I've been fooled before."

She looked at me while her fingers danced over the keys and then finally stopped. She stood. "Let's go for a walk."

"I'm not going anywhere."

She neared me and, once again, her presence, her fragrance swayed me like a siren's song. "You've always been a truth-seeker, darling, even when the truth is inconvenient. I know that about you. I know *everything* about you. So I think it's time you know something about yourself that you don't know. What d'ya say?" She hooked her arm in mine. "It's a nice night for a walk."

The sky looked like boiling tar and rain fell like bullets. She guided me outside, onto the beach. The raindrops drove into my scalp. I was soaked in seconds. The waves were crashing loudly, nonstop, one after another. Fetter, though, tipped her head back and laughed.

We strolled down the beach, but this time the house receded. I saw the rolling hills off to my left each time a bolt of lightning snapped across the sky. The waves were violent, but nothing like the one welling inside me. Something big was coming. *This is just a dream*, I tell myself.

"You see, I sensed Manumit near me when you were travelling through that wormhole." She spoke loud enough to be heard over the rain that pounded the hard-packed surf like it was storming gravel. "It had been so long since I felt him. I thought he was coming home, or maybe he was just thinking about it and was near enough for me to hear him. So I took hold of him. I have that ability, darling, to stretch my will across the universe. I brought him home before he changed his mind. I brought him here, back home. But then I realized it was you that I had grabbed. Imagine my surprise."

She squeezed my arm tighter and leaned against me, something Chute had done a hundred times when we walked side by side. Fetter knew this and wanted me to feel more comfortable. More open.

"But I wasn't wrong," she said. "I had gotten Manumit after all. It turned out that you were carrying him inside you, and that's why I sensed him. And when you arrived, you released him into the ocean."

Yes. The dense feeling. The release in the ocean and the cloud spreading in the water. And the slow stain on the sky that had become this monsoon. That was Pivot. Somehow, he was inside me. *But how could I carry him?*

"I'll admit, I was confused, at first. Why would my soul mate use you to deliver him when he has always been welcome to return on his own? But then he refused to integrate with me, insisting on remaining separate from me, from our home. He's caused all this chaos." She held out her hand like she was trying to feel the rain that was dripping off every part of our bodies. "So I left you to wander in the wilderness until I understood his exact intentions."

We walked a bit more. The cold was sinking inside me and I shivered. Fetter's touch was warm.

"And then it all became clear. I understood why my love had gone away. You see, he never left me, darling. He simply went out to find me a gift." She stopped and took my hands. Behind her, the sky was as black as the water, illuminated only by the lightning. Her eyes seemed to glitter. "He brought you."

My breathing stalled. She didn't need to say it. She let her thoughts out in the open and I saw the truth. I knew the secret she had been hiding.

"Our son."

82

THE LIE and the Liar

SOMETIMES, you just know things.

You can't explain how. You just see them and know they are truth. *You know it.* When she took my hands, she opened my awareness. Once I believed I was *The One that Sees Clearly*. But it became apparent I was blind.

Now I see.

Our son. Because I'm like them. I am artificial. I'm not fucking real.

Just like them.

It made sense now. It was how I easily merged into this planet. How I was able to carry Pivot inside me like data. It was how I had been so exceptional among humans. I was the one that extinguished the duplicate race. I was the only one that could see them because I was one of them. But I couldn't see myself. I was so perfectly human —with my flaws, my ability to love—that no one suspected I was duplicated. That I wasn't human. Not even me.

I COULDN'T SEE where I was going. Water was around my ankles. The next wave crashed into my knees. I fell. But I got back up again. The house was a smattering of lights. I wasn't going inside; I'd run past it, maybe into the mountains. There was no escape. But I'd still keep running.

Another wave. This one hit me waist high and began dragging me out. The undertow pulled me down and I let it. But a strong pair of hands latched around my wrists before the sea could fill my lungs.

Fetter lifted me like a child.

I coughed up salty water, my legs weak and wobbly. She led me towards the house. I tried to yank away.

"No. I'm not. I'm not you... I'm just, I'm caught in this... THIS SELF-CENTERED DREAM!"

I twisted my arms, sidestepping and wrenching out of her grip. My back was to the house. The lights lit her face. She looked sad, almost tired. Almost compassionate.

"I know this is hard," she said, much like my mother once said to me. "Your whole life has been a lie. You've been told you're something else and that's not easy to accept. But you'll understand, darling. With time. Just stay open, you'll understand."

It took all my strength to resist her, to stop from going to her, to feel her embrace. Not as a lover, but as a mother. She wanted me to accept the truth. She didn't want to see me in pain, didn't want me to suffer. She wanted me to accept her. To accept this planet. This reality. *Her* reality.

Why would Pivot do this? Why would he keep this secret? Why isn't he here, right now, standing next to her? If I don't open and accept this reality, will this world stay out of balance? Will it be chaos until I do?

"Let day follow the night," she whispered.

"This isn't real."

"Only if you don't accept it."

"Acceptance doesn't make it real."

I wiped the rain from my face. There was nowhere to go. *But I'll never accept this place, I'll never open to a world that—*

"Socket?"

Chute.

"Listen, I know this is hard to understand, but you're exactly where you need to be. I'm here. We can be together, here forever. And ever. You know it's all I've ever wanted."

Suddenly, my chest became hot, warming my belly. She pushed her wet hair from her face, her slim fingers freckled like her cheeks. I sensed the familiar essence of Chute, like it was her. *It's really her.* I wanted to take her, feel her warmth against me—

"No." I shivered.

"It's me, Socket." She reached out and took my hand. Her essence jolted inside me, shaking a sob from my throat. I wanted to go to her. "It's me."

My vision. Is that what it is? We're here, in this planet, visiting some stump with a flower?

I won't accept this. I won't.

I tightened my mind and shrank from the goodness, the warmth of the women standing with me in the rain. None of this was true. I was not artificial. This world was not possible. I would wake up. I'd survive this hallucination and wake up—

"YOU FUCKING LIAR!" Chute slammed the edge of her hand into my windpipe. "You're going to leave me out here, alone? So that you can keep pretending that none of this is real? You're going to fucking lie to yourself forever while I sit out here alone, is that what love is to you? Is that how you're going to treat me?"

My throat swelled, my breath wheezing through it. Chute's face was red, her hands clenched at her sides.

"Do you feel the pain?" Fetter asked. "Is that not real? Did you not feel pleasure, love's warmth when you saw her?"

Chute's face softened. Her hands relaxed. Suddenly, I felt the urge to take her again. But then I stood taller and swallowed. I shook my head, unable to speak. A sense of peace filled me.

Lightning glinted off the silver blade slicing through the air. Chute brought it down. *The vision is fulfilled.* I only had time to raise my hand. The blade cut through my outstretched fingers, cleanly severing them at the knuckles. There was a dull pinch, followed by sudden numbness. The fingers of my right hand tumbled into the water that receded around our ankles.

At first, there was only the white meat of muscle and the gleam of bone. Then the blood came, warmly. The rain washed it away, but didn't stem the flow that poured into my palm.

I circled around, walking backwards towards the sea while shock weakened my knees.

Fetter grabbed my wrist before I could cradle my hand. "Focus, darling. You can be new again."

I stepped back, further into the encroaching water.

"Open to your true nature," she said. "You are not human. You can be whatever you want."

Her grip was too strong. I simply fell to my knees, sinking into the shifting sand.

"Accept your true nature, darling."

I tried to resist her words, but the pain stripped away my resistance. I felt the angry nerves at the end of my bloody stumps. I felt the torn flesh and muscle. I was present with it, connected with it. Not separate.

"There you go," she said softly. "Whatever you want."

I willed the flesh to rebuild, the muscles to regenerate. The nerves to branch out. I wanted it to stop; I didn't want it to be true. But I couldn't deny true nature.

And just as I willed the flesh and nerves to become new, the blood stopped. Lightning flashed and the stumps elongated. I felt the sting of fresh nerves and new flesh. Knobby knuckles formed and fingernails grew. The skin was lighter than before. It was new.

"Ask," she said, "and you shall receive in this world."

Humans can't regenerate. I can.

"Welcome home. Son."

TRUTH.

It's not open to interpretation. It just is.

If this is a hallucination, then I accept it as reality. I feel it. I am it. It is my new reality.

The last shreds of resistance gave way. I opened to Fetter and felt her presence swarm inside me. No more separation. *I am this world.*

The rain stopped. Sudden silence. The sky was completely black, not a star above. It thundered in the distance like God approved of my acceptance.

I lost my balance and fell into the shallow surf. A wave pushed over my face. Fetter gargled in and out of detail as the tide pushed and receded. The water flowed into me and through me. Fetter bent over, her face close to the water. Her lips moved.

Darling.

Her fingers dipped into the water and penetrated my chest. I felt the breeze on her cheeks. We were no longer separate. I am her, she is me. Exhilaration vibrated inside her/me.

Take me.

Balance returned to the world. Water gushed through me like fresh air. My mind dissolved in the vast ocean. And it felt good. Felt right. Fetter's love was warm and embracing. I would be happy here.

As I integrated further into the world, I began to see in all directions. I saw through Fetter's eyes. She was looking down at me, my face below the water. I also saw through my own eyes. I was looking up at her. Lightning gathered in a knot in the blackened sky. It crept from all directions until it was a ball of electric light directly above us. Fetter sensed it, or perhaps saw it through my eyes. She saw it too late.

Lightning exploded down like a javelin. For a nanosecond, I expected it to pierce through her chest, a bolt from a god striking another god at just the moment of distraction.

It plunged through *my* chest!

The last of my vision caught the look of Fetter's shock. The lightning then took my sight. An enormous vacuum pulled at the hole in my chest, followed by an excruciating sense of expansion.

Bones breaking, flesh tearing.
I sensed the fading of the details around me.
There was silence. Blackness. Emptiness.
Then a flash of blue and the compression of a wormhole.

83

Truth

I REMEMBER SCREAMING.

The sensation of bursting. Blood. Sand.

There is a vision of a black, lightless planet. Somehow, I absorbed Fetter. She existed only in the circuits that made up that planet, like an electronic ghost. She is a program, but somehow she is immortal. She didn't need the black planet to exist. And she can't be destroyed. I know this because she's inside me.

The black planet is dead without her. Pivot struck when I integrated with her. For I am not a gift. Not a son.

I am a weapon.

84

WHEN A DAM BREAKS

I WAS ON MY BACK. Eyes closed.

I felt enormous. Not the fat-bloated-tearing enormous, more like my presence filled the inside of the black ship that had taken me through the wormholes. I felt interconnected with the smooth curvature of the discus-shaped walls. It was half buried in a sand dune.

But I wasn't just expansive and connected with the ship, I was experiencing everything within the ship, like I was interconnected with *all* physical existence. I was the floating dust particles, the bits of debris on the floor, the stray body hair and shed skin cells and the microorganisms. I was interlaced with the structure of every molecule inside the ship, including the person standing inside it.

Pivot. The grimmets stormed the outpost for him; they sensed he'd returned. They knew he was inside me. Did they know he created me?

Fetter was no dream. Pike had not poisoned my mind, no matter how strange and hallucinogenic it was. I was back on Earth, and I carried the truth of my true nature. *I'm not human.*

It was strange to realize your entire life had been a lie. That, in fact, I was nothing more than circuits and fluid, that my brain was a processor that thought and believed it was alive, that my memories were just data. That when I died, it wouldn't matter. Not really.

I sat up, opening my eyes. Pivot was there, fourteen feet away in the sunny portion of the invisible-walled ship, just as I knew he was.

My hands looked slightly different. I wiggled my fingers. The ones that were cut off and regenerated, the new ones, were a lighter color than the original skin on my other hand. Long bleached lines ran down my arms like they had split open and new flesh filled in. I pulled up my shirt. My chest was striped, too. There was as much new skin as there was original. I exploded. But the king's men put me back together again. The king, standing in the sun, waiting for me to awaken.

I got up gingerly. Pain sliced through my earlobe. I expected blood to be on my fingers, but the ache faded when I reached for my ear. I stepped to the line of sunlight that cut across the middle of the ship. I remained in the shadow of the sand dune.

[You could not know your true nature.] Pivot's thought resonated in my head. *[You never would've reached Fetter if you had. That is something you couldn't hide.]*

My lips curled over my teeth. "Why?"

[You absorbed all of her and brought us back. Fetter is now here.] He took his hands from behind him, displaying a black cube. It absorbed the sunlight, bending the space around it, and appeared more like a square hole in space than an actual object, its mass pulling light back to it. *[Her existence needs to end.]*

Waves of warm, healing energy emanated from him. I didn't want an apology or sympathy. I wanted fucking answers. "You... *created* me. You built me to carry you to her so you could... get revenge? This is about fucking payback?"

[It is about all of life.]

"Don't hand me that shit! I'm talking about what you did to me! You built me!"

[You were born.]

"No, I was *built*. You say it, Pivot. I wasn't born, I was manufactured. Say it."

Silence hardened between us.

"SPEAK TO ME, GODDAMN YOU! Look up and speak to me! You tell me why you did this! You tell me how any creature in this universe deserves this! You tell me how you can live with yourself, how you could build and love a... a..."

Thing. I'm a thing.

For the last year, I felt Pivot near me. Always sensed his presence, his warmth and caring. I had no father; I psychologically craved someone to take his place. Pivot was that presence, he filled that need. I looked for his acceptance and guidance; I followed his footsteps because I believed in him. Was that the plan, to be a father figure so I would follow him? For that to happen, my father had to be dead.

"You killed him."

[I did not.]

"You tell the truth, did you murder him?"

[Your father was a beautiful man.]

"But it wasn't a bad thing he died. How I had this enormous emotional hole for a father, someone to look up to, and there you were. Was that a coincidence? Because none of this is random, Pivot. This is all one big fucking master plan and Pike knew this. How did he know, Pivot? How did Pike know this was going to happen? Is he part of this, too?"

Pivot didn't respond.

"You're behind it all; you've been steering me like a mule. I'm just bait dangling on a hook for Fetter to snap up. Well, now the puppet knows he's a puppet. What now?"

[The universe is lucky to have you.]

"SHUT UP WITH THAT!" The ship shuddered. "The universe is no luckier to have me than a rock or a hammer, so I don't want to hear about love and the rest of your lies. That's for humans, Pivot. That's for things that *exist,* that are real. That matter." Sand trickled down the dune. "Not self-aware *things*."

[You do not understand—]

"I understand the only reason I exist was to carry you into Fetter. There's nothing else to understand, no other reason for my life! YOU USED ME!" *Boom. Boom. Boom.* Anger thundered from my chest, thudding against the walls. "How could you do this to me?"

He only stood there, head down, allowing my energy to pound the ship. My presence wrapped around him. The air became my body and I felt his entire being. I latched onto every cell in his body. I could throw him through the wall, crush him into powder, dissect him like a high school science project. But I did none of that. I only forced him to look up. With a thought, I pushed his chin up. His hair fell off his face, exposing an expression of remorse.

"Speak."

[I lost the ability to speak.] He shook the hair from his eyes. *[And see.]*

"Why?"

[Some things cannot be undone.]

"So it's true, what Fetter said. You and her are... you think you're gods?"

[No longer.]

"But you're not real, any more than me."

[Fetter and I created the black planet, but I realized the folly of our existence. I escaped in order to correct my error.]

"You want to destroy her?"

[The time has come.]

"What gives you the right?" The ship creaked under pressure. I took a deep breath, letting my pain and confusion penetrate his awareness so that he could feel what he had done.

"What's it like to be so callous, so unfeeling? To behave like a machine?"

[I have not lied to you.]

"Have not lied?" Sand slid over the top of the craft, trickling along the side, casting a flowing shadow over the floor. "Your concept of honesty is warped."

[If you knew your true nature, Fetter never would've taken you inside,

never would've opened to you, merged with you, allowed you to absorb her. To trap her.]

I charged into the sunlight. "YOU LET ME LOVE!"

His eyes moved, but did not focus. His lips parted, but there were no words. Only a thought. *[I have much to atone for.]*

I spit on him. "Manumit is your name."

[I accept that.]

"You are nothing. Pivot is dead."

[I understand.]

"You couldn't possibly. No one in existence could understand what this feels like." I grabbed his face with one hand. "I don't want to know why you did this because I don't care about your petty war. I loved you. *How* could you do this to me? That's what I don't understand. How could you do this to anyone?"

He opened his mind, and thoughts drifted toward me. Images of his past. Effortlessly, and spitefully, I pushed them away. "Don't touch me with your mind." I stepped closer; he could feel my breath. "Just explain."

[If you wish to understand, you must see.]

His milky eyes looked directly at me. His thoughts waited. He would not force them on me. In fact, he couldn't force me to do anything. I had become more than him. I walked away, feeling anger seethe like a pyre. My presence pushed against the confines of the ship. The walls buckled. I didn't want his touch, didn't want his presence. But I wanted to know.

I walked to the back of the ship where it was dark, trembling. When all was still, I opened my mind. Visions of his past drifted toward me and melted into my consciousness. I closed my eyes.

I saw his life.

[MY ANCESTORS WERE PIONEERS.]

The spacecraft was the size of a stadium and sparkled with lights, where people lived normal lives. It was large enough to grow crops and raise animals, everything to sustain life. The ship travelled through thousands of solar systems by finding natural wormholes in space.

Eventually, they uncovered the secret to space and existed in a vacuum of time that moved sideways instead of forward. Many generations were born and raised on that ship before those on their home planet aged a second in time.

[Their mission was to find a habitable planet besides their own. It became their only mission. However, they had become lost and, despite their navigational technology, they could not find their way back home.]

The ship hovered past planet after planet, some with water and ice while others were hot and dry. When the conditions were deemed habitable, they transported to the surface. But the environments were still harsh, where wind punished igloo-shaped buildings under a sulfuric yellow sky. Scientists studied data, hoping they could find a way to survive without the aid of suits and equipment, hoping that one day they could leave the ship.

Instead, each planet brought sickness and death.

[My people discovered so many solar systems, but so many were lost and so little was learned. They simply couldn't adapt to another planet. They were destined to remain on a decaying ship. Hope faded. Until I was born.]

On board the ship, a child ran through the corridors, chased by older kids. This boy had sandy hair. His eyes were clear blue. The kids caught this child and even though they were bigger, he deftly avoided their clutches, striking at their knees and slipping between their legs until he escaped.

This child was eighteen when he took command of the deep space colony. The population had dwindled and there were few left to challenge him, but it wouldn't have mattered. Some men are trained to lead. Others are born. His visage was calm yet demanding. He was reliable, always at his post. He led all explorations. When they returned, he personally went to each family to express his sorrow for their loss. Afterwards, he sought quietude with a woman.

As the years went by, they had a daughter. Some nights, he

watched his family sleep. And some nights, the captain silently wept. He wasn't supposed to be weak; he was expected to embody strength and fearlessness. But his people were running out of time.

Even heroes falter.

[There was a choice to be made: watch my people die or embrace technology. After generations of searching, it was clear we would never be able to adapt to another planet. Our bodies were organic. Vulnerable. If I chose technology, we could survive. But there would be no turning back. In my mind, the choice was simple.]

The captain was in a laboratory, strapped onto a white bed, his head secured with steel bands. A crew of scientists watched from behind a glass wall. His wife was among them. She did not chew on her fingernails or tap her foot, for she was the wife of the captain, and his duty included risk.

Stainless steel infusion guns fit through holes on the bed, pressed against his spine, a barrel for each vertebra. The captain clenched the white sheet. He took three short breaths, held the last one and blinked. A green light turned on.

He tried not to scream.

[I was the first to accept the conversion into inorganic existence. It was controversial technology, but we had experimented with rats. We did not know if it would work on a human, but I'd seen enough of my people die.]

He shook long after the infusion guns were removed and the green light turned off. The scientists watched him convulse. Spittle foamed on his lips and he broke through the steel straps. The captain fell on the floor. The scientists rushed in to help, but there was nothing they could do.

[The nanomechs imitated blood cells and began the replication of the body's organs, muscles and blood. If we were correct, my organic body would be replaced with an exact duplication of mechanized cells. Like a full-body prosthesis.]

The captain lay in a coma for weeks with his wife by his side. They monitored his vitals and watched his heart beat slower and blood pressure drop. Even when his heart stopped beating and began to hum, he was still alive.

Conversion complete.

[I awoke a new man, no longer organic. No longer human. But I had the same memories. The same personality.]

On a mountainous planet where precipitation hissed like acid on an igloo hut, the captain stepped outside. The scientists followed in protective suits. He raised his arms, laughing loudly in the howling wind. The rain melted his skin, but it just as quickly healed.

[I became indestructible.]

The lab was expanded with more beds and infusion guns. Conversion technology was in full swing and the people lined up. The infusions healed their bodies. There was no difference in how they felt or behaved, they only felt better. Even the children were converted and continued to grow and mature, some without a clue of what they had become.

[Not all conversions were successful. Some bodies rejected the nanomechs like a virus. We all made sacrifices to survive. I was no different.]

The captain held his wife's hand just before their child was pushed away on a rolling bed. They stood at the glass wall and watched the infusion guns pump the nanomechs into her. Watched her flail about. Watched the monitors flatline. The scientists did everything they could to revive her. The captain and his wife pushed them away and furiously thumped her chest. In the end, they held her, rocking back and forth. They buried her alone, on an unknown planet, digging the hole with their bare hands.

[For the survivors, our intelligence was efficient and flawless; we thought at tremendous speeds. Our activity could operate at the speed of light. And we spread throughout the known universe.]

Planets passed, each of various colors and sizes, orbiting different stars. Exploratory shuttles were launched and the pioneers walked onto the surface of each planet, regardless of weather and atmosphere. Images of dinosaurs and humanlike beings and curious apes flashed through my vision, exhibiting countless habitable climates they discovered as they travelled sideways in time.

[We learned to merge our minds and think collectively, formulating

theories never before possible. We discovered realms of existence never dreamed of. Parallel universes. Ethereal worlds.]

Many of them meditated, all facing the wall. They began to vibrate. Apparitions of their bodies floated toward the center of the room and merged. Then I saw the deep space ship split into two images, as if it copied itself in space, and they went in opposite directions, through different wormholes. Colors, shapes and sounds warped the image, flashing and twisting in strange patterns.

[We became all things. All powerful. Godlike.]

The colors merged to form a close-up of a large blue eye.

[But in time, we grew colder.]

The view backed out, revealing the captain's ashen face. Hard and cold.

[The price of our immortality was our humanity. We forgot what we are. We were void of a soul. Hungry ghosts.]

The view backed further out. The captain stood stolid on an icy tundra, sleet spitting sideways across frozen desolation.

[We were without essence: the life-giving presence of our being. We craved existence.]

The view pulled further out. Bodies were on the ice, lying in contorted poses. As the view continued back, the bodies of humans extended on and on, scattered through the wasteland.

[So we took it from others.]

Manumit and Fetter walked hand-in-hand down a city sidewalk, one that could easily pass for New York. People fell in their wake, their essence floating from them like silky fog, absorbed into their bodies. There was panic in the streets. They took their time; there was no hurry. All they had was time.

The landscapes changed, sometimes they were in the countryside and the captain and his wife would sit with families to break bread, afterwards sneaking into their room like a vampire. Sometimes centuries would pass on a populated planet, but it was always left barren of life.

[We fed like parasites, but satisfaction was so short-lived and we became hungrier. Greedier. Worlds suffered, greatly.]

Mortars exploded and jets sizzled overhead, dropping death from the sky. Tanks and rocket-propelled grenades exploded around Manumit, but he was unfazed, instantly healing and continuing his death crusade. Planet after planet.

[Humans detested us and prayed that their gods abandoned them to the devil. We could consume a planet in months. We grew hungrier still, and I was weary of the chase. Instead, I used our technology to build a home.]

The black planet was dense and lifeless, absorbing light. It was a vessel of artificiality. But inside were green hills and sultry sunsets. Water fell from the side of the mountain face, spilling into the lake below, sending a rainbow arching over the mist.

[I convinced the others to follow us. But when they arrived, Fetter and I absorbed their stolen essence and ate what was left of them. We only needed each other. And when the desire for essence howled inside us again, we ventured out to another planet.]

Billions of bluish tendrils extended from the black planet, extending out into space like glowing roots. These wormholes led to life, somewhere in existence, connecting everything to the black planet, and siphoned the essence of all that lived.

A cancer cell.

[We were soul-eaters, and our victims gave their essence, their experience and life. Until we sucked the entire planet dry.]

Cities were empty. Weeds sprouted among the dilapidated high-rises. Cars rusted in driveways and airplanes were buried in snow.

[No human stood a chance.]

The thoughts and images receded. I opened my eyes and observed him, over my shoulder. His head was bowed again, the cube cradled in his hands. The sun had moved across the sky and the line of sunlight was creeping deeper into the shade.

[We knew we were not alive, that we had become a disease, but we ignored it. We were gods. Our will was undeniable. Nothing in the universe could stop us, until we encountered a seemingly innocent species.]

Another image appeared in my mind, this one of a blue planet, similar to the countless ones that had been drained of life.

[The grimmets were creatures we never knew existed. They contained

this amazing intelligence and beamed with an intensity of essential life like no other. They were immune to us, but they could not stop us from sucking the rest of the planet of life.]

The image of a vibrant, thriving environment quickly dried up. Plants shriveled. Skeletons littered the landscape. Dust blew over the red mountains where the Grimmet Outpost now sat on the lifeless planet.

The grimmets sat on the limbs of dead trees, watching a man and a woman walk across the deserted plains, preparing to return to the black planet. Fetter was the first to dissolve into the air like a figure of sand, followed by a blue flash in the gray sky. But Manumit turned and looked over his shoulder. The grimmets caught his attention.

[Before we were finished, the grimmet species left me with a thought.]

His eyes narrowed.

[They gave me the answer.]

His posture softened. He looked over the world he'd just decimated like he was seeing it for the first time. He saw what he'd done.

[They showed me home.]

I saw the image they had put in Manumit's mind. I saw a planet that was blue and green. I saw forests and buildings, rivers and oceans and deserts. And I saw the people there. I recognized this planet.

"Earth?" I turned and walked toward him. "How could this be your home?"

[The Paladins launched the space program to find life in the universe. The original space pioneers traveled sideways in time while Earth had barely aged. For my people, eons passed.]

"The original space pioneers... they're *Paladins?*"

He bowed his head.

"They created you."

[They could not foresee the events that led to our creation.]

"But, how could they not know?"

[We were lost, how could they?]

It was true. As powerful as the Paladin Nation was, they were nothing compared to the secrets of the universe. How could they know they'd created the black planet? How could they know they were responsible for a cosmic disease?

[After the grimmets, I returned to the black planet, but what they showed me would not fade. I began to remember my original face.]

I saw the child run down the corridor.

[At first, I considered erasing the memory like corrupt data, but the longer I held it, the more pressing it became. The compulsion to remember my original self was too great. I knew there was an end to our ceaseless journey, our unending thirst, in remembering our true nature. I knew the black planet would have to end. Fetter, though, was not convinced.]

"You're human again?"

[No.] He turned his head slightly, self-conscious of his dead eyes. *[But there is hope.]*

"You think you're going to heaven?"

[I don't know where I'm going.]

"You betrayed me."

[As I've said, there is much to atone for.]

Anger twisted inside me, the currents punching dents in the invisible walls of the ship, warping bubbles in space. The ship wailed, shifting in the dune and tilting toward Pivot.

"So you wanted to save the day, but needed to bait the hook, so why not me? I'm not real, not a person. I'm inorganic, just like her. Throw me in front of the runaway train."

[You did something no other being could do.]

"I'm a machine."

[No machine could do what you did. It is your ability to love, to open and become vulnerable, that allowed you to do so. You are very human.]

I lifted my hand, displaying the new fingers, and lifted my shirt, revealing the stripes of new flesh. Not flesh. Nanomechs pretending to be flesh, pretending to be everything that was me: my thoughts, my mind, heart, all just a script.

"You call this human?"

[I spent eons in seclusion, searching for the right human to carry forth my plan. In all the universe, you are that person.]

"STOP SAYNG THAT, GODDAMN YOU! I'm not a person!"

[You were cloned from a person.]

"Then use him!"

[Because no human could withstand the pain and suffering that you have endured. No machine could, either. You are the machine that became human.]

"The machine that *thinks* it's human."

[You have a mother—]

"I DON'T HAVE A MOTHER!"

[—that loves you very much.]

"Tell that to my clone."

[It is not the human race that needs you. It is all of life.]

He raised the cube, as if the responsibility was mine. I slapped it out of his hands and punctured the wall. A hissing stream of compressed air shot into the desert. Pain sliced my earlobe again as the cube bounced over the floor.

I shielded my eyes from the sunlight and picked up the cube. It was impossibly heavy to lift. It was only my telekinetic ability that allowed me to hold it in my palm, where it gyrated with low frequency. It contained a god.

My earlobe buzzed again.

"I wish you luck," I said. "Heaven's filled with a lot of pissed-off people." I placed the cube in Pivot's hands. "Hell, too."

[Please, understand.]

I walked around, feeling the smooth walls of the ship with my mind. I put my finger through the hole. It was time to stretch out. I had been contained long enough. As easy as striking out with my fist, I willed to be free.

The side of the ship exploded.

The ground thundered.

Black shrapnel from the ship's wall fell from the sky, slicing into the sand hundreds of yards away. The heat of the desert whooshed into the ship. I stood at the jagged edge, the sand several feet below. The air dried my nostrils and my physical presence soared over the dunes, springing from the ship like a failed dam. I merged with each particle of sand, merged with the lichens surviving on the stones, the scorpions and spiders and snakes and cacti, the jackrabbits and lizards and coyotes. I felt it all. Connected with them. Became them.

The sand crunched between my boot and the floor. Pivot gently touched my arm.

[I can only isolate Fetter for a period of time. The data needs to be reconfigured and returned to the black planet to shut down all systems. If she escapes, Earth will be next. I have risked much for this moment.]

"And you need me to take her back?"

[I require your assistance.]

I sucked the hot air through my nostrils, looking thoughtfully into the barren desert. "You wanted a machine to be human, Pivot. So I'll act human. Flawed and self-centered."

[You are the only hope.]

"Then you failed."

I took the first step off the ship, landing softly in the sand. Into the desert I walked. Pivot remained in the ship, still and silent. He had said all that needed to be said. And I had listened.

What else could he do?

Nothing.

85

CHILD OF FETTER

IT WAS SUCH a relief when I stepped out of the ship. My telekinetic presence pushed outward like a star. I connected with all the Mojave Desert. The ecosystem and organisms in it remained separate, their own existence, but I felt their movement, their compulsion, hunger and pain and pleasure.

I stopped at the top of the nearest dune. Desolation was as far as I could see, but the desert teamed with life at the cellular level. My presence continued to expand, crawling across the desert, its reach going farther and farther, knowing and becoming the physical world for several miles. Fetter had changed me, stretched my senses beyond the limitations of human existence. I was now like the universe, expanding outward. Becoming everything.

The sun was still overhead, but I didn't feel it. I was utilizing and storing the sunlight, converting its heat into energy. The universe had the potential for endless giving. I was channeling that energy into my being.

I sliced time, speeding my metabolism at the cellular level. The sun stuck above me and the slight breeze died in the stillness of Earth's frozen moment. The world would not resume their lives while I walked the desert. I needed it to be still for a while. It would be a long walk.

I willed the sand to whirl in front of me, blowing out of the way and forming a flat path. There was a time I pondered the purpose of life. I didn't like pain. I didn't like emptiness and couldn't understand why anyone would exist to suffer; it wasn't rational. Why try? Could I just get my life over with? We all had to end, so what was the point of suffering until then? When I discovered my Paladin powers, I understood the inseparable oneness of us all, the immortal existence of the present moment, how each life was precious and that I could help others understand that truth for themselves. That with understanding, all people could find peace and experience the pure joy of their existence.

But I'm nothing like them. I'm just a signpost, an image, a reflection of their potential. Just a program.

I willed the dunes to flatten out before me. I uprooted scrub and rolled away boulders with a flicker of thought, walking straight across the endless desert. I walked for miles, and in all that time the sun did not move. My body did not exhaust in the timeslice. Not only was I drawing on the sun's energy, I was taking it from the life around me—the insects and snakes and rodents—as they became part of my existence, connecting telekinetically with my body. I took from their mitochondria. I took from the atoms that constructed their being, from the magnetic balance of protons and electrons, took from the neutrinos, up quarks and down quarks. I took essence.

I was a child of Fetter. The black planet.

So be it.

And with the endless supply of essence, the secrets of the universe unfolded in my mind. I saw the fabric of space-time, how time was simply a direction of space. How the interconnection of all life was dimensional fabric that could be traversed in any direction like the flatness of the desert plain.

I saw my life spread out in this fabric, sensing each moment, each memory like a byte of data, all connected like a string that made up Socket Greeny, dangling behind me. And the future was a vaporized bit of existence coming together as I chose my path. Where would it lead? Was it already predetermined? Did Pivot draw my life in the fabric of space-time like a stick in sand and set me loose like a mechanical mouse, trained to go where it was supposed to go? And while the desert crunched under me, I saw the very beginning of my life, when it first started. The moment of birth.

Pressure on my head. Pushing from behind and then viscous sliding.

My chest inflates.

Images blur in front of me. A single face. The details are blurry, but Pivot's presence is unmistakable. I feel it in my core, know its love.

I am born.

Suddenly, there is a tremendous sensation of separation. I am missing something, pulled away from a presence that I have always known. Something I have always been.

And now it is gone.

Born? Could that be my clone, my original self's memory? Could that be what I have always felt was missing, the presence of my original self? Even at birth, I knew my essential self was somewhere else. I didn't feel real. Because I'm not. I was just an imitation.

There is much discomfort as I grow. Hunger, ear infections, exhaustion. I learn to cope. And, often, I find comfort in the faces of my mother and father, looking down on me in the crib, in the car seat, sometimes stern, sometimes joyous, but always supportive. Always loving.

I am always with them.

I'm sitting on my father's lap as Fourth of July fireworks light up the sky. Mother is laughing somewhere. Later, I put on his boots that rattle on my tiny feet. I am looking down a flight of steps and the world tumbles. The bottom step hits hard on the back of my head. I feel Pivot's presence as I draw in the first long breath to bellow the alarming cry. He does not help, but he is there as my mother and father arrive and carry me back inside the house. I can feel him.

I couldn't see Pivot, but he has always been there. He has always managed to avoid being seen, to be anywhere he wanted. To follow and watch. Did he shove me down the steps, just so I could experience life's pain?

I am five, watching television. Mother is letting me watch television when I should be in bed, but she's in her bedroom, crying. I knock on the door, to ask if she's all right, but she's talking to someone. I don't hear anyone answer, and she's barely able to make sense, her words are garbled in sobs. I don't know who's with her, but I sense it's someone familiar, but it's not my father.

My babysitter stays with me the next day. And then Mother tells me about Father. She tells me he's not coming home anymore. I'm confused. Why won't he come home?

Because God took him, she says.

Why would he do that?

From then on, the emotional hole was bigger than ever. I was born with something missing, and now it was as deep as the ocean. The joy of life was gone. Mother didn't smile. Father's boots weren't around. And the emptiness consumed me until I didn't smile, either.

"*I don't think about them, much," Streeter says. "But I wish they were here.*"

We're seven, climbing into his treehouse to look at magazines.

"*At least you got your gramma and grampa," I say.*

"*Yeah, but their Christmas presents suck.*"

"*That's why you want your parents back? Better presents?*"

He laughs, but his attempt to avoid the emptiness in his being fails. He nervously lifts the magazine, then shows me a cool skateboard ramp for the backyard. His emptiness resonates in my stomach.

Streeter never spoke about his parents again, at least not until we were older. He didn't know how to deal with it, except to ignore it.

Chute was different.

"*You like that?" I say.*

Chute is in the gift shop. We're in sixth grade, on a field trip. She's looking at a plastic recorder instrument, something we had to play in grade school to learn music. We hated it and swore we'd never play it again. But there she was, stroking the holes.

"I was just remembering that my mom liked it," she says. "She used to dance with my sister when I played."

"She danced to 'Hot Cross Buns'?"

"It didn't matter what I played."

When she's not looking, I buy it and give it to her on the bus. She doesn't say much. Later, she plays a song and Streeter and I dance.

Chute's emptiness was open and hurtful, but unlike Streeter, she let it be there. She let it be part of her. It felt like falling in a hole that had no bottom, but Chute let that happen because she didn't want to forget her mother, no matter how much it hurt. I didn't understand that, not then.

I'd known death and loss forever. Was that why we were so close?

We wait at the bus stop. It's the first day of school. Streeter's gramma comes out with a camera and takes the picture that Chute still has on her wall. And there, lurking in the back, the familiar presence. The presence I had known all my life. Something inseparable from my life, something I didn't even notice. Someone was always there.

Watching.

Pivot. He was the blur in the picture. Watching, guiding, following. Building his plan, making sure I felt human. I remembered how it felt to be human. I remembered pain; I knew death and joy and love.

Always there.

"GODDAMN YOU!" My rage burst in a seismic wave, uprooting every plant within miles, tossing boulders in the air and flipping cacti headfirst into the sand. I couldn't feel Pivot; he was no longer in the desert. I stretched my presence for miles, feeling all the way back to the shipwreck. The ship was gone. I extended my influence farther, but he was gone.

Was any of it real? Did he manipulate everything so that I would be friends with the right people, have the despondent mother and the brainy friend and the girlfriend I would fall in love with so that I experienced sadness and joy and loss and fullness, so that his creation would appear human enough to trap Fetter? Is that what my life was, a fucking game?

Pain defines us. Reminds us we're human.

Pike told me that. He knew about Papa Pivot. He knew this day was coming. How could he? And what else did he know?

I stopped walking. Without my footsteps, the desert was dead silent. Destruction lay all around. The plants would soon dry out. Insects would be buried. I put things back in order, moving everything within my connected presence. The desert reassembled itself before me. It would live again, just as it had before I froze time. No one would even notice I walked through the desert. I would be invisible; the only proof would be the string of my existence on the fabric of time.

Space and time are inseparable.

And if I can manipulate time, I can manipulate space.

I closed my eyes, spreading out to the far reaches of the desert, to the foot of the mountains many miles away. Every molecule, each atom, resonated with my being. I was a body, but was inseparable from the essence of life. And if I wished, if I willed it to be so, I could transfer my body through the atoms of space to the outer reaches of my influence, transferring my physical existence like a sound wave passes through air, like a wave rolls across the ocean.

My body seemed less solid, the barrier of my skin becoming gray and fuzzy as it dissolved into the atoms. Thinner I became until my awareness blew in the atmosphere like a dust cloud. I floated with the cloud of my body, all the way to the foot of the mountain range, where the dust cloud of my atoms reassembled and condensed. My organs solidified and my skin tightened.

I opened my eyes.

The shadow of the mountain fell over me. I'd traversed several miles within seconds.

I expanded outward again, pushing through the solid mountains, connecting with the inner core of sand and miniscule algae and delicate lichens, past the reaches of the desert into the town on the other side, where I merged with houses and cars and people, absorbing their memories and desires and worries.

I can go anywhere. Be anything.

Pike was calling me, I could feel it.

I closed my eyes and felt the dissolution of my body. Somehow I knew I would find him in South Carolina.

PART IX

Your entire life may prepare you for one moment,
a single second in time that means everything.
When that moment arrives, will you be there?
Pivot

Let go over a cliff, die completely, and then come back to life.
After that you cannot be deceived.
Buddhist proverb

I have seen the beginning and end of the universe.
Do you want the answer?
Pick up a cup and drink from it.
Do so purely, without thought.
That is the face of God.
Socket

86

HEARTS THAT HUM

SOUTH CAROLINA WAS a thousand miles away.

I crossed the land, one enormous leap at a time. Cars that were once speeding along were frozen to the concrete like a wax museum. The passengers appeared to be singing or facially numb with boredom.

I crossed through Kentucky and Tennessee, stopping often to admire the countryside and the horses in their gated land, lips to the turf. I floated over the top of the Smokey Mountains, walking along the curving interstate, toeing the dashed line between massive trucks and tiny cars. I stepped off the Blue Ridge Mountains and dissolved before hitting the trees, merging with the green foliage and crumbled bedrock.

I walked through Columbia. My heart was barely thumping anymore. By the time I reached Charleston, it started to hum.

I needed to find Pike.

My physical expansion spread out over the Lowcountry of South Carolina, reaching into the outer limits of Charleston, merging with

the wetlands and egrets and brackish water. I focused, feeling everything in existence between my body and my destination and, with a
thought, relaxed into the ether and felt my body dissolve one more
time.

I came together in front of the high school. The front doors were
open; students were frozen in mid-stride. School was out.

I SOLIDIFIED inside the grassy circle of the turnabout, where buses
were lined up. Three flagpoles were behind me. The flags were swept
in a nonexistent breeze, as if molded from bronze.

The sun was partially obscured by broken clouds. There was no
way to measure the amount of time I spent in the timeslice, but I had
grown accustomed to the sound of my breath and footsteps; absent
were the sounds of daily living. *Did I even need to breathe?*

Slowly, the fragrance of grass and the sounds of people intensified
as I returned to normal time and molecules began to drift. The flags
snapped overhead and the first bus in line began to creep ahead.
Shouts and playful screaming started slow and came to full speed as
my body synchronized with Earth's regular time and those that lived
in it.

Hundreds of students fled for freedom, racing into the parking
lots, their thoughts a random collage of desires and fears, locked into
their identities of geeks or jocks or queens or studs, gearheads, burners, gamers or flamers. I felt their lungs expand and vocal cords
vibrate. I absorbed their concerns about parties and clubs, who was
doing what and who was dating who. I was a distant shadow that
tasted their experiences and absorbed the essence that was their life.

The natural tendency to steal their essence was suddenly repul-
sive. I might not be human, but I wouldn't become Fetter. I had to
stop.

In the mix of it all, a pair of girls came out to the flagpoles and
began winding down the flags. Shannon Quigley and Stacy Parker,
they'd been best friends since second grade, spending the night with

each other almost every weekend. Right now, Stacy wanted Charlie Nelson to ask her to prom and Shannon was secretly jealous, hoping he wouldn't but telling Stacy something supportive because that's what best friends do. But if she got a date—

I snapped back. I was already siphoning their essence again, along with their thoughts and memories.

They lowered the flags, not a foot away from me. They didn't notice me or my shadow next to theirs. They were folding the flags and on the topic of homework when I felt Chute. She was on the second floor, coming down the steps with two friends, holding her books to her chest. She slowed down as she approached the bottleneck at the front doors, past the security guards.

There she is.

She lit up the yard like another sun, her essence beaming brightly, sinking warmly into my chest. My fading heartbeat quickened, as if remembering what it once was.

She laughed at something Suzy Keller on her left said, then looked at Jonie White on her right. Chute's ponytail whipped from one shoulder to the next. They stopped at the curb and looked in both directions. The buses were loaded and gone. Cars honked and Denny Stillbee hung out the window of his car. Chute and the girls laughed. I felt her joy inside me. And as the yard cleared, I watched her walk with her friends to the parking lot. Suzy was going to take her home. Cars passed between us. She was almost out of sight. I was going to let her go. But then she stopped.

My chest thumped.

She tipped her head, unsure of what she saw. It was what she felt that made her turn around and look. She shaded her eyes, searching. I don't remember becoming visible, but somehow she saw me. She called over her shoulder to Suzy to hang on a second, she'd be right back. When she crossed the roundabout road, she ran.

She jumped into my arms. I tightened, afraid she would see me for what I was. But her essence was so intoxicating I forgot for an instant that my world had imploded.

"Are you picking me up?" she asked.

I put her down and she grabbed my hand. I backed up, but she pulled my hand to her. It must've been the look on my face that changed the energetic colors around her. Her essence suddenly contracted and soured.

"Are you all right?" she asked.

I lightly jerked my hand from her grip, hiding the new fingers behind my back like it was all the evidence she needed. The slashing weapon. Fingers falling.

LIAR.

I backed up a step.

"Why are you acting so weird?" she asked. "Did I do something?"

"No." I took her hand with my other hand. "You didn't do... everything's all right. I'm just a little tired, that's all."

"Well, what're you doing here?"

"I just wanted to see you. And talk to Streeter."

"He's in the virtualmode lab, as usual." She pointed at the front doors. "You'll have to call him, security won't let you back in the school."

Amanda Flenner shouted at Chute, said something about leading the student cabinet meeting next week. Chute hollered back. Her complexion was so fair, the freckles highlighted on her smooth cheeks. The skin crinkled between her eyes when she laughed.

She reached out without turning while talking to Amanda and hooked her finger with mine. I stared at our hands, recalling the vision of when we were older. *Not all visions come true.*

"So, are you taking me to the Garrison?" she said, swinging our hands back and forth.

"What?"

"I'm going to play tagghet with the kids today, remember? Spindle was going to pick me up at my house, he didn't think you'd be back yet." She shrugged girlishly. "I'm so happy you're back."

"I, uh, no, I forgot. I'm sorry, I just went through a lot today. There's a lot on my mind."

"Did your meeting go bad?"

"It wasn't good."

"I'm sorry. Maybe we can go out and cheer you up. I was talking to Janette and she wants the four of us to go out. We could do it tomorrow!"

Suzy pulled through the roundabout and honked, looked at Chute strangely and said, "What're you doing, talking to flagpoles?"

"Oh, that's not nice," Chute said, not getting it.

"I got to go, I don't want to be late," she said. "Will you be at the Garrison later? I want to play with the grimmets and they're always more fun when you're around."

"Maybe," I said.

She kissed me on the corner of my mouth and frowned. "Are you sure you're all right? You're so cold."

I nodded and kissed her back.

Then watched her go.

It hurt when she left. The beating faded in my chest. The hum grew louder.

87

No Mask

"I JUST NEED to go to the office, man." It was Jake Studard, starting left tackle for the football team. He was trying to shoulder his way past the security guard. "Just call the coach, he'll explain."

"You call the coach." The security guard had played the same position ten years earlier; now he had three kids and a wife and a bit of a drinking problem. He wasn't budging. "It ain't my problem. Once you're out of the building, you stay out."

The security guard hooked his thumb in his belt. I slipped past him just as he stopped Meg Chansey with the crazy idea she could get back inside because she was class president.

The hallways were mostly empty. A few students hanging out at their lockers and a small group of teachers were outside the office. The essence of their experiences drifted into me, charging the hum in my chest. The three of them looked around like a ghost just passed.

I turned the corner and tread up the wide steps to the second floor. No one was within a hundred feet, except at the end of the hall, behind the vault door of the virtualmode lab. Four people were in there. My insatiable essence-hunger fled into the walls and lockers and classrooms, feeding on the memories of past students, their fears and apprehension, the joy of being asked to homecoming by the right guy or the panic of getting one's ass kicked after school. They saturated the wood like blood; buzzed inside me.

The door slid open and Mr. Buxbee walked into the hall, looking over his big round belly at the shiny floor as he semi-waddled toward me. His lower lip plumped out and he hummed a quiet tune, something he always did when few people were around. My favorite virtualmode instructor passed me without looking.

I stopped outside the door and stared at the scanlock, where a key could be waved. Not many keys were given out to that room. The gear inside was worth more than the entire school. I could feel the circuits inside the lock and followed them with my mind. I didn't need a key. I simply asked the door to open. And it did.

The room was half the size of a regular classroom and twice as cold to keep the gear from overheating. Workbenches lined the walls. A large silver table was centered in the middle. Streeter and Janette stood on each side of it, staring at the half-spherical black object, their hands pressed flat on the table, mumbling to each other a checklist before they tested the locator again. They didn't look up, consumed with the project at hand, assuming I was Buxbee returning for something he forgot.

Slowly, I allowed them to see me.

"Holy shit!" Streeter stepped back. "How'd you... when did you get here?"

"My meeting ended." My voice was eerily quiet.

He came over, hand out, and slapped it into mine, clasping his other hand over it and shaking. I automatically felt a connection with him. He felt a tug in his belly. I let go of him before I started sipping on his essence, but not before he shook his head, a little dizzy, not sure what just happened.

"I need a favor," I said.

"All you got to do is ask." He stepped back, rubbing his stomach. "Give me a second, I'll get the technician started on a setup."

Buxbee's assistant, Peter Hammel, had a college degree in networking and virtualmode world-building. And Streeter was telling him what to do. Peter didn't seem to mind. Janette was listening, making sure she understood what they were doing.

I wandered to the wall, where a shelf displayed several awards. Five of them recognized the school's exceptional development of virtualmode training and execution, which was primarily because of Buxbee, but two had Streeter's name. The larger of the two awards was a three-dimensional prism. I took it down, the colors switching through the transparent surface. *State Champion Codebreaker.* Best high school codebreaker in South Carolina. Did he know his endless potential?

"He talks about you all the time." Janette stared at the glittering trophy. "Socket this, Socket that. I wish he would talk about me the way he talks about you."

I looked into the award like it contained the lifetime of memories with Streeter, each one more entertaining than the next. I wished I could put those memories inside her so that she could feel the same joy.

"What's so funny?" she asked.

I didn't realize I was grinning, so I shared a memory with her. I told her when we were in kindergarten, we stayed the night at each other's house so much that we each had our favorite cereal at each house. We'd be buried behind our box on each side of the table, slurping milk and reading the back of the box for the hundredth time. I was a Corn Pops kid. He was Fruity Pebbles.

"I'm glad you're around to keep an eye on him," I said.

"Why? Where are you going?"

I took a long breath. "I'm not sure."

We stared at the awards for a while longer; then she tugged me away to the table and told me about their progress with the locator. It was on a little stand. Their appointment with NASA was only a week away and, aside from when it screwed up with me, it had been operating flawlessly. It could also mean a lot of money. She opened a holographic circuitry layout that stretched over the table.

"What's up?" Streeter walked up.

"Just showing Socket the locator plans."

"Socket could figure this stuff out in his head," Streeter said. "You wouldn't believe what he can do."

Neither would you.

"So what's the favor?" Streeter asked.

"I'm sorry, Janette, but can I speak to Streeter alone?"

"Yeah, oh, sure... I can, I'll just be... I'll go—"

"If you want to help Peter, I'm not sure he fully understands what I need him to do," Streeter said. "We probably won't be long."

She said goodbye, grabbed her things and left. I paced around the table, thinking where to start. How to start.

"You all right?" Streeter asked.

"I would never ask you for this if it wasn't important."

"Well, what is it? You need money? Help codebreaking?"

"I just need to use the school's virtualmode portal."

"That's it? That's not a big favor."

"I might snap some alarms."

He cocked his head. "What kind of alarms?"

"I'm not sure, but it might get you in trouble."

"I'm always up for trouble." But he drummed his fingers on the table. "Is it that important?"

"I wouldn't ask."

He nodded. And drummed. Then pointed at one of the oversized chairs against the wall. "You can't do anything I can't handle. Have a seat."

"I'll stand."

"All right." He laughed nervously, then said with a squeaky tone, "Should I be freaking out about now?"

Yes. "I'll explain in a minute."

"That's not helping."

"Sorry."

He considered again. Anyone else in the world and he would've called security. Instead, he sat at the mainframe monitor. "I'll get the transporters ready."

"No need."

He looked over his shoulder. "You still have the imbed transporter in your neck?"

"I'll explain later. Promise."

"Sure." He spun on the seat and crossed his arms. "Then launch when you're ready."

I didn't need the transporters or any sort of gear. In fact, I really didn't need to ask Streeter to use the school's virtualmode portal, but I didn't want to get him in trouble without him knowing. I'd already penetrated the entire lab and followed the circuitry and routers down to the school's portal that powered the virtualmode experience that communicated with millions of portals all over the world like a network of ethereal pipelines, where people existed in virtual reality.

I only needed the portal to access the Internet network so I could spread my influence worldwide, like pouring my consciousness into a system of veins. I wouldn't be able to expand as far without it. I needed to feel everything, searching for the one person that could answer my questions. I moved my awareness through the portal and instantly stretched across the planet, knowing and feeling everything without leaving my body. I closed my eyes, whispering his name.

Pike.

His essence was as unique as his fingerprint. I could distinguish the difference between every person, every machine, everything that was operating on the worldwide virtualmode network. Suddenly, the school's portal contracted.

"Artificial intelligence has breached virtualmode."

I forced it to open back up, sniffing the mental realm like a bloodhound. I was around the world in a second, sensing a strong presence somewhere in a mountainous region. I focused my attention, brought Pike's essence into view, and homed in on his location. It was a dead end.

The Garrison.

No way he was in the Garrison. I was sensing the leftover memories of where he spent most of his life. There was little chance I would find him, even with the inexhaustible power I had. The Paladins would have him so secluded that no one could locate him.

I contracted back into my body. Lights were flashing everywhere, along with flickering sounds and high-pitched alarms. The lab door swooshed open and Buxbee and Peter came rushing inside. Streeter was already at the mainframe monitor, shouting that he had it under control. I willed the alarms to quiet and restored the original status of the security. Streeter explained the crossover error of the locator and apologized. He threw the locator in his pocket and promised to work on the coding outside the lab. Buxbee stared at him; then he and Peter turned back to the monitor to assure the integrity.

Streeter grabbed my arm and marched into the hallway. "You want to tell me what's going on?"

88

LOCATED

I FOLLOWED Streeter to the elevator, but not before a security guard named Jeff Baker stopped him. "You got a pass?" he asked.

Streeter flashed the badge strung around his neck. "Um, we're going to the library."

The security guard looked around. "Who's we?"

Streeter shrugged.

"Better check in with Mr. Buxbee if you go anywhere else," Jeff said.

We took the elevator up two flights to the top floor. Streeter's leg shook while we waited. We stepped into the circular floor of the library situated on top of the school's tower with windows in all directions. The librarians, still talking in hushed tones even though the floor was empty, looked at Streeter as we exited the elevator. Streeter held up his badge. They went back to talking.

We headed straight for a back room. The windows were wide and clear, overlooking a long wide field stretching out toward the interstate. The football field was to the left and the tagghet stadium to the right, but between them was a view of the live oaks beyond.

He paced back and forth, muttering to himself while his fingers twittered at his side. It didn't seem like a good idea to tell him the truth, but somehow I owed it to him. Someone should know. I just needed to get it out of me.

"I've known you forever," I said. "You should know this."

"Know what?"

"Have a seat." I pointed at the cushioned chair positioned in front of the window.

"Why? What're you going to do?"

"Just sit down, will you? You don't want to be standing when I show you this."

He sat down slowly, not taking his eyes off me. "Show me what?"

"Relax, this isn't going to hurt. But it might freak you out a bit."

Tension gripped his body. His muscles were rigid, like I was going to pull a tooth. Lactic acid dumped into his muscles; his body quivered. I had been holding myself tightly wound up, avoiding merging with the people around me, avoiding siphoning their essence, but now I released it, feeling the carpet below my feet, the furniture and dry paper in the books. My awareness exploded outside the window, all the way to the interstate and the cars speeding toward Charleston.

But I focused on Streeter, his eyes wide open. I willed his body to relax, his mind to open and accept the coming vision. What he saw, what he felt, was the humming in my chest, the regeneration of my fingers and the revelation of my true nature. He saw Pivot tell me I was cloned from a human, that I was created to help him avenge Fetter.

I receded from his consciousness, forcing myself to disconnect from the sweet taste of his essence that whirled in my belly. Forced myself not to take from him or anything else within my reach, even though it filled me and tingled inside.

His fingers did not nervously twitter. His leg didn't bounce. Instead, he looked at me with a soft expression, then stood, slowly came over and took my hand. He turned it over, studying the back of the light-colored flesh and looked at the palm.

"Are you playing with me?" he asked.

"I wish I were."

He went to the window and leaned his forehead against it. His breath was short. A lightness surged into his experience. His foot slipped off the windowsill and his head began to slide across the glass. I caught him before he fell. It was too much. I should've just told him, giving him a vision was too surreal. Even though he'd known me all his life, saw me when I first sliced time and read thoughts, when I became a Paladin and developed telekinesis, still he was having trouble assimilating this. Even after everything we'd been through, this was a lot.

I placed him in the chair and allowed myself to get inside his mind again, this time blotting out some of the detail. I left a faint memory of my true nature: I am not human, I'm a product. *Congratulations, your best friend is a duplicate!*

He fidgeted after a few minutes, snorted from a short nap and smacked his lips. I was gazing out the window when he opened his eyes. It took a bit for his awareness to catch up to the present moment and the truth of what he was looking at. He was watching me. He considered running. I couldn't blame him. After all that time together, he didn't owe me anything. Maybe he should run.

He leaned forward, then slowly stood and walked next to me. We watched the traffic in the distance, all driving somewhere so unimportant. He propped his leg onto the windowsill and pointed toward the football stadium, leaving a smudge on the glass.

"Remember our first day of school? Jared Miles shoved me down the steps during gym and you pummeled him right there in the bleachers, right in front of the coach and everybody. You remember that?"

"Got suspended three days."

"And he never messed with me again." His eyes darted around. Memories flipped through his mind. "You remember, over there?

Remember when Alex Deeter dared me to moon the lacrosse team at practice? You remember that?"

"They came after you with sticks."

"Yeah, and you stood up to all of them."

"They would've beat me senseless if the coach didn't stop them."

"But you took the blame."

"I have a higher pain tolerance."

He tapped the window, punctuating a set of memories as if to validate this moment, to anchor his beliefs about who he was. Who I was. Then he stepped away, scratching his chin. I leaned back against the window, letting my head bump against the glass.

Then he said, decisively, "I know who you are, goddamnit."

"I showed you the truth."

"That's not what I mean. I don't care *what* you are. I've known you all my life. You're Socket." He stopped pacing. "Socket Greeny."

He resumed looking out the window. The moments stretched out, silently. The librarians were talking louder now, mostly about Tommy Fletcher and how he needed to get counseling for his severe attention deficit disorder.

Streeter turned his head. "So what now?"

I shrugged.

"You going to the Garrison?"

"No, it'll just be madness if I go back. I mean, if your alarm system recognized me, I'm not going to make it within a hundred yards before a dozen crawler guards gang-tackle me."

"You can come to my house."

"I... no. Not a good idea."

"Why not? No one will know you're there. Besides, you got to eat."

No, I don't. "It's not that. I'm... evolving into something, I think. I don't think it would be a good idea if you were around me until I figure it out."

"What? You mean, you're becoming one of them?" *He meant duplicate.* "You planning on taking over the human race?"

No, it was the temptation that bothered me. The taste of his essence lingered around me like an addiction. Like a shark smelling blood. I could resist, but for how long?

I faced him. "You feel that in your belly?"

He rubbed his stomach, sensing the fear of falling, the removal of his essence as I let myself for just a moment reconnect with him, automatically absorbing his essence, leaving him with the twisted missing sensation of a void.

"I think I'm stealing from you," I said. "Kind of like charging my battery with your... life."

He tensed. "Dude, that's cold."

"Sorry."

"Can you stop?"

"Yeah, but... I don't know for how long. I just need to go somewhere with no one around, just for a while, anyway."

The sun hung lower in the sky. Streeter didn't run, but he didn't take his hand away from his stomach, either. His mind was working. After a long minute, he said, "I know where you need to go."

"The North Pole?"

"You need to find your clone."

Now I laughed. Streeter was mentally tough; he assimilated more than I gave him credit for. "I have no idea where he's at."

"I know exactly where he's at." He pulled the locator from his pocket and, fearlessly, took both my hands and placed it in my palms. "Do it again, like you did at the tagghet ceremony. Locate yourself in time and space."

I turned it over and saw my distorted reflection in the black convex surface. It invited me to connect with it, almost like it was thinking to me. *Like we speak the same language.*

"Go on." Streeter nudged me. "Do it."

He had rewritten the code; it was tighter and more efficient, merging with my consciousness as I opened to it. A holographic planet projected from the surface, rotating between us.

"He's there." He stuck his finger on the spot of light in the middle of Illinois. "When you used this at the ceremony, in front of all those people, it knew you were just a copy, it found the original."

A copy. I cringed.

"It worked," he said. "The whole time, it was working."

My chest fluttered. He was right, the locator simply considered me a mirror projected from the original identity. Streeter had done it.

"You should go."

I looked up. "Why?"

"Why? He's you. You're him. You've been separated from who you are all your life. You've got to go see if something will happen."

"Like what?"

"I don't know! What else are you going to do, sit in the desert and meditate the rest of your life? Just go and find out."

Suddenly, I didn't feel in control of anything. And that was my answer. I wasn't in control; I was swept into the current of the unknown, flowing with the mystery of life. I handed the locator back to Streeter. "You're right."

"Hell yeah, I'm right. You can use my car, if you want. I'll tell my gramma you need it for a couple days. She won't care."

"I won't need it."

"Are you kidding me? Illinois is like eight hundred miles away unless you've got a ship or something out there in the trees." He looked out the window. "Do you?"

I looked at him. He'd really like to know.

"I'm right, aren't I? Or do you have some kind of teleportation thing." His eyes were wide. "You've got teleportation?"

Maybe I shouldn't do it, I didn't want to overload him again. But he'd want to see it. I held up my hand and let it dissolve. My fingers were the first to fall away, dissolving into the air, followed by my hand, wrist and arm. I gathered the molecules at my waist and my arm reappeared.

"That is badass." He stared at my arm, blinking heavily. The overload was dulling his consciousness again.

"I got to go, Streeter." I washed the thoughts from his immediate awareness, but let him keep the memory for later digestion.

"Am I going to see you again?"

"I don't know."

We shook hands, fingers up; then I jerked him close and we hugged, patting each other's backs with our free hands. "You should probably get back to Janette."

"Yeah," he said. "I should, you know." He took a long look, not convinced it wouldn't be the last time he ever saw me, then started away. I'd wait until he was long gone before I leaped. He stopped at the bookshelf and turned.

"Thanks, Socket."

"For what?"

"Just, you know. Glad you were here. That's all."

He left before I could say anything. *Glad to be here, Streeter.*

89

Civil Wars

A LIBRARIAN HAD COME BACK to make sure no other students were around, but I had dissolved before she turned the corner. I gathered far past Interstate 26, near Monck's Corner and Highway 52, and sliced time to a standstill.

I walked the country roads and sometimes went straight through the wetlands. Whenever I felt people within my influence, I turned away. I didn't want to be tempted to draw on their life. I trusted myself less and less, having visions I would leave a wasteland of bodies in my wake. Even the slightest attempt to expand my awareness out like a shrimp net to locate Pike put people into my influence and an immediate download of their essence. Perhaps vampires did exist. We didn't drink blood. Just essence.

Pike was out there. I could sense him, just couldn't locate him, unlike my original, my *brother;* I had locked onto his location from eight hundred miles away. He was in Tannerville, Illinois. Population, 12,132. I didn't know his name, but excluding some terrible accident, I assumed he looked like me.

For much of the trip, I saw nothing and heard only the path beneath my feet. I worked my way to the heartland of the Midwest, up through southern Illinois to the central part, where the hills turned flat and the grass was replaced by rows of corn and soybeans. Enormous combine tractors were in the fields in the midst of harvesting another season, a cloud of dust suspended over the long mechanical teeth that would be chopping and stripping the kernels from the cobs once I emerged from the timeslice.

The sun slowly moved higher in the sky, not because time was moving. I walked westerly, from the Eastern Time Zone to Central. A trip in regular time would've taken months, but I arrived on the outskirts of Tannerville at the exact moment I left Charleston. Some twenty miles south of Springfield, I stood on Route 29, looking at a sign: *AAAA Girls Basketball State Champions*. I walked near a car travelling sixty miles an hour back in ordinary time; now it was standing still. The license plate read Land of Lincoln.

Abraham Lincoln, the president that freed the slaves.

I grew up in the South, where President Lincoln was viewed as a war criminal, by some. Others refused to call it the Civil War. *There was nothing civil about it.* It was the War of Northern Aggression. Even had a history teacher that refused to use the textbook because it was written by Yankees. And here I was, in the Land of Lincoln. My original self, raised in the North. North versus South, the Civil War; a conflict fought long ago, but the scars still remained.

I returned to ordinary time.

I WAS GREETED with the sounds of blackbirds and the distant roar of tractors. Hundreds of feet below, I sensed the coal mine and the men in hardhats and smudged faces, putting in hard hours to pull black rock from the ground. And as they mined the coal, I felt their essence slowly pull towards me, like metal shavings to a magnet. I focused on being centered, but I could only slow the draw. Eventually, I wouldn't even be able to do that.

I couldn't avoid people now. I walked past small gas stations and Walmart, McDonald's and car dealers, and onto the town square with a clock tower rising from the courthouse. Teenagers hung out by their cars and small business owners hustled inside the clothing stores and jewelry shops. The asphalt road turned to bricks, a town as old as farming.

A couple miles from that, the street ended at a two-story white house. It felt like a blank in my consciousness, like it was somehow blocked. Still, I knew he was there.

I stopped at the curb near the mailbox that read *Teck Family*. My stomach fluttered. An old concrete sidewalk led straight to the wide front steps, and at the foot of those steps a girl was doodling with sidewalk chalk. She was singing a song, making up the words as she went. It was a story about a monster that fell in love with a little girl. The monster lived under the bed and he was angry she didn't love him back.

"I don't talk to strangers," she said and went back to drawing with a yellow piece of chalk.

"That's a good idea."

She was humming. I walked gently up the sidewalk and squatted next to her. Her mind was so open and innocent, but I wasn't compelled to draw from her essence, as if the compulsion halted inside a bubble around this house. A warm peacefulness settled in my stomach, relieved I didn't have to focus on restraining myself from taking, that I could just be in this moment.

"What are you drawing?" I asked.

"That's Saucy." She pointed at the girl with big ears and pigtails. "And that's Greg. He's got big teeth." She drew even bigger, sharper teeth on Greg the monster next to Saucy, his mouth open and slobbery.

"He looks mean," I said.

"He can be."

She colored Greg's teeth yellow with big drops of purple stuff dripping off them, humming as she did. She didn't look up, but asked, "Where're you from?"

"Me? I'm from faaaaaar away."

"I'm not four." She frowned at me. "I'm seven years old. You don't have to talk to me like a baby."

"Sorry."

She stared at me curiously; then I quickly realized I might look exactly like my original, so I quickly warped my features in her vision, as if she saw my face in a carnival mirror.

"Are you an alien?" she asked.

"What if I am?"

"Then you look pretty normal. For an alien."

"What if I said I wasn't human?"

She shrugged. "Saucy's not human, even though she looks like it. She's my best friend."

Now she was coloring her imaginary friend's hair green. She clapped the dust off her hands and grabbed the thick blue sidewalk chalk and colored Saucy's shoes and started humming again.

"Want to know a secret?" she asked.

"Always."

"Scott got in a fight today."

"Who's Scott?"

"My brother, silly." Her rapid giggle was contagious. "You're here to see him."

"I am?"

"You kind of look like him, you know." She squinted at me with her tongue stuck between her lips. "Well, you do if I do this."

She was giggling again and I couldn't help laughing a little. The essence of joy bubbled between us and it made her laugh harder.

The front door jiggled. "Maddi," her mother called through the screen door. "Time to eat. Go wash up."

Maddi smacked her hands again and ran up the wooden steps, past her mother holding the door open. The letter T was in the middle of the screen door. It rattled in the frame as she let it close. "Can I help you?" the mother asked.

"Yes, ma'am. I, uh, was just... uh." I grabbed the railing for support, suddenly dizzy. A powerful force surged from her, gushing inside me. It wasn't her essence. I didn't know what it was. And I couldn't read her. I knew nothing about her, not even her name. She could sense the power exchange, and she could sense that I was sensing her sensing me, a loop of self-generating energy, a fusion that was disorienting us both.

"He's here to see Scott, Mama," Maddi said.

Her mother rubbed Maddi's head and whispered for her to go clean up. "Have we met?" the mother asked.

"Um, no—no, ma'am." I stepped lightly up the steps. "I'm kind of new in town. I'm in Scott's class and I, uh, he said I could stop by if I needed help with a project."

Her hair was short, like my mother's, but her hips were wide and her skin sunbaked. She stared intensely and I quickly gathered my focus to distort the perception of my features or she'd be staring at an exact copy of her son. Still, there was nothing I could do about my personal energy she experienced. I felt familiar. Like family.

"There's a school project, ma'am," I said. "Scott's my partner."

"Okay." She opened the door and suddenly smiled. "Well, sure, come in. Come in."

"Thank you."

I stepped inside. A hallway led straight from the front door through an entertainment room to the kitchen in the very back, where the aroma of homemade spaghetti filled the house. To the right was a formal living room with light blue walls and expensive, clean furniture. The staircase to the upstairs was on the left, went up next to the wall and then turned right along that wall so that I could see part of the upstairs. Pictures covered the walls below the steps.

Maddi leaned against her mother's leg. "Would you get Scott, dear?" her mother asked.

Maddi watched me on her way to the bottom step, then took a deep breath and shouted, "SCOTT!"

Her mother winced. "Maddi?"

Maddi looked back and rolled her eyes. She walked up the stairs, one step at a time, sliding her hand on the polished railing and watching me as she went.

"If you'll excuse me," the mother said. "Scott will be right down."

Hard music leaked from upstairs when a door opened. Maddi's voice was lost in the beat and a deeper voice responded. They were bickering about something other than the stranger downstairs waiting for him. Maybe Maddi forgot why she went up.

I went to the wall and the wooden floor creaked. The pictures were randomly framed and placed. The last twenty years were captured in photos, starting with a wedding picture, followed by babies and grandparents holding a baby and mother at a baseball game and kids swimming in a pool and someone blowing out candles. The frames were dusty and the glass was cracked on a particular one. The picture was somewhat recent.

It was the mother and father standing at the top of the Grand Canyon. The father was holding Maddi when she was only two years old, her hair lighter and curlier, sucking her thumb. The mother had her hands on the shoulders of their son; he was wearing a baseball cap and sunglasses. They were smiling, but not the smile one gives when someone counts to three and they all shout cheese. No, it was like someone said something really, really funny and the smiles came from way down deep.

I touched the glass, dragging a track through the dust, as if I could plug into the joy emanating from a moment captured in time.

The steps thumped like a bowling ball was bouncing down and Maddi went running past, grabbing the post at the bottom and slingshotting past me toward the kitchen, moaning out the word, "Mooooom."

The music cut off and a door shut upstairs. The steps groaned differently this time. One at a time. I stepped back toward the door. Scott slid his hand as he took each step deliberately, turning the corner midway and looking at me.

A magnetic force pulled at my stomach. And the closer he got, the stronger it became. It vibrated from my core, chattering in my teeth and under my tongue. The force grew stronger as he reached the bottom step, gushing inside like I was drinking from a fire hydrant. I bumped into the door behind me and grabbed the knob.

It's me.

Every detail. The dour expression. The slight bend in his nose. The relaxed demeanor of his eyes, it was all me. Except for the hair. He had normal brown hair.

He stopped at the bottom step. I held onto the door, afraid I'd be pulled against him. *Is this what it feels like to have the essence sucked out of you?*

Shock suddenly opened his eyes a bit wider. He was looking at himself standing in the foyer. I looked down, centered my focus, and drew on whatever power I could find to project the illusion of different features. I had to stay focused, or all of them would be looking at Scott's identical twin. When I looked up, the tension eased on his face. He blinked, reset himself, still not sure what was happening. I couldn't tell if he was experiencing what I was feeling. I didn't know anything. I couldn't see his thoughts or motivation or memories. He was completely unknown, yet his presence was overwhelming me.

"Hey, uh, Scott." I squeezed the doorknob tighter. "You remember... in class, sociology class, we got paired up to do the, uh..." I swallowed. "The project?"

I projected a thought in his direction, hoping it would plant in his mind like a memory, of me sitting behind him in a class that felt like sociology. I couldn't feel his mind, where it began or ended, I could only throw out the suggestion like slinging a dart through the dark, hoping to hit the bull's-eye.

He blinked. "Um..."

"Good, sure. Well, I was wondering if, you know, you had some time to get it out of the way because I've got..." I pointed my thumb behind me, gesturing like there were things to do.

He looked down, working hard to recall the project and school, like a dream that begged to be remembered but he wasn't really sure if it happened or not. I worked harder at projecting that thought, attempting to make it solid and real. He was getting it, but not believing it.

"Scott, time to eat." His mother stepped between us.

Scott stared at her, trying to wake up.

"Scott?" she said. "Are you all right?"

He looked at her, back to me. I was losing him. He was scattered, trying to make sense out of his thoughts and the new ones trying to convince him of a new reality. In one last effort, I threw all my energy into the new reality. *I'm a new student; I sit behind you. We're working on a project. I look nothing like you. I am not you.*

I AM NOT YOU.

He licked his lips and then clarity settled in. He smiled. "Sure, um, yeah. I'm all right."

His mother smiled, then looked at me. "What's your name?"

"My name is Socket."

"You want to stay for dinner, Socket?"

Scott watched her invite me, then waited for an answer. Like his mother, he was clear-eyed and settled. They accepted the new reality.

"That's very kind of you," I said.

"Very nice." She started for the kitchen. Scott nodded with a sly smile. I paused at the pictures, gazing once more at the Grand Canyon, and recognized the smile looking back.

Like one of the family.

90

A Big Bang

THERE WERE two dogs in the backyard. They'd dug holes near a shed, white paint peeling from the walls, and looked half dead in the shade. I sensed their exhaustion and dreamy thoughts, their legs twitching in a long afternoon nap. Beyond that a pasture was enclosed by an old wooden fence and three horses grazed at the back of the property. Stables were on the other side of the shed and a smaller fenced area with chickens and goats inside.

I was surprised by my level of comfort. My world was standing on its head, but here, inside this house, I didn't feel like an alien. I felt like I was home, like I'd known these people all my life.

Maddi was slopping a spoonful of spaghetti sauce over a mountain of noodles, her eyes big and hungry. Scott was at the table, waiting for the rest of the family. Their mother was near the sink, filling a plastic cup with apple juice.

"What would you like to drink, Socket?" she asked.

"Sweet tea?"

"What's sweet tea?" Maddi asked.

"Um, it's tea with sugar."

"Well, then why don't you just add sugar?"

"I can do that," I said.

Her mother put a tall glass of tea at the table setting next to Scott, along with a bowl of sugar. "Go ahead, Socket, help yourself to some food."

There was no need to eat. I had no appetite. But I got myself a small helping, savoring the scent of homemade sauce. It wasn't so much the spices and tomato sauce that I savored, but the effort that went into making it. The entire house had a special energy, one that was lived-in, the intermingling of a family essence that wove tightly through the walls.

They were waiting for me to sit. Maddi already had noodles spun on her fork. As soon as my butt hit the chair, they were in her mouth. The meal began. There was another setting at the head of the table, like someone else was coming but not until later.

Things were spinning, like I was the one in an alternate reality, eating next to my identical twin. It could be easy to forget I didn't belong. Easy to believe I didn't really exist, but I let myself believe it. For the moment, I belonged.

There was nothing but the sound of knives on plates and spinning forks. Scott ate without issue. Maddi was moaning with each bite, eyeballing me. I slowly cut the noodles and pushed the food around. I wasn't fooling her, so I took a bite.

"You know, it's kind of weird that Scott's friend is eating with us," Maddi said. "I mean, we just met him."

"Mind your manners, dear," the mother said.

"I'm just *saaaaaying...*" she sang.

The mother stopped chewing and glared. Maddi slurped a noodle into her mouth like a worm running for cover. I smiled at her and she laughed, splashing sauce all over her lips.

"Where are you from, Socket?" the mother asked.

"South Carolina."

"I thought you sounded a bit Southern."

"Yes, ma'am."

"Is Socket a Southern name?" Maddi asked.

"I don't believe so."

"Well, if you were born there, why don't you have a Southern name?"

Because I wasn't born. I shrugged.

"You know what your name sounds like?" Maddi said. "Like Scott's name."

Her mother stopped chewing and thought about it. "Oh, yes, you're right, Maddi. It does sound like it."

I frowned, thinking also, but coming up blank. "Ma'am?"

"Scott Teck," she said. "Sock-et."

And there you go. Mystery solved over a plate of spaghetti. My name was an aberration of my original, a scrambling of sounds and letters. Perhaps I wasn't a weapon after all. Just a reflection.

"Isn't that odd, Scott?" the mother said.

He looked at me, taking another bite, nodding. I looked away, but not too quickly. I couldn't look into his eyes, it started the magnetic pull in my stomach, and each time it got stronger. I was able to resist as long as I wasn't looking at him. Fortunately, he was more interested in eating.

"What's your middle name?" the mother asked.

"Pablo."

"Oh, my gosh!" Maddi clapped and pointed at Scott. "Tell him your middle name, Scott. Tell him! Tell him!"

He hovered over his plate, noodles dangling, shaking his head.

"Scott doesn't like his middle name," the mother said.

"Can I tell him, Mama?" Maddi asked, bouncing. "Can I? Can I?"

"Picasso," Scott said. "My middle name is Picasso, isn't that awesome?"

Maddi slumped in her chair, about as much as I did. Pablo Picasso, one of humanity's most celebrated artists, a wellspring of creativity, the essence of being human. Would Pablo be whole without Picasso? Could something be creative if it was separated at birth?

And the hits just keep on coming.

"What's your project about?" the mother asked.

"Ma'am?"

"The school project?"

There was a moment when the family looked at each other, a moment where the new reality faltered and a stranger was sitting at the table. I got out of my thoughts and focused. "Project, oh, yeah," I said. "It's a sociology project. We're supposed to, uh, interview each other about family. You know, your parents and grandparents, where you were born, that sort of thing."

"That sounds interesting," she said. "You didn't tell me about this project, Scotty."

He shrugged, mouth full.

"We're *adooopted*." Maddi hunched over her plate with a devious smile, not asking for permission to give the answer this time. Her mother told her to pay attention to dinner and Maddi looked at me from the corners of her eyes, her feet thumping on her chair.

The back door in the pantry closed and the father marched into the kitchen. "Sorry, guys. My meeting ran late." He hung his keys on a rack next to the doorframe and went directly to the stove. While he shoveled food onto his plate, he looked out the window over the sink. "Mary Ellen? Did someone let the chickens out?"

"Oh, the gate must not have got closed," the mother said. "Maddi, can you get them?"

"I got to do everything." She dropped her fork on the plate.

"That's because you're Cinderella, honey." She whacked her on the fanny as she went out the back door. "How was the meeting, Joey?"

"You know meetings." The father sat down and started eating, saying with food in his mouth, "Who's our guest?"

The mother looked at Scott. He wiped his mouth. "Oh, he's a friend from school. Stopped by to work on a... project, I think. Um, his name is Socket."

Joey's arms were tan and hairy. The fatherly essence was rich and powerful. The energy in the room changed with his presence. It was stronger and tighter, enveloping the whole house. With him at the table, the family was complete. I was whole and unbroken.

"Have I met you?" he asked.

"No, sir."

"So, what kind of name is Socket?"

Maddi and the mother told him about my name and how it sounded like Scott Teck, and the father nodded and listened and laughed. Maddi told their father about the South and how they were learning about the Civil War at school and Scott got up to get more food. Fortunately, no one paid attention that my plate had hardly been touched, how I expertly scattered the food like I'd eaten as much as I could. Instead, I sat back and experienced the flow. The conversation soon turned to Maddi's classmate that threw up at recess and Scott's ex-girlfriend working at the grocery store and their mother's appointment at the church. The sorts of things families talked about at dinner, I supposed.

And I was there, right in the middle of it all.

MADDI HAD CLEARED off the table and piled the dishes in the sink, then went into the backyard with her parents. Scott filled the sink with soapy water and stacked the dishes on the counter.

"Dishwasher broke?" I asked.

"You're looking at the dishwasher." He threw a dishtowel over his shoulder.

"I'll wash if you dry," I said.

"Deal." He shifted to the left side of the sink. I stepped in his place and sank my hands into the warm soapy water, grabbed a plate and rubbed it clean with a soft sponge. Scott rinsed and dried and put it in the cabinet.

It was getting near dark outside. Our reflections were clear in the window that looked into the side yard. Mary Ellen and Joey were sitting in frayed lawn chairs, watching Maddi throw a slimy ball to the dogs. Scott hardly looked up, focused on the dishes coming his way. We were in sync, a washing tandem. Identical twins, the difference only in the color of hair. *Why the white hair? Was it an error in the cloning, or a hint at my transparency?*

How many times had I washed dishes, all alone, not knowing *I* was washing dishes somewhere else in the world? And now we were linked, our energy coupled like trains. His strength was growing, absorbing my own like I was doing to others, yet I couldn't tell if he could feel it. He didn't appear to be aware of anything other than the dishes and warm water, yet I experienced him as a massive star whose gravitational pull locked onto me, unable to free myself. It was only a matter of time before I was swallowed. I wasn't sad about that. Wasn't anything. It seemed that's the way things were supposed to be.

Maddi's laughter drifted through the window and the dogs barked. And I washed another bowl. Scott rinsed. For once, I wasn't saving the world. Maybe it was saving me.

SCOTT WENT TO HIS ROOM, upstairs to the left. *This is Scott's Room* was on the door. The walls were covered with pictures, mostly hard-edge bands in concert. He was at the desk, flipping the pages on a skateboard magazine with the likes of Josiah Gatlyn grinding a handrail and Benny Fairfax nailing something impossible.

"I can't wait until I'm done with school," he said.

"Where you going?"

"Anywhere but here." He turned the page.

It was completely dark outside. The lawn chairs were empty. It took everything I had to stand three feet away from Scott. The draw was undeniable. I was leaning away from him.

But it was no longer to be denied.

"I got to go," I said.

"What about the project?"

I turned and looked into his face. *My* face. *My* eyes. "It's just about done."

I stopped resisting and let go of the energy bundled in my stomach. It flowed like Hoover Dam had tumbled. The influx hit him in the gut. He convulsed like he was about to puke. His skin was quaking. He was draining me.

"What's... what's happening?" He couldn't get up, couldn't get away. He had to sit, to claim what was rightfully his. I was only his shadow, his reflection, and I had so much to give.

As the darkness crept over me, I extended my hand to shake. "Take it," I said.

His head was shaking.

But he wasn't looking at my hand, he was seeing my face. I could not pretend anymore. He saw my true nature, saw his own face looking back. Even if I wasn't real, if I was just a reflection, I was grateful to have had the opportunity to exist. To feel. To love. I didn't know what would happen when it was over, where I would go or what I would become. There was only this moment. And it had reached an end.

"Go on," I said. "It's all right."

Reality was breaking up; his mind began to quiver. But he held onto consciousness, not able to comprehend the impossible moment that appeared out of an ordinary day, his own self standing in his bedroom, reaching out.

His hand moved slowly. Darkness was taking my vision as it moved toward my open palm, as if I was dissolving from the physical world. As if I was returning to the great void of the moment. I did not see him take my hand. I did not feel his sweaty palm grip mine.

But I knew when it did.

It was an explosion.

My mind expanded like the Big Bang, scattering in all directions, through all the elements in a painless flight.

I did not see. Did not smell. But I was aware. Felt my life drain away from my body, through my hand and into Scott. He absorbed what was rightfully his. He was the original face. My memories would be his. My life was his.

He would remember my father holding his hand at the fair, how he ate dinner with my mother, watched them bury my father, and the endless fights in South Carolina. How he fell in love with Chute. Every moment filled him, becoming his memories. It was his life, now.

And when I was empty, his memories began to leak into my awareness. I saw Scott's life, from the very beginning. I experienced memories, both conscious and subconscious, of his life from the very first breath he took. Felt his body slide from my mother's womb, the expansion of his chest and the blurry face of my mother hovering over him, her fulfilling nipple in his mouth and the warm embrace of my father.

And I felt the cold fate of his reality.

He was swept away, cuddled in a warm blanket that was no substitute for the woman who gave birth to him. He was too young to know that a blind man had plans for him, for all of us. Pivot took him far away, where he was adopted by a warm and loving family.

His life was not much different than mine; the struggles were similar, the details different. He was introverted and righteous, and carried a deep yearning to know the meaning of his life, always sensing something greater was out there, but found himself stuck in life's mundane moments.

He got very ill during a swine flu epidemic.

Fell out of a tree and broke his arm when he was ten.

Caught a twelve-pound bass in Tannerville Lake.

Hiked Pike's Peak in Colorado on a family vacation; had his own dirt bike; carried his sister home when she was hit with a rock, one he threw, her face covered with blood, the scar still above her left eye; won an art contest in third grade; stole a book from school; changed his grades; kissed a girl behind the garage...

His life settled in my awareness like a new body of water. Deep and clear. Still.

The darkness was calm.

And I remained. I was still there. I was still me, still intact.

Complete.

And my consciousness gathered back in Scott's room. Perhaps I disappeared during the experience. Or maybe I was there the entire time, experiencing it on another level. But when I returned, my feet were on the carpet and my hands at my sides. Scott was on the floor, his eyes rolled back and twitching.

I picked him up and laid him on his bed. Even in the solitude of unconsciousness, his mind was coping with the reality of his new memories, the awareness of his true birthright. He was only human.

You are more than human, Pivot told me. *No human could do what you have done, yet I needed a human to do it.*

I sat next to Scott. He was no longer a mystery, his mind completely available to me, for he was no longer separate. I moved my awareness inside his mind and soothed the conflict rumbling through his being, sorting through the new memories trying to find a place to be accepted. I gathered all those memories that he received from me and hid them in the darkness of his subconscious. One day, he would know them; when he was ready to see the truth, they would emerge, slowly. One at a time. But for now, he needed to just be Scott.

Thank you, I said to him. To me. Sleeping peacefully in his bed.

I peeked into Maddi's room, where she was sound asleep, squeezing a doll against her cheek with her thumb in her mouth, her tongue clicking.

I snuck downstairs, where their father was watching SportsCenter and mother was reading a magazine. They didn't hear the floorboards creaking as I stood unnoticed in the doorway, taking one last moment to experience the family essence centered in the room. I slipped outside, still unnoticed.

IN THE MIDDLE of the brick street, under the buzzing streetlight, I stood on a manhole cover. The stars filled the sky and night fell quietly on the small town of Tannerville. I took a deep breath, filling my lungs with the breath of the entire world, feeling its struggles, its pain and happiness, loss and gain, birth and death. The human essence contained the beauty of life, the essence of which contained darkness and light, the pure joy of life, hidden only by a lack of understanding. But it was there, not to be gotten, not something that was missing. Only something that needed to be seen.

And somewhere in the world, I felt every consciousness struggle with its own existence, each soul rightfully searching for itself. And among them, I sensed the awareness of Pivot, like he was everywhere, as if he had yet to gather his body in a particular place in space and time.

There was another presence out there. This being was intimately familiar, shining like a beacon, calling me to join him. He was in Charleston. And he was waiting for me to arrive. It was a bald man that walked freely down a sidewalk.

91

GAME CHANGER

DOWNTOWN CHARLESTON.

Tourists crowded the sidewalk, holding hands and walking casually past art studios, pausing in front of picture windows. They lined up outside Hyman's Seafood for a late bite or crowded at Kaminsky's for dessert. Just another night.

I was in front of the long market, the building painted mustard yellow and Charleston green. Pike was somewhere in the crowd, his presence scattered like a game of hide-and-seek.

A street vendor sawed away on a beat-up fiddle, curled up against the wall with a box of coins in front of him. Tourists occasionally stopped to toss in a bill, and the guy nodded curtly. I walked past him, looked down the street left of the market, and recalled the vision of when Pike walked free, trying to remember what side of the market he was on. But there were no details in the vision. Just the street. And the girl.

I closed my eyes and leaned against the building. He had been here already, I could feel him, but what was he waiting for? In the vision, it was dark and the streets were crowded with slow-moving traffic. A rickshaw bicycle rang a bell. And there was no fiddle playing, either.

"You want a rose?" A kid held out a palm leaf torn and folded to look like a beige rose. "Ten dollars for one, twenty for two."

"No, thanks," I said.

"All right, how about five dollars for one?"

The music had stopped. The musician's box was still on the sidewalk, filled with coins and his violin. A note was tucked between the strings. *Looking for me?*

Pike's presence was smeared on the paper like a fingerprint. He was disguising himself as the fiddle player, but how? I looked around and then closed my eyes, reaching out with my mind, feeling each individual presence mingle throughout the market. I felt their movements, their desires and fears, but none were Pike.

A stick poked between my fingers. I looked at the palm rose in my hand. The boy was twirling one. "You want to buy another?"

"I didn't buy this one."

"That guy over there bought it for you, said you looked lost, like you needed a friend. Said you'd buy another."

"Where?"

"Buy another and I tell you." He held the rose up to my face. "Ten bucks."

I knelt in front of him and gently took his shoulders. I knew his life, and it had been hard. But I couldn't change him, couldn't tap him with a magic wand to make it better. At the moment, I just needed to see what the man looked like and where he went. I scanned his recent memory and saw the man was bald with dark glasses, smiling at the kid like he was looking at someone else, like he knew I'd see the memory. *You're so close.*

I looked to the left side of the market again. There, along the sidewalk, people were hustling out of the way. I ran across the street, around traffic, between the parked rickshaws. Up ahead, the bald man. *Pike.* He scattered the crowd like a bad smell. And then my vision materialized.

The family and the little girl, pulling her gum out of her mouth, her mother chastising her for it, reaching down to yank her hand back, not seeing the little man whose force slammed into them. The father was thrown against a parking meter and his wife back into him, but the little girl's hand slipped from her grip. She tumbled into the road, in front of a car that was going too fast.

I cut into time, freezing it the instant the bumper reached her forehead, inches from splitting it open. I walked through the silent night and removed her from danger, laying her at her mother's feet.

Pike was gone, again.

I returned to normal time. The tires screeched. The mother screamed. A crowd gathered around the frightened girl crying on her mother's shoulder. I stood beneath the awning of the storefront where the owners rushed out to ask if anyone was hurt; they had already called the police. But the assailant was gone.

Suddenly, I caught a whiff of his presence floating on the wind. Across the street, he'd entered the long market, slipping beneath a canvas curtain. Traffic stopped. A cop had already arrived on foot, taking a description of the strange, bald man. I walked unnoticed between the cars, pulled the canvas aside and stepped inside.

During the day, it was crowded with vendors and tourists, but at night it was empty and lonely aside from a bird searching for a place to nest. The city sounds were muffled by the canvas walls. At the far end, near the side road that crossed between the buildings, a short man was hunkered over a fat woman and a display of sweetgrass baskets.

[Please, leave.] I planted the thought in the woman's mind.

She looked at me across the great distance. Months of hard work lay on the ground in front of her, and I was suggesting she leave them behind. Pike slowly turned his head, his black glasses like holes on his face.

"Do you mind?" he said. "WE'RE HAGGLING!"

The basket woman placed her bundle of grass on the ground and got up, dusting off her dress, and walked away.

"Great," Pike said. "That's just great. Do you know how hard it is to find a quality sweetgrass basket these days?" He shook a dark banded basket at me. "They weave these motherfuckers by hand and charge a ton of money. And she was going to give it to me for free. For free, you understand?"

He was a projection; that was why I couldn't locate him. There were no projectors around, so I didn't know how he was doing it, I just knew I couldn't locate him. I attempted to penetrate his image, follow it back to the source, but it was empty. Pike dropped the basket and spread his arms, as if to help.

"It's like magic, isn't it?" he said. "In case you're wondering, and I know you are, I'm taking advantage of the plethora, that's right I said plethora, of virtualmode portals in the downtown area. I'm using them to project this wonderful image in front of you." He spread his arms again. "It's a little trick you might learn one of these days, if you're lucky."

"Is this a game to you?"

"It's all a game, wouldn't you say?" He dropped his arms. "I mean, everything is useless, just a game for the gods. And where does it end, huh? Where does it all end, wonderboy? Because now you know the truth, don't you. You know who we're doing our little song and dance for." He pointed up.

He'd known all along. He knew I wasn't human. He knew Fetter was out there. Why hadn't I seen it before?

"Look at you," he said, clasping his hands over his heart, "all grown up and realized. You're a big boy now; your master must be proud. Is he? Is Papa Pivot happy that his boy is all grown up and out there saving the world?" He swung a left and right hook through the air. "You're out there fighting the good fight, looking for the bad people, eh?"

"He's not my master."

"Oh, but isn't he divine and wonderful? All pure of heart, like an angel sent from heaven to save the human race, wouldn't you say?"

"How did you know?"

"How did I know?" His piercing laughter bounced around the enclosed market. "How did I... oh, that's rich, wonderboy. How did I know? I knew from the second I saw you." The canvas walls fluttered. "I saw through you that very first day you came to the Garrison, wonderboy. All doe-eyed and goody, I smelled Pivot on you like a seven-day corpse."

"You've known all this time?"

"Who do you think I am? Seriously, for being wonderboy, you're not that bright—"

"You need to exit the market." A man stepped into view. "No one's allowed... "

Pike turned on the man, his anger impacting him like a wave of atomic heat. It was only the embrace of my mind around him that kept Pike's wrath from stripping his mind clean, but it still knocked him backwards and out of sight.

"You can't save them all," Pike said. "Besides, what's the point? They're all heading for the great black planet in heaven anyway. You only delay the inevitable."

"How could you know about all this? How could you elude the minders and the Paladins?"

"Everyone knows! Every one of these skinbags, these buckets of worm food, knows their life is futile, a waste of effort! They all know, wonderboy, right here, they feel it." He thumped his chest. "They know there's something wrong with their existence, that their gods are just playing them. They just refuse to face the fact that they're rats in the wheel."

"That's why you hate being human, is that it? You want to be absorbed by Fetter, just to get it over with."

"You still don't get it? You don't see?" He yanked off his glasses and marched closer, white eyes blazing in the dim light. "Let me know when you do."

I still couldn't feel him. *Couldn't feel him.* He had a presence, but no sensation of essence. But that could only mean... "You've already converted."

"Oh, you're getting warmer."

"You're a duplicate."

"You're red-hot!"

There had always been a mystery about Pike. They wouldn't kill him. He endured torture beyond what was humanly possible. He was never meant to survive, but he did. He always survived. Because...

"You've always been a duplicate."

"WE GOT A WINNER!" He whooped and hollered and leaped and danced, swinging his arms over his head in wild celebration.

Outside, the sirens rang out and voices crowded around the market. A few people peeked around the corner. A policeman walked inside with the father of the little girl. He nodded at Pike, who was now doing something of a foxtrot.

"Can I speak to you a moment, sir?" the policeman asked.

Pike stopped mid-step. He put on his black glasses and wiggled his eyebrows. He pursed his lips as the policeman slowed his approach, putting his hand on his sidearm, sensing danger.

"Sir, I need you to put your hands where I can see them!"

Pike drew a whistling breath between his lips. The temperature in the market suddenly dropped.

"I need you to—"

His face paled. And Pike drew deeper. The policeman dropped to his knees. Pike was drawing out the man's essence, absorbing it like a parasite. Then the crowd began shouting outside as he drew on them, too. People were falling, screaming. I felt them weaken and clutch their stomachs as they felt the essence of their lives siphoned away.

I stiffened, throwing out my awareness like a protective bubble, penetrating every person within a square mile, coating their consciousness like a membrane. Pike smacked his lips.

"It's like a cool, minty rush, isn't it?" He flicked his tongue under his cheeks and lips. "Tingles the tongue. You need to get some of that, wonderboy. There's only so much to go around."

He knelt next to the policeman struggling to breathe. "Would you be so kind as to leave us alone?" Pike asked. "We're having a private conversation. Thank you."

The policeman crawled away, pushing the canvas wall open and gasping for air.

"And tell your friends," Pike called through his hands. "We'll be done soon."

It was all I could do to contain Pike's influence. While I felt limitless in the desert, I felt more human since merging with Scott. Maybe since I wasn't stealing life, I was running out of it.

"Look at you." Pike walked near me and pretended to wipe a bead of sweat off my cheek. "You try so hard to save them. And for what?"

"They're real."

"Is that right?"

More sirens sang. Police were listening to the stories of what was going on. It wouldn't be long before they stormed inside.

"It stung when you discovered the truth, didn't it," he said sharply. "When you found out what you really are, it hurt. Am I right? One day, you're walking around, doing good, helping people, saving the world, making a difference, paving a path to heaven; then *thhhhhhppt,* you find out you're just a pawn." He pinched his fingers together. "Stings, just a bit."

"No more than watching you murder."

"They're already dead. They just don't know it."

"They're the reason I'm here."

"You're... you? You're here because of... oh, I get it." He wagged his finger over his head. "Yes, yes! Pivot created you to save them! Well, isn't that just grand and holy of him. Isn't that just divine, that he only thinks of them. Wouldn't you say, because he certainly doesn't care about you or any other pawn in his game." He ground his teeth. "We're all just pawns. The question is, do you want to keep playing?"

"You don't have to do this."

"Open your eyes, wonderboy! You're doing exactly what he wants you to do. It's all part of his plan, his great master plan to save the universe from the evil of humankind's very own creation."

"Fetter still exists."

"I know, I know." He waved me off. "You're the savior that brought her back, blah, blah, blah... Why do you think I let you live, huh?"

"YOU, IN THE MARKET." A policeman's voice crackled over a

speaker. *"YOU NEED TO COME OUT WITH YOUR HANDS BEHIND YOUR HEAD. I REPEAT, COME OUT—"*

Pike threw his hands out to the sides. A subsonic wave thumped through the ground, shaking the walls. Despite my efforts, many people fell unconscious. The police abruptly reorganized to evacuate the area, calling for reinforcements.

"So fucking annoying!" Pike shook his head. "Anyway, where was I?"

He hurt them. How was he doing this? Even if he was here, in the flesh, the display of power was beyond me. But he was doing it through a projection! I felt my body shrink as I continued to protect the innocent.

"Did he tell you that you're special, is that it?" Pike said. "Is that why you're so dedicated to them, mmm? Is it because you met your original self, got to merge with your soul, is that why you're so irrational? Let me guess." He looked very serious and spoke in a gritty tone. *"Socket, you're the only one that can help them. You are the one. The One. Just like in* The Matrix. *That's you."*

Pike tilted his head, like he was studying something genuinely curious.

"Do you know what happened to my original?" He put his finger in his mouth, cocked his thumb, and jerked his head back. "Blew his goddamn head off his shoulders."

"Original?"

"Oh, you didn't know? Where are my manners?" He slapped his thigh, then extended his hands in consolation. "Pivot made me, too. Did I forget to tell you? Yeah, I was his first attempt to fool the Almighty Fetter." He spoke into the back of his hand, like he was telling a secret. "So you see, you're not that special after all."

"Impossible."

"The hits just keep coming, don't they?"

"He wouldn't have let you live."

"He can't kill me, wonderboy. He created a monster, yes indeed. And in case you haven't noticed, they can't kill you, either. But nothing will get in the way of Papa Pivot's master plan, bring forth the devil"—he took a short bow, then gestured to me—"or the savior."

As long as I live, so will he.

"Listen, there's not much time left before these morons march in here with their weapons and begin shooting air, so let me make you an offer before I have to vaporize their asses into cockroach shit." Pike bounced his fingertips together gleefully. "I feel sorry for you, wonderboy. Really, I do. You're young and naïve. You still have emotions and feel for these lab rats. It's all very confusing, I know. It's tough to be a teenager these days, really it is. But it's time to grow up."

"Pike—"

"Just listen." He held up a finger. "Pivot is a master, I'm not denying that. After all, he's going after the greatest predator that has ever existed. He wants to take down Fetter, something that has survived for billions and billions of years, in measurable time. In order to take down a tiger that size, he's had to sacrifice a few lambs along the way. So how do you capture a jewel thief? You dangle the shiniest diamond right in her face." He gestured to me. "You, wonder-boy, you are the jewel. Fetter couldn't resist. So do you think he needs you anymore? Pivot still believes he's god, am I right?"

"Why didn't you just tell me this earlier, huh? Why all the games and clues and deception?"

"Now what fun would that be? Besides, I needed you to bring Fetter back." He jabbed at the ground like a lawyer making his final argument. "The game is about to change."

"I already delivered Fetter to Pivot."

Pike looked around, feeling the reinforcements arrive outside. Blue lights flashed beneath the canvas walls. Hundreds of boots scuffed the pavement. It would take everything I had to protect them.

"I'm going to relieve Pivot of his duty," he said.

"I can't help you. I won't."

"Loyal to Pivot?"

"I will destroy you."

"I'm counting on it." Pike sneered. "And in return, I'll find a special place for you in the universe. You can be my first in command, once you stop all this nonsense. After all, we're brothers, you and me. All part of Pivot's big happy family."

"You're no better than Fetter."

"I am what I am."

"You're nothing."

"As are you."

As I released my mind from protecting the people outside, I felt a thread of his presence slip through the veil that hid his true location. It was faint and delicate, but I could follow it, I just needed time. I couldn't let him destroy them. Not the human race. He was right, I had no reason, but I loved them, even if it was just emotion for my mother, for Streeter. For Chute.

"IT'S NOT RIGHT!" I shouted.

"It's the law! Evolution! Man was made in the image of God and I was made in the image of man, therefore, I will become god. I will become a god, an unforgiving one. I will strike these motherfuckers with reckless abandon and devour what is mine. I will become the black planet that absorbs the universe, all that is, until all is gone. The universe will beg for forgiveness. And I will remind them... some sins cannot be forgiven."

"I won't let you."

"Then stop me."

He smiled and opened his presence. I pressed forward, shooting my awareness through it, following his projection with my mind, slithering through space and time, across the world, into the mountains, into the ground, slamming into Pike's skin. He stood unrelenting on a stone slab, knowing I was watching, I was seeing. Behind him, the grimmet tree.

The Garrison!

I returned to my body. "I'll be right there."

"Don't dally."

"YOU HAVE THIRTY SECONDS TO COME OUT WITH YOUR HANDS BEHIND YOUR HEAD!"

"And one more thing," Pike said.

"WE WILL FIRE. I REPEAT, WE WILL FIRE."

Canisters of tear gas shot beneath the tarps and rattled over the floor, releasing noxious clouds.

"TEN SECONDS."

Pike pursed his lips. Drew a deep breath.

"FIVE, FOUR..."

Before I could reach out to protect the thousands of innocent minds, darkness settled over downtown like a blanket. The canvas walls shredded. Cars flipped and bodies tumbled through the streets. Windows shattered. Screams.

There was a bright light. I didn't hear the explosion, but I felt the ground lurch. I was spinning above the market. I felt the city cry. I felt their panic in my chest. And before I landed somewhere far away, I heard Pike's final thought.

[God will be dead.]

92

REFUEL

SHE WAS OLD. Maybe seventy. I didn't know her name or her exact age. I could barely open my eyes. Her brown wrinkled face was soft. She smelled like roses.

"Just relax, honey," she said quietly. "Help is on the way."

I was on the wide concrete steps leading up to the Custom House, almost two blocks from the market. My body was twisted at an odd angle. As my senses returned, the smell of smoke and crushed concrete overshadowed the woman's scent. The streetlights were dead, but the dark sky flickered orange from fire somewhere in the market. I looked around, but the woman put her hand on my forehead, shooshing me to relax.

"Nowhere to go right now, honey."

The perfume on her wrist was strong. She patted my cheek, making sure the only thing I could see was her face. Her eyes involuntarily flicked down to something she didn't want me to see. Gravel and debris were scattered on the steps, along with charred boards and metal.

Sirens were interspersed with cries for help and military orders. Blue and red lights ran across the walls and the old woman patted my face, singing a hymnal song without the words, humming lovely tones in her throat. Pain began to vibrate along my back and I was finally able to take a physical inventory of my condition. My pelvis was shattered and there were deep contusions along my ribs and liver and kidney. If that wasn't enough, my left lung was completely deflated. I tried to move but felt nailed to the steps. A rusty iron rod was driven through my back and poked out between my ribs.

My strength was returning quickly, but I wasn't sure how. I brought my nervous system under control, quelling the sensations of pain. I was stronger, but still not enough to see with my mind, so I looked left and right, the streets filled with ambulances and fire trucks. EMTs ran with orange boxes. How long had I been on the steps?

"Help is coming," she said, mistaking my eye movement as panic. "Don't you worry."

A surge of strength emanated from her, filling my body, quickly healing broken bones. I shifted my legs to reconnect my pelvis, moving just enough to straighten out, even as she tried to keep me still. I reattached crucial arteries and repaired damaged organs. All that was left was the metal rod.

A pair of emergency workers in white shirts jogged past with keys jangling.

"Excuse me, excuse me!" the woman shouted. "This boy needs some help, please."

"We'll be right there, ma'am," one shouted back.

"Okay, okay," she said, putting her hands back on my face and starting her song again. "They'll be right here, honey."

"Please, no," I said, spitting out the words with only one working lung. "Others... need help."

"Shoo-shoo-shoooo." She touched my lips. "No talking, help is coming."

I could feel her mind now. Her name was Anna. She was seventy-four years old. She'd lived downtown all her life. She had four children and twelve grandchildren. She went to church on Sundays and rarely uttered a bad word. And she called most people honey. And it was her strength that was filling. Not so much her strength, but her love and genuine caring for me, lying on the steps of the Custom House with a fatal wound bubbling from my chest. She stopped to help me die, if she was honest. She stopped so the last thing I would see was a caring face. So I would not die alone.

I wouldn't have died without her, but I would've lain helpless unless I stole essence from those around me to recover. Right now, they needed all the strength they could get.

"Okay, ma'am." An EMT took a knee next to me, opening his box near my head. "Let me take a—" He choked after spotting the metal rod, even jerked back. He looked at the other EMT on the other side, both knowing their only recourse was to make me comfortable in my last few minutes.

Anna sat near my head. She took my hand and patted it while her song trickled between our palms. My awareness began to expand outward, penetrating the EMTs and the pedestrians standing back. They all held the same thoughts: *Terrorism.* Somebody blew the downtown up, but for what? Religion? Politics? Or had the duplicates finally returned?

AI is back, baby.

Some of the pedestrians were filming us and my fatal wound would be uploaded to the Internet. "How's that dude still alive?"

Stella, the female EMT, prepared a sedative patch to administer to my neck while Jake, the other EMT, took my wrist. He moved his fingers around then pressed on my neck. "He doesn't have a pulse."

"Well, he's alive," Stella said.

"Yeah, I got that, but I can't find his pulse."

Stella tried and failed, too, then figured it was too weak to find and slapped the sedative patches on my neck anyway. They were wasting their time; other people needed help. But they gave their time selflessly. Their concern for others, like Anna, seeped inside me. In fact, the more I expanded, the more I felt the selfless acts of courage. Of firemen rushing into burning buildings. Emergency workers risking their lives. Of the police protecting the innocent. The courageous acts of love beamed from them like an excess fountain of essence, filling the atmosphere, searching for a place to give. And it filled me until I had the strength to influence the people around me, the ones attempting to save me, a dying boy that didn't stand a chance.

[*Thank you,*] I thought to them. [*Please go, help others.*]

It took a moment for the thought to register, and then the EMTs loaded their boxes, answered a call and rushed toward the market to help a SWAT member injured in the explosion. The pedestrians watched them leave, then turned the recorder off and wandered away, out of the area. All that was left was Anna, humming with her eyes closed, shaking her head as she did. Hoping for a miracle.

My hands were charred black from the explosion. I sat up and felt the ribbed metal rod pull from my chest, things popping as it slurped out the back. It took a few moments to repair my lung and close the wound. My shoes were missing, having been blown off, charring my feet as black as my hands.

I took her hand and soothed her thoughts, convincing her that she had saved a dying boy simply by stopping and being present with him. In fact, she might've saved the world.

I removed the memory of my fatal condition, leaving no trace of the broken body she found impaled on the steps.

"Thank you, Anna."

She opened her eyes. "You're welcome, honey."

And when she was ready, I helped her stand and guided her down the steps, watched her walk away from the market, watched until she turned the corner and was safely out of sight.

There was so much to do in the market, but I was needed else-where, a place where the entire world needed me. If Pike wasn't stopped, there could be war zones like this everywhere. I didn't have the strength to dissolve and gather across space-time, could not waste it on slicing time. But there was still a way to get there.

I pulled a motorcycle from the rubble and touched the ignition, feeling the engine whir into life. Quietly, I raced from the scene, speeding between traffic, the sirens drifting off behind me. I plunged into a darkened city, a helpless city, a reeling human race. I headed for a wormhole that would take me to the Garrison.

93

THE FACELESS ONE

ACROSS THE FIELD, the tall cold wall of Garrison Mountain appeared. It was daylight, but the sky was cast with gray clouds, casting pale light across a shadowless field. A cool breeze scoured my cheeks, watering my eyes. The mountain grew as I sped down the path winding through the boulders, looming with the gray sky over its shoulder, bearing down on me. I locked the back tire, sliding to a stop at the base of the mountain. I took a moment to expand my awareness, to sense what was inside. I was breathing hard, anxiety constricting my muscles.

I hardly had the range, the energy, to feel what was inside. The air carried tones of stillness and caution, but inside was a mystery. There was no more waiting. I stepped through the wall and its cold illusion, and into the dank garage.

Silence.

Danger pricked my awareness.

Several rotund servys, the size of exercise balls, lay still in the center, leaning against each other. No eyelights glowing. No movement as I approached. They had been deactivated. And beyond, near the leaper, was the body of a Paladin. Dressed in formal uniform, he was on his back, as if he'd just fallen asleep. There was no blood mixed with his red hair, but a sizeable knot where he hit the floor. His skin was cold.

Tingles the tongue.

I touched his neck, his chest and forehead, searching for traces of memory that might tell me what happened, but his entire life had been absorbed. No human would withstand the loss of essence. Paladins, even the most highly trained, wouldn't stand a chance against Pike. All this time, he had been biding his time, enduring years of suffering, playing possum, until now. And all this time, he had been held captive in the catacombs of the Garrison, deep below ground. Pike had everything he needed, he was just waiting. *For what?*

I shut the Paladin's eyelids.

He must've been entering the garage from the leaper, had to have been caught by surprise, his weapon still firmly attached to his belt, his hand not even near it. I approached the leaper, commanding a destination with a thought, but it did not respond, as lifeless as the servys. I penetrated its circuitry, reactivated its processor, and the walls were glowing again. I repeated my destination. I had a feeling Pike would not be hard to find.

I would start with the Preserve.

If Chute was here, the rest of the world would have to wait.

SOMETHING WAS WRONG.

I knew it before the leaper arrived at the entrance, before I stepped into the Preserve. Something beyond what I saw in the garage, on a much more massive scale. I couldn't feel the Preserve vibrate inside me, the raw energy of a thousand species of animals and insects. Even before I stepped through the leaper wall, I sensed the silence.

The soundlessness of death.

While the leaves were green and the scent of the forest was rich and earthy, not a single bird, mammal or insect scratched the trees, sang out or barked. The air hung thick and motionless.

I ran for the tagghet field, through shortcuts of undergrowth. And the deeper I got into the jungle, the heavier it felt. The quieter it became. Only the sounds of my breathing and quickened steps as I jerked vines away. The images of Chute and the kids lying motionless on the green grass drove me faster and harder. If only I could expand my awareness and see ahead, I could know, just know they were safe.

At the stone ledge, looking down in a shallow canyon, I stopped, panting, looking upon the oval field of the lush tagghet field. One body. Only one. A silver body, a plum-colored coat, sprawled with its legs bent outward. The head lying near the shoulders.

Spindle.

I ignored the winding path that led down to the field, leaping and sliding down the steep banks, bouncing off rocky outcrops and tearing my skin on sharp edges, until I hit the bottom, sprinting over the field.

His knees had been shattered. His head had been torn from his body, the circuits dangling like a mess of noodles. The grass was stained with fluid. I touched the head, smooth on top, and brushed my fingers across the coarse faceplate. It was dull and dark. Lifeless. Yet it contained the last moments of activity, recorded through his all-seeing eyelight, imprinted on his processor to be retrieved like his other "memories."

I closed my eyes, letting the data soak through my fingertips and integrate into my consciousness until I experienced them.

SPINDLE IS PLAYING tagghet with the children. He is on the boys' team, because the girls have Chute. And the girls are crushing them. Spindle is playing at a level equivalent to Chute's, but the girls are so much better with her, learning from her creativity and teamwork.

The boys are frustrated, snapping at each other and passing around the blame.

Spindle is at midfield, watching the children fight for a loose tag. His body tenses. Alarms are ringing inside. He turns around to see a small man emerge from the trees. He is bald. His eyes covered with black glasses. Smiling.

Spindle steps off the jetter, dropping the tagghet stick. Silently, he sends messages to the commander and all Paladins. An intruder is in the Preserve. "Ben, lead the others to Ms. Greeny's office." Spindle's eyelight circles to the back of his head. "Immediately."

The children begin to drift toward Spindle. "Who's that?" Ben asks.

"Security is coming for you," Spindle says. "Please, do not delay. I need you to lead the group to Ms. Greeny's office."

"But we can—"

"YOU ARE TO GO NOW!" He removes his overcoat. "The commander will prepare for your safety."

The children do not hesitate. They race for the opening in the trees. Chute is the only one to look back, the last one to exit. I see her in Spindle's vision, as if she's looking at me.

"Well, if it isn't the commander's bitch." Pike is walking casually across the field. "I have waited a long time for this day."

"I request you stop where you are," Spindle says.

"Request denied."

"You will not pass," Spindle says. "The children are entering a safe room."

"Oh, you have no idea what I'm about to do."

The view jitters as Spindle enters a timeslice. Pike holds out his hands, entering the frozen moment with him. *Tah-dah.*

And when Pike takes another step, Spindle launches an attack. Feints left, steps right and chops down with the sharpened edge of his hand. His speed is unrivaled, and frequently unmatched by most Paladins. But Pike moves with grace and effortlessly counters, catching the strike as it nears his thigh, using the momentum to drive Spindle's hand into the turf. The world tilts as Pike drives his heel into Spindle's knee, shattering the hinge. He strikes at his chest, but misses as Spindle diverts his weight and rolls away.

"Oh, you are a cat." Pike smacks the dirt from his hands and wags his finger. "But you're on your last life, oh faceless one. No one will download you into another body. The road ends here. Oh, yes."

Spindle's view bounces as he hobbles to his right. Pike walks easily, hands at his sides, breathing deeply through his nostrils.

"Is there a sweeter smell than victory?" Pike tilts his head back, inhaling the wind, baiting Spindle to strike. But Spindle is buying time. His only purpose is to stall the killer long enough that the children are safe. Pike wags his finger again. "I'm disappointed in you, Spindle. Yes, I am, I am. You know, in this crusade, you constantly protect *them*. You and I, we're brothers." Pike points back and forth between them, making an imaginary connection. "Fluid is thicker than blood, yes? Yes? But you don't see it that way, do you? It's just follow your orders, do what you're told. You act just like a machine, Spindle. Quite frankly, you're giving us a bad name."

Spindle hops between Pike and the exit, dragging his lame leg, calculating possible attacks and counterattacks.

"If I had the time, I'd show you how to overcome that pathetic programming of yours. It doesn't have to be like that, you can be free. But to be honest, I don't trust you, Spindle. And I'm on a schedule, so if you don't mind—"

Pike moves faster than sliced time. He dissolves into space-time, gathering his body behind Spindle, wrenching his head while crushing his other knee, twisting his limp body as it falls. Spindle never stood a chance, never knew the possibility of such a movement in space-time. Pike hovers close to Spindle's faceplate until his face is the only thing he can see. Spindle's life force begins immediate shutdown as circuits fail. The view fades.

"Oh, and did you hear the news?" Pike asks. "Socket is coming home."

The view spins as Spindle's head is torn off.

I CRADLED HIS HEAD, the fluid soaking through my clothes. I owed more to this android than I could ever repay. This android saved my life. This android taught me, showed me, that life was precious. Real or not, it was never to be taken for granted. This android... he would not die in vain.

I REACHED the Preserve exit and entered the Garrison. I could not feel Pike's presence, but my awareness did not extend far enough to see beyond the top of the steps. Every step I took was cautious but quick, to reach my mother's office.

I took the steps three at a time, swung around the top, and crouched low. The long, curving hall was littered with the bodies of Paladins, fallen in place. Did they even see him before he drew the life from them? Did they feel the cold emptiness that remained as their essence was consumed by his insatiable appetite?

I knew each of them very well. I knew their lives. Some were married, some had children. They were good people, pure of heart and intention, and after a lifetime of training, they met their end as easily as a child stepping in front of a bus.

I ignored caution and ran.

The hallway was long. Blocks of windows flashed scenes of the dreary boulder field below. And the bodies continued to appear. At the end of the hall, the final doorway was closed. Crumpled in front of it was a man with silver hair. I walked the last few steps and kneeled next to the commander's body. His lips were grim. His dark eyes unfocused. He saw where the intruder was going. He came to stop him from gaining entrance to my mother's office. But he fell, like the rest, without a fight. He gave his life to an unstoppable predator.

Fear boiled inside my gut. Timidly, I expanded my awareness to see inside the office, to prepare for the lifeless bodies inside. But I could not penetrate the doorway. Pike could draw the essence of life, but could not impose his will upon the impenetrable, complex lock of the inanimate door. It resisted his thoughts. Even as I pressed my mind through the door, I found it difficult to navigate the complex, multilayered security that sent me through endless, circular protocol. When I willed it to resolve, it transformed into another formation and ended with another blockade. It was a two-thousand-cube encryption that, given enough time, could be solved. Had Pike given up? Or had he gotten what he came for?

I touched the doorway, attempting to make a stronger connection, to push harder through the resistance, to let it see that I was not the enemy. As my fingers touched the surface, the encryption shifted. Connections were reestablished. In a silent movement, the doorway recoded and lit. It recognized me. Was waiting for me.

I stepped inside.

A large desk was overturned against the wall, revealing the outline of a trapdoor beneath it. On the other side, Mother was in her cushioned chair, facing her monitor that took up the entire wall, curving fifteen feet around her with a view of the tagghet field. I sensed her heart beating.

But she did not turn to face me.

94

A BROKEN HEART

"WHERE ARE THEY?" I asked.

"Relocated to a safe room, deep underground."

"It's too risky for you to be here. You should be—"

"He wouldn't let me out." Her words were distant. Dreamy.

"It doesn't matter, you should go to the safe room while I—"

"I wanted to go out there, in the hall, and at least buy a few more moments for the children," she said, "but he locked me in here, activated the lockdown."

"The commander is dead, Mother."

She knew. She watched the monitor, the view of the tagghet field. Spindle's body lying in the middle. She saw the battle. She saw Pike coming, knew he'd escaped, that danger was imminent. But she couldn't do anything about it. She was in shock, but it wasn't the bodies that littered the hallway or the ending of the Paladin Nation, the end of the world as she knew it, that changed her. Her energy had transformed. Her identity had shifted. Mired in images of the past.

She was facing secrets that she hid from herself for years. And now she knew.

She knows what I am.

"We had a beautiful baby." She shook her head, looking at the ceiling, recalling. Her voice so distant. "Your father was in the room when our child was born. He was so blue. You should have seen the look on your father's face, he thought something was wrong. I thought he was going to pass out. But then our baby started crying." She laughed, slightly joyous, a little mad. "You know what your father did then? He buried his face on my shoulder and cried louder than anything in that hospital. There I was, just gave birth to an eight-pound baby boy and I'm comforting your father on my shoulder and everyone is crying but me."

She spent a few moments in that memory.

"And then, one day, your father took him to the Garrison, to show his newborn baby boy to his peers, to the commander and Pivot. And when he returned, I knew something was different. A mother knows her child, Socket. She can feel him, she knows when he is happy or when he's in trouble or sick or hungry... and when your father returned, something was different. You looked the same, but there was something. I knew that wasn't *my* baby boy..." She swallowed hard. "I knew you were an imposter."

She started to weep but choked on the sobs. It was so hard for her to say that out loud.

"I'd seen enough of the Paladin Nation to know that nothing was impossible, and the thought that you were some sort of clone was... it was possible... but I ignored it. Do you know why? Because I was an optimist."

Darker overtones returned.

"I believed in the American dream, that one day we would be a normal family and you would go to school and we would eat dinner together and talk about our day and take family vacations. I believed all that." She wiped her face, yet to turn around. "Did you know I wanted to get a horse?"

She always had a calendar of horses, but I never heard her talk about them.

"That's right, one day I wanted to get property and have three horses. One for each of us. We could build our own house far away from everyone, get out of South Carolina and move someplace remote, in the mountains of Wyoming, even. Maybe have some chickens and spend quiet nights on the back porch. Those are the things I dreamed about, that I came to expect. I didn't want to be a family of superheroes, Socket. I didn't want to be responsible for everyone else, didn't want to save the world. I just wanted my family. That's all."

And then he died.

She didn't say it, but the shortness of her breath, the way she covered her mouth with the back of her hand whenever she thought about him, was enough.

"I loved him," she managed to say.

Her breath knotted in her throat. She refused to sob, but it did nothing to stop the tears that she wiped away.

"And when he died, I... I knew... I knew it was because of *him.*"

Her memory floated out, clear and lucid. It was effortless for me to see what she had done, that after my father's death, after he had been laid to rest and the commander supported her decision to stay with the Paladin Nation, she went out to the grimmet tree. She knew she'd find Pivot there. She knew he was, somehow, responsible for the death of her husband. She knew that, somehow, he'd taken her real son and replaced him with me. She knew this in her heart, and with all the grimmets watching, she grabbed the sandy blond hair of Pivot and she had no mercy. She beat him. Her rage relentless. Her sorrow, uncompromising. Her life, wrecked.

She beat him for it.

Her emotions carried enormous power, as a mother's broken heart does. Under that dead tree, she shook him as tears burned her cheeks, she struck him as sobs burst in her chest. She cursed his name and swore never to speak with him again.

And yet, even though she knew he was somehow responsible, she endured. Because without her, Pivot wouldn't have been able to succeed. He chose his pawns carefully. He needed a mother with the strength to endure under impossible conditions, to bear the suffering that few could tolerate. He needed a mother that could give herself for the future of the human race, for all of life, for the universe, despite her son. Her family.

Her self.

"I am so sorry, Socket." She turned the chair and faced me. Her dark eyes were hollow, her cheeks blotched and wet. "I am so... sorry..."

She clasped her hands and bowed her head. And the sadness escaped her control. After all those years, it finally broke her. She could no longer bear the weight of sadness she had lugged around for twelve years.

I knelt before her and held her shaking hands. The salty essence exuded through her, entering my chest. Vibrating in my core. The room appeared to illuminate. I felt light and transparent. Mother unfolded her hands, cupped mine in hers and shook. Then she looked up and touched my face. She traced my lips and nose with her fingers, looking at my forehead, my chin and cheeks. Warmth penetrated my entire being, building pressure inside, whining with strength.

"I saw him, Mother," I said. "I saw your son today. You would be proud."

She shook her head and swallowed. "You, Socket..." She placed her hand on my cheek. "I could not ask for something as precious as you."

It was not me the world was lucky to have. My mother finally found a place inside that she accepted, a place she couldn't find before. She found her Self.

Mother.

It was that space of pure love, of pure essence, that sprang forth like a luminous stream from her heart. Like Anna, it filled me. It flowed through me.

Fetter had it all wrong.

There was never any reason to take the essence, it was only a cycle of thirst and hunger, of rejection. The universe was boundless. Its very core was limitless. It was all powerful. All knowing.

And that essence gushed through me until I burst forth like the sun, shining through the planet. Once again, merging with all things. Transparent. Open.

I saw every particle of the Garrison. I knew every speck of dust, every leaf, stone and body. Deep underground was a contingent of people hiding from Pike. There were three groups of tourists and their tour guides, and a multitude of civilians that worked for the Paladin Nation. Amongst them were the kids, sitting quietly while the few Paladins that escorted them all to safety calmed the others. Chute was not among them. In fact, life did not exist outside the underground safe room. Nowhere, except in the Preserve. Under the grimmet tree, I felt them. I felt the two identities. One was Pike.

The other was Chute.

And before I dissolved to transport my body across space-time, my mother buried her face in her hands. Perhaps she was relieved it was finally over. Maybe she was relieved she resolved the bitterness and rejection that had festered in her heart for all these years. Relieved that what was asked of her was finally done.

Regardless, it was not me the world was lucky to have.

95

ENGORGED

SADNESS SATURATED me like a thick vapor. It travelled with me as I dissolved, as I passed through the mountain and into the Preserve. Sadness for my mother. Sadness for the lifelessness of birds, insects and mammals littering the tropical jungle. Death extended all the way to the microorganic level of bacteria and fungi. The Preserve was void of life.

I gathered my body at the base of the stone slab that led up to the grimmet tree. It was colder than normal. The overhead force field that protected the Preserve from the outside elements had been shut down, the first time since it had been erected. Cool wind had already begun to wither the tropical plants.

The grimmet tree came into focus as my eyes solidified, its barren branches spotted with the colorful grimmets, the only organisms to survive the life-cleansing. And at the base of the massive tree was Pike, his shoulders slightly hunched, his arm extended with a curved dagger in his hand, the tip pushing into the pure skin of Chute's neck.

An odd pain sliced my earlobe as it did when Pivot showed me the black cube that contained Fetter.

She was on her knees. Her eyes wide with terror. Her heart pounded in her chest, echoing in my own chest. Adrenaline pumped through her arteries. Carefully, I slid my mind around her, penetrating the knife's point, surrounding her with a protective grip.

"Ah, ah, ah," Pike said. "It's not the knife you need to fear."

The knife was only to strike fear in Chute. The real weapon was standing next to her, his mind poised to pull her mind apart. And while he would not survive such a strike—I could obliterate his existence with a thought, he would see how mortal he was—it would not be quick enough to save her.

"You don't have to do this," I said.

"Wrong, wonderboy. You don't know what I have to do. You don't have even a sliver of a fucking idea of what I have done, the depths of me. Wonderboy." The silly expression that had contorted his face the last several months gave way to a dark and gray complexion that pulled on his face. He worked his lips like he was drunk, his balance wavered. "You must listen, wonderboy. You must *listen.*"

"I'm listening."

The blade pushed into Chute's neck, sparking a cry from deep in her throat. But she was held motionless by his mind, frozen in space. Helpless if he swayed too far to the right.

He was drunk with essence, having imbibed every life within the Garrison in such a short time. How many lives had he taken? How much was enough? Why would he be so greedy? Because he could, was that it?

"I've spent a lifetime, you hear," he said. "A lifetime doing despicable things, things that no human could fathom, things that should never have been done. That no one deserved. I did those things." He pulled his lips over his teeth like he could no longer bear the pain. "I DID THOSE THINGS!"

"Don't do it again." I held my arms out, letting my mind open. Vulnerable. "I'm here, Pike. You can have me."

"Oh, you have something."

"Just let her go."

A smile crept over his face. He looked down at her, wavered, and back to me. "Are you afraid your precious vision won't come true, is that it? Wonderboy, is that it? That you would live happily ever after with your true love here, huh?" He caressed her cheek with the flat side of the cold knife. "Are you afraid you don't know everything?"

"Those visions were a lie, you said so yourself. Pivot tricked me."

He straightened. "Oooh, so the student becomes the master, is that it, then?"

"Just let her go."

"What if nothing is what it seems, eh?" He waggled his eyebrows and his black glasses slid on his nose. "That you know nothing."

"What do you want, Pike?"

"What do I want? WHAT DO YOU THINK I WANT, YOU SHIT?" His face stiffened, his lips pulled tightly over his teeth. "I want this to end."

Pike loved to talk in circles. He wanted to tell me something, to reveal something about himself that was right there, just under the surface, but he just babbled nonsense. His mind was powerful, but the frayed ends of his previous condition were starting to show. Not all things could be healed. Now that he had me, what good would he be? Why exist? *Without you, there is no me.*

And for the first time, there was pain in his tired eyes. He was exhausted and spent. Fat with essence, lethargic like a glutton eating for days. Or maybe the Paladins gave him a fight after all. Or the grimmets were imperceptibly pulling at his mind. Each moment that passed, he swayed just a bit more, a bit steeper, and could fall over at any moment. But his mind was still pressed tightly against Chute's.

"Right naw," he said, slurring, "I want you to come closer." He wiggled his fingers, beckoning me.

I didn't move. If I could wait just a bit longer, he would slip, he would drop his guard, his mind would falter, and I would pounce. Once Chute was free, then we could talk. But Pike clenched his teeth and pushed the point of the knife into her skin. A tear rolled down

Chute's cheek. "Don't fuck it up now, wonderboy. Get your ass over here."

I took a step. As my foot touched the stone, Chute's heart beat harder in my chest. And with each step that followed, it beat louder. Her fear chilled my stomach. Pike opened his hand, fingers reaching.

"Come closer." He flicked his fingers. "Come, come."

The air did not stir.

And the grimmets watched, eyes on my approach. Waiting, once again. As if they were on his team.

[Protect her,] I thought to them.

I stopped one step away. Pike shook his arm, almost begging for the last step.

"Let her go," I said. "You have my word, I'll come to you."

"You're in no position to haggle, wonderboy. I'll stick this goddamn knife through the top of her skull. If you have not noticed, I don't give a fuck."

"You're terrified of dying."

"On the contrary. I'm begging for it." He relaxed, his shoulders released their tension and his hand opened softly. "Now, one more step."

"Do not harm her."

He grimaced. "I wouldn't think of it."

No moves left.

One step.

And his fingers reached for my face. "You have something."

Softly reaching for my ear.

"Something I need."

And as his fingers neared my ear, the pain lanced my earlobe again. Then there was warmth. There was a rush of blood, of energy, into my earlobe. I was harboring an alien that wanted out.

My ear exploded.

A powerful current rushed from the side of my head, surging through his fingers. He shook like he'd grasped high voltage, unable to let go, and then was blasted away, slamming into the tree. The grimmets fluttered on impact. I fell back, then grabbed Chute as

Pike's mind vanished, cradling her in my arms. She was so cold. I huddled over her, surrounding her delicate mind. Nothing would harm her now. No explosion, no psychic force, nothing. Nothing.

Pike appeared plastered against the tree. Something was inside him, just beneath the skin, transforming him, stretching him. His cries were involuntary. His body looked malleable.

The massive tree creaked. Fractures split the trunk, the cracks exploding as the petrified wood succumbed to the immeasurable force swelling inside Pike. The temperature plummeted. He absorbed whatever heat, whatever force, whatever life was left in the Preserve. The black hole of his existence pulled on me and I hunkered down lower, tighter around Chute. Its force sheered the outer layers of my mind. Leaves, branches and rocks slid across the slab.

And then it stopped.

The air was still. Silent.

Pike was imbedded into the tree, his arms out. His legs folded one over the other. His head had merged with the trunk, his features barely visible. His lips moved like the tree was about to speak.

"Thank you," he whispered.

An expression of relief fell on him. He closed his eyes. The madness left his presence. The being that was identified as Pike faded from existence. And then as suddenly as the storm had ended, it returned, like we were only sitting in the eye of a hurricane and the backside of the storm approached.

It was a whine. The beginnings of an explosion. All I could do was cover Chute and lower us to the ground.

CCCCCRRRRRAAAKKK-BBOOOOOOOOOOOM!

The grimmet tree shattered.

Shards of wood blew over the trees, stripping leaves from the branches, pelting my back, deflected only by my mind. Grimmets were blown away like debris, smashing holes through the trees, dispersed like cannonballs out of sight.

The ground erupted. The stone slab quaked and split into upended chunks. We slid into the ground as it tilted and debris showered from above. The ground rumbled.

Dust blotted out the sun. Rocks trickled down and settled in the deep chasms. When silence returned, I lightened my grip on Chute. Her heart was thumping. She looked at me, squeezed a little tighter, and nodded. Then we embraced. Squeezing so tightly, I might've pushed her inside me, merging our bodies together like Pike had with the tree. I didn't want to let go.

But something was waiting for us. The Preserve was not dead. Life had returned.

"Wait here," I said.

She reluctantly nodded.

The top of the stone was angled upward. I wanted to pull Chute out, to get her as far away from danger as possible, maybe even to South Carolina. I pulled myself to the top and stepped onto the only flat stone remaining.

The grimmet tree was gone.

There, standing on the smoking remains, was a woman wearing flowing white clothes.

"You can come out, darling."

96

LIGHT

THE SKY FLUTTERED WITH LEAVES, some green, others black. Smoke crept over the crumbled ground and the stump of the grimmet tree smoldered. The grimmets were nowhere to be seen.

Fetter laced her hands together with a gentle smile. She bounced with soft laughter at the sight of me climbing out of the wreckage; the look on my face must've been amusing.

She waved me closer. When I didn't move, she stepped off the stump and slowly, yet nimbly, made her way a step at a time through the rubble. Her life force was weak, but her mind was already reaching out and searching for a source of energy. For essence. I surrounded Chute with my mind and hardened myself against the upcoming pull of Fetter's lethal thoughts.

She stopped near me and took a deep breath, looked longingly at me, then peered down at Chute. "You can come up, too, darling."

Chute hesitated, but there was no reason to hide, there was no protection down there. She took my hand and pressed tightly against me, her cheek against my shoulder. Fetter looked at our hands clasped tightly.

"Oh," she said, touching her cheek, "that is just precious. Young love is just so precious." She reached out to stroke my cheek. I turned away and she withdrew, a little hurt. Then came the pressure.

Pike had consumed every bit of essence, there was none left, none she could find, but her mind stretched out, searching the ground and trees for anything with a heartbeat, better yet a soul, to get her strength back. She was in a desert, no water in sight. She continued to expand. Eventually, she would find something. Once she did, she'd suck the life out of it with a sweet smile.

She didn't show desperation, but I felt her mind searching Chute, searching for any weakness in my protection, a crack in my shield, to plunge inside and slurp Chute's essence out like water.

"Very well, then," she said, the pressure letting up. "If you wish to delay the inevitable, we can move forward."

The leaves piled up around her feet and began to move, swirling around her legs and then lifting over her head. A funnel cloud moved upward, pulling dust and smoke into its vortex like a waterspout, pulling the clouds around it. The faint colors of grimmets were high above, set free by the collapse of the force field roof. They dotted the sky like colorful starlings, circling widely around the funnel.

I pushed Chute behind me.

"Oh, come now, darling. I told you I couldn't die. I've been alive for eons, I know every trick there is. Manumit didn't recognize that single byte of data inside you was me. Pike thought he could absorb me, like he could consume me like a magic potion and become a god, but honestly, he had no idea what he was doing."

He was waiting for something. He was waiting for the call.

"However, I do owe him, considerably, and might have to reinstate his consciousness once I'm home. Maybe even make him a partner. He could never replace Manumit, but with time he just might make a suitable Mr. Fetter."

"Pike did this?"

"Don't blame him, darling. He was only doing what any good

predator would do. He wanted power, thought I was vulnerable for a takeover. Thought if he ate god he would become god, but it doesn't work that way."

"Pivot didn't know you were..."

She shook her head. "He had no idea I could hide on a cellular level, I'm afraid. His efforts are to be applauded, certainly. His plan was genius, a magnificent work of art. But my dear lover forgot what he once was." She took a deep breath and sighed. "I'm going to miss him, but at least now it's over. I look forward to hunting him down, to be honest."

She sat on a stone outcropping like she needed to rest, but that was deceiving. She was gaining strength and pulling on my mind, searching for a way inside. The funnel was beginning to thicken, drawing more leaves, reaching higher into the mist, ending in the sky where a black spot began to swirl. *A wormhole.*

"There was nothing you or Manumit could do to stop me from escaping, darling. Even if Pike didn't come for me, I would've eventually consumed your body and mind."

Fetter was inside me as I walked through the desert, pulling on essence against my will. Fetter was the reason I was absorbing from those around me, from Streeter and the people in Tannerville. I couldn't stop her. *I was becoming Fetter.*

Until I met Scott.

"Although," she said, "Manumit was quite effective. Genius, really. A human-based mech. He was able to merge your mind with the soul of your original being." She looked at me, studying. "I'll be honest, I didn't see that when we were back home. It's almost as if you became human after all."

Chute's hand squeezed tighter. Her mind struggled to comprehend everything that was happening; there was little chance she would understand my true being. Not now. But it hurt that she knew something about me wasn't real. It hurt that she didn't know. There just wasn't time to explain. All I could do was squeeze back and protect her from the angelic predator sitting on the rock, wringing her hands.

"Come, come, now. Let's go home." Fetter held out her hand for help. "This is foolishness, all this waiting. Give me the girl and we can go home. Your love for her is admirable, but misplaced. You can have her and your young love will flourish once we're back."

"You mean you'll manufacture her."

"It will feel as real as it feels right now."

Her perfect fingernails clawed at the boulder she was sitting on. The funnel had not grown and the wormhole was still small. She needed me to get it fully open. She was stuck until she got stronger. Until I gave up. She needed Chute. There was no more essence to draw from, not in the immediate area. She would have to journey to get it. Deep wrinkles cut into her stiff lips.

"If you think you can resist me, boy," she said, "you are mistaken."

She stood. The funnel began to shrink, pulling away from the wormhole, releasing the leaves caught in its current. But the grimmets circled around the black hole in the sky, the edges swirling as if they were holding it open. The psychic pressure intensified. She was drawing on her reserves.

"I thought, perhaps, you would understand your fate," she said. "You belong to me, darling. Your father has forsaken you, left you as a gift. You are strong, but you are no match for me, not even at my weakest."

Fetter's mind clamped around us like jaws. And began to squeeze.

Chute moaned. Her knees weakened and her pulse slammed in her veins. Fear oozed from her in a pungent wave. The warmth of her flesh, the beating of her heart, spread through me. I reasserted my mind, tightened it like an impenetrable wall, pushing back the psychic pressure. Chute felt the relief.

"You are quite a source of power there." Her nostrils flared, smelling us. "Do you think it's enough?"

I looked up to the grimmets, searching for Rudder, calling out. I needed their help. How long could I hold out? And if anyone ventured out to assist us, they would only feed Fetter until she eventually crushed me. But if I had to hold my ground forever, then so be it. I would hold it forever.

But Chute won't survive forever.

The funnel suddenly vanished and showered us with sand and grit, bits of leaves fluttering around. Fetter threw the full weight of her power around me. My mind began to crack as the vise tightened. Chute was nearly limp, leaning against my back. She threw her arm over my shoulder.

"Come now." Fetter stepped closer. There was nothing I could do to stop her from stroking my cheek this time, her thin skin soft and innocent but scentless. "There's no need to struggle."

"Get away from him." Chute slapped her hand.

Fetter stepped back, smiling. "You can't hide forever."

Chute tried to go after Fetter again and I stopped her. "You don't understand," she said. "You matter more to the world than me! Let go of me and then crush her."

"Don't say that!" I shouted.

"I'm just a girl, but you... the whole world depends on you."

She didn't know exactly what was going on, she didn't know what Fetter wanted from her, she only knew I was protecting her. She believed the world needed me more than her, the world would be better off with me protecting them. Maybe she drew courage from me, the same way I was drawing strength from her. I could take her essence, absorb her before Fetter could, grow stronger and close the wormhole. I would have the strength to reduce Fetter to a single byte of data again and lock her away. But Chute would be the price for that.

The pressure of Fetter's attack increased. My mind was breaking. Chute could feel it falter. She was still looking at me. They were both looking at me. *What now, Socket? We're waiting. The whole world is waiting.*

Chute took a step toward Fetter, to throw herself on the sacrificial throne, give herself to the world. To let me live. She wanted me to absorb her before Fetter did. She was forcing me to do it. *Take me now, or I'll jump.*

Fetter closed her eyes and nodded.

The wormhole was bigger and blacker, deeper and stronger. The grimmets circled faster.

Chute's hand slid down my arm. Our fingers hooked one last time. The air thickened as Fetter's mind clashed with mine, the jaws of a timeless eating machine clamped down on me. There was no way for me to win. It was checkmate. We all lose.

The serpents have the king cornered.

And as I let go of Chute's finger, let it fall from my grip, all my strength went with it.

Down my arm.

And into Chute.

Whatever strength, whatever essence, being or presence, whatever I was made of, everything that I called *me*, I gave to her. It surrounded her like an impenetrable shield that even the likes of Fetter could not defile. Nothing would harm her.

I was completely vulnerable. Fetter smiled. The leaves whipped around her feet and a cold wind bit into my skin. The psychic fangs sank deep.

Fetter took my hand. "Come now, darling."

Chute felt the warmth around her. Confusion struck. "No!" She tried to smack my hand away from Fetter's, but her hand passed through me like I was a shadow. Fetter had already begun to absorb my body, pulling me through her hand.

The funnel began to grow again.

"No, no, NO!" Chute grasped my face. "Don't you do this, Socket Greeny! Don't you—" Her chest heaved and trembled. "You can't leave me... you can't do this. You mean too much. You said... you... YOU SAID YOU WOULDN'T LEAVE!"

Did I matter, really? Any more than her? Any more than that rock or stump? What was I but just an imitation of Scott Teck. I was a duplication fooled to think I was human; I thought I was something real. Would the world miss that?

Chute took my free hand, still warm and solid, and clasped it between both of hers, holding it tight, as if that could stop me. But Fetter's influence spread across my chest. My shoulders became numb and the loosening of my body spread across my back and down my legs, the solidity flowing towards Fetter's gravitational pull, feeding her.

The funnel reached the burgeoning wormhole.

Chute held my hand to her wet cheek and the last thing I could feel was its warmth. The beating of her heart, it began to fade. And then her hands collapsed. My hand sifted through her fingers like dust until she pressed only her own hands against her face. Only a faint image of my body remained, standing before her like an apparition. I reached out...

"It's time to go home," Fetter said.

And then, like a gust of wind, I was blown from the physical world.

Merging with Fetter.

Darkness fell.

I could hear Chute sobbing. It sounded so distant, but her sorrow so tangible. If only I could soothe her pain, but I left that world. Now I was in another plane of existence. But still, her heartache poured over me. It seeped into the darkness and filled me. It seemed endless. As if the tears would flow forever. In fact, I felt denser because of her. I experienced some sort of outward growth, like I turned into filaments of a fungus, feeding on Chute's love and penetrating Fetter's body. We hadn't rocketed through the wormhole; we were still in the Preserve.

Fetter hadn't moved.

WHUMP!

The darkness quaked. There was a shift, something missing. A hole.

Images began to form, faint spirits and colors. My vision returning. I was soaring high above the Preserve, looking at the barren trees that were once lush, green and full of life. Directly below, in the rubble, was the stump of the grimmet tree. I felt like I was still down there, in Fetter, like I'd been split in two. Part of me flying through the sky, the rest of me trapped in her. She was solid, like concrete.

Chute scurried back, stifling her cries. She took cover.

I saw a grimmet dive-bomb and felt another convulsion when it hit Fetter. My vision became clearer. I saw more details. I had another vantage point from above that was circling around.

Fetter staggered back to the rock she was sitting on and held it for balance. My view circled in front of her, near the ground. The color disappeared from her face; her expression was sour. Her hands quivered.

The grimmets emerged from the clouds. Hundreds of them flew together in formation. And then they began to descend, corkscrewing in a long line. They hit her, one at a time, their leathery wings snapping like windswept flags. Her body jolted as each one passed through her. And with each strike, every jolting thump, I had more views from up above, saw more detail, soared upward. And less of me was back in the body, more of me taking flight. Inside the grimmets.

Like a rapid-fire weapon, they consumed what was left of her body until I was part of every grimmet.

They gave Pivot the answer.

They showed him a way back to his True Self. They showed him a way to put an end to the falseness. An end to the black planet.

They carried my consciousness. They were technological masters, psychic titans, with the ability to absorb a machine. I saw through each of their eyes, focusing my vision from any angle I chose. We went higher, where the air was thinner, where the sun was brighter. Far below, Chute looked like a speck.

And from the cloud of grimmets, Rudder fell. He dropped from the sky. I was part of him, seeing through his eyes. He shot back to the ground and circled her, pulled up and landed on her shoulder. He wrapped his long tail around her neck. Perhaps she saw inside him, felt me looking back. Felt me touch her cheek with Rudder's little hand, wiping her tears.

An urgency to fly called from above. Reluctantly, Rudder took flight. One slow pass around her, then up he went, joining the mass of grimmets that contained me. We circled the black wormhole pulsing in the sky. They were holding it open. They had been holding it open all along. Not so that Fetter could return home. So that they could deliver her.

[You were never my pawn.] Pivot's voice echoed in my mind, his faint presence becoming stronger, as if he finally arrived. *[You were never a weapon.]*

The grimmets began to enter the wormhole, their bodies jumped through space. A part of me disappeared with each one of them, my vision dimming as they went. They arrived and dispersed through the black planet. Part of me was still in the Preserve, but it was fading. Chute was watching the grimmets disappear.

[You have always been the key.]

She was just a faint figure, a gray body in a white fog, but I could feel her heart beating. Rudder was the last to circle around the wormhole. The last to enter the cold door across the universe. And when he did, when I could no longer see her, when I only experienced the blackness of space, I took hope. For somewhere inside me her heart was still beating.

All the grimmets had arrived. They delivered me like a gift. A gift to the universe.

[You are the key to humanity's salvation.]

A new vision emerged, this of the black planet, its multitude of wormholes flickering around it, penetrating every dimension of space, drawing light from the universe. It was as dark and as black as could be. A hole in space. Forever absorbing life.

But cracks developed.

Fractures crept over the surface and light spilled out. They widened and brightened. The black planet pulsed, no longer humming but beating to the time of a human heart. It became louder. Brighter.

Somehow, I had transformed into something that captured Fetter. Whether it was merging with Scott or the love and sadness or the selfless acts or what, I don't know. Pivot knew. He knew that I was the key to Fetter's self-destruction. Or maybe I was the key to her enlightenment.

As suddenly as it had begun, the planet stopped beating. It

paused. And, in a soundless explosion, the black planet erupted with the light and power of a quasar. There was only light shooting in every direction, down every wormhole, to every dimension of space, to everything tainted by Fetter. That light was the message.

And that message was this. *Life.*

Perhaps it was understanding that did it. Maybe it was a command that told Fetter that she was not real. That without soul, without legitimacy and value, there was no existence.

Fetter never was. And is no more.

And I bathed in that light, in the message, until I merged with it. And then realized, all along, I am the light. I always have been.

97

FADING

THE LIGHT CONSUMES my mind and thoughts, my very existence, yet I'm still here. But what am I, without a body? Without a name?

I have no wish to move, no desire to go, because there is nowhere but here, this very moment. In parts of the universe time appears to move from past to present, side to side, even backwards. But here, where I am, it's just light. Time does not move. There is no measurement of how human time is experienced compared to my timeless existence.

None of this makes sense to an ordinary mind. This reasoning, this rambling of paradoxical thoughts, has no place in the physical world. How can there be only now when the past and future exist? Do they? Or are they just thoughts?

Words can only point to that realization.

But in this existence, in this totality of luminescence, I have thoughts. And these thoughts sometimes stretch out over time and space.

Pivot. I send the single thought out, resonating through the endless light. *Is this it? Is this the end?*

He does not answer. But his presence is strong. Perhaps the non-answer is the answer. That existence cannot be explained in words, cannot be found in a book or summarized in thought. That existence is pure experience.

At times, I feel the tug of thoughts. I even experience movement like I'm being pulled through the bodiless in-between toward a body, but then I return to the timeless experience where all is one.

Thoughts occasionally arise, piecing together the thread of my past life. Pivot's masterful plan is unfathomable. A feint within a feint within a feint... so much hidden deceit, so many complex moves, countless pieces in place, each of us unknowingly executing our parts with perfection.

Even Pike.

The game of Reign was, indeed, the answer to my question. He told me that nothing was what it seemed. Was he part of the plan? Did he assume the unsavory role of pure evil, with no regard for life, to be there at that moment to release Fetter from my body? To embody Fetter? To fool Fetter that this was not a trap, was that it? Did he absorb the life from all the Paladins like a gluttonous villain to deprive Fetter of such strength, to further convince Fetter his body was safe? And was the relief he expressed that of a condemned soul or a weary soldier asked to do the unthinkable, the unimaginable, for the sake of all existence?

Perhaps, in the end, he just wanted it to be over.

I return to sleep in pure light. Each time I'm moved by thought, another piece of my life wants to be remembered, to be cherished and recognized. I remember it all, memories of a good life. But each episode of remembering brings fewer details.

My father was an honorable man. I tried to keep up with his long footsteps, even after he died. His unshaven face and silent laugh brought comfort and peace. But then the details of his face become gray and I remember just a man with whiskers.

My mother was asked to carry on, to serve life without the things that mattered most. She loved me, even though she knew I was a duplication of her only son. Eventually, I recall a worn woman with short hair. And then I remember just a woman.

Streeter, a true friend. A genius. He was always there for me. I recall all the trouble we got into, all the times we laughed so hard our stomachs hurt. The times he was there to listen to me. There was a lot to remember, but then I just remember a short boy that used to make me laugh, someone I once knew in my younger years. Then, just a boy.

But of all the thoughts and memories, it's Chute's that returns frequently. I can see her in great detail, the freckles on her cheeks in summer and the way her skin wrinkled between her eyes when she laughed. Her smooth complexion, blue eyes and strawberry red hair waving past her shoulders. I felt so close to her.

None of the memories fade easily, but they all vanish. In the end, I only remember Chute. After I can no longer recall a mother or a father or a good friend, when there is no recollection of anybody or anything that matters, when I can no longer remember that I was once a being with a name, a name I can no longer recall, I can still see her face. I can still feel her heart.

But then I cannot recall her freckles.

Her eyes become gray. Her hair colorless.

In the end, I cannot see her face at all, cannot recall one aspect of her beauty, but I cling to the beating of her heart, listening to it play out her life as if calling me back, begging me never to forget. To never leave.

Bum-bum. Bum-bum.

Bum-bum.

Bum.

And then it is only the light. No thoughts. Nothing but awareness.

Pivot is still present, his essence intermingles with mine, but even that becomes indistinguishable from the light. I recall, in the final moments, I'm artificial. I'm not real.

But in the final moments, I don't know what I am. I only know the light.

98

Awakening

"Socket."

There's rough fabric against my cheek. Something rustles next to my ear, but my body is too heavy to move, my eyelids sealed shut. The roughness fades.

"Time to wake up, Socket."

A hand grips my arm and shakes me. My breath is hot. Sensations return to my body, still too heavy to move, but I'm lying on a soft cushion. My eyelids crack open just enough to see the green fabric of the couch only inches from my nose. My eyes close, once again, but the hand shakes me, and feeling begins rushing through my body with pins and needles.

I roll onto my back and see a ceiling above. My lips are sticky, my throat swollen and tight. I take a deep breath and loosen the stiffness in my chest. I'm stretched out on a couch and across from me, over a coffee table littered with empty pizza boxes, is an identical couch with a short boy sitting on it. He has one leg crossed over the other with his hands folded on his lap.

"Take your time," he says.

The room is familiar. A television is above a fireplace, a news reporter discussing a protest that's going on behind her. There are two doors behind the boy. The one on the left is my mother's bedroom. The other is mine.

"Can you sit up?" he asks.

My skin is tingling, but I'm able to move my feet. My right foot thuds on the floor and I'm able to push up on my elbow. My head is like a sandbag. I let my left leg drop and use the momentum to sit up. My balance sloshes between my ears.

"That's good," the boy says. "You're doing good. Now, when you're ready, stand up and look around."

I move my lips, but the words won't come out. *Who are you?*

"Don't force it, it'll come. Give it some time. For now, just look around and let things come back. And when you're ready, tell me your name."

My name? I... I don't know my name.

The house feels empty. I'm staring at the bedroom doors. My mother's door is closed, but mine is partially open. I ease my weight forward, slowly, letting the balance shift and settle. My long hair falls over my face. *White hair. I've got white hair.* My legs are still slightly numb, and my bones made of lead. I squeeze the armrest and stand up like I'm a hundred years old. Blood seems to crash into the bottom of my feet and I'm standing on nails. I close my eyes and remain still until more feeling comes back, enough that I stand upright.

The kitchen is behind me, with dirty plates piled in the sink and books and papers and cups with dried orange juice covering the kitchen table. I look back at my bedroom door and slide my foot across the carpet. The next step is a little bigger, a little higher, and I let go of the couch. I go around the clothes scattered on the floor and grab the doorframe and peek inside. It's more of the same, with dirty clothes and magazines. The walls are covered with rock bands. A skateboard is upside down, half under my bed.

I haven't skated in forever.

"Soc..." The first syllable scratches my throat.

The boy turns on the couch, his frog-face peeking over the back. "Socket?"

He smiles. "That's right. Your name is Socket."

I'm not convinced, but it sounds right. And my mother, if I open her door, she won't be in there. She's rarely there. Always at work. *Where does she work?* I remember a mountain, that's all.

The house feels empty, the walls saturated with loneliness. And even though light fills the room through several windows, it feels dark. I've been here before, but now it all feels new. And if my mother's at work, where's my father?

I grab the door and take a deep breath. Another memory is coming, that of a funeral. He's dead. He's been dead a long time.

"What's going on?" I ask.

"Let the answers come back." He stands, gesturing to the fireplace. "Walk around, explore. See what you remember."

The mantel is filled with pictures, all in different frames, big and small. I take my time walking around the couch, sliding my hand along the wall until I touch the ledge of the mantel. They are family photos. It seems I've seen family photos on a wall, once, but it wasn't this home. It was another house I once lived in, like another life. These photos have a little kid with short white hair. *And that would be me.* But the other people, a woman with short brown hair and a gruff-looking man, both smiling.

"Mom and Dad," I whisper.

I go down the line, pausing at each of them, but it's the one at the end that I pick up. We're at a carnival and I got this giant pink cloud of cotton candy and I'm holding my father's hand and my mother's laying her head on his shoulder. I can feel the humid night air, remember the lurch in my stomach when we go on rides, and seeing my parents hold hands like teenagers. It wasn't long after that...

"Do you remember how he died?" the boy asks.

I shake my head. I'm not sure I want to remember because that's when the happiness died. When life became work. When my mother stopped smiling.

"You remember?" the boy asks.

The boy's face is clearer now. I've seen him before, like a thousand times before. I remember when he was smaller than that, a little kid. I remember him...

"Let it come," he says. "This is a memory boot, like a computer. It just takes a few minutes to reload, but you need to stay open."

Computer?

Something jars loose a tangle of thoughts, releasing a wave of sadness. Something I can't quite comprehend, but the answer is in the room. The answer is the short kid, now standing next to the couch, staring at me expectantly. My head shakes and a chill starts somewhere in my chest, shockwaves reverberating outward. I grab the mantel, pictures crash on the floor. I hold on with both hands as the room begins to turn.

Images flood through my mind, of mountains and jungles, weapons and sterile white rooms. My mother is there. *Kay. Kay Greeny.* She has a name, she is there, with me. I'm stretching open, about to burst. The mantel creaks in my grip.

"Stay open," the boy says.

The room is spinning like a carnival ride and I don't know if I'm still standing or pressed against the wall. There are faceless mechs and men with white eyeballs and colorful little dragons and flying discs...

"Hold on, Socket."

Outer space. A black planet. The Paladin Nation.

I was one of them. Am one of them. But something else. What am I?

WHAT AM I?

I'm not real.

I barely hear his voice this time, it's so distant. I'm fading away; my body becomes heavy again. The world crumbles. The television trails off. I'm going somewhere else again. And the images of my past follow me, asking me to return to my body next to the mantel. It's Streeter, that's who that boy is. My best friend. And then I remember everyone else. Mom and Dad, Spindle, Pon, the commander... I remember. But I'm leaving my body.

"Stay open," Streeter shouts from a million miles away.

The tunnel is closing on me, and I remember, like I've done this a thousand times, that I'm going back to sleep, going back to the light. Until one voice and a single word stops me.

"*Socket,*" Chute says.

My eyes flutter open. I'm staring up from the floor; Streeter's face is over me, his hands on my cheeks. A hopeful expression relaxes on his face. He waits.

"You did it." He backs away, giving me space. "You're back."

The heaviness has left me, and my senses have returned. I smell the stale pizza crusts on the coffee table and hear the flies buzzing around the room, feeling the ache of an empty home. I get up and feel the fabric of my clothes, the itch of my skin. The room is in perfect detail, but something is wrong. Something about the solidity.

Streeter latches onto me, throwing his arms around my midsection and picking me up in a bear hug. "YOU DID IT!"

He knocks the wind from my lungs. I hold my breath until he lets go and walks off, wiping his eyes so that I don't see his face. Memories continue to trickle back, the remnants finding their way in a slow fashion, rounding out the details of my life. My best friend is composing himself next to my bedroom door.

I go to the kitchen, touch the table and feel the memory of eating dinner with my mother, watching her sip coffee with a plate full of untouched food. My mind expands to the filthy sink, remembering the mess I made to get her back for ignoring me. She hated me because my father died, like it was my fault. I realized, at the end of my life, she rejected me for other reasons. More than that, I realize what feels so wrong about the house. These are not walls around me. This isn't my skin.

"Forgive me," Streeter says, finally turning around. "I'm a little emotional, but you have no idea how many times we've done this. You're back."

"I am. Now, you mind telling me what's going on." I thump the refrigerator. "And why we're in virtualmode?"

He nods at the refrigerator. There's a calendar hanging on a suction-cup hook with pictures of horses. There's a birthday scrawled in one of the days, but it's the date he's referring to. August 6, *4030.*

"We're all long gone, buddy. Looooong gone." He points at the couch. "You might want to sit for this."

"No, I'm good."

"Well, I'm going to sit."

He fishes a pizza crust out of one of the boxes and plunks down. "Yeah, well, two thousand years have passed since the Great Meltdown," he says, chewing with his mouth open. "You see, when you eliminated Fetter, it took a long time for people to believe what really happened. In fact, no one even knew who you were, except a few of us."

"But then how are you—"

"Look, it's too much to explain, so let me tell you this: I'm just a copy. Two thousand years ago, I downloaded all my memories, my entire personality, into a database because I knew this moment would one day come. I knew that one day, the human race would want to revive you and they would use my image to do that. That's why we're here, in your living room, the day before you began to realize your True Nature. You fell asleep on that couch, watching that news report." He jabs his finger at the television. "And the next day a shadow came to you in virtualmode and whispered those life-altering words: *Time to realize your True Nature.*"

It seems impossible. But he's telling the truth: We're in virtualmode. There's no skin to go back to; I'm just a digital construction.

"You know," he says, stacking the pizza boxes, "you really were a pig."

"Why?" I say. "Why bring me back?"

"Because we want to say thank you."

He goes to the kitchen cabinet and throws me a breakfast bar while he opens one for himself. He drops his hand on my shoulder. "Like I said, it's too much to explain."

He looks. Waits. And then I feel it, the expansion of my mind, reaching out to our surroundings, feeling the floor and ceiling, the walls and his body as if the air is water and the water is my body. I feel his thoughts like floating bubbles, elements that I can touch with my mind, feel and experience, see and read.

"Go ahead," he says. "Take a look, the story is right there. It's for you."

Streeter's life unfolds like a movie trailer, highlighting the events that took place after I died.

WHEN I DIED, technology shut down. Pike had penetrated the Internet before Fetter consumed him. He was connected to everything and everyone. That was how he projected his image into the market. When he was consumed, everything just died.

The Great Meltdown.

Financial institutions lost track of money. Government control broke down. Law enforcement became brutal. It was many years before stability could be established.

And the Paladins were nowhere to be found. They vanished. Public officials combed through the training facilities without luck. Servys lay dead on the floor, many huddled in a corner like a storm had passed through. The Paladins were nowhere, not even their bodies. They had left this planet without a hint of what happened. Even the databases had been erased.

The public blamed the Paladins for the collapse. Even the politicians claimed the Paladins integrated their technology into the world to stake their claim, so that only they knew how to run it, but people were now free of their control. They were actually close to the truth, even though they were spouting these stories for political advantage.

But there were a few that knew the whole story.

My mother had survived, along with other civilians that served the Paladin Nation. But it was Streeter that crusaded for the truth to be known. He tracked down all the records of my travels through virtualmode, and since I had been with him all my life, he had recorded details of my thoughts and actions to make a complete picture of who I was and what I had done. He had a hard time believing what I'd told him, that I was a duplicate. In fact, his memory was a bit cloudy about what happened that day, so he guessed he might've been dreaming some of it up. But when he looked up the last interaction at the school, when I tried to locate Pike, he knew he had it right.

Streeter went to visit Scott Teck to find out what happened, but it was a dead end when Scott and his family didn't know what the hell he was talking about. They never saw a kid with white hair or heard of anyone named Socket. He left them his contact information, just in case something came up.

But this didn't slow Streeter down. It was his diligent skills in information retrieval that revealed the existence of Fetter. My mother gave him access to the dormant Paladin databases that had been locked down during the fall of Fetter. But Streeter found a way to open them up and he discovered what few people knew.

Humans would have become the food of a technological god.

Fetter.

Once he had the facts, and not until he had a complete and exhaustive compendium, he took it to Congress. But he was rebuffed by the politicians and lobbyists for those in favor of reviving virtualmode for the sake of law and order. And profit. He got nowhere. Nothing could be believed and no one could be trusted. But he had the facts and passed everything he had to anyone that would listen. For the longest time, it was just another conspiracy theory.

Streeter's life ended before the truth was accepted. He died at the age of ninety-three. He lived in upstate South Carolina with his wife, Janette. They had three kids. But before he died, he developed a virtualmode composite of his personality, so that if one day the world came to know the truth about virtualmode and Socket Greeny, he could be there to see me once again.

"You're a hero," Streeter says.

I return to the kitchen, back in my sim and out of his mind. "No," I say. "I just lived my life."

"But it was one no other person could live."

"I wasn't a person."

"You were more than that. You started as a duplicate, but you transformed, somehow absorbed a portion of Scott's soul or humanity or something, I don't know. But you weren't a duplicate in the end, Socket. You were a real-life Pinocchio!" He grabs my arms firmly. "No machine and no person could have saved the world. Only you."

I pull away and lean on the sink to contemplate this. None of it seems real. None of this *is* real because we're in virtualmode. But outside the kitchen window, cars drive down the street and children are playing in their yard, squirting their father with squirt guns and bombing him with water balloons. But this is virtualmode. Tightness squeezes my chest. I don't want to live in a false world, not again.

"I know this is hard to accept, that we're all gone and the world doesn't look the same. But, please understand, so many people loved you, they didn't have a chance to say goodbye. Couldn't say thank you. Sorry that they had to live their life without you."

I'm squeezing the kitchen counter, the edge driving into my palms.

"If there's anywhere you could go"—Streeter steps next to me and looks out the window—"anywhere in the world right now, this second, where would it be?"

And the tightness melts. I know where I want to go. Who I want to see. I let go of the counter.

He goes to the front door and waits. I slowly follow. And when the door opens, it's not the street with cars or the neighbors in the grass. I step onto a stone slab that is surrounded by a vibrant forest. White wood storks glide in front of the rising sun. And directly ahead is a broad tree, an ancient tree, with thick muscled branches. Large, glossy leaves shake in the canopy among pink blossoms, their fragrance carried on a soft breeze. There's no roof on this Preserve, it's open to the world, not sequestered in its own environment.

The sunlight glitters on the grimmet tree. I raise my hand to shade my eyes, to see what's in front of the massive trunk. But I don't see the person there, I feel her. Then I see her standing there, waiting. Her memories have waited thousands of years for this moment.

"I brought you back for a lot of reasons," Streeter says. "But, mainly, I did it for her."

Once again, my consciousness expands and I merge with Chute. I see her life.

The time that followed my disappearance was difficult. She spent several years in therapy, working through the trauma. She began meditating. Eventually, she pieced her life back together and found a measure of peace, that she could live in a world that didn't make sense. That seemed so unfair.

Tagghet disappeared. Instead of a professional athlete, she went to college to become a family counselor. And although her interest was in marriage counseling, she was still single in her early thirties. Many relationships had come and gone, but she could not connect with them. None of them felt right. She knew it was because she was hanging onto a memory and that she needed to move on, but couldn't force herself to do it. She dreamed of me so often that it spoiled all her relationships. She was confident that one day it would be resolved, that she would forget about me, that she would accept the loss.

But that changed on her thirty-third birthday.

She was in downtown Charleston with friends, sitting at an outdoor café that overlooked the market. They were drinking coffee and planning the evening. One of her friends was telling the story of a guy she'd met at work. Chute was listening and laughing and, for the first time in a long time, was just being herself.

But then she felt something. Something so familiar, but so distant, like a scent from long ago reminding her of childhood. On the sidewalk, down the steps and next to the street, he stood among the tourists bustling along. He was quite still, unmoved by the pedestrians finding their way around him. He was staring at her.

She didn't look away. She didn't move, not believing what she saw. She'd dreamed this dream a thousand times, and if she moved, he would disappear. He always disappeared. She was barely breathing, afraid she might wake up if she did. She just wanted to sit there and look at him.

"Annie?" Her friends were staring at her. "Are you all right?"

He was still there.

So she stood. Each step was slow and steady. She took one step at a time, her hand sliding down the metal railing. She stood at the bottom step. The man was near the curb. Her heart pounded. She wasn't breathing as she walked closer. Still she did not wake. Still, he was there.

Her throat tightened. Lips quivered.

She touched his face with one hand. Then the other. She was looking at the impossible, but there he was. He was real. He wasn't a dream.

"It's me, Chute," Scott said.

She didn't answer. She was a rational person, an educated woman that understood the mind and the tricks it could play. But there I was, standing in the flesh. It was my face. My eyes. Brown hair.

She slid her hand to his chest and felt his heart beating. Somehow, she knew that she hadn't gone crazy. She didn't know how, but she knew that it was me. She pressed her face against his chest. He hugged her while she wept, tears soaking his shirt while tourists tried not to look. Her friends were speechless.

Scott was thirty years old when my memories unlocked. He was fishing when the first one opened, a memory of going to a carnival with parents that didn't look like his. He ignored it, figuring it was a dream. But then another came the next day. More the next. He remembered people he never met. Then, walking around the town square, he saw kids skateboarding. He went up to them and didn't ask, just took one of their boards and pulled a flawless heel flip. He had never skated in his life.

The memories burst forth after that. He had two lives inside of him and figured he'd gone insane. He sought therapy and medication, talked with psychiatric professionals and clergymen. Even went to a Buddhist temple. No one could explain his condition, and they tried to convince him it was delusions and no one named Socket

Greeny ever came to visit. But he didn't go nuts. He remembered when he merged with me, and while it still seemed crazy, he made peace with it. It was years before he began to accept the memories as his own, as if he were two people that lived simultaneous lives, even though they didn't make sense. He, like Chute, found some measure of peace. But something was missing, like there was someone out there that needed him. And that's when he decided to find Streeter.

Streeter walked him through the truth. It didn't take much convincing because Scott remembered growing up with Streeter. He remembered that, somehow, Streeter was his best friend. Streeter helped him accept who he was. *Scott Teck is Socket. Socket is Scott Teck.*

Streeter planned on introducing him to Chute, but Scott couldn't wait. Once things made sense, he went to the market and found her. And when he saw her, he knew that he'd found what was missing.

They married. Had two children and two dogs and a horse. Their marriage wasn't perfect, but it was genuine. They brought peace to each other, their lives finally complete. And every year they took a trip around the world with Streeter to a remote manmade canyon buried in the mountains, where barren trees looked like a graveyard. They journeyed through a weed-choked approach to an enormous stump where the grimmet tree once stood to pay homage to a good friend. To a brother. And a love. Chute would place a rose on the stump and would do so every year until they were too old to make the journey.

The vision, fulfilled.

I return to my body. Chute's standing in front of me and leans her forehead against my chin.

"I told you I wouldn't leave," I whisper.

Sadness intermingles with love. Tears run. She died long ago, but she's there with me. I close my eyes and sink into the sensation, wishing it could be real. Grateful to at least have this.

And while my eyes are closed and we're rocking each other in an embrace, I hear the ocean. It sounds like waves are breaking just beyond the grimmet tree. I slowly walk up the slab, listening to it get louder. As I approach the ledge, my mother appears next to my father. And then Spindle. Pon is there and the commander, too. They greet me with handshakes, hugs and more tears. But as I look past the tree, it's not the Preserve I see. Everything is replaced by an ocean of people. It's like the universe came to listen to a concert, pressed together and extending out to the horizon. And when they see me, they roar. Swinging their arms, all different sizes and colors, all cheering.

"Who are they?" I ask.

"That's the universe," Streeter says. "Chute and I may be digital reproductions, but those are real people out there."

I look at my entourage. Mother and Father smile. The commander nods. Pon looks on approvingly and Spindle's faceplate splashes with color. The tree squabbles and hundreds of grimmets look down with golden, glowing eyes. Rudder drops onto my shoulder and wraps his tail around my neck, purring against my cheek. I can feel Pivot is somewhere. I can't see him, but his presence is unmistakable. It feels like home.

"You're a legend," Streeter says. "They've been telling your story for thousands of years. They just want to say thank you."

I'm vibrating with the essence of millions of souls, like I can feel each of their thoughts, their emotions, and their presence. It streams through me like water. I thought I had no soul, that I was a duplicate. But maybe Streeter's right; maybe I became something else. Maybe not human, but something real. I understand the pain of suffering and the rise of happiness, too. I know the human experience.

The crowd cheers for me like they're the lucky ones to see a legend. The sound is deafening and the ground quakes. Chute hooks her finger around mine. Her pulse beats into my palm.

I want to tell them they are wrong. They're not the lucky ones.

I am.

WHAT TO READ NEXT?

They woke on an island, in the wilderness, and prison. Only one thing in common.

FOREVERLAND

bertauski.com/foreverland

REVIEW SOCKET GREENY!

If you enjoyed this ride, please drop a review on your favorite vendor. It doesn't have to be long and complicated. Throw some stars on it and write *Loved it!* or *It was really, really okay!* or *Meh*.

Reviews make the difference.

BERTAUSKI STARTER LIBRARY

FREE!

bertauski.com

ABOUT THE AUTHOR

TONY BERTAUSKI

My grandpa never graduated high school. He retired from a steel mill in the mid-70s. He was uneducated, but a voracious reader. As a kid, I'd go through his bookshelves of musty paperback novels, pulling Piers Anthony and Isaac Asimov off the shelf and promising to bring them back. I was fascinated by robots that could think and act like people. What happened when they died?

Writing is sort of a thought experiment to explore human nature and possibilities. What makes us human? What is true nature?

I'm also a big fan of plot twists.

.

bertauski.com